The Making of
Incarnation

ALSO BY TOM McCARTHY

Remainder
Men in Space
C
Satin Island

The Making of Incarnation

Tom McCarthy

JONATHAN CAPE
LONDON

1 3 5 7 9 10 8 6 4 2

Jonathan Cape, an imprint of Vintage,
20 Vauxhall Bridge Road,
London SW1V 2SA

Jonathan Cape is part of the Penguin Random House group of companies
whose addresses can be found at global.penguinrandomhouse.com.

Penguin
Random House
UK

First published by Jonathan Cape in 2021

penguin.co.uk/vintage

A CIP catalogue record for this book is available from the British Library

ISBN 9781787333291 (Hardback)
ISBN 9781787333307 (Trade paperback)

The quotation on p108 is from the song 'Gary, Indiana',
with lyrics by Meredith Willson

Typeset in 12/15.25 pt Dante MT
by Integra Software Services Pvt. Ltd, Pondicherry

Printed and bound in Great Britain by Clays Ltd, Elcograf S.p.A.

The authorised representative in the EEA is Penguin Random House Ireland,
Morrison Chambers, 32 Nassau Street, Dublin D02 YH68

Penguin Random House is committed to a sustainable future for
our business, our readers and our planet. This book is made from
Forest Stewardship Council® certified paper.

MIX
Paper from
responsible sources
FSC® C018179

For Isadora and Alexis Lemon McCarthy

Incarnation is our grace. It alone creates colour, touch, distance, and music, the lithe resilience of the flesh and the desire that will not halt ...

Denis de Rougemont

Contents

Book Three

Prolegomenon

On the Dynamic Properties of Waves in Periodic Systems

From the S-Bahn, through shuttling latticework of tree branch and bridge truss, you glimpse it just below Tiergarten as you travel east-to-west, or west-to-east: a five-storey blue hulk. The building levitates unnaturally above the ground, jacked up on two giant, tubular pink ducts that protrude and curl downward from its sides then join together at its base, as though it were a crab reared up in fear, or anger, or some kind of mating ritual. What is it? It's the *Versuchsanstalt für Wasserbau und Schiffbau*, Research Institute for Hydraulic Engineering and Shipbuilding, outpost that Technische Universität Berlin has maintained, through a royal lease that's somehow weathered wars, land-value hikes and all the rest, on this small, elongated island around which the Landwehr Canal bifurcates into sluiced sections before merging back into a single flow out of whose grain all knots, spirals and other traces of past interruption or obstruction have been smoothed.

Or, scanned at a res higher than most S-Bahn riders have at their disposal: it's a complex of buildings, slotted into one another. The eye-catching, crustacean one's the *Umlauf- und Kavitationstank UT2*, its looping claw a conduit capable of pumping 3,300 tonnes of water round and round at nine metres per second – perfect for wake field and cavitation research, forced motion and propulsion tests and like manner of fluid-dynamic enquiry. There, amidst the roar of a two-megawatt ship diesel engine and vibrations of the vast pump's switch blades that shake wall and floor's sheet panels, dramas of rarefaction and compression, cyclic stress and supercavitation play themselves out on demand, putting model hulls, rudders and propellers through their paces, coaxing from these inception numbers and erosion-progress rates. Below this towering monster, strewn about its feet like strips of food or half-spawned offspring, lie a series of long, flat hangars. It's in one of these, the one housing the *Seegangsbecken*, the Seakeeping Basin or wave generator – intermittently replenished, like the UT2, by the same liquid mass diverted from and, eventually, released back into the Landwehr and thence onwards to the Spree – that today's action is taking place.

Here, Neptune's wrath is about to be unleashed on a platform supply vessel, an anchor handling tug and two oil rigs. Resident technician Arda Gökçek, Dipl.-Ing., VWS's Keeper of the Sea, stands at the basin's absorption end, moving his thumb and fingers round a MacBook's glide-pad, scaling metrics, modifying ratios, adjusting up or down wave height and stroke length, characteristic and gravitational velocities. When the profile on his screen, the rhythm of its curves and intervals, aligns with that of today's target values, Gökçek's hand breaks contact with the laptop, hovers an inch or two above its keyboard while his eyes cross-check the graphic contours one last time, then falls decisively back down on the space bar. More than a hundred metres away, at the basin's far end, the wave-generation mechanism groans; drive arms, pulleys and linkage arms, drive pegs, flange bearings and connecting rods stir, clasp and thrust, shunting a slanted flap repeatedly against the water's bulk. And then it comes, down the long, narrow stretch, peak doubling the ceiling's intermittent strip lights one after the other, raising each inverted, spectral light-line up towards its source before the trough swallows the reflection once more in its darkened vortex: the first wave. It's followed by another, and another, and another, soaking the green tiles along the basin's sides, redrawing the same high-water mark over and over with complete precision.

Do the boats and platforms sense them coming? Of course not; all propagation vectors of the medium they sit in have been plotted here, phase boundaries and resonant frequencies rendered

4

transparent; there's no wiggle room for ambiguity, and even less for fantasy – yet Gökçek still, each time he watches replica cities, dams or cruise ships, harbour walls or wind farms in the propagation section in the last, contracting moments just before the first wave hits, fancies that he senses, in the models' very composition, the clinging together of their atoms, an increased level of concentrated stasis; a *tensing* almost, as though they were bracing themselves; as though, somehow, they *knew* . . .

Now the waves are among them, tossing and convulsing them, sending them veering – laterally and vertically, longitudinally, transversally and every which way in-between – down paths that seem quite random but in fact are not at all, that's the whole point: cameras at the basin's sides are tracking and translating every heave and surge and sway, identifying, within the furious tangle of the lines, some kind of pattern to be viewed both retro- and prospectively, its fuzz transmuted into clean parameters that, once modelled, can be not only scaled back up for the benefit of future offshore installation planners but also, traversing their own vectors of circulation and displacement, transferred and extrapolated and fed into who-knows-what. Over the next sixteen months, today's worked-through data will be brought to bear on fields as variant as infrasonics and seismocardiography, the study of germ convection around airline cabins and the spread of rumour over social networks. Things are connected to other things, which are connected to other things. Yesterday, one hundred and three Asian miners died in a methane explosion; a small South American state underwent a coup; a large pod of whales beached itself off Western Europe's coastline. The pages of Gökçek's newspaper, lying open on a stool beside a half-drunk coffee cup, rustle as he climbs a nearby stepladder, borne upwards in his slipstream. From on high, the technician watches the boats lurching and bobbing drunkenly amidst the swells and currents, hurtling past the battered reefs of the oil platforms' legs and anchors. The elevation calms him; he's above the struggle, uninvolved. Visions of the Bosporus drift across his mind's back reaches, morphing through various formations – less a place glimpsed from car windows and mosque terraces on holidays, extended family visits, than a vague ancestral memory, an idea ...

The wave-generation mechanism groans; the flap shunts on to the same rhythm. The pillow-block journal bearings holding the driveshaft in place need lubricating: Gökçek can tell that from the note of irritation in its tone. On the smooth stretches of the basin's water, before the models break its surface, there's an outer coat of oil and dirt, a no man's land littered by corpses of the insects lured there by the mirrored swathes of airspace and bright rafters, the false promise of companionship. The anchor-handling tug, its prow of hardened paraffin, has got itself wedged in one of the oil rigs' leg struts. Computer modelling won't show you everything. Sometimes you have to actually *do* it, make a little world, get down amidst dumb objects and their messiness. From the basin's exterior, where it rests on J-hooks beside coils of hosing, wiring, torn canvas and string, Gökçek lifts a pike pole and leans in over the edge, trying to prise the vessel free. His right foot, raised behind him for stability, nudges the stool; coffee slops out, blotting the news pages. On a worktable beside the stool are an isopropanol spray can, a CD-ROM, a roll of toilet paper, an ice-lolly stick, a crumpled plastic glove of the type used for washing up, weights, floats, a fire extinguisher, an off-cut block of wood, a fold-out ruler, a hand-held torch, a tote bag, an external hard drive, a red marker pen, a plastic cup with small screws in it, a blue case of cross-point screwdrivers, a grease tin and a scrunched-up piece of tissue paper stained with a red substance. Further back, against the wall, models superfluous to today's scenario are stacked: a submarine, an ICE train, fifteen wind turbines, a life-sized emperor penguin and the city of Mumbai. In front of them stands a new prop, delivered to the Institute an hour ago from London in an outsize box, the unpacking of which has strewn about the floor styrofoam plugs and wedges that, being moulded to fit tightly round the model while it was in transit, now inversely (and disjointedly) repeat the outline of their precious cargo, also styrofoam: a spaceship with distributed, partitioned fuselage- and wing-configuration and a kind of half-detached, golf-ball-like annexe teed up just above its highest section. Gökçek's pike pole, finding its sweet spot on the tug's hull, prods it loose. The tug capsizes momentarily, spins on its side through a full clockwise circle and a third of an anticlockwise one, then, righting itself, glides round the leg struts to find open water. The flap shunts; the wave-generation mechanism groans. Gökçek returns the pike pole to its J-hooks and moves off in search of engine oil.

Alone among the props, the emperor penguin is not only replicated at a scale of one-to-one, but also (since the effect of turbidity on shallow-substratum colour was a subject of enquiry in the session in which it recently starred) painted black, yellow and white in the appropriate places. It's been cast in 'porpoising' mode: wings folded into torso, head held up in alignment with the body's central axis, feet wedged together and pointed down vertically to form a rudder. The meticulous streamlining has been undone, though, by its positioning: to stop its out-of-water bulk rolling across the floor, its neck has been rested across the roof of a train carriage, which (since the carriage has been cast at 1:22.5) not only makes the bird seem monstrous, gargantuan, but also angles it unnaturally, un-aerodynamically upward. Made to focus on the building's ceiling, its painted eyes seek out the skylight. Beyond this, the outside air is brisk, flushed by light breeze. Higher, much further up, two intersecting vapour trails have carved a cross against the blue – a vote cast on a ballot slip, the signature of an illiterate, an X marking the spot: *Here*.

Book One

1. Markie's Crime (Replay)

In the third of four school buses edging their way up Camberwell New Road sits Markie Phocan. The buses process in formation, a cortège. Taxis, vans, double-deckers, dustbin lorries and the odd rag-and-bone cart alternately hem them in and, turning, parking or reversing, create pockets for them to slip, if not through, at least into, claiming a few yards before they run up against hard fabric of immobile bumpers and exhaust pipes. Winter sunlight falls across the scene; if they'd been new, or clean, it would have made the buses glint, but since they're neither, it just coats them in a dust and diesel aura. Across the side of one someone has finger-scrawled the word *Fuck*; beneath this, somebody (the same person perhaps) has written *Thatcher*; but this name has since been scored through, substituted by *GLC Commies* – which, in turn, has been struck out and replaced with *You*.

Markie's sitting in the fourth row, by the window (driver side). Next to him, Nainesh Patel is thumbing through a set of football cards, picking out swaps. On the aisle's far side Polly Gould's tipping her head back, tapping space dust onto an extended tongue. Trevor Scotter leans in from behind her and, sliding his hand horizontally across the plumb-line between packet and mouth, interrupts the flow for long enough to grab some of the powder in his upturned palm. Polly spins round, but by the time she's facing him her outrage has already lost momentum. What's she going to do? They're not allowed sweets. Trevor throws his palm up to his own mouth, gloating at her. Then, swinging his eyes sideways, he brings both his and Polly's gaze to rest on Vicky Staple's head, above whose curly hair he rubs his hands, releasing a fine sugar and E-number fallout. He and Polly laugh.

'She got pink dandruff ...'

Vicky, staring at the seat in front of her from behind thick NHS glasses, says nothing. Paper planes and spitwads soar through the loud air. In the door-side front seat Miss Sedge sits impassive, shoulders sagging. No one's getting injured. They're crawling round the Oval now. Markie can see, over the wall, the scoreboard and the top rows of the upper stands; then, further round the ground's perimeter, rising above it, the gas holders. The tallest one is about two thirds full today, its green dome's convex meniscus giving over to a skeleton of interlocking diamonds. Vauxhall Gardens' hot-air balloon floats, tethered, to the gas holders' north, ropes on its underside converging on a flimsy-looking basket. Lowering his back and craning his head as the bus traces Harleyford Street's curve, Markie tracks the balloon across the windscreen until it slides from view beyond the upper border. The aluminium of the vehicle's carapace behind which it disappears is thin and translucent; the sun, head-on to them now, shines through it to illuminate the letters SCHOOL BUS stamped across it, broadcasting them to passengers in reversed form: *SUB LOOHCS*. Below this the same letters, smaller and similarly reversed, though this time through reflection of the front shell of the bus hugging their tail, run across the driver's rear-view mirror: SUB LOOHCS. To Markie, these are real words, drawn from a hybrid language whose vocabulary and grammar he can just about intuit; doubled, they present a header and subtitle, repeating a single cryptic instruction: *sub loohcs – look below* ...

Now the last two buses have got stranded in the middle of the Vauxhall Cross box junction, blue-and-white insects caught in a yellow web, old chassis shuddering while cars honk and weave around them. The driver of Markie's, unconcerned, leans on his outsize wheel and picks his teeth, ignoring other motorists' shouts and V-signs. As Nainesh murmurs 'Heighway ... Shilton ... Coppell ...', the lights release them. Markie wonders if the two events, the intoning of footballers' names and the release of buses, are connected; whether Nainesh has just *caused* the captive spell to break. To a last, long horn-blast, whose tone falls off as they pull away, they speed on to Vauxhall Bridge. Beside it, on the south side, a giant lot sits cleared, sticks and surveyors' string dotted and threaded flimsily about it. Nainesh looks up from his spread and, pointing at the empty space, announces: 'Going to be a secret headquarters for spies.'

'How do you know?' asks Trevor.

'My dad told me.'

'If it's secret, then how does he know?'

'He knows,' mutters Nainesh, burying himself back in the cards.

Polly tilts her head back and taps out another load. In the seat in front of her Bea Folco, headband knotted at right temple, stares out of her window. There's no rear-view mirror, nor any other reflective surface, showing Bea to him and vice versa, but Markie senses nonetheless a symmetry – both of them turned or folded outwards from the bridge's cambered spine, he facing east, she west – somehow connecting them. On his side, on the water, tugs from Lambeth River Fire Station are testing their canons. The water jets start at their bases bold and firm, then jag towards their apex, morph into a set of liquid hooks from which hangs a mist-curtain inlaid with small rainbows. Is this salute for them? For Lyndhurst Primary's four-bus procession? Markie, even at ten, understands that it's not, that the world goes on doing what it does when he's tucked away in classrooms; that this snatched peek at its weekday workings is a special and uncommon thing – almost illicit, as though he were spying on it: embedded in forbidden territory, reconnoitring the buildings and the traffic, the embankments and dilapidated barges, towers and cranes and church spires, Parliament downriver, though the haze; dispatching back (to whom?) some ultra-classified report, compiled in mirror-alphabet, or just in thoughts . . .

Polly, without warning, throws up. She pukes first on to the floor between her legs, then, turning in disgust from what she's brought up, out into the aisle. It triggers screams and raucous laughter, sudden drawing up of legs to chests, a simultaneous evacuation of all bodies from the event's epicentre and, pushing back against this from the seats on its periphery, a wave of curious encroachment. Miss Sedge has stridden over – a little too briskly, almost landing knee-length leather boots in vomit that is pink and lurid and still, as per the manufacturer's design, cracking and popping as the upthrown enzymatic juices release from melting flakes the pressurised carbon dioxide trapped inside them.

'She was eating Pop Rocks, Miss,' says Vicky.

Miss Sedge plants her feet on the vomit-lake's shores, leans over and winches Polly from her seat. As she's led to the front, the girl turns back and shouts at her informer:

'Four-eyed cunt!'

For the rest of the ride, the lake shape-changes with the bus's movement, spawning pools and channels, oxbows, forks and branches. Trevor, playing the joker, hooks his arm between two seat-backs and hangs right above it; when the bus, clearing the bridge, turns sharp right into Millbank, he loses his balance and starts to slip – or is this still part of the act? No one gets to find out: Miss Sedge strides over again and plucks him away too, slaps his face one-two with both sides of her free hand, then bundles him into the front row beside her and Polly. As he turns round to take a curtain call, leering back glow-cheeked at his classmates, his smirking eye catches Markie's; Markie looks away. The vomit's smell's coming on strong now; children start lifting scarves and collars to their noses. Markie wedges his gloves, conjoined by outward rolling of the cuffs into a ball, between his face and the window, seeking in their softness and sweet counter-smell a passkey to release him from this cabin, magic him outside to merge with cleansing spray, with light's extracted spectrum ...

They've arrived now. Into the parking bay the buses pull, two on each side of the *Mr Whippy* van that's blocking out the central stretch. In Markie's there's a rush towards the door, which remains closed while Miss Sedge shouts instructions for outside assembly. When it finally accordions back, children tumble on to the pavement and suck air into their lungs like surfacing free divers. High above them, from atop the Tate's stone portico, armed with flag and trident and flanked by her lion and unicorn, Britannia stares down like a disapproving headmistress. Orders go ignored as busloads mingle, bringing one another up to date: Cudjo Sani, on the lead bus, threw up too; on the second one a fight's left Jason Banner with a bleeding scratch across his cheek … Some children slink away into the garden; others hop up and down the building's steps. It's on these steps that teachers re-corral them into class-groups: four inclining columns that are led up past the Tate's vertical ones – only to crumble, bottlenecked by the revolving door. Beyond this, the marble atrium's an echo chamber, multiplying cries and whistles to unbearable cacophony; all four class teachers shout in an attempt to bring the noise under control, which only makes it louder. One of the Tate's guards, whose burly figure and demeanour mark him as an ex-serviceman, steps in, unleashing a deep bass that quietens the children less from obedience than from curiosity: his voice seems to rise from the whorled depths of the staircase down which the floor's two-tone mosaic disappears. Their attention won, he orders them to leave their coats in the cloakroom's group area, then oversees this order's execution, mess-inspection memories flickering across his eyes as arms wriggle out of anorak- and duffel-sleeves.

Markie hangs his coat up on a hook, but keeps the gloves. Holding them up to his face again, watching Bea drop her parka to the floor and step out of it (the zip's stuck), he starts experiencing a sense of overlay – the same effect as when Miss Sedge, back in the classroom, slides one sheet of acetate above another on her overhead projector to create across the wall an image not found on the individual sheets themselves. For a few moments, he's half here in the Tate's vestry, and half in the changing rooms at Peckham Baths – in *both* locations without really being in either. It's not just the mass transit and disrobing, nor that the same type of metal coat-hook lines both spaces' walls. No, this composite effect is pegged on something more particular: an afternoon, a little more than two weeks ago; Markie paired, as today, with Nainesh, two to a cubicle, peeling off socks and trousers – and realising, from the voices sailing past the flimsy metal panel separating their stall from its neighbour, that Bea and Emma Dalton were changing right next to them.

The understanding hit the two boys simultaneously; both suddenly fell quiet, eyes moving up and down the flaked partition, which rose far too high to allow over-peeping – *but* (eyes signalled one another) *its base* ... Its base gave off at shin-height, leaving a low, narrow void-strip. Nainesh, smiling, slowly crouched down to the floor, beckoning Markie: *Here, come* ... They had to press their cheeks right to the quartz-and-granite slab to reach the vantage point: from there, the hidden space swung into view around the panel-base's hinge; and, as though looking upwards while passing through some portico as lofty as the Tate's, they saw two sets of bare legs towering above them like the trunks of redwood trees, parallels playing perspectival tricks by narrowing *and* widening out into thighs before converging, at what should have been infinity but was in truth a mere two feet away, into unfoliaged waist-canopies, joins forming folds that bracketed more folds, all flesh-lines moving in strange synchronicity as Bea and Emma, oblivious to the perverse gazes being directed at them from below, marched up and down on the spot, singing the aria they'd been learning for the upcoming school concert:

> Toreador on guard now, Toreador! Toreador!
> Mind well that when in danger thou shalt be,
> Fond eyes gaze and adore,
> And true love waits for thee, Toreador,
> And true love waits for thee!

The angle prevented Markie from seeing Bea's face; Emma's either – but Bea was closest to him, and it's Bea around whom the visual conundrum has accreted in the fifteen-day interim: how to reconcile the two views, the two angles, the two vistas – trunk and visage – two parts of a whole whose *whole*ness he would love to somehow hold to him, clasp and sink into; but . . .

They're being handed over to one of the Tate's school-group guides. A slight woman in her twenties, she starts telling the children all about Joan Miró.

'Miró,' she trills in a voice full of what Markie instantly recognises as not enthusiasm itself but rather an intent to enthuse, 'learnt to paint when he was about your age. He loved the shapes and colours of his native Barcelona, which were bright and curvy and just full of life. He loved these shapes and colours so much,' she continues, 'that he's carried them inside him ever since. Although he's an old man now, and one of the world's most famous living artists, he still paints with the imagination and the vision of a child – which is why we're always *particularly* happy when children like you come and look at what he's done. Now, I'm going to pass round these . . .'

Worksheets are distributed. There are shapes to spot and tick off; symbols (sun, moon, woman) ditto; then questions about how the paintings make the children feel; a box to fill with their own bright and curvy drawings; and so forth. Trevor rolls his into a hardened tube and swats Jo Fife over the head with it; Vicky starts worrying at the edges of hers, tattering them. They're instructed not to touch the artworks, nor to stand too near. Then they're led, past two more sets of columns, through the polished mausoleum of the building's inner hall to the side galleries. Once in, they fan out through the rooms, zigzagging from wall to wall as they I-spy; clustering in twos and threes to compare notes and rates of progress; squeezing on to benches or planting themselves cross-legged on the floor to copy titles. Markie ambles his way past hangman figures, scribbled stars and charmingly imperfect circles, undulating harlequins, hanging pendula of heads and limbs, past kites and suns (he ticks that one off) and a snakes-and-ladders game that's left the board to take over a house – up, down, diagonal, the whole space – with cats and fish and jack-in-the-boxes joining in, while the game's die, which has mutated into a cuboid chrysalis, hatches a dragonfly or hornet or who knows what other manner of misshapen insect. He holds his glove-ball to his face each time he pauses in front of a painting, and breathes in its compacted softness while he contemplates the image. The glove-ball is misshapen too; not, strictly speaking, a ball – at least not a sphere – but elongated and with finger-tentacles, also turned felt-side outwards, protruding from its base, a fragile home-made teddy squid or octopus . . .

It's in the third or fourth room that he pauses for the longest. The schoolchild-spread has thinned right out by now; Markie finds himself alone in front of a big picture. The picture shows a kind of skittle-person standing on a beach, throwing a stone at a bird made up of a few basic shapes. The person has a single, massive foot on which he seems to rock; the bird, a punk shock of red hair, a rooster's comb. The person's face is featureless save for a single egg-yolk-yellow eye in which a red-flecked, black-dot pupil sits; the bird's head, similarly, is formed of nothing more than a blue circle with black dots for eye and nose. It also has a tail of crescent moon. Between the figures, bird and person, the stone is a kind of moon, too: pockmarked, half shaded and half bathed in pale-grey light. The person's throwing it at the bird by means of a thin black beam that serves him for an arm, pivoted around a black-dot navel in his skittle-belly: as he rocks back on his swollen foot, the beam seems to rotate or to be catapulted down to fling the stone towards the bird. There's even a dotted line showing the former's trajectory towards the latter, like a cutting dash marked on a dress maker's pattern sheet. The strange thing, even in this strange set-up, is that not only is the stone hurtling towards the bird; the bird, too, seems to be flying *deliberately* towards the stone, its head straining to meet it in mid-flight. Around this drama the beach stretches, empty and yellow as the thrower's egg-yolk eye. Beyond the beach, the sea is black, devoid of boats, swimmers or even waves and swells, patches of light and shade or anything that might communicate the qualities of water. It's not really trying to represent a sea at all – just oil, black and opaque, applied unmixed and undiluted from a paint tube, spread in a horizontal strip across the middle of the canvas. Above it, and above the beach, above the boy and bird and stone, a scumble-mass of dark-green clouds erupts and billows angrily, unfurling from their hems and underhangs more darkness.

Why does Markie stand in front of this one for so long? It's rich in I-spy targets (two moons), but he doesn't tick them off. There's something beyond odd about it, something not right, something – even by the game-rules of this painted world in which he's interloping – *wrong*. It has to do with the bird flying towards the stone rather than from it. With its flaring red coxcomb, its taut semicircle stick-wing, it seems to be springing from some brake or heather off the painting's bottom edge, to rise exultantly towards the stone; to be *willing* the collision. The whole space seems to be willing it. There's an inevitability about it; all the scene's routes and ranges, all its ambits, gradients and courses seem to have been plotted – lines and angles, dots and seams. It's not just that that's wrong, though: there's something else, too … On the beach, the barren and indifferent beach, its jutting shoreline where yellow meets black, two thorn- or fin-shaped sandy points are (just like the dot-eye of the thrower) daubed with red – that is, with blood. Which must mean that the bird's stoning, the event which the painting is showing, has *already* taken place – although it hasn't: this is lead-up, instant-just-before … *That*'s what's wrong – so wrong that Markie feels the need to plant his feet more firmly on the floorboards, to affirm some kind of stable ground or grounding. It could be, he tries to tell himself – it could be that the skittle-person stoned another bird before the curtain on this scene was raised; that he's a serial bird-killer, knocking off one bird after another, *thunk thunk thunk*, all day long; or perhaps part of a bird-hunting party whose other members we can't see … But Markie knows, even as he trots out the explanations inside his head, that they won't hold up: in this painting's universe there's only one bird, and only one person – nothing else. They *are* its universe, locked together in celestial terror, the yellow, lidless and black-centred sun in the thrower's face the only source of light, condemned to gaze unblinkingly, to shine in red-flecked perpetuity on its own crime ...

'Oi! Phocan!'

Trevor has materialised in the room. Has he just slipped in, or has he been here for a while? He, too, seems to have taken in the painting, and to have been taken in by it as well, but in a different way. He's sliding his eyes between it and Markie, back and forth, and beaming a malevolent, complicit smile. The two aren't friends, but Trevor's face, like Nainesh's back in the cubicle, seems to presume some kind of mutual understanding, to signal recognition of a co-conspirator. He's standing a few feet away to Markie's left – or, actually, crouching, head and shoulders lowered almost to waist-level and one foot extended backwards: set, spring-loaded, ready to jump upwards and across. His eyes point at the bird, then at the stone, then at the glove-ball Markie's holding in his right hand.

Markie knows exactly what Trevor wants; the clarity of the communication's almost psychic. It's not from mischievousness or a desire to break rules that he now straightens his right arm; it's the positions, distances, relations ... He's *obeying* rules, scored in the tablet of the canvas. He draws in his stomach, feels his navel turn into a vortex of dark energy, and, stretching his right arm back behind his head, rocks on his suddenly enormous-seeming heel, first back, then – fast, forcefully – forwards, bringing the arm pivoting around its point, the hand swinging down in a dot-arc whose geometric regularity he doesn't need a paintbrush to discern; it's written in the air, in the flight of the glove-ball that the hand releases, hurtling now through the gallery's empty space to meet Trevor's head – which, his legs having propelled his body into momentary flight, is gliding eagerly towards it ...

Thunk. The collision's softer, feltier than bird's and stone's. Nor does Trevor die: he falls back to the floor, feet landing out of sync with one another, torso thudding to a halt above them in a graceless, unaesthetic manner. His fists pump in celebration of some imaginary headed goal – but it's not about him any more: his part's completed; Trevor's body and entire existence can now fall away like spent booster tanks. What it's about now is the glove-ball, which has undergone both course-change and sudden acceleration: contact with Trevor's head has catapulted it back out again – not towards Markie, but across a new, third plane; the one that, in a painting, exists only in illusory or perspectival form, but, in a room, a real room like this gallery, is there, voluminous and light and dusty and traversable. Simply put: the thing is flying through the air towards the picture. For a stretch that lasts a fraction of a second but which Markie, returning to afterwards, will be able to enter and rerun from many, widely spread-out points, he watches, frozen in position (right arm and shoulder lowered in the casting's follow-through) and at the same time plunging forwards with the missile, straight into the clouds, their angry, black-hemmed green ...

Then, with another *thunk* – a clear one that reverberates around the gallery – the glove-ball hits the canvas. It strikes high up and centrally, above and to the right of the picture's own missile, near the arm-beam's apex. Does it actually remain there for a moment, or is this just retinal delay? For what seems like several seconds Markie sees it clinging to the painted surface. Figure, bird, stone, beach and sky and sea all shudder, unsettled by their world's off-centring. Then slowly, almost languidly, the glove-ball peels itself loose and, spent too, drops to the floor. Then nothing: total stasis – in the work, the room, in everywhere and everything. It's like a kind of vacuum. Markie's ears go funny; in the space between them, there's that loud absence of sound that brings with it a sense of vertigo, of cranial expanse beyond all manageable scale. Then, from all around, from every object and each surface – bird and figure, frame and wall, from lights and doorways, benches, exit signs and air, swooping and billowing and bearing down, zeroing in, accusatory and righteous, on him and him alone (Trevor has long since slunk away) – comes the alarm.

The next few things all happen very fast. Adults appear about him in a rush, their limbs and faces merging: Miss Sedge's leather boots are in there somewhere; so are guards' caps and jackets, and clusters of furious mouths working their jaws at him, words lost beneath the electronic wail, and hands grabbing his arms. Markie makes no attempt to evade these. He hasn't moved at all since the alarm went off. There are kids pressing in too: scurrying over to witness the capture, drink in the scene's red-handedness, grab a front seat to the dumbshow kangaroo court in session right before them, watch some ritual of punishment or sacrifice play itself out. They're to be disappointed, though. Markie is bundled from the gallery by a guard who parts the sea of gawkers with an imperious arm-wave; led through a side door marked *Staff Only*; then a fire door, and then down a corridor with concrete, untiled flooring; across a musty locker room in which casual shirts and trousers hang; and, finally, up some rather flimsy metal stairs into a chamber where two more guards – one white, one black – are sitting before a console.

Once here, the warder releases his grip on Markie's arm – and the boy starts to shake. The seated guards watch him for a few seconds; then the white one, turning from him with an air of cold disinterest, asks:

'Where's his mother?'

'He came here with his school,' the warder answers.

'Teacher, then.'

The warder leaves. The white guard turns back to the console, a banked set of TV screens with a control panel beneath them. The black one is still watching Markie. This one's older, with a thickset frame and wavy-electric hair that's greying around the temples. After a while he mumbles:

'Maybe he want some water.'

The white guard glances fleetingly at Markie, then at his colleague, who looks back at him expressionless but firm. They stay this way for three or four seconds; then the white guard clicks his tongue in irritation, rises from his chair and leaves the chamber.

The remaining guard shifts his gaze back leisurely on to the boy. It's an overbearing gaze – but calming, too: after a while Markie realises that the shaking has stopped.

'You want to see the replay?'

The man's voice is deep and slow: the same West Indian bass that Markie's heard on Brixton market stalls and jerk stands, from Rastas in knitted hats grouped around cab-office doors and cafe counters. The alarm's wail that has pursued him all the way to this chamber from the gallery falls quiet.

'You want to see, or not?'

Markie's not sure what the man means. He stands there stupidly, just looking back at him.

'Come.'

He's beckoning him over. Markie comes. The adult guides him to a spot beside his chair from which he, too, can watch the screens. There are nine of these, stacked in three rows of three: regular black-and-white TV sets, like you'd see in the window of an electronics shop – only these ones, rather than parading an array of makes and models to appraising customers, present a wall of identical, repeating units: pared-down, grey-cased monitors whose two black knobs are unadorned by channel markings. They seem, at first, to all be displaying the same scene: a silent room, shown from an overhead, slightly aslant angle. But this is an illusion, brought on by the uniformity of scale and setting: Markie starts to notice that some of the rooms have benches in them, some not; that some have doorway-openings at the screen's left, others at the right, or top, or not at all; that some have one or two people in them, others none, or many. The people move strangely: at normal speed, but with a motion that's somehow imprecise and fluid at the same time, as though they were immersed in water, and the rooms were aquaria. Ever since he passed the restricted staff and fire doors, Markie's had a sense of being backstage, amidst the scaffolding and props not just of the museum but, somehow, of the entire experience he was supposed to undergo here today. This vision now – multiple, partitioned into cubicles whose occupants can't see each other but into each of which he, like an unobserved Britannia, can peer down, or up, or both at the same time – compounds this feeling. It's as though he were looking at another world – another world that is still recognisably *this* one. There are children milling around three of the screens; there, on one of them, is Polly; on another he picks out Nainesh, Vicky … there's Miss Sedge … and there's Trevor, standing alone, trying to busy himself in his worksheet while glancing up from time to time towards the camera, wondering if it has found him out …

The guard switches a button on his console; one of the screens goes blank, then jumps back into life as lines flicker and jag across it. The man's creating this effect by pressing a lever, a small joystick; when his thumb eases off the stick, the jagging stops – and Markie sees a small boy, whom the rolled-up gloves in his right hand as he stands before a figure, bird and landscape drained of colour identify as no one but himself.

'But how … ?' he starts to ask.

The guard pauses the joystick and raises an eyebrow to elicit the question's completion.

'I mean …' Markie tries again, 'I'm here.'

The guard smiles for the first time now.

'I said we'd watch the *replay*,' he tells Markie. 'Look.'

His thumb nudges the joystick to its right. The boy on the requisitioned screen does nothing. He continues to do nothing for some time. The guard nudges the stick further rightwards, scrambling the screen into jagging lines once more; then releases it as a change in the lines' texture betrays the presence of a second figure, entering to the boy's left.

'Here's where it hot up,' the guard murmurs.

Unscrambled once more, same-but-different Markie's arm comes back and forwards, and the glove-ball travels towards same-but-different Trevor's rising head and on into the canvas, all with the dislocated liquid motion everything on these monitors has. The guard is slowly nodding. When he turns once more to face him Markie sees approval written in his features.

'Nice action,' he tells Markie. He pronounces it *ak-shun*. 'Now we go slow' – ditto – 'motion.'

There's more nudging, and more jagging, then the boy stands in the gallery impassive once again. This time his arm comes back in incremental shifts whose constituent units, morphing from one position to the next, seem to arrive in place before each new position's image has established itself – then, no sooner than it has, slink off towards their next position, with the result that the arm, at any given moment, appears to occupy at least two phases of its transit simultaneously.

'Charlie Griffith in his prime,' the guard says fondly. 'Open shoulders, planted feet, head down ...'

Markie's not sure what he means. On another screen another guard, perhaps the one who brought him to this chamber, is talking to Miss Sedge, then gliding discontinuously off with her out of the picture. His guard here is replaying the throw again, pausing it just after the release, as though to contrast Markie's action with that of the figure in the painting that still hangs there as a backdrop. Markie's gaze, though, is drawn away from this by the scene shown on the screen at the stack's bottom-left corner. Against the wooden floorboards of an otherwise deserted gallery, a single person stands: a girl. Her face is turned away, but the headband tells him that it's Bea. Not just the headband: as she breaks now into a walk, away from the camera to her screen's, and the whole screen-bank's, outer border, something about her motion transmits, even through the fish-tank time-lapse of this circuit, clearly to Markie – so clearly that it seems to him almost deliberate, a call ... The monitors are silent, though. The chamber's silent. The West Indian guard has drifted into memories of inswingers in Bridgetown. Miss Sedge and the white guard are gone too, lost in some corridor, some stretch of in-betweenness. It's all happening, and not, in greyscale, here and somewhere else, draining away.

2. Distance Creased

The first thing disgorged by File C16 of the Institute for Industrial Psychology's archive once its binding ribbon has been loosened – the first object to slide from the card folder and lie face-up on Monica Dean's allotted table here in LSE's bright library – is a photograph of women working among tall plants. They're reaching, holding shears up, cutting fruit, which, bending, they deposit in large baskets. The plants (hops or giant runner beans) are tied to poles and laid out in neat rows, beyond which other poles, still taller, hold a net in place around the whole enclosure, sculpting its mesh-pattern into sags and apexes, like ones you get in circus tents or radio cages. On the photo's reverse side there's a handwritten caption: *Agricultural labourers, England, 1882.*

The file's next photograph shows women feeding cotton into machines that scutch, willow and gather it on spools which, arranged in a ring, themselves feed a larger, central twist-spool. In the next picture – same year, 1889 – this twist-spool, or one like it, has in turn become a spinning chorus girl alongside scores of others: circled layers of spools stacked in a tower that looms above the solitary woman tending to the doubling winder, threading its central bobbin, making sure each fibrous tendril's tautened to the correct stretch and temper. For a second, this operator (faceless, since her back is to the camera, hence to Dean) takes on the look of a performer, mastering a harp or piano. This impression quickly passes, though. Her posture has nothing commanding about it: bowed head, outstretched arm and crooked back seem held by the cords, not the other way round – governed by them, like the limbs and torso of an old marionette.

Each file has the same type of ribbon round it, pink. They make them look like gifts, like chocolate boxes, perfume cases – or the briefs that Dean's used to preparing for D&G's barristers. If there's a ritual element to legal procedure, there's one also to these holdings' presentation to her: how the wooden elevator bears them up from hidden stacks; the slow glide of the archivist from the dispensing station through the waist-high turnstile separating restricted and (by prior appointment) public zones; the way Dean has to don white gloves to handle them ... Then image after image of these century-and-a-half-old people planted in rows, on floors, in trestles. Most of them, buried in their tasks, seem unaware they're being recorded; occasionally, one will look back at the camera in a manner that seems neither defiant nor inquisitive, but just resigned: one more piece of equipment ...

Here's a line of women on high stools beside a workbench, peering through stand-clamped magnifying lenses at cogs and gears they've picked at random from a belt that trundles by in front of them. It's more recent: 1925, a caption, typed this time, informs her ... *By increasing stool-distance from bench to 18 inches, shadow on working point eliminated. Strain reduced by 5% through consequent adjustment in arm-angle* ... There are more like this in the next file: women at benches, tables, spindles; belts and cables all around them – horizontal, vertical, aslant; wire, rollers, wheels and hooks. There are men, too, stranding, vulcanising, cooking, pressurising, insulating, braiding; reeling lengths of cable on huge turntables that, like the cotton feeders' spools, feed onwards, up to huger wheels; working with iron, rubber, lead. They're making bridge-parts, painting cookers ... *25% of painting time saved by introduction of flat for round brush having wider spread* ... They're fitting diodes into speakers and assembling batteries; assembling hoovers, fridges, tractors; moulding golf balls, aeroplane tyres, rubber gloves they quality-control by slipping on to cast-iron testing-hands that run in a saluting guard-of-honour line above the conveyor (also rubber); truing bicycle wheels by turning them in automated stands whose mechanisms are driven by belts wrapped around more bicycle wheels ...

Here's a strange one: female workers at a hairbrush factory, perched beside buffers. They're taking almost-completed brushes from wheel-mounted bins that sit just to the left of each of them and holding these up to their buffers (set into the workspace's back wall at the same, regular interval as the workers: twenty women, twenty buffers) – which, Dean deduces from both the blurred texture of the buffers' surface and the scene's implied mechanics, must be spinning: the women are distress-texturing the reverse-side of each hairbrush's head, thereby preparing it to double as a clothes brush. Attached to the photo is a sheet of text that's typed, but not directly: there's no dent or imprint in the paper, and the lettering, faint and purple, suggests an early form of photostat-ting – incorrectly executed, since the text's column has been sliced right down the middle, its left-hand portion censored or redacted:

> ed the buffer to sit comfortably at
> s were adjustable in height and distance
> creased by 12%

Dean holds the sheet up, draws photo and caption closer to her, then extends her arm again. It makes no difference: the women keep their backs turned, and continue plying their buffers. Their own hair is covered by cloth hats, from beneath which the odd wisp snakes out to curl across a cheek. Phantom images, sediment left in Dean's mind by childhood bookshelves full of harems, handmaid-ens and vestals, hover about the picture, transforming these drab factory girls into ladies-in-waiting tending to an empress, combing and re-combing untwined tresses, chaste and decorous through afternoons in the royal bedchamber, an enclave closed off from the world of men, of time, soft music drifting in from neighbour-ing rooms, from halls and ballrooms, foyers, cabinets, saloons . . .

She's been holding this buffer photo for a while now. Why? Not sure. What does it tell her? Nothing. On, then: she has work to do. She has instructions.

3. The Ten Commandments for Depicting Space Travel in Movies

Or, just: *The Ten Commandments* – the rest is self-evident, from the context. The title's new; the format is more punchy. It runs, as it stands, like this:

1. Physics – condensed, applied, particular, molecular, atomic, photonic, planetary, plasma, nuclear, nano-, astro-, geo- and etcetero- – this shall be thy Lord and God. Physics has built your spaceship; it has raised it from the bondage of the earth and is propelling it to wheresoever you boldly are going. It is a jealous god: make graven images to other ones – particularly to the god of aesthetics, whose idol is the harlot of sensual perception – and it will visit the iniquity of the fathers upon the children, unto the third and fourth generation, yea even to the end of thy franchise's line.

2. Thou shalt not show thy astronauts perambulating over alien planets as though they were strolling through Central Park. Just look at Arnie (slide 1) wandering about the Martian landscape here: even a body as solid and muscular as his would weigh about a third of what it does on Earth. Ever wondered why Armstrong and Aldrin bounce around on those Moon-landing films? (If some smartass quips *Because they're faked* then I shall commandeer his body and dispatch it to the Marshall Space Flight Center's Antimatter Lab for instant condensation and annihilation!) On Jupiter, the scales tilt in

the other direction: there, you'd weigh in at almost three times your terrestrial load. Each time you raised your thigh and knee to take a forward step, it'd be like (slide 2) training on a leg press pegged to max.

3. Thou shalt not let thy FX boys create giant, billowing explosions every time a starship fighter or space station is destroyed. That they're being overpaid to cook up stuff that looks cool isn't an excuse for contravening basic laws of possibility. For an explosion, or any form of combustion, you need oxygen – and there is no oxygen in space. Look at these (slide 3) flames in *Starship Troopers*: they're even licking upwards (flag on that too; there's no 'up' or 'down' in outer space) round the vessels' hulls. And when the vessels deflagrate completely, we get huge booms – which, by dint of the aforementioned lack of oxygen or similar medium through which sound-waves might travel, is equally impossible. Kubrick, by contrast, gets it more or less right in *2001: A Space Odyssey*: when Bowman (slide 4) blows *Discovery One*'s hatch to re-enter the ship, there's an *im*plosion, playing out in a vacuum, and in silence ...

Ben Briar turns his face to the plane's window. Outside, through the triple membrane, he can see the transatlantic predawn stretched round the earth's curvature, a triple membrane too: haze, cloud, permafrost landmass. They must be somewhere above Newfoundland or Greenland. Troposphere and Arctic gauze, whisky on ice, his PowerPoint presentation. In *Interstellar*, on the scientist Mann's ammonia-rich planet, frozen clouds furnish an upper ground that can be walked on – which is bullshit too: ice couldn't hang suspended like that. He should add this; maybe in Commandment Number 9, the gravity one ...

4. Honour the laws of speed and distance. A radio signal from Earth would take twenty minutes to arrive at Mars, our next-door-neighbour planet. If you're being a little

more adventurous, and sending missions to the far end of the galaxy, you can extend that period to months, or even years. Instantaneous telecommunication, back-and-forth *deploy-the-heat-shield/how's-the-wife/are-the-fish-biting* repartee between Mission Control and Canis Major, is a major no-no. If an astronaut picks up a message while careening through Andromeda or Triangulum, it's a safe bet that its sender died more than a century ago.

And on that note:

5. Thou shalt not have thy hero travel back in time. As Einstein showed us, time can warp and stretch, but neither he nor any other scientist with an ounce of credibility has ever claimed it can run backwards. The only property capable of moving across dimensions is (q.v. Commandment Number 9) gravity. Even if time travel *were* possible (and once again: it's not), to effect it would require more that the sum total of all energy existing in the universe. Having journeyed to the past, you couldn't do anything when you got there, and there wouldn't even be a 'there' to get to and do nothing at. The fantasy that you can go back to a 1930s high-school prom, screw your own grandmother, stop World War Two from taking place and change the outcome of the 1953 World Series is precisely that: a fantasy ...

Is the grandmother bit too risqué? It isn't Disney he'll be dealing with in London. Degree Zero are hip's *ne plus ultra*; or as hip as you can be with a turnover north of fifty mil a year. And judging from the specs, this project itself must be budgeted at roughly double that. It's a grand space opera in the *Star Wars* mould, with princesses, kidnappers, pirates, smugglers; imperial federations gathering tribute from surrounding vassal-planets, rates for which are renegotiated every solar cycle at galactic councils in the recesses of whose auditoria, corridors and ambassadorial docking bays secret alliances are proffered, struck, betrayed ... Briar's got the treatment right here, wedged beneath his whisky glass. It's written by one Norman Berul, and it's crawling with cardinal errors. Take this scene, in which the lover of a dowry-bearing, peace-cementing bride-to-be signals his paramour (said betrothed – though not to him) by means of lasers flickering in the sky above her royal chamber, projected from his ship lying just outside the stratosphere of her intended's (who is also his adoptive uncle's) planet … Setting aside the fact that, if the pining bride can see it, so (presumably) can the cuckolded king and all his courtiers, servants, general subjects, right down to the space drunk pissing in the alleyway outside the planetary dive bar – even overlooking that fact, the scene is a non-starter, since … Briar sets the printout, water-marked by the glass-base's condensation, down again and moves Commandment Number 7 up one place:

6. Know this: lasers cannot be seen in space. The laser-pointers stoners whip out when they're tripping at Dead concerts –

change Dead reference; these kids weren't even born

– at techno clubs are visible because the air in auditoria and warehouses is saturated with dust particles. Same in your bedroom: it's because you never vacuum that you can amuse yourself by making your cat (slide 5) overbalance as he clutches at the red or green line he can see but not touch. You bastard. But in space – no dust, no cats, no line. That room's been vacuumed: it's *all* vacuum. Weapons-grade beams might blow holes through your spaceship's hull, but you won't see them. Even if you were a Jedi warrior, you wouldn't see a laser beam, let alone be granted the reaction time to parry it with your own sabre. Light travels at the speed of … yes, light. A reflex that kicks in before the thing to which it is a reflex has been registered by the reflective agent isn't a reflex but a temporal conundrum that (q.v. Commandment Number 5) is an abomination in the eyes of Physics.

7. These things matter. One hundred and fifty years ago President (slide 6) Lincoln helped charter the National Academy of Sciences. Why? Because he grasped that an understanding of science by the populace was of prime importance to modernity and progress, to the republic, to democracy itself. The other road, the path of ignorance and superstition, leads straight back to Salem. And maybe, just maybe, Lincoln also intuited the role that speculation, entertainment, the imagination would play in the new republic's future. After all, didn't its creation both demand and entail one giant imaginative leap? Physics, for all its evidence-based leanings, is a creative journey too, a plunge into the far-flungest –

farthest-flung

– farthest-flung reaches of imagination. We fold space inside out in an attempt to picture how the universe is shaped. We tease parallel worlds from the peepholes of boxes that have cats inside (we're bastards too). We smash particles together at insane speeds just for the thrill of seeing what will happen. And all these activities cost (slide 7) money, and (slide 8) more money, and (slide 9) more money. We scientists burn our way through so much money as to make your own extravaganzas' price tags look like collection-box spare change. Where does our money come from? Government. And what shapes Government's budgetary policy? Public opinion. If Joe Public ain't excited by the prospect of discovering the Higgs boson and unlocking multiverses, Congress don't send us the tax dollars to discover and unlock them.

8. That's where you guys come in: you are our interface. Through you, we seed the public with a love of science. And we're your interface as well: to credibility, to disbelief-suspension, to all that Aristotle-101 shit. If the set-up in your flick doesn't look *plausible*, your viewers aren't transported,

or enchanted, or even willing to part with their own cash to see your movie in the first place. Which is bad – for you, for us, for everyone. We're your safeguard against that eventuality, just as you're ours against our own supply-chain cut-off. It's symbiotic: hummingbird and bee balm, gut and good bacteria, pilot fish and shark. Which, to bring things back round to our own point in the multiverse, our current fragile patch of space-time, is why you've invited me here to your lovely and impressive studios – and why I, as Two Cultures Consultancy's Senior Partner, have accepted said invitation. Which brings us . . .

Briar lifts his glass again, takes a sip, then eases back into his seat, lumbar-support pads rising to meet contours of his spine and ribs. NASA never used to fly him first class. Fifty-eight, he's a boy in a toyshop in this setting – has to suppress an urge to press each button, plug some lead or other into every socket, find skin surfaces on which to smear each of his courtesy toiletry-pouch unctions. He part-lowers his laptop's lid and activates his pod's free-standing entertainment console. Comedy. *The Big Bang Theory*: why not? Here's the Aspergic Sheldon in his living room, debating with his neuroscientist girlfriend Amy rules pertaining to dilemmas thrown up by some hypothetical Dungeons and Dragons game-turn. Amy is, as always, cold and logical. Sheldon, by contrast, plays it camp and passionate: he's genuinely hurt that she can't see the in-play permutation his way, paces agitatedly about the set, holding back tears. Behind him, there's a whiteboard, covered with the algebraic shorthand Sheldon and his pals are always scrawling. Briar hits *pause* on his armrest-set and, squinting, peers at the image closely, scrutinising the notation.

It's a Feynman diagram, with straight, arrow-bearing black lines and wiggly, plain blue ones modelling the procession of fermions and photons through an interaction sequence. Someone's done their homework: all the vertexes have one arrow line travelling in to meet the sine line and another travelling out again, slanted at forty-five degrees. Positrons are labelled $e+$, electrons $e-$, photons with a gamma, γ. Briar thrusts out his lower lip and nods approvingly, tilting his drink at the screen as he raises glass to mouth once more. Just as the liquid hits his tongue, though, the satisfaction it's about to consecrate is rudely snatched away, evaporated from his very palate, by the sight of ... What's this? At the whiteboard's bottom right we've got a kaon, composed of both up and strange antiquarks (u, $\bar{s}$: fine), breaking down into three pions ($\pi+$, $\pi+$ and $\pi-$: fine too), with two intermediate steps that involve a W boson (blue $W+$: good) and a gluon (green g: all good) – but the gluon, whose procession should be indicated by a spiral, is instead being represented by a zigzag that in turn spawns branches to which arrows have been added willy-nilly, like so many sprouting leaves ... which, as any Caltech nerd would know, is totally ridiculous. It makes a mockery of the diagram, the characters, the scene, the show's whole universe. To go that far, do all the research, then ...

Briar swallows, but it's tasteless. He raises his laptop's lid again:

9. Black holes. Don't get me started on black holes ...

– but finds that he can't concentrate. He throws the remnants of his whisky, watery by now, ice caps all CO_2ed, down his throat's hatch and pings for service, orders up a new one. Zigzags. When the stewardess has left he flips his laptop lid shut, stows the thing away and scrolls on through his in-flight entertainment system's menu, settling eventually on the cartoon channel.

4. Corydon and Galatea

Dr Mark Phocan, M.Sc., C.Eng., shunning the quads and cupolas and college lawns that pull the disembarking trainloads eastwards, drives past Oxford station, dips under the tracks and heads away from the town centre towards Botley. A minute or two later, somewhere past the hump of Osney Bridge but before Binsey Lane bus stop, he crosses the unmarked boundary beyond which the city's aura, like a Wi-Fi signal, stops transmitting: from here onwards, church halls and day schools are no longer photogenic; restaurants are unable to charge heritage supplements; lamp-posts, paving stones and bollards lie abandoned to their unaugmented there-ness. When the drab parades of newsagents, launderettes and betting shops in their turn taper off, to be replaced by megastores set back behind vast lots, generic signage – Currys, Jewson, Pets at Home – more vibrant than the saplings planted around each concession's border, Phocan's mood shifts, as it does each time he makes this journey, to the kind of neutral that's brought on by the awareness that he could be anywhere at all in Britain; anywhere, at least, that's nowhere.

Beyond this, it's park-and-ride and ring-road territory – plus, not for Phocan, who's been trundling down this route for several years now, but invariably for first-time visitors since the side road hasn't been uploaded into TomTom, Garmin or CoPilot, a confused spin round the McDonald's drive-thru or three-pointer in the Enterprise returns zone before retracing in the opposite direction, west-to-east, the stretch just prior to the large inter-section of A420 and B4044, cab driver asking if they're sure they've got the right address, *ain't nothing else around here*; then, just as the phone's coming out, emails are being popped open, thumb-tapped signature-address spawning a blue pin that seems to hover, what the fuck, above their very car – *that's* when they generally spot the turn-off, unnamed and un-signposted, for Finns Business Park. It's an estate un-parklike as they come, consisting of a main drive from which offshoots lead either to dead ends or, looping, back round to the drive, flanked or plugged in either case by plain industrial units. Phocan's pulling up and parking beside one of these units now: a low-lying semi-prefab, ground floor brick, upper corrugated iron, entirety dwarfed by an electricity pylon whose wires run above (but not quite along the same axis as) its long rectangular roof. On the main door, beneath a logo that depicts a sheep and stick, words legible only to those who, like him, have already approached them announce the unit's occupant as Pantarey Motion Systems, Private Limited Company no. 4037859, Est. 1982.

The sheep, yes ... A story goes with that. It seems Pantarey's founder, Anthony (Tony) Garnett, suffered from insomnia. Since adolescence he'd been fed the old canard about sheep-counting, which piece of trite folk-wisdom he'd summarily dismissed as nonsense – until, during a trip to Western Australia on which he was (as you'd expect) beset with jet-lag, he found himself replaying across the inside of his eyelids well into the small hours images of sheep that he'd observed moving through gates, into and out of dip-troughs and so forth about his cousin's farm the previous day. These images weren't really painterly, or even cinematic: they were more – let's say – *schematic,* their schematism in its turn presenting a conceptual quandary. What most stood out for him was the way the movements, the displacements – the real ones from which these night-time shadow-plays were drawn – were at once beyond a certain point quite unpredictable *and* governed by a general drive or aim: that of Cousin Dermot to manoeuvre the animals from Point A to Point B. Garnett pictured dots in space – the location of such-and-such animal at a given moment, the corresponding location of such-and-such another one at the same instant, then another (animal/instant/both) – conjoined by lines: of transit, detour, switchback; lines themselves dictated by the general flow of the collective, or collected, mass and by the less mechanical yet no less operative strings of need, fear, rivalry and yearning linking one sheep to another, to their power-of-life-or-death-commanding master and his dogs – a set of shifting hook-ups that, while chaotic and perhaps so endlessly self-modulating as to fall within the category Random, paradoxically displayed, when taken at the level of the whole, the spectacle of order and control in action, of harmony unfolding across the gradient field of a muddy and fly-saturated pasture. There must be, Garnett told himself as the first wisps of daylight crept in round the curtains, some way of *comprehending*, or at least of capturing, not simply at the level of the field's totality, but also at the scale of its constituent parts and moments, its haptic and recursive structure, the temporo-spatial information hiding, like so many Ithacans, beneath the wool and bleats and nervous little leaps, of somehow *rendering* this information, setting it to work. For Western Australian farmers? Perhaps not – but Garnett sensed immediately that the implications of his dawn ruminations had far wider scope. For the next week, the sheep, the real ones, much to simple Dermot's chagrin, were fitted with reflectors, magnets, paint-drippers, track-scoring styluses and all manner of passage-indicating prostheses. Garnett's insomnia remained unresolved (it got worse) – but Pantarey grew from these preoccupations, these antipodean gambols. Whence the logo.

Phocan, like all his colleagues, has served up this foundation myth repeatedly to the clients he leads through, or pauses beside, this door. Is it entirely true? Who cares? The man's a father to the company, a shepherd to his flock. The stick was depicted, for Pantarey's first three decades, as a staff or crook (though Garnett toyed with the idea of showing it with keys and stoppers, like a flute). On the logo's redesign in 2012, it turned into a non-specific object, evocative of data wands, airport-security sticks and the like;

the sheep itself grew semi-abstract, half a cloud. 2012 was also the year that Pantarey's IT Officer Yusuf Hossain implemented, company-wide, the security protocol (for scanning foreign drives, writers and the like for viruses and malware) known as Sheep Dipping – unconnected (that software's ownership lay elsewhere) to the firm's origins; but for Garnett the coincidence served as a confirmation, token that some kind of wheel, in running through its generational revolutions, had carved his personal iconography into the columns of the industry's own temple, laid down his intellectual sediment in its very bedrock.

Past the door, in lieu of a lobby or reception, there's a cube-shaped space inside which sits, atop a wooden plinth, a glass display case that, in turn, contains another cuboid frame, a rudimentary box that's been built around yet one more box: a Pentax camera – Garnett's, circa 1978. This last, innermost object always, even to Phocan, born long enough ago to vaguely recall parents' necks being strung with such albatrosses, never mind to the dig-nat majority who traipse past it, appears as eerie and outlandish as would (say) a similarly encased hand-cranked chocolate grinder, copper steam-iron or Canopic jar. Behind the first layer of transparent glass, the camera's lens, opaque and Cyclopic, passively malevolent, holds both Phocan's figure and the small blocks of Finns, sky and general daylight that have wandered through the door with him into the entrance chamber captive on its surface, flattened in gnomonic whirl. VGA leads that seem as thick (proportionally at least) as early transatlantic cables emerge from the innermost box, snake their way through purpose-drilled holes in the extra wooden casing, then coil and gather against the display's outer border, fraying into skin-shedding cross-sections. When Garnett first designed the thing – and that is what this is, no model but the very one, his prototype motion translator – these led to an IBM processor larger than this whole room, the display of which component on the plinth would, naturally, present a certain obstacle of scale. Instead of trying to surmount or circumvent this, the space's designers have opted to affix to the wall above the cabinet, in vinyl lettering, a passage first in Greek:

λέγει που Ἡράκλειτος ὅτι πάντα χωρεῖ καὶ οὐδὲν
μένει . . . δὶς ἐς τὸν αὐτὸν ποταμὸν οὐκ ἂν ἐμβαίης
(Πλάτων)

then, below, in English:

Heraclitus says: Everything flows and nothing remains still . . .
You cannot step into the same stream twice
(Plato)

Garnett himself provided the translation. His first discipline, before Engineering, was Classics: he studied it right here in Oxford – up the road, back past the station, sherry and spires and 1890 issues of *American Journal of Philology* that you had to blow the dust off before reading in a library that (as he has often told his incredulous staff) you could actually *smoke* in, Corydon proclaiming his doomed love for Galatea in dactylic hexameters, Magdalen's own deer-park pastoral ... A world not Phocan's: he's straight kinetics, Bristol to Imperial to Pantarey. Streams may be one-use-only, but the staircase leading on beyond the entrance chamber he's ascended many times, passed again and again the photographs that flank it, framed pictures of sensor-fitted athletes, soldiers, actors; of drones, robots and virtual assembly lines, all culminating in an upper landing-level picture that shows nothing more than strings of data, jiggling luminescent on a screen. Past this, behind another door, a corridor zags sharply, first one way then another, through the upper floor, like a right-angled maze; and, maze-like too, it seems to defy spatial logic, spawning rooms that extend further than they should be able to before bumping against the passageway's next parallel or perpendicular avenue – offices, workshops, server-repositories ... Phocan, navigating the dark space with ease, glimpses in one of these rooms a collection of dummy heads and torsos in various stages of completion and/or demolition – sight which, though familiar, always makes him cast his eyes about in search of a frustrated Q who'll cluck impatiently *Now pay attention, 007 …*

It's not Q or his spectre he'll be meeting today, though: it's M – the man himself, sheep-contemplator, motion- and ancient poetry-translator, temple-inscriber, bedrock-impregnator and, more prosaically, employer. In the most well appointed of the labyrinth's chambers he finds Garnett at his desk, perusing diagrams of satellite dishes from which phalanxes of numbers (all Arabic) and letters (some Latin, others Kanji) radiate.

'Mark.'

The *Markie* disappeared some three decades ago, about the same time as his glove-ball. Still, there's something strangely infantile about being addressed in this way, first-name, by this older man. The informality's not bidirectional:

'Mr Garnett. You wanted to see me.'

Garnett motions for him to sit down.

'Have our lovebirds arrived yet?' he asks.

'I don't know,' Phocan answers. 'I just got here myself.'

'You drove from London?'

'Yes. I could have given them a lift; or picked them up from the station – although I don't know what they look like.' He tries to picture the awaited guests sharing a taxi, performing the habitual lost divagations – which prompts him to ask: 'Are they a couple? Have they even *met* before?'

'Not sure,' says Garnett. 'All I know is they're students. At it all the time, couple or not.' He chuckles to himself, then asks: 'How's Lucy shaping up?'

The question takes Phocan aback. Lucy's the intern, the apprentice. It's not Garnett's enquiring after her that's disconcerting; it's the segue. Before he answers, he scrutinises the worn face across the desk, probing its eyes for some flicker of innuendo, or … There's nothing. If there's a proxy wish written there, it's one less carnal than concerned, in a *paterfamilias* way, with the moulding of charges, shaping of futures.

'Fine,' he eventually responds. 'She's curious.'

'What's curious about her?'

'No, I mean she shows an intellectual curiosity.'

'That bodes well,' Garnett says. 'She went to Tokyo with you?'

'Yes,' Phocan nods. 'The JAXA work's advancing nicely.'

'So I see.' Garnett taps the satellite-filled pages on the desk in front of him. 'Talking of outer space: how's the Degree Zero project panning out?'

'Good too,' Phocan reports. 'I'm visiting them next week. *Incarnation.*' He speaks this last word in false deep-tone, as though voicing a trailer. 'It's actually three or four projects: there's the modelling of objects; there's the plotting of various movements – in one scene, movements perhaps not unlike our target ones today ...'

'Perhaps not.' Garnett now taps his nose. 'Always good to keep an eye open for lateral applications ...'

'And then,' Phocan goes on, 'there's a disaggregation scene: a spaceship, super complex. They've got the water-tank people at VWS working with initial gross models. But I thought that we might also try to sound out NW, the wind-tunnel crowd, when I go there next month with the Austrians, the ...'

'That's exciting,' Garnett cuts in.

'What is?'

'The wind tunnel. First time we'll have trialled PIV. It could be a stepping stone to going fully markerless in high-precision situations.'

'Let's hope so,' Phocan says. 'I was at BAE again just a few days ago, and tried to discuss using markerless on unmanned aerials with your friend Pilkington, but couldn't get much from him – certainly no commitment to expanding contract terms. He doesn't talk much.'

'He's a complex figure. Lots of skeletons.' Garnett's face turns contemplative, slightly melancholy even. 'But in any case,' he picks up, brightening again, 'we're way out in front. Nobody's close to us on pose-estimation and deep learning-based tracking ...'

'There's still lots of noise inside our data,' Phocan cautions. 'Even Physis 6. With markerless, mean absolute error goes right up to thirty millimetres – way too much.'

'And with markered?'

'Less than ten – mainly due to skin artefact. When we do skin-less, with cadavers, error drops to almost zero; though cadaveric evaluation has its own limitations, in terms of movement ...'

'Kasper thinks ...' Garnett begins, but this time Phocan interrupts:

'Kasper's put all his eggs in the T-pattern basket. The problem with that is ...'

'I know, I know,' Garnett holds up a stilling hand. 'I've heard you out on this, just as I've heard out Kasper on the pitfalls of your faith in quintic and spline fillers. You two,' he chuckles again, 'are my Jacob and my Esau, tussling over inheritance – which makes me like Isaac, old and blind ...'

'I wouldn't call you blind,' Phocan dutifully reassures him.

'We all are.' Garnett brushes the offering away. 'That's what makes our whole schtick possible. We're shooting photons through the darkness, hoping for some bounce-back, for some ping of ...'

The sentence tapers off. He seems distracted, as though listening to something only he can hear.

'Of what?' prompts Phocan.

'... of something,' Garnett answers vaguely. 'Certainty, enlightenment ... I don't know ...'

Now Phocan can hear it too: the sound of the building's front door opening again, of voices in the entrance chamber, new arrivals being regaled with anecdotes of restlessness and sheep. That Garnett, despite the diminished aural powers that go with age, should have picked it up before him must be down to an attunement, to some sensory affinity with the very passages and walls, the bricks and girders of this complex that he's built from his own head, spun out of half-sleep. Rising now, his boss announces:

43

'That's our amorous pair.'

The two of them step out, process past rooms in which more dummies are dotted about. The heads are black and featureless, the torsos, too, their 'skin' being formed of tightly knitted cloth to which are affixed silver nipples – not, in the cause of realism, on the pectoral area, but everywhere, prolifically, bubbling like plague boils out of arm, buttock, midriff, thigh. More nipples lie around: in plastic drawers, on workbenches, strewn all across the floor. They've been both hand- and purpose-made by guests of Her Majesty lodged on the other side of town, HMP Bullingdon – markers, new 'pearl' ones, perfectly spherical (the old type, mummified in reflector tape, presented folds and rifts that broke light up into divergent planes – good enough for first-pass overviews but about as helpful as a broken lens or randomising feature when it comes to more exacting capture). Some dummies are mounted on bases, upright; others lie prostrate where they've fallen, like Pompeians; in one corner of a workshop a whole mound of them is piled up in a crate, victims awaiting resurrection by some situation, some scenario, however temporary, of approximated life ...

They'll have to wait, though: the humans have their own scenario to bring to life today. Phocan follows Garnett on towards the capture studio. This comes after two more turns, beyond another set of doors: the building's central and most cavernous space, known simply as The Cell. Velveteen, rubber-floored, rectangular, The Cell is draped at intervals with black cloth – sometimes stapled in large redacting squares to its white walls, sometimes hanging down from hooks, like arrases or theatre curtains. Theatre-like as well are the long aluminium rails that run along the border of the wall and ceiling like an offset and unornamental cornicing – and run perpendicularly to this too, brace-affixed to each of the room's transoms, while a central length of the same railing, held in place by longer pendular bracing, cuts along the ceiling's middle, intersecting with each of the cross-rails so that the overall rail-structure forms an enclosed and enclosing frame, a kind of involuted exoskeleton. Hanging in turn from this, their wires coiled round their beam-trellis in creeper-like profusion, are a set of light-emitting cameras: Pantarey's own HDI220s, upgraded this year to incorporate FGPA and DSP, 120 fps with 16-megapixel sensors and four LED-rings with 850-nanometre spacing – in short, the latest word in sensing-recording tech.

Phocan glances at the numbers on the cameras, printed large and white on the black surface of each: 1, 2, 3, on up to 12, as laid out in the specs that he and Kasper Sennet handed the technicians three days ago. Sennet's already here in The Cell, talking to Biomach's emissary. The cameras are positioned round the aerial boundary of a square that has been formed within the larger rectangle down on the floor, its edges demarcated by white tape. To one side of this square, they've set up several chairs and two desks. On the latter, spread out in a phalanx, are five monitors, on each of which the surface area of the taped square that they abut is shown – not in a photographic manner, but rather as a topographic layout. The depiction varies from screen to screen. One represents the nipple-studded objects lying within the square; another the same objects and arrangement twelve times, from twelve different angles; a third homes right in on a single marker, both enlarging it and placing it in cross-hairs at whose intersection point its pixels shimmer, like a desert sun or target in a sniper's long-range viewfinder. A fourth portrays the sight-lines issuing from each of the feed-cameras, and their points of intersection – multiple, converging in the air above the floor into ever tighter clusters round the bed and bedside table and flowers. Despite their differences, one feature all screens have in common is their division of the floor-square into regular white sub-squares that overlay its plain black rubber surface with a grid. The fifth screen simply shows this grid, aslant and foreshortened, from above – from right above: not only, that is, from above the grid but from above the overhanging cameras as well, such that the cameras themselves are rendered as numbered square-cone shapes hovering in a ring about the scene: twelve Olympians gazing down bright-eyed, *glaucopis*, on the stage.

45

Was a bed mentioned? There's indeed one here: the largest of the floor's three objects. Though represented on the screens as no more than a rectangular parallelepiped, it is, in its material reality, a genuine queen double: memory-foam mattress, white Egyptian cotton sheet (200 thread count), two Siberian goose-down pillows – subject of debate, these, when they configured the space: Sennet argued that they'd break the sight-lines; Phocan countered by affirming their necessity to some of the requisite, you know, *manoeuvres*. Next to this, the bedside table, plain, white, unadorned save for – third and final object (objects really) – a vase bearing flowers. Yes, flowers: a bunch of freesias. Why not? Romance lives, even in the grid. Besides which, they don't want the scene to be too arid or (despite its end) too clinical, lest other flowers droop or fail to spread and blossom. What they need is a warm, intimate setting – or a set, laid out here before the *theori* both human and *ex machina*, awaiting only actors for its drama to begin.

And here they are, being led in now by curious Lucy Diamond: a woman and a man, mid-twenties. Their arrival has provoked much interest here at HQ – no mean feat, since they've had lots of famous people through these doors over the years: top football players, pop stars ... Nothing quite like this, though. Neither face is recognisable, and their names, were they known to the general staff, would garner no reaction – but somehow, not long after Garnett had picked up their presence, everybody else had too, the knowledge travelling from floor to floor. A professional demeanour's been maintained by all whom the two visitors passed in the corridors or workshops; faces set to neutral-friendly, welcoming nods nodded; but there's still a *frisson* that can't be suppressed, hanging about the air. Are they good-looking? Sure – but not strikingly so. The woman has brown hair, wavy and shoulder-length; the man's is black and short, matching the stubble on his face. He's wearing jeans, jumper and jacket; she has culottes, trainers, a loose-hanging shirt ... They're both Caucasian; she has slightly darker skin than him. Students, Garnett said: Phocan wonders what type. He and Eldridge, the Imperial gang, never looked that insouciant. Maybe art students. *Are* they a couple? If they've just met for the first time – on the train, or at the station, on the platform, in the taxi as they whipped their phones out, popped their blue pins – then it would have made for quite an interesting conversation ...

Once Diamond, same age as the pair (perhaps the reason, it strikes Phocan now, for Garnett's thought-progression in his office a few moments ago) has deposited them in The Cell, it's Sennet who takes them in hand. He explains how motion capture works, shows them the nipples, trying to be as deadpan as he can as he pronounces the word, *nipples*, but he can't today and breaks into a smile, which thankfully both visitors return. He then introduces them to Jayani Perera, Hip Specialist at Biomach, this session's client. Perera, in turn, explains today's field of enquiry – namely, the stress that's placed, by the positions commonly (or indeed uncommonly) encountered during heterosexual intercourse, on femur, ball and acetabulum (how much, precisely, by each varying position, where, and for which partner), the concomitant risks of impingement, or even dislocation, in sexually active (and why shouldn't they be?) beneficiaries of total arthroplasty. As she talks, she first sculpts hip-joints in the air, running her palms round globed caput femoris, ringed zona orbicularis and the outlines of ischia and ilia, sliding her fingers up and down greater, lesser and third trochanters, all spectral. After a while, her hands default to her body, pointing at her own hips as she pushes them forwards and withdraws them in a manner as innocuous and unsuggestive as the context allows, which is not very. But at some point these hands start travelling – first to the man, whose loins she draws slowly forward through their thrusting range, then to the woman, whose waist she leads through its inverse and corresponding motion.

The pair allow their bodies to be guided by Perera: a seal's been broken, border crossed; from here on in, they're part of the equipment. Phocan and Diamond are now able, without any awkwardness, to convey them to their respective changing areas, formed by the hanging from the rails of more velvet sections.

Phocan takes the man, Diamond the woman. Having invited his charge to strip, Phocan starts sticking markers to his skin: around the waist, across the thigh, the buttocks, in a column up the backbone to T-junction at the shoulders and perform a switchback down each arm; then a few outliers – on calves and ankles, cheeks and forehead – to help mark overall bodily outline.

'Won't some of these come off when we … you know, with the movement?' the man asks.

'Don't worry,' Phocan tells him. 'We've got plenty on you. We can afford to lose a few.' It is a problem, though – one he's discussed with Sennet, failing to find much of a solution other than this overcompensation, this profusion that makes of this poor student's flesh a nipple-cushion as densely studded as the dummy-torsos. 'But if you notice one has come off,' he adds, 'leave it on the bed; don't stick it back on. It would have a slightly new position on you, which would feed us bad coordinates.'

'Will you be here?' the man asks. 'In the room, I mean?'

'Normally we would,' Phocan answers. 'But in this instance you'll be left alone. The sensors will be on, the disks recording. But it's not a film: they're just transcribing movement. Nobody will see your faces; nobody will *see* you at all. And it's not recording sound …'

He pauses; in the silence muted gasps, imagined sighs of pleasure flitter about their ears. Phocan looks the man up and down, checking the distribution. The legs are thin and hairy, turning smooth and waxy at the hips. He pictures the woman's thighs wrapped around these, which prompts him to remove from each the highest marker. Of the two he's just unpicked, he retains one but – final touch – sticks the other to the man's lower forehead, like a bindi on a Hindu bridegroom: Vedic third eye, intuition … He hands him a bathrobe – a kimono, still virginally plastic-wrapped, compliments of Tokyo's Chofu Creston in which he and Diamond stayed two weeks ago while there installing the space agency's HDI220s – which the man unfolds, shakes out and slips about him, holding in the sides the better to admire embroidered storks and fountains. Phocan parts again the velvet curtain and they leave the cubicle – at the same time, it turns out, as Diamond and her charge emerge from theirs. The young woman sports a matching complimentary kimono, Diamond's; on catching sight of one another thus attired, man and woman simultaneously pinch a fold between their thumb and forefinger, holding the pattern and soft fabric up to view, a plumage-display, stork to stork, fountain to fountain, smiling. For a few seconds, the seven of them – man, woman, Diamond, Sennet, Phocan, Garnett and Perera – stand in meditative Shinto silence. It's Diamond who breaks it:

'I hope I've done the marker-distribution right,' she says to Phocan. 'I concentrated on frontal and antero-posterior axes.'

'Sounds good to me,' he tells her. Speaking, he's conscious of the silent Garnett's gaze on him. It's an approving one. He, in his turn, gazes at the couple, at these stand-ins called upon to underwrite a thousand marriages, a thousand renewed couplings. Diamond's had the same idea as him: the woman's forehead has a bindi-nipple on it too. For a fraction of a second, Phocan senses one more act of standing-in or substitution at work here; the presence, veiled, redacted, of a coupling unconsummated, of a bride uncaptured – too young, a child almost – exiting the frame. Sennet's briefing the students further:

'Once you take your bathrobes off,' he says, 'the cameras will detect the markers, and, through these, your exact positions. As long,' he adds, pointing at the floor's tape-demarcated central area, 'as you stay within the borders of this square – that is, inside the white lines. Of course, you've got the bed, but ...'

Perera picks the thread up: 'As discussed,' she tells them, 'we want to ascertain the stress occasioned by a wide range of positions.' Her diction, coupled with the Sri Lankan accent in which they're delivered, makes Phocan wonder whether these words are reproduced verbatim from her research brief or whether she always speaks with such lilting formality. 'To that end,' she carries on, 'we ask you to engage with one another in as many variable

49

configurations as you are able. You can move about the bed, the bed's edge, floor or table ...'

All eyes follow her prompts, jumping from each area to the next, before coming to rest atop the bedside table. Freesias? Sennet, clicking away at the screens' settings, running them through their own configurations, pauses to add:

'Obviously there's no duvet or top-sheet, since they'd block the reflectors and defeat the object. We've set room temperature to 23, so hopefully you'll feel quite comfortable. But if you need us, or need anything, just ring.' He points to a buzzer next to the doors.

'Nobody's following us live?' the woman asks in a variation on the question that the man posed to Phocan. 'From another room, I mean ...'

'No,' Sennet answers. 'Only the sensors. You have total privacy.'

The woman nods slowly. Is she disappointed? Is she just taking in the information? Or is she trying to reconcile the two terms in her head? *Privacy, sensors:* odd coupling, bedfellowed together in a conjugation as strangely contrived as this whole set-up. The only term that really seems to find its fit, to have a place here, is *total* ...

'Any more questions?' Phocan asks.

Woman and man shake heads.

'Well,' Phocan beams a broad smile at them, 'we'll leave you to your own ...'

His voice trails off. He turns to Garnett, inviting his boss to sum things up before the session proper starts. But Garnett raises his hand once more, delegating commentary to his charges. It's Sennet, stepping back slowly from his monitors, who completes the sentence:

'Devices.'

5. Client A

An hour or so into the Old Street meeting, Dean finds herself experiencing an acute sense of déjà vu. It's not the vague type, trace levels of some half-remembered episode contaminating the admixture of the present, jarring it, for a brief moment, into a blurred double-vision of itself ... No, this is sharp, precise and instantly identifiable: what's inserted itself between this conference suite's long board table, leather swivel chairs, occupants thereof (on the one hand) and (on the other) her *apprehension* of these surfaces and personae is a photograph, a picture from a bundle she was served up on the second day of last week's stint in the LSE library.

The photo, taken some time in the 1950s, showed a managerial scenario: seven executive types – five men, two women – seated at three long tables set up in a U-shape round a hanging screen. On to the screen a film was being projected: it (in turn) showed a male worker, or perhaps experimental subject, sorting objects into a series of compartments, while beside him an imposing clock kept time. In their office, or laboratory, or cinema, the manager/scientist film-viewers seemed to be assessing the man's skill at this task, and hence (Dean surmised) his aptitude for such-and-such a post. She passed over the image at the time, angling for larger catches – didn't make a note of it or snap it with her phone; but now ... now it seems to hang about the room's corporate air, both spectral and enlarged, a frame and backdrop for today's whole gathering.

The set-up: a 'symposium'. Dorley and Grieves, law firm in which she, as junior associate, serves, is offering, for a consideration of one thousand pounds and change an hour, its services to Peacock, a consultancy. Despite this contractual relation and – to Dean – confusingly, Peacock are not D&G's client in this interaction; rather, they're acting as intermediary between the IP-specialists and their *actual* client, whom both parties, in all correspondence, documents and (now) verbal dialogue alike have followed the convention of referring to as *Client A*. Blind council: when a party's feeling shy, if you perform due diligence, check they're not gangsters, terrorists, what have you, it's all kosher, from a legal point of view at least. More than mere intermediaries, Peacock are *staging* the symposium, in the full dramaturgical sense. They laid down the rules of engagement some weeks ago: D&G's team have been instructed to present 'encomia' into which they, the Peacocks, are permitted, frequently and at will, to interject, interrogating their theses, premises, presuppositions and so on; the D&Gs, thus challenged, will elaborate, expand, extrapolate – and out of all this back-and-forth, like fragile truth wafting about the Agora at the end of a Socratic dialogue, to be breathed in and feasted on by all, will arise some peerless understanding of the current state of patent and copyright law; or at least of the parts of it falling within today's (disorientatingly vague) remit-parameters – namely, those of 'gesture'. It's being filmed, the whole exchange, recorded for eventual viewing by other consultants back at Peacock and, presumably, this Client A themselves, who'll trawl its contents for strategy prompts or market-recognition tools or whatever else it is they're after. Whence Dean's apprehension of this other, older scene, this object-sorting skit: in both scenarios, the players are simultaneously acting and not acting, doing what they're doing both because they're doing it for real *and* as a show, put on for post-hoc viewing by an audience that's lurking out of sight, beyond the frame ...

There are, needless to say, big differences too – not least the props: in this state-of-the-art conferencing room, it's on not a canvas pull-down but a 65-inch back-lit LED that the embedded scene is appearing. A video-clip, it shows a dancer in great bat-like silken wings twirling her arms, causing a web of floating ribbons to gyrate around her.

'Loie Fuller,' Dean's colleague Julius Leman, mid-encomium, is telling Peacock's delegation. 'Creator of the "Serpentine Dance" she's demonstrating here. She managed to patent the chemical compounds she used in her colour gels; and the salts that gave her cloths and stage sets their strange luminescence; but she never managed to patent the dance itself.'

'Why not?' Robert Elsaesser, Peacock's point-man, asks.

'The US Copyright Office,' explains Julius, 'denied her suit – in 1892, against an imitator, Minnie Bemis – on the grounds that her, Fuller's, performance, irrespective of its groundbreaking uniqueness, had no overarching structure, wasn't "about" anything ...'

In the short pause while notes are jotted down, the dancer continues to twirl and gyrate. The gif, a digitised transfer from celluloid, has jumps and flecks, birthmarks of the old medium; like the spinning silks, it loops back on itself, over and over.

'1892 ...' Elsaesser's teammate Roderick picks up the baton. 'Seems like a long way to track back.'

'Copyright's a long game, my friend,' Clive Dorley, QC, murmurs across the table at him.

'Naturally,' Roderick concedes. 'But maybe we could focus more on where the legislation's going, not on where it's come from.'

A collective under-the breath chortle, indulgent and patronising at once, issues from D&G ranks. The Peacocks, looking slightly hurt, retreat into the kind of silence that demands an explanation.

'Law,' Dorley provides one, 'works on precedent.'

'It's Janus-faced.' Juliet McKraken, Senior Partner, backs him up. 'Looking backward to discern the future ...'

Roderick's objection overridden, Julius ploughs ahead by jumping back three centuries.

'This lady,' he announces as the screen gives over to a pale figure swathed in ermine and red velvet – static this time, jpeg of an oil painting – 'is Queen Anne. Her 1710 decree, modestly titled "The Statute of Anne", is technically to do with publishing, in that it endorses an author's rights over and above those of the printer who puts out their book. But what it *really* does is set out a whole raft of statements and provisions tying landed property to immaterial thought, paternity to "personality", private work to public interest ...'

Dean, listening, fidgets with her own speaking notes, which seem trivial and unworked-through by comparison. She draws an arrow in their margin with her pencil for no other reason than to make the others think she's annotating, fine-tuning some insight ...

'... via the legal deposit scheme.' Julius is still in flow. 'Very of its time. Part and parcel of the era of enlightenment and revolution. Seven decades later, the framers of the US Constitution more or less copy and paste the statute: Article 1, Section 8 – the "Copyright Clause" – applies at first to books and maps and charts; then printed music gets tagged on in 1831; then dramatic works in 1856 ... photographs 1865 ... movies 1912 ... sound recordings 1972 (this one surprises people: you'd have thought sound would have come much sooner). Then – and here, perhaps, is what most concerns us – in 1976 a new Copyright Act extends protectable status to choreographic works and pantomimes.'

'And that's the latest upgrade?' asks Elsaesser. 'That's where we're at now?'

The D&G crew once more let loose a volley of indulgent-patronising chortles. Dorley quips: 'If things were that simple we'd all be out of work.'

A pause, while Peacock's delegation wait for the missing information to be supplied. Julius lets it run on for a few seconds, for effect, before taking up again:

'This is what happens: after that last Act is passed, you start getting instances of litigation that, in turn, set precedent. So in 1977, the producers of a Broadway musical successfully sue a Hollywood studio when a dance is reproduced without permission in a film. But over the following years, several other suits fall flat. People find that when they try to copyright individual moves or "steps", it doesn't work.'

'Why not?' Elsaesser asks.

'A step,' Julius answers, 'is an isolated unit, not a sequence. Think back to Queen Anne's authors: they could copyright a book, but not a word. So a composer, now, can copyright a symphony, but not a note; a painter a painting, but not a brushstroke. It's the same with movement. The devil's in the detail, though: thousands of hours of court-time have been spent arguing about the exact point at which a unit *turns* into a sequence. It's still up for grabs. And then, it gets more complex, on two fronts.'

He takes a sip of water. He's got the floor, and wants to hold it for a while.

'Firstly,' he resumes, wiping his lips, 'there'd already been successful acts of registering and litigation *prior* to 1976, the year choreographic copyright takes hold. Hanya Holm, a German émigré, managed to register her choreography for *Kiss Me Kate* in 1952. But that was thanks to having documented it in Labanotation – Rudolf Laban's system for codifying dance moves, for recording them in scores: it was covered by the older law protecting written manuscripts. By the same token Johnny Hudgins, an African American, won compensation three decades earlier for blackface tributes to him performed here in London, on the grounds that they were drawn from a "dramatic composition". That was an outlier, though.'

'How so?' asks Elsaesser.

'This,' Julius informs him, 'was back in the 1920s – an important period, given the rise in stock of African-diaspora culture: Harlem Renaissance and all that ... It brought two separate world views into conflict. The folks sharing moves in uptown New York ballrooms hadn't inherited the same proprietorial notions as their European-descended counterparts. They'd *come* from chattel, after all, not held it. So they turn up at the Savoy and the Apollo on Saturday nights, tap and swing around together, unpacking and tweaking one another's steps, and – *hey presto!* – the Lindy and the Charleston are born. But no one owns them. Then a downtown Broadway maestro gets inquisitive, or brave, and ventures north of 120th Street; and his eyes jump from their sockets; and before you know it all the sequences have been incorporated in some musical – whose producers copyright it. This pattern will continue in the entertainment world for decades: think of rock 'n' roll, or hip-hop. Crudely put: white people nicking stuff from black people pretty much describes the history of popular music.'

A reflective, or perhaps embarrassed, silence follows. There are no black people in this room. Elsaesser moves things on by asking:

'What's the second front?'

'The second front,' says Julius, 'hinges round a single word: *derivative*.'

'*Derivative*,' repeats Elsaesser.

'*Derivative*,' confirms Julius. 'Copyright grants to its owner a bundle of entitlements: to display, perform, distribute and reproduce a work, and to create' – he raises his fingers in inverted commas – '"works derivative of the original". What does "derivative" mean?'

He pauses again. Was that a question? The Peacocks look at one another awkwardly before Elsaesser, spreading his palms, hands the unsolved riddle back to D&G.

'Everything's derivative of something else,' says Julius. 'Nothing comes from nowhere. Copyright disputes, in the choreographic field, have traditionally been argued on a genealogical basis, rather like paternity suits: if Work A can be demonstrated to have been the "father" or "grandfather" of Works B, C or D ...'

On the long table, water glasses stand untouched, bubbles in them fewer, slower, smaller than before – third-generation stragglers, great-grandchildren of some lost spring. From ermine and velvet, Queen Anne looks on palely. It takes a few seconds for Elsaesser to frame the obvious question:

'And how is that demonstrated?'

'By having the best lawyers.' Dorley's older, wiser voice floats up from his chair's recesses.

There's a round of laughter, which, since Dorley doesn't join it, soon dies out. He wasn't joking.

'Show them the K-pop case,' McKraken instructs Julius.

Obediently, Julius calls up a file that's lying minimised on his docking station. On the LED, Anne crumples out of view, a genie returned to her flask, to be replaced by a troupe of contemporary, floppy-haired Asian boys advancing in syncopated steps across a lunar landscape, chasing an elusive alien girl. These in turn are sucked away to docked oblivion as Julius pops another file and the scene changes – or, in fact, doesn't: here, in grainier texture, is a striped and blanche-faced *mimique* performing, in similarly extraterrestrial environs, more or less identical movements.

'D&G took on this case ourselves, three years ago, and won,' Julius overdubs. 'We acted for the estate of Jean-Louis Barrault, the French mime artist this band were ripping off. That they're doing this is obvious. Self-evident. But in *law*, that's nothing; it has no significance. What allowed Barrault's descendants to prevail, despite the migration in medium, vaudeville to video-streaming, and the quite considerable time-lag, over fifty years ... What swung it for them was the fact that Barrault, prior to his death, had – unusually – bought back all rights to his own work from the various producers who'd contracted him over the course of his career. If not, proprietorship would have been corporate rather than individual – and, to further muddy the waters, dispersed; it would be a matter of tracking down whichever outfits had acquired or inherited the holdings of whatever other outfits held them prior to that.'

During the last few moments, the Peacock gang have, in some kind of Pavlovian reaction to the content of his spiel, been sitting up straighter, straining forwards, eyes lit up with new levels of attentiveness. Are they actually breathing faster? It seems so to Dean, although it could just be the overheated ventilators on their laptops, or an uptick in the suite's AC ...

'This,' says Elsaesser, voice charged with more directed purpose, 'is intriguing – in point of view of where Client A's interests lie.'

'Can you be more precise?' McKraken asks.

Elsaesser, weighing his words, answers:

'In corporate, rather than individual, ownership ...'

'... of movement, yes,' says McKraken. 'So we've understood – which is why we've asked Julius to paint the spectrum for you ...'

'A task he's doing admirably,' Roderick jumps in again here. 'But I wonder: why are we hovering around dance and music? I mean ... entertainment's certainly part of the picture; but it's not the *focal* point. Client A, as we've outlined, is more interested in these questions as they pertain to what we used to call "the industrial arena".'

Dean, sensing that she's going to be called on soon, tenses up.

'The law,' Dorley's benevolently chiding voice weighs in once more, 'works not just by precedent, but by analogy as well.' The Peacocks look confused, so he continues: 'Choreography may seem like a niche subject; but it's the paradigm for all fields in which flesh and bones, bodies in motion, meet with the legal codifications that both support and constrain them; as such, choreographic legislation should be seen as the umbrella for *all* argument involving movement. Which, if I understand correctly, is precisely Client A's concern.'

The Peacock team, quieted once more, sit back. Dean scrutinises them. Besides Elsaesser and Roderick, there are two others: a young woman about her age and a man in his mid-thirties who's been taking notes continuously; plus the three camera people, two male and one female, filming the proceedings – one front-on, one from each side. They're all got up in smart-casual attire: slim chinos, open shirts or jumpers topped by blazers for the men, jackets over patterned dress or jeans for the women. She's checked Peacock's website: they have lavish premises in Hammersmith – brainstorming studios, hospitality suites, summiting pods ... D&G's own offices in Goodge Street have two large rooms set aside for just this type of pow-wow. Why have they been Ubered out here, to this new-build Old Street flexi-hub with spaces hireable by month, or day, or hour? Despite the first-name informality, the free-flow format, the light, glassy airiness bathed in aroma of fair trade, she senses that this meeting has been crafted, from top down, not only to ensure that things are rigidly hermetic, but, beyond that, to confer upon itself, its own occurrence, a degree of anonymity, or – is it too much to think this? – of *deniability* ...

McKraken says: 'The principal difference between the worlds of dance and the more commercial applications that form Client A's zone of enquiry is that, in the latter realm, it's usually *technology* that's patented; not human movements.'

'Well, yes. Let's ...' Roderick flips through his notes and, finding what he wants, strikes out on a fresh tack with newfound confidence: 'Let's take the scenario – the everyday one – whereby a person swipes a smartphone or a tablet. Right?'

McKraken nod-shrugs acquiescence.

'Could we not,' Roderick asks, 'see that person *themselves* as the tool that opens up the file or application? The sweep of the hand or fingers, their particular configuration, could be thought of – in principle at least ...'

'As proprietorial?' McKraken asks.

'Why not? The action's been devised by the device's engineers, designers, programmers ... In effect, it's the true "content" of their work: the soft- and hardware are just trappings – props, or prompts. So although *you* perform the action, it's *their* creation – the designers'; just as a given dance sequence is its choreographer's. And yet, as we all know, a hand-motion or a gesture – even ones instantly identifiable as associated with a certain product or personality – isn't afforded the same, or any, level of protection. Not yet ...'

'It's a non-starter,' Dorley cuts him off. 'That line of thinking has reared its head from time to time over the last few years, and promptly had its bottom smacked and got sent to bed early. Heavy-metal singers trying to register their devil-horn signs, stuff like that ... Those cases always fall at the first hurdle: frivolous, dismissed.'

'Those ones, yes,' Elsaesser concurs. 'But at the more sophisticated – the more *technological* – end of the spectrum ...'

'Gesture-based interaction in HCI systems,' Roderick starts reeling off a list he's been holding back, powder-dry, until now.

'Hand-topology and skeletal-data descriptors, encoded via Fisher kernels and multi-level temporal pyramids ... Linear SVM classifiers applied to feature-vectors, computed over presegmented gestures to pluck recognition moments from continuous streams ... We're thinking of the type of work that companies like Bewegung and Kinect and Pantarey are doing.'

'We've advised Pantarey,' McKraken interjects.

'We know you have,' replies Elsaesser.

The dynamic's shifting – Dean can sense that. Now it's the D&G team who find themselves quieted by the Peacocks' knowledge of the field, wrong-footed by their having kept it under wraps until this point, as though playing dumb had been a strategy to draw out their interrogees. She recalls vaguely the Pantarey contract, for which she prepared some of the secondary paperwork: it involved pre-emptive registration of a gizmo, some kind of high-speed, light-projecting camera. Are Client A a company like that? It seems unlikely: the length and expense to which they've gone in orchestrating this whole formalised exchange would place them further up whatever chain D&G find themselves part of here – a larger operator, tweaking cords from a far higher stratum, an atmosphere more rarefied ...

It's Elsaesser who lets the silence run on this time, then decides when and how to end it.

'In all kinds of fields,' he says, 'gaming to manufacturing to warfare, gestural operation's taking over from the joystick model that in turn replaced the hands-on one. What Client A is interested in interrogating – interested in *speculating* on, let's say – is how this, over time, might impact our legal understanding of specific hum-tech interfaces. Not the *gestures*, but the *interfaces*; the configurations.'

'If we move,' Roderick again, 'beyond the old dichotomy of man/machine, of operator/tool, and begin to view the whole thing instead as a ... as a kind of *constellation* ... held in formation by a force-of-gravity specific to its own context: a specific task, a particular design-moment, a uniquely-codified relation ...'

He lets the thought hang in the air, held in formation by the force of its own logic. On the 65-inch, Barrault's still alien-chasing on the moon, eyes round and bulging from the combined effects of atmosphere, lust and intoxication. McKraken, trying to wrest control of the proceedings back to D&G, turns towards Dean and says:

'This might be a good moment ...'

This is it. Julius is vacating his chair, yielding both floor and laptop to her. The slides are in there, uploaded already; still, there's a false start while she toggles between thumbnails, reddening ... Then it's up on the widescreen: the first of the ancient photographs she's copied, cropped, enlarged – though not enough, she's sure, to make them anything other than small, flimsy offerings at this high table ...

It shows a woman sitting next to a vast vat of chocolate. The woman herself, her form, is imprecise: her shoulders and arms have doubled, tripled, run into a blur of motion-shimmy, while her face has been erased almost completely, leaving discernable just the outline of a nose and sunken eye socket. Beside the vat, there's a tray; on the tray sit thirteen little coils of chocolate – a baker's dozen, bite-size dollops neatly laid out in two rows. Unlike the blurred human figure, objects – vat, tray, dollops – have remained in perfect focus; you can even see the craters and escarpments in the huge, half-set mass of unscooped chocolate, the declivities and trenches carved into its mudflat as it's quarried. Running between vat and tray – slicing between them in both directions, just at the point at which the woman's arm blurs most – is a streak of light so sharp that it looks solid: a continuous line, a track swerving and jagging as it races back round to rejoin itself and form a circuit.

'A Cadbury's worker,' Dean tells the assembled company. 'From the Gilbreth collection. This one,' she continues, clicking to the next slide, 'is a spanner driller.'

'What collection?' asks Elsaesser. 'What is this exactly?'

On the screen, a ghost-figure, the wispy remnant of an over-alled man, hangs between a crate of spanners and a fixed drill head. While the worker's no more than a pall, both machine and spanner-crate have kept their form; hurtling electrically between these last two, where the ghost's transparent fuzz of arm ends in a smoke-puff hand, there is – once more – a light track: multiple tracks this time, pursuing roughly but not exactly the same course, each one as bold and vibrant as a neon tube.

'Gilbreth,' says Dean. 'Lillian Gilbreth. She worked first with her husband Frank and then alone, from the teens right through to the nineteen sixties, rationalising workplaces: shop floors, assembly lines, eventually whole industries. Back in their day, the Gilbreths were minor celebrities; there was even a film made about them, their family life. Now they've lapsed into obscurity, but ...'

'What are those light tracks?' Roderick asks.

'They're called cyclegraphs,' Dean tells him. 'She – Gilbreth – developed the technique of attaching a light-ring to the finger of a seamstress or machinist, and allowing this, through long-exposure photographs, to trace the shape their hand made as they went about their task.'

'Why's this one broken?' asks Elsaesser as, in the next picture, an ectoplasmic haze of laundry woman floats above two stacks (one crumpled and one tidily arranged) of handkerchiefs. This time, the tracks of light running, just off the midriff of her dwindling body, to and fro between the sharply defined linen piles are formed of Morse-like dots and dashes.

'Gilbreth,' explains Dean, 'has used an interrupter here to have the light blink on and off – quickly, ten times per second. That way, the long exposure will reveal not just the path the woman's hand makes, but also how long it takes to make it. That's the point, the object of the exercise. Manual labour is repetitive; a hand-kerchief folder, or lathe operator, or what have you, will perform the same action again and again, thousands of times a day. With her cyclegraphs, Gilbreth could demonstrate that each "doing", every iteration of the action, involves the worker's hand travelling (for example) three feet and two inches, and takes 4.1 seconds. More importantly, it allowed her to work out that, if the worker's employers were to lower the workbench by an inch and a half, and move it a little closer to, or further away from, the machine, or tools, or product, then they could bring that action's cycle down to two feet and eleven inches, and 3.6 seconds. Multiply that saving by however many thousand for each worker's day; then by three hundred for their year; and then that figure by the company's roster ...'

'But ...' Roderick's not convinced. 'A photograph is flat. How can it measure *distance*? You'd need depth.'

Dean has the answer to this quibble at her fingertips, one of which brings up the next slide.

'Stereoscope,' she comments – unnecessarily: the picture is a dip-tych, showing an index card-stamper's action (an arced light track, like the outline of a trout or salmon leaping up a stream) from two sides, front and profile. 'But,' she presses on, 'Gilbreth went further: once you have what she called a "stereocyclegraph", then you can make a three-dimensional model of the action. Look ...'

Now there are four boxes on the screen: cut-away boxes, black, whose three sides (always the floor and two right-angled walls) are wallpapered with white graph squares. Mounted inside each box is a careening light track; this time, though, these tracks appear solid not just through a trick of shutter-time, but because this is what they are – genuinely solid, shaped from moulded frames of metal fixed in place with little hooks which, if you squint, you can just see. In one of the four tracks, the bright metal circuit has dark stripes painted at half-inch intervals around it to recreate the interrupted blink-effect seen in the last-but-one image.

'By producing physical iterations,' Dean says, 'Gilbreth could help workers learn the best way to perform their action – by run-ning their hands along the moulds cast from their most efficient colleagues, for example ... She could also tweak the casts, the wireframes, themselves, to improve the modelled action further – often in collaboration with the workers, with an eye to their own comfort. It's no good having a more efficient hand-path if it makes the woman's back give out after three years. More enlightened companies like Cadbury's, a Quaker family business, understood this. Plus, if the woman's back lasts ten years rather than three, then she's more profitable, too: you don't need to keep training up replacements.'

She clicks through two more photos of assorted wireframes in their boxes. Their shapes morph through a large range: some are suggestive of a roller-coaster track, others of cowboy hats with rims and peaks, others of trunked or long-necked creatures – elephants, giraffes – or antennaed insects, or snakes uncoiling, frozen in mid strike . . . At the base of every picture there's a string of numbers and letters, squiggles that look like miniature sketches of the outline beneath which they're scrawled.

'How big are these boxes?' asks Elsaesser.

'Like shoeboxes, I guess,' she answers. 'The action's modelled at scale, one-to-one.'

'And how many of them are there?'

'I don't know. She kept on producing them for decades. But lots of them were discarded after they'd served their purposes. From what I could make out from the records I saw, it looks like the Smithsonian have gathered up a few. MIT, too. But the main Gilbreth Archive's held at Purdue, where she . . .'

'With who?'

'The University of Purdue, Indiana. They helped facilitate her research, after 1940 at least . . .'

Dean's finger hovers on the mousepad, itching to click on to the next picture. But there's no next picture; that's her lot. She's played her hand, got nothing else. She reddens again, unsure of what to do with the display, control of which she's now relinquishing; then decides to revert to Julius's last slide, the gif of the moonstruck Barrault. No one in the room says anything; the Peacock people don't even seem to be taking notes. Dean senses that her presentation's been a flop; she's about to excuse herself, to slink off to the toilet, when Roderick asks:

'Would you say . . . ?' He pauses, then reformulates the question: 'Would you see these models as a kind of "first citation"?'

'Legally?' she asks.

Roderick nods.

'I suppose that would have to be argued, like the K-pop case – although it's not the same. I mean ...'

'Maybe,' Elsaesser adds, 'they could be viewed as an alternative form of Labanotation – sculptural rather than written. They *record* a sequence.'

'Yes,' says Dean. 'But ...'

She finds herself too flustered to pay much attention to the rest of her faltering answer, which in any case is drowned out by other conversations striking up around the room, a mishmash of exchanges, crescendoing, separating out and coming back together.

'... that with music,' Julius is saying, 'it's more codified: since the Dubset Agreement, streaming's become standardised, IP-wise. You've got your MixSCAN algos scanning traffic, distributing royalties and so on ... But *movement*, of the type Client A's interested in ... We're still in Wild West times in terms of any generalised ...'

'... when legislation's going to come,' Elsaesser's reasoning. 'It has to: might be two, five or ten years downstream, but ...'

'The notion,' Dorley's still in pooh-poohing mode, 'that one could apply the same criteria universally to movement as to music-downloads is quite fanciful. How would you ... ?'

'Sure: but the *constellation*,' Roderick trots out his buzzwords again, 'the *moment*, the designed *relation* ... Now, with motion-capture heading markerless, and viewing capability pretty much everywhere – why can't the algos scan that too, in all types of ...'

'... in on the ground floor,' Elsaesser's impressing upon McKraken. 'Future patenting, or maybe retrospective acquisition ...'

For the remaining minutes of the meeting, Dean finds herself picturing, once more, the spools she saw a week ago: the circled layers, stacked like orders or committees, each layer overseeing the one below, reporting to the one above, but unable to see the one above that, or the next ... The image stays with her on the ride back to Goodge Street, and all afternoon – and resurrects itself the following week, when Dorley summons her into his office.

'It seems,' he tells her, 'that your little wireframes struck a chord.'

'With whom?' she asks.

'With Peacock,' he says. 'Client A. Whomever. They want more.'

'More what?'

'More,' Dorley repeats. 'I'd like you to explore that avenue a little further. I thought you could take up where you left off.'

'Explore ...' she starts, then falters. 'What exactly should I do?'

'I think,' says Dorley, 'you should get yourself a plane ticket to Indiana.'

6. Stagings

They sit in rows, all facing the same way. Light – fluid, synthetic, over-spilling from the screen in front of each – coagulates in spectacle-lens glass before draining away over skin that, no matter what ethnicity box (optional) its owner might have ticked on Degree Zero's application form, in this room is recast in grey. All of them wear headphones, thick and padded as the walls of sanatoria. Some have sandwich packages open in front of them, others rice-noodle concoctions composted in plastic tubs; every desk sports, standing sentinel beside its glide-pad, a lone porta-bottle with an inbuilt perma-straw extruding from its lid. In many ways, it's a generic office scene – with one divergence.

It took Phocan a while to put his finger on it last time he came here to Berners Street as well; but passing through this outer room packed full of low-grade modellers, concentrated airlock between public-facing, poster- and award-draped lobby and the Art Dept's inner sanctum, just before reaching the keypad-operated door to whose code sequence this room's denizens aren't privy, he recalls Eldridge mentioning it to him on that other visit too, at the same exact spot he's twigging on right now: none of them have phones. Not charging on the desk, nor peeping from pockets, nor even sprouting cables from the recesses of shirts and jackets: they're *verboten*. Slip one out, or even have its ring crow from your handbag to betray you, and you're gone – no grace, no first-time pass, just your P45. These guys don't even have an internet connection: beyond DZ's intranet, or more precisely narrow avenues of this (the CAD, Maya and Autodesk files to which they've been given individual clearance), their isolation is complete. It's non-stop lockdown in here, one that's met not with the racket of tin mugs rattling on bars and catcalls ricocheting down corridors, but instead with quiet mouse-clicks, *insert components, line, repeat line, circle, pan, zoom, centre, undo, save*, as edges are laid down and rotated, surfaces rolled out, objects created, their mosaic patches willing themselves into definition, landscapes unwrapped – and, simultaneously, rewrapped, cooped within strict geometric confines, parameters and ratios recalculated with every mutation, several times a second: a collective, restless and resigned sketching, in variously transposed or extrapolated versions, of cell walls.

'They've all done vocational degrees,' Eldridge tells him this time, barely bothering to lower his voice as his tapping fingers tease open the inner door. 'For them, coordinate space began in 1982, with *Tron* – a decade before they were born. Try talking to them about soil mechanics, dead loads or cadastral surveys, and they'll go completely blank. This stuff,' he thumb-jerks back dismissively, 'is all they know.'

Memories, shared, follow him and Phocan as they step over the threshold: Imperial College's banked lecture halls, Fluids 21, Bernoulli and Boundary Layer equations, Hyde Park railing-hopping, drunk 2 a.m. dips in the Serpentine, a roast chicken carcass left out on the table of their digs' kitchen for so long that a new carapace grew right across its quadripartite rib-vaults ... They remain unvoiced, though, Eldridge contenting himself with quipping:

'Fuckin' kids.'

They laugh – but there's a double edge, an unease, to their laughter. Is the coders' youth the actual gag? Or is it the fact that this group's baby-facedness allows these two men in their prime to cast themselves as old that furnishes the punchline? They *are* old: in this world, forty's ancient; not having a command of Blender, Topsolid or Tekler wired into your neural system places you in not simply a previous generation but, beyond that, an entire evolutionary category that new mutations have consigned to oblivion.

Isn't *that* the real joke? Phocan's ilk thinking they're midwifing the future into being, when all the time they're navigating their own obsolescence? Eldridge, despite the bohemian tendencies he harboured even fifteen years ago, now realised or at least half-realised in 'creative-industry' employment, has always had a sharpness Phocan felt he himself lacked: call it self-awareness, insight … Perhaps his irony today's a roar against extinction – fading now, dying off too as they enter the inner room.

This space, although no larger than the outer, equally devoid of natural light, seems instantly more airy, spacious and just generally patrician, a field marshal's CIC. To its walls are pintacked scores of photographs and diagrams of spaceships and space stations, both real and fictitious: docking bays and sleeping quarters, exercise pods, gyrodynes and probes. Beneath these, lying on the floor, hand-drawn sketches sample and remix the elements and features of their vertically arrayed source images: a solar panel here, an observation window there, the axels of a centrifuge set one way, rubbed out, relaid along another axis … On a large table in the centre of the room, just where a papier-mâché landscape of the battle terrain would be if this really were a military HQ, there sits a scale (1:72) model of the Kern Federal Starship *Sidereal*. It's incomplete – partly because still under construction, partly because Herzberg, *Incarnation*'s art director, is using the old cut-away effect, the better to facilitate understanding and corroboration between all involved parties: graphic designer, construction coordinator, set dresser, screenwriter, prop builder, costume designer, VFX supervisor, CG director (Eldridge), cinematographer, first, second and third assistant directors and, end of the line, apex of this particular food chain, director (Lukas Dressel). Right now, a core triumvirate of the above (first, second and fourth listed) are conferring round the carved and whittled styrofoam ship, soliciting, or fending off, a set of interjections from their Special Technical Adviser Ben Briar.

'Which bit's the CC?' Briar's asking.

'CC?' repeats Herzberg.

69

'Crew compartment. Where they live.'

'We kind of thought they'd live all over,' Herzberg tells him. 'The stokers, Tszvetan's crew, his homies, his lieutenant smugglers, can be quartered below deck, under these giant propellant tanks. The Princess gets the guest suite, which is adjunct to the *Sidereal*'s main body. We've made it that way to accentuate her purdahed status. Tszvetan himself we'll see mostly pottering about the navigation deck. That's where we need shoe leather from you.'

'Shoe leather?' now it's Briar's turn to be stumped.

'Stuff to do while he's speaking his lines. Buttons to press, levers to pull ... that kind of thing.'

'There haven't been "levers" on spaceships since the 1967 Soyuz,' Briar coldly informs him.

'Well, whatever,' Herzberg counters. 'Touchpads, vocal interfaces ...'

'Tszvetan's a pilot,' Berul, *Incarnation*'s screenwriter, pipes up here. 'A navigator, captain, helmsman. He steers his way. It's important to frame him like this: at the bridge, in command of his direction, of his fate – until the thanadrine episode, at least, when he'll veer wildly off course ...'

Federal Starship Commander Tszvetan is what, in the industry, they like to call an *archetype*. His bloodlines run far back: through Han Solo to Rick Blaine to Drake, Raleigh and such licensed privateers. Throw a little pinch of Pete 'Maverick' Mitchell and Huck Finn into the mix and you've more or less got Tszvetan's character pool: rebellious, independent and, by virtue of these traits, through choice rather than duty, fiercely loyal. His rich back-story, worked up through weeks of research conducted first in parallel and then amalgamated in a Dorset hotel to which the whole scriptwriting team had, like a jury, been sequestered, involves loss of parents, kidnapping, being set adrift in a small space-pirogue that washed up or rather (pace *Superman*) crash-landed on a 'random' planet, Kern, upon whose populace the strapping if barely bridled colt, reaching maturity, made such a strong impression (winning the Tagel Races three years in a row, notching up endless kills of enemy pilots during

the Third Saraõnic War, etc., etc.) that Kern's ruler, Louis Q, conferred upon him the effective status of a nephew – ironically, since
unbeknown to both, they are *in fact* related, by occluded blood. As
ranking federal officer and decorated ace, and royal ward to boot,
Tszvetan has been granted quite a bit of leeway to conduct his own
free galaxy-wide enterprise – enterprise that, in a star system as wild
as this one, borders at times on rampant criminality; although it's
also vital, given the tangledness of inter-federal treaties and alliances,
to be attuned to the nuance of any given situation, each chance
deep-space encounter, and to tailor one's behaviour accordingly.
Nor should this buccaneering interfere too much with his official
duties – which, of course, it doesn't: wise Louis Q understands, like
the Felipes and Elisabeths of yore, that these activities go hand in
hand, each acting as a spur and tonic to the other.

At *Incarnation*'s outset, we find Tszvetan guiding the *Sidereal*
into Doon Leer, giant harbour of the planet Argeral, erstwhile
foe of his adoptive Kern but now, post-Landis Détente, its trading
partner and uneasy 'ally'. Due to various subplots put in solely
for the sake of complicating things – i.e. of signalling complexity – the *Sidereal* has been posing, through its three-moon-cycle
voyage over from Kern, as a scientific mission sent out to observe
various celestial transits; but, once clocked and hailed by Doon
Leer Port Authority, it casts aside this cover, announcing itself as a
vessel full of smuggler-traders – which is true, but not the whole
truth. In reality, Tszvetan has been sent as Louis Q's own proxy,
under orders to advance the latter's suit of tendering to Argeral's
Crown Princess Tild an offer of betrothal.

'You're losing me,' says Phocan as Eldridge recaps the plot for
him. 'Tendering proxy what suits?'

'He's delivering a question-popper – a marry-me-baby: Louis Q
wants the heiress-apparent as a trophy bride who'll cement the *pax
romana* between his kingdom and hers, Kern and Argeral. *That's*
why Tzsvetan's pitching up now in Doon Leer ...'

It's over at a second table, in the corner of this room, by
an elite detail of Eldridge's own lieutenants, his most trusted

modellers, that Doon Leer is being designed. These modellers, too, are stealing freely from the pictures pinned up to the wall; but they're transcribing straight to screen without the intermediary of paper. Their overriding brief is simple: Go Big. Dressel wants the film's depiction of Argeral's port to be iconic; to not only serve as source, reference and gauge-stick for all future sci-fi *auteurs*, but to loom in the imagination of a whole civilian generation too, haunting their dreams and colouring their experience of a hundred real-world spatial interfaces – their era's *Strangelove* War Room. Argeral's the big boy in the B-Roth star system: the actual seat of military power (although, like several other former vassal planets, Kern, due in no small part to Tszvetan's prior heroics, has managed to inflict local defeats on the imperial fleet, thus carving out small pockets of resistance) and the *de facto* economic hub. Everything passes through Argeral; no matter from what dark provincial back reach of what sub-planetary shithole they've been mined, traded or plundered, through the zones of which provisional or regional authorities they've passed in contraband form, it's upon arrival here that material, goods, services, etc., become converted into credit – in *Incarnation*'s lingo (the writers have compiled a phrasebook), 'charged'. And Doon Leer, being the administrative, military and fiscal portal through which each and every vessel, soul and item entering or leaving Argeral must be processed, is the feature of the planet that first greets voyagers as they press their eyes to viewfinders and windows: glowing, throbbing, tractor-beaming their small ship, whatever orders they might relay to its puny motors, down towards it. Dressel wants this whole economico-galactico event field, this politico-spatial set-up, translated into establishing-shot tableau, into a wide-lens ballet of tugs, giant cargo freighters, tiny pilot drones gliding up and down beams cast out by port traffic-control towers, avenues and corridors of light and movement all converging on this greatest of all harbours; to render perspectively the city's power and majesty, vectorially the fascination its approach occasions: all lines lead to Doon Leer.

Accordingly, the Art Dept boys and girls have pilfered their way through Canaletto, Cole and Turner, not to mention Berkey, Paul and Hoesli: a gondola-sprinkled grand canal here, a network of citadels and lookout posts joined by ribbed generators there, funnel-clouds swirling at their edges, all projected in one-point. For their main template, they've lifted the bare bones of the vista that greets Dorothy and her friends as they skip down the yellow brick road to the Emerald City: Doon Leer, in the preliminary sketches, rises crystalline from grey-zone conurbations that proliferate about it, from the outlying agro- and industrial sectors feeding into and off it, buffer zones between its glory and the unkempt wood and desert lands that stretch for miles around Argeral's surface before giving over, past the planet's rim, to the abyss of outer space. The city's composed (at this distance, at least) of squares, or rather rhomboids, stacked atop each other like innumerable slanted bricks – slanted, and electrified too, since they glow. All of which gives the metropolis the look of somewhere in a perpetual state of assembly, a throbbing compact of great crystalline slabs, an expanding vert and azure chessboard.

This is easy for the modellers to render, since squares and rhomboids are their building blocks too. What's not so simple is the port's multitude of aerial ingress and egress routes: make them too straight and the whole vision will look rigid and anachronistic; too wavering and the core vanishing-point optics will get lost.

'We were picturing,' Eldridge is telling Phocan now, 'the way bees come and go from hives. There'll be infinite variations in the routes, but overall, since they all eventually pass through the same tiny hole ...'

'It's funny you should think of bees,' says Phocan. 'Just last week we were working with the Institute of Zoology, tracking exactly that. I got stung twice.' He folds his left sleeve back to show two swollen patches on his forearm. 'We decided in the end,' he continues, buttoning up again, 'that you can devise algorithms just as good from PIV.'

'PIV?'

Phocan holds a pinched thumb and finger to narrowly opened lips; for an instant Eldridge thinks he's miming toking on a joint, as was their wont back in South Ken – before, realising that Phocan's *blowing*, not drawing, he deciphers the charade:

'Ah – bubbles. You mentioned that – also in relation to helping model the final sequence, when the ship begins to ... with the wind ... Holland, right? Sledges ...'

'Bobsleighs,' Phocan corrects him. 'Next week. I can sound them out about staging a break-up, get quotes, and so on.'

'I mean, we've got a basic model with the Berlin water people, as you know, but ...'

'Sure. And with the bubbles: I'll be watching them through tug-, freighter- and drone-tinted lenses. If anything good comes up ...'

He tips Eldridge a wink, to let him know their shared past buys him certain privileges, sneak peeks at material that, strictly speaking, should remain, like the *Sidereal*'s royal passenger, partitioned off, restricted. Eldridge nods gratitude, and moves them onwards past the next block of collaged source-pictures. Dressel and Herzberg, as one would expect, want the establishing shot's wide-frame to evolve into a slow zoom into the metropolis itself, mirroring Tszvetan's POV as the *Sidereal* is guided down to its assigned docking station. Then a ground-level pan across large swathes of processing bays, weighing houses, custom-filter basins ... This horizontal realm is the domain of Doon Leer's chargers – 'chargers' being the name for the army of navvies and low-ranking port officials who load, unload, tariff-rate and zap ('charge') the contents of each vessel's manifest (and of course, anything else they might find stashed behind the floor- and ceiling-panels) with Argeral's own special brand of radium-tinged sub- or supra-electricity. In Argeral, energy is the unit of measure: goods, services, credit – all just names for, varying modes of, charge. Charge may now be galaxy-wide standard, exchangeable and leverageable all over; but only in Argeral can it be conferred upon an entity and thereby (as it were) 'minted', a transformation that's effected by its formal passage through Doon Leer – which passage's most basic, sweaty, greasy nut-and-bolt work is conducted by the aforementioned dockworkers. These chargers are a race unto themselves – several races, several species: they're made up of itinerant labourers from all corners of the B-Roth system. Swarthy Arwaks, pointy-headed Tallians, three-handed Girodeans and such like: nomadic populations who've migrated here but never really settled; who sleep in Doon Leer's inns and brothels, or on mattresses in dosshouses, or in makeshift lean-tos purposed from discarded cargo shells. They work under the protection of their charismatic foreman Ourman, in whom Tszvetan will recognise a kindred spirit (a sequel, already in the pipeline, is to follow the heroic-but-conflicted Ourman as he conveys, amidst the chaos of a bloody uprising or coup, the entire charge-reserves of Argeral to safety). Although (not only in the obvious phylogenetic sense but also in a civil-legal one) aliens, these chargers are typical of Doon Leer's general population, which is also largely made up of outsiders – migrant traders, brokers, diplomats, spies, slaves, charge-drawn here from all over.

'That's the thing with great imperial capitals,' Berul, whose team have case-studied a trans-historical selection of these, is impressing just now on Briar, Herzberg and whoever else will listen. 'Empire, whether Roman, Inca or American, is always about movement, you see. If a place gives off a "rooted" vibe, if its inhabitants all look or talk the same ... well, then you're signalling to your audience its parochial, small-planet character. But if you want to convey real heart-of-the-beast centrality, engine-room levels of power – then you have to show a restless scrum of wildly different bodies: haggling, hustling, darting and colliding their way across every urban surface.' His hands haggle and dart about the air in illustration, before hovering beside his ears. 'And you have to lay down a soundtrack brimming with a cacophony of languages ...'

Berul, Dressler, Herzberg, granted the power to generate a universe, are gods. The rules governing all *Incarnation*'s actions and events, from most momentous plot reversal to least consequential background filler, are compiled in a big, fat tome entitled, quasi-biblically, *The Book of Incarnation*. The designers and coordinators are their priesthood; the modellers, their clergy. Briar's a kind of one-man Inquisition, wheedling out sacrilege and apostasy – though from time to time, when theological debate arises, it becomes clear to the true faithful that the Two Cultures man is (as he himself put it in as many words on his arrival here in London) acting as the enforcer of his own church's dogma. They may birth worlds, but these worlds must be underwritten by the possibilities laid out in the big Book of Physics he's constantly waving at them. Underwritten, too, in a more literal sense, by backers and producers, who'll oblige the crew to send them rushes at the end of each day's shooting, run barely edited scenes past button-pressing focus groups, then demand reshoots and re-edits, rewrites. They've already put the script through seven drafts. Gods or not, Dressler and co. have no illusions about this, know all too well that they exist in a closed feedback loop with baseness and stupidity. Their deck on the trireme might be a little higher, oars and benches softer, but they're galley slaves, just like the kids stuck in the outer room. Beneath their feet, the render farm hums, sending vibrations from the basement up through the whole floor, as though the entire building, like the *Sidereal*, were being held in the tractor beam of something larger than it, an inexorable, if opaque, process.

'For the thanadrine scene,' Eldridge is explaining now to Phocan, 'we'll need – I'm running ahead – some kind of mechanical rig.'

'To move around the performers' bodies?' Phocan asks.

'No. Well, yes and no: to move around their bodies and to move their bodies themselves around. It's to take place in zero gravity.'

'Cool.'

'The setting for it,' Herzberg says, diverting Phocan back to the styrofoam *Sidereal*, 'is the Observatory – this chamber here, with glass walls all round it. The lighting's the main thing: the spaceship's own lamps will all be off, but the two actors will be lit by the reflected glow from moons and other planets, coming through the glass. The scene takes place at the end of the voyage back to Kern; the end, too, of a long solar night, just as the predawn rays of Fidelus are creeping round the edge of Ardis Minor, into the home-planet's atmosphere. We want the light to glide around their bodies in a way that looks good *and* is consistent with the solar-planetary layout we've constructed.'

'In that case,' Phocan reasons, 'we should build two rigs: one for the human figures, and another for the light and camera. Car-plant robots are good for this. And we can model it all first with ray tracers.'

'What's that?' Briar wants to know.

'You fire rays from a camera,' Phocan explains, 'to a point you've designated as the light source in the take, and track the photons as they ricochet around whatever surfaces and objects you want in there. That way, you can see how light will spread and dissipate across the scene – by reading its path backwards.'

'You're going to put Joel Reney and Rosanna Wilmington into a car-building machine?' says Briar.

The Degree Zero gang and Phocan all giggle at this notion.

'No,' says Eldridge, 'we'll use mo-cap performers.'

'From Bergen,' Phocan adds. 'The Movement Underground.'

'From what?' Briar's confused now.

'Bergen. It's in Norway,' Phocan tells him.

Eldridge explains patiently to Briar: 'Most of the actual *filming* in a film like this is done with stand-in bodies – when we use real bodies at all, that is. Your Joel Reneys and Rosanna Wilmingtons just turn up at the shoot's end, speak a few lines, let us film their faces so that we can paste them over to the performers' craniums ...'

'... pick their cheque up ...' Herzberg adds; then, catching a glance from Eldridge, adds: 'Here, I meant to ask you ...' and leads Briar off to the room's far side.

'That guy's scary,' Eldridge confides *sotto voce* to Phocan and Berul.

'Special Technical Adviser?' Phocan whispers. 'And he doesn't know about ray tracers?'

'He's more Realism Tsar than STA. If NASA didn't use ray tracers on the Shuttle or the International Space Station, he doesn't want to know … Talking of craniums, though: we might need some help from you with the skull-blade alignment episode.'

When Phocan stares back at Eldridge blankly, Berul prompts: 'Scene 25 …' His listener's face showing no uptake, he adds: 'Please tell me that you've read my screenplay.'

'I don't believe,' says Phocan measuredly, 'that Pantarey were sent a copy …'

Berul turns away in frustration. Eldridge rolls his eyes. 'Paranoid retards. I'll take care of that.'

Unclipping a small walkie-talkie from his belt, he orders a sub-ordinate to send him Soren, Degree Zero's runner, whom in turn he tells to go forth and amass the NDAs and restriction waivers requisite to the procurement, in a format either hard or soft, of *Incarnation*'s script for Phocan. Soren, who's got tiny whiskers on his upper lip, velveteen threads as yet untouched by any razor, scurries back off through the outer room, then through the lobby, out of the production building and across the courtyard to the mews in which the stable conversion that accommodates DZ's legal department is housed. On his way, he sees two junkies ambling towards the staircase leading to the render farm basement. He passes Deli Svevo's blue delivery cart, purveying the ranking staff-ers' lunchtime sandwiches, and passes also couriers wending their way by pushbike, motorbike and foot across the cobblestones, darting up and down narrow staircases leading to offices and workshops of DZ and other companies, picking up envelopes and packages, pulling others out of Velcro-fastened bags, scanning their barcodes, flashing e-pads up for signature, then radioing dispatch for their next assignment, haltingly conducting conversations over FaceTime and WhatsApp all the while in Russian, Polish, English, Arabic and Spanish. Amidst its transience, its impermanence, there is a durability to all this that Soren, if he wants to progress in this business, or perhaps simply in life, would do well to note. Empires will crumble, Death Stars will explode, but scurriers will always be there.

7. Ground Truth

Diamond, like Briar, has been tutored by Phocan on the ins and outs of moving photons around. She shadowed him her whole first week at Pantarey. On the Monday, as technicians set up a pommel horse in The Cell's gridded area, it was he who laid out for her the fundamentals of passive optical motion capture.

'What a marker does,' he pinched between his thumb and fingers the small, cream-coloured silken sphere he'd picked up from a table, one of thousands that seemed to sprout about the company's HQ like tiny mushrooms round a forest floor, 'is reflect light back to a camera. The camera's LEDs send the light out and the marker, the "nipple", bounces it back, thereby providing a position, or coordinate. One marker, one position; two markers, two positions; three, three; and so on. That's all it does: reflect – which is why we call it "passive". With me so far?'

She nodded. From a doorway on The Cell's far side a short, muscular gymnast was emerging.

'Here, though,' Phocan continued, 'is the paradox: the marked position's not the final goal. It's not the spot you want.'

'How do you mean?' she asked.

'The spot you're interested in, the one you *really* want, from a kinetic point of view, is the true pivot-point or centre – what we call the "root". In a human motion, this is almost always hidden from sight. The markers serve as stepping stones or way stations towards unearthing this elusive root. With four of them, we can build point-clouds round it, extrapolate it and reconstitute it.'

The abstract formulation began to make sense once the gymnast, about whom Sennet had been busily attaching markers, mounted his horse and started swinging and scissoring around it. On the screen before which she and Phocan sat, Diamond watched lit dot-squares loop and gyrate in repeating sequences.

'You see them here.' Phocan's finger skipped from square to moving square. 'If we take these four, round his wrist, and draw them out' – his mouse clicked its way through these actions as he described them – 'then set this box up ...' With five or six more quick-fire clicks he'd built a rectangle out to the wrist's side and reproduced the dots (still moving, cutting out a small, repeating sub-step of the body's larger dance) inside this, their original arrangement expanded and enlarged; then, scurrying across a set of side bars, pull-down menus and the like, he made the duplicated dots fire out, like laser canons, four beams that, meeting at a fifth spot lying within their boundary, caused this last spot – itself moving on the screen, tugged back and forth by the four marker-derived dots' movement – to blaze into visibility, and Phocan to announce triumphantly to Diamond: 'There's our root. That's the wrist's core.'

He went on to unearth several more roots from various passages and junctions of the gymnast's body, building rectangles off to the side, replicating marker point-clouds inside these, shooting rays out from them to bring to light new pivot-points.

'The goal, most of the time, in close-up body mo-cap,' he told her as he did this, 'is solved skeleton.'

'What's that?' she asked.

'Think of your clothes,' he told her, 'relative to the skin beneath them. A *person's*' – he corrected himself as he caught her peering, cross-eyed, at her own jumper – 'clothes. They're moving all the time. A marker on the former, on a T-shirt or whatever, won't give you a precise indication of the exact location of a mole on the surface of the latter. Just as a marker on the skin itself won't pinpoint a joint's coordinates beneath it, since skin's also highly mobile: as far as we're concerned, it's just another layer of clothing.

What we're after is the base, the bones under it all: solved skeleton. In clinical situations, at least. With entertainment, it's a little different: there the emphasis is more on augmented effect.'

'And here?' she asked him, pointing to the swivelling figure.

He had to think a little before answering:

'Here's somewhere in-between. It's not so much the *skeleton* we want as the whole circuit of force and counterforce, balance and its limits. Here the root's neither bone nor muscle, but something else, something more systemic ...'

Diamond, staring at the screen, let her gaze lose itself in the proliferating boxes. Shifting it back to the real gymnast, she was greeted by the sight of yet another box: the pommel horse around which he was circling, spindling and flairing. It was elongated, leather-finished, cambered on its upper surface, like a coffin. That all this motion, all these sequences, this ultra-formalised display, was orchestrated round positions that themselves remained interred ... The thought perplexed her; over the next weeks, it was to cloud her world view: everything she saw, each scene or situation she watched or participated in, she'd start extrapolating, reproducing, root-pinpointing, building boxes for, always off to the side ...

The Tuesday was spent off-site, down in London. In the basement of Guy's Hospital, Wing A, Lift C, she and Phocan were admitted to a gait lab on whose wall were painted sting rays, octopi and mermaids, all cavorting round a sunken treasure chest that Diamond at first glance misinterpreted as a flight recorder. Around an ethanol-dispensing tub and bandage box on a low table next to an examination couch were crowded soft-toy dinosaurs, ducks and gorillas; above them, half-depleted sheets of *Paw Patrol* and *Peppa Pig* stickers magnet-clamped to a whiteboard, figures peering in bemusement at its diagrams. The patient (in the management idiom printed on the dossier Dr Cromarty, Chief Clinical Scientist, was perusing as they prepped the room up, *client*), waiting outside when they arrived, was designated by the string *MA2703*.

'*MA*'s Male Adolescent,' Cromarty explained. 'This is his third visit.'

He handed Diamond the dossier. Flicking through it, she found page after page of episodic record, interspersed with boxes across which tricoloured contours (violet-orange-grey, now shadowing, now cross-cutting, now diverging from each other) depicted foot-progress angles and degrees of ankle torsion.

'I devised this format myself,' said Cromarty. 'The consultants who have to parse it to extract their cues for surgical decisions hate it. They just want a story, with a simple moral: *Do this, don't do that* … But pathologies aren't fables. My task is to break each down to its constituent parts.'

MA2703's was pretty broken down: it contained dramatic peaks – femur-fracturing and calf-twisting interventions of the previous year, for instance – but these were few and far between: mostly it was subplots – abductor tension drop-off and knee-range expansion – whose bearing on the main arc, or even on each other, seemed quite tendentious; overall, it offered scant development, imparted no sense of heading to a climax or *dénouement*, happy or otherwise.

'Cerebral palsy's non-progressive. That's what makes it such a rich adversary, or quarry, or' – Cromarty looked around and lowered his voice to a whisper, as though not wanting to pronounce the word within the *client*'s earshot – 'muse.'

'Here, Lucy,' Phocan, sitting at a monitor-decked table with the gait lab's technologist, one Agnieszka Czajka, called her over. 'You can test the pick-up. Walk around waving this about.'

He threw her a calibrating baton, and she paced about the floor turning first one way then another, gyrating the baton's T-boned end in small loops through the air, as though to consecrate the space with holy water, or perhaps to dowse for water in the first place. As the corresponding loops and spirals etched themselves across the surface of their screens, Phocan talked Czajka through the pathways, shortcuts and (he seemed ready to admit this even if Pantarey's own help page wasn't) pitfalls of Physis 6™.

'The most important difference between this version and 5 is that you don't have to manually label each articulation point: the software does it for you. When it comes to the eventing, this will save you lots of time.'

'We ready for him?' Cromarty called out from beside his couch. Phocan gave the thumbs-up.

'Showtime!' Cromarty, turning ringmaster, raised and oscillated an imaginary top hat. His second, Dr Winter (same job title as him minus the *Chief*), exited the room, re-entering with a boy and (Diamond presumed) his mother.

'What's this?' Cromarty, turning from his couch, threw a mock double-take, and stared at the fourteen-year-old with friendly-astonished eyes. 'They must have sent Nathan's big brother!'

The boy smiled, blushing. Cromarty waved him over, and he left his mother's side to cross the floor on pointed, scissored toes. Cromarty kept his faux-shocked spiel up while MA2703 approached him, instructing Winter to check that they hadn't mis-prescribed super-strength growth hormones, screwing his face up Quint-like as he announced in his best sea-dog drawl *We're gonna need a bigger gait lab* ... Behind it all, though, Diamond, standing right next to him, could see his eyes running metrics, taking stock.

'Nathan,' he announced when the boy reached him, 'our eyes are giving science the lie. We're going to have to measure you, to bring your growth spurt back under the canopy of reason. Strip down to your underpants.'

Nathan, still reddening, obeyed. Cromarty steered him down on to the couch, extracting from his upper reaches waist-circumference and wrist-to-elbow figures with a measuring tape, while his second noted knee-to-foot and toe-abduction scores from the couch's base, where, like a surveyor hunkered in the shadow of a cantilever bridge, he crouched holding a goniometer between one opened eye and the bent legs which towered above him. This completed, they swabbed the boy's calves and thighs down and attached to these EMG electrodes, flesh-toned discs from each of which a miniature box hung, flashing intermittently, a tiny distress beacon. Their batteries, or perhaps his own nervousness converted into electricity, sent small local spasms through Nathan's leg muscles, rippling the skin's surface, and he reddened again, embarrassed by this subcutaneous excitation that was briefly, before Winter veiled its modesty with the bandages he coiled around his legs to hold the EMGs in place, visible to all – and even then still visible to Phocan and Czajka on the screen, across which they watched rows of fuzzy soundbars etch their way horizontally from left to right, jumping seismically with every quiver. Winter then, with Diamond's help, dotted about Nathan's metatarsals, thighs and kneecaps the Pantarey markers.

'To the Catwalk!' Cromarty commanded.

Winter now led Nathan to the gait lab's central area, a narrow strip or runway.

'If you pull the P6 window up,' Phocan was saying to Czajka over at their side table, 'you should see …'

There it was, on her screen: a set of light-points moving in conjunction with each other, as they had with the pommel-horse gymnast.

'Now,' said Phocan, 'click on *spline fill*, and …'

As soon as Czajka did this, lines – green, red and white – sprung up between the white dots, weaving a cat's cradle of intersecting, if irregular, triangles set on two perpendicularly adjoining planes; a configuration that, while purely geometric, nonetheless communicated unmistakably the hip-to-heel formation of MA2703's lower torso. When Cromarty, still playing ringmaster, had Nathan walk from one end of the runway to the other, this formation also ambulated: a complex pipe-cleaner figure, or the bottom half of one, whose constituent vertices and edges shifted and reconfigured with each movement. Occasionally, a line between two points would vanish, then flash up again between two other points, trying to forge a plausible connection that, in turn, would either stick or, overridden by the software, vanish again.

'I thought it knew which spot was which,' said Czajka as the figure's left thigh flickered out of visibility.

'Well, it does most of the time,' responded Phocan. 'Especially when it's been told once. If you just label that spot RTIB for right tibia, and that one LHEE for left heel, it should retain the designations as it moves on.'

Czajka pulled the labels from a menu on her screen's right, and dropped them on the dots tracking the positions of the markers that in turn showed the locations of the boy's tibia and heel; as his passage down the Catwalk continued, she performed the same click-and-drag manoeuvre for RTOE, LASI, RASI, LPSI ... Once MA2703 reached the strip's end, Cromarty, with a spinning gesture of the finger, turned him round and sent him back; then back again once he'd reached the other end; then ditto once more, and again. Phocan was right: after three or so passes, the lines joining the dots stopped fading, retaining their integrity instead from phase to phase.

'All labelled,' Czajka said, impressed. 'Can we go for strikes now?'

'Absolutely.' Phocan nodded. 'And it'll tell you when you've got a good one. Hit *Show Pads* ...'

When Czajka did this, the runway depicted on her monitor separated out into three rectangular sections, labelled *1*, *2*, *3*, each corresponding to a strike pad set in the real strip's floor. On MA2703's next pass, as his heel hit the first actual pad, on screen an arrow jumped out of the first rectangle, thrusting upwards from the floor in line with the stick figure's thigh.

'That's a hit,' said Phocan. 'You don't need to mark it; it'll auto-tag.'

'How are we doing?' Cromarty called pantomimishly across the room.

'One strike on that pass,' Czajka called back to him.

'Nathan,' Cromarty exhorted the boy, 'we're going to have to work you further. Keep it up. Imagine you're a sentry, pacing up and down before the palace gates.'

On the next pass they got strikes on Sections 1 and 3. The middle pad, though, didn't seem to want to register one: could have been reduced sensitivity from wear and tear, or how it lay within the boy's gait cycle ... Finally, after eight more to-and-fros, Section 2 pinged for them in concert with the others. Czajka, reprising Phocan's earlier gesture, held her thumb up to her boss; Cromarty informed Nathan that he was a star, instructed him to relax, to put his clothes back on, to take a bow, conducting all the others in the room in a round of applause that caused the child to redden yet again.

'Now,' Phocan, Diamond at his shoulder, told Czajka when the clapping had died down, 'you event it. Rerun the sequence; if you hit the notch marking each event, it'll prompt you with ...'

She was already gliding the cursor to the first, most leftward-lying notch; as soon as this reached it, a *Create Event* box popped up, with *MA2703 right foot strike* pre-entered inside it.

'Click *Confirm* ...' said Phocan.

Czajka did this; then confirmed the next *Create Event* box's default content as *MA2703 right foot lift*; and the next *MA2703 left foot strike*; and so on, moving rightwards down the runway, until the cycle was fully marked.

'Now we plug the holes,' said Phocan.

'There are still holes?' asked Czajka.

''Fraid so. Even Physis 6 can't prevent markers going into blind spots, clashing with each other, and the like,' he conceded. 'What it *can* do is give you the tools for overcoming this ...'

For the next fifteen minutes he walked her through the program's various gap-filling options. While he murmured instructions, Czajka rotated the stick figure round on her screen like a clay pot on a wheel, combing it for parts where body-lines, despite the software's interventions, were still missing; when she found one, she swooped down on it, zooming in to enlarge single points, threading these with wavy filaments she fed through needle-eyes of cones and onwards to the next enlarged point, which she cone-threaded too, the frazzled braids floating around the figure in a loose gossamer web until, tightening the filament to pull it straight, she bridged the void between the paired points once again. On completing each fill, Czajka road-tested her fix, running the tibia- or thigh-formation of which it formed part backwards and forwards through sub-segments of the event in which they, in turn, played their own micro-role or function: the quarter-second following right foot-strike, while the metatarsal was straightening, or the two-tenths preceding lift off, when it was curving up again ...

Diamond, not having much to do at this point, found herself staring at MA2703's mother, who'd been hovering around Phocan and Czajka's station, watching the accumulated data being fed into the gait lab's server, amalgamated with cached readings from his previous two sessions and fed forward to the online cataloguing systems of CMAS and ESMAC, to be worked through by the matrix of five continents' and heaven knows how many leading institutions' interlinked, cross-indexed CP research. Canopy of reason. Under this woman's gaze, the processors, blinking synaptically beneath the table, seemed to take on the status of boxed hierophants, oracles which she had ventured, suppliant, down to this grotto to consult; the wires linking them to one another to become black naval cords that, dipping from view behind gun metal, wound their way back to dark secrets, mysteries of origin, her child's sad incunabula. Her eyes, tracking them until they disappeared, were filled with a look not just inquisitive but also pleading – as though somewhere, among the labyrinths of circuitry, printed on some nanometric stretch of RAM-card, there lay the key to *fixing* Nathan, fixing the whole situation: something as simple as a switch that might be thrown, a feedback loop reversed, a line of code rewritten ...

'So,' the mother haltingly asked Cromarty when he, too, sauntered across to the processing station, 'what's your current thinking?'

'On what?' he enquired back.

'Rhizomoty.' She spoke the word carefully, as though its very syllables contained an incantation.

Cromarty pulled a face. 'The trouble with SDR – rhizomoty,' he said, rolling out what Diamond could see was his standard lecture on the subject, 'is that it's based on the belief that you can simply isolate a problem from the body that it's part of. Edit it out, as it were. It doesn't work like that. Bodies are systems; complex networks; parts all interlinked. This is especially true in the neural field. Just slicing through the nerve-roots in the spinal cord won't stop the overstimulation in the upper brain: the ataxia's caused by a million other channels and transmitters, all of which are over-firing. Look, here's how …'

He began to sketch her, in the margin of his dossier-pages, a motor neuron. When Diamond dropped back in on it two minutes later, the lecture had broadened out to embrace the entire history of hyperkinetic disorders – their social reception, the attendant attitudes and *mores* – through the eras.

'The Ancients held sufferers in esteem, thought them possessed of second sight; and the Medièvals attributed to them the votive fervour of the followers of Vitus, shaking in rhapsody before his statue: *choreia,* choir, a chorus. You don't have to see it as a curse.'

'I don't,' the mother countered in a half-indignant, half-found-out tone.

'Besides,' Cromarty added, 'the surgical decision, ultimately, won't be mine …'

His words trailed off, and he tapped his pencil's end against the paper, as though marking out a rhythm – to the process of decision-making, or of illness, or simply of time, its non-progression. His sketch's neuron had a core from which grew tentacles that trailed beneath it, like a jellyfish's. Diamond, feeling like an interloper, looked away, towards the gait lab's wall, where cephalopod limbs danced lithely with the fronds of seaweed woven all around them, with the happy crabs, the concupiscent mermaids.

Wednesday, it was back to HQ, where she progressed from single- to multi-body capture. Arriving in The Cell, she found its area divided by foam building blocks into a kind of floor-plan, with walls reduced to stubs that stopped at shin-height.

'It's an embassy,' Phocan explained.

'Which one?' she asked.

'Generic,' he said. 'SG are building a training tool for police forces around the world. The old embassy-storm scenario: terrorists, hostages, window-shattering abseils, boom, et cetera.'

SG was Serious Games plc, a regular Pantarey client. They'd brought both terrorists and captive embassy personnel with them – all, Diamond discovered when she chatted with them over greaseproof-wrapped brie and chutney sandwiches whose lustre was fast crusting over, junior SG staff.

'I feel like a dickhead,' a young man called Darren told her, standing beside the trestle table in a gluteally unflattering, nipple-studded black bodysuit. 'Pearly King in a gimp outfit.'

'It could be worse,' his colleague and her counterpart, the SG intern Michael, added. 'Last time it was loonies for ...'

'Mental health system users,' Darren corrected him.

'Mental health system users,' Michael, in mock naughty-schoolboy voice, repeated, 'wriggling and slithering about the walls and floor, to train nurses and orderlies to talk them into taking meds or standing still while straitjackets got pulled over their heads.'

'At least we don't have to do facials,' murmured Darren.

Diamond saw what he was getting at when, unfinished sandwiches abandoned, Darren, Michael and the other bodies were directed through their various routines, terrorists shuffling sideways across rooms with hostage-shields clasped tight in front of them, or jumping out of doorways to point guns at absent SWAT teams, or, touched by the latter's prospective bullets, crumpling to the floor. They executed these actions and others in a matter-of-fact, quite undramatic manner: dying, they expressed no shock or sorrow; threatening death, they exuded no menace; suicide vests, detonated with motions as banal as those deployed to release seat belts, produced no explosions. There were neither shouts nor screams: the actions all took place in studious silence punctuated only by the squeak of trainers on the floor, or SG's line manager and the ex-SAS man he'd brought with him calling out instructions. Since these were generally to repeat a certain shuffle, dart or crumple, or to move to another section of the floor, there to perform an action unrelated, or at least non-sequent, to the one they'd just been doing, there was no continuity, nor coherence, nor even any sense of anyone pretending, at a level either individual or collective, to be actually living out the situations and events they were depicting.

'The face stuff gets added later,' Phocan explained to Diamond when she asked about this. 'We have a trove of expressions – fear and anger, and so on – that we'll provide them with. For dialogue specific to this tool, we've got two actors coming in this afternoon.'

These actors, when they appeared, were transformed into over-grown teenagers, faces marker-pustuled, and then made to utter lines such as *Get back*, *I'll kill her*, *I've got a bomb* and *Save me*, all with the requisite look of desperation, terror and determina-tion – but ultimately, since Phocan had instructed them to speak the words out clearly and, what's more, *slowly*, to facilitate good capture of mandibular and labial modulations, in a manner as strangely denatured as the morning's movements.

'It's not really acting, is it?' she commented to Phocan as he extracted roots from jowls, temples and cheekbones, reconstituting a snarl's pivot-points inside another box.

'Oh, it is, though,' he said – then, raising his voice to address the male performer, called out: 'Peter, come over here a minute.'

Peter, still silk-acned, ambled across and, when asked by Phocan to tell Diamond what he'd studied, announced proudly:

'German Expressionism. Did my thesis on it.'

Seeing her look blankly back at him, he added:

'The stuff you see in the old silent movies – how the villains scowl and cackle, and the heroines expand their mouths and eyes into huge gaping circles, to convey a state of mind that'll be rec-ognised by any audience. That's what acting was about in those days: facial showjumping. You had to ride your skin and muscles through a course, negotiating obstacles, like troughs and fences: joy, shock, menace …'

'Do you do theatre stuff as well?' she asked.

'You mean contemporary theatre? Do I act in it?'

She nodded.

'God no,' he snorted. 'Naturalist bullshit – like the *twentieth* century had never happened, let alone all ... this.' He gestured round The Cell. 'This,' he repeated, smiling at Phocan with what seemed to Diamond a mixture of affection and gratitude, 'is where the action's at. It's the real deal.'

'Faces,' Phocan explained to her as he manipulated Peter's feature-dots after the actor and his leading lady had retired, 'are landscapes. They've got peaks and ridges and ravines, which can be surveyed with absolute precision. Once you've got the contours, you can start manipulating them – like landscape architects ... you know, Capability Brown ... Anything's possible. Look ...'

A couple more clicks and Peter's upper lip started to curl back on itself, unwrapping his left cheek. Moving the pointer over to the right ear, Phocan then peeled back the other cheek, folding it down over what was left of the mouth and pinning its apex (now its nadir) to the long, underhanging ledge of the submaxillary passage where chin curves round into neck. He continued this origami until what had previously been Peter was no more than a cubistic scramble, resembling more a quarry or a bomb site than a face.

'For lots of applications,' he told Diamond, 'you don't need an actor in the first place. You can build the features up from scratch, then flesh it out. Look here ...'

Shuffling windows, he called up a file named *Annabel* and popped open a girl's face – a child's, no dot-point reconstitution but, it seemed, a gif filmed on a webcam: she was smiling, brushing hair out of her eyes and blinking shyly.

'This one was made for Interpol,' Phocan explained. 'A honey-trap for paedophiles. There was no original, for ethical and legal reasons. But she *looked* authentic; and she could even hold short conversations with the marks; so they thought that they were FaceTiming a real child, and would stay online for long enough for police to trace their IPs.' Closing the file, he added: 'Poor Annabel. She never got to exist, other than as a composite built around general metrics: long lashes, thin arms, brown hair, whatever ...'

He sat in silence for a while. Diamond watched him, waiting for him to continue with her priming. But he'd slipped into a kind of dazed hiatus, staring at something she couldn't discern, his mind trawling files inaccessible to her. The first time she'd been introduced to him, she'd misheard his name as *Focal*; and the elision, the corrupting metonym, had stuck – wasn't he, after all, inducing her into the world of focusing, of looking? His own look, she'd since noticed, was sometimes jumping between distances and depths of field, as though trying to lock on to two or more focal points at the same time – and, as a consequence, finding itself stranded between staging posts, lost in some interstice whose vagueness spurred it on towards new acts of focusing at once more strained and more vague; as though, like the earliest photographers out of whose bellowed, velvet-curtained clutter his whole discipline had hatched, he'd been conjuring his subject into visibility by use of multiple and staggered lenses, both inverting and reversing, and through not just apertures but also veils. He had that look now, seemed to be staring not so much at the actual screen in front of him as at some absent, offset one that floated spectrally a few inches in front of, or behind, this. She found it intriguing, and compelling, and somehow, in ways she couldn't quite articulate, as instructive of the pursuit to which she found herself apprenticed as any concrete or specific knowledge of it that he might confide to her.

Phocan, Phocus, hocus-pocus. They spent the last few hours of Wednesday cleaning. Multi-body capture turned out to be a nightmare in terms of its sight-lines. Limbs and torsos of one figure, passing in front of those of a second, or a third, as terrorists clasped to their breast or ducked and scuttled behind captives, produced weird and grotesque mergings: bodies seemed to mutate, sprouting organs and appendages in every which direction, then to slough them off again – a fluid orgy of construction and dismantling that ran simultaneously, at a range of speeds and rhythms that were unaligned yet still conjoined, processing at the same overall pace. Phocan's (and Diamond's) job, then, was to separate the bodies out again, to subjugate the schizoid carnage to the strictures of fixed individual identity, in which a leg, head or shoulder was assigned to a single person, and that person was determined as either an aggressor to be vanquished or a victim to be saved.

'We're like the rugby referee,' he said, 'who has to dive into the maul and strip the players from it one by one, to work out whose hand the ball's lying in, where another player's hand or leg is relative to that and to the ground, and so on. Come to think of it,' he went on, turning from the screen, 'sport's even worse than this. I've got to go and pitch our software at a sport-science trade fare in a few weeks from now, in Rome. We're supposed, before then, to have come up with a tool that can untangle football post-goal celebration pile-ups.'

'And will we?' she asked. 'Come up with it, I mean?'

'No,' he answered. 'It's impossible. What we can do, though, is fill the gaps, the unknown – unknowable – blank areas, with what, based on the possibilities, are the most plausible conjectures. So, with this hostage situation,' he turned screenward again, 'you've got – just as with the single-subject capture in the gait lab yesterday – your spline-fill, pattern-fill, rigid-body and kinematic-fills, then cyclic and quintic spine-fills …'

Moving vertically along his drop-down, he ran all these options through their paces – one after the other, and with varying success. Sometimes a scrambled mass reorganised itself into the same number of clear, differentiated bodies as had entered the mix in the first place; at other times, though, the reconstituted figures would gain an accessory, hanging in the air beside them – neither gun nor handbag, nor any other prop that had been present earlier in the day, but such incongruous paraphernalia as umbrellas, party balloons and top hats.

'Artefacts,' smiled Phocan.

'Artefacts?' she repeated. 'Like handcrafted things?'

He nodded.

'But,' she said, 'aren't they the opposite of that? Not things at all, or even images of them … Why do they call them that?'

'I don't know. I suppose because they're artificial – not there in reality, just generated, "crafted", in the interface between the object and its rendering. They're the mirages of our profession. You get them a lot in UAV work.'

'UAV?'

'Unmanned aerial vehicles. We're doing it tomorrow. I'll have to get you clearance.'

In fact, they spent both the Thursday and the Friday at BAE's headquarters outside Farnborough. The site was huge, ringed by two layers of reinforced green fencing; at the entrance, beside a security post whose personnel took fifteen minutes to admit (their preferred term, sent back and forth down radios, was 'verify') them, a Union Jack hung limp from a giant flagpole.

'Is this a company or a military base?' she asked him as they crawled past various fighter jets and helicopters planted in the verges and roundabout-islands.

'The distinction kind of blurs here, I'd say,' Phocan muttered as he parked by a gargantuan hangar. Pointing to two figures who'd emerged from a minute door at the foot of this, he added: 'Ah, here's Roger. He's our guy.'

Roger was the younger of the two; the other, smartly dressed, austere, the other side of sixty, wasn't introduced to them and, after murmuring some kind of order or instructions to Roger soon after they'd entered the building, retreated down a corridor into what Diamond took to be an even more restricted area. Unmanned aerial vehicles turned out to mean drones. In the sector of the hangar to which Roger led them, three or four of these were buzzing round a demarcated cube of airspace not unlike that of The Cell: black rubber floor, one fixed wall, string-mesh curtains making up three floating ones, HDI220 cameras clamped to rails establishing the control area's effective 'ceiling' (the hangar's actual ceiling was a good hundred feet higher). The drones were kite-sized, like the ones she'd see hovering above Port Meadow of a Sunday, play-things of children and hobbyists – only these ones came across as sharper and more waspish. They'd accelerate across the space then stop right on a speck of airborne dust without seeming to have to brake or slow down first; or turn one way then another in figure-of-eight patterns that recalled for her the gymnast's moves about his pommel horse. Their sound, undissipated here by any meadow's wind, was sharp too: an insistent and vindictive whine.

'With drones,' Phocan informed her as he hurled one roughly from his hand into the control zone's midst, where, after weaving around a little, discombobulated, it eventually re-stabilised itself, 'responsiveness is everything. Roots have to be recalculated several times a second – which removes much of the human interface.'

'How so?' she asked.

'We're too slow.' He smiled back at her, as though her question, and the computational inadequacy it betrayed, had furnished its own answer. 'These quadrators have IMUs to measure ...'

'Have what?'

'Sorry: inertial measurement units, to sense angular velocity. The idea is that they should be able to pitch and twist their way through doorways, vents and all manner of cavities, taking requisite decisions onboard, autonomously.'

'Hey,' called Roger from the far edge of the cube. 'Now the Ancient Mariner's gone, let's show your friend the Buzzby Berkeley skit.'

'Ancient Mariner?'

'Pilkington.' Roger jabbed his thumb over his shoulder in the vague direction of the inner warren into which his grey-haired boss had disappeared. 'What say?'

Phocan smiled indulgently. Roger and his sidekick Josh strolled over to a bunch of drones lying to the control zone's side and, crab-zagging around crouched, from one spot to another of the demarcated area's floor, arranged them symmetrically about this. Retiring back out past the white tape, they gathered round a laptop with a Beastie Boys sticker on it, Josh looking on with eager anticipation while Roger typed in commands.

'... and ... Enter! Now sit back, enjoy ...'

He stepped back, and the drones all lifted off in sync. Once airborne, they, too, started a crab-dance, a quadrille, with pairs cutting parallelogram-figures around other pairs, then splitting to form new pairs that in turn would cut new parallelograms, knitting intangible chain mail in the air as the block glided diagonally, overall shape intact, from one corner to another. That corner reached, the drones all wedged themselves into a tight-packed bud inside its right angle, then, like stamens of a wind-blown dandelion, turned outwards and detached again, one row after the other, shooting off to the cube's furthest reaches.

'That number's called "Little Web of Dreams",' Josh told her.

'And,' Roger, still in announcer mode, added as each of the web's dreams wended its way back to an assigned spot on the floor, there to await further orders, 'I'm afraid it's the finale as far as you're concerned.' Then, to Phocan, by way of explanation: 'Reaper guidance system next. This one's Level Two.'

Diamond, too, turned to Phocan, for a translation.

'I couldn't get you clearance beyond Level One,' he told her apologetically. 'You'll have to sit this bit out.'

'Try,' Roger chipped in as she traipsed down her path of exile, 'to pump Aidan in the next room for state secrets. He'll be happy to spill the beans.'

Aidan was, indeed, talkative. Like Josh and Roger, he was dressed in jeans and trainers; his demeanour, though, was slightly stiffer, less at ease – the consequence, it turned out, of a military background.

'I used to fly those things,' he told her.

'Quadrators?' she asked.

'No,' he said, opening his own, stickerless laptop. 'Predators – the predecessor of the Reapers you people are helping us with. They look like this . . .'

Diamond peered past him at a picture of a long, windowless tube whose several short wings, like those of insects, were arranged about the thorax in a range of positions and angles, some pointing up, some down. If it was insect-like, it was aquatic too, its smooth, grey carapace reminding her of the skin of seals, or the large, featureless underbelly of a whale as it passes a tourist boat. There was, as with the whale-glimpse, something incomplete and unsatisfying about the sighting – as though, even when viewed in close-up, the creature's face, or character, its centre of intelligence, had stayed submerged.

'It doesn't have a head,' she said.

'I'm its head,' Aidan told her. 'We'd fly them from the ground.'

'Where?' she asked. 'In Afghanistan?'

'Yes,' he answered; 'I mean no. The *Predator* was in Afghanistan; but I'd be flying it from a field in Hampshire.'

'You'd be standing in a field?' She still had pictures of Port Meadow in her mind.

'A hangar in a field,' he said. 'Like this, but smaller. A box in a hangar; freight-container size. On a base, of course. I'd be there in full uniform, reporting to and liaising with various officers in other rooms: mission intelligence coordinator, director of operations, all the computer support personnel. But it was me and one co-pilot, or sensor-operator, in the box itself, flying the thing.'

'From a joystick?' she asked.

'Well, not just,' he said, sounding taken aback. 'We had six or seven screens around us: live-feed, instrumentation, flight data, terrain maps, ground-truth intel uploaded from the troops – photographs, basically … Then chat boxes, so you could talk with the ground forces and with your own superiors – on the base, in London, Kandahar, wherever – directly, in real time. We'd be there at the controls for nine hours at a stretch.'

'Just watching?'

'Sometimes. Once I watched a house for a month straight, while people wandered in and out, or not; nothing important happened there. Or sometimes we'd scour roads for IEDs: hidden bombs, booby-traps. Troops can't see these, but we can, because metallic objects have a different temperature to the soil they're buried in. So do the cords that lead from them to detonators: they leave bright heat-signatures that run straight to the insurgents waiting to trigger

97

them off when a Humvee or squadron comes along. When you've pinpointed these guys, then you either tell the ground troops where they are or send a strike down yourself, from the bird.'

'What bird?'

'The drone. You whip a Hellfire missile off its rails, and take them out.'

'How long did you do this for?' she asked.

'Two years,' he answered. 'Then I got discharged.'

'Why?'

'PTSD,' he said. 'Pilkington took pity on me, brought me in here, and ...' He stopped and, mistaking her confused look for incomprehension, started annotating: 'Post-traumatic stress disor ...'

'I know what it means,' she said. 'But you weren't ...'

'Weren't what?'

'You weren't ... I mean ... in a war zone ...'

'Wasn't I?' He smiled, then added: 'Aren't we?'

Diamond made no response. From the restricted area next door a quadrator banked or accelerated, its tone crescendoing aggressively, then, just as suddenly, diminishing to no more than a liminal hum, like lights or fridges make. For half a minute, neither of them spoke. Then Aidan, keen to keep the exchange going, outed with:

'Guess how I and the other sensor-operators spent our out-of-theatre time.'

'What theatre?'

'The war zone. Guess how we passed our time between shifts.'

'I don't know,' she shrugged back. 'Sleeping? Drinking?'

'We played video games,' he told her.

'You're kidding.'

'Not at all,' he said. 'I'd even sometimes do a flight-simulator one. You could pick different eras: pilot a Handley Page Victor or a de Havilland Mosquito, all the way back to a Sopwith or an RE8. I found it relaxing; even therapeutic. Nobody was getting killed ...'

Silence, laced with modulating background whine, set in again. Then Aidan, suddenly animated, said to Diamond:

'Hey: you wanna see the Light of God?'

'I'm sorry?' she replied.

'Here, look.' He beckoned her towards his laptop, cursor skipping between folders. The file that he eventually clicked open was an mpeg; it showed a terrain, rendered in night-time vision: houses, trees, a deserted street ... The scene was being filmed from the ground, from something (she deduced from the slight movement, a slow heave and fall, as though the picture were breathing) like a body-camera. Nothing was happening – until a broad and brilliantly shining column burst out of the heavens and planted itself on the earth a hundred or so yards from the filmer.

'That's our beam,' Aidan announced. 'The laser that we send down from the sky. Our ground guys put their goggles on and *pow!* they see it, showing them the spot they need to hit. Only them: to the bad guys, it's invisible, but to our people it shines like a holy apparition: Light of God. When it reaches the floor, it blossoms.'

'Into what?'

'A square shape, usually.'

'God's a square?'

'Apparently. This is one of my own missions: I beamed the Light down on a sniper I'd located, and the Captain thanked me after they'd wiped the guy by sending me the video, a keepsake. Here, I've got another one that I can show you ...'

The new mpeg he opened had been shot in daytime, from the Predator itself – or rather, Aidan explained, from its Hellfire missile. Watching it, Diamond was at first reminded of generic YouTube parachuting clips: it showed, from POV a descending body that itself remained unseen, this same body's passage through the air. First there was blue sky, then, at the picture's base, the flat horizon line; then this last tilted upward like a trapdoor opening around a hinge set just beyond the frame, pushing the sky away as though the latter were a cushion or tarpaulin lying atop it, sliding off to be replaced by a single dry-brown surface that filled the whole screen. This new surface was approaching fast, and gaining definition as it did so, pixels refreshing at a rate that matched the speed of the descent. Eventually, out of its earthy gauze, a form emerged, an image: of a settlement or conurbation, perhaps no more than a village, whose white edifices were arranged around a central opening, a yard or plaza. In this opening a group of people in white robes stood, clustered loosely together, engaged in some kind of congregation. As the ground rose nearer it seemed to accelerate, and all the clearing's edges raced away, the opening opening further, flowing out, its borders running while its centre, too, expanded, growing ever clearer: white-robed men, locked in their confab, unaware that they were being observed – until the mpeg's final frames, in which they turned their heads up to look straight at the camera, and at Diamond, for the fraction of a second just before the screen went blank.

'I think that it's okay to show you this,' Aidan reflected. 'It's my own; never got classified. I say "my own", but actually, it was the software that rumbled the baddies this time: it detected sequences of movement and alignment that implied a probability of 95.6 per cent that something insurgent-linked was going on. Above 95, a strike usually ends up being called. All I did here was send the thing down, save its video-feed as a keepsake. I've got a whole bunch more that I could … Are you staying in Farnborough tonight?'

Phocan arrived at that moment and whisked her to safety. She found herself excluded from the inner hangar's sanctum for a stretch of the next morning, too, but managed to confine Aidan to showing her pictures of artefacts (she had retained the term, and impressed him now by using it) thrown up by drones' remote-sensor software: of rainbow-cars and aeroplanes, their outlines doubled, tripled and quadrupled, daubed in glorious, RGB-separated technicolour; of the glacial and crystalline terrain-effects produced by vignetting and mosaic blurring, by relief displacement, colour balancing, chromatic aberration, bi-directional reflectance … She spent what seemed like ages staring, captivated, at these glitches. It wasn't just that they were beautiful; beyond that, in their abstraction of a battlefield, of snipers, IEDs and doomed village summits into pointillistic billows, scumbled glazes, dribbles, splashes, smears, they offered her relief, a kind of psychic camouflage . . .

Thus passed her first week. That was a month ago. Today, she finds herself doing PM analysis. The clients in this case are Ruff, an architecture firm, who've been commissioned by the City of Bedford to redesign one of the town's central shopping areas. Pantarey's brief is tripartite, and alliteratively so: transit, entanglement and tempo. The shopping strip is outdoors but, being divided from the street itself by retail outlets, steps and bollards, carless; whence today's mode of enquiry (PM stands for 'Pedestrian Motion', although in-house, they prefer the trade-term 'Pedestrian Flow in Urban Corridor', whose acronym, if you remove the linking preposition, never fails to prompt a giggle). They're to notate, in terms of not just route but also rhythm, the passage of self-selecting, if unwitting, subjects through the area of enquiry, translating every eddy and coagulation, every bump, swerve and dispersal into data-clusters that will form the basis of a model that in turn will inform Ruff's, and Bedford's, reconfig-uration of the space under investigation. In lieu of white tape, this space's borders are defined (although not marked) by T40Ss, nestled furtively under the eaves of facades and the bracket arms of lamp-posts – cameras that, instead of bouncing rays off reflectors stuck to the bodies of their subjects (who today, naturally, aren't wearing any), deploy laser-detectors to register depth of field. It's a new system, a new method, one in terms of whose hard- and software Pantarey have (as Garnett likes to boast) opened up clear blue water between them and their competitors, thus maintaining in their industry not only market advantage but, beyond that, a heroic status tinged with traces of the mystical. Markerless is the holy grail of mo-cap.

If she's progressed to markerless, she's become Markless too: Phocan's off purchasing gallons of bubble-mixture, to waft at a bobsleigh when they go to Holland next week. She's not tagged to him any more exclusively, in any case; these days she's farmed out to whoever needs an extra pair of hands. Today it's Sennet she's assigned to. He's had her climb a ladder, tweak a camera's angle, talk the cashiers in the precinct's Pret a Manger into letting them charge two iPads and a Mac whose batteries were running low and, now, dip back into the same Pret to buy Danishes and coffee so that she and he can ensconce themselves at the outdoor tables incognito: just two folks doing whatever they're doing here in St George's Walk, two grains of sand or pebbles on a beach, lost amidst all the others sitting, walking, idling, clicking, eating . . . though, of course, they're not. These grains of sand also contain the world: their little screens, like the Quaker Oats packet in the hand of the Scot on the Quaker Oats packet, are feeding them the entire strip, captured and enclosed, from above . . .

'What's interesting about the way people move in public space,' Sennet mumbles at her through pastry-flaked lips, 'is that they don't do what they're meant to. They don't follow the paths laid down for them. The planners envisaged shoppers leaving the Waitrose and the smaller concessions, then resting a while on those benches before moving on down the strip. But the benches get nabbed by the tramps, who take up residence there permanently, and create a natural exclusion zone around them; and besides, the spot under the willow tree's much nicer, as it's shaded in the summer – and warmed by low sun in winter, thanks to the gap between the supermarket and the cleaners to the south. Then the steps provided as the corridor's main exit: see how no one's using them. They like to cut between the bollards and the optician's instead . . .'

On the laptop, the veracity of his claims, unascertainable to the naked eye, is instantly self-evident – all the more so when a heat-trace filter's applied, uncovering the accumulated smudge-tracks of each passage since recording started half an hour ago.

'By contrast,' Sennet continues, 'certain interventions produce certain predictable effects. Our trestle tables here, for instance: people don't climb over them, they go around. Even so, you notice how most of Pret's customers prefer to carry their snacks over to the empty market traders' stalls, and requisition these for picnic spots.' He cancels the filter before adding: 'That stuff we can all chart, though. What's really hard to get a handle on is self-congestion.'

'What's that?' asks Diamond.

'People instinctively move to spots where other people happen to be gathering. These spots are themselves as often as not intermediary – that is, they spring up in the gaps between "actual" or landmarked spots. But once they've sprung up they *become* a kind of landmark, temporarily at least. Which means that they, too, get offset on to other spots that spring up between them; and so on and so on, recursively. The only constant is the gap-structure, the "gapping". Outdoor life takes place in intervals.'

Sennet's got two hobby horses. One is talking down Phocan:

'Mark doesn't get this,' he continues. 'You can bring a joint or femur or torque-increment into definition, right down to the micrometre and beyond – but what does that tell you of the flux and reflux of the bigger-picture, the temporal-pattern set-up? I'm surprised Garnett can't see that. He loves Mark, treats him like his own son ...'

At times like these, she senses, with a tinge of excitement mixed with squeamishness, as though the vision were a secret whose unveiling is almost obscene, Pantarey's own solved skeleton creeping into focus. Sennet's other hobby horse is Markov chains. His conversation defaults to them in every second gap imaginable – and, the rhythmic sensitivity inculcated in her by today's task hints at her now, is about to again. 'A discrete-time Markov chain in countable state space is what we're dealing with here,' he tells her between sips of coffee. 'Although I suppose that you could argue for this corridor being viewed as a continuous or general state space ... Either way, the transition matrix is composed of the same jumps and holding times. If you take just one metric – length of pause between each burst of forward movement, for example ... Here, let me try to pull that one up ...'

Diamond, masticating leathery apricot, tunes out and runs her eye along the shopping precinct's floor. A section of its paving stones has been replaced by slabs – or not so much 'replaced by' as 'converted into', since the slabs have been cut from the paving stones themselves, in blocks whose edges don't align with theirs, placed in thin metal frames then returned to the paving, each block reset in its original position but removable so as to afford access, when required, to beneath-street-level pipework and cabling. Eight of these framed slabs run, one after the other, from a spot parallel to where her table ends to where the Waitrose starts: a strip within the strip, like old-style unspooled film, narrowing as it runs away from her, perspective accentuated by the rows of columns on each of the avenue's sides. A woman in a dress is entering this sub-strip now, being hit side-on by sunlight falling through the gap that Sennet pointed out a moment ago. From somewhere behind her, out of view, accordion music carries on the air: a slow, repeating tune that's full of minors. At the precinct's far end, by the bollards, a man leaves the optician's, holding the door open for a policewoman who's peering at a notebook as she enters. On the window by this door a diagram shows a cross-section of the eye, with sclera, retina, cornea, iris, aqueous humour, extra-ocular muscle and retinal blood vessels all labelled. Beside it, smaller diagrams contrast a healthy eyeball (spherical cornea, single focal point) with an astigmatic one (oval cornea, multiple focal points). A group of men in ties cuts between Diamond and this poster; as they pass her table, one of them says, *When I see that, it's time to go*; another answers, *It was time already*; they all laugh. The first man retorts something back, but the accordion music drowns his words out as they cross paths with the woman in the dress, replacing her within the sunlit zone ...

Here's a strange one-two-three: a moment ago, a bald man with a backpack on his shoulder cut sideways through this zone towards the cleaners. As he entered it another man, bald but without a backpack, exited. Now, not half a minute later, a third man, also lacking a backpack although this time hirsute, is making his way in through the door. Diamond knows, because Sennet has told her, that the patterns they extrapolate from these comings and goings will be used not just by Ruff as they reshape the precinct; they'll also be harnessed, transformed and further monetised by Pantarey, deployed to other contexts and assignments, birthing algorithms for crowd scenes in movies, background movement in games ... But what's creeping into her mind now, metabolising with the sugar in a buzz of whimsical conjecture, is the apprehension, the suspicion, that some algo's at work here *already*, moulding this space's tempo, orchestrating all its paths and modulations; some source-code hiding not, like skeletons, beneath layers of skin and clothing but (quite the opposite) in the transience of its relay to the surface and beyond, the stealth of its convection up into ephemerality. She looks back at the ground. The paving to the framed slabs' right has painted signs and numbers running over it, instructions to the workers who will drill it up next week, or the one after that: algebra-strings of ciphers, as though it had come pre-annotated. She looks up again, right up towards one of the T40Ss, whose cold gaze tells her nothing. Beneath it, on a ledge, a pigeon's staring back, ostensibly at her and Sennet's Danishes; to Diamond, though, its concentration has a complicit air about it, as though, at some level, on some animal frequency, it (unlike her) had worked this stuff out, learnt to ride the streams and thermals of the algo's sequence – whence the superior, disdainful gaze it's sending back at her.

'They're memoryless, naturally,' Sennet's saying. 'That's the defining Markov property: absence of hysteresis. The amount of time between this movement-burst and the last one, or the one before that, has no bearing at all on how long we'll have to wait until the next. Only the present counts – or, if you want to be exact, the "stopping time" ...'

Diamond's not memoryless, though. Her thoughts are starting to ride back, like homing birds or web-dreams, to that first week, and Aidan's video: the second one, the mpeg with the village. It comes on suddenly, and quickly grows: the incongruous insertion, plane by plane and frame by frame, of the foreign scene into the precinct's tableau, to the point that soon it feels as though she were watching the former episode all over again – not on her screen but right here, in the space itself, replaying across its surfaces and textures, accelerating as it heads towards its lethal end. Is it some shared formal character that's causing the strange superposition, this overwriting of a Bedford plaza by some clearing in Afghanistan? It seems unlikely: that other space was square, while this is elongated; and the buildings were quite different, and the clothes ... Besides which, Aidan's mpeg had no audio: no human chatter, hum of background traffic or accordion notes emanating from behind the market stalls; and no smells, neither of Danish nor of tobacco, nor of the perfume coming at her from a woman stepping off the sub-strip now, out of the lateral light-block, depositing about the air a Roberto Cavalli vapour trail that spreads and dissipates ...

No: it's the above-thing, the above-ness, that's prompting this hysteresis in her. That she can see, with naked iris, cornea, etc., the whole doomed area from down here on her bench, and *at the same time* from on high, translated into topographic layout, sliced by the passage of its movements into clefted sections pieced together like some weird confection – this splitting, this doubling, is asking her mind to spindle and flair in ways it's just not trained to. Small tension-spasms start to scurry outwards from her spine. She senses her own presence as a threat: to buildings, people, life itself, to the whole atmosphere and habitat in which she finds herself embedded – unsuspected, deadly, fingers caressing the interface, the packet, the command-screen that's calling destruction down; senses in the very act of watching it this way a violence so ruinous that nothing, up to and including vision itself, will escape it. As the sequence playing out at the cleaners' entrance is brought to completion by the emergence of a new man with *both* hair *and* backpack, Diamond's mind supplies what neither file nor precinct has managed to show: the explosion – screams, cascades of glass and concrete, slabs and bodies opening, faces unravelling, space peeling and crumpling. Would this crowd, haphazardly assembled civic body of which she's just one small sensory organ, even *know* it had been hit? Or would these people carry with them to eternity this snapshot of drab market stalls and benches, perfume and accordion music, shopping trolleys being shunted by old ladies past the tramps, and eke out some kind of afterlife inside it? Who's to say that's not what's happening *right now* ... ?

Diamond's never had a panic attack before, and isn't sure this is one coming on – but there's a shortness to her breath, a need to tell someone, let them know ... know what? The policewoman's emerging from the optician's again, folding her notebook closed. She glances towards Diamond, and then up, towards the bird. Diamond, for her part, looks down, and fixes her gaze on the paper bag her Danish came in. Are you meant to breathe into it? Her right hand, reaching towards the table for this prop, detours (through either instinct for self-preservation or just hunger) at the final moment to the pastry – and it's this that saves her: raising it to her mouth again, she senses in its freighted texture and solidity, its leathery resistance, a guarantee of life that's strong enough to override the spectre of destruction, firm enough to steady now her breathing, calm her muscles; biting into it, she understands with growing confidence that whatever crisis she felt coming has been averted. By the time she's pushed the final mouthful in she's laughing inwardly: at the absurdity of the whole episode, perhaps, or perhaps with relief. She runs her gaze once more across the paving stones. Downtrodden wads of chewing gum in the illu-minated areas glimmer like markers; in the darker patches they sit dullened, faded stars. Apricot tangs her lips. These, starting to move, mouth silently: *It's okay, nothing's happening, everything will carry on.*

8. The One Best Way

Skirting Lake Michigan beneath Chicago, Interstate 90 makes a Gilbrethian kink, veering eastwards to pass laterally through Gary, from whose junctionery Interstate 65 resumes the southbound line to Lafayette. Floating on an elevated section past the miles of ruined factories and boarded houses, Dean starts murmuring, in tune with the rental engine's hum-key, half-remembered snatches of a song from an old film she watched one rainy Sunday afternoon back in an era, more remote than childhood itself, of fixed-schedule programming: chirpy, folksy lines rhyming *Indiana* with *Louisiana*, *Rome* with *home*, *syncopation* with *hesitation* – or was it *explanation*? ... By Remington she's pieced together the pre-chorus and refrain:

> There is just one place that can light my face:
> Gary, Indiana, Gary Indiana ...

– but no more. The lyrics stick with her right down to West Lafayette; and, as she rides the lift up to the fourth floor of the Hilton, takes a bath, falls straight asleep and then, inevitably, wakes at 4 a.m. to watch predawn grey seeping through cheap lacquered drapes, they're still there, echoing within the rhythms of the hotel's heating system, void spaces and interstices of her jet-lag: *syncopation, hesitation, ana, ana, home ...*

Dorley has sent her out here, to consult the Gilbreth archive, with a view to ascertaining ... what, exactly? Her remit's vague: to dig around the holdings, see whether the idiosyncratic modelling technique devised by an industrial time-and-motion pioneer a century ago might be construed to constitute, its iterations to lay out, a set of 'first citations' – might be construed to do this to the extent that these could form a legal basis for … for something. On whose behalf is she conducting this enquiry? Client A … via Peacock … although her first, and indeed only, point of contact, the post she reports to, mothership, control, is D&G, on to whose server she's to upload daily all her research files, the paragraphs and pages of her interim report …

Her remit is so vague, in fact, as to preclude, in terms of methodology, the rigour into which a Dip Eng Law, a clerkship and a junior associateship have trained her. In this rigour's absence, she's jumped randomly, as off a pier into a lake, into a wide expanse of Gilbrethness. This Gilbrethness washes and laps across her desk, sequence determined by the order in which folders happen to arrive. Here are four things she's learnt about Lillian Gilbreth in her first three days:

1. That her family spent their summer holidays in Nantucket. Her husband Frank taught their children to sail by marking out a boat-shape on the ground, etching gunwale, bow and stern into dry earth, laying pieces of rope for main- and jib-sheets, moveable poles for boom and tiller, and drilled them in the art of jibing, tacking, heeling and running before the wind until they'd attained an advanced level of seamanship without ever having set foot in an actual boat. The local drugstore, where they'd go for ice cream, was called Coffins.

2. That she had the idea for the cyclegraph technique while hired by Remington (firm not city) to devise methods of increasing typing speed and accuracy: looking at the way the typists' fingers flexed, extended and contracted, jumping up a row or two before recoiling back to rest above

their home-keys – never along a simple up-down vector but (she suspected, and the cyclegraphs confirmed to her) in circuits, buckled loops in which no single position other than the resting one was passed through twice; how entire hands shot up to platen knobs and carriage-release levers then fell back again, in similarly asymmetric and yet fluent, self-enclosing paths ... Later, on the back of this, she would be hired to work on more efficient firing of machine guns, which Remington made too. The mechanism, it turns out, is pretty much the same.

3. That she was a lifelong Republican, who even flirted with eugenics – but that, despite these rightward leanings, Lenin so admired her methods that he rolled them out across the Soviet Union, hoping they'd help smooth the way towards state socialism. She met Russian delegations, and American trade unionists. *If everyone just worked together*, she opined with a flourish lost on almost all her readers, *class conflict would melt into air, into thin air.*

4. That, as a child, she went to school with Isadora Duncan, Jack London and Gertrude Stein –

– this last fact being divulged, to Dean's amazement, by a school yearbook: Oakland High, 1891. One of its pages bears a photograph of a prize-giving ceremony: there's a rickety-looking stage, and a gowned lady handing medals out to children, three girls and a boy. *From Left: Gertrude Stein (rhetoric), Lillian Moller (grammar), Isadora Duncan (gymnastics), Jack London (math).* The girls are bunched together, in a kind of huddle; the boy, smaller, stands facing them, holding his medal outwards, as though deciding which of them to dedicate it to – less London than Paris, dumbstruck by three goddesses. He looks ill at ease, as though the lines of a short life-script had been pre-stamped on his face: the restless yearning, the stumbling around backwoods, the search for a moment never quite possessed, for some lost eighteenth century ... The girls, meanwhile, look confident, as though they know already that, departing this photo, they'll call into bloom the twentieth.

Here, in File 27, is a letter to her sister Vera, written a few days after Lillian's wedding:

I've exchanged,

she muses,

not only my name but, it seems, a whole *mise-en-scène* – high-ceilinged rooms with gilt-framed mirrors, stiff black sofas stuffed with horsehair, music boxes and wax flowers under glass domes, our *hoch-Deutsch* Moller *habitus* – for this new upstart world. Frank *is* America.

What does she mean? Frank is an upstart, to be sure: a short and self-made man who had no business courting her; bricklayer who so infuriated his successive bosses with his disquisitions into the efficiency or lack thereof of each hod-carrying style, of every path of trowel to wall and hand to brick and brick to wall, etc., that they kept promoting him just to get rid of him until he found himself devising streamlined operation protocols for entire sites, then companies, and now already, at just twenty-seven, industries. They're honeymooning in the St Francis, just off Union Square. She recounts to Vera, in some detail, how the bellboy, carrying in the breakfast tray, tripped on the door sill and spilled the tray's contents:

I retain a picture of it in my head: the tray flying through space, the cups and coffee jug, glasses of orange juice, plates of egg and bacon all gliding away from it, bodies no longer glued into a unit, each following its own trajectory.

III

Frank's in the middle of a contract with the New England Butt Company; he decides on the spot to remove sills from all shop floors within his purvey. Lillian continues:

> The strange thing is that, every time I call the episode to mind, I see it not in motion but quite still, as though each part were frozen, hanging in the air, above the threshold ...

The marriage produces thirteen children, of whom twelve survive. Frank runs the household like a training camp, like a laboratory – a showroom, too – for his cult of time management. He films the children eating, table-laying and -clearing and, on analysing the developed footage, devises more efficient methods for these tasks; methods which, once instituted, he films too. He films their tonsil and appendix operations, extracting new surgical protocol: nurses should act as 'caddies', placing requisite woods and putters in the doctors' hands, ensuring that play runs uninterrupted, tee-box to fairway to green, incision to resection to suture ... Various-sized Gilbreth offspring, blinking in magnesium glare, slide out on to Dean's desk now and again; but mostly it's pictures from the 'betterment rooms' set up by Frank and Lillian in their employers' factories, or their own Purdue lab, shop floors' and workstations' meticulous duplicates. Here, in File 14, are some blown-up film frames showing workers – seamstresses, meat packers, telephone-exchange operators, each wearing a light-ring – performing their tasks against a grid: in some cases an actual gridded backdrop, in others a penetrating screen imprinted on the film through multiple exposure. They're heavily annotated, snags circled, arrows injecting comments – *work rhythm broken here* – into the spots, the 'knots', that need untangling. A handwritten draft passage is attached by paper clip to one of these:

> Each unit divided into subdivisions/cycles of performance.
> Each cycle then divided into subcycle = micromotion.

The full, typewritten draft, contained in File 31, continues:

Once all micromotions are identified and modelled, methods
of least waste can then be synthesised.

The sentence will end up in *The Quest for the One Best Way*,
Lillian's magnum opus. Frank likes to film his subjects at full speed,
a clock-hand racing in the background, measuring off hundredths
of a second. But Lillian has understood the paradox that's central
to their entire project: that motion can be mined – interrogated,
made to spill its secrets – only when its territory, its dark interior,
has been colonised by its inverse, by stasis.

Here's another scene of arrested motion, in File 7: a photograph
showing a roadside picnic. The Gilbreths' open-top Pierce-Arrow
has pulled up in a small clearing by a wood; hampers and rugs
and children, like so many micromotions, have been unpacked, laid
out across the grass. Lillian describes this picnic, or one like it, in
another letter, also to Vera, from File 9: Frank, map-reading, getting them lost, she murmuring behind the steering wheel beneath
her breath:

> *Nel mezzo del cammin di nostra vita*
> *mi ritrovai per una selva oscura*
> *ché la diritta via era smarrita …*

Beside the blankets, they find an enormous anthill. Frank
presents it to them as a paragon of streamlined labour. Lillian
counterbalances his sermon with her own, more nuanced portrait
of a highly complex social structure held together, ultimately, not
so much by efficiency as by belief – in service to the queen, in
colony's totality; belief that's wired in, pulsing at an irreducible,
base level, neural electricity itself …

Frank, on his own base level, hates waste. He abhors it, an
abomination in the eyes of his one god, efficiency. Wasted food,
wasted water, wasted energy, money or motions: all these offend

113

him, sting him to the core. Waste is pollution; waste is dirt. A large portion of his time-management rituals turn around cleaning, cleanliness. At home, the bathroom walls are hung with instructions for washing:

> Soap in right hand, on left shoulder; run down top of left arm back up bottom of left arm to armpit; down side, down outside of left leg, then up inside of same leg; then ditto in mirror-version for the other side ...

If, afterwards, one of the children leaves a tap dripping and the tub fills up again, they're made to take a second bath, *teach them about wasting water* ... One summer, in Nantucket, they're all set to work on a research project into the best way to pack tins of detergent. Deliberations about whether or not to buy a family dog turn around calculations of the reduction in garbage-man-motions to be brought about by lowered household food-waste levels. For bodily evacuations they're allotted a fixed time to purge themselves. Here at this picnic, they'll be banished, when they need to unload their own waste, in twos, into the woods that loom silver-gelatinous behind them: clearings must be kept clear, unwholesome motions buried down in earth and darkness. Lillian, summarising Frank's thought, writes that the elimination of waste will result in 'Happy Minutes', in time 'saved'. Saved for what? *From* what? *Might Frank's real drive*, Dean finds herself jotting down in her notes,

> not be towards some kind of time so sanitised it's empty – time devoid of motion, of all content other than itself? – And would this empty, voided time be *pure* time, or just ... void?

The archivist who's taking care of Dean is one Ms Bernadette Richards, MA, MLIS, CA, Processing and Public Services Officer (Archives and Special Collections). Portly and black, cast in the timeless mould of middle age, she treats Dean like an aunt who hasn't seen her for a decade: calls her *Honey*, expresses amazement that she's high-tailed it *all the way over from England!*; ushers her each day into the dedicated reading space she's reserved for her. She serves up to her additional material not held in the Gilbreth files, more general-circulation items. There's a book, long out of print but a bestseller in its time, written by two of the grown-up children, Frank Jr. and Ernestine; also (as Dean informed the Peacocks) a film. Both are as folksy as the 'Gary, Indiana' ditty, full of quirky anecdotes and screwball vignettes – run-ins with exasperated servants; toll-booth attendants, wide-eyed at the sight of twelve kids packed into a car, waving them through *gratis* ... And both play up Frank, presenting him and him alone as source of the whole Gilbreth *Weltanschauung*, artesian well whence its initiative and dynamism gush. But Dean can see after her first hour in the holdings that it's Lillian, all Lillian, who upscaled Frank's narrow ergonomic vision, teased it out across fields and dimensions that he didn't even know existed. After her first day she can see, too, that it was Lillian, not Frank, who penned the essays and the books for which, sometimes with her, sometimes alone, he's credited as author. Could Frank have come up with this passage:

> Growing to realise the importance of the slightest change from a straight line or smooth curve, the worker comes to think in elementary motions. Tracing and retracing, with our models' help, these motions – motions refined through changes to chair and work-bench placement, table height and inclination angles, through study of the most efficient workers' models (other workers running their own hands along the model's wireframe track, over and over), and through further refinement even of these – all this will bring about a transformation from awkwardness to grace, from hesitation to decision ... ?

Of course not. A psychology degree's made Lillian understand that operators have to *own* the movements they perform. Frank never got this; he's a Taylorist, thinks that the employee has to be shown – told – what to do. But she can see the value in a machinist *knowing*, both kinetically and intimately, through repetition, like a lover, every curve and bend and twist of their own action, in aspiring to the perfect line, *desiring* it. Again, could Frank have written:

> The importance of rhythm was recognised in the Assyrian and Babylonian pictorial records, which perpetuate the methods of their best managers. By the same logic of perpetuation must the machinist be trained until his eye can follow paths of motions, judge their length, speed and duration, and thus cultivate an innate timing sense, aided by silent rhythmic counting, that can estimate the times and routes of movement with instinctive accuracy ... ?

Überhaupt nicht. She's learnt this through studying poetry: ranges of metre, cadence, rest. Before psychology, her BA was (like Dean's) Eng Lit; MA dissertation on *Bartholomew Fair*. Literature's threaded through the fabric of all her deliberations. When she writes, in *The Quest*'s first waste-attacking chapter, that *true conservation contains thought of neither waste nor niggardliness*, she's got Shakespeare's *mak'st waste in niggarding*, from *Sonnet One*, pulsing, surround-sound, in the background. When designing for workers the relaxation areas she's identified as vital to output's beat, she fills them with books – a different selection for each space, but always one that includes a dual-text *Divine Comedy* (she slots this into all her waiting rooms too, picturing impatient or distracted eyes falling and lingering on Purgatorio IV's *attendi tu iscorta, o pur lo modo usato t' ha' ripriso?*). She writes her own poems. Here, in File 27, is an elegy to Gantt:

> He preached the Gospel of real leadership,
> In quiet words, with stress on facts and laws
> Showing the goal and pointing out the way,
> Nor dreamed his words would found a Fellowship
> Of those who held him Leader in a Cause, —
> The winning of a new Industrial Day.

It's rubbish, sure – too corseted, too measured – but that's not the point. It's the *mechanics* of the process she appreciates. Writing's an operation, just like sewing, cutting steel plates or assembling boxes. Lillian has studied Marey, knows that *le père de la chronophotographie*'s work began with sphygmographs, pulse-writers, etching blood's own cadences and meters on smoke-blackened glass; that some of his earliest motion photographs, alongside ones of bayonet points swirling as they traced the outlines of the perfect thrust, recorded cursive hand-styles, carved in air. Killing and writing. Her annotations in the margins of her battered copy (File 20) of le Prof's *Du Mouvement dans les Fonctions de la Vie* try out various translations for his neologism *chronostylographie*: *the writing of time ... time-writing ... time-as-writing ...* During their first Remington contract, when Frank guinea-pigs the children into testing out his touch-type learning system, covering the keys with a blank sheet to force them to internalise the letters' layout, he gets them to copy out a passage of *Moby-Dick*. He's never read the book – just seized on a Harper & Brothers edition he's found in their rented holiday lean-to, vaguely aware that it has something to do with Nantucket and the sea. But Lillian has, and spends two days dissecting in her mind the episode on which the tome, by chance, has fallen open in Frank's hands: the Polynesian harpoonist Queequeg, also transcribing – in his case the tattoo-pattern from his skin over on to his (for now) redundant coffin:

Many spare hours he spent, in carving the lid with all manner of grotesque figures and drawings; and it seemed that hereby he was striving, in his rude way, to copy parts of the twisted tattooing on his body. And this tattooing had been the work of a departed prophet and seer of his island, who, by those hieroglyphic marks, had written out on his body a complete theory of the heavens and the earth, and a mystical treatise on the art of attaining truth; so that Queequeg in his own proper person was a riddle to unfold; a wondrous work in one volume; but whose mysteries not even himself could read, though his own live heart beat against them; and these mysteries were therefore destined in the end to moulder away with the living parchment whereon they were inscribed, and so be unsolved to the last . . .

Needle, harpoon, pen; white whale, white paper . . . That summer, concurrently, they're also working for the Automatic Pencil Company. Frank stages a publicity stunt, filming the children building a casket, filling it with old-school, fixed-lead pencils and, with decorous and solemn faces, burying it in the sand. They all get double scoops as a reward for this one, lining the bar at Coffins, shooting thumb-propelled graphite at each other between licks. The druggist's name, Lillian learns in conversation with him, has been passed down from carpenter-undertaker forebears. Nantucket wood has a distinctive colouration, its own shade of black. Back in the house, too busy to keep notebooks as she darts from bedroom to pantry, porch to bathroom, she has a Dictaphone installed on every floor; the tape-rolls, emptied daily, are sent down to two stenographers installed in a small room beside the lounge. This prompts a small epiphany about a book that's long been part of Lillian's mental landscape: *Dracula*. 'There is,' File 34, a letter to her mother,

> so much *secretarial* work in that novel – all that typing out and duplicating of the other characters' notes and confessions that Mina busies herself with, even as her vampire-tainted blood turns on her. I always wondered, when you read it to me as a child: How does she find the time?

Now, though (June 1924), she *gets* it; gets that this is what the story is really about; that all the earth-boxes inside which the Count walls up and ships his territory and domain from Transylvania to London via Whitby, death-lair crates with which he sends himself from half-life to revived un-deadness, serve as doubles, satellites orbiting the *real* box within whose walls life becomes deadened and revived:

> This, Mother, I now see: the true vampire's casket is Dr John Seward's Dictaphone.

Three days after this letter's postmark, Frank, standing in the phone box from which he's just spoken to her, suffers a massive heart attack. After the funeral, Lillian pens another too-stiff elegy:

> Go on, My Dear, I shall not faint or fall,
> I cannot know, but I can sense your way.
> God speed! You must not swerve or wait for me.

She thinks back to that summer, all its typewriters and secretarial pools, three decades later when she's hired by Macy's. Beneath floors stacked full of toasters, stoves, refrigerators (the demand for automated kitchens has exploded, due in no small part to her own work), she installs felt padding round the long pneumatic tubes through which notes shuttle from the ground-floor tills up to the safe room and change clatters in the opposite direction – eight hundred of them, powered by air drums whose vibration was sending a constant roar around the shop floor. *Pneuma*, breath of God; now muffled. Filming the cashiers at work day after day, week after week, extracting first one then another of them from the line-up to isolate and metal-cast their motion in the on-site betterment room, then tweaking the positions of the tubes, the chairs, the tills, then gazing down, from the store's mezzanine, over her new configuration, she perceives, once more, a kind of secretariat, expanded twenty-fold: these women rhythmically striking their keys, transcribing some great work, a book taking on shape, right here, before her very eyes. If Borel's monkeys are destined, eventually, to write *Hamlet*, what would the character and content of the cashiers' opus be? Perhaps this one will never have a name, is bound to hover just beyond the edge of legibility, eternally suspended in the act of being composed ...

And then there are the boxes. On her fourth day of research, Dean's led by the kindly Ms Richards down to the stacks from which the files have been brought up to her; and then beyond these, out into a courtyard – a sizeable one, more like a loading bay or depot – inside which sit rows of corrugated-iron containers of the type used on giant cargo ships.

'This is where we keep oversize holdings,' the archivist confides with a wink, as though letting her in on a secret. 'You'll want Number 7.'

Ms Richards fumbles in the pocket of her skirt, pulls out a plastic fob and holds this to a corresponding plastic-coated patch on Number 7's door. The patch, or possibly the fob, emits a small beep; the soft, rubberised sound of smart cylinders and latches disengaging follows, and the door pushes back automatically to allow them ingress. There they are, in rows and layers and columns, as in the storeroom of a shoe shop: a supply of little boxes sitting in a big one. They look at once the same as in the pictures Dean saw back in London and completely different. Same because they're plain back boxes with two sides and the roof cut away and, rising from the floor of each, a thin metal track that crotchets and streaks about the air to loop back round to where it starts, its bows and swerves thrown into relief by grid squares marked across the box's whole interior. Different because here, amidst dust flakes idling through weak shafts of sunlight, the twisting bars' implied speed, their kinetic vibrancy, has been both retained and (as it were) stood down, switched into standby mode. They're flaking too, grown bulbous with oxidising, like old skin. In the physical objects, she can see not just the hooks that anchor the wireframes to the boxes' floors but also, in the more elaborate or 'off-balanced' of these wireframes, thin vertical support armatures tucked away behind them. The painted background squares, so luminescent in the photos' black and white, seem fainter in the real air's chromatism; besides which, they're genuinely faded with time. But as soon as Dean steps forward and scrutinises one and then another from close up, the tubular iterations, as though reactivated by proximity alone, seem to zing back into life; she can not only see but almost viscerally *sense* light-rings' trajectories: so many lathemen's or seamstresses' action-signatures retained, fragments of time and motion held against oblivion ... Lillian's preferred term was *embodied data* ... Instinctively, Dean finds herself, like the models' first users, looping her thumb and fingers round the tracks, gliding her hand along their winding path, repeating some hundred-year-old moment – reinhabiting, perhaps even re-*living* it, skin stroking metal ...

'How many of these are there here?' she asks.

'Says in the record three hundred and eighty-five,' Ms Richards answers, flipping through a print-off. 'That's here. The Gilbreths' own inventory lists more, in other archives ...'

It does indeed. Lillian has been meticulous in indexing each one. The Smithsonian has eighty or so; MIT a score; Stanford a handful, in the Muybridge archive. Hundreds more have been lost or destroyed – but they're still inventorised. They all are: every box the Gilbreths ever made. Lillian was quite unflinching in her determination to capture each movement, not to let a single one slip her recording net. Once an action was wire-modelled, the model was photographed – in stereoscope once more, reverse-engineered into a little pair of thumbnail snapshots, photographs of models made from photographs, that in turn were assigned a number and, along with a short title or description of each action ('shelf-assembling', 'switchboard operating', etc.), entered in the record whose print-off Ms Richards has in her hands now. *That's* what was represented by the squiggle-strings scrawled at the base of the photos that Dean showed the Peacocks: one riddle, at least, solved. Dean spends the next two days working out which of the eight hundred and fourteen inventorised movements have their corresponding models extant here, in Oversize Holdings 7, matching them up, thumbnail double-photograph to box – task helped by the inclusion of each number on the boxes themselves, written in white paint, also now faded but still legible, on their floors, near the front edge ...

There's a Five Guys on the strip-mall just off campus, and, next door but one to it, a Tender Greens. Breaking off, alternately in one or the other of these, each day for lunch, Dean finds she's watching people eat – or carry food across the restaurant, settle themselves at tables, remove coats, hang bags on backs of chairs, head to the bathroom, open doors – through penetrating screens and chronocyclegraphs now grafted to her visual faculties, invisible prostheses. The passage of fork to mouth, of hand to napkin, arm to sleeve or hip to door-jamb – all becomes ergonomics, choreography. In spinning hems and shawls, amidst the smell of burgers and seared tuna, she sees, once more, Julius's grainy and post-coloured Loie Fuller gif re-looping. Isadora Duncan: Lillian stays intermittently in touch with her until she (Isadora) dies. File 24 contains a 1913 letter in which the diva thanks her old friend for the condolence note after her children's drowning. *You would like their father: he's the scion of machinists* ... So does File 25, from 1927: *Down in* le Midi, *cheri, frolicking with Desti and Chatov* ... Lillian, in her own journal from that year (also File 25), comments that it's Chatov's scarf that, catching in an Amilcar's rear axle two weeks after the postmark on this one, snaps Isadora's neck and sends her *à la gloire* ... Gertrude Stein stays on her radar too – hard for her not to: by the thirties she's packing out concert halls around America, intoning publicly to rapt audiences

what was the use of my having come from Oakland it was not natural to have come from there yes write about if I like or anything if I like but not there, there is no there there

and privately to Lillian

You'd love what they've turned our old neighbourhood into: an industrial park ...

There's reams of other correspondence. Dean returns to it when her matching of inventory to boxes gets held up. Here, in

Files 42–5, are Soviet-stamped envelopes bearing tributes from the Russian Taylorist Alexsei Gastev, telling her she's

> set the worker on the path to the one best way; helped unleash him from the shackles of his body; through your light-rings consecrated his new matrimony with the liberating dynamism of the great machine ...

Or here, File 46, from Vassar's President, inviting her to the opening of a hall of residence named after her

> the better to inspire our students to find the one best way through the great challenges that face them ...

This phrase, *the one best way*, crops up time and again throughout the articles, the books, the letters. As the projects scale up, and as Lillian grows older, the words appear to change their meaning, or at least their range, until it seems that she's no longer looking for the one best way to pack five hundred toys into a crate or move a thousand chocolate lumps from a conveyor belt into the variegated moulds of an assortment tray: she's after bigger fish. *Might there not be*, she writes (File 61) to Powel Crosley, autumn '54 from Sarajevo, *a one – a truly one – best way? For everything, I mean ... ?* The more she delves through these Purdue files, the more Dean starts discerning – in the writings or, perhaps, between them – the outline of an idea taking shape in Lillian's mind, as though the archive were itself, in its totality, a wireframe model down whose kinking path Dean's thought-hand, little palmer-pilgrim, is now gliding:

> From the mid-forties,

she writes in her report to Dorley,

> terms such as 'perfect movement' and 'pure original motion' start cropping up in Ms Gilbreth's notebooks – often

free-standing, out of context, but nonetheless (to my mind) indicating a turn in her thinking towards the possibility of some form of 'higher' or 'absolute' movement not yet modelled, perhaps even (if such a thing may be imagined) derived from no source other than itself. This turn coincides with Ms Gilbreth's newfound fascination with the sightless workers she was helping train. Having started from the premise that such physically disadvantaged people could, with help, be brought up to the capability levels of the able-bodied and thus granted assembly-line and even artisanal roles, Ms Gilbreth ended up believing that, despite appearances, blind people stood at an *advantage*, not a disadvantage, to their fellows.

(Dean likes 'fellows': it's a Gilbreth kind of word.)

For the blind, she reasoned, all movement is *de facto* already abstracted from extraneous context and surroundings; and, at the same time, embodied as action that has no exterior correlative it's imitating. From the late fifties, when she found herself consulting for first NACA, then that agency's successor NASA, Ms Gilbreth's utterances, growing rarer, started drifting in more fanciful directions, as though the prospect of entering outer space had expanded the frontiers of the possible, or thinkable. Towards the end ...

Dorley calls her from London two hours after she dispatches this email, audibly excited. 'NASA?' he barks. 'You mean this lady, Gilbreth, is instructing *astronauts* on how to *space-walk?*'

'Not exactly space-walk,' Dean replies, voice full of sleep (it's 3 a.m. West Lafayette time). 'More like just move about the module, whose designers had drawn heavily from her work on domestic ergonomics. From the early days, she'd get her children to follow her around the kitchen with balls of string and pin-tacks, marking her passage from sink to bin to cutting board, or cupboard to bin to door to bin again, until the room became its own cat's-cradle model box.'

'That's insane,' chuffs Dorley. 'Neighbours should have called in Child Protection …'

'Not really,' replies Dean defensively. 'It worked: it led to her designing better kitchens. Later, after her blind work, she made modified ones for people with reduced mobility: simplified, refined, more closed-in and all-surrounding. So the progression on to NASA-consultancy makes sense: if you think about it, a space module is just a kitchen or a living room for people whose motility has been conditionally altered.'

There's a long pause while Dorley takes this in. The line, too, seems to stop its crackling and hold, like a breath, the scratch and buzz that has been riding with their voices like a dirty aura. Then, smudging the quiet's cleanness with new static-bearing speech, he says:

'You told me there's an inventory of all the motions that she and her husband modelled?'

'Yes,' she confirms.

'Send it to me,' he orders her. 'By the way, stop sending unencrypted files. Use CounterMail or Proton from now on.'

'Okay,' she tells him. 'I'll do that tomorrow. I'm matching the numbered inventory entries to the physical models in this collection. There's a little glitch, but it should be cleared up by then.'

In fact, there are two glitches: Dean's path through the archive has acquired its own pair of snags, its 'knots'. The first seems trivial: the inventory's entry-numbers skip from 807 to 809 – there's no 808. Clerical error perhaps – uncharacteristic, though, from the diligent Lillian. Dean wouldn't get too hung up on this, if it didn't come in tandem with the second snag-knot. This one's vaguer, harder to pinpoint: it consists of a change in the demeanour of the holdings' staff. Ms Richards, so benevolent and helpful for the first few days, has grown more distant – or, to be precise, evasive. She's still there, tending to Dean, supervising files' delivery to her; but a reticence has crept into her manner. Twice, in the last two days, request forms have come back with 'in use' stamped across them. When Dean asked 'by whom?' the archivist seemed to recoil, snatching the chit away as though even allowing her to see it were too much. Bizarrely, as they left the building after the second of these episodes, Dean heading off through the dark car park back towards the Hilton to file her daily report to London, Ms Richards called after her:

'Take care!'

The words weren't spoken in an offhand tone of voice, nor colloquially proffered; it sounded as though the archivist were actually warning her to be careful, as though she'd perceived some imminent threat lurking among Purdue's lawns and footpaths – ejaculation strange enough to make Dean turn around to ask what she meant. Too late: Ms Richards' hairbun, coat-wrapped frame and stuffed leather bag had slipped away into the darkness, and the question died in Dean's throat. The next day, when she raised the issue of the missing 808-entry, Ms Richards answered, almost curtly:

'I can't help you.'

No *Honey*; no beamed smiles; Dean was left to stare morosely at the gap on the page (there is one, a double return – she pictures a hand at the typewriter's lever, Lillian's or one of her secretaries', undulating in a double fishtail side-swipe, left to right and back again) between the photographs and short movement-descriptions of Box 807 and those of Box 809. It could well have been a simple error, after all: these entries are among the last ones, made at a point when Lillian's eyesight, like her memory, is fading, letters and notebook entries starting to wander off on their own divagating courses, handwriting kinking and wavering as the end, in all its shapelessness, heaves into view ...

Lillian spends her final three years in a retirement home in Phoenix, Arizona. It's called The Beatitudes. The name suggests to Dean some kind of girded region, like the Temperate or Torrid Zones, the Tropics or Antipodes, Indies or Maritimes; it's not until she looks it up that she realises it comes from the Gospels. Matt. 5:3–11: *Blessed are those who ... etc. ... etc.* Lillian, nominally, is agnostic – but she nonetheless believes in upward passages, apotheoses, transformations: hesitation to decision, awkwardness to grace. By this time she's phenomenally famous. Invitations (all declined) to speak, or at least to come and pick up honorary degrees, are pouring in from all around the world; there's talk of statues being erected, of becoming the first woman (Liberty aside) stamped on a US banknote ... In the Soviet Union, Lenin's veneration of her has taken deep root, outlived Lenin and moved on two or three generations, beyond Gastev, on to Rozmirovich, rationalisation associations, *ob'edineniia* ... Her children visit her, tell her about the moon landing for which her work has been so instrumental, but she doesn't really understand. She makes final, sporadic entries in the notebooks, though, and keeps up intermittent correspondence. It's among the tail end of this latter category, spread over the final two files, that Dean comes across the Vanins letters.

There are two of them, folded up in envelopes that, like Gastev's, bear Soviet postmarks – in Vanins' case, from 1969 and 1970. The paper inside is letterheaded with Cyrillic writing and an image that seems to depict some kind of university or research centre. The writing itself's in Latin script, though: handwritten English. It's quite hard to follow, partly by dint of not being very neat, partly due to a propensity to give over to diagrams or algebraic shorthand. The letters' author is one Raivis Vanins – name already familiar to Dean: Lillian has mentioned meeting him a few years earlier, in ... a quick flip back to File 32 retrieves this datum: Zürich, the Fourth International Symposium on Applied Kinetics. Lillian's diary entry of 26/2/65 records her being impressed by the young physicist, whom she saw as *taking my work somewhere interesting, quite unexpected* ... The letters seem to be part of a series; they refer to previous correspondence (not contained here); on top of which, they're incomplete, missing whole pages.

In the first letter, deploying a familiar tone (he uses her first name), Vanins thanks Lillian for her enthusiastic response to the work he's 'been conducting in light of the T.T. episode'. He outlines, through sketches and calculations so incomprehensible to

Dean that they might, with equal plausibility, represent a formulaic disquisition on the nature of dark matter or the flightpath of some kind of insect (there's a kind of cone, two directional arrows corkscrewing around a straight vertical line and, beside them, the same letters, *T.T.*), his thoughts about said 'episode'; and informs her that, with her permission, he'll attempt to model it. Of the second letter, only page two is preserved inside the envelope: beginning and ending mid-sentence, it communicates what Vanins calls 'my shock – amazement, and perhaps delay ...' *delay*? No, there's a dot and then a cross: the word's *delight* ... 'my shock – amazement, and perhaps delight – at the implications of this labour, which would seem to transform all the tenets and' (illegible: *assumptions*?) 'of our ...'

Here the page ends. Paper-clipped to it, though, is a photo of a wireframe model – a little snapshot, like the others Dean has seen, the thumbnails in the Gilbreth inventory; but in contrast to these just a single, not a stereoscope, image; slightly skewed too, since it's been taken (presumably by Vanins) in a different setting, from a different angle, and printed with different chemicals on different paper. In the model, in its open-sided box, the metal track rises and turns first anticlockwise and then clockwise before plunging once more to the floor. At the top, on to the photograph itself, are written, once more, the doubled initials *T.T.*; at its base, *Box 808*.

It's not the air conditioning that sends a chill down Dean's back as she looks at this photo – more the sudden recognition, morphed into a physical awareness, of a missing part's insertion. She finds herself flipping back and forth between the files now with real vigour, driven by the sense that something's taking shape here: something solid, perhaps almost *sayable* – but, if so, only silently, in this scrawled idiom of pictorial and alphabetic cipher, doodle-hieroglyphics ... nonetheless, by virtue of these same, somehow *recoverable* ...

In the last file, there's a journal that she hasn't thumbed through yet, Lillian's final one. It, too, is full of doodles, letters, symbols that might, together, amount to some form of mathematical notation, or might simply represent the dying unravelling of a mind whose frame has lost all traction, warp- and cloth beams tumbled from their axes, fallen prey to woodworm and decay. Even amidst this fuzz and visual shipwreck, though, there are still words: fragments, snatches of recalled or uncompleted thoughts ... *name for force that holds all things in motion? ... praxis* (energeia), *work* (ergon), *potential* (dynamis) – *but contemplation ...?* A jumble of these snatch-fragments appears in the notebook's final entry, peppered about (as though to annotate) a drawing that Dean recognises as a shaky copying of one of the cone-and-corkscrew sketches from Vanins' first letter. Some of the words that Lillian has added, perched amidst the springs and arrows, look like names: *de Honnecourt, Maricourt, Bessler* ... Others, lower down, seem to be written in an archaic form of Italian: *fattore ... farsi ... fattura ... legato con amove in un volume ... geomètra misurar lo cerchio ... l'amov che move* ... Three crayon-drawn circles cut across these lower fragments, each circle gradiently coloured so as to partially reflect the others. Below these, in English, runs, in bold, penned letters, like a kind of tag, the line: *Box 808* – is that *charges?* No, it's *changes* – *Box 808 changes everything.*

In the time it takes Dean to flip forward through nine unused, virgin pages to the notebook's cover and then back again to this page, one thing at least has become clear to her: the inventory's omission of the eight hundred and eighth box is no accident or oversight, no numeric typo. There's a thing – a something, or an *everything* – behind it. That something has a name, or rather number – 808 – and an embodiment, a box, a low-grade pho-tograph of which she, Dean, is holding in her hand. It's in her right hand; her left, meanwhile, is hungrily (and blindly) padding the desk around it, feeling for a copy-permission sheet – vainly too, it turns out: she's used up all the ones Ms Richards gave her. She considers going over to the archivist's station to ask her for a new one, but holds back, as though afraid of leaving these open files alone, of letting the alignment into which she's nudged and coaxed them – alignment that, like that of stars, seems to portend some great event, some revelation, but just fleetingly, when viewed at the right moment from a certain point and angle – slip away again. She stays there until closing time, first noting all the words down, then just staring at the pages, eyes darting from diary to photograph to letter, letter to diary to photograph, as though to string-and-tack them, to cat's cradle the whole set of scenes and movements, or at least their traces, on to which they open – and, in the same movement, close again …

After being kicked out, she races straight back to the Hilton, and stays up most of the night drafting a new report for Dorley:

Somewhere,

she writes, excitement and the lateness of the hour extending her a license for rhetorical indulgence that she wouldn't normally permit herself,

in the relay between Ms Gilbreth and her young adherent on the far side of the world, the far side of the Iron Curtain; in the transfers and translations, in the unexpected redirections of the type that only geographic distance and generational difference and, above all, chance's vagaries can occasion, something cropped up that seems to have beguiled, fixated and surprised them both – certainly, to have consumed Ms Gilbreth to the point that, in a final and quite counterintuitive move, she redacted it from the index of her life's endeavour. The significance attached by her to Box 808 is, despite the host of unknowns hemming it in on every side, beyond all contestation. For her, and in her own words, it 'changed every-thing'. For my part, I'm convinced that, despite the enfeebled

too strong – and prejudicial

that, despite her weakening general state around this time, the recognition on her part of some kind of breakthrough

130

achieved by her cohort Vanins (himself at the peak of his professional and intellectual powers) was effected from a robust inner mental enclave, a castle keep of absolute lucidity …

Does Dean really believe this? She does. Despite the shakiness, the incoherence, there's a conviction emanating from the penstrokes, from the words, a certainty that no doubt, not even the confusion of senility, can undermine. The question follows, though –

The question follows: what new ground did this box breach, that hundreds of other boxes hadn't? A course-shifting event, insight or understanding must have emerged from what first Vanins and then Ms Gilbreth called 'the T.T. episode'. As to the nature of this episode, I remain entirely in the dark. Perhaps more research, this time into Vanins' own archive, should such exist, is called for. How this last might be tracked down, given the disintegration of the state under whose auspices he worked, is …

She sends this, as instructed, in encrypted form, over the firm's safe line. She then steals a few hours' sleep beneath whose surface dreams – of boxes sent by ocean liner to the wrong location, Five-Guy and Tender-Button shake-straws twisted into wireframes modelling some momentous action taking place offstage (behind the counter, in the kitchen or some other non-specific backroom), tardily submitted copy-request slips that, doubling as hotel-guest towels, blot, sog and disintegrate – are never far submerged. Morning finds her in the strip mall's Au Bon Pain, then, ten minutes prior to opening, staking out the Holding Center's entrance, willing its staff – custodians and doormen, even janitors, but principally Ms Richards – to appear round the corner, jangling keys.

Her willing doesn't work: Ms Richards doesn't come today. In her place, when the Holding Center does eventually open, there's a man: a little younger, possibly late thirties, white, neat moustache sitting on a grey, clean-shaven face. She senses, as soon as she nears his workstation (he's reordered it; it's *his* today), a new charge in the air. He rises to meet her, but it's not a friendly rising; more like – *almost* like – a blocking of her route.

'Can I help you?' He utters the words coldly, in a tone that makes it clear that helping her's the last thing he intends to do.

'Oh,' says Dean. 'I'm working here. I mean ...'

'You're staff?' he asks.

'No, no,' she starts to tell him. 'I'm a reader. A researcher. I've been here – just here ...'

As she tentatively points over his shoulder to her little desk, she sees that her nest of files and papers, which Ms Richards usually leaves out for her, has been cleared up.

'Oh ...' she says again.

'You have a pass?' he asks.

'What? Yes, of course,' she answers, feeling for it in the pocket of her handbag. As she does this, the man's face, despite its attempts to remain expressionless, is briefly lit up by a micro-smile, a flicker of pleasure furnished by a foreknowledge of what's about to happen.

'Please touch in,' he instructs her.

Ms Richards issued her the pass and showed her how to do this on her first day here, but subsequently always buzzed her through herself, so Dean has never used it. Pressed to the electronic reader now, the card's met with a sour beep that, if she'd been sinaesthetic, would have presented to her vision the same colour and tone as this man's skin.

'Oh ...' Dean mutters for a third time. 'Shall I ... ?'

The man doesn't answer, doesn't help her out in any way. After what seems like an interminable pause, he says to her:

'Your card's not good for entry to this centre.'

'What can I ... ?' she begins; then, again, 'Maybe I can ...' But these efforts don't get any uptake. Eventually she tries: 'I mean, I'm a registered visitor.'

This last clause he latches on to. 'Any visiting privileges you had,' he informs her, 'have been rescinded.'

'How do you mean?' she asks.

'You are no longer welcome here. You'll have to leave the building.'

The next few minutes, when she'll look back on them, will remain stubbornly blank, as unretained in memory as long-past movements never modelled. She must have turned and walked back down the corridor, past the concierge's booth, opened the door and exited – but these actions seem to have evaporated along with her access to the world of Lillian and Frank and Vanins and the curves of sculpted light and moulded time and all the other magic toys that have been placed beyond her reach. All she'll remember is standing alone in the Holding Center's outsize car park in the bright indifferent sunshine, listening to the middle-distance trundle and whirr of vehicles passing by on Interstate 52.

Book Two

1. And Down We Went

You don't hear the fan start. There's no slow and ponderous *thwop . . .
thwop* notching up to *thwop-thwop-thwop*, then accelerating through
the *thwopthwopthwopthwop* layer before emerging on the other side
as an undifferentiated liquid roar. This is due, in part, to the positioning of motors and compressor at the point of the circuit furthest
from the test section and the control room; in part also to the electric
buzz that, spilling from the motors' dedicated substation, covers the
whole site. The engineers know when the fan is on, though. The
first thing they pick up is the ripple-pattern on the surface of their
tea; then comes the windows' rattle, and a general blurring (or is
it a *sharpening*? van Boezem duck-rabbits from side to side on this
one) of all edges: desktops, monitors, drawers, whiteboards. A few
seconds after this, flesh joins the vibratory awakening: you feel it
in your gut, in pressure waves, like bass – only, you realise as the
frequency now finally resolves itself into a sound, it's high, not low;
soprano, an urgent and indefinitely prolonged *fermata*, drawn from
the fraught diaphragm of some mechanical Rhinemaiden.

Most wind tunnels have two control rooms: one for synchro-
nising the activities of the various aerodynamic subsystems, the
other for model-handling. Here at Nederlans Wind NV (formerly
Nederlans Lucht- en Ruimtevaartlaboratorium Luttelgeest), these
functions are amalgamated in a single space, which, consequently,
has assumed almost cathedral-like proportions. Under a giant halo
light that seems to hover, flat and round as a benevolent spaceship,
are two rows of pews, all white, with screens interpolated down
their length at regular intervals like prayer books. Right now,

several of these screens are showing temperature readings from the stilling chamber, second throat and contractor, pressure readings from the strain gauge balances and blow off, or voltage readings from the heat assembly, all topographically arrayed. Others show the outline, geometric and abstracted, of the model. The actual model, the physical object, is being nudged and shuffled into place atop a force plate set in the test section's floor, which is raised by half a metre from that of the control room and separated from it by a partition wall whose central stretch is inlaid with a thick window. The elevation and the framing, not to mention the illumination from the lights embedded in the test section's surfaces, infuse the model and the men around it with the look of figures in an altar scene or stained-glass panel: a master image to which the smaller, lowlier boxed pictures votively refer. The model seems (and not entirely without cause) to give off its own light – no model at all in lay terms but the thing itself, full-scale, fully dirigible, fibreglass cowling and steel parabolic runners (eu.4,000 a pop) freshly scored by the Igls ice it shot down just two days ago: a bright-red bob-sleigh, BMW, fifth generation, and the Österreichischer Bob- und Skeletonverband (Zweierbobdivision)'s pride and joy.

'There will be no movement.' *Cheftrainer* Otto Ebner, ITK, M.Sc. (Linz), peers nervously towards the precious vehicle as the NW engineers lock the force plate's crown into position.

'Well,' van Boezem grants him, 'the *bobsleigh* won't move. The air will move around it.'

'*Ja, natürlich*,' Ebner says impatiently. 'That part I understand. But what I mean is that there'll be no *Friktion*. *Reibung*. It only stands above the board, with runners still on the same place. On the *authentisch* track, over the ice, the runners move.'

Van Boezem pinches the bridge of his nose. No Lorentz-transformation algebra required to work out that this session will be long. 'Ground friction was not one of our parameters,' he gently informs Ebner. 'Only air drag. If you'd requested it, we could have placed a moving belt under the model, although not one made of ice – and then, the speeds at which …'

'No, no: is fine,' Sven Medosch, the Verband's *Statistiker*, slips his svelte arm across Ebner's shoulders and leads him away from van Boezem towards a spread of clipboards, casting the Chief Technician a wink as he does so. Ebner won't be that easily bought off, though; he still peers out, hawk-like, at the bob, the engineers, his half-naked riders, upper portions of Elastan suits hung from their waists, the spread arms lolling downwards, limp and sacrificial ... From the moment this Dutch visit was first mooted, he insisted on verisimilitude. He's told the riders not to look at or even think about the wind-tunnel environment around them, but to fill their heads instead with sights, sounds, smells of the *Bobbahn*: rushing white walls, rooftops of Badhaussiedlung flashing into view beyond them, scrapes and crashes, the refrigeration plant's ammonia ... Everything counts. They're dealing in thousandths and ten-thousandths on overall times, which translates, at any isolated moment within that continuum, to micro-, even nano-seconds. At this level, the molecular comes into play: of this he's sure. Just thinking something (*Here's a banked turn ... It is cold ... Ice whips my cheeks ...*) will fire off neurons that will cause changes in muscle tension, inflate neck and thigh nerves, trigger a contraction of the shoulders; and these things, all these voluminous, if to the naked eye invisible, arrangements, reassemblies – well, these too must register at some scale, present surfaces and edges to be touched, resisted, dragged, no? ... *Wer weiß?* It all forms part of the picture.

And here's Phocan, set back by several rows of monitors and NW or OBSV personnel from the test section's glowing shrine. He's standing guard, with Lucy Diamond, over a trolley on which several large cases are stacked. PIV: particle image velocimetry. It's new, for Pantarey at least, assayed successfully with ventilation fans, about as powerful as a stack of hairdryers, back in The Cell, but otherwise as yet un-road-, or rather tunnel-, tested; this will be its first real application. Phocan, running this thought through his mind, finds himself tripping, or at least stumbling, over the word 'real' – not for the obvious reasons (setting's artifice, speed's simulation, etc., etc.) but because it forms the tail end of the space-ship's name that's wedged itself into his various mental door frames ever since that jaunt to Berners Street, to Degree Zero's office, the whole *Incarnation* project. *Sidereal*. He had to look it up (*adj*: of or pertaining to the stars; time measured relative to same; motion as well; from *sidus*, star) and even press the online dictionary's little *speak me* button for the right pronunciation. *Side-ear-ial*, stress on the *ear*. In his own ear, though, in its echo-chamber, he still hears it as *side-real*: two words, standing beside each other, speaking of adjacency – their own, sure, but also of adjacency in general, of things set to the side of other things. Would that, he muses as he, too, watches the riders kit up, mean *un*real things, turfed out of the real's kingdom, made to stand in some ignominious corner of deceptiveness and falsehood? Or might it mean real things *themselves* cast aside, rerouted, drifted leeward, hiding in a kind of quantum sidebar to the world, to time? At the film's climax, the ship's supposed to start disintegrating: *that's* what he's meant to be asking van Boezem about today, when the right moment drifts by, an aside: *Would it be viable to model the disintegration sequence here?* They're already doing it in water, in Berlin; but a wind tunnel would give them another POV on it – it is wind, after all, that's meant to tear the thing apart … And if the answer's *Yes*, he'd not only be helping his friend Eldridge; in drumming up more business for the firm, he'd also be earning Brownie points with Garnett: two birds, one stone. Meanwhile, there are the lasers and the delay generators – and, most importantly, the bubbles …

Suits have been pulled fully on now, BMW and OBSV logos puffed up into legibility by forearms, pectorals and deltoids. When the riders stoop to gather up their helmets, Katja Avanessian, team *Krankengymnast*, extracts two small plastic packets from her tracksuit pocket and hands one to each. They're ear-plugs, polyu-rethane, designed to compress then re-expand to fit the contours of a given ear canal. As Oskar Luksch squeezes his in, he feels their noses slide over cartilaginous *Startkurven*, ride up fibrous walls of first, then second *Hohes S*-turns, before getting wedged somewhere in acoustic-meatal speed traps. It prompts him to begin his visualisation: for the next 54.25 seconds, while Brakeman Eward Miessen performs box jumps and calf raises, Avanessian clears away discarded water flasks and Engineer de Veen preps up his smoke gun, Navigator Luksch stands in the same spot, eyes closed, hands clasping spectral rings that hover just before his waist, swaying first one way then another as inclining shoulders set a line for chest and stomach to pursue, hips twist and calibrate, then the whole torso twitches, readjusts, pursues another line ... To van Boezem and his staff, Phocan and Diamond too, he has the look of a *sensei*, or *senpai*, an adept or apprentice in some esoteric martial art; or maybe just a madman.

'High speed leg good; compressor good; vanes positioned; temperature stable ...' Second Technician Roussel's eyes hopscotch about three screens as he checks off the functions.

'Wind-flow up to .4,' van Boezem instructs him.

A palpable excitement spreads across the Austrian contingent; they all look at the test section, expecting ... expecting what? Leaves to scurry along the ground, branches to whip and dance, riders to grab at lamp-posts as their umbrellas evert and fly away? None of these events, of course, occur. But there's a stirring – one that seems to come, like the visceral tremblings and the singing (which they clock as something not *new*, but rather familiar yet until now unnoticed), as much from *within* as from the tunnel's recesses: an eerie and exhilarating apprehension that what's meant to happen here is happening already, all around, invisible.

Van Boezem nods to Medosch, Ebner, Avanessian. 'We'll start slow.'

Ebner holds his index finger up towards his riders: First Position. Luksch, standing at the bob's left side, retracts the push-bar from its slit and holds his open hands eight or so centimetres from this, as though warming his palms on it. Miessen stations himself half a metre behind and slightly to the right of him at the bob's rear, hands similarly raised above the fixed twin push-bars on its fins. The riders remain still and silent for a good half-minute, letting their breathing synchronise. Then Luksch starts intoning the cadence:

> *Ach, du lieber Augustin,*
> *Augustin, Augustin*

After the first two lines, Miessen joins in, and the two of them rock back and forth in unison as they chant:

> *Ach, du lieber Augustin,*
> *Alles ist hin!*

– their voices rising more and more with every beat until they hit both *hin!* and bars with a loud shout, throwing the full force of their minds and bodies at the word, the metal and – ultimate target, to be rushed, ambushed, blasted to oblivion before it has a chance to scramble its counterforces – stasis. Or that's what they *would* do if they were on the starting ramp at Igls; here at Luttelgeest they can't *actually* push. They know exactly how to manage the discrepancy, though; Ebner has been very precise in his instructions: they're still to fling every last joule of energy towards the bars – but then, at the precise juncture where the force would (in the normal sequence of things) pass from hand to metal, they're to freeze the instant. Not relax, *versteht ihr – gar nicht!* – but to freeze, or to arrest (*verhaften*) the action, keeping it in such a state that the force remains present, concentrated, even active; but restrained. The two men do this now, and hold the posture, the required exertion doubled by the dual demands of pushing *and* holding back.

'Now,' van Boezem tells the Austrians, 'we seed the air.'

He nods to Engineer de Veen, stationed by the tunnel's wall two metres upwind of the riders. De Veen presses a switch on his smoke gun and holds its wand out so its nozzle sits right in the centre of the flow. The propylene glycol vapour first emerges from it as a wispy dribble, unsure where to go – then, elongating as it slithers from the aperture, raises and weaves its head from side to side as it advances, a snake charmed by the tunnel-*pungi*'s single, drawn-out note, its body rippling along behind until, taken complete control of by the stream, it hurries in a straight, brisk thread towards the model. When it meets the bobsleigh's nose it curves around and hugs this closely, without losing either form or (it seems) speed; to the Austrians' untrained eyes, the cowling even appears, in raising and kinking the vapour, to accelerate it. Hitting first Luksch's and then Miessen's bodies, though, the thread – halted, rebounding, crushed by its own continued onrush – frays into a jumble of irregular patches which in turn break up and dissipate into a formless cloud around the riders' helmets.

'You can see,' van Boezem commentates unnecessarily, 'that standing is not aerodynamic.'

'*Ja*,' says Medosch, 'but is unavoidable. How else can they get quickly moving? And besides, the speed is low in this phase – so they are not creating much resistance, I think. *Oder* ... ?'

The Chief Technician gives him an approving pedagogic nod. 'The Reynolds number round the bodies at this point is ...' The statement floats, unfinished, towards Roussel, who, plucking the figure from his left screen's right-hand column, tells them:

'1×10^2.'

'What's Reynolds?' Medosch asks.

'Inertia-to-viscosity ratio,' van Boezem answers. 'It's a dimensionless quantity, so we can use it to scale up or down a given situation, or to establish dynamic similitude between different positions – in this instance, of the riders ...'

Luksch and Miessen, in their test section, know nothing of Reynolds numbers. Luksch, as per Ebner's instructions, is gathering mountain peaks around him – Patscherkofel, Serles, Kreusspitze, Speckkarspitze – stacking them, nearer and further, in the smoke-haze. Miessen, meanwhile, is running through his split-times: .1 seconds off the leading pace at fifty metres means .3 over the course; .2 at fifty stretches to .7; .3 to a gaping 1.5 ... This, too, is seeding: by the time you've hit the first mark, the eventual delay's already bedded in the present moment's soil, the end-time's genetic destiny written in the roots and tendrils that grow out of this, a code that no twisting contingencies of skill or luck will ever fully manage to erase or override. Miessen, like all brakemen, has grown strong under the load of this responsibility. It weighs on him regressively: if the jump-on spot is where, handing the reins to Luksch, he gifts to the navigator a future that, *at the hand-on point itself*, is largely set, then this point, too, is seeded, predetermined – by the first steps of the push, the tightness of the cadence prior to that, his limbering-up before that too, the training before even that; regimes of exercise, nutrition, general formation stretching back for weeks, months, years. Gripping the push-bars tighter still, he summons through the vapour memories of his first ever descent: his cousin's fourteenth birthday party, Königssee run glowing in winter darkness under arc lights whose meter had been well fed by the coins of Onkel Lukas (*privat vermietet* for a whole two hours: Tobias's branch of the family, flashing across his horizon in biannual starbursts of Audis, dressage horses and Antiguan holidays, always seemed like aristocrats next to his); and he, not knowing the other guests (all Kalksburg classmates of Tobias), lurked in the background, poor relation – until Tobias, on his fourth or fifth go, pushed a boy wearing a brand-new Schöffel ski suit from the sleigh and beckoned him instead into the back seat, shouting pink-faced *Hold tight, Eward ... Hold on tight ...*

Ebner, level with and perpendicular-facing to his riders on the far side of the viewing window, lets his gaze slide from their visored faces and Elastan-coated shoulders, hips and knees, on upstream (down imaginary run) into the smoke-flow. His lips, cracked and blue-veined, are open, moving almost imperceptibly, intoning what van Boezem, glancing sideways at him, presumes are his own quantities and scales, the Reynolds numbers of his discipline's arcana. Wrongly: what's actually being mouthed into the air is the continuation of the cadence:

> *Geld ist weg, Mensch ist weg,*
> *Alles hin, Augustin!*

Ach, du lieber Augustin,
Alles ist hin!

The words, both carried and smothered by the tunnel's song, start colouring the scene's bizarre abstraction: its transposition of sleigh and riders from their ice-groove twelve hundred kilometres away to this empty tube; their simultaneous doing and not-doing of their actions; their frozenness in time while time still visibly flows on past them … As folk-rhythm and arrhythmic, monotonal fan-note fold into and out of one another in the space around his ears, Ebner senses, seeping out from the test area with a consistency against which no thickness of glass could insulate, infusing the control room's air, filling his lungs with every breath, a kind of melancholy. He pictures the cadence's author, the drunk minstrel Marx Augustin, set down (as recounted by the stanzas) in a grave that isn't his, a plague pit, stripped of money, friends, clothes, even a floor to lie on, clutching the only object he has left: the bagpipe, outlandish paraphernalia of his errant craft, this plaintive sack of wind …

'Otto. Hey, Otto!' Medosch has been saying his name for a few seconds now. Ebner grunts, shuddering himself back to attentiveness.

'What?'

'Ready for Second Position?'

'*Ja, selbstverständlich.*' He waves to Luksch and Miessen; when, seeing this gesture, they uncrouch and loosen, shaking hands and feet and rolling heads, he holds two fingers up. Obediently, they climb into the sleigh, Luksch at the front, Miessen behind. Once in, the brakeman doubles over, bowing his head forwards till it's buried in the small of Luksch's back; the navigator, meanwhile, slides his legs down the interior of the vehicle's front cowling, right down to the nose, hands feeling for the steering rings while torso sinks until only the visor and the helmet's crown protrude above the fibreglass's rim.

'You can increase the speed now,' Medosch tells van Boezem. The Chief Technician nods and instructs Roussel to ramp wind-flow up to 1.5. Again the Austrians all peer expectantly towards the test section, inside which (again) nothing looks any different – until de Veen once more fires up his smoke gun and holds out its wand: this time the wind snatches the thread immediately, whips it straight along to the sleigh's nose and over its upper body towards Luksch's helmet – meeting which it kinks a second time, as smoothly and continuously as the first; then, curving back downwards as it clears the crown, traces the outline of his upper back for a few centimetres before peeling off, re-finding its horizontal and, ignoring Miessen crouching far below it, racing on unfrayed to the tunnel's diffuser.

'Like a silk tight over a waxed leg, no?' van Boezem smiles to Medosch.

Unobserved by any of the men, the eyes of the two women present, Avanessian and Diamond, meet and roll.

'What groundspeed is this simulating?' Medosch asks.

'About seventy kilometres per hour,' replies van Boezem.

'They do this speed,' the *Statistiker* tells him, 'for the run's first half only. By the second they're at 120, even 140.'

Van Boezem half-turns towards Roussel, floating this figure onward to him too. Roussel's hands slide about three keyboards, pipe-organist fingers pressing keys, initiating tracker actions, pumping bellows, pulling stops. Inside the test section, de Veen plants his front leg more firmly and leans back into the wall. The smoke is hurtling over model and riders now, honing them, like a belt sander perfectly aligned with razor's edge. The Rhinemaiden's becoming more and more worked up: her pitch, still emanating from all quarters – walls, desks, objects, air – is growing higher, louder, faster. A minute or so into this new flow-rate (3.1, Roussel announces to the room), an effect so eerie and (it seems) miraculous occurs that all but the NW personnel turn and cast about them looks of bewildered fascination, like enchanted sailors.

'Where are those coming from?' Ebner speaks for all of them; 'those' being the voices (plural, contrapuntal) into which the single note is separating out and multiplying. More than a duet, it's a madrigal, with Aeolian minors, tritones and ascending sixths – all slightly *off*, but off by intervals that, while not uniform, seem coordinated, each one's notch of off-ness corresponding, by some system which no earthly musicology could parse or measure, to that of the others. The image comes to him of electric pylons singing in the wind: lattices, cages, gantries, crossarms, wires all oscillating, voices humming each at their own frequency but intertwining, a hermetic *cantus firmus*.

'From the fins,' van Boezem answers Ebner, pointing. Directing their gaze back at the test section now, they see the smoke-thread being chopped up around the bobsleigh's tail into short snippets, each of which twists and cringes, as though trying to flex its way back upstream, to a time before the cut, the sudden birth, this traumatic discontinuity, but succeeding only in taking up its place as one more in a set of disconnected, curling vortices.

'*Le tourbillon*,' Roussel says knowingly.

'What?' Medosch asks.

'The engineer's old friend the whirlpool,' annotates van Boezem. 'Your bobsleigh's strolling down von Kármán Street.'

'Reynolds is up to 90,' Roussel states, much too contentedly for Medosch's liking; 'which means drag coefficient .075.'

This figure Medosch understands. Turning towards van Boezem, he mutters: 'Not good …'

'No, no,' the Chief Technician answers soothingly. 'It is good. This turbulence you must think of as the sand in which the treasure you've come here in search of has been buried. Here is where we start to dig, take readings, help you make improvements … Our machine' – the helix-swirl his hand makes at this point expands the reference area of this rather old-fashioned term, *machine*, so that it circumscribes both the test section and the out-of-view stretches of the tunnel; also the control room, the entire site and, beyond all these, some mysterious, or perhaps dimensionless, quantity forever destined to exceed the sum of its constituent figures – 'will be your map and shovel all in one. We even do the digging for you …' NW has paid a brand consultancy firm eu.50,000 to come up with this analogy. It seems to get some purchase on the Austrian.

'Yes. Yes, of course,' he says. 'What do they need to do?'

'The riders?' asks van Boezem. 'Nothing. We will run the wind-flow right up to the top speeds the sleigh reaches, and keep it up there for as long as they can hold position. During this time, we vary the angle of attack, by changing ...'

Medosch begins to frame a question, but van Boezem whips the answer out before a word is uttered:

'The angle, that is, between the model's reference line – its chord – and the oncoming flow. This we achieve by changing the inclination of the force pad. Thus we can ascertain not only drag but also lift, lateral force, yaw, roll and pitching moments over a range of attack angles.'

'You can *see* all these?' Medosch asks.

'Some of them we will see in the smoke and on the chalk; and' – here he nods towards the British delegation – 'the bubbles. But what we see with the eye will be a sketch, no more. The gold will come to the surface later, when the data's processed.'

Roussel digests the figure that van Boezem proceeds to murmur to him – 5.2 – with a kind of avarice. As he opens the valve yet further, they all feel the gut-roll growing, waves spreading outwards from their abdomens, across the room, the air, the other people's bodies – and inwards too, vibrating down through muscles, fluid, bone. The choir are screaming now, fugue-permutations veering and careening to the outer limits of the field where *any* ratio of intervals or pitches might hold sway: tonics swapping with sub-dominants within the space of single notes that seem to play out in three octaves all at once, false entries, inversions, retrogrades and diminutions running riot through all keys – until, suddenly, these fall away, like clouds, and the accompanying mute throbbing in their inner ears lets them know, like the calm, triumphant silence that fills airline cabins in the first few seconds after take-off and ascent have been successfully completed, that they've passed the hearing threshold.

Phocan and Diamond took the early flight today: Stansted, 5.45. With no duties to perform yet, Phocan's gazing at Roussel's screens, their digit-clusters and their thermal patches, outlines and auras pulsing in peristaltic rhythm as the feed-data replenishes itself. If Roussel is sifting lines and figures, sorting shuffling movements into groupings and translating colour-swarms to information, Phocan's simply hypnotised, Medusaed. On the central monitor the bobsleigh's silhouette crouches in vivid blue, innermost doll of a *matryoshka* set, with ever-larger silhouettes repeating all around it and each other, grading from green to yellow as they multiply. No fixed shells, though, these dolls are living – or maybe dying. Their bodies, as they tumble escalating outwards, are forever breaking open, pixel life-blood gushing from one level to the next, which ruptures too, ditto the next layer – on and on up, in lurid flows that radiate towards some vague periphery, then, when it seems all form and structure *must* have ebbed away, turn round and radiate back in again, the two-way current generating in its midst small, transitory islands, intermediate thresholds that, no sooner than they're formed, start bleeding too. Somewhere, around the borders of his own dazzled thought-screen, he senses an intuition trying to stake out a provisional ground, or at least drop into the flood tide a sea anchor; senses at work within these flows some kind of *logic*. Not the fixed one under whose protectorate Roussel's operating and within whose jurisdiction the processors and hard-drives are accumulating rates and indices ... No, Phocan's starting to suspect the presence of some *other* kind – an *illogical* logic, whose nebulous, endlessly mutating grammar would be formed not of fixed terms but of its own very mutability, pure drift ... One, though, at whose core, or outer border (since these two are shifting places constantly), there lies a proposition ...

Which – elusive and perhaps ridiculous, but this morning, in NW's gargantuan contraption, filtered through the gauze of his cognitive dissonance, no less insistent – proposition, plainly stated, is: that this display, this lurid animation, has been crafted, tailor-made, for him, specifically *for him* – if only he might ...

if he had the wherewithal to ... It's the acetate effect again, the overlaying, simultaneity: this looped drama of shape-finding and shape-loss, of coagulation and disintegration, seems to gather and disperse, to draw into discernibility even as, in the same motion, it scrambles it again, a process – is it too much to say a *struggle?* – to which Phocan, though he never willed or planned it this way, has been dedicating his whole life. The pixellated dumbshow, pregnant with itself, seems to affirm this to him on repeat, performing, in encrypted, mute language of shade and contour, a long quest he's never quite managed to *name*, all its encounters glimpsed in passing but not realised, some seduction whose full consummation might be glorious but would (the rupture and the blood-gush hint) necessitate, or at least stand *adjacent* to, a scene of monumental and inexorable violence. Now Phocan senses, tingling in his gut with the great fan's vibrations, a dual feeling of purpose and of guilt – guilt for an act of which, even if he's never *executed* it as such, he's been, since long ago, entirely culpable.

'Mark?' asks Diamond. 'What are you ... ?'

And just as suddenly the intuition and the understanding which it seemed to be drawing, in pulses, to the edge of clarity both dissipate, spilling past the on-screen *matryoshka* bobsleighs' and his own mind's outer lip, conjectures carried and transmuted beyond recognition by the unforgiving lines, inferences all unravelling into their dance ...

' *'ch habe eine Frage.'* Ebner, three feet closer to the test section than Phocan, has been similarly lost in musings – in his case directed to or prompted by his contemplation, through the glass sheet, of the actual bobsleigh, or rather of the smoke-laced air flowing around it. He murmurs his remark in German as he's really just thinking aloud; but, since a question's signalled, van Boezem asks him what he wants to know. The *Cheftrainer* hesitates at first; then, switching to English, outs with it. 'If I am understanding right, your' – he opts for that quaint word again – '*machine* ... is leading back round to itself.'

The Chief Technician, despite the obtuse phrasing, understands what he's getting at. 'Yes,' he answers, 'it's a Prandtl tunnel. A fixed loop.'

'This means,' Ebner continues, 'that the wind that passes my men turns a corner, and another, and another, and eventually passes them again a second time; and then a third; a fourth; a fifth ...'

'Well, yes,' van Boezem says.

'Then, my question: once it contacts with their bodies, with the sleigh, it is changed. It is ... marked. Its shape, as the smoke shows us, has been altered; and this alteration is a point of information.'

'Yes, exactly,' van Boezem's face beams teacherly benevolence again.

'So this bit of wind then moves onwards, down the tunnel, *all the time still shaped this way*. It is no longer just a neutral piece of air: it is an *Abdruck*, an ...'

'Imprint. Impression,' Avanessian prompts.

'*Genau*: impression, of my navigator's elbow or my brakeman's cheek, or of the bobsleigh's nose, or of this whirlpool by its fins. And not just of that body: it's a *Stempel*, also, a "stamp", of that moment, of that point in time, *nicht wahr*?'

'Yes, but ...'

'So: when it comes around the second time, already shaped and *stempelt* this way, and it hits the nose or cheek or elbow once more, which once more should make a mark, an information-point – well, I am thinking ...'

The others wait indulgently for him to formulate this – his own team, too. He's won three Olympic golds, four silvers, six bronzes. Method in madness; he has leeway.

'... I am thinking that this second *Abdruck* cannot be a pure one. It is not imprinting on to blank, but on to an already-imprint. After it has gone round the first time, every particle of air is like this: a two-, or three-, or thousand-time already-imprint. And the moment-*Stempel*, too, is carried round to the next moment, which so then is *stempelt* on already-moment ... which is a big problem for me, because ... because when ...'

This one, medals or not, he can't quite formulate. It's there, though, lucid in his head: the vertiginous suspicion that this instant of perception on the riders' part (of coldness, being whipped by ice, seeing the turn's edges loom), and, with it, a newly generated piece of *now*-ness, is being funnel-looped round, folded back in on itself, to replay, like Marx Augustin, from the hollow spot of its wrongful interment.

'But,' van Boezem breaks the awkward pause, 'it's not like that. There are the honeycombs in both the settling chamber and contraction area, and meshes, which remove swirl and lateral variation as the air passes through their cells. And the diffuser's screens, that break down eddies into smaller ones, which decay faster. All these are turbulence-suppressing mechanisms; through them, we are able to deliver to the test section consistently clean air.'

Ebner digests this sceptically, then asks:

'Where do *you* get the air from?'

'In the first place, you mean?'

Ebner nods.

'We take it from the ambient, just like an open Eiffel tunnel does.'

'The ambient?'

'Outside: the fields, the sky ...'

'From the ambient it comes and to the ambient it returns,' Roussel intones, lifting his eyes up to the halo-light.

Van Boezem fixes Ebner with a reassuring smile, which is half-heartedly returned. The physics lesson's settled the *Cheftrainer* for now; but small, undecayed pockets of disquiet are still there, swirling downstream in the honeyed silence. Van Boezem senses a tiny perturbation in his own mind, too: something to do with his elision, unchallenged by Ebner and so let stand by him, that casts the Luttelgeest air as the ultimate blank slate: uncompressed, unfiltered, free as the birds that dart about it. Disingenuously: he knows all too well – as engineer and *polderburger* – that the air about these fields, this sky, is anything but neutral. It, too, is *stempelt*. This landscape has been made: lines laid down, sections divided by right angles, flows turned and diverted down braced channels. *God*, as the old saying (unattributed) would have it, *created the Earth – but the Dutch created Holland*. A century ago there wasn't any earth, or even air, here; only water. Lying three metres lower than the sea it has (for now) evicted, polder land is scooped-out, hollow land: one giant wind tunnel. And in all Dutch polders, right from the beginning, it was wind that did the scooping and the empty-ing: cap-mounted sails pumping water through *duikertjes*, into Archimedes screws the windmills also powered ... And when the polders grew and bumped against each other, and the water bailed out of one threatened to overrun its neighbour, rather than fighting and sabotaging one another's works (as villages in Bangladesh still do), municipalities, like children pooling Lego, let their individual polders become chambers in a huge, amalgamated polder-circuit – which, in turn, called for joined-up governance, a national control room operating subsystems of *baljuws*, *heemraden* and *dijkgraafs*. Three of van Boezem's ancestors were *baljuws*; one of them is mentioned in Leeghwater's *Dagboek*; his paternal grandfather, the one he knew, worked directly under Lely. Environmental manage-ment is in the blood that pumps around his body: regulated flows, each cycle marking out a generation ...

And so is disquiet – or, to give it a simpler name: fear. For there's that other wind, even less neutral, whistling off the Noordsee, from Rhein-, Maas-, Schedlt- and Eems-nymphs all conglomerated (gods, too, can pool Lego) into a monstrous Zuidermaiden, furious and vengeful. You can't always hear her, but she's still transmitting on some frequency or other, even when the storm-fan's idle: in previ-ous triumphs written on the ground, circular *wielen* scored by the screwing movement of inland-boring water; or carved, like the name of van Boezem's maternal grandfather, the one he never knew, into memorial-stone beside those of the grandmother and two uncles he never knew either, drowned in their sleep in '53; or in the dreams that, despite the Delta Project's realisation and the sealing of all exits to the sea (the polder-circuit, too, is closed-loop now), despite the EUMETSTAT- and FOAM-linked, MPP-enabled weather-tracking systems to which every *stadhuis* in the whole of Flevoland is hooked up, still come to him, as to all *polderburgers*, at least once a year – dreams of water rushing, vertical as the dyke-wall it's just breached, thundering and boiling as it spreads out at its base, a giant brush lifting trees, cattle, houses, people, sweeping them away ...

The tunnel has been running at 5.2 for half an hour. Roussel turns from his screens and signals to his boss that he's got what he wants for now; van Boezem does the same to Medosch; Medosch looks enquiringly to Ebner, who nods back at him, then signals to his riders to stand down – or, rather, up. All their ears pop as they drop back through the hearing threshold. De Veen has downed his smoke gun and picked up a camera; he's taking side-on photographs of the bobsleigh's rear section, on to which he painted, just before the session started, a monochrome layer of kerosene mixed with fluorescent chalk. The wind has evaporated the former and coaxed the latter out into a boldly contrasting set of vortices and sinusoids smeared luminously over each fin, abstract geometric paintings. Van Boezem, turning to the Pantarey duo, announces:

'Bubble time!'

This is Phocan and Diamond's cue to unpack their trolley-mounted cases. They extract, from cut foam lining in which the objects sit like the articulated parts of saxophones or rifles, a range of angle-poise arms, cameras, lasers, goggles and a plastic bottle of car-battery size from which a pipe protrudes and inside which a greenish liquid sloshes as it's carried to the test section. While Phocan helps de Veen fix lasers and cameras to the tunnel's walls and ceiling, van Boezem explains to the Austrians:

'You will be the first NW clients to benefit from this particular flow tracer.'

'The goggles are for us?' Avanessian ask Diamond.

'No,' she answers. 'They're for the riders. But if anyone is epileptic, you might want to leave the room.'

The wisdom of these words becomes apparent when, be-goggled Luksch and Miessen crouched back in their cabin and the wind flow ramped up once more, Phocan activates the lasers, which strobe purple round the bobsleigh and, more strangely, green round the periphery of the observers' vision. Still stranger is the way the beam, in the test section, separates into three sharply defined, if porous, walls: one at the bobsleigh's nose, another at its tail and a third half a metre downstream of it, each one a thin light-plane cutting the flow crossways, like a sluice gate. Strangest of all, though, is the spawn of bubbles that the plastic bottle, sitting upstream of the model, tirelessly brings forth and launches on the air: a bubble-throng of biblical proportions – exodus, horde, frantic pilgrimage – more and more of them, all rushing and stampeding down the tunnel, bouncing off the cowling, skipping over Luksch's helmet, dancing reels and circles in the wake-turbulence before eventually scurrying, like a crowd of lemmings, to cast themselves from the diffuser's cliff-edge to its meshes' rocks, on which they burst.

'Why the three laser planes?' Medosch asks Phocan.

'They translate the drag field down the tunnel,' he explains. 'Each plane is an interrogation area. The bubbles give specific index points from which value can be derived across a diachronic stretch.' Leaning over de Veen's shoulder, he starts talking him through the tomographic software, the lasers' bandpass filter presets, the delay generators' resolution-timing scales ...

Ebner, staring into these translation planes, which seem to catch the helium spheres even as they zap unpausing through them, coquettishly offering his eyes presence and stasis while with the same gesture whipping the illusion away again, dissolving it back into wind, sees something ghostly in their *Nachglut*. Van Boezem, noticing the *Cheftrainer*'s gaze lost in the bubbles, smiles:

'It's like a children's party, no?'

Ebner makes no response. He never had children. Athletes young enough to be his offspring, then his offspring's offspring, have passed through his arms, a new batch every three or four years: he's got them, then they're gone, down the ramp, out of sight round the first bend, leaving as after-image trophies, photographs,

the next batch in whose faces their faces are ghost-stamped, like
the previous batch's were in theirs. Now it's the bubbles' dance
that's tapping out the folk-song's rhythm in his head, twitching
his cracked lips into silent motion once more:

> *Jeder Tag war ein Fest,*
> *Und was jetzt? Pest, die Pest!*
> *Nur ein großes Leichenfest,*
> *Das ist der Rest.*

– and he sees, framed and dissolving in each plane, day after day,
the remnants of the last day's party: held in stillness but rushing
headlong nonetheless to the next day, the next party; till all planes,
ghoulishly aligned, present the spectacle of plague-corpses feast-
ing on plague-corpses, pausing in their chewing now and then to
gaze straight back at him, their new companion, and to chant in
undead voices:

> *Augustin, Augustin,*
> *Leg' nur in Grab dich hin!*
> *Ach, du lieber Augustin,*
> *Alles ist hin!*

Navigator Luksch's visions, too, are reaching a finale, or at least
a coda. He's gone down the Igls circuit – threaded both needle-eye
and labyrinth, set a line through Höcker, Fuchsloch, Hexenkessel,
Weckauf – in his imagination at least twenty times in the last ninety
minutes, slide-carouselled his way through every mountain range
in Austria. He's physically and mentally exhausted – but the bubbles, infusing the air with lightness, are granting him a little uplift:
he finds his thoughts wandering, not from the Hafelekarspitze and
the Patscherkofel, but from winter to spring and summer. Although
the exercise does not, strictly speaking, fall within the remit of
Ebner's instructions, he starts dotting the pictured Tyrolean hills
with flowers, whose names he reels off from a list that he was made

to learn by heart in fourth grade: Alpine aster, lady's-slipper orchid, purple saxifrage and two-leaf squill; true lover's knot, anemone, blue moonwort and the stemless gentian stamped on the back of one-cent coins ... then lady's mantle, wolf's-bane arnica and eye-bright augentrost; spring gentian, yellow dock, globeflower, false helleborine, mouse-ear hawkweed, maidenstears, bitterwort and (rarest of all, jewel of the Sonnenspitze with its own, dedicated folk song) edelweiss ...

What machine, operating at what scale or dimension, through what overlay of planes, could tell this congregation – render or make visible to them, carved into what flow tracer or the undulating contours of which screen – the following: that the litany which Luksch is silently reciting was originally written, back in 1583, by one Carolus Clusius? What of that? More than a little. There's a closed-loop circuit at work here, conveying the Low Lands to the heights of Austria and Austria back here to Holland, slipstreams in whose turbulence this afternoon's whole episode is held, all passing through the needle-eye of Luksch's reverie. For the Flemish-born Clusius not only compiled, while serving Maximilian as Prefect of the Imperial Medicinal Garden in Vienna, the definitive taxonomy of Austrian flora; he also, summarily dismissed by Maximilian's successor Rudolf, wended his way to Leyden, in whose *hortus botanicus* he set to work studying the strange permutations of a new variety of flower. Plucked from the Himalayan fortieth parallel – the slopes of Pamir, foothills and valleys of Tian Shan, Kunlun, Karakoram – and meandering its way, via the silk undergarments of Ottoman warriors, the double-tasking executioner-gardeners of Süleyman the Magnificent, and Ogier Ghislain de Busbecq, Dutch ambassador to his court – or alternatively (the data's weak here) via Ceylon, through the usurping offices of Governor Lopo Vaz de Sampaio – to the unknown Flemish merchant who, finding a set of bulbs tucked in a fabric shipment, mistook them for onions but didn't like the taste so planted some instead, inviting to admire the bloom come spring his neighbour Joris Rye, a botanist, who wrote immediately to Clusius ... Riding whatever magic carpet of history it was that wafted it down here, the tulip, with its long stem, large leaves and boldly woven petals (*tulipan*, like a turban, the Turks said), elicited from gaping Hollanders a reaction so immediate that cod-psychologists would later speculate that the flower's form, through a quirk of chance or fate, presented to the 'national mind' some kind of visual cipher to which it was just *programmed* to respond . . .

Respond, of course (this part's well known), it did, teasing the genus out into a range of species – *Admiral Liefken*, *Admiral van der Eijck*, *Viceroy*, the eponymous *Tulipa Clusiana* – which, being Dutch, they traded. It was 'breaking' they prized: erupting trans-formations, brilliant scarlets and swarthy almost-blacks running in sharp-edged stripes, or flames, or flares, along the centre of each petal, staking out clear borders round its edges, rendering the genus supreme among flowers *in the same way* (Charles de la Chesnée Monstereul now) *that humans are lords of the animals, diamonds eclipse all other precious stones, and the sun rules the stars.* The thing was, that no breaking pattern could be duplicated, nor, despite the tricks the nurseries deployed (grafting, soil-depth variation, manure-starving, manure-glutting, freezing, scorching; some even turned to alchemy), breaking induced: it happened, or it didn't, and it ran its course. It was, Monstereul mused, as though the flowers, in finding their true lines, were *self-perfecting* – the logic of the occidental horticulturalist cross-fertilising at this point with that of the oriental poet (Khayyam's tulips sup, as do we all, on Heavenly Vintage until Heaven chooses to invert us back to Earth, like empty cups) or, indeed, theologian, for whom the tulip (*lale*: same Arabic letters as *Allah*), bowing its head when in full bloom, embodies the essential virtue of modesty before God . . .

But not before the market. By 1634, a *Viceroy* bulb is fetching 3,000 florins, a *Liefken* 4,400. The famous tulip-trading marts are set up on the Stock Exchanges of Amsterdam, Rotterdam, Haarlem, Alkmaar, Hoorn. As the Revolt sends waves of bulb-packing immi-grants and refugees up from the south Netherlands to the United Provinces, the pool swells; traders grow rich; their *handelhuisen* start investing in land-reclamation schemes, carving out room for gardens in which new bulbs can be cultivated, reinvesting profit from these in more polder-schemes; round and round, the centripetal cycle pushing outward: space, money, space, all held in an expanding membrane of liquidity … Thus Clusius, Father of the Tulip, fathers Holland.

Breaking will later turn out to be caused by the Mosaic Virus. Aphid-borne, it may make lovely patterns – but it reduces the flower's reproduction rate at the same time. Which means fewer flame-streaked tulips – which, *natuurlijk*, makes them all the more valuable. By 1637 a *Rosen* bulb is going for ten times a craftsman's annual salary. Bigwig investor Adriaen Pauw's got a giant bed of them blooming in his castle grounds, or so it seems – but it's a layout of earth-mounted mirrors, angled to multiply half-bunch into cornucopia. Do you, Pauw wonders one day as he directs his gardener in shifting the mirrors around for greater effect, even need the half-bunch to create the illusion? Do you need *one*? After all (he tells himself), the rarest and most precious *Rosen*, *Semper Augustus*, has grown so scarce that no one has actually *seen* one in three years. There are supposed to be twelve of them in existence, all held by … by this *man*, this man who's meant to live in Amsterdam, but whose *identity* … No matter: we don't need the flowers or bulbs, the traders say; we'll sign contracts for future delivery. The buyer doesn't need the cash; the seller doesn't need the goods; nor will they when the date comes round – they'll just exchange the price-difference between now and then. With prices fluctuating daily, and these fluctuations having rhythms that, to cannier traders, are discernible (and, it goes without saying, manipulable), you're trading in the pattern not on the flower, but *of the fluctuation*. Same thing: it's still pattern. Index and value. Might there be a navigator, crouched down in the *Beurs*' cowling, tweaking with imperceptible mastery the steering rings? Might its lines, too, be self-perfecting? The traders reckon so; they dance around its slipstream, spinning out options, futures – even as the plague, the human one, starts cutting their own reproduction rate, their stock …

And then the slipstream turns into a vortex. Shorting, bear-raids, rumours swirling left and right ... Here's some motherfucker selling *risk on credit!* Here are angry 'florists' hammering at the *Eerste Kamer*'s doors, demanding payment on all contracts executed before 30 November; then pleading for twenty per cent buyouts; then (*come on, guys!*) for at least *ten* ... No dice, the politicians say: enough's enough. We've got a name for what you *klootzaks* have been playing at: *windhandel*, trading in the wind. We're banning it. All contracts (sub- and forward-contracts, swaps, exchanges) void. At which point, as you can imagine, pandemonium breaks out: you've got speculators chasing each other through the cobbled streets, ripping up contracts, dropping the shreds from bridges into the canals; and you can't even give the bulbs (the common types of bulb, the only ones in actual circulation) away; the true line, all lines lost, steep-banking turns and labyrinths now unnavigable, the crash's inevitability finally revealed in all its naked obviousness as seeded from the very push-off, its anticipation the only thing that lets you know it hasn't come quite yet, until ... *Pop!*

The fan has been switched off now; the riders dispatched to the storage room to change back into civvies; lasers dismounted, angle-poise arms unscrewed from the walls; bobsleigh zip-bagged and borne off to a waiting van. Roussel's screens are still lit, but they're static. Beneath them, under the desk, the hard drives hum. They know stuff, but they don't know what they know yet; it will be a week before the fully processed findings are presented to the OBSV. De Veen has got a mop out, and is cleaning up the viscous film that's sticking to the tunnel's floor. The bubbles have marked the diffuser's vanes too, peppering their mesh with dull grey patches that, over the following weeks, and months, and years, will grow duller and greyer as they merge with one another and with newer patches; a thickened and composited stain ledger that will never be read, even if someone were to try (why would they?), but will nonetheless record, in muffled, incoherent scrawl, that something, at some time or times, has taken place.

2. Love Philtre

Aboard the KFS *Sidereal*, things are hotting up. Tild, the ship's royal passenger, upon whose safe conveyance to her fiancé hopes for the future well-being and security of Kern, Argeral and pretty much the entire B-Roth star system largely rest – as, too, does the honour of Commander Tszvetan, her conveyor – is voyaging (as protocol demands) in an isolation that is splendid but no less solitary for that. For the first moon cycle or so of the long trip, she flops around the immaculately contoured repos, ottomans and hanging eggs that deck her suite. Now and again she ventures out to traipse the *Sidereal*'s long, empty corridors; if a crew member tries obsequiously to return her to her quarters, she rebukes him for presuming to tell *her* where she may wander, tossing back as she spits the words at him black hair that's streaked with radium-coloured zigzags. Despite her haughtiness, the crew are all in awe of her – star-struck by not her status, but her spunk. Early on, soon after they'd left Doon Leer, she would turn up in the engine rooms, play Atcheque with the stokers and swap some of her philtres for the amphoras of 'kwavit they're carrying back to Kern ('back' as in back again: the liquor, native to their planet, only acquires its character when it's transported twice across the Kwador boundary line, one time in each direction, the resulting chemical mutation generating its distinctive taste and potency). When informed by blu-text that such fraternising was forbidden to the crew, she merely shrugged; but on learning that the stoker who'd been friendliest to her had received a beating for his kindness, she halted the visits. So now she just flops and lounges, lonely, homesick and, above all, bored.

It's not until the middle of the second cycle that she finds her way to the Observatory. This chamber sits above the *Sidereal's* uppermost starboard trusses – hovers almost, an appendage, communicating with the main body of the vessel only through a spiral staircase coiled around the fixing arm that alone prevents it from detaching itself and drifting into space. The chamber is perfectly spherical: a cyst, or fishbowl, or giant helmet, floating eyeball, whose wall (feat of engineering) is formed of a single tempered sapphire-glass sheet. Inside, torquetums, dioptras, astrolabes and spectrohelioscopes nestle in soft velveteen moulds around a central standing console to whose upper surface is affixed a second and much smaller vitreous globe, a 'reader' capable of both ascertaining star positions and ascribing to newly encountered constellations, when its memory's up to the task, tentative designations, whose names it, when required, projects across the larger dome's interior, thereby aligning territory and map. On stumbling across this room, Tild, not one for reticence, starts making free with instruments and console, holding to her eyes and twiddling the discs and flanges of the former, slowly moving downturned hands above the latter, as though warming them (the reader's operated like a theremin). It's while standing thus cocooned by astral coordinates both actual and projected, light sliding across her face and adding new transversals to her hair's angular geometry, that her immersive reverie is rudely broken into by a male voice issuing, it seems, from space itself:

'You're not supposed to be here.'

Tild spins round. He's standing behind her, near the hatchway to the staircase – although not that near: he must have been observing her unnoticed for some time. Counterweighing shock at his presence, fury at his voyeurism and a need to reassert authority, the Princess, raising back to her right eye the astrolabe her hands almost let drop when he first spoke, enquires disinterestedly:

'Says who?'

The question is rhetorical: the voice was Tszvetan's. He, too, has spent much of the last moon cycle flopping about the *Sidereal*'s navigation deck and wandering its corridors, the most recently trekked of which has brought him to this eyrie. Is it anxiety about fulfilling his obligation to his 'uncle' (in fact, uncle) Louis Q, or lingering grief at his parents' loss, or simply solitude induced by years of long celestial voyaging, that lends him such a sad and contemplative air? Or is it something more immediate? Taking a step forwards, he tells Tild:

'You're holding it wrong. Here, let me show you ...'

Thus begins the first Observatory Summit. He explains to her the reader's software, talks her through rotation of styluses, alignment of tabulae quinoctialis, interconversion between horizontals and ecliptics ... To his surprise, she demonstrates a complete understanding of the mathematics involved, even correcting him when he mis-states the off-set of the axis of rotation of the planet closest to which they happen to be passing just now, Gallon, as 25 degrees (it's 23.5).

'Your computation's weak,' she scolds him teasingly.

'It served me fine during the Saraõnic War,' he quips back.

The atmosphere inside the chamber changes instantly, as though the thermo-gauge had yanked the temperature down several notches.

'The Third one?' Tild asks.

'I was too young to fight in the other two,' he answers.

'My uncle died in that war,' she tells him.

He pauses for a while, then says, without any affect or inflection:

'I'm sorry.'

'Are you?' She sets the sextant she's got in her hand down roughly, hairline fracturing its index mirror. Looking for some other object to take up, her hand's drawn towards the rapier he removed (the better to facilitate his taking up position right against the reader's console stand) from his waist and laid down moments ago, which is now humming softly on the deck.

'Don't touch my rapier,' he says measuredly and quietly – and the Princess, despite being unused to obeying orders, even less interdictions, freezes inches from the weapon. Sensing his control of the situation, Tszvetan presses his advantage home by adding, in a voice tinged with cruelty: 'It's killed people.'

These lines bring the Summit to an abrupt close. Tild storms from the Observatory, and spends the next three or four diurnals beaming large 3-D projections into her suite's stale air. She beams two Atcheque pieces she finds in her pocket, prisoners held over from an uncompleted and now uncompletable engine-room game. She beams a dead cigala she finds rigor-mortised amidst pumps and sandals in a desiccated wardrobe. She beams scans (of objects, faces, scenes) that friends have blu-texted from Argeral. The *Sidereal* turns out to have a good on-board projecting system, capable of both fast streaming and high-magnitude upscaling without sacrificing definition. Placing her text-compact, or just any object, on the jack-pad, Tild moves around the simulacrum it builds hovering before her, gazing at it from all sides and angles, even underneath: she spends hours splayed on the floor in dreamy study of various forms, their curves and masses – study made still dreamier by her ingestion of the contents of the philtres she's brought with her. Back on Argeral, Tild was both wild child and decorated student, first of all her year in quadrive and alkimia; until Tszvetan and his crew turned up to head off her diploma-path with Louis Q's proposal, she'd been a magisterial candidate at the Academy, investigating for her *disertatiõ* the mineral and molecular composition of her planet's signature power source and medium, breaking charge's field down into components, teasing from these integrants derivatives several of which turned out, when ingested, to produce effects that, from a psychoactive point of view, could be called *interesting* ...

Nor is she all brain, though. It might seem like whimsy, or a fascination with its structure and articulation, that prompts her to spend more time perusing the projection of the pendant hanging by her neck than she does the beamed likeness of anything else – but there's a darker reason for this. The pendant casts, in intimate anatomic detail, the skull of her uncle Merhalt – uncle who, as she has just had cause to inform Tszvetan, perished in the most recent conflict between their respective planets. Merhalt was just three years older than her, more a brother than an uncle: they grew up together, frolicking in royal *brinquedotecques* and *gzhiardini*. When she learnt that he'd taken his place among the millions of other victims of this pointless space-grab out in Saraõ, she cried for weeks on end, refusing to leave her boudoir, shunning all visitors. What brought her out eventually was news that Merhalt's body had arrived back, in full state, to be accorded its due funerary rites – prior to which she obtained from the crown pathologist a skull scan (he had died – unusually – in close combat, his skull's staving by an enemy rapier bringing about his demise), which she had the royal *mettalourgon* cast for her in rare blue osmium.

There's no precedent for this in Argeralian custom; it was her own eccentric plan entirely, realised by operating way beyond the limits of her royal prerogative. But realise it she did, and the pendant, intricately modelled relic, has hung from her neck ever since. Here in the *Sidereal*'s ambassadorial suite, she sets it down on the jack-pad and beams it out again, breaking the seal on one more philtre, the contents of which she swallows (the philtre's aperture being small and narrow) in small, pucker-lipped sips. Then, as the skull sculpts itself out once more at waist height, larger than life-size in the room, she again sits, then lies, then slides around it, staring at the meticulously rendered set of planes, plates and panels all conjoined around a central suture running down it like a stitch before abruptly giving off to a large crater, a concavity that seems to suck into its void all planes, all lines – and yet, being formed of beamed light no less than the projection's other areas, is as 'present' as them, as filled in as this whole luminous sphere that, were she to beam her own face in like detail, she would see reflected not only in her eye's curved outer membrane but also in the tear forming against this now, just on the verge of dropping . . .

For the stretch following the first Observatory Summit, then, a stand-off sets in and takes hold, a kind of stalemate or (as with Tild's Atcheque match) hiatus, interregnum, period of suspended play. The Princess mopes about her suite, gazing at formless forms; Tszvetan mopes about the upper quarters, fiddling redundantly with cockpit settings (for the most part automated), meandering along corridors that seem to multiply and grow the more he treads them, heading back again and again to the even more isolated Observatory, leaning his face against the cupole's glass and staring into space, letting his eye rest on one point, on a planet or a vulcanoid, a tiny giant or hypergiant or subgiant, then moving it backwards to a further-outlying, tinier-still detached binary or nebula, with the effect that all the stars and clusters seem to be in constant retreat from him, from the *Sidereal*, each other ...

'Chill of intergalactic distance,' murmurs Herzberg, leaning over the shoulder of Eldridge, who himself leans over that of his star coder Charlie, working keyboard and glide-pad down beneath them at his table. 'Is there some way to, you know, *accentuate* ... ?'

'What if you take each one of the star points,' Eldridge suggests, 'and increase the space between it and the next by a measure proportional to ... I don't know ... time elapsed or something ...'

'We can do that,' says Charlie. 'With Parergon you can set relational distance-augment/time-diminish gradients. It gives you a kind of infinite perspective.'

'But ...' Herzberg isn't entirely happy with this idea. 'It's not so much *infinity* we want; not disappearance at the edges or the limit. More like ... an *invasion* of what's near by far-ness ... Like all surfaces and edges are retracting, dwindling even from their own position ...'

He's thinking, partly, of the staircase scene in *Vertigo*, or the reverse-pull shot of Brody on the beach in *Jaws*. But even more he's dredging up deep-sedimented memories of childhood meningitis: how the room, his little bedroom, seemed to fill with a voluminous expanse that simultaneously emptied it, ate it away, as though some cosmic road digger were scooping out whole chunks of *there*-ness, filling them with *not-there* craters. These craters would swell, pregnant with an absence to which his delirium acted as midwife, birthing it in sweat and whimpers right above the carpet – and then cupboard, desk, toybox and even bedside lamp would take on the aspect of unmanageably distant objects, even though they were right next to him. The illness seemed to open up a peephole on a universe of expanded vacancy, laid out somehow beside or maybe even *within* this one, waiting for its opportunity, its chink, its moment …

'… a monstrous remoteness that has got all close-up,' he's telling Charlie. 'Outer reaches transposed to the inner sanctums … Or as though eternity had wormed its way into each second – that's the look I want: helpless, cold and neutral. Definitely cold.'

'Parergon can do that, too,' Charlie says confidently; 'no probs.' He types *c-o-l-d* in his sidebar.

The onset of the third moon cycle brings with it a change of mood. Tszvetan and Tild, quite separately but in sync, as though the course their surges, ebbs and bores will take were set by mechanisms they're no more aware of than a tidal body is, find themselves – almost literally – crossing swords once more in the Observatory. It's she who interlopes on him this time; unlike her, though, he notices her entry straight away, but lets her circle him a couple of times before addressing her:

'Not far to go now,' he comments, pointing through the chamber's glass wall to a spot lying somewhere beyond her left ear. 'We're passing Acephalus already.'

She turns round and sees the planet, with its signature blue ring, but ventures nothing in reply. Eventually he adds:

'You must be happy.'

To this line, too, she offers nothing back. Her silence, like their terse earlier exchange, seems to dictate the chamber's gravity: the air feels heavy. After a long time she turns back from the glass to face him.

'Are you married?' she asks.

Tszvetan shakes his head. 'To my work, maybe.'

'And just what's that?'

He gestures round the chamber, or perhaps beyond it, as though indicating all the galaxies and nebulae. 'I navigate.'

'And smuggle,' she adds with a smirk that is aggressive but not hostile. 'Your hold's full of zeletrion and 'kwavit.'

'It's all charged,' he says. 'I've got the manifest.'

'Sure,' she laughs. 'And if . . .'

The second Observatory Summit is cut short at this point by the loud wail of the *Sidereal*'s alarm system. It will turn out to be triggered by a short in the composting tank, easily fixed. But Tszvetan's not to know that yet; he hurries from the chamber – leaving, as Tild notices when she, too, makes towards the hatch, his rapier on the floor. Of course, she picks it up. And, after turning it over in her hands just as she did the torquetums and dioptras during her first visit to this room, she takes it with her, back down to her suite.

Why does she do this? Hard to say. Perhaps because, since childhood, she's got used to taking what she likes. Or perhaps, on the contrary, as not a manifestation of her birthright's license but a reaction against circumstantial powerlessness: if she's, effectively, a hostage to diplomacy, to realpolitik's exchanges, then she'll take her own sub-hostage, turn this glowing, humming thing into an object as symbolic as the Atcheque pieces. Or perhaps . . . perhaps because the object *itself* fascinates her. It's not just the aura lent it by its lethal function; there's something else, too, something about its shape that speaks to her, that seems to whisper the familiar, even the intimate . . .

In this last intuition, she turns out to be half-right – or (more correctly phrased) *exactly* wrong. It's not the rapier's *form* that she was recognising, but the *inverse* of this. When she lays it on the jack-pad and beams it out all big and holographic in her suite's dry air, the blade's physical qualities – its pronounced distal taper and the deep off-centre fuller running from its point of balance to its centre of percussion, or the grainy, light-martensite *niye* jagging in layered contours down its side – take on the aspect of the imprint left by something else. Or, rather, of the block that *made* that something else's imprint in the first place, of the negative of all its pleats, folds and declivities. Instinct tells her immediately what that 'something else' might be. Tugging at her neck, she sweeps the rapier aside and lays the blue osmium pendant on the jack-pad in its place. Scaling up the projection, homing straight in on the skull's fracture, she can see straight off that its topology's the same – that is, the unequivocally corresponding opposite. And if she slides the rapier back next to it, and aligns the two together ... just so ... There it is, an exact fit: all of the dents and shards and pockmarks that define the skull's deep crater, its fatal concavity, slot in precisely (*amphichirally* – the term jumps out at her from ghosts of lecture notes abandoned back on Argeral) to the visible units that together make the blade; they're mirror images of one another. This is the weapon that killed Merhalt; and the hand that wielded it belonged, and still belongs, to none other than her pilot and protector Tszvetan.

This is the plot's first crisis. And its second: it's a double-crisis. Why? Because it's been growing glaringly self-evident to Tild, despite all efforts to camouflage awareness of the fact amidst the billow of projected objects and the fuzz of philtre-daze, that she's in love with Tszvetan. It started as they left Doon Leer, among the pageantry and splendour of departure, courtiers lined up in gold and scarlet robes, hautboys and tombours filling the bay with noise: the way this self-possessed but sad figure stood alone on the ramp of his vessel, half-detached, like the room in which she's since met with him twice, from the whole ceremony, and (by extension, as though the ceremony acted as a baroque stand-in for this) from life itself. In her long, drawn-out pacing of the *Sidereal's* labyrinth, she's been both trying to lose the object of her fixation and, at the same time (as if by chance, round the next corner, on the far side of an airlock), to run into it. As has he. It's mutual: Tszvetan, too, has grown fixated with this jag-haired princess who acts like some sister he never had, who seems to hold all rules and custom in contempt but who nonetheless can see a higher value in this royal marriage, her submission to it almost, at some scale or level, a defiance. His roaming, and her roaming, de-centre the labyrinth, have turned the *Sidereal*'s corridors into a Kepler field in which binary planets waltz round each other in anxious ellipses, each seeking the elusive focal point that would, if ever actually reached, result in a collision guaranteeing its cataclysmic end. Now, though, an extra weight, a Schwarzschild element, has been thrown into the mix: she's got the rapier. At some point he's going to have to come and get it, from her suite ...

And when he does, she'll be obliged to kill him. To do anything less would be to spit on Merhalt's grave. As far as Tszvetan's concerned: to follow his desire for her to its conclusion would, same thing, defile *his* uncle, feed him through a mangle worse even than death's. Still, the ambassadorial quarters' draw on him is irresistible. He reasons, knowing even as he runs the argument through his head that it's plain bullshit, that he *has* to go and get the rapier, and do it discreetly; that to send one of his crew, or in any manner formally acknowledge her theft of it, risks sparking a diplomatic incident. That part is true; what's spurious, bullshit, about it is that he knows all too well that if he goes down there and allows the inevitable to take place, a situation will blow up that's ten times worse politically than any rapier-snatching episode ...

Consequently, a second stand-off sets in, one far more charged than the last, as the stakes are now much higher – and are about to increase, since Tild, among her ottomans and eggs, has taken a decision. Out beyond Acephalus, out past even Gorgon and the Lethe Nebula, there lies a planet called Nocturnis. Beneath the hydrogen clouds of its atmosphere and the kaolinite layer of its topsoil sit compacted (and eponymous) mineral belts of noctural. Since 742 (ironically, as a consequence of the Third Saraõnic War, a sub-clause to the Landis Armistice that brought it to a close that year), Argeral has held the exploitation licence for these belts, revamping the small mining concession (noctural has niche industrial uses) that was sitting all dilapidated on the Granchap Fields, sole foothold of life, let alone civilisation, on the uninhabited outcrop. It was in Tild's own research group at the Academy that noctural was first seriously analysed, its elements identified; and Tild herself who baptised the previously unknown one '*thanadrine*'. This compound – denser even than the osmium she wears around her neck – turned out to contain an admixture of thebanum and chalcanthitus so concentrated that its ingestion, even in trace quantities, would be guaranteed to bring about a dreamy, carefree and perhaps even fantastic but for that no less inevitable death; whence the name Tild assigned to it. Ever the student, or perhaps the danger-seeker, she's brought an extract of it with her, a philtre-pent tincture that she's kept, for safety reasons, separate from all the others. Digging this out now and laying it on the jack-pad, beaming it up large, moving around its replica and marvelling at its strange colouration – dense black laced with blue, not unlike the swathes of interstellar void extending all around her out beyond the *Sidereal*'s walls – she wonders if she'll gain some kind of experience of these abyssal spaces, some *awareness* of her entering and merging with them, of oblivion itself, when she ingests it. For this is her decision: to drink the thanadrine, to rejoin Merhalt, thereby staying faithful to both her brother-uncle and, since she can neither kill nor love him, Tszvetan.

It's back to the Observatory that she repairs in order to see the plan through. She doesn't want to do it in the confines of her suite; far better here, amidst the constellations she'll soon join. Stripping the philtre's seal, popping its cap, she holds it up towards the galaxies and clusters and blank patches, toasting them all with her final gesture; then (unable, due to the philtre's shape, its narrow aperture, to down its contents in one gulp), begins to suck-sip the thanadrine. It's yet another sign of the extent to which their thinking, not to mention moving, has become entwined that Tszvetan bursts in on her as she's halfway through this, and immediately (from her pallor, or the fatalistic and determined look on her face, or if not those then the convulsions starting to rack her lower body) understands exactly what she's up to. As she stares straight at him, piercingly, defiantly, he rushes up to her and, snatching the philtre from her fingers, suck-sips its undrunk half. Even in what she takes to be her death throes, she's astonished by this act. The two of them stand face-to-face for a few seconds; then, as Tszvetan's calves and thighs start shaking to the same irregular beat as hers, they throw themselves into each other's arms to wait for death.

Death, though, has other things to do. It will be several cycles before Tild, from a chance conversation she'll have with one of Louis Q's barons at a banquet during which her royal health is toasted repeatedly with 'kwavit, realises what has (at a bio-chemical level at least) occurred: just as the ship's transit through the Kwador boundary line alters the composition of that liquor, so, too, has it changed the make-up of the thanadrine they've just imbibed. While the thebanum element seems to have been unaffected, the chalcanthitus has become, not exactly neutralised, but rather *catalysed* into something more akin to cantharidinus or rhodotoxina – to put it in lay terms, into an aphrodisiac. As the *Sidereal* rounds Ardis Minor, moon of its destination planet, and as Kern itself, sunk in the final stretch of the long night from which the rays of Fidelus will soon awaken it, heaves slowly into view, Tszvetan and Tild find themselves floating naked, clasping at each other, joining, separating, joining again as they tumble slowly through the chamber from which, Tszvetan having disabled the charge, gravity has, like duty and concern, been exiled.

This is the difficult bit. Modelling it all was relatively easy: you just build the room in CAD, drop in two bodies, set the parameters for movement, and the program does the rest. As far as lighting goes: the ray tracers have done their job, marking (in reverse) the trajectory of photons as they squirt from Fidelus, bounce off Ardis Minor and the by now far-away Acephalus, wash around the sapphire glass of the Observatory's dome, then pass through this to be deflected or occluded by the console and the moulds of various instruments, or by the floor, or by discarded clothes that drift, course logarithm-plotted, about the chamber's air; plus, naturally, by the floating and migrating limbs and torsos of the dis- and re-entwining lovers. That all works just fine. The difficulties start when you go analogue; when human bodies, with their flesh that knows nothing of asymptotes and their parabolas, enter the picture and start wobbling and flapping over the whole equation. They've brought in the finest, the industry apex: mo-cap performers from the fjords, from Bergen, whom they've rigged up and manipulated through the movement sequences the software scripted. But it looks awful, even if you discount all the straps and cages. For one thing, their skin and muscle, toned though these may be, still sag downwards at every opportunity – we're not in zero gravity *here*, after all. The A.D.s have tried all kinds of fixes, even stitching threads into flesh-coloured leotards and pulling upwards at the spots where droops are most egregious; but this just gives you a chicken-skin look whose repulsiveness runs counter to the scene's required eroticism. For another thing, even when they've adhered to their assigned paths with what to the naked eye may seem complete precision, there's still massive deviation. Actual bodies just won't do what's asked of them; even complying, they set up folds and kinks and barriers in all the wrong places, which plays havoc with the light path, which in turn trashes the whole set-up that Eldridge's guys have been, meticulously and at great expense, constructing for the last few weeks. And then, above and beyond all that, it just doesn't seem *right*; the movement, taken as a whole, doesn't in any way suggest that all this tumbling and twining's *really* orbiting around a central and impassioned act of coitus.

'Looks like a puppet porn show!' Herzberg shouted when he saw the rushes.

'The window of a butcher's shop during an earthquake,' Eldridge concurred. 'Haunches and carcasses all bumping up against each other!'

'Rag-dolls spinning' – Herzberg again – 'in a dryer!'

So they've defaulted, on the sly, back to the virtual; or at least to the virtual archive of a pre-existing scene they never them-selves staged, nor even witnessed. No one did – discounting the participants, who didn't really 'witness' it as such. Phocan has slipped them, in the strictest confidence, some files that he said were gathering dust on the Pantarey server, out-takes from a previous job whose purpose Eldridge and his team can only guess at. What they show, in fully captured and evented detail, is two human figures, male and female, copulating in every position that might be imagined, plus a few that none of them ever thought possible before viewing this cache. What's so useful about it from the DZ team's perspective is that, rather than try to push two floating bodies, virtual or real, together – that is, to do this from a starting-point of their not being conjoined, and to make their conjunction seem convincing – they can instead, like the ray tracer, work backwards, throwing the whole process, its causation, into reverse: *start* with bodies plausibly (because actually) joined in coital union, and work *outwards* from that point in order to extrapolate approach and exit angles and trajectories, a bit like they did with vessels entering and leaving Doon Leer's harbour. It's a canny move: since they'll only be using Pantarey's off-cuts as a foundation stone, embedding their core moments beneath layer after layer of morph and render until the original's completely (in terms of recognisability) buried, there's no danger of anyone crying IP-infringement foul downriver. The team isolate positions, movements, thrusts, and build outwards from these, constructing graceful, tender sequences, elaborated to the point that they can drop both Bergen mo-cappers' and CAD-programmed bodies, or at least parts of them, back in. *Then* comes the light: twenty coders are right now, in one way or another, helping to reintroduce this into the newly configured mix, splash it back over fresh topologies, a newfound land of curves and edges either roving on their own or set in motion by the POV that roams in loops and gyres round the Observatory's chamber and beyond the dome of this, out into space, now looking in on the two lovers through the glass, now turning outwards, flaring into rings and starbursts as it rotates to face Helio-D directly, now graining up as it rolls onwards away, back round towards the *Sidereal*, Kern's arced and hazy surface in the background ...

'Hang on a minute,' Ben Briar smells another rat here. 'What the fuck is that?'

'Lens effect,' Herzberg informs him.

'It looks really good,' adds Charlie.

Briar purses his lips, as though he, too, had been necking some bitter philtre. Choosing his words carefully, he enquires:

'And why ... ?'

It falls to Herzberg to step up and defend the visual aberrations:

'I'd have thought you would approve: it's realistic – these blemishes are what you'd actually get if you stationed a camera just there.'

'So,' Briar snatches at these incriminating words, 'we're to suppose that there's a *camera*, a real, actual camera, in space, floating conveniently next to these two lovebirds' nest? Is that part of the plot? If so, then why not show its gantry, or its stabiliser, or just have the time-code flashing on the image?'

In fact, he's not a million miles off here, although not in the way he thinks. A camera *is* part of the plot – several cameras, some protruding bulbously from ceilings of the *Sidereal*'s corridors, their presence plain for all to see, others less evident, or not evident at all, secreted grub-like inside wall panels and rivets, rails and hanging tubes, or even hovering in plain sight yet, being nanoscopic, underneath perception's radar. Tszvetan's no fool; he knows that the Kern authorities, and Louis Q himself, are keeping tabs on him – and knows, too, that his uncle has turned a blind eye to most, if not all, of his previous misdemeanours, that a degree of wilful ignorance has always oiled the cogs of their relationship. But this ... He sensed something quite strange about this mission from the outset, almost as though it had been set up, planned, like some kind of experiment in which both he and Tild would serve as lab rats, their maze-navigations constantly observed. Later, lying in quiet post-coital reverie beside her on the floor of the Observatory to which gravity has been restored, he'll even wonder whether Louis Q was *willing* this to happen; whether he's actually watching in real time and, if so, whether it's in fury or benevolence, like a kind, indulgent god gazing down on his creatures who, imperfect (since He made them that way), have (as His great plan prescribed) screwed up ... That's later, though. Right now (to the bemusement of the crew, who know when not to reason why) he's turned all charge off: there's no energy, no recording or transmitting capacity; the vessel's powerless, hanging suspended between Ardis Minor's pull and that of Kern, whose outer atmosphere it's grazing. Everything's suspended – not least time, which seems to partake of the quality of light, groundless or levitated, far-flung, outcast ...

Diamond, during that long week of technical induction, got all hung up on the question of instantaneity. As Phocan talked her in more detail through Pantarey's cameras, with their four circular rows of LEDS emitting infrared at 850 nanometers, he explained the principle of 120-degree illumination, and of passive optical motion capture generally:

'You've got to *throw* the light out and then catch it back again,' he told her. 'These LEDs pulse at the frame-rate of the camera, which is anything from thirty to two thousand frames per second. The speed doesn't matter: what's important is that whatever speed it's running at, the pulse-rate of the LEDs is set the same.'

'Why?' she asked.

'Think about it,' he said. 'The camera throws the infrared out to the markers, and the markers bounce it back at the exact rate as that at which it's thrown out; *and* at the exact same rate as that with which the camera snaps the light back and records it. That makes for ... makes for ...'

This was a prompt: he was waiting for an answer. She knew the one he wanted, and supplied it:

'Instantaneous capture?'

'Instantaneous capture, spot on. You don't look convinced.'

She didn't – wasn't. After chewing on her tongue for a few seconds (a trait her girlfriend liked; it opened up a window, she said, on her cogitative processes), she ventured:

'It's just ... If the light has to travel out towards the object, then bounce off it again, then travel back towards the camera ... Well, doesn't that take, you know, time?'

Phocan laughed.

'But Lucy, it's travelling at the speed of *light*. That makes it instantaneous.'

He'd still said *then* and *back*, though. And *again*: throw the light out, *then* catch it *back*, *again* ... But that was just words. To all intents and purposes, he was right: she saw that. Yes. And yet ... it worked fine, the logic held tight if you were capturing the motion of a gymnast swinging round a pommel horse two yards in front of you, or hostage-taking extras dragging hostage stand-ins round a simulated embassy, or even a control drone in the sky two miles up. But what if you went deeper than the sky, further away? Each photon from the sun takes eight minutes and twenty seconds to reach Earth; sixteen-forty to bounce back. So light from Sagittarius, Auriga, Cassiopeia ... ? Years, centuries, millennia, immeasurable stretches: by the time *those* LED-ringed cameras have snapped their bounce-rays up again the Earth probably won't even *be* there any more. The principle's no different with the gymnast; the distance may be shorter, but the mechanics are the same: emission, then recapture, all conducted at a pace that's ultimately no less limited than that of sound, or of molasses, or cars crawling up Finns Business Park's drive, over the bumps .... She kept her counsel, but retained the quibble henceforth as a grit of secret certainty: that structural delay is built into the process; that, even when it's playing out at a level beneath the detectable, the measurable, it's still *there* ...

This is the level Tszvetan and Tild are occupying right now, the time-zone they're inhabiting: the zone of the delay, of light's slow transit. Since there has been no bed, nor couch, nor even floor beneath her during this magnificent and weightless tryst, Tild's had the impression that what's supporting her, providing base and traction every time she pulls Tszvetan down towards and into her or, hovering above him, descends once again to dock on his set body, is nothing other than the planes and cushions of the light that's reconfiguring itself around them so accommodatingly. It hardens into banks and columns when required, or billows out, when that's what their movements and positions ask of it, into soft, downless pillows, undulating waves that in turn dissipate when heads or arcing backs no longer need them. The light's both prop and medium of their lovemaking; at one point, opening her eyes suddenly as she throws her head back, seeing a beam shoot out through the dome's sapphire glass and break into a fine scintilla-dust beyond it, she's struck by a conviction that this light is pleasure itself, reified. If it plays that role for her, it also plays the role of safety: swaddling them, holding and hiding them inside its dazzle, it keeps consequence at bay. What law requiring plain, diurnal optics could penetrate this fine-mesh cradle to disturb its frequency, undo its tangled luminescence? In the last moments before Kern's tractor beam locks on to the *Sidereal*, as she drifts off into sleep, this luminescence seems to open up still more around her, and grow deeper: an abyss that, even as she sinks into it, bears her up.

3. The Norbert Wiener Appreciation Society

They do this thing at Canard where they wrap a poached duck in soft clay and fire it in a kiln for half an hour. To liberate the roasted bird, whose juices the tightly fitted carapace has kept intact, removing any need for basting, they smash the hardened earthenware embalming with a hammer – right before you, at your table. It's a Celtic recipe. The clay comes from the Evenlode by Charlbury a mile away, thick mud borne down there from the Cotswolds, sedimenting as the river winds its way past Ascott-under-Wychwood, Chadlington, Stow-on-the-Wold ... The waiting list for tables seems to wind for just as long; Garnett tried once to get a reservation, and was offered an early-evening slot six months away. But Pilkington ... Pilkington's managed to grab a place for them in the two days since dropping him a line, asking to 'pick his brains'. The man's hooked up in many ways, through channels Garnett has learnt over the years not to enquire about too much. He's waiting for him in a quiet little enclave, a snug almost, in the corner. It's the best spot in the restaurant; they won't be overheard.

'My Anthony. Still tying paintbrushes to sheep?'

'Things have progressed a little since then – as you know ...'

Their hands unclasp and they sit down. A waiter passes by with bread. After he's gone, Garnett enquires:

'How's Thérèse?'

No small talk, this – more of a plunge in at the deep end. Pilkington's wife was diagnosed two years ago with Parkinson's. Her state is not improving: tremors, cogwheel rigidity, pill-rolling fingers, festination ... Pilkington uses the medical term for each of these symptoms, not bothering to translate or annotate, since he knows full well that Garnett understands them.

'It's ironic,' he says when the list's exhausted, 'us two talking about this.'

Here, too, Garnett can follow perfectly, no need to gloss: they're on the same page – same pages. *The Human Use of Human Beings*: the passages devoted to Parkinsonianism. Voluntary feedback regulating a main motion fails to establish equilibrium with postural feedback working in the opposite direction ... oscillation levels spiral out of control ... the patient reaches for a glass of water, and his hand overcorrects, swings too much, draws a too-wide arc ... For Wiener, everything was feedback. When I pick up a cigar, I translate into action nothing other than a feedback mechanism, a reflex turning the amount by which I've not yet picked up the cigar into an order to the lagging muscles. When I shoot down a plane, my limbs on the ack-ack gun and the wire along which the firing order hums its way towards the earphones clamped round my head, the vacuum tubes that plot the plane's path on a radar screen, and thus the timeline from which approach gradients to the spot of air it's occupying right now can be extrapolated to predict the spot that it will occupy two seconds hence: all these make up an integrated circuit, in which servo-mechanism isn't just the mode of mankind, but his measure also. And not just of mankind: elevators, steamboat engines, jellyfish amalgams, the whole architecture of abstracted systems such as economics or the law – these, too, are birthed and structured by (and therefore legible within) the matrix-womb of cybernetics. They were so excited by it, he and Pilkington: atheists both, it was as close as either of them came to having a religion. Spectres float between the two men now, kinking round curves of wineglasses and side plates: ghosts of two young engineering postgrads with wide collars, bushy sideburns, flaring cords, all fired up by the new world leaping at them from the pages of Nash, Bateson, Geyer and von Glasersfeld. But it was him they came back to, again and again

– prophet, messiah and apostle, all contained within a single name and figure: Norbert Wiener. There was something in his vision that transcended informatics, systems- or game-theory; something Garnett thought he'd left behind with Aeschylus, Catullus, Sappho: a condition best denoted by the old, unscientific label *poetry*. *We are* (Garnett had this line taped to the wall above his ZX Spectrum's screen) *but whirlpools in a river of ever-flowing water; not stuff that abides, but patterns that perpetuate themselves* ... Or (this one from a passage that was read at his and Amber's wedding): *To be alive is to participate in a continuous stream of influences from the outer world and acts on the outer world in which we are merely the transitional stage* ...

'It seemed so optimistic, then,' Pilkington muses as he swills Malbec around his large-bowled Waterford. 'Wiener was offering us a path to justice, knowledge, the unlocking of closed structures ... What did he call it? *Irreversible entry into a ...*'

'*Irreversible movement into a contingent future which is the true condition of human life*,' Garnett supplies the words.

'Exactly. Man as open system. Society as an endless process of unfurling and cross-pollination. Life itself as file-sharing *avant la lettre*.'

'Yes – to an extent ...' Garnett inspects his wine too, as though it, and not the proposition, were the suspect element. 'But ...'

'But ...'

'Wasn't the vision always tinted darkly, blood-tinged? All that Manichaean talk: the universe abandoned, running itself down ... technocracy casting human responsibility to the winds, to have it come back seated on the whirlwind ... the arms race, business, advertising rowing us into a maelstrom of destruction, or just floating us quietly on downstream, to the waterfall ... He called us *shipwrecked passengers on a doomed planet*. You look like you're about to kill us.'

These last words are spoken to the waiter who's raising a mallet just beside their heads. Used to such quips, the latter brings his weapon down to fracture the upturned hold of the duck that's lying on the tray stand he's unfolded by their table. The casing falls away, as do succulent legs and wings and fillet at his carving knife's light touch. With tonged fork and spoon he serves these to them, lays some sprout tops on the side, refills their glasses and departs again.

'For Wiener,' Garnett mumbles after a few moments through cheeks filled with sweet brown flesh, 'life was all about denying death. God's, Santa Claus's or your own: the need to alleviate the disaster of mortality is what fuels belief in progress, and the endless generation of bigger and better things, or "products" ... The death-drive offset on to the assembly line ...'

'This,' says Pilkington, 'is what I wanted to ask you about.'

'Death?'

'Assembly lines.'

Garnett, mouth refilled, whirrs his knife-hand mechanically: *Go on* ... Pilkington, setting his own knife and fork down, asks:

'Do you recall the work of Lillian Gilbreth?'

'Yes, of course,' Garnett responds. 'I looked at all her time-and-motion studies when I was setting up Pantarey.'

'Lillian and Frank ...'

'Lillian and Frank: correct. Their methods laid the groundwork for what people like us do. Our Norbert even mentions them, in passing. They bridge the gap between the nineteenth-century – Marey, Taylor – and the world that would emerge with Ford: mass automatisation and, later, digitisation. Without them, there'd be no mo-cap.'

'She made boxes, didn't she?'

'That's right: light tracks sculpted in metal and set in cutaway black boxes. Each one showed the path of a worker's movement cycle. I've got one at home.'

'An actual Gilbreth box?' asks Pilkington.

'I presume so. I found it in a storage cupboard in an old Birmingham factory that ...'

'Does it have a number on it?'

The urgency of his old friend's tone takes Garnett aback. He, too, sets his fork down, and answers:

'I don't think so. Never looked. She made scores of the things. Hundreds, probably.'

'Eight hundred and fourteen.' Pilkington flashes a bridge-player's smile, the type that might accompany the partial revelation of a hand.

'Well,' Garnett smiles back. 'Seems like it's I who should be asking you the questions. Are these extant?'

'The boxes?'

'Yes: the eight hundred and fourteen boxes – the eight hundred and thirteen I don't have ...'

'Not all in physical form,' says Pilkington. 'Some are in collections; others will be knocking about basements, like yours was. Others just got thrown out once they'd served their purpose. But she catalogued them all. Itemised them.'

'How?'

'Stereoscope. Essentially, by reverse-engineering the process that she'd used to build them in the first place. And these records, almost all of them, are "extant". Every motion, every iteration she cast has been "stated", as it were ...'

Pilkington's cards take on material embodiment now, as he pulls from a folder nestled in his corner's recess a set of papers which he spreads across the tablecloth.

'Have a look ...'

There are two stapled stacks. Garnett leafs through the one with pictures on it: column after column of black-and-white double-photographs of Gilbreth boxes, all numbered and labelled, much as Pilkington has just described. The other's full of text: the paragraphs of some kind of report in which the name 'Gilbreth' pops up every five or so lines. Its diction's not quite academic, not quite scientific, certainly not journalistic – closer in style to a government white paper or internal dossier that might circulate within a corporation ... *Bearing in mind the importance Ms Gilbreth attached to the abstraction, or perhaps better to say extraction, of kinetic sequences, we might speculate that* ... Typeface is Times New Roman ... text is broken into sections, the division following a logic less of subject, theme or chapter than of patchwork assembly, legible blocks alternating with long strings of ciphers, or commands, or code, typed in a different font that reminds him of old JavaScript or ASCII: *01mdean02cdorley03crypt04decrypt7text102 ...*

'We came across this,' Pilkington comments after letting Garnett flip for a while through the pages, 'last week. I'd be intrigued to know your thoughts.'

'*Came across?*'

'Yes: noticed, stumbled on to, picked up, were appraised of ...'

'You make it sound passive.'

'It is. Just like what you do: passive ... what do you call it?'

'Passive optical motion capture.'

'Right. We passively captured this communication while it was in motion.'

'You people ...' Garnett tries to strike up a mock-chiding tone; but duck and greens start to taste different in his mouth; the air seems to take on an altered texture, infused now with obligations, with embargo, with the shadow of officialdom. Is it called *MI5* or *MI6* now? Or some other name that's never even written down or spoken? 'First thing I'm going to do when I get home is get my IT guy Hossain to upgrade my security, install a better firewall ...'

'My friend,' Pilkington fixes him with a pitiful gaze, 'use a typewriter.'

With a quiet nod he invites Garnett to skim his way on further through the stack. The first few pages precis Gilbreth's life and work; they contain nothing not already known to him, bar a few details about family circumstances (*twelve* children); her husband's abhorrence of dirt; the extent to which NASA leant on her work; her penchant for writing sub-par verse ... It's several sections in, after a range of ASCII interjections (the *mdean* part of the cipher-string keeps popping up), that the meat of the report starts peeping through, passages highlighted in yellow marker, either by Pilkington or by whatever *us* is lurking behind him, behind these pages' digital purloining, this whole afternoon's encounter ...

It seems to involve correspondence carried out by Gilbreth with a young Latvian physicist around 1970. Parts of the correspondence, two letters from him to her, have been scanned – by now, double- or triple-scanned, print much degraded. More scans, of what Garnett understands to be pages from Gilbreth's jotter book or journal, are reproduced beside these. Here, too, the handwriting is hard to parse – all the more so due to its tendency to give over now and again to doodles; the physicist's letters also break off intermittently for diagrams or sketches. The report's author has tried to summarise the correspondence (no mean task, since even the physicist's side of it, the only side included in the file, is incomplete); also to gauge this correspondence's effect on Gilbreth, as surmised from her reactions to it contained in this same jotter book or journal. *The significance attached by Gilbreth to Box 808 . . . what he persisted in calling 'the T.T. episode' . . . what the acronym 'T.T.' might . . .* This acronym's recurrence sends Garnett flipping back to where he first encountered it: the partial scan (it begins with the second or perhaps third page) of the first letter, whose author also refers to 'the T.T. episode', proposing to model it according to Gilbreth's own light-track wireframe technique (for good measure, he includes a kind of drawing showing a cone-shaped object swinging round some type of pole, though in the absence of the letter's opening page, or maybe pages, the actual, un-abstracted or -extracted content of the 'episode' remains obscure). It's only then that Garnett registers the name of Gilbreth's correspondent, though his eye must have flitted across it several times.

'Vanins? Raivis Vanins? I knew Vanins.'

Pilkington's still fixing him with his bridge-player's smile. Of course . . .

'Oh,' says Garnett meekly. 'You knew that already. Is that what . . . ?'

'In part,' Pilkington answers. 'Why not? Let's start there. Tell me about Vanins.'

'Well . . .' Garnett sighs resignedly. 'I met him twice. Once at a Paris congress in the mid seventies . . . Then in Delft, ICAM, 1988 or so . . . We had a drink together, corresponded for a little afterwards . . . He was director of the Solid-State Physics Department in Vilnius or Tallinn or – what's the capital of Latvia?'

'Riga.'

'Right: at Riga's Technical University – a post he got at the ripe age of thirty-eight or thirty-nine.'

'Something of a whizz-kid?'

'He was viewed that way, certainly,' says Garnett. 'He seemed to have a whole body of papers to his name ... light-particle sound pulses, shear-wave imaging, self-focusing, the work of Askaryan, Sarvazyan, Osipyan ... He was one of the few Russian – Latvian, Eastern Bloc, whatever – scientists allowed to travel; I guess he acted for us as a kind of peephole on to the whole world of Soviet physics. Not a particularly open one ...'

'Even after perestroika?'

'He went quiet around that time; I think he'd retired. But rumours seemed to swirl around him, even in his absence: a kind of mythomania born of ignorance instilled by decades of the Cold War; all that weird shit we'd imagined going on in Soviet labs and research institutes – I don't need to tell you ...'

Pilkington grunts acknowledgement. It was weird shit: para-magnetic resonance, synchotron radiation, superconductivity ... They knew, from leaks, defections, propaganda, that advances, even breakthroughs, were being made – but sifting all this traffic, trying to separate the signal from the noise, to work out which development was actual, which just paranoid projection ... The speculation, at its outer reaches, skewed weirder than weird, veered into the realm of sci-fi: bioradiation, pondemotor forces, Z-rays, ESP ... In the late eighties, after Albatross, Pilkington was loosely involved with a counter-research unit that had been set up in Cambridge for the sole purpose of establishing the efficacy or otherwise of 'instrumental psychotronics' *à la* Beridze-Stakhovsky, just in case ... And then, when the whole Soviet house of cards collapsed, this, rather than bringing clarity, a giant reveal, just saw the archives dissipated – shredded, lost or siphoned off to private holdings ...

'One of Vanins' big things, like mine, was kinaesthetics,' Garnett's saying. 'He was Gastev's heir, essentially. Saw the ends of practices like Gilbreth's stretching far beyond assembly lines, or even spaceships. Once his writing started getting out, translated, circulated, well, it struck – like Wiener's had – a chord with people in all kinds of areas, not only physics.'

'And the rumours?'

Garnett shrugs. 'The usual type – in the biomechanics world, at least; that township's age-old urban legends: that he'd come up, behind his institute's walls, with a means of generating torsion fields, or proof of Tryon's zero-energy hypothesis, or some such philosopher's stone ... Perhaps nobody quite believed these *literally* – but on states of equilibrium, particularly, he was streets ahead.'

'That subject,' confides Pilkington, 'or one like it, seems to provide the topic of his correspondence with Ms Gilbreth. Here, on page twenty-four ...'

He helps Garnett leaf through to the nominated page, which contains, set side by side as before, printed scans of two handwritten papers: on the left, a page from a further letter, or perhaps the same one, from Vanins to Gilbreth; on the right, another page from the jotter book/journal of the latter. In the left-hand scan, Vanins describes his *shock – amazement, and perhaps* (illegible) *– at the implications of this labour, which would seem to transform all the tenets and* (assertions?) *of our* ... In the right-hand one, Gilbreth seems to have copied in her own hand the diagram that appeared on Vanins' previous letter-page. Here, once again, shakily rendered, is the cone, or cone-shaped object, or perhaps just cone-shaped field of vectors, circling the upright line, or pole. The circling movement's bi-directional: double-headed arrows at the cone's base, its swing-zone's lower rim-circumference, make this clear. About the figure Gilbreth has added several other little sketches: of cogged mechanisms, mill-wheels, spoked and levered automata; also some coloured circles. Across the whole page are dotted a few words and phrases in Latin or Spanish, and some names.

'*Maricourt?*' Garnett reads. '*Bessler? De Honnecourt?* The wheel-and-hammer, spinning-rings-that-need-no-winding, pendulum-decked-gravity-disc charlatans? Is Gilbreth in her addled dotage starting to buy into the old perpetual-motion scam?'

'Not at all.' Pilkington lets out a short laugh. 'Although you'd be surprised how many of physics' big beasts jumped down that rabbit hole before: Wolff, Bernouilli, even Leibniz ... They set out to demonstrate the notion's folly and, somewhere along the line, flipped over into obsessive believers, drunk on a conviction that the very work they'd done to dispel any credence in the possibility of endless movement proved its viability ... which "proof" the next scientist in line set out to debunk, only to find himself converted – while the first, meanwhile, had apostasised back again. You could say the perpetual motion's there: these self-renewing waves of scepticism and credulity, reason and fantasy ...'

He takes another sip of wine. Watching him, Garnett pictures a toy, a gizmo he once gave to his young nephew: a Sullivan drinking-bird that, as methylene chloride rose up its long neck-tube, tilted its felt-covered beak into a glass of water, the absorption of which caused the cooling chloride to sink down its neck again, which in turn pulled its head up for a breath of air before the process started over.

'I've become convinced,' Pilkington dabs his lips, 'in my own state of addled dotage, that our work, at base ... The great contraptions we come up with, all the engines and the interfaces and the operating codes – that these are nothing more than prompts for our own supposition and projection, stand-ins for some ultimate machine we'll never build but nonetheless can't stop ourselves from trying to ... Jacquard looms, the Internet, crackpot time-travelling patents or those influencing engines sketched by generations of psychotics: whether they get made or simply trawled up from the depths of some delusion is beside the point. All machines are imaginary. Doesn't our Norbert say as much, somewhere?'

'He does,' Garnett murmurs distractedly; he's scrutinising still the copied journal pages. From the shakily redrawn sketch, the coloured circles, the scrawled names and Latin / Spanish words, an arrow leads down to the page's base, where, in a hand that appears purposeful and strained, as though accomplished only through a monumental act of will, more words, in bold, are written:

'*Box 808 charges ...*'

'It's *changes* ...'

'... *changes everything*. Which one is 808?'

'Have a look,' Pilkington answers knowingly, pushing the other paper-stack towards him once more. Garnett flicks through the pages, eye moving top to bottom, down the photographed and numbered motion boxes, through the seven hundreds, then into the eights, 805, 806, 807 ...

'Oh!'

'Exactly.'

There's no 808: it's missing. The stretch of paper where it should be leers back blank and empty, glaring as a razed section of forest or a patch of wall from which a painting's been removed.

'Why,' Garnett wonders aloud after a few moments' silence, 'does she go on about it so much when – this other person too ... ?' He's flipping through the pages of the second stack again, the scanned notes, letters, journal pages, the anonymous author's summary and gloss of these. It's everywhere: ... *that Vanins' experience of 'the T.T. episode' led to the creation of Box 808 is highly* ... page nine; *808 seems to have excited her so much that she revised her entire* ... ten; eleven: *Box 808's supreme importance to her project is attested by* ... 'What do you think it ... ?'

'That,' Pilkington responds, 'is the big question. That's what's generated all the noise.'

'Noise?'

'In my ... community. We're not the only ones to have picked up on this. There seems to be a general buzz all round. Consensus is that there's something worth looking into ...'

'What kind of something?'

Pilkington reflects a little, then continues:

'Vanins was, *inter alia*, an important figure in the field of Soviet aeronautics. I've seen files, whole stacks of files, on him. If he did, as your colleagues liked to fancy, chisel a Northwest Passage through a stretch of the hitherto theoretical-physically impossible, even if it didn't lead to any direct application we became aware of, but got lost amidst the clear-out, overlooked, misplaced ...

Well, MOD will want to know about it – as will several other outfits we could think of ...'

'But why would he tell Gilbreth? She wasn't a *physicist*.'

'No. But she, more than anyone else, understood kinesis. Bodies in motion. And she'd used this understanding to transform the world – feat for which he, and many of his ilk, revered her. I think they saw her as a kind of Darwin or Linnaeus, capturing and freezing movement's every sub-species and class and phylum: folding napkins, pulling levers, loading guns ... all part of the same general ballet. With the boxes, she'd attempted to amass a general taxonomy of act and gesture. To amass, and to improve – for practical reasons, partly: efficiency, well-being of factory workers, housewives, astronauts ... She always wanted to work out ...'

'The "one best way".'

'The one best way,' says Pilkington, 'exactly. But – as the author of the report you're holding explains so lucidly – the meaning of those words changes with time. It starts out signalling the leanest path, the most economic and productive route a worker's hand or body can cut through the space around it in the execution of its task. Later, though ... Later, the idea sprouts wings, grows all-encompassing and vague at the same time. There's something abstract – almost devotional – about it all. She seems to come to believe that there exists, somewhere, hidden from our view, a *perfect* shape for every act – essential, almost preordained. And beyond even that, that there might be a kind of *absolutely* perfect motion-circuit hovering concealed behind even the perfect ones – the kingdom, as it were, containing all the phylums; sum of their possibilities, their infinite- and zero-point, alpha and omega ...'

'So she *was* a mystic,' Garnett murmurs.

'Yes and no,' says Pilkington. 'Isn't that what ... ?'

'Isn't what what?'

'Isn't that what you do?'

'Me?'

'Pantarey. All your kinetic typologies, which you scale up and down from keyhole surgery to war to silly films ...'

'I wanted to ask you something about silly films. We want to use a wind tunnel to stage ...' Garnett begins, but Pilkington waves the interjection off:

'Isn't your work – our work – all about accessing and deploying underlying sequences and patterns? Mapping particulars on to great universals? Isn't that the art to which, in one way or another, we've both devoted our best years?'

Garnett, out-argued, grants the point in silence.

'And our Norbert, his Augustine visions – isn't that a form of mysticism too? He saw inductive logic as a supreme act of faith. Call it physics, metaphysics or theology: it doesn't matter ... And I'm wandering. We want to know what Box 808 is, and what *everything* it changes.'

'You really think there is one?' Garnett asks.

'A Box 808?'

'An *everything* to be changed by it.'

'Gilbreth,' Pilkington deflects the question, 'clearly thought so. But then, she was very old; the diaries and the notebooks show a mind stumbling. Besides, whether there *is* or not – an *everything*, a box, an either – is beside the point. There's noise. Which means our view on this, like Gilbreth's photographs, is stereoscopic: focus is partly on the actual givens, the reality, whatever this might be, and partly on gaming the speculation. If someone else thinks *we* think it's important, or if a third party thinks that we think *they* think it's important, then ...'

Garnett can see this: it's straight von Neumann, basic game theory ...

'Even,' continues Pilkington, 'if this box had nothing in it but a pair of old shoes, or was empty – if it exists, we want it to be us that has it and not one of the someone-elses and third-parties ...'

The waiter comes to take their plates and hand them dessert menus. Garnett orders a crème brûlée, Pilkington a slice of chocolate tart, and brandies for them both.

'It's a pity,' Garnett muses when they're left alone again, 'that you can't ask Vanins what it's all about.'

Pilkington's face, the flow of its expressions, shudders to a sudden halt; he looks at Garnett's own face now intently, scrutinising it. Garnett, uncomfortable, adds:

'He is dead, I presume.'

'Not at all!' Pilkington sits back suddenly. 'I thought you knew that.'

'No. I hadn't heard from, or about, him in so many years, I just imagined ...'

'He's living,' Pilkington informs him, 'on a dacha outside Riga. In his upper eighties, but still ... *extant.*'

'Then why don't you ... ?'

The other's look as the sentence trails off underscores the thought's naivety. In a tactful, almost diplomatic tone of voice Pilkington tells him:

'A head-on approach from *us* doesn't seem, in this instance, quite appropriate.'

Garnett can see that as well – but not what's coming next. Pilkington picks up his dessert fork, taps its tines against the tablecloth – twice, a little Morse-code rap – and says:

'We thought that maybe you ...'

'Me? How on earth could I ... ? I mean, if your own people couldn't ...'

'Precisely because,' purrs Pilkington, 'you're not one of our people. Or anyone else's. With Pantarey, you struck off on your own. Makes you a *bona fide* member of the same old guard as him: the pioneers, trailblazers ...'

Garnett looks down modestly, bathing in praise's warmth. His friend continues:

'You could renew contact with him: shared field of interest – states of equilibrium, perhaps ... revisiting an old line of enquiry ... compare notes ... steer it onwards from there ... He'd respect you. He'd *trust* you.'

'And,' Garnett looks back up, 'I'd betray that trust?'

'For a purpose. For a purpose. And it's not even betraying. If this 808 stuff was nothing, a delusion of Gilbreth's senility, then what harm is done? If it was something, then that's knowledge shared – *unboxed*, brought out into the light. That's a good thing, surely – scientifically speaking …'

'I'm not sure I view it the same way as …' Garnett starts, but Pilkington cuts him off.

'Your man Mark Phocan has been visiting us at Farnborough.'

'Well, yes,' says Garnett, not quite seeing the connection. 'After all, you're a client.'

'For now,' Pilkington says. 'The contract's coming to an end. There's been talk of renewing it, taking it to another level, with markerless tracking …'

Garnett stares at his friend, trying to work out what he's getting at – as though his words, like a report encrypted, were keeping their essential content wrapped, embalmed, sarcophagaed beneath a carapace of manner; leaking out, though, now, through cracks skilfully wrought, with just the right amount of pressure … Mixing together too: imaginary machines, markerless tracking – and now this: beyond the perfect movement, beyond movement itself, some kind of 'absolute', a disembodied circuit, hovering, concealed, everything-changing. Taken together, what would it all bode? The 'kingdom', as Pilkington would have Gilbreth hoping? Or another type of dispensation, far less kind or to be wished for: a regime of total capture – one with which he, Garnett, is, always has been, complicit … Latching on to Pilkington's *un-boxed* and groping into memory's back reaches, to some passage filed away with deer and sherry, he now pieces together half-remembered shards of Hesiod, *Works and Days*: ἐκ γαίης πλάσσεν κλυτὸς Ἀμφιγυήεις παρθένῳ αἰδοίῃ ἴκελον, *moulded clay in the likeness of a modest maid … Pandora … took off the great lid of* πίθου, *the box … then earth was full,* πλείη μὲν γὰρ γαῖα κακῶν, *of evils, and sea too … Aloud now, he recites:

'μούνη δ' αὐτόθι Ἐλπὶς ἐν ἀρρήκτοισι δόμοισιν ἔνδον ἔμιμνε: *Only hope remained …*'

'What's that?' asks Pilkington.

At this point in their meeting, before Garnett can respond, a strange interlude occurs. Swing-doors arc open, wafting smells of melted chocolate and burnt sugar to them, prelude to their waiter who glides, back first, through the entry to the kitchen then rotates mid-floor to guide their desserts smoothly down towards their tabletop. As Pilkington's plate taxis across the last few centimetres to its assigned slot beside the small fork he's still playing with, Garnett notices his friend's hands tensing suddenly, fingertips simultaneously digging into and pushing away from the tablecloth.

'What's this?' Pilkington's voice has real aggression in it, tinged with what sounds to Garnett like fear.

'Chocolate tart,' answers the waiter. 'Isn't that what you ordered?'

'Yes,' Pilkington responds; 'but not with this ... this ...'

Both Garnett and the waiter peer down at his plate. It's white, and circular, as plates generally are. A portion of its surface area has been filled by the dark slice of tart – a sector whose two radii are connected at their separated ends by an arc inset from but aligned with that of the plate's circumference, while their meeting point precisely coincides with the plate's centre. Coming from the plate's far hemisphere to intersect this tart-slice sector at an obtuse angle – intersecting it so as to rest partially atop it – is a wafer: light-brown, slightly smaller than the slice itself and shaped not as a sector, even a displaced one, but a triangle whose base sits on a chord the endpoints of which lie at roughly three and six o'clock (POV Pilkington). This wafer, like most wafers, bears the mark of the iron in which it was formed, a grid pattern stamped across its surface. To its side, lying in the final sector of the plate, the one covered or crossed by neither slice nor wafer, sits a scoop of ice cream – high-end, in-house-fabricated ice cream within whose spherical mass fragments of ground vanilla are embedded, like small graphite flecks in marble.

'... *assemblage*!' Pilkington, alighting on the right word, almost hurls it at the waiter. 'I ordered the tart! There was no mention of ice cream or wafer.'

'We mark it with both *D* and *G* on the menu, Sir. If you're dairy- or gluten-averse, I could ...'

'That's not the point!' Pilkington cuts him off angrily. 'I just want to know what's ... what's coming to me ... without these ...'

His sentence fades out, possibly because he realises as he speaks it that it makes as little sense to him as to the waiter or his friend. These two both stare at him, wanting to help remediate the situation while quite unable to because they're at a loss to understand it.

'I can have it,' Garnett offers. 'We can swap.'

'No.' Pilkington nixes the idea gruffly. 'It's not that. I'd rather you just ...'

'I'll take it away,' the waiter picks his cue up here. 'We'll take it off the bill, of course. And if there's anything else we can offer you to ...'

'Nothing. The brandies. Make them doubles.'

'Absolutely,' says the waiter. 'On the way.' As smoothly as he set it down he whisks the plate off the table and guides it back through the kitchen's swing doors out of sight. Garnett makes to say something, but Pilkington, regaining his composure, waves the episode away.

'Vanins,' he says. 'You'd be helping me immensely. Have a think; let me know.'

Tentatively, Garnett shatters his crème brûlée's glaze and starts to eat it. Brandies come; they drink them. Pilkington, relaxed and meditative again, muses:

'Shipwrecked passengers on a doomed planet ... I remember that bit now. But – doesn't he say something about salvation, too?'

'Not exactly,' Garnett answers. 'He says that even in a shipwreck, human decencies and values don't all necessarily vanish.'

'That's it. It's true: not *necessarily* ...'

'We're going down, he says; but we can do it *in a manner worthy of our dignity*.'

'To dignity!' cries Pilkington. He drains the remnants of his brandy, then announces: 'I'm paying. Let's go.'

Outside, there's a car waiting – smart, executive, unliveried. Pilkington instructs the driver to go first to Charlebury Station, where they drop Garnett. As the car pulls off again, he winds the window down and calls out:

'Use a typewriter! And burn the ribbon afterwards.'

4. The Girl with Kaleidoscope Eyes

Noam Webster, keeper of the skulls, runs his hands up and down the row of crania lined up on the shelf. His fingers tap the parietal bone of one, linger on the orbital plate of another, jump past two more and touch down on the zygomatic arches of a third: his little warm-up, loosening the ivories, prodding them into attentiveness while he decides which tune to play, which key to play in. Lucy Diamond, standing just behind him, scours them with her eyes. Their shapes and sizes are so variant that it's hard to see them – and Webster, and her – as belonging to one species. Some have bulging frontals, others flat ones – straight-up, windscreen-slanted ... some temporal lines are raised, others regressed ... sutures each scrawl their eccentric signature, their wavering graph-curves, on calva-rial parchment. Plus, each one is damaged – chipped, indented, notched, trepanned, depressed – in its own way ...

'The thing with high-velocity impact – say, when a bullet travels through a skull, especially when dispatched from up close, what we might call the "execution scenario" ...' Pinching the sphenoids of the skull on which it's currently resting between thumb and little finger, Webster's right hand lifts it; the fore and middle fingers of his left, meanwhile, turn into a gun's barrel jammed against the occipital bone. 'The skull's so fragile,' he continues, 'that, as soon as the bullet' – his cocked thumb-hammer crooks in simulated pin-strike – 'enters it, it starts to splinter, with the lines of fracture spreading out in all directions, in proliferating branches, like a rail-way network sprawling over a whole territory – to the point that there's no territory any more: it's all just fracture network. When the splinter lines run up against each other, they remake the skull in their own image, as a set of void channels, of fissures; at which point the skull disintegrates. This process takes place with extraordinary speed. It sometimes runs its course, entry to disintegration, more quickly than the bullet travels: the cracks tear around the cranium's circumference so fast they beat the bullet to the other side. By the time it arrives at the frontal plate, there *is* no frontal plate there any more, hence nothing left for it to exit through. Which poses certain challenges to subsequent investigators ...'

'I see,' says Diamond, trying from the off to strike a balance in her tone between receptive and imperious. This is her first solo outing since being upgraded to full Pantarey staff member (Associate Technology Officer, ATO: she's just handed him her card). Last time she visited Forensis, it was as Phocan's sidekick; now, she has to signal brief-command, client entitlement. She informs Webster: 'But in this case, it's not a bullet. It's a rapier. The character's already got a model of her uncle's staved-in skull, and when she finds the rapier that did it, she's able to ...'

'What's a rapier?' Webster asks.

'It's a long, hand-held weapon for close-quarter combat. In this film, they're full of energy. They glow.'

'Like a lightsaber.'

'Kind of. But it's solid, made of martensite. Maybe the closest approximation would be a samurai sword – one infused with plutonium or some like form of radiation.'

Tokyo: Chofu. Images of dogwood spray in Jindai Botanical Gardens spread round Diamond's own cranium, of *ume* flowers, whose long filaments, extending radially from deep-red central stigma to wave laden anthers at incoming airborne traffic while bright petals fanned open around them, seemed to duplicate in softer form the satellites that she and Phocan were helping JAXA to configure. Their hosts took them, one afternoon, to visit the Yoshihara swordsmith workshop: endless rhythmic hammering and bashing of the smelted *tamahagane*, breathing of the wood-fires, rasping of the bellows, fire-spark blossom drifting through the air, about the floor ... Even when drawn out into billets in which the *katana*'s final shape could be discerned in embryonic form, the steel still held within its body molten pockets, hot as planetary mantle. *Charge*. From the Creston's high windows she'd look out over the night-time city, its unquenchable illumination, the magmatic neon flows, and see a unit – like a battery-pack or memory plug-in of unspeakable complexity – continually recharging. And the people ... She read on the plane an article describing Fukushima's aftermath: whole populations radio-iodinised, buzzing with enough isotopic discharge to work Geiger counters up into a frenzy. If the Yoshihara visit stuck with her it was, perhaps, because the precious, volatile bars plucked from the furnace seemed to reify that sense of chargedness – that, and the way bandanaed and kimonoed swordsmiths held them up for reverential scrutiny, or passed them on between themselves, from tong to tong, or laid them out to cool, polished and dusted them, less artisanal than ceremonial, forensic ...

'This,' Webster has set the skull down now and moved to a computer, 'is a PBR, made with our latest toy, a Faro laser scanner, of one of these specimens – the third one from the right, to be precise. We could provide you and your movie people, Double Zero, with ...'

'It's Degree Zero,' she corrects him.

'... Degree Zero, with this very scan, or one much like it. It's made with the same flyover method we use with the Pitt Rivers and British Museums, digitising ethnographic artefacts.'

'Artefacts as in ... ?'

'Statues, fetishes or handmade bowls, what have you ...' he tells her without taking his eyes from the screen or fingers from the glide-pad, moving about which they spin the radiant green cranium around, enabling multiple flyovers, each from a new angle, of its wound-crater, a detailed survey of its pleats and ridges.

'This is more or less exactly what the character does,' Diamond says.

'She has a Faro scanner too?'

'Version 20.0,' Diamond smiles back, 'with screen-independent holographic render ... Hey, what's that?'

She can't help herself slipping back into ingénue mode: the printouts covering the wall behind the monitor are too intriguing. They seem to depict a kind of urban grid: an irregular one, with arrows indicating various jagging trajectories across it.

'What's ... ? Oh, that: Sarajevo,' answers Webster. 'Twenty-eighth June 1914. It's the route that Archduke Ferdinand's car took across the city. Collaboration with the History Department at UCL. Apparently, the century since the assassination has produced a thousand theories as to why the anarchist Princip did it, or why this particular event sparked off the biggest tinderbox in human history – but no one's ever thought to carry out a basic time-and-motion study.'

'And ... ?'

'And what?'

'And what has it revealed?'

'It has revealed,' Webster proudly announces, 'that it all boils down to a three-point turn.'

'A three-point turn – like in a car?'

'Indeed: not *like* but *actually* in a car. The Archduke's motorcade, driving down Appel Quay, here' – he's over at the wall now, pointing out the road in question – 'turns right toward Franz Josef Street so as to deviate from the back-up route to which it has, as a precaution, switched (a bomb has been thrown earlier, and hit a secondary car; the pages of the speech Franz Ferdinand reads just prior to his assassination are flecked with blood) – a double-deviation, back to its initially announced route. Which isn't very safe, given the day's threat level. So, when the security implications of this dawn on the Archduke's bodyguards, they decide to switch back a second time; which re-rerouting necessitates a three-point turn. Now, think of three-point turns: what do they all, no matter how swiftly or deftly they're executed, entail?'

Diamond thinks back to her driving test: angles and distances, protocols and sequences, mirror-signal-manoeuvre ... 'Toggling between forward and reverse?' she tries.

'Well, yes ... But that dictates another basic quality: that every three-point turn contains, at – *as* – its pivot-point, a static moment. Here in Appel Quay, this moment takes place right by where Princip is standing. So, naturally, he pulls his pistol out and offs his sitting-duck duke quarry.'

'What are the chances?' Diamond murmurs.

'Chance,' says Webster, 'is a can of worms this project has pried open. The more you look at it, the more you start to see a sort of correspondence – of *symmetry* almost – not only in the layout of the streets, the doubled routes, the switchbacks and retracings and so on, but also in the larger field of the event's contingencies. Take just one sample area, for example: the lead actors' titles. On one side, you've got Franz Ferdinand, the Archduke; on the other, Princip, the anarchist. *Archduke*, like *princip*, means 'prince' – from *arc* or *arche*: prime authority, but also curve plotted in space; and *dux*, or leader, plotter of a route. The Archduke's people plot a route through space; the anarchists launch their counterplot, a plot against arch order, against structure. But their plotting is defective – as you might expect: they don't believe in arcs or arches, that's the whole point. But – here's the twist, which perhaps isn't such a twist after all – an arc comes to their aid: a double-arc, embodied in a three-point turn. It's like a kind of doubling-up, a folding. And the street towards which the Archduke is heading doubles his own name, halfway at least: Franz Josef is his uncle, who's dispatched him off to Sarajevo – like a double, to die in his place.'

'So are you saying ... ?' Diamond begins; but Webster cuts her off:

'I'm not saying anything. Just tracing out a set of lines; a fracture network. That's all I do. I have a hat in this ring, too.'

'Professionally?' she asks.

'Titularly. Staying within the same interrogation boundaries, names and their meanings: *arc* comes from the Greek *arkheion*, house' – he opens up his hand to indicate their environs – 'of records. In Ancient Athens, they had *archons*, magistrates, guardians and interpreters of the public archive; through their collective analyses and deliberations, the *archons* oversaw the workings of democracy and justice.' He pauses for a while, then adds: 'Archives were held in chest or *arks*, made of acacia wood.' His finger gently slides down from the diagrams and route maps and swings back towards the skulls as he continues: '*Arca* can mean *coffin* too ...'

Diamond's middle name is Sky. It was her mother's maiden name. Her parents were second-wave hippies, early-nineties flower children. In tribute to the tangerine streets and marmalade skies, the plasticine porters with looking-glass ties of the song – as well (she suspects, reading between the lines of the foundation myth they fondly peddled her) as the fact that they were both tripping when they met – they named her Lucy. Are there arches at work there, too, plotting, from base coordinates of nomenclature, the paths and switchbacks, folds and doublings, assignations both fortuitous and unfortunate, even catastrophic, that her life will follow? Or is it something older, routes laid down prior even to that, some vast mechanism as inevitable as the engine movements of open-top motorcars, or newspaper taxis appearing on the shore, waiting to take you away? Here, in Forensis plc's back office, one of the many darkened rooms that she now seems to spend the lion's share of her time in, Diamond finds herself struck by a pervasive sense of powerlessness, of freedom from volition. It's neither a particularly bad feeling nor a good and liberating one – it just is what it is. It comes to her, she shrugs it off and turns to Webster as he says:

'This is the other thing I meant to show you.'

He's back beside her at the screen, shutting down the luminous green cranium and popping open in its place a LiDAR file depicting, in equally rotatable projection, a modern urban or suburban living room. The space is illustrated colourfully and schematically, in architect-diagram style. Between orange and yellow blocks and cuboids labelled *closet*, *bench press*, *TV*, and so on, a green human avatar lies stretched out, the circle of its head distended into a long oval seeping red across the floor. Cutting aslant the room, a conic section, also red, depicts a projectile's flight path, door to facing wall, passing above the backrest of an armchair at whose base the human figure's feet lie, pivot-points around which it, too, has been doubled, folded out and downward, vertical to horizontal. Diamond recognises the scenario at once: it's a case Pantarey have taken on for a humanitarian NGO, the shooting of a Guatemalan dissident. They modelled the whole thing two weeks ago back in The Cell, with markered extras moving through various scenarios, the files then being passed to Forensis who, like them, are offering their services *pro bono*.

'This is a sneak preview,' Webster tells her. 'We're still working on it. But – spoiler alert – the *Policia Nacional*'s account is holding up about as well as this politician's hairstyle.'

'Trade unionist, I think,' she corrects him again. 'How can you tell?'

'If it had been a random break-in, as they claim, the victim would have moved either towards or away from the point of entry, to confront (if he was feeling feisty) or (if he was minded for self-preservation) flee from his assailant. On top of which, objects and furniture would be displaced. If they'd even wanted to make it look as though it *might* have been a break-in, they could have knocked over the stereo or bench press, or rifled the closet. But they didn't. The position of the victim's feet – hinged round but otherwise unmoved from by the armchair – suggest he had no inkling of his killer's presence in the house. And then the gunman has chosen the angle most propitious for a straight-up take-out: a clear line of sight, good reference points in the door frame and far wall's cornice boundary. If I apply all the axes, you can see . . .'

He clicks a side-bar option, and the depicted room becomes a kind of loom all of whose yarns converge on the shooter's position, as though its contents and dimensions were being knitted by, from or around this single point, the muzzle of his gun. The geometry's so clear, so perfect, that it seems to Diamond inconceivable that the space, the living room, could ever have been designed for anything other than this one event; seems that the converging warp-lines were all there already, and the conic section too – not over- but *underlay*, integral design-key announcing: *This is the bullet's trajectory, and always has been; this is the point at which Plane A is intersected by Line B ...* If this trade unionist has died, it's for the simple reason that he drifted into this trajectory, transgressed the plane, the point of intersection – occupied, however transiently, a certain spot within the grid.

'Their timeline's off, too,' Webster's telling her.

'Sorry? How do you mean?'

'The *policia*'s. From their crime-scene photos that they say were taken two hours after the supposed break-in,' he pulls up a screen of thumbnail snaps in which the loom's symmetry and order have been lost, neutralised or at least camouflaged by the actual room's banal grey surfaces, 'you can see, through the window, the exact lie of the shadow cast on to the ground by the house's outer wall. Cross-referencing that with the building's original architectural plans, which we got hold of, and with Street View, and with easily obtainable sun-tracking tables for Guatemala City on that date, March the fifteenth ... Well, you get a time-reading of more than three hours earlier. It's clear the time code on the photographs is falsified, or at least wrong ...'

Now Diamond's thinking of another room, with freesias, and *ume* flowers; of a bed, a furnace, stars, a spaceship, Chofu, Sarajevo ... In the Creston's bedroom, on the wall, a line from Basho had been printed: *Days and months are travellers of eternity*. As thumbnails, blowing up and shrinking, follow one another in quick, flickering procession, she sees once again the pulsing lights, synaptic spectacle of death and continuity, flat screen in which all actions are contemporaneous, replenishing each other endlessly.

'These people,' Webster clucks, 'don't get it: everything is information. It's being sensed, being recorded, stored and studied all the time. The entire world's an arc ...'

He's picked up the skull that he was holding earlier; it's resting, like a sleeping kitten, in the cradle of his left hand held to his warm stomach while the index finger of his right hand runs and reruns down its suture, like a blind man's scanning lines of Braille.

5. Critical Interval

On the apron, as the Alitalia Airbus A320 is being pushed back, Phocan watches a small drama playing out. Beside a jet bridge that's accordioned down almost flat against a terminal itself shrinking with increasing distance is a hawk. It's hovering about the corrugated metal, almost, but not quite, in place; every few seconds it tweaks its position, shifting two or three feet to the right, or left, or up or down, returning to a spot it occupied a moment earlier, or else establishing a new one in the gaps between all these. It does this neither languidly nor playfully but with intent, wings beating fiercely, head and neck twitching their way through minute readjustments that keep its vision locked on the same focal point.

Working his own gaze backwards down the eye beams, Phocan sees what's in the cross-hairs here: a sparrow flapping gracelessly against the tarmac, making abortive take-off bids in one direction, then another. At first he thinks the sparrow must be wounded, grounded by a broken wing; that the hawk has picked it out and is just waiting for its energy and will to ebb away, for surrender to set in, before swooping down for the kill. When the sparrow rises ten or more feet in the air, though, he realises he's wrong: this ascent was perfectly competent; calling it off and turning back again was a decision, as deliberate as the hawk's studied readjustments. It takes a few more strike-outs by the sparrow and adjustments by the hawk before he understands what's going on: the hawk's controlling the whole area without needing to patrol around it; closing off vectors of airspace, blocking swathes and columns of potential flight, each mooted escape path, simply by angling itself towards them. The two birds understand each other, and are operating in well-calibrated synchrony; a chess game they'll carry on playing, move and countermove, the one snuffing the other's future out, until the sequences have all been run through, endgame drifting on to the inevitable resignation, just a matter of time ...

A few feet from the sparrow, there's another scene unfolding. A luggage cart's trundling across the pavement, four dolly compartments coupled up into a train pulled by a small tractor. As the driver plies the narrow staging-area channel hemmed in by red restraint lines to his left, white vehicle-corridor and yield lines up ahead of him and, to his right, the aeroplane, perched on its yellow taxi lane, to which his consignment is to be delivered, then pulls a tight U and draws to a halt across (but not within) the red and white rectangle of the loading box, the dollies snake from side to side, each taking its cue from the one in front, so that the carriage as a whole seems to be partly following, partly digressing from, routes of the boundary markings over which it's slithering. *Bedbug, moth*: the words take shape amidst the verbal babble spilling out of cabin speakers and the open in-flight magazine. Yesterday in Finns, Garnett called Phocan to his office again. Entering, he discovered his boss watching a YouTube clip. It was an old one, digitised TV footage from the sixties or even fifties; it showed a man advanced in years demonstrating to an awkward, crew-cut child the operation of some kind of robot with a painted insect carapace.

'Palomilla.' Garnett's tone was full of fondness – for the insect, or the boy, or Phocan; or, perhaps, for the avuncular, robot-controlling man. This last was holding a small flashlight in his hand, directing its beam straight on to the dog-sized, beetle-mimicking contraption, which responded by advancing with a whirring sound across the studio floor. But not in a straight line: it meandered drunkenly, turning a little one way then the other in a kind of ponderous slalom, as though undecided which of two approach angles to pursue towards a beacon-wielding summoner who, like the wind, could not be steered directly into but demanded constant tacking.

'It's his Tropism Machine,' said Garnett. 'He built it – that's Wiener there – with Singleton at MIT in '49. They called it Bedbug-Moth, or Palomilla.'

'Funny names,' said Phocan, to say something.

'The Bedbug-Moth's because it's phototropic. There's a tiller,' Garnett beckoned him near, as though explaining a model train set's workings to him, 'underneath the cover, which controls the single steering wheel beneath its nose. The tiller's set up with two modes of action: one positively phototropic – programmed to do nothing more than seek light out, like a moth – the other negatively phototropic, as monomaniacally' – he cut the word into insectoid segments, *mono-ma-nia-cally* – 'intent on fleeing any and every light source, like a bedbug. See?'

On screen, the cyber-beetle carried on its restless battle with itself, veering first, dog-to-bone, towards the torch, then in revul-sion, Superman from kryptonite, away again, which made the positive impulse kick in once more, which in turn triggered the counter-impulse – on *ad infinitum*, or at least the mpeg's end.

'He built it to help army neurologists.' Garnett's voice was meditative. 'Battle-worn troops were coming home displaying pathologies ranging from the shakes to full-blown neurasthe-nia . . .'

On his desk, between the keypad and the monitor, there was a kind of shoebox. It was old, black and wooden – more the type of box you'd keep brushes and tins of polish in than shoes themselves. Two of its sides, and the roof, were missing, thus affording (whether by chance or design) a view on to an abstract diorama: from the floor rose a kind of sculpture, a thin metal tube that veered and swerved about before dovetailing back to its beginning spot. This misshapen diadem was held in place, at its lowest point, by a crude staple and, at a point not its highest but presumably the most propitious balance-wise, by a column planted unobtrusively in the scene's background, a dark obelisk whose pinnacle rose to meet it. The interiors of the sides that hadn't been removed were covered with white grid squares like

The Cell's; on the floor, near the front edge, the number 374 was handwritten in thin white paint.

'It's my own,' said Garnett, watching him eyeing it. 'A Gilbreth box.'

Phocan, drawing a blank with this name, stared at the twisting metal loop some more. The supporting obelisk made him think of Cleopatra's Needle on the Victoria Embankment; by extension, of a raft of funerary, sphinx-like forms, as though the floating circuit had been mounted on some monumental, if miniaturised, riddle.

'It seems,' Garnett continued, 'that they've started to become collectible.'

'What have?' asked Phocan.

'Sit down,' Garnett instructed him.

When he emerged from the office two hours later, he'd been handed a bunch of papers, and told he was going to be dispatched to Riga (*It's the capital of Latvia*, Garnett informed him helpfully) to hunt down a box – a box much like the one he'd just been shown, but with a different number. He'd also been chastised for knowing nothing about his own discipline's pre-history.

'But,' he objected, letting the rebuke, unjust though it was, slide in order to address the more pressing implications of the order he'd been given, 'I've got Rome' – phone out, fingers leapt into action, swiping and expanding iCal entries, summoning up schedules – 'then Bergen, then ...'

But Garnett's hand, raised in paternalistic override, cut him short.

'You've got time,' he reassured him, soothingly but for that no less authoritatively. 'I still have to prepare the ground for such a visit. You'll need a plausible excuse; some line of enquiry not linked to the box itself – not directly, at least. In the meantime ...'

In the meantime, Phocan has been reading up on Raivis Vanins. Seems that the guy came of age during the height of 'Soviet Taylorism' – or, to use its more generic name, of 'scientific management': the wholesale adoption, and adaption, of the capitalist

West's newest industrial labour protocols, not least universal standardisation of not only shop floors but all metrics by which work was both conducted and assessed. A million steelworkers, shipbuilders, car, washing-machine or aeroplane constructors stretching and reaching, bending and swivelling their way through sequences so near-identical as to be assessable at scales macro and micro, Omsk to Ufa, Krasnodar to Tolyatti ... If the deviating tendency of a single Voronezh double-roll rotary-press operator or Chelyabinsk MINSK-2 circuit board assembler could be nixed the moment it arose, ironed back into ergonomic conformity with the actions of the other ten-thousand-odd rotary-press operators or circuit board assemblers, so, too, could deviations – good ones, beneficial tweaks and upgrades, from the minutiae of belt speed or switch position right up to complete equipment overhauls, metrification, even digitisation – be rolled out in unison across the Euro-Asiatic board, and, once unrolled, evaluated with complete precision, increased yield-to-man-hour (-week, -month, -year or -five-year) ratio determined to the third decimal figure. Where Taylor's only frame and *telos* had been growing factory-owner and shareholder profit, his Soviet cheerleader Alexsei Gastev saw in Taylorism's rise an opportunity to liberate the worker from long serfdom, from an evolution trapped in nineteenth-century neoteny; to release him from the shackles of his very body, or at least the bourgeois-humanist conception thereof, its small-minded designation as a skin-bound monad separated from the roaring and erupting dynamism of the great machine. The first unlocked by, multiplied and networked through the second, though, a new man (this, as far as Phocan can make out, was Gastev's main thrust) would arise, and with him a new proletarian culture – singing, joyous, epic, in which noisy cavalcade of work will bring about both individual self-oblivion and collective self-determination; where in generators' running transmissions, furnaces' gurgle and hiss, the rhythmic clang of blows, our thirst for life will gain titanic force. *Comrades,* he bellowed in 1920 on being handed the Central Institute of Labour's inaugural directorship, *raise up your hammers to forge a new world!*

Gastev fell foul of Stalin, and was shot in the Great Purge of '36–'38. Vanins, luckily, was still in nappies then; he entered adulthood and, not long after, took his master's degree as the second Soviet-Taylorist wave was breaking, implemented through the Ordzhonikidze EEI, in plans for a new Statewide Automated System, *Obshche-gosudarstvennaia avtomatizirovannaia sistema* … Safer, if soberer, times. Besides which, Vanins was a scientist – physics, pure and, if not neutral (nothing was), then at least emanating from a source so far above syndicalism or the vagaries of party faction as to occupy an abstract plane of absolute relations from which Soviet science and industry were compelled, by destiny as much as edict, to take their cue. He seems, though, to have shared his predecessor's zeal for ergonomic transformation, to have been convinced that something bigger than production figures was at stake in the labourer–tool coupling. Phocan's reading a selection of his papers now, as Norman beaches slide beneath the wing:

Work, therefore, should best be understood as a state of kinetic absorption in which the operative's entire essence is given over to the rhythm of his apparatus – and, in being thus surrendered, is remade as an unbound potentiality: fluid, morphing, never finished; spirit realised as rhythm …

The rhythm motif's big; it keeps on cropping up: *rhythm of historic sublimation … rhythm and time …*

Thus we, as the work terminal's architect, create – in the true revolutionary tradition – a new mode of world-time, one in which the flux of being pulsates …

'That's bullshit,' Sennet, peering over Phocan's shoulder, annotates. 'You can't impose a tempo at the scale of history: only detect it.'

'You're not really meant to see this,' Phocan tells him, turning the page window-ward. It's true: Garnett was quite stern about this – uncharacteristically, since Pantarey staff always operate under professional *omertà* anyhow, research, data, files all covered by a large NDA-shroud that each of them has signed, if not in actual blood, at least in lifeblood of continued salaried employment-prospects. That's external, though: the company culture, generally speaking, positively encourages in-house chatter, note-comparing, the cross-pollination of ideas and applications. But *internal* muzzling? Phocan's only guess – two guesses – are that either it's a personal matter, Garnett's indulgence of a box-collecting hobby about which he's slightly coy, or else that Garnett, here, is playing the role of gauze or interface, screening off other players in a game whose stakes are higher than whatever level to which he, Garnett, let alone he-Phocan, has been cleared ... There was an urgency to his employer's tone, a sense that he was passing to him (yes: to *him*, not Sennet) an important baton, harnessing him with a task allotted not so much by Garnett, or even by whomever it might be that he was hiding, as by some abstract force of pure necessity – that Phocan was, like Soviet science and industry, being assigned a *destiny*: to find this box elided from a cataloguing system fifty years ago. This urgency, which he dismissed at first – just as he dismissed, for the first few days he swotted up on it, the box number's elision as a small clerical error – has been infecting him, too, merging with the sense of purpose he experienced in Holland, in the wind tunnel, and (by association although there's no rational reason for this) with the intimation of guilt that, like a vapour-outline, swirled into shape and dissipated again around that. Encountering Vanins' utopianism now, the physicist's gaze fixed on a bright, pulsating future, compounds this intimation: Phocan's own future, by contrast, seems to somehow lie already in his past – to loop back through it like a Gilbreth motion circuit, to some point, some stretch of time, some *act*, lodged there even if yet to be passed over ... And encountering the Latvian's clarity of insight, now, reprises his own sense of nebulousness, of occupying a field of vision that's at once both luminescent and as opaque as these thickly packed, sun-impregnated clouds they're flying through ...

Sennet blows a silent raspberry and turns back to the talk that he's to give tomorrow. Phocan has a presentation to make too, but he'll do that on auto-pilot: it's just software demonstration, sales-pitching. This stack is more enticing. It's infused with a real fervour. At one point Vanins casts himself and his colleagues as *the new Phidiases, sculpting and modelling the fine ivory of Soviet man* ... He seems to have had his fingers in a range of pies, not least that of aeronautics: several of the papers Phocan's been handed by Garnett are concerned with flows – compressible, transonic, incompressible; with aeroelasticity and flutter; with divergence and control ... Clouds fade out over Northern France; Paris scrolls past; later, Alps. Their pleats and folds, for Phocan, chime with the words *sculpting and modelling*, make him think of topography, of CAD and LiDAR ... Here's the old AI, Aeroplane Introspection, kicking in again: the other week, in Berners Street, he felt *old*, felt that he and Eldridge were like dying magi, sole repositories of their subject's mysteries. Now, though ... Now, after Garnett's (perhaps, after all, not so unjust) admonishment and errand-assigning, and while reading Vanins, he's struck by a feeling of *youngness*, of being granted a geological view across a landscape that was formed generations before his arrival, strata crinkled and stacked, each one atop the other, like the plates and ridges of these mountain ranges over which they're flying; or, perhaps, an *archae*ological view, as of the sedimented levels of the city towards which the plane's beginning its descent now, new announcements spilling from the speakers triggering a scurry of tray folding and seat repositioning, of paper stashing, leaving just time before the bump-down for a last unanswered question to pass through his mind: *Why Palomilla?*

They're booked into Hotel Cardano, in the Celio. Lots of the IACSS delegates seem to be holed up here; an easel-mounted noticeboard stands in the lobby, giving dedicated shuttle-bus departure times. The graphics, this year, depict a CGI footballer levitating upended in mid overhead-kick, the letters *I-A-C-S-S* flying from his feet like clods of turf – stellar rather than dirty clods, as bold and glittering as movie-poster titling, with smaller subtitling below word-fleshing out the organiser's acronym: *International Association of Computer Science in Sport*. The player is fictitious, image-source generic – politic on the part of the Association, who can't be seen to promote or favour any one of the many brands and outfits represented by the conference's attendees; although the level of the membership subscription taken out by each of these does, not unreasonably, bring concomitant dividends in terms of line-up and slot-allocation, sideline hospitality, favourable stall-positioning and dinner-seating, and so on. Generic or not, Phocan can instantly identify the picture's provenance: a project Pantarey worked on for FIFA 18. It was Ribaldo who came in, blacked-out limo bouncing its way up Finns, to do the mo-cap for the special moves (run-of-the-mill dribbling and passing and formation-holding had been grabbed weeks previously in Vancouver, from the UBC varsity team). He was uncooperative to the point of obstreperousness: didn't want to do the tricks he thought of as his 'own'; even tore the markers off and stormed out to sulk in the car while panicked handlers whispered into phones. Electronic Arts' lawyers prevailed: a mo-cap obligation clause was written into the contract that in turn underwrote the revenue-stream keeping his car parked, motor idling, outside HQ right then. Someone must have explained this to Ribaldo; after an hour he re-emerged scowling, submitted himself to nipple reattachment, and, eventually, performed stepover, chop and scissors – but badly. It was obvious he was doing it half-arsedly: a little *fuck you* that he'd thought up in the back seat. Phocan and co. had to spend the next two weeks patching the moves over from match footage, pixel by pixel, thread by thread and fill by fill ...

The conference centre's in the Borgo – close enough to walk, which Phocan does. The first morning's sessions are all about pattern analysis. In the spirit of supportive comradeship, or adherence to its motions maybe, he drops in on Sennet's. It's a panel discussion; besides Sennet, there's a German *Informatik* guy, a statistician from Slovenia and (as chair) a Texan dynamical systems theory prof – all male. It's Sennet holding forth when Phocan slips, coffee in hand, into the side-room:

'... into four main schools of thought: perturbation (Hughes, Dawkins, David), relative phase (Walter), chaos (Lames) and, lastly – and conversely – self-organisation (McGarry). What my team at Pantarey, in collaboration with Loughborough's Sports Science Department, have been developing in relation to football – soccer – both draws from and supersedes all these conceptual frameworks ...'

Phocan has heard this before: complex human-behaviour streams, of which those found in football are exemplary ... hidden temporal-sequential structure ... detection beyond the 'narrow reach' of standard statistical analysis ... whence ...

'Whence,' Sennet's rounding the pitch off now, 'Pantarey's new T-pattern model.'

The statistician, understandably, has been bristling at these assertions. As soon as the chair signals open discussion he jumps in:

'We have a good track record. Since the advent of sabermetrics to the world of baseball, statistics – even in what you call its "standard" form – has managed to ... I mean, you won't find a major-league team that's not signed up to PITCHf/x. The diamond's been transformed into a mathematical matrix; strikes, singles, doubles, home runs into data points; coaches can reset their field to account for such-and-such a batter's tendencies, to leverage the probabilities ... I'd call that pretty *wide* reach ...'

'I'm not,' Sennet cuts back in, 'denying any of that. But the *time* element ...'

'The "time element" just happens,' the Slovenian scoffs. 'It's a set of dots and clusters laid out in a line.'

Now it's the *Informatik* man who's taking umbrage.

'I cannot agree with this. Frequency of occurrence – even probability – is not coterminous with, much less equivalent to, relationships between discrete events within a sport performance; or any other type either ...'

'Exactly!' Sennet bows his gratitude across the table's velvet, bypassing the chair, who's happy to let play run on uninterrupted. 'And that's where our T-pattern analysis comes in. If I could demonstrate …' He fiddles with his desktop, still the projector's prime feed; a string of letters pops up on the screen behind the panellists. 'Here's a short stretch of play, extracted from an English Premiership match last season. Each event type – pass, tackle, interception, shot, save, throw-in – has been assigned an alphabetic value: a letter, in other words. So here, you get the sequence *p a n b p j c n j d p n p a p j p b n c n d n j p j a b n n c p n d*. No pattern there, you might say – but you'd be wrong. There *is* one, but it's hidden by redundant letters. When you extrapolate it on a lower line' – he does this with the next slide – 'and strip out all the *ns* and *ps* and *js*, you get the sequence *a b c d* – repeating twice.' He pauses, to allow his listeners to see the truth of this claim for themselves, before continuing: 'Frequency counts wouldn't have detected this; neither would lag-sequential or time-series analysis. T-pattern, though, allows us to unearth repeated temporal strings, even when various other event types pop up in-between the pattern's elements.'

The Slovenian's stumped. The German is impressed. Sennet presses home his advantage with a third slide:

'You can see here that, after an occurrence of *a* at moment *t*, there's an interval $[t+d1, t+d2]$ $(d2 >\_ d1 >\_ 0)$ that tends to contain at least one more instance of *b* than you'd expect from chance alone. We call the temporal relationship between *a* and *b* the *critical interval* – a concept that lies at the centre of T-pattern thinking. Determining or ascertaining it – plotting, that is, both critical interval itself and also interval between each of this interval's instantiations – will place a manager at a distinct advantage. In a nutshell, that's where the extra goal's going to come from.'

Now the chair enters the fray:

'How is it different from the algorithms that the hedge-fund wonks are running?'

'It's the same principle,' Sennet concurs. 'Mapping chance over a temporal continuum, deducing from that map a strategy for profitable intervention. The difference is that, unlike trading, football is zero-sum: one side's successful intervention is the other's catastrophic loss.' Shifting in his seat, he adds: 'Of course "chance", being circumstantial, isn't actually chance at all. What we discovered is that, even when there's *no* pattern, there's still a pattern. The small patterns no longer in evidence have been subsumed by larger and more complex ones – that's why they've disappeared. Which is good: you *want* to constantly upscale your detection from partial to larger strings. So here,' he clicks his next slide up to reveal new letter-chains, 'if $Q = (ABCDE)$ could be partially detected as, for example, *(BCDE)* or *(BDE)* or *(ABCE)*, you discard the *A*s to *E*s and scale to *Q*; after which you'll have to consider a newly detected pattern – *Qx*, say – to be equally or less complete than an already detected pattern, *Qy*, if *Qx* and *Qy* occur *equally often* and *all Qx*'s event-elements are *also* present in *Qy* (but not vice versa). At which point, you eliminate *Qx*. We call it "completeness competition". It's a kind of brutal evolution – Darwin on steroids, a fight to the death: the only pattern standing at the end is the one for which no critically related pairings can be found to feed the hungry Moloch of a larger pattern.'

Sennet's won the room: people are scribbling notes. He drinks his victory in, then adds:

'Some patterns are acyclical. In other words, the temporal distances between their occurrences – the patterns', not their events' – may be irregular. The *within*-pattern intervals between events can still remain invariant, or not: it doesn't matter. What counts is the *overall* pattern occurrence ...'

Phocan's attention's drifting now: he's looking at the delegates, their lanyard-mounted name-tags, the IACSS tote bags hanging from their chair backs, draped across their knees ... Gilbreth and Gastev met one another at a conference: Prague, 1924, ICSM – the Industrial Congress of Scientific Management. He was head of the Soviet delegation; she part of a forty-strong American one. Did they have tote bags then? Or lanyards? Did attendees cultivate a studied air of boredom as the default look to bring into each room, or scan the rows of seating ranking delegates according to desirability? And what of 1965, Zürich, where a now-ancient

Gilbreth met a Raivis Vanins not yet thirty but already throwing quite a swell out from his MIPT lab? Had he felt bold enough to stride across, announce himself, start holding forth about kinetic hypostasis? Or had he edged up to her nervously, threaded his way between rings of minders and admirers, meekly pressed a paper or a card into her hands? However it occurred, he'd got her attention: their correspondence started soon afterwards, and lasted five years, until she was too gaga to write anything to anyone. Phocan's got, in his own tote bag, the passages of it that Garnett passed him, copies of surviving scraps, incomplete sub-strings of a larger pattern time and loss have rendered undetectable; he was up half of last night reading and rereading them. *T.T.* ... That doubled character, like the ones on the screen now, seems to have codified some sequence or event, what Vanins and Gilbreth both referred to as an 'episode' ... And then the mention of a box, the number, 808 – the same number absent from the stereoscoped inventory. There does, as Garnett took pains in his office to convince him, seem to be some link: the two terms – *808*, *T.T.* – keep popping up together. But it's what accompanies them that's intriguing: *changes everything* ... There's an apperception, from Gilbreth's end at least, of some grand divulgence taking shape, its form and outline growing lucid, even as her mind fuzzed over ...

The chair's opened the panel up to contributions from the floor – all of which, confirming Sennet's clean sweep of the session (panel discussions are as zero-sum as football matches), are directed to him. A sharp-faced young man's asking a nerdish question about completeness-competition equations; Phocan tunes out again, and looks through the window. The jalousies, controlled from the same master panel as the beamer, were angled so as to render the room dark enough for slides to be discernible, although not so dark as to obscure the speakers; now, with the onset of the Q&A phase, the technician has notched the slats another fifteen-odd degrees towards the horizontal, to illuminate the questioners. Their upward slant sends Phocan's gaze into the sky above the Prati, where starlings are flocking in large numbers. There's a name for it, which he can't remember. Back inside the room, Sennet's explicatory voice has given over to a woman's – an Italian woman with (Phocan discovers when he turns back inwards) black glasses and a headband. She's asking Sennet about something she's describing as the 'event border':

'Where do you set this?'

'Set it?' he asks back.

'Yes,' she responds. 'Where is it? What's inside the event field, and what's not?'

Now Sennet understands the question. 'The groundsman has kindly set this border for us,' he answers, 'in bold, white, painted lines. When players and the ball lie within these, they're pattern-legible; outside them, they're anathema. They don't exist.'

He looks around the room for the next question, but the woman's not done yet:

'This cannot be so,' she informs him. 'Even with one of your own event examples – *la rimessa*, "throw-in" – this border is surpassed or ruptured by both ball and player. Besides, think of the stadium layout. Beyond the touchline are the dugouts. The substitutes sit here; and the manager, effecting active interventions. And behind this, more importantly, *la folla* – the crowd. You'll know as well as I that home-field, home-crowd advantage generates, within the English Premier League, a sixty-four per cent home-win rate.'

Sennet, initially dismissive of her quibble, is brought to attention by her command of this statistic.

'And then,' she's warming up here, 'there are other factors. How long before the game did the team eat? Did they arrive together at the stadium? Did the Catholic players pray ... ?'

'Ah,' Sennet thinks he's seen a weakness in her attack line, 'T-pattern makes no judgement on causality – not at the gastronomic scale, nor at the theological. It merely detects patterns.'

'*Si, si,*' a conference-centre staffer's holding out his hand to take the mike from her, but she's not surrendering it. 'This issue of causality's a *falsa pista;* it has no bearing on my point. My point is that these factors, too, stand in relation to the *a*s and *b*s and *c*s.

They, too, are in the pattern. If we can highlight' – she pronounces this word with the Italian *h*-drop: *eye-light* – 'one particular event type – say, the goal kick … What is the "event" here? Kicking the ball up the field? Okay. But what about the bouncing of the ball before the kick? Three bounces? Four? Does the goalkeeper wipe his glove against his forehead, to clear away perspiration? Does he evacuate his throat, mutter a phrase, or even speak the phrase's words inside his head as he starts on his little run-in to the kick? Or does he glance at the stadium's seating, towards where he knows his girlfriend or his mother or his son is sitting? What if he catches sight of a particular banner in the stands, or recognises, just before his foot touches the ball, the odour of an hot' – the dropped *h* again – 'dog …'

'Are you suggesting,' Sennet asks her, 'that we should assign values to each of these … *micro*-events?'

Now it's her turn to smile.

'*Perché no?*' she shrugs.

'But then …' Sennet's victory lap has turned into a marathon, in which he's starting to show telltale signs of exhaustion, of cramp's onset. 'If you brought all those in, your equations would be hopelessly unwieldy. I mean, where would it *end?*'

Nobody seems to have an answer to this question; for an uncomfortably long stretch, the room is quiet; then the chair, the Texan systems-theory man, outs with a quip about *this* event field's end, its border, being dictated by the schedule, the odour of biscuits waiting for them in the lobby, etc. There are chuckles, but the atmosphere's deflated. Delegates shuffle out. Over amaretti, Phocan gets talking to the awkward questioner. Her name's Rafaella Farinati, and she's with the Università degli studi di Milani, *Dipartimento di Psicologia dello Sport*.

'Were you just trying to knock him off his horse?' he asks her.

'An *orse?*' she asks.

'To take him down a notch. Demote him.'

'Ah! *Affatto non*,' she answers. 'We are also making our equations for completeness – though I think we understand the term

218

in different ways. Five years ago, we started to examine the cases of *nevrotic* sportsmen and sportswomen, ones who can't hit the ball until they've gone through a routine: of touching some part of their body, for example, or brushing their eyes on one spot of the stadium, then on another – same sequence again, each time. We have concluded that these people were *non aberranti ma esemplari* – not perverse, but typical. Through them, we come to understand the field and range of data that a player's processing at any given moment.'

'Don't they shut that out, though?' Phocan asks. 'The excess stuff?'

'Exactly wrong.' Rafaella Farinati pokes his shoulder with a floury finger. 'It is central to the data-architecture of their whole performance. Like yours now.'

'Mine? What performance?'

'You're exchanging conversation with me,' she says, 'but what's really in your mind? The taste of your *biscotti*, and the colour and texture of this carpet that we're standing on; the various other carpets it reminds you of; the rooms they lay in, what you experienced in those rooms; your anxiety about which *sessione* to attend next, or where to go for lunch – that's what you're thinking, what's determining your actions and decisions. If we want to understand event fields then we have to be *olistic*, start appreciating all the channels on which information is being processed, not a fraction of these only ...'

Actually, what Phocan's thinking is that Rafaella Farinati's cool. It's not just what she's saying, or gratitude to her for having granted him this dose of *Schadenfreude* over Sennet; there's something about her whole demeanour, her ensemble – most of all the headband, which is stirring vague associations round the peripheries of his own recall, ones that he can't quite assign a value to, not yet, *rimesse* held up just beyond the touchline ...

'Where are *you* going to lunch?' he asks.

She snorts derisively, as though to say: Anyone could have seen *that* event type coming. 'I visit the Forum and the Palatino each time I'm in Rome,' she tells him. 'I'll take something on the way there. I think you have your *presentazione* on body-separation now, though … no?'

He wonders if she's memorised the schedule, or if she harbours a professional curiosity for kinematic-filling software, or … or what? She's giving off an air not just of knowing Phocan's business, but, beyond that, of knowing it in a *knowing* way, as though aware of more than she's been letting on. Before he can reply, she brushes off his shirt the micro-crumbs, but not the flour, left by her finger's prod, then smiles – not at him, it seems, but at something over his shoulder – turns on her heels and disappears into the general IACSS throng.

He cranks out his own talk distractedly. Artefact reduction … quintic interpolation … Pantarey … Physis 6™ … and done. He lunches with Sennet, bad linguine in a tourist trap on the bank of the Tiber, then decides to skip the afternoon session and head to the Forum too, even if he won't be able to pass off bumping into Rafaella Farinati as a quirk of chance. The bumping-into doesn't happen anyway; she's departed by the time he gets there, if she ever went there in the first place. A meeting does occur, though. Phocan's leaning on a railing by the sunken water garden of the Domus Augustana, looking down on its fuzzed labyrinth whose shape reminds him of a QR code, when he becomes aware of someone at his side. It's the kind of proximity that straddles the border between normal and invasive, measurable not in standard inches but through incremental calculi that would relate the distance between people to amount of space available around them. This guy's three or so feet away from Phocan – on the tube or at a football game, T-pattern parsed or not, this would be plenty. But they're not on the tube; there's hardly anyone about now; three feet is too close. What's more, the guy is looking at him, smiling. Pick-up? No: Phocan sees, peeping from his jacket-front's top pocket, a plastic protuberance that he recognises from its colouration as the upper corner of an IACSS delegate card.

'Quintic filling,' his companion murmurs. 'Liked your presentation.'

The accent's Italian, or maybe Swiss. Phocan doesn't recall seeing him in his talk.

'Just standard stuff,' he answers unambassadorially. 'Who are you with?'

The interloper smiles again, his gaze directed ever so slightly to the side of Phocan's face this time, pulls a card from the same top pocket and passes it over. It reads: *Alain Pirotti*; then, below this: *Cassius First Motion*. No job title, nor logo, nor company tag-line with obligatory present participle (*making, bringing, streamlining . . .*); just these words, an email address and a phone number.

'Your project touched,' Pirotti tells him, 'on an issue spanning our discipline's whole field.'

Phocan waits, politely, for the thought's completion, the reveal, which Pirotti now provides:

'I mean,' he says, 'the gaps. They've plagued our business since the outset.'

'What,' asks Phocan, eyeing the card, 'does Cassius do?'

Pirotti, still smiling slightly off-centredly, waves away the question.

'For decades – long before the markers and the processors arrived; as you know . . .'

'I'm not quite sure I follow . . .'

Pirotti fixes his eyes firmly back on Phocan's face.

'It's in the report.'

'Which report? Mine?'

Pirotti smiles back silently by way of answer. 'For almost a century now,' he says eventually, 'the capacity has been in place to plot the curves and stretches of a movement-segment at its outset; to describe its structure; to enclose it in a form that's folded back into itself, contained and perfect; like . . . let's say, a figure-eight. And then to do the same for the same segment's end-stage: another *eight* . . .'

He pauses, gaze still fixed on Phocan as he speaks, observing his reaction.

'So,' he resumes, 'we have two bookends, carved with an artisan's precision: start and finish, *eight* and *eight*. But then, between these, at some point – between two given points within that stretch, the more we zoom in and interrogate it – there will always be a patch of unmapped territory: a hole, big and round, or oval, or who-knows-what shape: a *zero* ... What are we to do?'

A breeze, rising up from the sunken garden, ruffles Phocan's neck. Pirotti, seeing him tense up, presses:

'Eight; zero; eight ...'

Phocan stares back at him, uncertain what to say. Up in the sky, the birds are at it again: starlings, clustering in spheres, columns and conjoining funnels – giant masses that billow and contract elastically as their internal volume redistributes itself. Pirotti, still smiling at him, asks:

'We live in a time of information-sharing, do we not?'

He pauses again, waiting for an answer. Hesitantly, Phocan says:

'It depends what information's being solicited, by whom.'

'Okay,' concedes Pirotti. 'Of information ... *exchange*: an *economy* of knowledge. Our world, unfortunately, is not open-source. But people will pay well for much sought-after insights, or packages.' Then, as though it were an afterthought: 'Or boxes ...'

There's that breeze again, that ruffling. Phocan looks down at the labyrinth, trying to discern its source. Pirotti, at his ear, continues:

'We should keep in touch. We understand, my people just as yours, that correspondence can be ... fruitful.'

My people? Now he's feeling dizzy. It must be the height, the angle or the labyrinth's pattern, triggering some reader-response in him, some reaction. Phocan closes his eyes for a while, head resting on the rail. When he looks up again, Pirotti's gone; the Palatine is empty; then a group of Chinese tourists in bright anoraks starts trickling across the hilltop's green. Before he, too, leaves, Phocan's granted two small, if sudden, insights. Firstly, that Pirotti's smile was not so much intended for *him* as responding, albeit with a certain delay, to another smile directed at its bearer earlier: Rafaella Farinati's. He couldn't explain how he knows this, but he does: the second smile fitted the first – *completed* it, as both prompt and response, Phocan's shoulder a mere way-station or relay post across which it was beamed. Secondly, that it's *murmuration*: the word for starlings' clustering and flocking. He should have had it on his tongue-tip: it's been modelled over and over, after all ... Reynolds ... Delgado-Mata ... Hartman ... Benes ... Hildenbrandt ... subjected to bin-lattice spatial subdivision, transposed to a spread of fields: multi-channel radio-station programming, weather-simulation software, dispersal/concentration ratios of crowds fleeing in panic from the source of gunfire ... What's this instantiation of it, this bird ink-blot, murmur-modelling for him? It's hovering above the Basilica now, thickening over Caesar's temple, elongating over Vesta's, before trickling up the facing hillside to pulse in the air above the Tarpeian Rock, which sits denuded, awaiting new traitors.

6. DYCAST

In the next room, Thérèse is sleeping. She sleeps several times a day now. At first it was structured – *morning nap*, 10.30 to 11.15; *afternoon rest*, 2.15 to 3.30 – but as things advanced it started to just happen when it happened. Where it happened, too: chair, sofa, bench ... It's almost narcolepsy. This time, at least, she looked vaguely comfortable, propped up by cushions in a window seat, well covered by a shawl, and the heating's on. Pilkington, post-prandial, thought he'd catch some himself, but got diverted, *intercepted*, passively or not, en route through his study, where, best part of an hour later, he still finds himself. He's trying to compose an email, response to a request that Garnett's sent him: his old friend wants pointers as to how a spaceship might start to collapse when placed inside a 'solar wind'. *For comparison*, Garnett has written, *think of a fighter plane in a Mach 25 environment: what panels would give first? How would they peel away? Is there a formula for determining the brittleness of sheet-metal and rivets relative to age, stress factors, pressure? Etc. ...* It's for a film Pantarey's working on, some sci-fi blockbuster. A little quid pro quo. He's jotted a few notes down, but for the last twenty minutes he's been ruminating, letting his thoughts glide idly back to last week's Canard meeting: the clay-wrapped duck ... the ice cream ... the damn ice cream ... with the wafer-grid, no less ... That kind of detail always brings it on: old Project Albatross. It's as if people knew. *Do* they? Those little jabs and accusations seem to follow him around, to hang or coalesce around him, rumour-cloud of smirks and whispers, words so familiar they don't even need vocalising: *How do you lose an aeroplane ... ?*

He's seated at the secretary. Both the object and the term have come down to him from his grandfather. As a child, he'd spend hours playing with the cubbies and the drawers, the slant-front opening, the small under-the-counter catch that, once depressed, released the hidden recess from mahogany depths. In the first weeks of their marriage, when they moved into the house, shuffled the furniture around, it confused Thérèse when he spoke about it. *You make it sound like a person – like a mistress with whom you slink off to spend your time*, she told him. *Call it an* escritoire *instead. Or just plain* desk. But he persisted stubbornly with *secretary*. The word, for him, is less suggestive of humans – stenographers, PAs, what have you – than of secrets, recessed, catch-protected; or, perhaps, at some more bodily scale, of secretion, moist, dirty and shameful. Pilkington's hand slides furtively around above his knees, making its way towards the button. It still works: he feels the spring-load mechanism give, hears sprockets, rods and chain crank through their paces, waits for the small compartment to slide out from behind its thin facade, Potemkin panel … About once a year he undertakes this ritual, akin to prelate flagellation or to Filipino auto-crucifixion. *This* is why he thinks that, on the balance of probabilities, it's a good bet that Vanins has some notes, some records, *something* of the sort Thames House are so keen to get hold of, stashed away: because *he* does, in defiance of all acts and contracts, interdictions, vows … This residue he's held out or held back, held *to* him, siphoned off and buried like toxic waste, or dark, disgusting treasure, serves as his private autobiography, his unpublished confession, scrawled in code, a hieroglyphic alphabet of sine and cosine, channel-filter frequencies, glide-path degrees, strain-gauge transducer settings and transmitted pelvic loads …

He sets the disgorged recess on the desktop, covering Parkinson's carer support information packages, reunion invitations and phone bills, and lifts the notebook from it. It's a Silvine memo pad, red, 10 by 16, the brand name slicing cursively across an empty shield around whose sides two laurel branches curl on the front cover;

pages lined, not graphed, inside. Pilkington's surprised, each time he thumbs them, at how un-aged they are: thirty-plus years on, they should be yellow, crinkled, like old parchment. But, as though the secret drawer contained a humidor, the paper, the card binding, the whole book is soft and pliant to both touch and eye; the jottings could be yesterday's, today's ... The agelessness brings on a double recognition: not just of the notes, but of the nature of the memory for which they serve as peg and cipher. Hasn't it, too, stayed forever young? Rather than obeying the rear-view mirror optics that dictate all mental objects must retreat down one-point avenues of time, dwindling and fading, the whole thing has become fixed by the perspective, drawn into sharper focus – not shrunk but compressed, infused with greater density; through concentration, made to loom larger. Wasn't that the whole point in the first place? A compression that was also an expansion? Four years into a single second – a second that contained a million others, and as many lives and deaths ...

He got the gig six months into his posting. Not through the normal chain, his MOD line-manager or the one above him; no, it was McReady, his old supervisor back at Edinburgh, who tapped him on the shoulder, took him to tea in the Four Seasons, introduced him to Sir Ronald, figure who loomed large, if spectral, in the military-aeronautical imagination: MOD's Chief Scientific Adviser, full member of both Defence Management Board and Defence Council ... And to Dashell, Langley's Vice Principle of Research Projects, who found tiered cucumber sandwiches and scones perplexing.

'Are you meant to eat bottom-to-top or top-to-bottom? Why do they cut the crusts off, anyway?'

'For symmetry, I think,' opined Sir Ronald. 'Given that they're triangular, two sides with crust and one without would seem a tad off-balance ...'

Then they got down to cases: a collaboration, hook-up, joint-planned and -conducted, between NASA, British Aerospace, the FAA, Marconi Avionics ... There were others, junior partners, outliers, subsidiary parties ... The idea was to stage a CID – the first of a civilian aircraft. Dashell's people in Virginia were interested in acquiring baseline structural crash-dynamics data; BA and FAA in testing out an antimisting kerosene they hoped could not just fuel a plane but also prevent fireballing when spilled at impact; Marconi in the validation and improvement of their nascent structural-mathematical aircraft model; all parties in load measurements and load transmissions, fuselage acceleration, occupant human tolerance and the various sliders linking these to one another and a host of subcats, all interrelated. CID stood for *Controlled Impact Demonstration*. Simply put, they were to crash a plane, deliberately, on a beach out in the Indian Ocean.

'Project Albatross,' Sir Ronald informed Pilkington, cleaning a spot of clotted cream from his cheek with the back of his little finger. 'So named for the bird's wingspan, and the Tristan of that family's presence – admittedly quite rare, often through misadventure, which you could say complements the one-off nature of our test – in the region.'

'And what role would I ... ?'

'Navigation,' replied Sir Ronald. 'It's quite simple – just a big remote control, really. We need to guide a Boeing 720 safely to its doom.'

'Emphasis,' Dashell leant in, 'on *safely*. The impact footprint will be tiny. And the interrogation window – the one *we're* interested in – is the first second after impact.'

'The first *second*? But the fuel ... the antimisting agent ...' Pilkington turned to McReady for professorial support – and was met with a look of detachment, the three years of tutelage, the entire scaffolding of academia revealed now as a sideline to the *real* work the Prof. Emeritus had been doing when he reared his charges, falling away now as the intellectual vessel was delivered to the orbit of this higher purpose. On his own, he turned back to the other two, and asked: 'Won't that play out over an extended period – say, half a minute or so? And the load transmissions too, as they react to one another while the plane ...'

'Exactly,' Dashell told him. 'There's so many factors that it's basically random, or as good as, two, three links down the event chain. Our good friends can throw their private-sector money on that bonfire if they want. That initial second, though ... We're banking on it giving us a pretty stable metric in terms of the data traces it could generate, if intelligently primed.'

Thus began the next four years – four years which, if their destiny was to be swallowed and consumed by just one second, prepared for this fate by gorging themselves on the previous two decades. All transport accident files, company and govt., from Boeing, Lockheed-California, McDonnell Douglas, the FAA, the CAA and all the rest, were gathered, sifted, strained; each passenger jet crash between '58 and '79 broken down, stripped, fed into the accumulative database that in turn produced, after eight months, a Venn diagram revealing that, of 993 disasters in this period, 176 were both well documented and within the catchment area for survivability; which special crashes were then evaluated in great detail: context, cause, collision-nature, outcome ... Every wing detachment and tail break-up, every stabiliser loss and slat retraction, tail strike, stall, fuel-tank explosion, pressure bulkhead failure; the whole spectrum of fuselage deformation following impact, conflagration timeline, crumple pattern and debris trajectory, injury-type distribution and row-based survival odds – all these were cross-indexed, each factor bringing with it, like so many plane shards, patches of its originating context and scenario, the pieces joining together in the manner of a jigsaw puzzle made from piles of other puzzles, mixed, scrambled perhaps but now quite neatly reassembling into a new image that, instead of just remaking one of the originals, creates a new composite in which each of the old ones stays recognisable even as it's wiped. Call it the *Ur-crash* (or, in Gilbrethian style it occurs to Pilkington in reverie beside his secretary now, the *one best crash*); the one that hasn't happened yet *as such*, but that nonetheless has underlain each of the ones that *has*, rulebook and blueprint, sum of possibilities, totality that hovers spectral above every partial iteration, haloed blur or maybe heat mirage – and hovers, too, above the spectres of its victims, past and future, open ledger always full yet always holding space back for new entries.

By March '82 this ur-disaster had been planned and plotted. Statistics, magicked up through rounds of filtering and cross-indexing, revealed that 54.5 per cent of mishaps happen during approach and landing, which dovetailed neatly with the practical requirement that the thing descend on to a strip of beach. Glide slope would be a representative $3.3°$ to $4.0°$; nose-up attitude $1.0°$; sink rate 17 ft/sec; no roll or yaw attitude; longitudinal velocity 150 knots ... It got so Pilkington could actually *see* it, see the plane descending, again and again, guided by nothing other than his own volition, held in the phase-lock of his mind's variable frequency; and hear, on repeat too, not just the roar of its approach, but also static crackling around this channel's edges, taking on the character of voices – hundreds, thousands of them, filling the bandwidth with their cries ...

His first visit to Septentrion was in the autumn of '82. He was flown commercially via Lagos to Mauritius; onwards on a military plane, a giant propellered Atlas, to the Diego Garcia base; from there, on a Short C-23 Sherpa to the atoll, touching down in the footprint itself. You see it long before you reach it: this distended pretzel floating in the sea, emerging in a patch you could have sworn you'd stared at for some time already and had thought was empty, like an anamorphic image in a painting or germ culture in a petri dish. Its shape, folded and curled round a central lagoon, earns it its designation as an atoll, but to all intents and purposes it's a bank – a set of sandbanks ringed together, elongated white-tack lumps pressed on to a blue wall. Ground-side, the white takes on an even whiter quality. Grabbing a handful of beach as he stepped out of the Sherpa, letting it trickle back between his fingers, Pilkington noticed the people waiting to greet him exchange appreciative glances, observing the eager act of a professional – material analysis, soil-sampling – and felt fraudulent: in reality, his gesture was simply an attempt to clasp, to get to grips with this consuming *whiteness*, with the pigment not so much of a mineral as of a concept, a condition. The sunlight was white, not yellow; the sea-glare too; and so, apart from one black private, were the personnel, American and British servicemen and engineers. No locals: they'd been shipped out forcibly two decades earlier; their own catastrophe, a crash no one would model. White: sand, people, light itself were blank and virgin, plasmic surfaces awaiting first impression. Then blue: sky, sea, electric matrix of emergence, of potentiality – blueprint indeed ... If this small, narrow strip would be Ground Zero, then this moment he was engineering two years hence, this charged and stretched-out second, would be not only his, but (it seemed to him, somehow) his whole epoch's founding instant, the explosive *now* from which the futures of both would billow, find their mass and shape ...

'We'll be acquiring,' Dashell was also on the atoll with a spotty-faced assistant, Briar, overseeing the NASA side of things, 'over three hundred and thirty time histories. Fuselage accelerations normal, transverse, longitudinal; wing (inner, outer, bridge and tip) accelerations normal and spar longitudinal; bending moments wing and fuselage vertical ... Then loads: seat, dummy, lap-belt, shoulder-harness, bin-support link ... Dummy accelerations normal, transverse, longitudinal – head, chest and pelvis ...'

'Pelvis?'

'It's where most of the body load goes, typically. The plane crash-lands, and everyone performs a giant synchronised hip-thrust.'

He wandered off whistling 'Ain't Nothing but a Hound Dog', leaving the Marconi man, Anderson, to bring Pilkington up to speed on anthropometric modelling:

'Thirteen of the dummies will be instrumented – triaxial accelerometers, restraint load cells and the like buried in their various cavities, to ascertain whether the load transmissions and accelerations stay within parameters of human tolerance – of liveability, in other words. These ones will be diffused about the cabin, to maximise coverage; some upright, others set in brace position. Then seventeen more, non-instrumented ones, your basic CPR types, will make up the numbers, keep the smart ones company; just like in life.'

'And how will they relay their intel?' Pilkington asked.

'Transducers,' answered Anderson. 'Four hundred of them, transmitting from the dummies, engines, fuselage, you name it ... Gain ranges from one to one thousand, with full-scale output of 5V into the pulse code modulation system, which has a frame format: 129 8-bit words per frame at one megabit per second; 60 words assigned to the 180-Hz channels and 58 words to the 100- and 60-Hz ones. We keep word size down at 8 bits to allow for the high sample rates, and send the whole thing through a low-pass four-pole Butterworth filter before sampling, to stop aliasing errors ...'

Anderson had lost him with *pulse code modulation* ... Daydreaming, Pilkington found himself mixing the term in his mind with *human tolerance*: the idea of a pulse, a pulse-beat, persisting amidst all the wreckage, sending out its signals past the barriers that death, aliasing errors and all other weapons stockpiled in oblivion's arsenal have set up in a bid to stifle it ... It was when Anderson got on to describing the aircraft structural mathematical model they were developing that his attention was reined back:

'... that this will be the takeaway: whether DYCAST gives us an accurate view, or not ...'

'What was that?'

'Whether it gives us an accurate ...'

'No, the bit before: die cast ...'

'It's the finite-element code the model runs on: DYnamic Crash Analysis of STructures. If this little outing ends up validating it, we won't need to keep smashing aircraft on to beaches.'

Pilkington tracked back to the Four Seasons meeting, Dashell's spiel: *so many factors ... basically random ... two, three links down the event chain* ... Now, in his mind's eye, he saw a pair of dice, flung down on to a table of white sand, striking and bouncing, glancing one another, every new collision upsetting whatever spin axes they'd – if just for a millisecond – settled into, diverting roll paths into new ones which would lead to new collisions, on and on, chance multiplying, mushrooming exponentially, infinity reached by the first tenth ... It was, indeed, random. But that *first* strike, that initial contact ... *that* could be willed: the angle that the dice are held at, how hard they're thrown, which side is upwards-, downwards-, sideways-facing ... So it was with the plane's impact: scale the dice-throw up a thousand-fold, milli- to second, and you've got the time-frame of the crash – the same proportional relations, same progression into randomness, but also the same window for control. Glide slope, velocity, sink rate: if well primed, these could, as Dashell said, provide a stable metric, generate a set of numbers that were unique, finite, *true* ...

Whence his own role: die-primer, off-vessel helmsman. *Kubernetes*: wasn't that where Wiener dug up the name *cybernetics* in the first place? If McReady, playing pilot himself, had steered Sir Ronald to him it was because he knew that the Ph.D. he'd midwifed into being contained the most up-to-date overview of the field. *On the Use of Emulator Software in Remote Navigation Systems*: most cited thesis in the department's history; earned Pilkington his stripes – and now this. Armed with Sir Ronald's seal, he got to hand-pick his team. Back in the UK, they designed this project's tailored remote navigation system – thirteen channels, one per servo – plotted the 720's path from NSF Diego Garcia's runway (Septentrion's strip wasn't long enough for take-off) over the sea, the banking turns – first left, then right – that it would make, worked out the wiggle-room it had to dampen oscillations, realign with target centreline, the final approach angle. Like (it strikes him now here in the study, duck and wafer still crowding his mind's stage) a Gilbreth wireframe, yes ... Then Vanins. Garnett said that he'd put a man on it already. Others are on the trail: Thames House knows that, through its own various feedbacks. Everything leaks. Typewriters and ribbons, word-size, sample-rates ... The pulse code modulation data on four of the channels of the airborne tape recorders, Anderson informed him, would be digitally delayed by 256 milliseconds, to ensure data acquisition in the event of a momentary tape-speed perturbation during impact.

'Think of it,' the Marconi man said, 'as a kind of memory glitch, but in real time.'

Pilkington did, and more: wasn't the entire project like this? An instant held back or diverted from itself; a second that's both more and less? Where *was* that second, then? Where is it, now – where did it go? Nowhere and everywhere, perhaps: for him, it's turned into an overwhelming presence that's eternally ungraspable; totality that's incomplete; destination missed, elided; moment cut out from the flow of time and exponentially enlarged, like some eternal frame ...

A small disturbance comes from the next room: a murmur, breaking the surface of Thérèse's sleep. The pamphlets, the online support groups say anxiety can be precursor to dementia. Maybe it's just the heat: the radiators are on full. Out on the atoll, it was always hot, even at night. On his return there, February '84, he found the strip transformed: cameras, landing lights, lines like yard-markers on American football pitches or shove-ha'penny-board guillotine slats ... Two rows of heavy steel wing-openers had sprouted in the landing corridor itself, ten or so metres past the tyre-kiss spot.

'They're slicers,' Anderson, on whom the intervening eighteen months had incised their own trace, a slight jowl-lengthening, announced. 'They'll cut the thing wide open, spill the AMK fuel at a guaranteed rate of between twenty and a hundred gallons per second. Here, have one of these ...'

He opened a pull-top metal beer tin and handed it to him. To Pilkington's amazement, it was cold. Last time round, they'd spent all day glugging warm water out of Osprey bottles that, if you could be bothered, you could tie up, trail in the lagoon and reel back like a fishing line to drink tepid at best. Now, the Americans had fridges. Besides beer, they kept ice cream in them, industrial-sized tubs of vanilla, strawberry and mint-choc chip, which they gallantly shared with their English partners. Among all the men (they were all men), both officer and private, military and civilian, a mood of camaraderie gave over, as April approached, to one of palpable excitement, laced through with a lubricating joviality, with transatlantic banter about cricket, baseball, hockeys field and ice (relative merits of), the edibility or in- of Marmite, what in heaven's name hominy grits were, speculation about why dummies were orange, why Septentrion was so named when its constituent sandbanks clearly numbered six, why the first of April had been chosen for Impact Day ... *April Fool!* they took to calling out to one another, to the sky, horizon, or whatever surface they could find to hurl the call at. It became their password, their shared in-joke, unofficial project title. *Who're we foolin'?* they'd bark and howl over beers and ice cream of an evening, endless stars spread out across the blue-black dome that seemed to curl not just above but around and even below them as well, as though their atoll were set in the middle of a glass-ball paperweight, a snow-globe, bone-chip particles still riding thermals generated by a contact, a shaking, that had taken place long ago, before time began ...

The joke, of course, turned out to be on them. Preventing accidents indeed ... The most enduring laugh, the bitterest one, would be Pilkington's, and his alone. They didn't, they still don't know: it was *him* ...

7. The Movement Underground

There's a joke all Bergeners know: a tourist and a ten-year-old local kid find themselves next to one another at a bus stop/shop counter/cafe table – in whichever version, staring through rain-bleared glass at streets along which rivers of rainwater gush. The tourist asks the kid:

'What's it like here when it's not raining?'

The kid looks back at him as though the question were the stupidest he'd ever heard.

'How would I know?' he says. 'I'm only ten.'

Rain here is post-Newtonian: it can fall down, sideways, even upward. Stepping out, first morning in town, Phocan picked up an umbrella in the hotel lobby, and was puzzled by the receptionist's enigmatic, slightly condescending glance. The riddle was resolved within two minutes. No one carries the things here; they're useless. The rainwater swirls in hazy streams, auratic drifts around you, finding out your every port of entry: gaps between coat fastenings or shirt buttons, between sleeve and wrist or trouser-leg and ankle, weft and warp of jumper-knit. By the time he'd reached Sardinen he was saturated: not just clothes but (it felt) skin as well, as though some strange inversion of this country's vaunted sauna ritual had just taken place, a reverse sweating, and the atmosphere, not he, had shed its moisture, millions of nebulised drops that his body, like a sponge, had thirstily absorbed. His hosts' first act was to have one of their number, an acrobat named Trine, lead him to a *klær buttikk* to purchase a full-body anorak that, like a scientist in a film involving mass-contagion or (as with *Incarnation*, although Ben Briar – oddly – hasn't flagged this up and called for the characters to wear similarly prophylactic outfits) alien contact, he now dons automatically each time he ventures outside.

MU's housed in an old canning factory, whence its informal title. MU stands for the Movement Underground, but everyone just calls it (building, company, employees) Sardinen. In the vaulted workshops, hooks from which the daily catch was hoisted by the barrelful before being upended, sloshed down ramps on to conveyors that led millions of fish a merry dance through grading, brining, nobbing, seaming and eventual cartoning now secure ropes and bungees, aerial straps and nets, *cordes lisses* and *volantes* to and from which acrobats hang, swing, split, piston and basqule, while up towards and even sometimes on beyond them other bodies rise, shot from the trampolines with which patches of floor have been inlaid. Still others fall, from beams and loading doors, in dives by turns gracious and willed, evocative of Acapulco cliffs, and (conversely) passive and unshaped, as though the faller had been shot or pushed or simply lost their footing, on to blue crash-mats that boom as they implode under each impact, upper surface crumpling before rising once more, yeast-rich dough on speed-play, to assume its previous volume although not topography (the exact distribution through the plastic of folds and creases never, Phocan's concluded, the same twice) as they await the next free-falling mass. In one corner of the room a human pyramid reaches almost to beam level: a misshapen one that's crumbling and collapsing even as it forms, discarded body-blocks scrambling to their feet and stumbling on across the floor to form new, smaller mastabas as they clamber over other fallen, stumbling bodies, groping their way forward ...

The scenario's as follows: Tszvetan and Tild have been found out. It was always bound to happen; even at the state reception in Kern's harbour, as the *Sidereal*'s doors groaned open and the bride-to-be was led down the long, rose-draped walkway, face emerging from the clouds of dry ice with which the vehicle had been doused (Herzberg's, not Briar's, idea) – the way her escort led her by the hand, the way he *held* her hand, a lack of stiffness to the grip exuding more familiarity than ceremony ... Courtiers' tongues started wagging right then, and haven't stopped since. One of their number, a weaselly commandant named Marloe who's long harboured a grudge against Louis Q's protégé (they're the same age; Tszvetan was a better racer than him, and outnotched his kills during the War by two-to-one), has been constantly dreaming up ways to blow their cover. He's activated route tracers and communications spyware, body-signature detectors, crypto-shadows; he's let slip, Iago-like, insinuations at each opportunity – none of which ruses have achieved their goal, partly because the lovers have been on to him and taken appropriate precautions (trace-erasure software, phoneme-scramblers, shadow-diffractors, etc., etc.), partly due to Louis Q's unwillingness to see, or to acknowledge having seen, what's obvious to everyone else.

And obvious it is: no one-off, the thanadrine-fuelled episode has tapped, in Tild and Tszvetan, inexhaustible reserves of passion. It's an addiction; they get actual, i.e. somatic, withdrawal symptoms if the tryst isn't re-consummated every day or so – high temperature, nausea, the shakes ... For venues they've been using semi-public spaces: the Botanical Garden, Natural Science Museum, Tentirn Tower – assignations thought up on the hoof and messaged via ad-hoc interfaces immune to deciphering because devised by the lovers themselves, intuitively, idiolects almost. He'll drop chips into her blu-ray stream at certain frequencies, or project flickering laser-beams on to low-hanging clouds above the palace, or flash over an iconogram showing a *caprifolio* tree, none of which symbols have been pre-infused with a fixed meaning by them – but each time, she knows exactly what he's signalling. The others – courtiers, servants, populace-at-large – know merely *that* they're signalling, and trysting, but can't place this knowledge in the forum of decodable enunciation, hence of record ...

Marloe, no fool, has thought the situation through, and tweaked his strategy accordingly. He's come to understand that, as far as his aims are concerned, his goal isn't the *uncovering* of the affair, since this was hardly covered in the first place. Nor is it convincing Louis

Q that the affair is taking place: if what the ruler's seen already isn't evidence enough, then nothing will be – they're virtually screwing right in front of him. No: what he, Marloe, needs to do is to uncover to the *populace* Louis Q's awareness of the state of play; and beyond that, to uncover to him, Louis Q, the populace's knowledge of his knowledge of their knowledge of the tryst – a loop of knowing feeding back into and energising itself, galvanising the whole situation from its stupor. Once all separating curtains, all snug-walls have been torn down, all blind alleys razed, the partitioning of acknowledgement eradicated, then ... *Then* Louis Q will *have* to act: his own head, crown, sceptre, his *authority*, will be on the block. Marloe's been dreaming up some fitting form of *mise-en-scène* through which the requisite tripartite viewing – Louis Q of lovers, public of lovers-and-Louis-Q, Louis Q of public-viewing-him-viewing-lovers – might be orchestrated ...

Events, or at least the court calendar, conspire with him: on Kern, from the Second Kingdom onward, to mark each new moon cycle a royal hunt's been undertaken. With much sounding of tambours and waving of draps, the regent and his entourage mount an armada of five-cylinders and *kjarabancs* and chase down the *radjars* that proliferate around Kern's veldt and wetlands. The excursion lasts a whole diurnal – an all-male affair, one in which Tszvetan, in the normal run of things, would not only feature but also star, bagging more of the elegant, antlered beasts than anyone else (though, as protocol demands, tributing to Louis Q the excess of his tally over and above that of his liege). But this time he's crying off, pleading an old injury, a Saraõnic shoulder-wound that's playing up – which is (to use the old Kern idiom) *kwatsch*: he and Tild will take his uncle's absence as free pass for an uninterrupted nocturnal of *coup*ing. This they do, imbibing between bouts a range of cocktails that Tild's mixed for them – nothing so all-consuming as thanadrine, none of which in any case remains (they knocked it off in one go that night on the ship), but nicely complementary to such drawn-out sessions nonetheless: rhodontrine, porphyridion, mandragal, draughts that double the effects of darkness, swathe them in the intimacy and security of what seems the first, or maybe final, night, inducing a forgetfulness, obliviousness even – to danger, to the risks of discovery and of forgetfulness itself. Eventually, passion and bodies spent, they drift seamlessly off into a deep and peaceful sleep. When Louis Q, led on by Marloe (who is easily, once Tszvetan's DF software's been reactivated, capable of tracking them) and with the entire hunting party in tow, arms laden with *radjars* in a state (it seems) no more limpid or inanimate than that of the two lovers, stumbles into the *palazzo's* Sala Rosa just as dawn, once more, peeps round Ardis Minor and creeps over the Kernwinal Hills, projecting Fidelus's light on to the golden threads of the room's darkened tapestries, it takes a full minute of shouting, prodding, tugging and, eventually, slapping to wake Tild and Tszvetan up.

This, then, is the state of play: Louis Q, apoplectic at his bride's and nephew's joint betrayal of him; at having himself been found out finding out; at having (consequently) to do something about it; at the tawdry symbolism of the antlers being clasped all around him, proffered like so many mocking mirrors – and Tszvetan and Tild, blinking in the hostile daylight, shamed and naked but at the same time silently defiant. They stare back at the assembled company with eyes so piercing that courtiers avert theirs; to Louis Q, the eyes say: *Yes. You willed it, and it happened. What are you going to do?* The regent has no choice. He decrees that Tszvetan and Tild be executed in the public square come the diurnal's zenith. Marloe, though, who truly is a shit, ventures to suggest to him that Tild instead be handed over, straight away, to Kern's *leperosi* – poor sub-citizens who, afflicted by a meteor-borne virus that both disfigures and cripples them, causing rank lesions to erupt across their skin before eating its way down into their flesh, which in turn causes toes, fingers, sometimes entire limbs to auto-amputate … These creatures, shunned by employers, landlords and just about everyone else due to the highly infectious character of their disease, find themselves condemned to endless wandering about Kern's empty precincts, waste grounds, marsh- and border-zones, from which they emerge intermittently, en masse, to shove mendicant, insufficiently digited hands at passers-by who recoil in revulsion from them. Why not, urges Marloe, hand Tild straight over to the group of them that they saw camped out in the disused old port as they rode back from the wetlands, and let them have their way with her?

In this, too, Louis Q is cornered: any temperance of his ire, ebbing to humble love of his revenge's violent pace, would be viewed as a sign of weakness – from a political, never mind personal, POV, ill-advised messaging. Tszvetan is popular, and the *plebeiani* seem to be taking Tild to their collective heart as well; a delay or commutation that leaves the two intact could birth a dangerous ambivalence in terms of public loyalties, open an interregnum in which fealty might start swinging, see the younger couple take on the aspect of a parallel royal household, a new court-in-waiting . . . No: it behoves Louis Q to be swift and brutal, and accept Marloe's baroque proposal. So it is: Tszvetan to be burned, today, in the *piazzo*; Tild to be gang-banged to death, gangrenously, by Kern's *leperosi*.

'You're sure you want them climbing over each other like this?' Phocan asks Herzberg as the two men watch Sardinen's *akrobater* mounting one another's backs and shoulders, then, formations grown top-heavy, tumbling off again to roll about the floor before once more finding their feet and seeking out newly forming masses to join up with.

'Absolutely,' the AD decisively responds. 'It's what Lukas wants. The *leperosi* manifest as a collective body. They *represent* collectiveness – a counterpoint to the heroic individualism of the main characters; and . . . there was something else too . . .'

'Okay,' Phocan says. 'It's just a little difficult to . . .'

'Also,' Herzberg continues, recalling Dressel's involved lecture on the matter, delivered to him by the great director back in London on the eve of his departure here, 'disease, infection and affliction: these are low embodiments of the desire that's overtaken the two lovers. He mentioned *Death in Venice*: how the plague, you know, all the collapsing bodies, symbolise the moral downfall of the upright and respectable composer, his "abandonment to longing's putrefaction" ...'

Phocan hasn't seen *Death in Venice*. But he knows that markering and mo-capping a 'collective body' is going to be a headache – paradoxically, since a gangling, multi-limbed monster is precisely what you often get before you extricate and allocate the portions; that latter task (extricating, allocating) being the very one to which he's just last week been trying to convince the IACSS crowd that Pantarey's Physis 6™ is perfectly suited. Here, though, the sequence is reversed. The production *to order* of an artefact, of tangle and confusion, isn't as simple as you might presume – unpredictable or indeterminate conglomerations being characterised, after all, by indeterminacy, unpredictability ...

'Let's,' he tells Herzberg after thinking for a moment, 'get them markered up, and have them do their tumbling and re-amalgamating as per your directions, and we'll just see what we get, take it from there.'

Watching the sequences three hours later, rain playing against Sardinen's corrugated roof the only background noise now *akrobater* have been stood down and decamped, collectively, to a bar round the corner named *Sardinkan* (with effusive hospitality as buoyant as their leaps and bounces, they urged Phocan and Herzberg to come join them once they'd finished what they 'had to do'), Phocan is pleasantly surprised at the results. The mass of future *leperosi,* as yet featureless and unadorned with poxed and lacerated skin, limb-stumps, lecherous grins, and so on – they'll acquire those in London, at DZ – do indeed seem to function as one single, if unusually configured, organism, whose decentralised intelligence flows around it in a current as it, too, wends simultaneously one way and another, coalescing like continuous rainfall round the body of the girl – as it happens, Phocan's raincoat-selecting assistant Trine – who's standing in for Tild, or rather for Rosanna Wilmington.

'I like it.' Herzberg nods approval over Phocan's shoulder. 'I think Lukas will too. Let's go join our friends in the Sardine Can.'

Herzberg's satisfaction with his little pun deflates as soon as they arrive to find that *Sardinkan* does indeed mean 'sardine can': a graphic of one, hanging over the bar's entrance, leaves no room for doubt on this front. Inside, it's as packed as one, acrobats crammed around tables, perched on barrels, windowsills and ledges, straddling the wooden beams that run beneath the hostelry's low ceiling. They seem to have quite a heat on already; there's a jovial air about them; some of them are singing; others laugh as they pass phones around. Drinks are ordered for their guests, along with a new round for the Sardinen. When Phocan asks Trine, who's made space for him beside her, what they're looking at on the phones, she hands the one she's holding to him, and he scrolls through scores of snaps of acrobats in various states and shapes: crumpled, starred, falling, swallow-diving, flailing, rising, soaring, catapulting ...

'How do you know who's who?' he asks. Most of the jpegs show them in bodysuits, or with head tucked under legs, or stretched back upwards so the face is turned away.

'We don't,' she shrugs. 'It doesn't really matter. What's important is to find new figures and new permutations.'

'But ...' he starts – then finds he can't find the words for his quibble.

'Yes ... ?' Trine prompts, wiping a giant beer-head tidemark from around her mouth.

'I mean ... Aren't you proud when it's *you* who's found one?'

'That's not how we think,' she tells him. 'It's never about *us* finding something, or *us* owning a particular action ... We're trained to see our bodies as the place where the action occurs.'

'And your face?' he asks.

'What about it?' Trine asks back.

'When Rosanna Wilmington's is plastered over it ... Won't you feel, you know, kind of cancelled out?'

'I was never "in" in the first place,' Trine replies.

Phocan's about to ask her what she means, but just then another round arrives, ordered this time by Herzberg.

'Half the film's budget gone right there!' he shouts as he passes out the tankards. 'Pantarey can get the next one.'

This Pantarey does – after which Phocan's at least half-cut, as are the company in general: their bodies seem to glide from beam to ledge to chair to bar counter more fluidly, without definite outlines; bar counter and beam seem to be gliding too, their borders shifting, realigning. Then it's out again into the acrobatic rain, surging and turning, hovering and bouncing. Trine's beside him, holding his arm, and the cobblestones are running till they're back at his hotel; then somehow he, like Bergen's rain, has managed to fall up two flights of stairs to his second-floor bedroom, sadly without Trine it seems, although someone is holding forth to him on the subject of anonymity – or is it just him, talking to himself, lying face down, forehead intersected by the raised wooden threshold between lounge and bathroom … ?

The threshold mark will stay with him, forehead-imprinted, for most of the following day; in his scrambled state he'll associate it, every time he glimpses it in rain-blurred glass, not simply with Trine – that is, with Trine's absence – but also with vaguer, modulating sequences, chains of imperfectly reflected episodes that regress backward, passing through Rafaella Farinati, telescoping off into some dark recess that memory, at least his right now, isn't up to the task of illuminating. Now, waking up still splayed across the doorway, the rain still crackling out a constant background static on the walls and windowpanes, its aquacity crowing at his dehydration, he drinks all the bottled water in his minibar, then refills the container from his bathroom tap. Flipping his laptop open, he finds awaiting him amidst the inbox clutter two emails of note. One has a *.lv* address: Latvia. It's from Raivis Vanins' office, and it bears, prefaced by a *re:*, the header (*Possibility of Jumelans visit?*) of his own email from four days previously. It reads:

Dear Dr Phocan,

Professor Vanins thanks you for your interest in his work. His research into states of equilibrium was principally conducted

several decades ago, and has not until quite recently elicited the type of curiosity you communicate. The Professor
draws your attention to the holdings of Rīgas Tehniskā
Univerisitāte's Solid-State Physics Department, where the
bulk of his archive is kept, and suggests you begin by consulting these. He asks me to add that, should you still wish
to meet with him in person, he will, in deference to his old
acquaintance your patron Dr Garnett, be prepared to make
time for you. Should such an interview be desired, he suggests a date after 13 September.

Yours,

Lazda Krūmiņa
pp Professor Vanins

Patron? Nice word: paternal. No mention of black boxes: why
would there be? They weren't alluded to in the overtures to
Vanins made by first Garnett and then, once the channel of communication had been opened, him. Reading this Lazda Krūmiņa's
response, Phocan feels fraudulent, borderline criminal – an impos-
tor, even if he's not, his sense of alienation from the straight path
of his calling amplified by this appalling hangover. Maybe he
played up his strategic fascination with the states-of-equilibrium
stuff too much: is there an edge of suspicion to the surprise
expressed by her, or perhaps through her by the Professor, about
his Trojan horse, his *violon d'ingres*? He's not able, this morning,
to gauge innuendo levels. What does *until quite recently* mean ...?
The second message comes from a generic account, no national
suffix – but the address grabs his attention straight away: it's
a.pirotti@gmail.com. The header: *808*. It opens with the same
salutation as the other:

Dear Dr Phocan,

It was edifying and encouraging to meet you in Rome. I
wonder how your enquiries into the subject we discussed

up on the hillside are proceeding. Do keep me up to date. Perhaps we could connect in Riga, should you find yourself in that neck of the woods at any point in the near future.

I remain your friend and well-wisher,

A.P.

Now, just as when he met Pirotti in the flesh a week ago, Phocan feels disoriented, vertiginous. It's more than just the toxins and potassium depletion: it's the sudden groundlessness induced by overlap of territories that should find themselves far apart, unconnected – as though, in their fibre-optic relay to him, or perhaps within the very silver casing of his laptop, two separate fields had intersected, *read* each other, breached whatever barriers had been put in place, by geography, technology and just plain reality, to keep them separate and unrelated. *Riga*: how on earth ...? In London, as soon as he'd returned from Rome, he looked up Cassius First Motion, and found nothing; he scoured online directories of mo-cap companies, not that this was necessary: the industry is small, he knows them all, but there are always fledglings, start-ups ... nothing; then of general tech, CGI outfits *à la* Degree Zero, sports-science labs, data-security firms – still nothing. Cassius didn't exist. There was, of course, the number on the card – but to phone *that* would have entailed a step beyond another threshold, the betrayal one. Industrial espionage. Why didn't he report the tapping-up to Garnett or Hossain immediately on his return? He doesn't know the answer to that; but for some reason, he didn't. It seemed too intimate, a *peccadillo* almost. And then Farinati's role, if she was part of it ... Should he have read her over-the-shoulder smile? Her pointed marking of his lapel? Or seen through her proffered not-quite-assignation on the Palatino, the most obvious place in all of Rome? Now this ... He throws on his anorak and heads out into the rain.

The day at Sardinen is spent, once more, capturing tumbling, dis- and reassembling bodies. Once his nausea's been quashed by sugar-intake, Phocan settles into a quiet rhythm, watching leprous forms advance with an irregular regularity, a faceless multitude that seems to sense and think and measure time through its collective body: Lukas's formulation, planted in his mind by Herzberg, repeats itself for him as he sits editing sequences after the live-capture session's finished, playing the same short stretches over and over ... *liberating dynamism of the great machine* ... in the rain's crackle and his laptop's hum, Gastev's lines take shape too. Or was it *erupting*? The more Phocan watches, the more abstract the sequences grow: pixels, shearing from the mass's body to form new blocks, take on the aspect of cells, plasmatic units in search of new clusters and new designations. *Non aberranti ma esemplari* ... Farinati's words to him also seem to ricochet around the cannery's airspace. In his addled state, reason all but capsized by great waves of glucose-level fluctuation, Phocan, for some reason, finds his mind drifting back to the extensive disquisitions that Diamond, when she was still wet behind the ears, Pantarey intern, drew from him on artefacts, subject that seemed to fascinate her. No matter how much he tried to impress on her that these were nothing more than the result of glitches, bugs, shortcomings in the code, she kept pushing her homespun thesis that they might in fact be caches for 'a type of information that we haven't yet learnt to interpret'.

'How do you mean?' he asked, bemused.

'You know, like in the old days, when rheumatics' knee-joints foretold thunder-storms. Or with PTSD'd veterans like my friend Aidan' – this man's name, ever since Phocan's knightly rescue of her from his clutches, had become a kind of bonding joke between them – 'how some weird, neurotic quirk they keep repeating, that makes no sense, is really a symptom that encodes a trauma-scene too awful to be captured as "official" memory but, thanks to the, you know, encoding, manages to sit right in the open, hidden in plain sight ...'

He mock-swatted at her head with the data wand he was holding.

'Doesn't work like that. They're glitches. Software failure. End of story.'

Today, though, he's suddenly not so sure, finds himself prey to an inversion as total as that of yesterday's Acapulcan plungers. What if ... what if artefacts, rather than marking a limitation, an inadequacy, were ... What if, contrary to all evidence, to logic itself ... if they were the very thing most *true* in all configurations – tokens, splinters of a stratum of reality so deep, so sedimented, that it hasn't yet been charted, let alone assigned grid-coordinates, a vessel or a form, but ... ? And if ... then ...

No, the thought won't take shape, probably because it's *kwatsch* as well. Fuckin' kids: Eldridge was right. Phocan closes the *leperosi* file and pops open another, *falling.vp*. There are those plungers: a body, male or female, tightly clad in a black, marker-studded bodysuit, is dropping from one of the loading doors towards a mat. Phocan's got seven versions of the plunge: some clumsy, others more streamlined and aerodynamic, some neither-nor; same body, or different ones, performing each – impossible to tell, and doesn't matter. It will eventually become a fleeing Tild, plummeting flailing from a cliff edge to be caught in mid-air by a pirogue-riding Tszvetan; also *leperosi* One, Two and Three, and perhaps Four and Five, too, hurtling to their deaths as they lunge and grope after her. Phocan runs the flailingest dive-sequence through several times; then a more placid one; then, for no reason besides whimsy, he freezes this second dive in mid-fall, runs it backwards, then forwards, then backwards again, so that the figure yo-yos up and down, before eventually freezing it once more in mid-air. Thus arrested, its kinetic panic is transformed, communicating now a kind of serene unconcern that Phocan finds soothing. Spreading outwards from his screen, it seems to overtake not just the space here in Sardinen but beyond too – Rome, London, Riga; to usher in a general state in which things, all things, find themselves caught up in the same general, if unnameable, contraption, and the world, its stakes, its struggles, all hang in the balance.

Book Three

1. *Cidonija*

Like the cracked skin of *leperosi*, the Gulf of Livonia's surface is stretched by the wind and furrowed by the wakes of ferries plying their corridors between Riga and Stockholm, Riga and Helsinki, Riga and St Petersburg. There are larger ships too – tankers bearing freight-stacks, corrugated blue and red and yellow boxes piled five-high. In one of her dispatches, this woman (he presumes that it's a woman for some reason) whose name has been blacked out in the *01mdean02cdorley* printouts he's been handed mentions *Dracula*: Lillian Gilbreth's fascination with the novel's boxes, with the Count shipping his earth-lair in a set of crates from Transylvania to England ... Phocan's got boxes on his mind. The first Latvian houses that slip into view beneath the wing, laid out across a strip of sandy beach or dotted amid trees and inland waterways, look like the cargoes' freight containers, colourful and wrinkled through their overlay of plank strips. The same type of wooden house lines the road into town, strangely anachronistic next to glass towers of banks and international hotels. Above his taxi, like the streaked track of a wireframe, tram cables run – always in duplicate, a double line bending and kinking as it traces, in advance, his one best way towards this assignation with Vanins, with Lazda Krūmiņa, with (whisper it) the possibility, the spectre, of Box 808.

But not all the way; not yet. The vagaries of airline scheduling have deposited him in Riga two days before he's to be received at Vanins' dacha, which seems to lie a few miles out of town on a commuter train line. Lazda, with whom he's by now had enough rounds of correspondence to be on first-name terms, has given him detailed instructions for getting there, and even mooted the possibility of a night's stay, but on the date she's been inflexible: the Professor will be available on 14 September, not a day before. As soon as he's dumped his suitcase in his eighth-floor room at the Intercontinental, Phocan makes his way, through empty squares guarded by old orthodox churches whose gold roofing seems to splay itself out, disco-ball-style, in the yellow of autumn foliage on branches, lawns, paths, steps and gutters, past ornately corniced civic buildings alternating with dilapidated work yards, telecoms outlets with vacant lots, towards Tehniskā Universitāte's archival and administrative building. It's a dark grey edifice with opaque windows, sitting on a square that's given over to a Red Guard monument, several bus stations and a taxi stand, and separated from the city's broad and charmless river by a four-lane carriage-way. The lobby's full of frescoed portraits, men Phocan has never heard of: Konstantīns Pēkšēns, Vilhelms Ostvalds, Etjēns Laspeiress, Eižens Laube, August Toeplers, Alvils Buholcs ... There's a frescoed map, too, charting these savants' diaspora to the Americas, Australia, the vast swathes of Soviet Europe, Soviet Asia ... None of them seems to have stayed in Latvia.

A lone receptionist in a glass booth is unsure where to send him; after a few calls on her internal phone she directs him to a third-floor office. But he gets lost on his way there, finds himself wandering long, empty corridors whose marble slabs embed what looks like a circuit-pattern, pared down and abstracted, stripped of all resistors and inductors, switches and capacitors and any component that might impede its linearly superimposable advance along the floor, past vacant leather armchairs, unappreciated plants and columns both of plaster and of dusty sunlight. Occasionally, emboldened by the solitude, the absence of mounted cameras, Phocan interprets a door's ajarness as an invitation, and intrudes soft-footedly on empty studies in which test tubes and retorts, loop tracers and lab flumes, interferometers, resonance tube apparatuses, polarimeters, ballistic galvanometers, Van de Graaff generators, pipettes, burettes and barometers lie around workbenches beside open notebooks whose pages give off in mid-scribble, as though suddenly abandoned – not a half-hour ago, nor a day, or week, or even year: these rooms are musty, full of age and obsolescence, of hypotheses and theorems dissipated without being distilled, embryonic worlds that never found their frequency or form. In one room a chipped wooden ladder leans against shelves that seem to have been ransacked, their books strewn across the floor or toppled, domino-like, over one another, box files tipped back, spilling photos, letters, pamphlets. On another's windowsill, old Soviet quarterlies are precariously stacked. Phocan palms through them, finds an English one, flips open to an article: *Electrolyte Solutions: Literature Data on Thermodynamic and Transport Properties*, by Victor M. M. Lobos and I. Quaresma, 1956. Beside the windowsill an old machine keeps watch, a buttoned, dialled and tubed contraption at whose function he can't even guess; it has gauges and needles on it, maybe a sonometer – but there's nothing that might serve as pick-up. To its upper surface has been taped a kind of crib-sheet, but the lettering's Cyrillic . . .

The archivist, when he finally locates her and hands her his card, reacts with surprise not only to his visit but also to the idea that there might be archives, in this building, of the sort he's looking for. Vanins? Phocan's dropping of the name, by now infused for him – as, it seems, for quite a few others – with magical, totemic qualities, falls flat. Perhaps it was the way that he pronounced it. He tries *Var-neenz*, but to no avail. The archivist, if that's what she is, prods about her own internal phone (like the receptionist's, an old push-button auto-dialler) and, after two short dialogues in Latvian, informs him that most faculty documents from the sixties and seventies have been moved to a storage facility on the outskirts of town. She gives him an address, which he then thrusts at one of the taxi drivers waiting at the Red Guards' feet.

It starts to rain during the drive – a rain more gravity-observant than Bergen's. Soviet-era housing blocks run into one another, streaking and reforming in the windscreen wipers' screen-save. The facility, lying off a road that turns to mud as prefab office blocks give over to decrepit warehouses and car breakers, is fenced, barriered and gated; but there's no one at the gatepost and the barrier is up, so they drive straight into the compound and crawl hesitantly past ramped loading bays and shuttered entrance windows. Above these, and them, a bunker-type building rises five storeys tall; large metal signage, battened to its roof, spells out the storage firm's name: *RIGASTOCK*. Beneath the letters, draped all the way back down to the first floor, a billboard optimistically flashes Rigastock's phone number and URL to passing trade. A woman walking, umbrella-less, from one of the building's side doors towards her parked car scurries past Phocan when he jumps out of the taxi to accost her; a large man in overalls smoking a cigarette, though, similarly unprotected from but seemingly untroubled by the rain, cranes his head down to listen a minute later. He appears not to understand a word that Phocan says to him – but, answering in what sounds like Russian, leads him up one of the loading ramps, then through another side entrance, then down a corridor towards a lift. This conveys them to a fifth-floor storage space whose concrete walls are lined with ventilation ducting, fire extinguishers and buckets, two of which have been moved out to spots around the floor, also concrete, to catch the drips falling from the ceiling. Eventually, they arrive at a wooden door; the large man knocks on this; a woman, opening it, welcomes Phocan into a carpeted office hung with pastoral-idyllic paintings showing *radjar*-like antlered deer cavorting around forests of a lurid, almost psychedelic colouration. The large overalled worker bows his head and retreats, leaving them alone.

This woman turns out to speak no more English than the worker did. She asks Phocan if he understands Russian; he tells her he doesn't. They eventually establish that they both have a few words of German – enough for him to convey what it is he's after and for her to tell him that if that's the case he's not allowed to be here: it's a private storage company; and besides, if the archives he wants to consult come from a Soviet-era state facility they'll have a seventy-five-year embargo slapped on them; on top of all which, she now has to close the office, to go pick her daughter up from school. She more or less frogmarches him downstairs and outside again; but, seeing him scour the compound for his taxi, which by now is long departed, she takes pity on him and, telling him he'll never manage to summon a new one out here, offers to drive him back to town. Thus he returns, wetter but no wiser than he was when he left it three hours ago, to the Intercontinental.

'Why're state archives being held in commercial storage spaces?' he asks an American tech worker on to whom, two drinks in, he's unloading – in generic, unspecific form yet still perhaps, it strikes him the next morning, in view of the tendency of Pirottis to pop up in places where you're least expecting them, imprudently – his frustration in the hotel's bar. 'Or, more to the point: why are they being held in private storage, but still covered by the censorship laws of a state that no longer exists?'

'This place is kind of schizophrenic,' Kyle (the name's still pinned to the guy's T-shirt) tells him. 'After independence, they privatised everything, but didn't overhaul the infrastructure or even the personnel. A third of the banks went bankrupt; the owners of another third are now in jail; and the last third are making hay as money-laundromats. *Their* owners would be in jail too if they weren't in government, or at least pally with it. The censorship is from the new regime: they don't want all the dirt on who was shopping whom to come out while the shoppers are still skipping around in public. Plus,' Kyle, also at least two drinks in, is warming to his subject, 'what you have to appreciate is that almost half the population here are ethnic Russians. They speak Russian, call the Latvians "Nazis" – which, during the War, they were – see the Soviet Union's collapse as a catastrophe and keep nagging Putin to send back the tanks.'

'I can't work out,' Phocan twists his straw reflectively, as though the answer lay amidst the ice cubes, 'whether the vibe here's ultra-modern or just retro, left behind.'

'Both at once,' Kyle says decisively. 'Riga's always looked both ways, ever since its Hanseatic League days, when it served Peter the Great as gateway to an open, i.e. unfrozen, seaboard. It's skimming distance now from Scandinavian comm-techs, and at the same time still tied umbilically to swathes of Steppe and centuries of peasantry. If you go down to the covered markets by the train station, you'll see old women from the countryside sitting all day long, each at their own little table or beside a tattered quilt their grandmother made, trying to sell five shrivelled turnips, staring into space.'

He turns to the barman and orders more vodka tonics. When they come he picks up where he left off: 'During the Cold War, Riga was an intersection point for spies. This hotel,' he lowers his voice, 'would have been rigged up with microphones – not to mention pretty girls to drink with, take up to your room, whisper restricted info to. Now,' he concludes, scrutinising him through vodka spectacles, 'it's just us.'

Phocan excuses himself and retires, alone, to bed. Next morning, as he's heading to the market to see for himself the Stoic turnip sellers, he receives a call from the first archivist, the Tehniskā Universitāte's one, who has not only kept his card but also gone to the bother of doing some ferreting around for him. They have some Vanins-related items in their building after all; he's welcome to come look at them. These transpire to be mainly articles he's authored: *Resistance Gradients in Mesospheric Flight*, 1968; *Benefits and Disadvantages of Delta Wing Configuration*, 1964; plus several more in Russian. There's a folder full of notes, too – drawings, sketches, jottings, and so forth. No letters from Lillian; no sudden *T.T.* enigma-solving key or cipher; but – gold dust it seems at first, then, as time wears on without any actual revelation, let alone *eureka!* moment, ensuing, just dust – he does come across the number *808*. It's written – more exactly, drawn – beneath a chart listing dynamic properties of the Tu-144 aircraft: the two figure-eights separated by the not-quite circle (Pirotti was right: it's more of an ellipsoid). 'Drawn' as in doodled – whimsically, as though Vanins had been daydreaming during a meeting, let his mind drift in the middle of some computations … And repeatedly: as it progresses, it rotates until each of its digits is lying horizontal on the page, one beneath the other, *0* under *8*, two

8s beneath each *0*, the whole sequence hanging vertically, like a flourish underneath a signature, a spring, or possibly (perhaps he wasn't daydreaming at all) the type of flight-path that the figures given in the chart might produce in the Tu-144. For an instant, Phocan's back at Farnborough, surrounded by the whine of Roger's air-decorating drones. They called it *Buzzby Berkeley*, two zs: 'Little Web of Dreams' ... That Aidan character hitting on Diamond in the outer room ... the austere and elusive Pilkington ... Phocan's alone: the archivist's left him the side-room to her office. Glancing at the door, he slips his phone out, turns the sound off, takes a quick snap of the page and pockets it again; then steps out, thanks her for her help and heads back down the circuit-patterned marble corridor feeling cheap and treacherous, a spy in a hotel ...

Next morning, finally, he hops on a commuter train to Jumelans. The carriages are quaint: blue-yellow-orange on the outside with steep steps to their high doors, decked out with wooden seats wide as park benches inside. The conductor can't be more than eighteen; he's got up, *Saturday Night Fever* style, in a uniform consisting of side-lapel skinny blazer and large-collar shirt unbuttoned to the base of his ribcage. They trundle out along a spit of land bordered by inlets, past old wooden houses camouflaged by foliage of spruces, ferns and taller trees he can't identity, past fishing dinghies lost in reeds, stopping at single-platform stations for two, or four, or no passengers to board and alight. Most have wooden ticket offices or waiting rooms, the same plank-strip overlay he noticed from the plane, with faded signage in both Latin and Cyrillic. One, though, the last stop before Jumelans, a place called Siliciems, sports a new, asymmetrical steel station house topped with a racing quiff or 'accent', whose implied speed matches the building's slant – a construction of the type that calls attention to itself as architecture, as commission.

'It's for the super-rich who come from Russia to Siliciems for the New Wave Festival each year,' Lazda will tell him when he comments on it in the car. 'A waste of money, since most of them arrive by limousine, with chauffeurs, or even by helicopter; never train. They stay in the spas, which get guards at their entrances, and the town's suddenly full of plastic lips and boobies, and for one week of the year a cappuccino costs ten euros. The whole festival's a cover; no one's interested in New Wave; they come here to do business deals off Moscow's radar.'

Lazda speaks near-perfect English with a heavy Baltic accent. She's the only person waiting at Jumelans for the Riga train. She's wearing jeans and a light army-surplus jacket, standing beside a Skoda's open driver-side door.

'Phocan,' she says, pulling off, pronouncing the two syllables inquisitively. 'It is a typical English name?'

'It's anglicised,' he answers. 'It refers to Phocis, a region in Greece – to Phocans, who come from there. I suppose I must be ...'

'I read your papers,' she cuts him off, changing gear.

'*My* papers? I haven't ...'

'*Bodily Differentiation in Haptic Event-Modelling*. Also: *Sequence Layout for Generic Simulations* ...'

'Wow. I didn't think anyone knew about those. That first one was my thesis.'

'It's all online,' she tells him as they pass a small, derelict factory whose brickworks are being reclaimed by the forest. 'I like to know who comes to see my grandfather.'

'He's your grandfather? I thought you were just ...' But this thought is swallowed by his second question, which, turning to face her, he lets loose too quickly: 'Many people come?'

She pauses before answering, scanning the rear-view mirror. 'Sometimes they come, and go again. Then others come; then no one for some time, then several close together. I don't think they find what they're looking for.'

Is there a mocking tenor to the words? An accusation in them? Her voice isn't hostile; there's a kind of knowing irony to it, though. It prompts him to defend himself pre-emptively:

'I'm interested in his work on states of equilibrium. Are you a scientist too?'

'No,' she says. 'Art History. I'm an assistant professor here in Riga.'

'But you serve as his secretary?'

'No one else provided him with one,' she says – then, turning the tables, asks: 'Who are you working for?'

'Pantarey,' he replies defensively. 'I laid it all out in our first email exchange; and the research param ...'

'Yes,' she cuts him off dismissively. 'I know. Who are they working for?'

It's as though she'd slammed the brakes on, or they'd pulled up at some kind of road block or control point. The conversation restarts, but a threshold has been passed.

'Several clients,' he says, feeling paradoxically less, not more, defensive – not because the question's not aggressive but because, in this instance at least, he genuinely doesn't know. 'We have partners of all types – universities, medical research firms, sports science, entertainment, aerospace ...'

'Partners,' she bounces the term back at him.

'Our founder,' he tells her, both illogically (since it doesn't follow) and (since she already knows) redundantly, 'knew the ... your grandfather.'

She sniffs and turns off the main road on to a small track lined with narrow ditches and with houses, some no larger than allotment cabins, others more elaborate, but all bearing the marks of having been assembled on the hoof, as patchworked as the foliage whose colours blend and jar around them. The track intersects another, similarly ditch- and house-lined, then, almost immediately, a third, into which Lazda makes a right turn before pulling off, just opposite a tiny and abandoned-looking children's playground, into what he takes to be the Vanins property.

It's an old place – several places, more a complex than a single building – built around a garden. There's a two-storey main house of light blue wood, to which a one-floor brick extension has been added; lying across a lawn from this, a kind of hybrid barn or greenhouse whose unpainted wood strips alternate with glass and corrugated plastic rises as high as the house it faces. Further in, at the garden's far end, its base obscured by an overgrown vegetable patch, a treehouse stands, cubistic and irregularly proportioned, its undulating roof of small wood tiles inset with non-aligned, oddly shaped skylights. Phocan's eye darts, as he steps from the car on to grass whose texture has a softness his shoes haven't felt for a long time, from one place to another, wondering which opening, which plane or vista Vanins will appear from; wondering beyond that just how this *name*, this presence that till now has manifested itself to him only in sentences on paper, as report and rumour, ubiquitous but unlocatable reverberation, might be translated into and embodied in a frame of roughly, give or take a little, the same size as his. It seems almost unthinkable ... There's movement in the greenhouse-barn – is that him? It's in the upper stretches of the glass and plastic; and the lower, and all over: dark patches flapping, shadows sweeping and retreating, at a scale too big, it seems, to issue from a single human, a formation too dispersed and mutable to come from humans at all ...

'He's sleeping,' Lazda says. For a moment Phocan confuses this snippet of information with the shadow-puppet show he's watching, the strange silhouettes – as though the flickering were Vanins' dream, the glass and plastic membranes his translucent mind-scrim. They're both wrong, though: Vanins is awake, and walking from the low-lying part of the main house towards them. Phocan knows it's him and not a gardener or housekeeper from the wave of care that sweeps through Lazda's body once she's caught sight of the thin man in the light-brown pullover, diminutive against the bricks: the way she opens her whole stance towards him, takes a half-step forwards, as though to assist him as he steps on to uneven lawn, then, catching herself, holds the motion, keeping it in check or in reserve, her muscles still alert, on call in case they're needed. They're not: the old man proceeds steadily, diminutive against the grass his feet don't seem to flatten, diminutive still as he reaches Phocan and holds out a light and fragile hand.

'You are Garnett's missile.'

The voice, too, is light; if not exactly fragile, it's still textured, grained by age.

'Missile?' asks Phocan.

'I mean missive. Garnett's envoy.'

Phocan nods. 'He sends best wishes to you.'

Vanins unclasps his hand, then, prompted by the sight of something beyond Phocan's shoulder, asks:

'You like *cidonija*?'

'I'm sorry ... ?'

Vanins says something in Latvian to Lazda. She disappears into the house. The old man holds his arm out, inviting Phocan to follow her; they traipse inside. *Cidonija* turns out to be quince, dried, sliced and sugared. They eat them from a china bowl, with milkless black tea, also sugared. Lazda is quiet while Vanins floats Phocan general enquiries about Pantarey's projects, his own background, the state of kinaesthetic and fluid-dynamic research in the UK ... About the more specific reasons for Phocan's visit, the equilibrium-state stuff, he asks nothing – either because he's taking it as understood, established between them already, or perhaps because he senses, on some frequency, that, like the New Wave Festival, it's just a front, a cover. Behind her look of disengagement, Lazda's listening carefully: Phocan can tell, can feel her scanning his responses as though they formed a long, unbroken printout being cranked out by a polygraph. Eventually Vanins rises and says:

'Come with me to the aviary. We can talk there.'

Back across the lawn, the greenhouse-barn reveals its secret, or at least one of them: the patches and silhouettes are made by birds' wings flapping against the glass and plastic. There must be scores of them in here, large and small: swifts, plovers, waxwings, crakes and sandpipers and wrens, wagtails and pipits, all the way down to the common thrush and sparrow, flitting from wall to shelf or darting in and out of the small birdhouses dotted about the beams. There are plants, too, pushing against windows, trailing twines from rafters, drawing finely woven curtains round two or three armchairs and a sofa spread about the floor.

'I built it myself, in the sixties,' Vanins tells him. 'It was not easy. In Soviet times you couldn't buy materials; but you could *get* them. You had to negotiate: you went to a sawmill with your own wood and asked them to cut it for you in exchange for three litres of homemade apple brandy, or a kilogram of courgettes. Now,' he adds with a laugh beneath whose sugar coating bitterness is stored, 'you can buy anything; but no one can afford it.'

'How long,' asks Phocan, 'have you had this dacha?'

'It was my father's,' Vanins answers. 'Normally, under communism, it would have been confiscated; I could even have been exiled or shot for owning private property. In my case, the state took it, but they let me lease it back, since I had dispensation: my position at the Universitāte ... The *aviary* I said I needed in order to carry out research into bird flight, in the tradition of Marey.'

'Did you carry it out?' *Marey*: Phocan's been learning about him these last few weeks, since he in turn loomed big (as *01mdeanetc.* also records) in Gilbreth's formative prehistory – first person to translate into sinuous curves captured on paper, glass or, later, photographic plate the movements of soldiers, patients, cats and all manner of subjects locomoting, pulsing, flowing, flying. Diagrams of birds rigged up with harnesses and *stylographs*, hallucinatory negatives of each stage of the wing's transit superimposed in single-frame simultaneity, float now from the textbooks Garnett pressed into his hand and flap around his mind.

'I observed them,' Vanins smiles wryly. 'I looked after them, and still do.'

His hand sweeps a few seeds scattered about a counter into a small pile, which he then pinches in his fingers and holds up to feed two wagtails and a thrush who perch just long enough to snatch one each before darting away again. Vanins' eyes follow them as they disappear into one of the birdhouses, then turn back to Phocan as he declaims, in frail but steady tones:

'*How do you know but ev'ry Bird that cuts the airy way / Is an immense world of delight, clos'd by your senses five?*'

'I'm sorry?' Phocan asks.

'Marey's biographer chose those lines as epigraph. Do you like birds?'

'I like movement,' says Phocan. 'And I like equilibrium.'

'So you have said,' Vanins replies. 'I invite you to stay for supper. In which case, you should remain here overnight; there are no trains back into Riga after seven. You can stay in the treehouse.'

'I would be delighted,' Phocan answers. 'Perhaps then we can talk a little more about your work on ...'

'Later,' Vanins tells him. 'Now, I'm tired.'

He motions Phocan to the aviary's door, and out across the lawn. On the far side of this, the treehouse's skylights are lit up. Lazda emerges from beneath them, folded pillowcase in hand. Has she been preparing the place for him? Was the decision to have him stay already made? As they approach the main house Vanins stops in his tracks and says:

'Marey, as you know, was fascinated by it.'

'States of equilibrium?'

'No,' Vanins looks bemused; 'tiredness. That was one of the main goals of all his research: to eliminate fatigue. He saw it as a moral – as a *spiritual* – affliction, scourge of a nation exhausted by defeat to Germany, by absinthe and hashish, by *ennui* ... His *Station Physiologique* was set up to re-galvanise the youth, to bring the clerk or manual labourer into alignment with the soldier and the gymnast, infuse them, and the body politic in general, with the energy and dynamism of the locomotive – or the bird ...'

He closes the aviary's door gently behind them, before adding:

'But me, I'm tired.'

Later, as he lies with Lazda on the aviary's sofa, sweat cooling on their skin, Phocan will ponder this exchange again, wondering if Vanins' words held some kind of accusation, or acknowledgement, or resignation ... Wondering, too, again, on whose behalf he's been sent here. *Missile*: was the malaprop really an error? Like his granddaughter, the old man speaks English with a heavy Baltic accent, but the grammar's perfect ... These reflections are for later, though: tomorrow afternoon. Now, grainy and imprecise as the gloaming that surrounds the house's faint but warm electric haze, Vanins' utterance doesn't solicit a response.

2. Frisch Weht der Wind

'You can get away,' Herzberg finds himself explaining, 'with a lot more in a situation that's unfamiliar than in one that's familiar. A spaceship is not – to most people, most *other* people – familiar.'

Ben Briar, his addressee, holds fire, contrarian impulse overridden by the qualifiers *most* and *other*. Herzberg, sensing a few more seconds of indulgence unfolding in front of him, continues:

'Now, you might think that this lack of a comparator, of an experiential reference point or authority, would whip the rug out from beneath the possibility of empathic identification. On the part of the audience, I mean. But, paradoxically, it doesn't. Or rather, it creates an opening, the chance for a swift one-two. What I mean is, that you counteract the defamiliarisation by introducing, however incongruous they may seem, the *most* familiar, mundane objects of all, to make the whole scenario credible. So, here, we've thrown a simple fork in ...'

On the BenQ PV3200PT 32-inch 4K IPS Post-Production Monitor at which the two men, and a host of others grouped around them, stare, the fork, CGI rendering of your basic IKEA Livnära (chosen, for its generic tine spread and wood handle, over the more narrowly Scandi-connoting Förnuft), drifts languidly in mid-air down the *Sidereal*'s engine-room corridor, rotating as it passes the POV.

'*This* object, though,' Herzberg cautions in a stern tone, '*has* to be convincing. You must really go to town in terms of detail: where it shines, the metal's granularity, how aged it looks ...'

The fork continues its slow passage down its gravityless vector, emitting, like an isotopic sheen, the memory of every *castaplane* and *stoumpot* mouthful it has borne from plate to mouth – and not just those of surly and unmannered stokers, nor even the refined crockery and lips of such as Tild and Tszvetan, but also of each of its viewers here in this room and, beyond that, in the world at large, the universe outside these walls to which it seems to slowly inch, awaiting its launch through some hatch as yet unseen.

'The best lies,' Herzberg commentates as soon as he feels the allure of the fork's lustre fading, 'are ninety per cent truth.'

He teaches a design course at St Martins; it's a line he feeds his students. Here, though, the dynamic's different, the authority reversed. It's like a viva, or tenure-track meeting, or even disciplinary hearing. It's as though he were *pleading* for Briar's approval – framing everything in the man's terms, his Aristotelian metrics. *Realism Tsar*. He gets more nervous about, sleeps less each night before, having to interface with the adviser than he does when making presentations to people with actual executive power over him, the power of contract-termination, fingers resting on the levers of professional life and death: *they* treat him with the reverence due to a craftsman, defer to his artisanal expertise, whereas this guy ... The Two Cultures man is like a gruff version of Yoda. He may not be the Emperor, nor even a Sith Lord or Darth, but he's the keeper of the Force – and in this universe the Force, like charge in Argeral, is everything. Now Yoda's gearing up to speak, rolling his shoulders, grunting, as though inconveniently roused from a deep sleep.

'Before we start with forks,' he croaks, 'perhaps we could establish where this "wind" is coming from.'

It's a fair question. Herzberg has an answer, though:

'It's coming from the *Sidereal*'s prow, and rushing down towards its stern.'

'But how's it moving *down* it? Wouldn't it just sweep the *Sidereal* along *with* it, like a piece of chaff?'

'That isn't the effect we ...' Herzberg starts – then, self-censoring, tries again: 'Tszvetan is driving against the wind, head-on, engines full blast. He's also using the C-Anchors, which lock on to a coordinate and set the ship's position to that, rather than just relative to ...'

'Do you even know what solar wind is?' Briar witheringly interrupts.

'Well, sure. It's a ... it's a discharge,' Herzberg desperately tries to reconstruct the Wikipedia entry he glanced at a month ago, 'a stream of electrons, particles, and so on, discharged by a star when it ... when it, you know ...'

Briar cruelly lets the silence ring for a few seconds, before stating, in a casual, almost bored voice:

'It's a plasma-stream released by a sun's upper atmosphere. Its corona. As you say – correctly, if incompletely – a discharge of electrons, protons, alpha particles and other agents that have managed to amass escape velocity. It travels supersonically across the heliosphere until it runs into the termination shock – hitting which, and despite dropping to subsonic speeds, it propagates in front of it a bow wave that wreaks havoc with magnetic fields and gravitational configuration and incoming cosmic rays of any planetary atmospheres unlucky enough to find themselves in its path – indeed, that subjects planets without strong magnetospheres to complete atmospheric stripping.'

'That,' Herzberg jumps back in eagerly, 'is kind of what we're going for: stripping. We want the solar wind from Fidelus to *strip* the *Sidereal*, take it apart. That's why it needs to stay in place: so that the wind can unpick it, right down to its skeleton – and beyond, to nothing.'

Briar ponders this statement for a moment, then, surprisingly and to Herzberg's enormous relief, pronounces:

'That can work. Your ship would have to approach Fidelius ...'

'Fidelus.'

'... would travel through Fidelus's heliosphere, inwards from the heliopause towards the heliosheath, until it nears the termination shock. That's when the wind will hit it. But you have to understand: it isn't just a wind. As I've just intimated, it's a general cosmic fucking with all terms and values: gravity, polarity, attraction, radio-wave intensity, light ...'

'That's even better.' Herzberg's really happy now. 'Exactly what we want.' His hand moves across the desktop to *Incarnation*'s leather-bound, Post-it marker-swollen treatment and rests for a while atop it. It's not there for consultation or for prompting – the whole team know it by now almost by rote – but rather as a prop, a crook, a totem whose mere presence can gird and stabilise all realms, even the ones in which disastrous destabilisations are to play out ...

Tszvetan is indeed driving against the wind, in every sense. At the end of a string of plot-twists no less acrobatic than the MU acrobats performing in them – leaping, still shackled, from the flames licking at his feet from the lit pyre in Kern's *piazzo* on to the pirogue on which his friend and sidekick Govnal, gatecrashing the execution, whisks him away to safety; scything his rapier through scores of horny *leperosi* as he clears a path for, and then plucks from free-fall, Tild; fleeing with her to the Marais wildlands where, befriended by the hermit O. G. Rin, they live, royal clothes worn down to Tarzan-and-Jane strips, as hunter-foragers; then, as Louis Q's DF drones close in on them, making a bid for lasting freedom, re-entering Kern's citadel disguised as (what else?) *leperosi*, breaking into the docking-bay in which the *Sidereal* has been impounded, rapier-scything a few pound guards in the process (Govnal, meanwhile, has spread word among Tszvetan's loyal stokers, who are standing by to reman the vessel – after, naturally, doing a little scything of their own); and, finally, blasting their way (the harbour's tractor beams having been sabotaged by these same stokers) free of Kern's atmosphere, back up past Acephalus, beyond Ardis Minor, out into deep space.

Or, more precisely, towards Fidelus. The crew, preparing to set course for Patagon or maybe Nova Z once they've passed through the Sirin belt, are caught off-guard by Tszvetan's orders to keep bearing straight ahead. Tild, too – but neither she nor they say anything. With each passing diurnal a tacit understanding grows; and with it a complicity, a fatalist conviction, sets in. There's no habitable planet out there: only more asteroid belts, then empty interstellar medium, then, at the end of this, the heliosphere around the massive star. To enter that, to drive on through depletion and stagnation regions to the termination shock, can only be a one-way ticket – no one on the *Sidereal*'s in any doubt about that. If they go along with it, if they decline to mutiny or even comment on the starship's ill-boding trajectory, it's because their minds all seem to have coalesced around, been drawn into alignment by, a single intuition – unarticulated, perhaps inarticulable, but nonetheless as forceful and attractive as the monstrous conflagration towards which they're hurtling. It's tied in with the whole set-up of their tryst: its history, its circumstances and condition. For Tild, coupling with Tszvetan wasn't simply an *alternative* to being faithful to Louis Q, one possibility or option among others; it was a rejection of *all* options, of all possibilities, the very category – a plunge into the impossible. For Tszvetan, reciprocally, Tild was never just a quarry, Argeralan *radjar* to be hunted down, new entry to be jotted in his amorous kill list. Nor would it be correct to say that his desire for her was simply 'bigger' or 'stronger' than his sense of duty towards Louis Q, than his adherence to convention, his respect for codes of honour and the like. No: it, too, involved a bound beyond all binds and codes and underpinnings; it required the crossing of a threshold past which there exists no stable ground – just void. The void called them, and they came. What new ground, then, what planetary terrain, what minerality of soil and subsoil, could sustain this shadow-coupling, feed this love birthed through, of and into groundlessness? None: only the void might host it. If, on the voyage from Argeral to Kern, they found a habitus in light's delay, amidst the ultraviolet and the infrared of its obstruction, now, once more, it's to the spectrum's break-up, to the ravaging and disentanglement of light itself, of photons separated and expelled, transformed into a material force, to wind, that they will turn to find the non-place of their dwelling, found their kingdom of non-being. After the tenth diurnal they can spy, from the Observatory, diffracted through the viewfinders of astrolabe and spectrohelioscope, the strange flickerings of Fidelus's current sheet, rippling like a ballerina's skirt; then, with naked eye two diurnals later, aurora, swirling ghostly in the star's magnetosphere, celestial will-o'-the-wisps, beckoning . . .

The modelling here's complex – even more than for the first seduction scene. Light-waves will need to be not only bounced around but also separated, broken down, unthreaded. That will come later. For now, the DZ crew just need to figure out how the *Sidereal*'s to be stripped. They've started with a gross model – with three, in fact: one digital, CAD, low-spec, the basic form and outline of the vessel; the other two physical, if equally basic, iterations, duplicates each of which has been immersed in its own fluid-mechanical environment. NW have allowed use of their wind tunnel for flow tracing and yaw/roll/pitching-moment measurement, but they flat refused to submit the thing to wind speeds that would actually break it up, since flying parts of a spaceship, even a scaled-down one, would have dented, gnarled and lacerated delicate, expensive honeycombs and vanes (van Boezem's indignant email, sent via Phocan, informed them that they'd 'have to meet all costs for the destruction of not just your spaceship but also our livelihood!'). So, for the full, catastrophic sequence, or at least its gross, undetailed version (analogue), they've stuck with the Germans, who dunked into the *Versuchsanstalt für Wasserbau und Schiffbau*'s Berlin cavitation tank a month or two ago a 1:96 *Sidereal*, VWS being less squeamish about such propositions due to a long history of simulating nautical mishaps, their UT2 containing strong, debris-catching nets affixed downstream of measurement section but up-flow of pump and filter parts. ('The irony,' Eldridge told Herzberg, who tells Briar now, passing the quip off as his own, 'is that, to simulate wind, even when wind's itself a simulation – or, let's say, approximation – you need water.') Eldridge has got sequences from all three of these first, tentative modellings up on the BenQ now, running in multi-screen. In the left-hand-side video, the tank one, broken water-flecks dance furiously round the ship's hull, rising to form lips and wedges as they run across its winglets, landing struts, disruptor banks and stabilisers. The watery medium in which the camera also sits, in tandem with the unabbreviated proprietorial label, *Versuchsanstalt für Wasserbau und Schiffbau*, overlaid across the film's upper-right section, makes Herzberg, every time he watches it, think of U-boats chugging through the depths of the Atlantic. The right-hand-side video, the CAD one, shows an analogous, or rather non-analogue, version of the process taking place in the cavitation tank, pixel-flecks and lips and wedges forming and dispersing, flaring and contracting round the *Sidereal* as they pass it in a stuttered virtual flux from which fury, this time, seems quite absent. In the middle video, the NW one, the wind tunnel's smoke tracer wraps the ship in a fine-mesh cocoon while bubbles bounce and ricochet about its slipstream.

'We've established,' Eldridge says, 'the movement round the vessel's hull. In both the CAD and the water tank we ran the sequence on until it starts to break up, as you'll see. But in a way, that's a red herring. It might give us prompts, suggestions; but our task here's not so much to record the way an actual or simmed vessel broke apart on such-and-such a day, as to decide how *we* want *our* one to do this, in a way that maxes the event's spectacular potentiality *and* is consistent with the flow-parameters enveloping the object – and, of course,' he finds it politic to round off with this small gesture of tribute, 'all the laws of physics that, in turn, envelop those.'

The gesture works. Briar slowly nods assent, but asks:

'How will you decide, when you haven't got all the details there yet? It could be that it's the tiniest piece of a truss segment, EVA rail or radiator panel that gives first – which fragment then tears a small rip in down-hull cowling, which causes depressurisation in the avionics or the storage bays, which ...'

'Ken Pilkington,' says Herzberg, 'thought – he's at the MOD, in aeronautics – that it would most likely be ...'

'Ken Pilkington?' Briar repeats, incredulous. 'How in heaven's ...?'

'He slipped us some advice, through Pantarey ...'

Briar's gaze, for a brief moment, seems to disengage – from them, the screens, the room, the task at hand – and to transfer itself on to some other figure that, like a ghost at a private feast he's hosting, only he can see. Eventually he murmurs:

'If anyone knows about dematerialising aircraft ...'

He doesn't complete the sentence. Herzberg, cautiously, continues:

'He suggested having something towards the front give first: a payload bay door or forward bulkhead ...'

'Pilkington!' Briar whispers – then, realising that the others are all staring at him now, shakes off whatever phantom he's confronting and, authoritative voice restored, informs them:

'Yes: bay door or bulkhead are both possible. But it could equally be near the back, if there's more drag there: say, an aft body flap or stabiliser could pull a whole segment of fuselage off with it as it ...'

'We like front best,' Herzberg tells him. 'That way, you can see the event-chain progressing down the vessel, both structurally and dramatically: people racing around as the damage spreads, trying to batten down communicating hatches, seal the airlock modules and so on ...'

'Yes – but for that, surely, you need details.'

'To a degree. You just have to be Jesuit about it. What happens if we start by making this communication mast snap off and plough on through the solar sail, then having sections of the engine blow? You start the run that takes the ship apart from there, or there, or *there* – just "peel" a bit back, let the computer do the rest. But you do this in gross, not fine. You don't need every ventilator duct and odour-filter canister factored into the model at this point. That would take months to work out, even with the procs we've got. You only need to fake a bit of detail – which is where our fork comes in. So, here, we've primed up three scenarios ...'

Charlie, who like a faithful stoker has been waiting for this moment, pulls up now on the BenQ the first of these. It depicts, as intimated, a front-to-rear event-chain of destruction: nose sensor, gyrodynes, elevons, correction engines, thrusters peeling off the simulated model one by one, colliding with each other and the hull.

'We've put seams through the structure,' Eldridge explains, 'and assigned each surface properties: tensile strength, brittleness, elasticity, and so forth. Just to get an idea ...'

'Doesn't look very realistic,' Briar says.

'Well, not yet. There's no part-sim in it at this stage, and ...'

'Part-sim?'

'No particle simulation: smoke, metal confetti, things that go *pow* and *pouf*, like dust from beaten rugs. And, of course, no light. Those come in at the render stage. Now, here's Scenario Two ...'

This one, not wildly different, starts by unpicking a thin telemetry, or perhaps approach and rendezvous, antenna from the *Sidereal*'s upper fuselage; the antenna then embeds itself, like a knife thrower's decorated blade, in the ship's starboard solar panel, which begins to shred, decompositing itself as its shards rush on downwind. The third scenario begins with the same initial detachment, only this time the antenna, like a twig being fed into a shredder, finds its way into the port-side engine, which explodes, not only ripping out whole segments of the cargo bay and armoury but also sending what's left of the ship careening sideways, fishtailing as it tries to right itself.

'The great thing with Houdini,' the screenward-facing Charlie tells them, 'is that it knows the wind's not constant: you can factor in the gyre and gimble. And the spaceship will correct as it gets buffetted – which, in turn, informs what part it exposes and, by extension, what might go wrong next.'

Briar nods more, acquiescent if not humbled.

'Of course,' Herzberg jumps back in, 'we won't show the whole thing. Just some moments from its progression, to narrate its timeline – the best bits. With wide-shots, you don't need to get all details right – on close-ups, though, you do. That's where physical modelling's useful: showing how a screw works its way loose, or how cracks spread across a heat-tile ...'

'There we can take cues,' Eldridge adds, 'from the cavitation tank, and feed them into the simulation.'

'Where's this extra sail appearing from?' asks Briar as, on Charlie's screen, a new wing flickers into view out of abyssal darkness and adapts itself spectrally to the span of the first one which is listing down to meet it.

'Glitches,' Charlie answers.

'We'll catch them all in rendering too,' says Eldridge. 'We'll have wranglers round the clock, twenty-four/seven.'

Now the scenario's gone interior: we've got fire extinguishers, pneumatic panels, contents of medicine chests all drifting loose inside the module – plus, again, the fork. Herzberg, sensing a kind of truce with Briar, starts telling him a story.

'There was once, a few years back – not here at Degree Zero but at one of our competitors, in London perhaps, or perhaps it was in the US, I can't remember – a man named Decebal Călugăreanu.'

Eldridge, Charlie and all the others smile; they know the story. Briar nods again, awaiting the next part.

'Călugăreanu,' Herzberg continues, 'was Romanian, a whizz-kid coder, brought in by this post-prod company for a specific purpose: plotting the passage of an object (a royal sceptre or magic crystal or Moses basket or something along those lines) down a stream, a strait of quick-flowing water in a scene in some big-budget fantasy or other ...'

The day (so the story goes) Călugăreanu arrived in London/ LA/Wherever, the FX department's head – Herzberg's counterpart – introduced him by rolling his eyes and saying 'I'm not even going to *try* to pronounce this guy's name ...' The staffers looked at their feet awkwardly, embarrassed by their boss's xenophobic boorishness; over the next day or two, they learnt to pronounce the name without much problem. It's not that hard: Decebal, like *decibel;* Călugăreanu, like the Sardinian city. The dept head never learnt it, though – for the next few weeks he kept the eye-roll up, called Călugăreanu *D.C.* each time he addressed him, and so on. Călugăreanu, meanwhile, set about plotting the sceptre/crystal/Moses basket's passage downstream. Let's imagine that the sequence was to run for about twenty seconds: it's a matter of defining a trajectory that's both dramatic and consistent with the givens – water flows at such-and-such a pace, rocks here and here, object dropped here ...

'Like Poohsticks,' Briar says.

'Exactly,' Herzberg concurs. 'Same as what we're doing: fluid simulation. With rapids, or with wind, a thousand micro-factors come into effect with every frame. The better the simulator, the better you can calculate where the thing is in twenty seconds; and the better you can do that, the better your water will look. So Călugăreanu gets to work. He works alone. He's a hard worker: always at his desk, first in, last out. In fact, he's never out. They find him in the office every morning, punching the keys, clearly not having slept all night. The weird thing is ...'

The weird thing was, he never invoiced for his overtime. The FX dept head would prompt him, ungraciously, calling across the floor *Hey, D.C., don't you guys want to be paid?* 'You guys' perhaps being coders, or Romanians, or just people with non-waspy names. Călugăreanu would just smile back quietly. He knew why he wasn't invoicing for the night-time labour. A day or so into his coding, the thought had struck him that, if he could work out where a sceptre/staff/Moses basket will be in twenty seconds in a river, he could also work out where pork-belly futures will be in the morning on the Chinese Stock Exchange, and spent his nights building an algo to do just that. On the day before he signed off on his Poohstick task, he sold his algo to Salomon Smith Barney for 500,000,000 dollars. It was all over the feeds; the staffers cheered him to the door. But Călugăreanu wasn't quite done: on his way out, he paid a quick last call on the dept head, and made him an offer: if he, the head, could say his, Călugăreanu's, name, right now, then he, Călugăreanu again, would pay him, head, ten million pounds/dollars/euros – instant transfer, on the spot.

'The guy actually tried,' Herzberg rounds off the anecdote. *'Cala-gear-something ... no, Kalloogerena ... Calarea ...'*

'Supercalifragilistic ...' Charlie joins in.

Even Briar is smiling. There's a coda to the story, though.

'The really interesting bit about it all,' Herzberg in full-on lecturer mode, authority restored now, adds reflectively, 'is that Salomon Smith Barney only got three or so months' use out of Călugăreanu's algorithm. Which was fine – they made their 500,000,000 back several times over. But it turned out to be so good that it influenced the entire pork-belly future-trading system. It became *part of* the system, its macro-machinery – like a lock, a weir ...'

His gaze, and Briar's, turn back to the BenQ. The model videos are playing again now, snips from further down the files. In the Berlin cavitation-tank one, angry lips and wedges have now prised struts loose, caused stabilisers to hang off like broken wings, the hull to flap autocorrectively from side to side – which, in turn, hastens its destruction. Below this, the CAD simulation runs through the same scene disinterestedly, flecks moving without rancour or intent around the shredding ship. The wind-tunnel footage, as before, shows a smoke-swaddled *Sidereal*, cradled by the flows that hold destruction, and it, in abeyance. Inside the vessel, similarly passive, Tild and Tszvetan stand amidst untethered medicine boxes, fire extinguishers and fork tines, awaiting their consumption, their apotheosis.

3. Jamalac Scoop

Gloucestershire in September: willowherb drooping and flaking in weak sun against the wall, meadowsweet's last flowering in the ditch, cut grass composting in the pile, and Thérèse sleeping. Now she sleeps more than she doesn't. At some point in the summer it flipped over; he didn't record it then, nor could he put his finger, now, on the precise week, let alone day, on which it happened – but a tipping point has been reached, passed, left behind, and sleeping has become her main state, her default mode. Doctors are hopelessly reluctant to commit, endlessly pussyfoot around his questions, no matter how circuitously phrased (*How might we begin to plot ... ? In terms of temporal parameters ... So what type of trajectory ... ? ... timeline from here on in ... ?*) – but the chatrooms, the support groups seem to give her three to six months. Speech is going; so is taste; smell's gone already. She doesn't admit it, but she's seeing and hearing things, hallucinations: he can tell that from the way her eyes, last part of her that's still alert and active, fix on the empty space above his head, or on a spot of wall beside the door-jamb, then dart off again towards an edge of cornicing or stretch of carpet and hover there, fiercely attentive, by turns frightened, bewildered and enchanted. What are they saying to her? What magic lantern shows is she being treated to? They've upped her Levodopa levels, to deal with the cramps and neuralgia, but her dopaminergic transmission is degenerating, and toxicity is setting in. Incontinence, too. Human tolerance finds its own boundaries, its limits: illness is a way of tracing, rubbing and redrawing these, over and over, an endless experiment, blueprint drafted on the body's foolscap . . .

Pilkington's in his study, and he's got it out again: his secret ledger, laurel wreath that brings with it no public office, manifesto that no joyous crowds will ever hold aloft, Red Book destined to remain unread. Strangely, his anxious dreams nowadays concern it, and Albatross, as much as her. The two scenes seem to have merged together: it's her arm, her shoulder, or the casters of her wheelchair that he's trying to steer round, realign with target centreline, guide safely to their landing corridor, their kiss-spot on the sand. *RLOS*: the acronym's scrawled on the page open in front of him, above a sketch showing the signal-command chain he set up to lead the 720 from Diego Garcia to Septentrion. Radio line of sight: a terrestrial-oceanic network, simple as Ancient Greek beacon towers or games of pass-the-parcel, with each post receiving from the last one temporary jurisdiction over the plane, giving it a little airborne left-and-right to check the telemetry, keep the old thing responsive, then handing it onwards to the next one. There they are, each station's sign: *DG, LV Siren, RPS Sept* . . . the letters float about the page, reanimating for him metal pylons rising from cement set into sand, or from the deck of the light vessel bobbing just beyond the fourteenth parallel, the *Siren*. The mast beside the landing strip, beside home base, Ground Zero, was a triangular guyed lattice, red and white, with tensioned steel cables set at various angles, Lilliputian bindings pinning it down to the beach. Beneath it, the green tents; the generators; the recording vans; the instrument stations of Marconi, BA and the rest, arrayed in complex subdivisions like a desert sheik's encampment . . .

And, between all these, orienting their scatter, attracting them around it like so many shavings round a magnetised lead bar, the landing strip, evacuated main street of a western town awaiting its high noon. With static cameras planted all about so as to cover every angle, to provide shot-reverse-shot capacity for each phase, each moment of the action, the beach reminded Pilkington (who'd never seen one but held in his mind the same popular image of them as everyone else) of movie sets. And the plane heading towards it ... that, too, was like a film set: less protagonist than mobile studio, equipped with its own cameras and mikes, lead players, extras, props, all bound by their adherence to a script whose first draft was – is – written down right here; whose final typescript, shooting version, had been photostatted and distributed in various modified, partial forms, like an orchestral score adapted to each instrument. Turning the page, he finds, spread out across the next two, a block diagram of the data acquisition system: Time Code Generator (IRIG A) feeding Tape Recorders #1 and #2, Camera (IRIG B) and Syst 1 PCM, which last box is also fed into by Signal Conditioner and in its turn feeds two more Tape Recorders, #3 and #4, Delay Memory and S-band ... The arrow-headed flow lines bi- and trifurcate as they run left to right, verso to recto, kink as they dip into the notebook's central gutter. The plane, too, was meant to slide across the boundary between each control zone, pass eventually the margin separating sea from land, and hurtle in, an arrow to its mark, transducing multi-channelled secrets to the giant IBM housed in Dashell's and Sir Ronald's tent, the largest, greenest, shadiest one: master converter that would process all the multiplexing input cards' sequential data, filter and sample and make legible once more – to them, to him, the world and all posterity – the millions of words hurtling their way, 8 bits at 129 per frame, across the great unworded silence, the blank space.

Outside the study, a small gust draws from the meadowsweets white spray eruptions, puffs that hang about the air like smoke when canons have been fired. Above them, birch trees rustle and shed leaves. First breath of winter, of a future with no Thérèse in it. On the first of April 1984, a light breeze skimmed Septentrion, fuzzing the atoll's sand. Beaufort would have ranked it 2: the vane beside the landing strip was stirred but not priapic; wavelets on the sea were glassy but not broken. By quarter past nine, everyone was at their posts, although there were still two hours to go until the kiss-down; mood was busy but informal, people calmly and good-humouredly getting on with what they had to do, zapping about by jeep and foot, or radioing from one station to another, or, when stations were adjacent, just calling across: *Hey, fool, get your ass over here* ...

The beers, at such an early hour on this day of all days, were confined to their fridge-barracks, cooling beside champagne bottles that they'd had to bribe (with other champagne bottles) Diego's quartermaster to enter in the manifest as 'technical hardware'; but ice creams were out in force. No one in the command chain had objected: they kept the men cool, and happy; Dashell was himself partial to them. Anderson, some time in February, had started experimenting: now, beside the pre-fab chocolate and vanilla, there were mango and papaya, coconut and litchi, guava, starfruit and jamalac on the menu, scooped out of a Gaggia gelatiera (inventoried as 'counter-antifreeze device') that, like a commercial airliner with instant turnaround, was kept in non-stop operation. *Albatross Ice Cream*, Anderson called it; *Comes in seven deadly flavours* ... Pilkington, like most of the other senior personnel, had a scoop in front of him more often than not: working his way through the sins, sloth to envy, litchi to guava, one at a time, held in a small glass beside his console, although not for long; in these temperatures, you had to polish them off quickly. Today, he was downing more than normal – out of nervousness, perhaps, or perhaps because he garnered comfort, reassurance even, not so much from the ice creams' taste as from their form. With an old Japanese Nevco serving spoon on the inner cranium of whose aluminium scoop-head flaking blue paint had produced a surface that resembled, it struck Pilkington, that of the atoll-flecked Indian Ocean if viewed in gnomonic projection from on high, the Marconi man, like a cosmic magician pulling newly formed planets from his hat, managed to turn out compact globes of coloured coldness that, time after time, came up impeccably, exquisitely spherical. Pilkington must have gone back for a new serving every half-hour, small rewards to help him tick off each task: copying the pre-fires, clearing the frequencies with each guidance station, checking flight-path coordinates yet once more

... In the last stretch, the final minutes just before Hour Zero, it was a jamalac scoop that stood in front of him – most exotic of all the flavours: wax apple, *syzygium samarangense*, white with a pink blush. Beyond this scoop, his radar screen, gridded, green and empty; beside these, the book.

At two minutes past eleven, on Diego Garcia, the Boeing took off. Twenty-one and a half minutes later, it was handed over to the *Siren*. In another twenty-three, it would come within range of Septentrion. Pilkington was to bring it down himself. Any of his team could probably have done it, but the final approach seemed, from a symbolic point of view, consistent with the rites and pro- tocols of nautical tradition, to demand his individual pilotage, his personal conveyance. *Kubernetes*: he'd plotted its route and relay; he would carry this Olympic torch through its last few steps, sink it in the bowl, the cauldron of its final conflagration. On the landing strip, the heavy steel wing-opening blocks gazed seawards, impassive as Easter Island statues. On his screen, the plan-position indicator's radial trace swept its way round the grid's concentric circles, drawing swathes and segments out into an afterglow that faded and returned with each new sweep. At 11:45:32 he glanced at the scoop: it needed eating, but he didn't dare divert his hand, his eye, one jot of his attention from the console on which, from one instant to the next, a new dot would appear, and grow into an outlined shape: wingspanned, an albatross, his very own one, coming home to roost ...

'Hey Pilko!' Anderson hailed him from the Marconi tent. 'Turning up fashionably late. Is that an English thing?'

They were a little past handover time: forty-five seconds ... now a minute ... now two ... Pilkington felt, for the first time since coming here, effect even the ice cream never gave him, a chill spreading outwards from his skull, down the back of his neck. He radioed to LV *Siren*, who said the plane had left their zone four minutes ago.

'But you can see it on your radar still?'

'Negative that.'

'Then why can't we?'

In the loud silence riding the waves back to him, he heard fear massing, finding its inchoate frequency. His walkie-talkie buzzed: it was Sir Ronald, 'checking in', voice calm and measured, deep bass over which Dashell's more dramatic baritone soon cut in:

'Where's our fucking airplane?'

On Pilkington's second monitor, a message appeared: *Integrity Event*. Could mean just about anything: antenna obscuration, interference, doppler shift, clock error, or some kind of drift ... They were using extended Kalman filter; nowadays, it would have been unscented, with all arbitrary non-linear functions replaced by derivative-free higher-order approximations and their Gaussian distributions, sigma points furnishing state vectors and uncertainties, all propagated via state transition model. The drones at Farnborough have IMUs and built-in geodetic systems, little onboard globes with their own prime meridians and tropics ... That's now, though; this was then. A big remote control, just like Sir Ronald had said. On his main monitor, the radial trace continued sweeping, drawing into luminescence the plane's absence, the grid's emptiness. In front of it, the scoop was melting: sagging, crumpling, sloughing off its symmetry. Out on the runway, slicers stood brutal in their unusedness. Over the next few minutes, hours and days, they, like the pylon and the generators, like the vehicles and the tents, would transform themselves in his eyes, without actually changing their form or appearance, from idols issuing exultant summons to their god, a living deity who any second now would manifest himself, into mute testaments to their, or to the world's, abandonment. It was the physics, though, not metaphysics, that would imprint itself on and stay with him. Not the advanced aerodynamics of forces and moments, of wind axes and velocity, of drag and side-force coefficients; but the simple physics, so child-simple it was colour-coded, of the radar screen's vacant web (green), the sky's undotted upper plane (blue) and the beach's undisturbed lower one (white), all arranged around this pink-blush sphere that was dissolving, and dissolving with it all the other shapes too, running them into a flat, continuous surface on which nothing was and always would be taking place.

There was an inquiry, of course. It took two years; and, like Albatross itself, it kind of fizzled out. It was in no one's interest to bruit the affair about. All documents and drives, all screeds and scripts and transcripts touching on, feeding into or output by each phase of the operation were commandeered. His own station, every monitor and floppy disc of it, was impounded; the red notebook, though, remained, like the 720, off-radar. Hiding in the light, perhaps: everyone had grown so used to seeing him clasping it that it had become, for them, a part of him, not of the project, like a pair of glasses hanging by a strap around a person's neck, a wallet in their hand – or, in previous centuries, a monocle or ladies' fan. Irony of all ironies: the inquiry reproduced the fatal error of its subject of interrogation, as though ritually replaying, in a blind spot, its own blind spot. They pored over the printouts, looked at the transmitting hardware, at the sampling rates, the signal-to-noise ratios, the onboard sensor-switching frameworks … They checked and rechecked the flight-path coordinates, tracing the chain of copies and transferrals all the way back to the first typed pages. But the error, as he could have told them right from the beginning, from Hour Zero – *April Fool!* – wasn't in the reproduction from one typescript to another: it was there *ab ovo*, in the first ever typing-up. On the lined Sylvine pages, for coordinate conversion, geodetic to ECEF, he'd used Newton-Raphson iteration to determine the meridian arcs that, in their turn, specified the reference ellipsoid. For the third flattening, he'd gone with Bessel-Helmert series; for the evaluation, Clenshaw summation. Typing his cipher out for distribution by the project's secretariat, he'd substituted, for convenience, Jacobi ellipsoidals – which substitution, he'd presumed, would be self-evident to everyone, all down the chain. It wasn't. He'd seen that within two minutes of the plane's disappearance, or (more correctly stated) of its failure to appear, and understood immediately what had happened. The numbers and equations that had been uploaded might, on their own terms, have been completely sound; but between the *Siren* and Septentrion, they'd lost traction – on the stations and the masts, on one another, on the territory they were traversing – and, cut loose from their fixed moorings, embarked on a frenzy of auto-conversion that had rapidly transformed the onboard navigation system into a random event space. Like a dice roll. He *had* given them a crash, after all: a pure, numeric crash, so perfect it negated any external enactment. Within two and a half minutes, he'd also understood that this sequence of causation would never, in the absence of the notebook (whose scrawled cipher was, in any case, illegible) be traced back to him.

They never found the plane. Two spotters, an RAF Poseidon and a US Navy Orion, flew around, first north, then south of the four-teenth for a week, scouring the sea for wreckage; for a week after that they extended their search westwards, to Mauritius and the Seychelles; for a third week, eastwards, towards Cocos, Christmas Island and Jakarta. Then they gave up. Amidst all the tech, the hardware, all the data acquisition tools, no one had ever thought of installing a black box. Why would they? In the 'normal' run of things, if the experiment had gone to plan, it would have been superfluous: the whole plane was a giant flight recorder. Possibly, years later, parts washed up on beaches – in Oman, or Pakistan, Australia, Holland, Norway, who knows where: a fragment of tail section or a tape machine head, an accelerometer's dial, the arm or pelvis of an instrumented dummy ... Would these scraps have found their way into a database, been locked on by and steered to the restricted section, laid to rest, in name at least, in some memorial archive? Or would they just have been prodded by child combers, like lumps of jellyfish and mermaid's purses, plastic bottles, hunks of styrofoam and all the other spawn of cargo-spillage, sea-dumping and general world-discharge, draincocks and drowned dolls, bath ducks and deformed squishies, curtain hooks, door hinges, dehumidifier grilles and baking moulds, ball valves and parts degraded beyond thresholds of their name, the host of things released from purpose-contract to meander pointlessly from zone to zone? He wouldn't have known one way or another; he was well out of the loop. He pictured the plane, though, over the months and years that followed, as having found a kind of berth, a gate slot, somewhere, in some spot for which no geodetic data point existed: an aporia, blind alley, cubby-hole or nook ... He still does now: he sees it, sometimes on the ground, at rest, and sometimes flying, still, after all these years, a white bird gliding in a parallel and empty sky, above a darkening flood.

4. *Assassiyun*

On his first morning in the dacha, Lazda takes Phocan on a trip to the Jumelans store, to help her with some shopping. It's a ten-minute drive. Old wooden houses alternate with woods for the first stretch; then, as they near the town, new-builds pop up, great mansions lurking behind walls and electronic gates.

'A Russian oligarch,' says Lazda as an icing-sugar-pink palace slides by, its cameras eyeing their little car suspiciously. 'And that one,' she continues, pointing to a mock-Arabian confection on the road's far side, 'belongs to a pop star.'

Past these two, in a giant, dilapidated compound, a five-storey structure set on stilts, with terraces and balconies and long rows of tall windows half of which are broken, wrestles with the trees that have pushed into it, or even in some case grown inside it, their roots finding sustenance and purchase in cracked concrete and exposed iron beams.

'This,' Lazda tells him, 'was a hotel for well-behaved Soviet workers. Only the good ones, party members, were allowed to holiday in Latvia. The rest had to go inland, away from the border. And this one,' she slows the car down as they pass another gutted behemoth, 'was an institute for Soviet chemists ...'

On the way back, they detour to the beach. Phocan thinks he recognises the small factory they passed en route to the house yesterday, the derelict one whose brickwork shrubs and creepers are reclaiming. He's right.

'It's the old *stikla fabrika* – the glassworks,' she says. 'It closed in the mid-eighties, before I was born. Here we are.'

They've come to the end of a narrow, overgrown track whose mud has given way to sand. Beyond it, unkempt marram grass dotted with more brick foundations, these ones crumbled right down to ground level, leads on to a beach whose sand looks large and smooth, almost transparent. The shoreline, hemmed by a long fringe of this marram grass on one side and black kelp and sea-wrack on the other, broken only by a little inlet thirty or so yards to the north of them, runs in a thin strip for several miles in each direction before jutting, to the south, the Riga Gulf side, in a point on which a lighthouse stands and, to the north, the open Baltic side, in what looks like a military installation or perhaps observatory, an array of satellite dishes and domed roofs silhouetted against the pale sky.

'A listening station,' Lazda says, seeing him peering out towards the latter. 'This area was full of them. They were all decommissioned in the nineties – now, though, they're up and running again.'

'You must have come here as a child, to swim,' says Phocan.

'I did, but not my parents or my grandparents. It was forbidden. A good swimmer could get to Sweden from here, if the water wasn't too rough. Along the entire Baltic coast, they kept the sand completely smooth, with brushes pulled by tractors, so that they could see if anyone had tried to cross it.'

Phocan squints towards the horizon, trying to make out some kind of bump or jag that might be Sweden, but can't pick out anything beyond the normal sine-wave of the sea's background frequency. When he looks back again, Lazda's vaporised, collapsed into an empty jacket, shirt and pair of jeans lying at his feet. He picks her up again ten yards away, racing in underwear towards the water. September; fuck it; why not? He strips down to his pants too, streaks along her fugitive print-trail, past kelp margin and wavelets, on into a sea no Gulf Stream current seems to have warmed up. She's a good swimmer; by the time he's caught up with her she's carved a big loop out beyond the surf line, parallel with the shore and back in again, plus run up and down the beach a few times to dry off.

'You won't,' she tells him as he crumples to the strangely vitreous ground beside their clothes, 'catch anything at that speed.'

Re-entering the car, before she starts the engine up again, she pulls a headband from her jacket pocket and slips it on, to keep her wet fringe from her eyes. Phocan, shocked by the cold and the exertion, undergoes a moment's dislocation; slunk down into the passenger seat's faux-leather, he forgets where he is, what he's doing, what year it is. He might even doze for few seconds on the way back to the house; he's not sure. Images of Lazda, her parents and her grandparents, of Lazda *as* her own mother or grandmother, head covered in a handkerchief or headband similar to the one she's wearing now, face turned away towards the sea, the whole thing greyscaled like in old home movies, telescope away once more along vague avenues of memory, or of forgetting, merge with other memories perhaps his own, or perhaps not, flicker and fade into and out of focus with the houses new and ruined, institutions, wooden shacks all flashing intermittently through a rainbow-veil of autumn foliage. By the time his circulation has restored itself, his consciousness re-found its bearings, they're gliding down the almost-intersecting tracks once more, then, passing the abandoned playground, pulling back into the garden, with the light-blue dacha looming above them to the left, aviary to the right, cubistic tree-house at the far end beyond the vegetables.

'He'll be in his study,' Lazda says as they carry the supplies into the kitchen. 'You can go there.'

Vanins is indeed in his study. It's housed in the low-lying extension to the main house. Phocan knocks, and is called in. On a worktable are laid out several box files and bound manuscripts.

'I've dug up some papers,' Vanins informs him. 'Some of my work touching on states of equilibrium. You're welcome to consult them.'

For the next two hours, Phocan does so. They're not wildly different from the ones the archivist found for him at Tehniskā Universitāte. There's an article on Hamiltonian vs. Langrangian formulations; another on fictitious forces, non-inertial reference frames, the implications of the Coriolis effect for aerodynamic engineering ... There are some lecture notes – in Latvian and Russian, but the diagrams and mathematical notation he can follow. From time to time, he looks up from them, out of the window just above the worktable. Through its panes, which have irregular consistencies, as though they'd come from different glaziers, he can see the stretch of garden lying between the vegetable patch and his misshapen treehouse. There's a well that seems to still be in use, since it has a rope-coiled winch and bucket; next to this, a tree stump with an axe lying on it; behind this, a stack of chopped-up firewood about which small birds, presumably not Vanins' but wild ones, hop and dart before retreating back into the furze of spruce trees that delineate a smudgy, incremental border between the property and the surrounding woods, which are made up of larger trees that Phocan can't identify.

'Aspens,' Vanins tells him when he asks. 'They're general around here. For paper. You'll have seen paper mills dotted around the countryside on your way out of Riga. Have you found,' he continues, 'what you're looking for?'

Phocan hesitates before answering. Vanins is looking at him fixedly. He ventures tentatively:

'There was something I saw back in Riga, in Tehniskā's archive, that I didn't quite understand ...'

'Go on,' Vanins coaxes.

'It involved,' Phocan continues, 'a small note you'd made, beneath a chart ... dynamic properties of such-and-such an aircraft ... I saw you'd drawn,' he tries to keep his breathing steady, to suppress the tremor in his voice, 'the figure *808* ...'

Another roadblock? There's no measurable pause, no slowing of the pace, but still there seems to be a kind of a glitch or stutter in the passage of the words, the information, through the air.

'Maybe I had,' says Vanins. 'What of that?'

Phocan has thought through, both in dialogue with Garnett and alone, various scenarios, ways a putative conversation on this topic might go, the kinks and switchbacks down which it might cut its path. This one hasn't been modelled, though. It seems as though Vanins is challenging him, inviting him almost: *Go on, ask me for it* ... Or is this openness a kind of judo move, a going-with-the-flow, to let his opponent's force expend itself, draw him off-balance? It's too late for Phocan to pull back; before he's even scripted the words in his head, he finds himself saying:

'You knew Lillian Gilbreth ...'

Vanins looks up, towards the window and the garden, before answering:

'We met only once, in Zürich.'

'But you corresponded.'

Vanins pauses again, then answers:

'You are not the first to have enquired about this recently. And I suspect you will not be the last. What is it in my correspondence with Mrs Gilbreth that appears so important, now, for all of you?'

Phocan steels himself, lunges in further:

'She seems to have grown excited about some of the research that you were conducting around 1969, '70 ... Something you both refer to as "the T.T. episode" ...'

Vanins lets him run on, waiting to see how far he'll go. It's as he feared; the tactic works – before he knows it he's completely lost his balance, hears himself blurting out:

'Then there's the mention of a wireframe motion model, one you made yourself after her method. I think it might even have been assigned a number in her own cataloguing system – you know: *Box 128, Box 275,* and so on ...'

Now Vanins has him trapped, arm-locked: despite his slightness, the old man seems to tower above him, to demand submission as he asks:

'And if this box existed, what would it change?'

Phocan returns the only answer he can think of:

'Everything, apparently.'

Is this capitulation, or a counter-punch? Does this all-but-straight citation of the diary entry manage to wrest some of Gilbreth's authority, to tap into it, enlist it? It's having some effect: Vanins seems to be stepping off him now. After a while he asks Phocan, more gently:

'Do you believe this?'

'Did you?' Phocan asks back.

Now Vanins really eases off, withdrawing into himself, lost in thought. Eventually he says:

'We believed a lot of things. In this respect, we Soviet scientists were like *assassiyun.*'

'Like what?' asks Phocan.

'*Assassiyun.* Assassins,' Vanins answers. 'The young men of Arabia who joined the Old Man of the Mountain's cult, after they'd been lured up to his hideout, drugged and woken in a garden where wine gushed from fountains, music spilled about the air, and maidens, nymphs, attended to their every need.'

'I don't quite follow ...' Phocan says.

'The young men,' Vanins runs on, 'thought that it was paradise, entry to which only the Old Man could guarantee; and so they joined his cult, became assassins. But it was all fake: a stage-set, levers pumping wine and sound-tubes piping music from an unseen chamber. The *assassiyun* themselves would have been operating it: last year's recruits, the year before's ...'

'The same ones,' Phocan plays along, although he still can't see where this digression's heading, 'who'd been tricked by the illusion previously?'

'Exactly,' Vanins nods. 'Why would they do this? Once they'd seen how it all worked, how *they*'d been fooled, why didn't they turn on their deceptive master and denounce the whole arrangement?'

'Maybe,' Phocan tries, 'the stage-set operators got a kind of upgrade: better perks, more wine, regular access to the nymphs ...'

'That,' concedes Vanins, 'would be an explanation – a cynical one, though. And besides, an "upgrade" is small compensation for the loss of paradise. No: I like to think that at some level, on some scale, they must have carried on believing *something*. That, even if the larger story wasn't true, they saw it as a useful fiction, that enabled something else to operate: something good and necessary – something even miraculous, perhaps …'

He looks out at the garden again for a while before continuing:

'The Soviet era was a good one for scientists – those of my generation, at least, who weren't threatened with imprisonment. We, too, believed in something. Not the Revolution, nor the truth of Lenin's vision, nor whichever five- or ten-year plan we were engrossed in: it was something bigger and more abstract. Maybe it was the orchestration itself, its implicit promise that society, the world, could operate as one giant apparatus – that this apparatus, this intricate machinery, could transform experience and knowledge, elevate them to a higher state …'

'… *remade as an unbound potentiality*,' Phocan quotes.

Vanins starts, surprised.

'I see you've done your homework.'

He's quiet again for a while, as though running the old article's phrases through his mind. Then, slapping its remembered pages shut, he tells Phocan:

'You're too late, though. All that was a long time ago. Whatever elevation, transformation … whatever "miracle" we thought we might be bringing about – that has evaporated now. Like fountains when their pumps have been shut down once and for all.'

He turns his hands out, palms up, as though to come clean about their emptiness, his generation's bankruptcy, and adds:

'Everyone stopped believing, and the apparatus ran itself down. By the end the only question was what bits of the machinery the operators, or their supervisors, could steal …'

The two men stand in silence by the desk, beneath the window. Then Vanins asks:

'What do you believe in, Dr Phocan?'

Phocan answers without hesitating:

'Geometry.'

Vanins, scrutinising him with a mixture of interest and something approaching affection, repeats:

'Geometry?'

Phocan nods.

'Same as Mrs Gilbreth.' Vanins smiles approvingly. 'You may stay tonight as well, if you wish.'

In the afternoon, while Vanins siestas, Lazda takes Phocan to the aviary. She trots on ahead of him, ducking behind bird boxes and plants, then reappearing in another spot off to the side, behind him or further ahead still, as though she knew a set of worm-hole shortcuts linking disparate parts of the space together. It becomes a kind of game, a hide-and-seek or catch-me-if-you-can, just like the morning's beach chase. This time, he catches up with her beside a sofa set into a little nook surrounded on all sides by leaves.

'Did you find what you're looking for?' she asks.

'He's reticent,' he says, thinking that she's referring to his research-note quest, or, since all pretence otherwise seems to be collapsing, directly to Box 808, the T.T. episode ... His answer makes her laugh – either because that's not what she meant or perhaps because it *was*, but not what he was meant to understand, or to acknowledge having understood, or ... The sense of dislocation's coming on again. This time, when he reorients himself, she's got her arms around his neck; they're kissing, sinking to the floor, the beach, the sofa, and the clothes are crumpling in a pile again, underwear this time joining them. Afterwards, they both briefly nap. The aviary's birdsong infiltrates his dozing; in his dream, the twills and chirps are voiceovers laid down by commentators, or accusatory statements made by prosecutors, at a trial, or in a newspaper report, or a similar kind of post-hoc assessment that, through some quirk of anachronism, is being applied even as the scene that it assesses is playing out. The sound of a buzzsaw wakes them: aspens being cut down, perhaps, for paper in the woods nearby, or maybe just a neighbour chopping logs. Sunlight's streaming through the windows; the birds dart around it, vanishing into their boxes, perching on the white-streaked tops and ledges to peck seeds and chirp more.

'How come,' Phocan asks her, tracing with his index finger the outline of a birthmark on her back, 'it's you taking care of him?'

'My parents,' she tells him without turning round, 'both died when I was young. He and my grandmother raised me.'

'And when did she … ?'

'In 2001. Since then it's just me.'

This last reflection seems to snap her back into the present. She swivels to her feet and says:

'We should get dressed; he'll be up soon.'

At dinner, Vanins seems sombre. Does he know what they've been up to while he was asleep? Over small glasses of black-balsam liquor, he reminisces about Jumelans neighbours; he and Lazda speculate as to which of these were KGB-conscripted; together they decry the lot of academia in Riga, the state of its libraries and halls of residence …

'The Tehniskā's archive building, when I visited,' says Phocan, 'seemed quite empty.'

'Everyone's left,' says Vanins. 'Or they're leaving.'

Lazda collects the plates and carries them through to the kitchen. When she's gone Vanins leans close to Phocan and murmurs:

'You could take her with you.'

'To Riga, you mean? When I go back? Are you happy for me to stay just a little … ?'

'You won't find it,' Vanins cuts him off.

'Won't find … ?'

'It,' Vanins repeats. 'There's nothing.'

'I don't …'

'Equilibrium … suspension … stasis … all of that. It's just bodies, in space …'

His words trail off and he sits quite still, looking ancient, voided, shrunken, hands folded in front of him in mortuary style. Then he adds, as an afterthought:

'And geometry has its assassins too.'

Phocan's about to ask him, again, what he means; but Lazda comes back in bearing a *cidonija* pie, and Vanins leans back and looks away from Phocan, placing their last exchange under embargo. He retires to bed soon afterwards. Lazda and Phocan spend the night together in the treehouse. She speaks Latvian to him as they make love – small words and phrases here and there for which he doesn't request a translation; they seem kind and happy. They sleep for an hour or so just before dawn, then set out early on another outing to the little general store in Jumelans.

'A third dinner,' she says, 'then I'll drive you back to Riga. I go there tonight as well. You can stay with me if you like, in my flat.'

They stop by the beach again. It's colder than yesterday: the sun is gone; the autumn's pressing in. Chasing her out past the kelp- and surf-lines once more, he wonders if she'd come to London with him. Is that what Vanins meant? Maybe he'll try to press him in his study, if he's welcomed there again when they get back; or over dinner – revisit his mutterings, unpack them, see if they can be rearranged into some kind of sense. Stasis, suspension; waves and sand ... He catches Lazda sooner today; maybe she's letting him; this time they warm up one another, looking out towards a Sweden that's still un-discernible, although the water's calmer, blacker ...

There'll be no third dinner. Turning off the ditch-lined track into the garden this time, they observe, first little sign that something's out of place, two plovers and a sandpiper idling about the lawn; then, that the door to the aviary is open – not unlatched or ajar, but agape. Birds of all kinds are spilling from it freely. Lazda, whose sudden paleness he attributes, like his disorientation yesterday, to the sea's coldness, jumps from the car without turning off the engine and dashes towards the building – he presumes to seal the door and stem the birds' flow, their mass breakout. But she runs straight through it, leaving it wide open: her concern isn't the leakage but something beyond, within. A shrill squawk issues a few seconds later from the high-windowed barn's recess – a birdlike, or at least not human-sounding shriek, that Phocan thinks at first might be a peacock's, though he can't remember seeing any in there. Reaching over, turning the ignition off himself then stepping from the car unhurriedly, he ambles through, clos- ing the door behind him slowly, as though casualness might set up its own roadblock, bar disaster from its hatching, or at least its broadcast. But it can't: after two turns he comes across her, and him. She's kneeling on the ground inside their little bower; he's floating above her like a saint or cosmonaut – or, rather, since the rope running between him and the beam, quite visible, belies the illusion of weightlessness, a Bergen acrobat, if you subtracted all the energy and motion.

Over the next few hours, lots of people come. There are ambulance crews from Riga, like their vehicles seasonally streaked in brown and yellow; more sombre blue-clad *policija* personnel; white plastic-sheathed forensics teams; pathologists and miscellaneous others. It's Lazda who deals with them. He's asked to give a statement to some kind of sergeant who speaks English, to corroborate (although there can't really be any doubt about what's just occurred) the statements being constantly solicited from her. She's surprisingly composed: organising and receiving seems to keep her going, to infuse her with purpose. Phocan, redundant, is reduced to brewing the strange black tea that they drank on his arrival and serving it out to any takers; then, when there are no more of these, to hanging about the lawn. By mid-afternoon he has recorded, mentally, a) that Latvian ambulances, like London school buses three decades ago, bear their labels, their descriptors, in unreversed form on their fronts; (b) that the treehouse in which he's sleeping is skilfully constructed, using stay rods and tension fasteners to grip its beams to the trunk, thereby avoiding any need for bolts and kingpins; and (c) that quinces, on the tree, are all but indistinguishable from pears.

How much significance does he attach to these small observations? About the same amount as the pathologist, who, mounting a ladder to undo the rope from its beam, does to the fact (visible only from this elevation) that the bird box closest to him, one of dozens dotted about the aviary, differs from the others in having only two (rather than four) walls and no roof. Inside, a kind of bird-nest shape has calcified: a central twig that rises from a brackish mass of smaller ones, droppings and seed-husks and, once risen, banks into an anticlockwise turn; then, on completing this, reverses its direction to bank back the other way, clockwise, thereby describing in the air a kind of double-helix before dropping to rejoin its starting point. Beneath this twisted mass, on the bird box's floor, three curvy white lines, lying side by side near the front edge, describe their own loops: one, the central of the three, a distended circle, or ellipse; the two bookending it more convoluted figure-eights that traverse their own paths and curl back, like the twig above them, to their own beginnings. These lines are old and faded, grey as much as white. As for their constitutive material, their 'medium': it could be paint, or it might just be bird shit.

5. The Beatitudes

Back to the grind: Goodge Street, D&G's offices, rooms full of stale sunlight and old leather, shelves that sag beneath *Halsbury's Laws of England*, every volume since 1907; beneath them, bound editions of *All England Law Reports, Scots Law Times, Session Cases* ... Dean's here mostly these days, or at Gray's Inn, or the British Library, Social Sciences (Law and Legal Studies) Section. She's working on two briefs right now, side by side. One involves straight-up infringement, of an anti-spillage mechanism for baby bottles: the copier is citing an equivalent contraption predating not only the litigant's patent application but also the institution of patent, or almost any other kind of, law *tout court* (the Ancient Egyptians used it, their defence goes). The other's a tad more complex: a music streaming service themselves under siege from a class-action test suit brought by twenty artists, suing a derivative (or just con-temporaneous) streaming service for interface-duplication. She's wading through A&M vs. Napster, MGM vs. Grokster, PMR vs. Spotify, Spotify vs. Deezer ... Buses, taxis, Clerkenwell and West End sandwich outlets seem imposing and oppressive, London accents ugly and anomalous: her mind's still in Purdue – or should that be Nantucket, Oakland, Riga, Arizona? Or somewhere *between* all these, blank spaces on a map or on a page, omissions from a catalogue, a set of letters ... She caught herself yesterday writing, in a mail to Dorley: *Since I came back from Perdue* – and let the typo stand, cementing with it her take on events, recasting the whole sojourn, those ten days, as *temps perdu* ...

In reality, of course, that time, its content, has been not lost but redacted: *that*'s the term best suited to the inexplicably aggressive reticence she first encountered in West Lafayette, and which then trailed her back to London. Peacock, D&G both went from wanting to know everything there was to know about the Gilbreth archive to not only wanting to know nothing more but, beyond that, demanding that all previously confided content, and all trails and records of their, or her, ever having carried out such research be erased – quite literally: she was to delete her copies of the dispatches, surrender working files, wipe all notes from her laptop. One Tuesday morning, two weeks after her return, a man from GCHQ turned up at the office and enquired, in friendly tones, if she could fill them in on anything she thought might turn out to be *sensitive* (his term) in any legwork she'd conducted for, say, recent clients – specially if this legwork touched on, subject-wise, the history of time-and-motion studies, or kinetics, or exchanges between East and West sides of the Iron Curtain on these subjects during the Cold War, which ...

'Hang on there,' Dorley cut in, sending straight back out of the door an intern bearing in three teacups (she, he and the spook were the only ones participating in this meeting, which had not been scheduled). 'If it's work that Ms Dean, or any other member of this chambers, has conducted for a client, then it's – as you surely must know – confidential.'

'Yes, absolutely,' the GCHQ man replied. 'Absolutely ...' He was about the same age as her, late twenties, and he looked as little like the avatars of MI5 that she could summon to her mind as possible: mild-mannered and light-humoured, quite informal ... 'This is all completely off the record. We could start bouncing terms like *Investigatory Powers Act*, *UKUSA Agreement* and so forth around, but that might seem a little ...' As though struck by a side-gust, he shifted direction, and said: 'Although, in fact, while legal advice privilege protects all communications that make up formal (as its name suggests) legal *advice*, and litigation privilege covers research conducted for the purposes of actual *litigation*, neither of these cover the fact-finding enquiries and general proddings-around of the type you've been ... the type we're interested in: strictly speaking, these aren't – as you'll know too – governed by ...'

'If you want,' Dorley was rising from his seat, 'to take this any further, you can come back with a subpoena.'

No subpoena was forthcoming. Three weeks later, though – three days ago, that is – she had a strange encounter in a restaurant. It was a small place in Southwark, a converted workshop in the narrow brick-street warren south of London Bridge where bearded, tattooed chefs bounce *bacalhau* and *camarão* in copper dishes amidst leaping flames just feet away from diners perched on stools at a zinc counter curving through the space – a tapas bar. She'd been summoned there by a friend who stood her up, breathlessly recounting down the phone an incomplete, or incompletely worked-through, story about someone's child needing to visit A&E – but not before she'd got there and sat down. Having informed the waiter-greeter-host she'd be eating alone, she found the seat beside her occupied five minutes later by a man whose accent, when he ordered, sounded vaguely Alpine – Austrian, Swiss, Tyrolean, a *Sound of Music* kind of hybrid. On sliding in, he flashed a smile her way (not straight into her eyes but slightly to the side of these, as though at something just behind her), then left her alone for the next forty or so minutes – until, plates cleared, she was scanning the *doce* section of the menu she'd been handed back, vacillating between *torta de amêndoa* and *peras bêbedas*. Then his voice, friendly, intrusive, invaded her airspace.

'Try 808.'

The stools were swivel-types. She swivelled hers round so she was facing him.

'I'm sorry?'

'808. It's the best thing they have here.'

She flipped the page forwards, to the sherries, then back again, to the *cursos principais*. The dishes were numbered, but ...

'There is no 808,' she said.

'I know,' he answered, smiling straight at her now. 'But if there were …'

She felt a sudden heaviness, the counter and the copper and the flames all pressing in on her. Deliberately and slowly, she asked him, already half-knowing the response he'd give:

'If there were, then what?'

'It would change everything,' he completed the sequence.

'Who are you?' she asked.

He slipped a card across the zinc towards her. She glanced at it but it was turned face-down; she didn't want to pick it up.

'I'd like to pay for your meal,' he told her, smiling more aggressively.

'No thanks.'

'We'd like,' he ploughed on, switching person, 'to pay you a large fee for an hour or so's consultancy. It shouldn't present any problem, any … conflict. Your contractual relationship with Peacock is acquitted. There is no embargo.'

She pulled her credit card out hurriedly and waved it at the waiter-host.

'Or even just your notes,' he said. 'Your old ones, that you didn't use. We'd pay you handsomely for those.'

She hadn't managed to attract her target's eye. Gathering her things – bag, phone, book, glasses case – she slid down from her seat.

'I shredded them all,' she told him, and made for the exit, paying on the way out. She kept to Bermondsey Street, which was crowded, and walked quickly north, not looking behind her until, just before the long tunnel underneath the railway line, she found a taxi. Safely installed and moving down St Thomas Street, she turned round then to see if he was following her – which he wasn't, didn't need to: if they knew about 808 and Peacock, then they'd know where she lived too. His card, she discovered after she got home, had found its way into her handbag after all: she must have swept it up in her haste to escape. Pirotti. Cassius First Motion. She burned it immediately, on her gas hob, washing the ashen remnants down the sink.

She wrestled, over the next forty-eight hours, with the question of whether or not to tell Dorley about the approach, the tap-up. Not having decided one way or the other after three sleepless nights, she reasoned that her delay in divulging, if divulging were to take place now, would itself constitute a culpable withholding. Nor would it be the first one: in her deleting, wiping and surrendering, she'd neglected, or omitted, or just not *happened*, to volunteer two files that she was never asked for – her own small act of reticence to match, or counter, Purdue's. On what had turned out to be her last day in the archive, in defiance of the reader regulations, of the signed covenant between her and Ms Richards and the Gilbreths and who knows whom else, Dean, after a quick left-right peek, had slipped out from her trouser a muted phone and snapped two pages of Lillian's jotter-book journal – the last two, the ones with all the doodles and the letter-symbols, the Italian fragments and the crayon-drawn circles and the English tag-line this Pirotti was to quote at her. She could, supposedly, have done it above board: put in a scan-request form, got her copy the next morning, but ... She'd sensed by then the change in atmosphere, a coldness issuing not *from* the archivist but *through* her, from stacks hidden and expansive and, above all, somehow sinister; sensed things closing in, a quarry bright, delicate and rare slipping away. So, furtively and with a shame-defiance cocktail burning in her gut, she'd done it: *snap, snap,* minus *snap*s. Now, back here in Goodge Street, New Kingdom anti-dribble threads and Dubset clauses she's not interested in splayed out before her, she slips the phone out, pulls the pictures up again ...

She must have stared at them a hundred times. The doodle hieroglyphics, then the strings of letters, symbols, not-quite algebra; the lines and vectors that seem to connect one fragment to another, bind them all into some kind of tapestry of reason, or at least of correspondence ... and the colours, morphing, flecks of one contained within another like faint visual echoes, a whole chromatism of epiphany whose key ... At the bottom once more, in bold letters, *Box 808 changes everything*. Floating above it to the right, tethered by connecting penstroke, the initials *T.T.* Constellated all around it, like saints, cherubs, satellites, those scrawled Italian snatches: *fattore ... farsi ... fattura ... legato con amove ... geomètra misurar lo cerchio ... l'amov che move ...* They were penned in Lillian's Phoenix rest home, The Beatitudes: shaky hand, fading eyesight. The imprint of the pencil, impregnation of the paper by the ink seem weak, washed out and faded by first time, then reproduction. In Purdue, Dean typed the sequences into her laptop, saved them to a file that she no longer has. Now, here at D&G, she strikes up a more haptic, analogue relation with them, even if it's mediated by the touchscreen of her phone: dragging her way around the pictures, finger-stretching them to zoom in on one patch of cursive penstroke, sliding them to follow its path on into another, she finds herself clutching her own pen, transcribing the shapes of words and letters out on to the back of her printed note pages ...

Fattore ... farsi ... fattura ... legato con amove ... She took Italian in school, and knows that *fattore* is author, maker or creator; *farsi* the thing that's made, and *fattura* the act of making; *legato* means tied up or bound together ... *amove*, though, doesn't mean anything. The term is half-repeated in *amov*, which doesn't mean anything either – unless it's a first go at the word popping up a little to the right and just above: *move*, moves, sets in motion. That, she's reasoned since Purdue, would make sense, its doubled presence here explained by the word's naming of Lillian's lifelong preoccupation. Now, drawing the figures out, retracing the lines as they jag and curve, doubling again their divagations in the manner of the legal scriveners of old, or the monk-scribes of even older, she comes to notice for the first time that the *v*s in *amove* and *amov* are different from the one in *move*, their right stalks more upright, curled over at the top, like the *r*s in *cerchio, misurar, geomètra* ... and *fattura, farsi, fattore* – which, in turn, leads to a realisation: they're not *v*s at all, but also *r*s. The words are actually *amore* and *amor*. *Con amore*: with love; *amor che move*, love that moves ...

Reverting to digital again, she enters this second sequence in the search bar of the desktop monitor in front of her and, 0.41

seconds later, is presented with the source of not just this but all the other fragments, too. It's Dante, *Divina Commedia* – which she should also have known: she had to study that in school as well. The final, sign-off line, the 'out': the poet or his stand-in, after passing all the way through Hell and Purgatory, through the spheres of the Inconstant, the Ambitious and the Wise, then onwards through the Contemplatives and Fixed Stars right to the *Primum Mobile*; after plotting the entire machinery of circles driving other circles, wheels within wheels, then passing even further, on into the centre, the Empyrean, *finally* gets to behold, face-to-face, *l'amor che move il sole e l'altre stelle*, the love that moves the sun and other stars …

Dean, slumped into her chair, lets forth a kind of sigh, or grunt – a sound of neither triumph nor relief, but simply of the type you let out when, too late, you've got the punchline to a joke you should have worked out several stages back. It seems so obvious: what else would it have been? Lillian's favourite book, the one she planted in the workers' common spaces and rest areas, all the waiting rooms that she designed; the one that must have seeded her mind in the first place with the notion that each action has its best way, its *diritta via* – and the one that, at the end, old eyes turned up, beatitudinous, towards the fading stars, the moon that she'd helped conquer, bobbed back like a patch of word-wrack, half-remembered jetsam to be clung at while she, too, waited to be called into whatever other room was being readied for her …

Setting the pencil down, Dean looks out of the first-floor window. It's dusk; in the street, a lamp is flickering on – and off, and on again. It's been that way for some days. D&G and several neighbouring tenants have complained, citing distraction, epilepsy-trigger risk, ratepayer shorting … Camden Council have promised to repair it later this week. The pole looks old and rusty; it might also have to be replaced. For now, though, it stands blinking intermittently, a fragile finger raising to the sky its bulbous matrimonial band.

6. The Molecularity of Glass

Phocan is leaving. Lazda might join him later, in Riga, or perhaps in London. Or she might not: he might stay in, or return to, Riga – quit Pantarey, his jostling with Sennet for ascendency, the lot ... Or they might both move somewhere else entirely: Berlin, Rotterdam, Helsinki, start afresh ... Or none of the above. Everything is possible and nothing certain. There's a kind of vertigo, exhilaration almost, that comes with moments like this, born of knowing that an old order of things has ended, that the world-as-was must be remade, or at least reconfigured. Lazda's great-grandparents, their generation, would have felt it with the People's Council's declaration, 1918: amidst all the violence, the catastrophe and death, vertiginous exhilaration of the new, of independence ... Last night, he thought she'd want to sleep, but they made love instead, repeatedly, she sobbing between each bout, clinging to him, scratching him, in passion or in anger. Did he *cause* Vanins' death – precipitate it, bridge the final gap between the deed's potentiality and its conversion into action? Maybe. If he did, though, he's a bridge for her as well, between this new time into which she's entering and the previous age in which her grandfather was still alive. And he *understands* Vanins: he's read his papers, knows what he was all about. Other bridges she seems to be burning: she decided straight away to sell the dacha; and the aviary, site of the cataclysm, the old order's end, she's going to have pulled down almost immediately, once the birds have been rehoused or just released ...

A taxi has pulled up. Phocan's getting in; it's pulling off, passing the abandoned playground, turning into the nearest of the three narrow, ditch-lined tracks. Its engine, still in low gear, makes the window of Vanins' study rattle. The taxi disappears; the window, of course, stays: it isn't going anywhere. It's a wood-framed window with four panes. The panes, as Phocan noticed two days ago, seem imperfectly matched to one another. And with reason: they're not just of different ages but of different constitutions too. Three of them (from garden side: bottom left, top left, top right) are made of float glass – soda-lime-silica-constituted, batch-mixed, tin-bath-poured, roller-lifted, lehr-cooled and strainlessly annealed, machine-cut rectangles displaying a regularity, indeed a sharpness, of light propagation with refraction kept right down at <1.5 per cent and scattering, reflection and such manner of distortions similarly minimised. The fourth, though (bottom right), has been cut from different quartz-cloth: cylinder-blown sheet glass, trench-swung, stand-cooled, heat-scored, flattened and hand-measured – tailored, as it were, to order, to the frame's dimensions. Where the other three panes are replacements (occasioned by, in chrono-logical progression: one frost-crack wrought by an exceptionally cold February; one quince, thrown by a young Lazda at a darting cousin whom it – obviously – missed; and one tawny pipit lured, *assassiyun*-like, by the artificial flowers and sky and general depth-illusion laid across its surface by the guileful Old Man of ray optics), the fourth is original: an 1896 piece, putty-set into fresh aspen timber by Vanins' father when he built this dacha.

He, Kārlis, the father, obtained this pane from the glassworks beside Jumelans – no longer, as Phocan saw, operational, nor even really present, its batch-house, furnaces and packaging huts discernible now only as brickwork footprints in the unkempt marram grass through which summer bathers traipse on their way down to a beach whose sand they might still notice is laced to an unusually high degree, a point of saturation almost, with glass fragments, smoothed and coarsened edges posing no risk to their unshod feet. There is a circularity to the beach's mineral constitution: for decades it was its own sand that, shovelled, winched and chuted, fed the glassworks' doghouse, where it mixed with sodium and calcium and magnesium and barium landed by the sack-load from the vessels that once plied the inlet – and, contrafluvially, the blown cylinders' off-cut fragments, the crushed alkali or cullet, that was spat back out to lie around the beach until it was scooped up and thrown back down the batch-feed's gullet once again: sand turning into glass, glass into sand, an endless loop. Or so it seemed, until the glassworks closed in 1985. This one veteran pane, though, still bears witness, through the variant, and varying, texture of its vitreous mass, its imperfect transparency, to the old Jumelans *stikla fabrika* character. How? Unlike the newer ones, it contains bubbles, waves, inclusions, reams and pleats. Looked through from study side, it introduces to the garden little folds, occlusions, doublings – each one near-imperceptible alone, but in amalgam overlaying the flow of branches, well and wood stump with a set of tiny visual hiccups, backwashes or eddies that's at once bewildering and quite hypnotic. All windows around here (since they all came from the *fabrika*) used to produce this effect – which is to say that, viewed from the inside of houses, churches, offices and schools, the entire region, all its scenes and people, used to hic and eddy like this, pause and run and gloop to these same quirky Jumelans rhythms …

There's been debate in recent years, in the more speculative fora of the world of academia, nebulous zones where physics, palaeontology, even musicology start unravelling across one another, about whether or not certain objects and materials could – in theory, at least – be viewed as ready-made or 'inadvertent' recording devices. In 1968, the normally placid proceedings of the International Congress of Classical Archaeology, co-hosted by the Deutsches Archäologisches Institut and the Berlin Ethnologisches Museum (Abteilung Materielle Ethnologie), were ruffled by the presentation of one o. Prof. Friedrich Kelpler, who'd dropped in from Karlsruhe – or, to the ears of his fellow delegates, another planet – where he held the Chair for Ästhetik und Theorie der Medien. What caused all the kerfuffle (picture scowls, snorts and disruptive muttering, even – unprecedented – walk-outs) was o.

Prof. Kelpler's claim that potters' ribs, needles and fluting tools would etch into the wet, receptive surface of thrown clay as, spinning, it was coaxed into the form of bowl or amphora a set of furrows very similar to the grooves carved into lacquer by the heated stylus of a gramophone recorder; furrows that, just like the stylus's, would impregnate the clay with sonic vibrations of the atmosphere surrounding them – which vibrations, clay once hardened, would become immortalised, at least for as long as the ceramic object lasted. Thus, in effect, or retrospect (this was the o. Prof.'s central thesis), an Attic potter's workshop served as a two-thousand-year *avant-la-lettre* recording studio. To yelps of incredulity, Kelpler ran a reel-to-reel of sounds (crackles and scratches set against a whistling background) that he claimed to have picked up by 'playing' an Apulian krater using a hand-held crystal cartridge.

Two years later, after Kelpler's 'findings' had, against the wishes of most of its editorial board, been published in *The Journal of Archaeological Science*, a second article appeared, in *Ethnos*, this time co-authored by Yale anthropologist Kent Foster and Lund acoustician Åke Engström, both well respected in their fields. They claimed to have verified Kelpler's hypothesis, or at least its mechanical possibility, by recording, by means of a vane whose impedance at attachment point into wet clay was ZM(12/11)2 (groove modulation velocity thereby being set at vg = 2 pS/(ZM(12/11ss))), their own voices singing '*Ja, må han leva*' (it was Engström's birthday), and then subsequently reviving these voices with a custom-made tone arm and off-the-shelf Euphonics U15P pick-up.

This second article opened the floodgates: from '75 onwards, archaeoacoustics research labs sprung up in universities around the world; Mycenaean kantharoi, Corinthian alabastrons, Thracian mortaria, pithoi and pelikai and pyxides from Syria to Hibernia were off-mastered, pressed and distributed. Words, phrases, whole stretches of dialogue in Aeolic, Doric, Latins Classical and Vulgar were detected, intercut with barks of Roman dogs, cries of Athenian street-merchants; one archaeoacoustician, in Chicago, even claimed to have eavesdropped on Homer trying out his *Rhododáktylos Ēós* line while stopping by to watch a kylix being spun ... The craze came to an abrupt end when no-nonsense Columbia emeritus Wade Gudron Jnr detailed, in the spring 1982 issue of *Hesperia*, the counter-experiments in which he'd reproduced the playback element of Foster and Engström's (and most subsequent archaeoacousticians') sessions but – devastatingly – not their recorded-content one: in place of ceramic objects, he'd run arm and pick-up over bricks, sandpaper, a table top, a pair of jeans and even, with the level cranked to max, thin air. When he demonstrated, both in sound and sine-wave visuals, near-identical 'voices', 'barks', 'cries' 'phrases', etc. (not to be outdone, he rendered audible not just one but three lines from *The Odyssey*), produced quite evidently from no more than a combination of random static and the listener's imagination, the game was up.

Or rather mothballed: funding streams may have atrophied, but a life-line, a clutching-straw of sorts was thrown out in the form of a postscript- or addendum-article, placed in *Phoenix* (1984, fall issue), by Cameron Blaine Ph.D., Reader in Linguistics at Laurentian, Ontario. Blaine argued, quite correctly, that, while archaeoacousticians' putative ability to separate the signal of antiquity from the noise of contemporary hardware and enthused projection had been thoroughly discredited, nonetheless the *existence*, and indeed the buried *presence*, of the signal in the object had, by Engström, Foster et al., and even by Gudron Jnr, been adequately established. The melodies might be, for now at least, unheard; and, until the requisite hardware (one, admittedly, with needle<haystack signal-magnification ratio) came along, they would remain inaudible; but they, and their immortal words, were *there* – 'if,' as Blaine signed off, channelling George Herbert, 'we could spell ...'

And glass? Is it not, as much as clay, a 'plastic' artefact? In the absence of oscillation-inscribing ribs and needles, the gramophone-analogy may not, in this case, hold – but here the science, if anything, is stronger. While a stylus merely translates into spiral grooves the sound-waves captured in its feeding diaphragm, blown glass is formed by – *as* – the direct imprint of the human diaphragm itself: *Atem*, πνεῦμα, breath of life. And after setting, flattening, cutting, even installation, its 'solidity' is no more than apparent, an illusion that takes in the short-term contemplator only. To the *longue-durée* gaze it is perpetually fluid, molecules migrating over decades, even centuries, about a three-dimensional plane: top to bottom, side to corner, outer to inner surface, all about the swirling Equatorials and Gulf Streams of its oceanic body. This process is reactive: glass is super-sensitive. In 2009 MIT engineering professor Dave Able and his team, in partnership with Microsoft and Caul Research, using equipment that made cartridges and pick-ups look as ancient as the potter's studio that Homer did or (most likely) didn't visit, filmed, without any audio input, an empty tumbler standing on a drinks-table beside which one of Able's graduate students was declaiming 'Mary had a Little Lamb'. While to their naked eyes the tumbler was quite still, when replayed at a speed of 4,300 fps, motions, caused by sound-waves hitting its surface, of one tenth of a micrometer, or five thousandths of a pixel (infer-able through boundary fluctuation, or just changes in the pixel's colouration as one region encroached on another), were rendered visible and, through Caul's algorithm, translated back to sound, until *And everywhere that Mary went her lamb was sure to go* warbled back out of a speaker half an hour after its first, natural iteration. Although, in this instance, it was the real-time disturbance in the glass's form that furnished such a level of retrievability, the glass, as Able's team knew all too well, would have continued its displace-ments far into the future at levels lower and more micrometric still – in terms both of its edges, their vacillation through the air about them, *and* of the internal scurry of its sound-shocked par-ticles within the confines of their gathering-containing cylinder, up and down the sides, along the rim, the convex pools extruding from its base-plane: so many pinballs ricocheting endlessly off solenoid-filled bumpers, kickers, slingshots, off each other – and then, even after that, the bumpers' *memory* of being hit, replaying in quivering aftershock, detectable on no seismograph perhaps but solidly, materially, at nano-scale, the scale of atoms, *happening* ...

And if sound, why not light? Do photons, too, not bounce and multi-ball around? *Light*, the fifteen-year-old Phocan was made to recite mantra-like in GCSE Physics class, *travels in straight lines until A Level.* Even *air* can bend and warp it, send it arabesqueing into mirages, *fata morganas*, floating castles. So windows ... windows are to light what mazes are to rats, or pots to lobsters: looming edifices full of switchbacks and blind alleys, forks and three-way junctions, secret passages that magic travellers to far parts of the labyrinth, or even duplicate or triplicate them till they occupy two or more stretches at the same time – but, like all enchanted palaces or funhouses, exact their toll, a levy measured in the photons that are doomed to traipse about their corridors for ever. *Absorption* (as Phocan's teacher informed him when he turned sixteen, popping with one thrust his optics-cherry) is the term for this entrapment: not, strictly speaking, *loss* of light, but rather its snaring, and eventual conversion into heat – which, just like sound, wreaks havoc with those flows and currents, spreading its own interference waves, disturbance patterns that in turn spark new disturbance patterns, chain reactions, on and on. Viewed from this perspective, isn't every window a light-capturing machine? An event recorder, like the murder victims' eyeballs said to retain imprints of the acts they've witnessed? Even ones with low refractive indexes, like Vanins' study's three newish, float-glass panes, claim as many as fifteen of every thousand photons seeking safe passage through them. And the fourth: the kinky, stuttering, gaze-tripping Jumelans *stikla fabrika* pane? This one's voracious, swallowing *seventeen* and up, a Scylla and Charybdis furnace-fused into one giant, vitreous monster whose very flesh retains the heat-conversion traces of innumerable devourees.

If we could spell ... What would this pane divulge? The light residues of which histories does it store up? No murders, certainly – just visits to the well; the stumping of the birch that once stood next to it, then the stump's service as a platform for the chopping into firewood of smaller birch and aspen logs; proliferation of the spruce branches, their annual pruning; springtime growth of grass, its summer scything; rain, snow, more rain, sunlight, moonlight, starlight, the accumulated meteor-streaks of a hundred and twenty-two Augusts and Septembers; ditto those of (averaging out to account for species variation) forty-three generations of birds darting, pausing, swooping, in one tawny pipit's case for the last time; mainly, nothing more than tiny oscillations in grass blades and twigs ... And somewhere, lodged in the still-shifting contours heat-marked by those billions of levied photons, broken, scattered and kaleidoscoped to a degree no high-speed camera or algorithm yet devised could reverse-engineer, one scene, from 1969: of Jesēnija – Raivis's wife, Lazda's grandmother – standing in the garden, moving and not moving simultaneously.

She would be planted, feet apart, between stump and well, playing a novelty game better known in the last few decades by the proprietary title 'Swingball' but in those days referred to as 'tether tennis' – playing on her own, with (or against) herself. The set, purchased by Vanins on a recent trip to Zürich, consisted of a pole whose whittled base was sunk into the earth and to the upmost portion of whose mast a coil or spiral was affixed; to the coil, in turn, a ring clip had been fastened – fastened, that is (being looped around rather than welded on), to the coil's overall helix although not to any one spot of this, thus enjoying (if that's the word) free reign to corkscrew its way up and down the spiral's length. To the clip a string was tied; the far end of the string, a metre away, fused into a tennis ball. Jesēnija Vanins (née Lazdiňš) was hitting this ball with a racquet: first with one side, forehand, then, as it swung on its leash round the pole back to her, with the other, backhand. It was April; in the Atlantic Ocean, the Apollo 9 had splashed down some days earlier; in the sea of Japan, a US EC-121 reconnaissance plane had splashed too, downed by a North Korean MiG-21; in Britain, the first vertical take-off jet had just been trialled; in Riga, at the Universitāte, the entire administrative board had resigned under student pressure, replaced by new and more permissive blood. A handover, or changing of the guard, winter to spring, seemed to hang in the texture of the garden's air as well: a finer and more grainy quality of light, a dotting of the visual field with midges, dragonflies and bees, whose buzzing laid an intermittent base note underneath the *thwock, thwock* tenor of the racquet's strikes ...

It was the mechanism that had made Vanins buy the set: this curved metal bar along whose length the ring clip glided had instantly reminded him, when he'd first caught sight of it in the *Sportwarengeschäft*'s display window, of Lillian's models; of hands tracing their turns and loopbacks, again and again, the repetition copying the same paths over to the tracers' bodies, consigning them to memory of limbs and muscles. On this spring morning (mid-morning, that long stretch of unconcern that sets in an hour or so after breakfast), it seemed to Vanins, watching from his study (he was writing a paper for the *Soviet Physics Journal*, on the reasons for the N1 programme's failure), that Jesēnija was playing the tracer's, the path-learner's, role, performing movements programmed into and dictated by the core form of the coil, as though she and not the ball were its final extension, gliding in locked orbit. With each of the ball's anticlockwise loops her shoulders would reach with the arm and racquet to greet its return – and with these, in their wake, the segments of her back would take off, one after the other, like so many cohorts of an army obeying orders to decamp, to strike out on a march, each unit moving separately and yet in conjunction with the larger troop formation; and, as though chasing these, her hips, too, would rise, hoisted on thighs that in turn were driven by soft knee-hydraulics, by articulated calf-and-ankle mechanisms further down; all in the space of half a second. Then, the ball being met and dispatched on its clockwise counter-loop, her arm, in each second's remaining half, would sail back, wrist bending the other way to reset hand and racquet angle, a boat smoothly changing tack, easing its way through calm, compliant water to the spot (unmarked on any chart yet implicitly, through seamanship so ancestral it's become almost genetic, *known*) at which it would once more bump up against the yellow buoy or, more accurately, fellow (if counter-directional) voyager, *sputnik*, this small sphere that on contact always found itself, if not in the exact same location, then at least in the same place relative to its circumnavigation's compass ...

The window was, of course, integral to this scene, to these effects. As Vanins watched her through it – that is, through three old Jumelans panes (the frost-cracked one had already been replaced), the main part of the action framed, as circumstance of height and desk-placement dictated, within the pane that now survives – its glass not only stretched Jesēnija's movements; in its glucose thickenings and accretions, it seemed to expand the duration of these movements too, doubling each moment and replaying the doubled passage in a kind of simultaneous slow-motion. Jesēnija, twenty-six, was already expanding on her own, waist and bust widening as she laid in fat in preparation for Dagnija's, Lazda's mother's, birth (the pregnancy, having one week earlier cleared the three-month hurdle, was no longer secret). Her body, as she swivelled one way then the other, seemed to store up and replay for him a wider set of movements and positions, their associated scenes, from early courtship onwards: a gesture made when greeted in the street on one chance meeting; the way she'd once set a cup down in a cafe in Alberta iela; how she'd reached for her coat afterwards, flung a scarf round her neck; or flung the neck itself back, laughing, when he'd told her a joke one day on the bridge in Bastejkalna Park; had done the same each time he kissed her in a certain spot, under the chin ... These and scores of other moments, transposed and repeated, merging with his own partial reflection in the glass, sparked in him a sudden awareness of synchronicity, of processes all happening at once – or rather, being re-melted, blown into and held within some new formation, an arrangement relegating the time of their actual happening to insignificance. Nor was he observing this from outside: he was held by the formation too, gathered and absorbed in its consistency: watching, remembering and anticipating fused together, rhythm and suspension merging, *thwock, thwock*, with his pulse-beat …

How long did he watch for? Hard to say, in light of these reflections. It would be wrong to call the episode 'timeless'; that is, to try (rhetorically at least) to place it out of time. It was packed full of time, and times – so saturated with them, though, as to defy all measure. Vanins was, it's true, entranced – but even in that trance, amidst its swirl and billow, he maintained a sharpness, a keen perspicacity. As the parts of the kinetic symphony presented by Jesēnija and the tether-tennis set seemed to detach themselves, to wander from their posts while still somehow ensuring that each post continued functioning, he started seeing racquet, ball and figure (torso, elbow, thigh, etc.) not as what they *were* but rather as objects in a long celestial dance, all acting on each other: racquet attracts ball, which attracts figure, which carves rhomboids, sinusoids and gyres into the air, which in turn draw racquet – all of this drawing and holding his attention, which in its own turn (was Jesēnija aware that he was watching?), fuelled and sustained the dance, sent all its parts careening round their orbits and meridians once more: another cycle, and another … Vanins thought – how could he not? – about his work: of states of equilibrium, sines and cosines, vector sums and net force. But, rather than being harnessed as correlative for these, a prompt for new practical applications, the tether-tennis symphony seemed to take hold of them and send them into orbit too. Everything – work, the world, politics, even physics – seemed suspended, flipped into a mode of operation in which operation itself has been stood down and, in that very passiveness, that *uselessness*, been opened up to every possible new use. At one point it occurred to him that he was watching nothing less than life, in its pure, concentrated form, unhidden by the camouflage of purpose – but he put that thought on hold, since to name, to give a label to the phenomenon he was engaged in contemplating would have gone against its nature, nature of which his abandoned contemplation, contemplation for its own sake, was a merging, doubling and careening part …

He did, though, even in abandonment, experience a sense of urgency, of mission. Over the next weeks, and months, this urgency, this mission, would act on him like a coiled helix, dictating his activities. Right now, though (now, then, whenever – ask the windowpane), its first motion took the form of his right hand reaching – slowly, cautious not to frighten off a thought so delicate it might take flight, or just evaporate, at any second – down to ruffle the pages of his essay draft in search of a clean sheet. Failing to find one, he turned over the most recently composed page, covered on one side only, and, on its virgin verso, wrote in English, beneath the heading *T.T.*:

Dear Lillian,

I think I've made a discovery ...

7. The Wrangler

Under the mews's cobblestones, below buildings that, prior to their conversion into advertising, architecture, investment-portfolio management and film-production company offices, slept and fed and watered Fitzrovia's draught and livery horses; off the courtyard, past an iron door whose perfunctory chain lock persistent junkies are continually unpicking; down a stone staircase on which both light and oxygen levels noticeably decrease every two or three steps; beyond another, state-of-the-art double door that neither addict nor anyone else not armed with trifecta of swipe card, RFID tag and daily-generated pin code has yet managed to outsmart; in an expansive if compacted basement whose humidity and temperature are recalibrated every five and a half minutes lies Degree Zero's render farm. There, behind glass dust covers, eighty-two motherboards denuded of their casing and arrayed either upright in long lines, like after-dinner mints, or horizontal, one above the other, like shelves built to store nothing but shelf, flicker and blink in restless computation. Between these and across floor, walls and ceiling snake two hundred and eight yards of cabling. Tower fans, also shelf-sized, rotate sentinel among them. Their modulating roar, the motherboards' relentless hum, the general tremble of electric overcharge all rise through earth and bricks above; below, they shake plasma and membranes of all plastic, metal, glass and wood and, not least, the lone human who's on duty here tonight.

Do we know him? We do: it's Soren, he of the velveteen hairs. He has, as hoped, 'progressed'. No longer a mere runner, he has been promoted to the post – still entry-level, but a salaried one nonetheless – of render wrangler. His job: to monitor, from dusk to dawn, the passage of the endless gigabytes that make up each of *Incarnation*'s images, through the SVN-filters into the server; to assign to each frame's cluster a processing pen fenced off from all the others yet at the same time, inasmuch as they all feed off and into the same source and output channels, conjoined; to see to it that these pens don't become overcrowded, blocked, stampeded; to ensure the welfare and, indeed, to verify the basic genetic purity of each one's charges, checking for scripting errors, unforeseen corruptions and all manner of infirmity that, if not picked up and isolated at this stage, will mutate and multiply through the next, and the one after that – contagion that, worst-case scenario, will eventually erupt across the skin of the released film in an outbreak of glitches and anomalies that would cost DZ their reputation and (needless to say) Soren his job. More specifically: this job entails watching, on his desktop, logged into the server through VNC client, the revision numbers roll past and refresh themselves; checking how much memory each processor, or 'proc', is using, and reallocating a portion of its labour to another when the figures go too high; updating the SVNs; running system admin ... Sometimes Soren moves methodically, from one proc to the next; sometimes he darts between them randomly, spot-checking, keeping them all on their toes with the element of surprise. From time to time he pulls up all the procs' vital statistics simultaneously, lays them out side by side in multi-screen, columns of numbers and figures all jiggling together: a muster-parade roll-call, to ascertain whether there's been any slacking off. If he spots sloppiness or snags, he brings offending stragglers back into the fold by issuing an shh command. He does this manually, types into the Blender script the letters *shh* – as though he were some kind of whisperer, lulling and soothing not a single restless animal but hundreds all at once. This render farm has more processing power than most countries. It's managing calculations that would take a human a whole lifetime – to work out the position of a hair, the passage

317

and rotation of a piece of dust, the luminescence of a fork's tine, frame by frame by frame ...

Incarnation's render has been scheduled as a twelve-week task. 44,928 frames, to be rendered at an average speed of sixty-one minutes and fifty-six seconds per frame, with twenty-three being concurrently processed at each given moment, equals 2,016 hours. It's running round the clock, every day of the week, no breaks for public holidays. Soren is one of four wranglers – the most junior, which is why he's got the graveyard shift. So here he is, tonight: corralling, *shh*shing, verifying, updating, cross-checking, plucking sample lines of code out of the millions that shuttle past like (if you want old-school, analogue comparators) newspapers on the conveyor of an offset press, or reels of cross-weave rolling off the loom of some giant fabric plant – the difference being that each of Soren's interventions, rather than carrying the process forwards, helping to fire the morning edition off to waiting stands, newsboys and breakfast tables, or to bring the tapestry closer to completion, sets it back: it's an unpicking, registered by a small back-tick on the aggregated progress bar that has its own dedicated screen both here on the farm's wall and on the remote desktops of the many supervisors and coordinators, editors, compositors, accountants and so forth who track it like impatient suitors to whom an answer, yay or nay, *some* kind of resolution, is long overdue.

To unpick or back-tick ourselves: *Incarnation*'s render *had* been scheduled as a twelve-week task. That figure's been revised to fourteen. It will go up further: no one doubts that. We're in Week Eleven. Right now, most of the frames working their way through the procs are drawn from the film's final, seven-minute sequence, which depicts the KFS *Sidereal*'s break-up as it drives manically, suicidally, towards Fidelus. As the ship powers its way past the star's outer heliopause, into its heliosheath and on towards the boundary of its termination shock, the plasma-discharge sloughing off the sun's upper atmosphere, racing at supersonic speed from its corona, proves too much for the vessel's constitution. Screws and rivets bend and elongate and shoot off like so many poppers on a baby's one-piece; panels of sheet-metal sheer away and tumble down-hull, gouging into heat shield, wing and skirt new gashes where their jagged sides make contact; stabilisers, banks and a whole storage bay detach themselves and, rather than simply hurtling away, hover, vortex-held, expanding and imploding simultaneously, their forms, dimensions and properties, the very laws by which they're bound, gone haywire. The bow wave has indeed, as Briar proposed, brought on a general fucking with all terms and values. Basic oppositions – up/down, attraction/repulsion, togetherness/separation, even inside/outside (of an object, of the ship, of people's bodies) – seem to be collapsing. A rapier (maybe Tszvetan's, lethal implement that stove Merhalt's skull, that led to the seduction and thus, indirectly, to the present pass, or maybe just a random rapier whose history we can only guess at – either way, denuded now of all pasts, which slough off particulate as well), moving of its own volition, lunging and patinandoing in mid-air down an auxiliary corridor, is shattering into ten thousand shards but still managing to sear through the jugular of a stoker whose own vital frame, though similarly crystallising and disintegrating, writhes in affliction, as though each of its newly minted fragments retained the memory of the whole of which they until recently formed molecules; the stoker's blood, spilling, mingles with distant stars, *becomes* the stars that are now fully visible through the *Sidereal*'s hull although the hull, somehow, is still there, both contained by and containing the external space that it was built to keep at bay. Things proximate – grid-panels, ring-latches, attenuators – seem to stand at infinite distances; things far or forgotten – distant nebulae, *brinquedotecques* and *gzhiardini*, relics of Argeral childhoods – seem to be close at hand: it's a catastrophe happening here, sure – an annihilation, an extinction – but there's also, ultra-paradoxically, a counter-movement of formation, of *emergence*, going on as well, a sense of something edging its way, through all the chaos, to the threshold of the visible, the comprehensible ...

Tszvetan and Tild, like salmon fighting their way upstream to the pools from which they spawned, have pulled and scraped and lunged themselves back to the place where it all started: the Observatory. They've writhed and threshed their way through hatches, slid along conjoining tunnel walls to which gravity has at first pinned them down, then, suddenly reversing its direction, thrust them onwards, as though willing them towards their goal. From time to time they've had to push aside a stoker's body, or observe a dying one being vacuum-sucked into the interstellar void. The stokers' faces, both alive and dead, all have the same expression carved across them: never terrified or anguished, but satisfied, contented, *happy* even, proud of having seen through to its endgame and beyond a fierce devotion from whose pledge they drew their strength and purpose, drew their very essence as retainers. Death, conjunction with the stars, cements this essence, renders it eternal. Even amidst the carnage, Tszvetan and Tild register these attestations of a faith oblivion can't snuff out; vindicated and spurred on by them, they plough on through disintegrating airlocks and equipment bays, battery modules, water-storage tanks, up past what used to be the *Sidereal*'s starboard trusses; tumble up, down and along the geometry-defying, now semi-fluid double-helix of the uncoiling spiral staircase; and, finally, find themselves spat, internally vomited, into the viewing platform's spherical and cyst-like chamber.

The sapphire-glass dome – perhaps because it was so thin and provisional in the first place, scarcely more solid than a bubble – has held up to now, although it's only a matter of time before it, too, disintegrates. The instruments, the spectrohelioscopes, astrolabes, dioptras and torquetums, are flying through the air, colliding with each other and the central console, with the globe-within-globe reader whose controls are running all amok, casting out names, coordinates and legends, defunct cartographies dredged up from unravelling memory, on to a territory also unravelling, buckling, shredding. The radium-coloured zigzags in Tild's hair are tangling and unravelling too, transversals warping and distending with the globe's schizoid projections. The G-force is playing tricks with her and Tszvetan's facial muscles, tautening and stretching mandibles and orbitals and infraorbitals, setting them in arrangements that are manic and yet also strangely calm – like the stokers' expressions, acquiescent, *happy*, utterly committed to a process that's been willed and dared, and that's now daring them. Tszvetan, wrenching at Tild's shoulder, turning both their bodies round so that they're facing outward, bulging eyes pressed right against the sclera of the dome's own bulging eyeball, says to Tild:

'It's waiting for us.'

Despite all the roar, the splintering and smashing, he doesn't have to shout. The magnetospheric overhaul, the atmospheric stripping brought on by the solar wind, has imposed intimate acoustics in which the sound-waves carrying his voice convey it to her as directly as if he'd spoken straight into her skull, or in the dome, the whispering gallery, of a silent cathedral. At the same time, propagating without amplifying it any more, they carry it all over: along each of the *Sidereal*'s tunnels, corridors and bays, up and down its sump-tanks, masts and vent lines, skirts and cones and baffles – and beyond, over Fidelus's termination shock, throughout its heliosheath. The intimacy's general. It encompasses way-distant clusters, all the hypergiants and subgiants, binaries, deltas and cepheid variables, the furtive aggregates of dusty clouds, the welcoming abyss into which, willing the dome to shatter, he and Tild are preparing to leap. Is that what Tszvetan meant by 'it'? Is that what's waiting for them? The abyss? Or did he mean the leap itself: the doing of it, the enactment of its moment, the split second at which time makes contact with eternity? His words, replaying now like a universal echo, vest all power of decision in the *it*, not in the lovers: it's the *it* that's clasping them within its holding pattern, offering them their only course of action, the choice of doing what they have no choice but to do: to yield, to surrender to this omnipresent and elusive place, this instant whose happening can take place only as a pause, a waiting ...

Motherboards hum. Tower fans' roars modulate as they rotate. Soren checks the time: 3:21 a.m. He does this on his desktop, since he's not allowed to have a phone down here, nor any other interface with what's beyond the door. The upper world could end without him knowing it; could *have*, somewhere between frames 37,204 and 37,275, between the last SVN update and the one before, between a dust fleck's impetus towards a new rotation and the putting of this into motion, the conception of a shadow cast out by a fork tine and the shadow's generation, ended. Soren often finds himself entertaining – running, updating, revising – fantasies of emerging, blinking, into the next day's light to find that London has been nuked, zombie apocalypsed or fire-and-brimstoned from existence. He was raised Methodist, taught to believe in the end of time, in rent and rapture. *Render*: the word, now, still carries echoes of his first encounter with it, Mark 12: 17 – *Render therefore unto Caesar the things that are Caesar's, and unto God the things that are God's.* And of his second, also in the church in which he sang each Sunday, surpliced and cassocked choirboy, number 103 in the Welsh Hymnal: *All laud we would render: O help us to see …* He hears, from time to time, more frequently the tireder he gets, the hymn's words, the tune, its cadence, slinking through the farm's background, foreground and surround sound, replaying in his head, an ear-worm:

> Immortal, invisible, God only wise,
> In light inaccessible hid from our eyes …

… then *Something, blessèd, glorious, Ancient of Days*, then more light: *unresting, un-something and silent as light … pure Father of light; Thine angels adore thee, all veiling their sight …* and *clouds which are fountains … something …* and then back to light again: *'Tis only the splendour of light hideth thee …* It's not just him remembering, half-remembering, them: the lines are being sung to him actively, it seems, by voices not quite human – maybe super-, of a higher order, angels, dancing in the circuitry, light inaccessible, wisdom pronounced in muffled tones, in shh code; or maybe sub-, the half-formed tongues of entities themselves only half-formed, half-thought, held within some limbo of not-quiteness: foetus-beings, unbaptised, unsaved, their fallenness surrounding them like artefacts, RGB-separated halos of imperfection. In the last fully rendered sequence, committed to SVN as avi file 7,021, light from Fidelus, its corona's plasma-stream, is washing the *Sidereal*'s command antenna, pouring into and through it, liquefying it while, reciprocally, the antenna, its assembly mount and the surrounding fuselage are pouring out too, shedding their forms to flow, proton, electron, alpha particle, into the sunlight, like gold melting. Rendering, as Soren knows full well because it's what his mother thought his job involved when he first told her about it, can mean smelting iron, lead or brass; also reprocessing (this is what his *grand*mother understood his new métier to be) the overspill of slaughterhouses, the already-butchered carcasses of cows or chickens: grinding, steaming, crushing them still further to extract the fat or tallow, to squeeze out a tiny bit more profit, one last ounce of mulch ...

On his desktop, through the VNC window, Soren watches frame 37,289 go through its one hundred and sixty-fourth render pass. The physics, the material properties, the specular qualities and a dozen other factors have been overlaid, grafted on one another, and the finished image is now looming into view. It's a close-up of Tszvetan's skin: his bulging forehead pressed right up against the now almost impossibly overpressured sapphire glass. Skin is translucent; it's notoriously hard to get the balance of fleshiness and luminescence just right in a normal setting (sitting in a bedroom, walking down a street or even riding a horse or spaceship into battle in a stable light environment), let alone when you've got multiple reflections and a general collapse of the physical field in which both light and skin reside. And then the porousness, the hairs ... One integer, one digit off the mark, and suddenly you'll have great clumps of thick-weave pushing through the membrane like diseased rabbit fungus. In those instances he has to pull the frames out, send them back into production, and the progress bar back-ticking too. Those are the easy calls: the harder ones come when it's just one or two pixels, one fragment of flesh or hair or shadow in the wrong place for a fraction of a second, miniature sub-error no one's going to notice – until someone does, not necessarily his line manager, nor even Herzberg, Dressel, *Incarnation*'s ten or twenty million viewers; it's that twenty million and first, that nerd who spots it on his fifteenth streaming, pulls it out, posts it on badrender.com, and the shame wends its way slowly but surely back to Soren, settles on him like a rash. Even harder: if the *image* is fine but he can see an error in the code behind it, inactive for now, but ... Does he wave it through since no one else is going to know; or will this error, like a bullet in an unused chamber, work its way round eventually, a few roulette turns on, and splatter brains, his or someone else's maybe but his *fault*, forensically retraceable to him, to this decision or avoidance of, this moment of deferral ... ?

Tszvetan's temple, although bulging and stretching to the limits of epidermal tolerance, is intact. Its underlying code is sound. Tild's skin, too, tautening in manic yet calm determination, retains its integrity; her hair's geometry may be going wildly wrong, but it's going wrong in a way consistent with the render code, the *right* way. Stokers, too, and grilles, airlocks and panels are flying apart *correctly*, each of their parts following trajectories consistent with those of each of the other parts, the collisions between, the currents and back-swells acting on them generated by the previous currents and collisions, the trajectories and back-swells plotted by the software. As each frame completes its final pass, it's posted on the same screen as the progress bar, remaining there until the next completed frame replaces it. The order of succession follows that not of the film itself, its narrative, but rather of the sequence in which each of the twenty-three frames being worked over in each batch is spat out of its rendering pen, assigned an avi number and held up for scrutiny both here and in DZ's linked spaces, like (to go old-school once more) a newly developed photographic print being pegged up dripping on a darkroom clothesline. The last one out, the one drying on the progress-bar screen right now, shows, in close-up, a pressure-gauge dial mid-eruption, glass face cracking like sheet caramel, the needle detaching, propelled outwards on its spring like an ejector seat. The next, replacing it now, shows, in wide-shot, a long jet of light that was correction engine similarly leaping from the ship – initially as a coherent streak, then fraying as its wavelengths fluctuate and part, then finally, at the shot's far edge, being reamalgamated as the colour-threads are gathered and subsumed, like candyfloss strands, by the larger clumps of light spinning and amassing in Fidelus's heliosheath. Here's that Livnära fork again, free-floating trimaran cast loose from the *Sidereal*, ploughing its way hungrily towards Fidelus as though to devour it, to *be* devoured. This is an orgy of consumption, cosmic autophagia, space eating itself, chucking itself up, swallowing itself again, viscera and linings involuting to ingest whatever's just ingested them: plasma-wave, loading bay, dome, termination shock, temple, abyss …

Tszvetan and Tild are through the Observatory's pane now – through it *and* within, both *here* and *there*, as though they'd broken through the boundary not just of the sapphire glass but also of their bodies, of their senses, at once dispossessed and occupying the other side of them, looking at both themselves and space, all space, from any and all points, possessing each of them convulsively. Seeing is touching; light is vision; *laud we would render; 71 per cent complete* … And, most miraculous of all, amidst the deformation and the involution, there are forms: there is consistency; faces and landscapes – eyes, smiles, zigzags, outlines of Kernwinal Hills and Marais wildlands – still, flying in the face of possibility, persisting …

The sequence-file Soren's got open on his desktop, playing and replaying through the speakers, is the one containing Tszvetan's line: *It's waiting for us*. As it loops, it, too, breaks down: *swaitingf … swaitingf … swaitingf* … It's 4.17. The splendour of light hideth. The adoring angels are speaking in tongues now, echolalia. The room, like the *Sidereal*, like termination shock and heliosheath, is melting and reforming. In the choir, they kept their vestments in the sacristy off to the side, on hooks, beside the albs and stoles and cinctures of the clergy. Reverend Edwards always liked to watch the boys change, their white flesh. Shh. Soren's dozing. Photons shoot off the corona. In The Beatitudes, Lillian's eyes are blighted, cataract-occluded, lenses glazed and clouded. Faded colours, halos, rays of that deep light which in itself is true, *nel suo profondo vidi che s'interna*, saw gathered together, *legato con amore*, bound by love into a single volume, leaves that lie scattered through the universe, *squaderna*, shh, substance and accidents and their relations, I saw as though they fused in such a way, that what I say is but a beam of light.

Out past the double door, on the stone staircase, halfway up or maybe halfway down, two junkies are, like Soren, on the nod. Do they have names? Of course – but these will only show up near the end of some long credit roll nobody ever bothers watching, least of all them. The farm's noise carries to them, but out here it's less aggressive, its roar muffled, almost lulling. It's still physical, though, a buzz and tremor rolling out in waves, washing their crumpled bodies, holding them in place. As each new wave crosses the unmanned border of their consciousness it ripples slightly, bending and diffracting; then it, too, starts to disintegrate as it heads further in, towards the lower reaches, to a blackness neither rays nor traces penetrate.

Acknowledgements

The Making of Incarnation's composition benefited from start to finish from the willingness of various technical experts to submit their wind tunnels, water tanks, mo-cap workshops, gait labs and post-production studios to my scrutiny — an act all the more generous given the often sensitive or redacted nature of the work carried out therein. To Mark Quinn, Marvin Jentzsch and Christian Navid Nayeri, Adam Shortland and Caspar Lumley, Andy Ray and Richard Graham I'm very grateful. Also, for extramural tutorials on CGI, physics and copyright law, to David James, Martin Warnke, Donn Zaretsky and Alison Macdonald; for Greek guidance, to Penny McCarthy and Daviona Watt; and to David Isaacs, for research and assistance throughout. I would also like to acknowledge the financial support and hospitality of the DAAD Artists-in-Berlin Program, who gave me a year-long fellowship.

In wider-lens view, the novel's contexts and trajectories both arose and found their shape, as always, in dialogue with a host of other artists, thinkers and friends. Ruth Maclennan first directed me towards the Institute for Industrial Psychology's archive. Melissa McCarthy opened my eyes to the significance of Queequeg's tattoo-copying antics. Mark Aerial Waller pulled the world of archaeoacoustics onto my radar. Omer Fast shared his drone-pilot interview notes with me. Ieva Epnere and Kristaps Epners snuck me into restricted faculty buildings and storage bunkers all over Riga. Florian Dombois directed smoke and lasers around me in his exquisite contraption on the roof of Zürich's Hochschule der Künste. The St George's Walk episode of 'Ground Truth' grew out of a workshop with five pupils — Rosa Brennan, Carina Clewley, Milla Kahl-el Gabry, Annie Stables and Leah Swarbrick — at Prior Weston Primary School in London; Webster's speculations in 'The Girl With Kaleidoscope Eyes' out of a live-writing session in Berlin's K Gallery for 'The Death of the Artist', No. 7 in *Cabinet* magazine's '24-Hour Book' series. To these, and many other collaborators, I'm indebted – as I am to my excellent editors on both sides of the Atlantic, Dan Frank and Michal Shavit, and their colleague Ana Fletcher; to my magnificent cover designers Peter Mendelsund and Suzanne Dean; to my tireless agents Melanie Jackson, Jonathan Pegg and Marc Koralnik; and to the even more tireless Eva Stenram.

More WEST *Highland* TALES

Orally collected
BY THE LATE J. F. CAMPBELL

*Transcribed and translated from
the original Gaelic by*
JOHN G. MACKAY

Edited by
W. J. Watson, D. MacLean
& H. J. Rose

VOLUME 2

Birlinn

This edition by Birlinn Ltd. 1994

Birlinn Ltd.
13 Roseneath Street
Edinburgh EH9 1JH

With thanks to the Department of Celtic
Aberdeen University for use of original editions.

A CIP record of this book is available from the British Library.

ISBN 1 874744 23 8

More West Highland Tales Volume II was originally published
in 1960 by Oliver and Boyd.

Chuidich Comhairle nan Leabhraichean am foillsichear
le cosgaisean an leabhair seo.

Printed in Finland by Werner Söderström OY

TO THE MEMORY OF

JOHN FRANCIS CAMPBELL OF ISLAY

IAIN ÒG ÌLE

THE GREAT MASTER OF FOLK-TALES

29th December 1822—17th February 1885

PREFACE

THE first book of this series contained two tales from MS. Vol. viii., and tales from the first half of MS. Vol. x. of the MS. Collections of the late John Francis Campbell of Islay.

The present book contains tales from the second half of MS. Vol. x.

The Abbreviations employed in this book are the same as those in the first book.

J. G. McKAY

NOTE

A good many years have passed since Volume I of *More West Highland Tales* was published, and a word of explanation seems called for. J. G. McKay worked for many years on an edition of all those numerous Highland folk-tales from J. F. Campbell of Islay's collection, now in the National Library of Scotland, which the latter had not already published in his great *Popular Tales of the West Highlands* (Edinburgh, 1860) ; at the time of his death in 1942 he had several volumes ready in manuscript. The first of these was published in 1940, under the auspices of the Scottish Anthropological and Folklore Society, with the co-operation of Professor W. J. Watson, the Reverend Professor Donald Maclean, and Professor H. J. Rose. These editors got Volume I finally ready for the press, and did some preparatory work on Volume II ; among other things, Professor Watson, who was to oversee the Gaelic text, availed himself of the assistance of the Reverend William Matheson in revising McKay's sometimes rather inconsistent spelling in both volumes.

It had been McKay's hope that Volume II would follow shortly on Volume I, but his own death, the war, and then various other unavoidable circumstances have delayed its appearance till now. After the war the manuscript was placed in the hands of a general editorial committee, which included Major D. C. Crichton, Mr R. Kerr, the late Mr J. B. I. Mackay, Mr T. J. M. Mackay, S.S.C., the Rev. J. Mackechnie, Mr Samuel Maclean, Professor Angus Matheson, and Professor H. J. Rose, and to these gentlemen the Society now extends its 'warmest thanks for their valuable help. In particular the four mentioned on the title page have played a major editorial part in revising the manuscript ; and something may be said of what this part has been.

Campbell's original collection was made partly by himself, but to a much larger extent for him from the folk-tale tellers by a number of collectors, men of a greater or lesser degree of

education and ability to write Gaelic. As a result the Gaelic
texts are very uneven, and J. G. McKay adopted a policy of
editing and normalization. If the work had been intended
solely for scholars it would no doubt have been preferable to
print the originals exactly as they stood, but since it was planned
to appeal to that much wider audience who had already enjoyed
the *Popular Tales of the West Highlands*, McKay's decision was
no doubt wise. Nevertheless, even after 1940 there still remained
much to be done to the Gaelic texts ; spelling apart, there were
obscurities, cruxes of interpretation, and much else. This part
of the work has been undertaken, with great skill and with his
usual profound scholarship, by Professor Angus Matheson, to
whom the Society is particularly indebted. Professor Matheson
appears on the title page as editor of the Gaelic text, but the part
he has in fact played, at various stages in the history of the
book, has been much more far-reaching than that. A number
of notes by himself are printed in square brackets with the
initials 'A. M.'

Secondly, the translation as prepared by McKay was felt
not to be entirely satisfactory. There were some inaccuracies,
and these were dealt with by Professor Matheson. But in
addition, the style of the English used seemed by this time
rather unsuited to the present day. In McKay's youth an
archaising diction was the fashion for translations from ancient
literature and folk-tales, but tastes have changed, and this is
so no longer. The task of editing and revising the translation
in accordance with modern ideas of style was entrusted to
Mr John MacInnes, for whose labours, partly under difficult
conditions of military service abroad, the Society is especially
grateful. He has produced a very smoothly readable and
accurate English version, and corrected some slips ; but in
addition he has undertaken the troublesome task of seeing the
whole work through the press. All the editors have read
proofs, but Mr MacInnes has taken the responsibility for all the
mechanical work involved.

Thirdly, the Society has been fortunate in having for
Volume II, as for Volume I, the invaluable help of its Honorary
President, the distinguished folklorist Professor H. J. Rose, who
has edited and revised the folk-lore notes, and has made some

additional comments given here in square brackets with the initials 'H. J. R.'

Lastly a word on the present writer's part in this volume. McKay's Notes and other commentary were apt to be longer than necessary, without adding anything of proportionate value, and moreover sometimes contained certain personal ideas, developed at length, which modern scholarship would probably regard as doubtful or obsolete. Such changes in outlook are natural if only with the passage of time. It was felt desirable, therefore, to do a certain amount of pruning, particularly as the great increase in the costs of publication since 1940 made it essential to reduce the size of the manuscript where practicable. I was therefore commissioned by the Society to undertake this task. I have treated it almost solely in a negative way, removing only that which seemed to be of small or no value, keeping anything that appeared even moderately worthy of inclusion, and deliberately adding almost nothing on my own account, though much might often be added—one or two brief notes in square brackets with the initials 'K. H. J.' are the only instances.

If the impression given by the above remarks is that the edition of Volume II is scarcely now the work of J. G. McKay at all, this would be quite erroneous. Apart from the translation, and the above-mentioned corrections of the texts and Gaelic spelling, little has been changed and very little indeed added, the alterations being almost all by way of subtraction. Hence the book remains essentially McKay's, and the debt owed to him by folklorists and students of literature everywhere for the years of laborious, enthusiastic, and single-minded toil which he devoted to these unpublished Gaelic manuscripts is now considerably increased. Volume II is indeed his memorial.

The Society wishes to express its warm gratitude to the McCaig and Carnegie Trusts for generous financial grants-in-aid towards the expenses of publication. The Society is grateful to the publisher, Messrs McLaren of Glasgow, for permission to include three tales from *The Wizard's Gillie.*

KENNETH JACKSON
President, the Scottish Anthropological and
Folklore Society

CONTENTS

LIST OF TALES

'83.1. UIRSGEUL, No. I

A version of part of the Mermaid [*recte* The Battle of the Birds, *W. H. Tales*, i., No. 2] with a new incident about a woman fallen in love with by another [the incident also occurs in No. 113, this book]. Ann Darroch [of Ballygrant, Islay], reciter. Hector MacLean [transcriber]. Recd. June 1, 1859.'

Across this, Islay has written—" Abstracted at the Battle of the Birds. The Gaelic need not be printed." The Gaelic MS. is bound up in MS. Vol. viii., near the beginning. It is therefore not given here.—On the lower half of the flyleaf, Islay has listed the next—

On the back of one of the last few pages of No. 105, Islay has written—
'No. 105. The Merchant—[Patrick] Smith—Arabian Nights.

    106. The great uarisgeul—Macfie—A version of the King of Asair
        Ruadh [=Easaidh Ruaidh, *W. H. Tales*, i. No. 1] but very
        curious—The good old language lost—Referred to in Note on
        No. 1, Ia[nuar]y [18]60.[1]

        107. Fiachaire Gobha. [See] the Collier [No. 348, English List]—I
           heard this—(?) a book story.'

MS. bears no number. Not mentioned in Islay's Gaelic List.

A flyleaf occurs here, on which Islay has written—
    '118. Mac a' Chìobair.
    119. Cù Bàn.
    120. Na Trì Rathaidean Móra.
    121. An Cat Glas.'

The MSS. of Nos. 119, 120 are bound up in MS. Vol. viii., and are therefore not given here. A version of No. 119 appeared in *Zeitschrift für Celt. Phil.*,
i., p. 146. No. 120 appeared in *The Celtic Dragon Myth*, p. 149.

---

[1] See *More West Highland Tales*, i., notes to No. 1.

A gap of no less than 23 numbers occurs here, and a gap of numbers after No. 129 in Islay's Gaelic List, *W. H. Tales*, iv., end, where he has an apparently irrelevant remark about 20 tales which had been bound together, etc.—I cannot understand this at all, but suspect that the 20 were all published, but under different numbers. The Gaelic List, and the other lists at the beginning of MS. Vol. x., which is superseded, indicate that Islay numbered his material in some cases three times. This makes it sometimes very difficult to trace them.

with which is fused No. 165, Cogadh eadar Sliochd dà Bhràthar, 'A Battle between the Descendants of Two Brothers.'

ADDENDUM TO LIST OF TALES

Disconnected and unintelligible, and therefore not given here.

Of no merit, and therefore not given here.

Bound up after No. 67c. Abstracted, *W. H. Tales*, i., No. 10, Var. 2. For the Gaelic, see *Béaloideas*, iv., p. 398. See also *Waifs and Strays*, iii., p. 301.

Of this, Campbell says—'Poor wit about a Laird of Islay.'

To be published later.

Fused with 53a, q.v.

A version of *W. H. Tales*, ii., No. 45. Professor Watson has some interesting notes on Mac Rùslaig in *Scottish Gaelic Studies*, i., pp. 210-211.

Sent by Hector MacLean. Not given here.

In Islay's Gaelic List, 'Mac na Bantraich,' the Son of the Widow.

Abstracted *W. H. Tales*, ii., No. 30, Var. 2. For the Gaelic, see *Béaloideas*, iv., p. 399.

---

[1] [*sic*].

More West Highland Tales

MAC IAIN GHEÀRR

 [*MS. Vol. x., No. 62*]

BHA siod uair ann, fear ris an canadh iad Mac Iain Gheàrr ann am Muile, agus chaochail a athair, agus cha d'fhàg e de chloinn ach Mac Iain Gheàrr is a bhràthair. Agus bha cuid mhór aca a dh'fhàg an athair. Agus phòs am màthair an sin duine eile, agus is ann air tìr-mór a bha e. Agus an ceann ùine, dh'fhàs a' bhean gu tinn agus coltach ris a' bhàs. Agus bha Mac Iain Gheàrr is a bhràthair ann am Muile, agus char fios a chur chuca gun robh am màthair gu tinn. Agus dh'fhalbh iad, agus rànaig iad, is bha iad treis ann, agus cha robh am màthair ach tinn.

B'fhada le an oide a bha iad a' fuireach, agus thuirt e gum faodadh iad a bhith dol dachaigh. 'Thoir dhòmh-sa do làmh,' arsa Mac Iain Gheàrr, 'gun cuir thu fios orm dar a chaochlas mo mhàthair ;' agus gheall e sin da. Ach cha robh dòchas mór aige as, agus rànaig e caraid dha fhéin, agus dh'iarr e fios a chur chuige dar a chaochladh a mhàthair. Chuir am fear sin fios chuige : 'ach,' arsa a charaid, 'is fheàrr liom thusa a dh'fhuireachd gun tighinn.' Dar a chuala Mac Iain Gheàrr seo, rànaig e a bhràthair, agus dh'innis e dha. Agus thuirt a bhràthair, gum b'fheàrr leis fhéin gun iad a dhol ann. 'Cha bhi sin ri aithris,' arsa Mac Iain Gheàrr, 'nach d' rachadh sinne gu tìodhlacadh na màthar ; is thoir leat an gunna.' 'Cha toir,' arsa esan. 'Chan iarr mise ort a toirt as a' bhirlinn,' ars esan.

Dh'fhalbh iad agus rànaig iad, agus chuir iad a' bhirlinn air laimhrig. Agus dh'fhalbh iad gus an taigh an robh am màthair marbh. Agus bha an oidhche aca a' ruighinn. Bha òl gu leòr an siod. 'Stad thusa,' arsa Mac Iain Gheàrr ri a bhràthair, 'ach an cluinn sinn gu dé tha iad ag ràdh 'san taigh.' Chuala iad fear a' cantainn, 'Nan tigeadh a nis Mac Iain Gheàrr, cha bhiodh e toilichte gus an tugadh e a mhàthair gu Muile g'a tìodhlacadh.' 'Ùbh, ma thà,' arsa am fear eile, 'bhiodh cuid a mhàthar aige' 'A bheil thu 'ga chluinntinn siod, a bhràthair ?'

2

MAC IAIN GHEÃRR

No. 41.   [*MS. Vol. x., No. 62*]

ONCE upon a time there was a man in Mull called Mac Iain Ghearr. His father died and the only children he left were Mac Iain Ghearr and his brother, and they inherited a good deal of wealth from their father Then their mother married another man who lived on the mainland. After some time she became ill, and it seemed she was going to die. Mac Iain Ghearr and his brother were in Mull, and word was sent to them that their mother was ill. They set out and arrived, and were there for a time, but their mother remained poorly.

They made a long stay, it seemed to their stepfather, and he suggested they should go home. 'Promise me,' said Mac Iain Ghearr, 'that you'll let me know when my mother dies' ; and he promised. But Mac Iain Ghearr had no great confidence in the man, so he went to a friend of his own and asked him to send him word. His friend sent word, 'But,' said he, 'I would rather you did not come.' When Mac Iain Ghearr heard this he went to his brother and told him. His brother said that he himself preferred that they should not go. 'It shall never be said,' says Mac Iain Ghearr, 'that we would not go to our mother's burial—and bring the gun.' 'I will not,' said he. 'I shan't ask you to take it out of the ship,' said Mac Iain Ghearr.

They set off, and arrived and moored their ship, and on they went to the house where their mother lay dead. When they arrived it was night. Drink was flowing there. 'Wait,' said Mac Iain Ghearr to his brother, 'till we hear what they are saying in the house.' They heard someone say : 'If Mac Iain Ghearr came now, nothing would satisfy him until he took his mother to Mull for burial.' 'Ah then,' said someone else, 'his mother's property would be his.' 'Do you hear that, brother ?' said Mac Iain Ghearr. 'Yes,' said his brother. So Mac Iain

arsa Mac Iain Gheàrr. 'Tha,' ars esan. Agus tholl Mac Iain Gheàrr an taigh troimhe, agus thug e a mach a mhàthair, agus dh'fhalbh iad leatha, agus rànaig iad far an robh a' bhirlinn air laimhrig.

Agus bha uamhag ann an sin, agus chuir iad chuige teine, agus chuir iad fear de shiùil a' bhàta eadar iad fhéin is am màthair. 'Nis,' arsa Mac Iain Gheàrr ri a bhràthair, 'tha easbhuidh oirnn. Chan 'eil boinne stuth againn. Có as feàrr leat-sa, falbh no fuireach ?' 'O, is fheàrr liom,' ars esan, 'gun duine againn a dh'fhalbh.' 'Cha bhi sin ri a chantainn,' arsa Mac Iain Gheàrr, 'gun rachainn gu tìr ann am Muile gun bhoinne a bheirinn do na daoine a choinnicheadh mi.' [1] Is dh'fhalbh Mac Iain Gheàrr, agus thug e leis buideal a bha anns an taigh far an robh a mhàthair.

Am fear a dh'fhuirich, a bhràthair, chunnaig e an seòl a bha eadar e féin 's a mhàthair a' gluasad gu làidir, agus loisg e urchair, agus lìon e an gunna a rithist : agus loisg e naoi mun tànaig a bhràthair. Agus thànaig Mac Iain Gheàrr, agus buideal làn air. Agus dh'innis a bhràthair dha mar a dh'éirich dha, gun do chuir e naoi urchraichean 'na mhàthair. 'Ùbh,' arsa Mac Iain Gheàrr, 'chì thu gur e a tha agad fortan.' Dar a dh'fheuch iad, bha aca naoi biastan-dubh.[2] Agus dar a chunnaig iad an là, dh'fhalbh iad agus rànaig iad tìr ann am Muile. Agus chunnaig iad a' tighinn 'nan déidh cóig eathraichean làn de dhaoine, agus bha an t-sabaid ann dar a thànaig iad cuideachd. 'S cha do thill air an ais ach triùir.[3]

Bha taobh dubh agus taobh geal do'n bhirlinn aig Mac Iain Gheàrr, agus bha dà sheòrsa sheòl aige dhi, feadhainn dhubha agus feadhainn gheala. Agus bha e 'na mhèirleach mór, agus bhiodh [4] e a' goid a' chruidh leis a' bhirlinn as na h-eileanan. Ach oidhche char a dhà dheug a ghoid air Mac Gill'-eathain ; agus rinn na seirbhisich a mach gu cinnteach dha gur e Mac Iain Gheàrr a ghoid iad. Agus is ann a bheireadh iad Mac Gill'-eathain far an robh Mac Iain Gheàrr.

---

[1] The use of whisky at funerals was universal. The funeral cortège was sometimes preceded by a piper, and another man. The latter dispensed oatcakes (or other food) and whisky to everybody whom they met on the way to the burying place. See also *W. H. Tales*, i., No. 15, Notes.

[2] For the luckiness of otters, to which Mac Iain Gheàrr refers, see the notes

Ghearr bored a hole through the wall of the house and brought his mother out and came to where the ship was moored.

There was a little cave there and they kindled a fire and placed one of the ship's sails between their mother and themselves. 'Now,' said Mac Iain Ghearr to his brother, 'there is one thing we lack. Not a drop of liquor have we got. Which do you prefer, to go or to stay?' 'Oh! I'd prefer that neither of us went,' said the other. 'It shall not be said,' says Mac Iain Ghearr, 'that I would land in Mull without a drop to give the people who met me.' [1] And Mac Iain Ghearr went out and took with him a cask that was in the house where his mother had been.

The one who remained behind, Mac Iain Ghearr's brother, saw the sail that was between himself and his mother moving violently and he fired a shot and reloaded. Before his brother returned, he had fired nine. Then Mac Iain Ghearr returned with a cask full of liquor, and his brother told him what had happened, that he had fired nine shots at his mother. 'Ah!' said Mac Iain Ghearr, 'what you will find is that you've got a fortune.' When they looked they found nine otters.[2] When they saw it was dawn they set off, and came to land in Mull. They saw five ships full of men coming after them, and when they met a fight started. There returned only three.[3]

Mac Iain Ghearr had a black side and a white side to his ship, and two kinds of sails for her, some black and some white. He was a great reiver : he used to carry cattle off from the islands in the ship. But one night twelve cattle were stolen from MacLean ; and MacLean's servants convinced him that it was Mac Iain Ghearr who had stolen them. And so they insisted on bringing MacLean where Mac Iain Ghearr was.

to this tale ; and for another story of firing at a corpse and an otter's coming forth, see *Robertson*, MS. 460, p. 101.

[3] The tale (which fails to say whether they brought their mother to Mull and buried her there), is obviously defective here. The relation between the dead woman and the otters is obscure, and it is not said what became of her body.

[4] This word is the last on the 8th page of the MS. At the foot of that page, the scribe has written '30th July, 1859.'

Chuir Mac Gill'-eathain fàilte air Mac Iain Gheàrr, is chuir
Mac Iain Gheàrr fàilte air.   Agus dar a ghabh iad naidheachd
d'a chéile, thuirt Mac Gill'-eathain gun tànaig call air a raoir,
gun deach dà mhart dheug a ghoid air.   'Cuiridh mi geall,'
ars esan, 'gun robhas 'ga shamhlachadh sin ri Mac Iain Gheàrr.'
'An tà, bhà, a bhròinein,' arsa Mac Gill'-eathain.   'An tà, cha
ruig thusa [a leas] sin a chreidsinn,' arsa Mac Iain Gheàrr.
'Ach bho'n a thàna' [1] tu,' arsa Mac Iain Gheàrr, 'fuir'idh [2]
tu cuide rium fhéin an nochd.'   'Tha mi deònach,' arsa Mac
Gill'-eathain ; agus char na fir a bha leis dhachaigh.

Agus rinn Mac Iain Gheàrr an t-ullachadh a b'fheàrr a
b'urrainn e do Mhac Gill'-eathain.   Is dar a bha iad gu math
ann an dòigh, thuirt Mac Iain Gheàrr ris, 'Chan 'eil àite agam
an cuir mi a laigh thu ach an sabhal : agus théid mi féin a laighe
cuide riut aig do chasan.'   Agus dar a thànaig an t-am, char
iad a laighe 'san t-sabhal.   Agus thug Mac Iain Gheàrr leis botal,
agus bhuail Mac Iain Gheàrr air sgeulachdan agus air òl cuide
ri Mac Gill'-eathain, agus an ceann treis, thuit Mac Gill'-eathain
'na chadal.   Agus air a bhuinn a bha Mac Iain Gheàrr.   Agus
bha sgiobadh aige an còmhnaidh dar a dh'fhalbhadh e a'
feitheamh [3] na birlinn.   Agus ghoid e fichead mart air Mac
Gill'-eathain an oidhche sin.   Agus chan fhacas e féin riamh air
féill a' creic cruidh : ach bha buidheann eile aige 'nan com-
panaich a bhiodh 'ga dhèanamh sin air a shon.   Agus ged a
chìte a' bhirlinn geal ùr air an dala taobh a' dol air a h-adhart,
chìte dubh sean i a' tighinn air a h-ais.[4]   Ach mun do dhùisg
Mac Gill'-eathain, bha Mac Iain Gheàrr 'na laighe cuide ris.

Agus dar a dhùisg Mac Gill'-eathain, dh'fhaighnich Mac
Iain Gheàrr ris, 'A bheil thu blàth ?'   'O, is mi thà : a bheil
thu fhéin blàth aig mo chasan ?'   'O, is mi thà,' arsa Mac Iain
Gheàrr, 's e a' toirt làimh air a' bhotal : agus shìn e air sgeulachdan dar a shìn iad air gabhail an drama.   'An tà,' arsa Mac

<hr/>

[1] MS. *thànaid thu*.

[2] MS. *fuir ead*.

[3] *faomh* in MS. which would mean *consenting, assenting* (*Celtic Review*, x., p. 356)
and could not therefore be the word which the reciter meant.   Reciting tales induces
slumber in *Waifs and Strays*, ii., p. 487.

[4] *Tha taobh dubh 's taobh geal air, mar bha air bàta Mhic Iain Gheàrr* ;   'He has a
white side and a black side, like the boat of Short John's son.'   Mac Iain Gheàrr

MacLean greeted Mac Iain Ghearr and Mac Iain Ghearr greeted MacLean. When they had heard each other's news, MacLean said he had suffered loss the night before : that twelve cows had been stolen from him. 'I wager,' said the other, 'that was represented as being like Mac Iain Ghearr's work !' 'Well, as a matter of fact, my good fellow, it was,' said MacLean. 'Then you need not believe it,' said Mac Iain Ghearr. 'But since you've come,' he added, 'you shall spend the night with myself.' 'I should like to,' said MacLean, and the men who had accompanied him returned home.

Mac Iain Ghearr made the best preparations he could for MacLean. When they were comfortably settled, Mac Iain Ghearr said : 'I have no place for you to sleep in but the barn ; but I myself will go and sleep with you at your feet.' And when the time came they went to lie down in the barn. Mac Iain Ghearr took a bottle with him and fell to reciting tales and drinking with MacLean, and in a little while MacLean fell asleep. Mac Iain Ghearr was on his feet at once. When he was abroad, Mac Iain Ghearr always had a crew in attendance on the ship. And that night he stole twenty cows from MacLean. But he himself was never seen selling cattle at a fair : he had another band in partnership with him who did that for him. And although, going one way, his ship was seen white and new on one side, on her return she was seen as old and black.[4] However, before MacLean awoke, Mac Iain Ghearr was lying down along with him.

When MacLean awoke, Mac Iain Ghearr asked him : 'Are you warm ?' 'Yes : indeed I am ; are you warm yourself at my feet ?' 'Oh, yes,' said Mac Iain Ghearr as he brought out the bottle, and when they started drinking he began to tell stories. 'You know,' said MacLean, 'I believe I was hearing

(or Ghìorr)'s proper name was Archibald MacDonell. He was a noted reiver, and followed a known practice of pirates in having his boat and sails of different colours on each side. See *Teachdaire Ùr, Jan.* 1836, p. 52 ; Nicolson's *Gaelic Proverbs*, p. 362 ; *Ged is fhad a mach Barraidh, ruigear e,* 'Though Barra be far out, it can be reached,' said by Mac Iain Ghèarr, one of the Mac Ians of Ardnamurchan, to MacNeill of Barra, who had been very hard on him at a Court of Justice ; *ibid.,* p. 200.

Gill'-eathain, 'tha mi an dùil gun robh mi cluinntinn sgeulachdan
'na mo chadal an oidhche a raoir.' 'An tà, tha mise 'ga do
chreidsinn,' arsa Mac Iain Gheàrr ; 'lean mi treis orra an déidh
dhuit cadal, is mi an dùil nach robh thu air cadal cho luath.'
Ach mun do sguir iad de bhruidhinn is de ghabhail an drama,
thànaig teachdaireachd gu Mac Gill'-eathain gun deachaidh
fichead bó a ghoid air a raoir. 'Nach cumadh sibh rium roimhe,'
arsa Mac Gill'-eathain, 'gur h-e Mac Iain Gheàrr a bha a' goid
a' chruidh anns a h-uile àite ; ach a nis, tha e soilleir, an duine
bha 'na laighe cuide rium fhéin, nach robh e a' goid a raoir ?'
Agus cha do chreid Mac Gill'-eathain facal de dhroch-bheairt
air Mac Iain Gheàrr tuille gu bràth.

6th August 1859.

NOTES

MS. vol. x., No. 62. In Campbell's list, the title is not given ; instead of
a title, the words 'Historical ; pretty good' appear.

The scribe has written in the MS.—'A Story related by Roderick McKenzie,
Strath of Gairloch, Ross-shire.' Against this, Islay has written—'Good :
quote [?] history [?].' The scribe was probably one of Mr Osgood H.
MacKenzie's schoolmasters.

Another account of this celebrated pirate which agrees in several points
with No. 62, though not so wild, will be found in *An Teachdaire Ùr Gàidhealach*,
1836, p. 53. The name is there spelt 'Mac Iain Ghìorr.' See also *Witchcraft*,
p. 47 ; *Superstitions*, p. 181 ; *Sgeulaiche nan Caol*, pp. 19, 21 ; *Trans. Gael. Soc.
Inverness*, xv., p. 162 ; Nicolson's *Gaelic Proverbs*, pp. 200, 362 ; W. Livingstone's
Gaelic Poems, p. 74 ; Marjorie Kennedy-Fraser, *Songs of the Hebrides*, Oran
Buaile, or Milking Song. [*Celtic Monthly*, xv., p. 233.—A. M.]

'When a dairymaid in Mull was milking a young cow, of whose pedigree
she was proud, she sang to her, saying—

> "*Ogha Ciaraig, iar-ogh Duinneig,
> Chan fhaigh Mac Iain Ghiarr a Muil' thu.*"

Mac Iain Ghiarr was a wild reiver of the seas on the West Coast. He was
of good family, being of the MacDonalds of Mingarry in Ardnamurchan. His
mother had been early left a widow, and she married a farmer in Mull ;
and one of Mac Iain Ghiarr's feats was—in after years, when his mother
died—to steal her body away by night, in order to bury her with his own
father. He had a boat painted white on the one side and black on the other
which gave rise to the proverb—*Taobh dubh is taobh bàn a bh'air bàta Mhic Iain
Gheàrr*. This was the boat that was so useful to him because no one that
saw a white boat go up the loch in the morning thought it was one and the
same with the black boat they saw returning in the evening. Mac Iain

tales in my sleep last night.' 'I quite believe that,' said Mac Iain Ghearr, 'I kept on reciting them for a while after you slept, thinking you hadn't slept so soon.' But before they finished talking and having a drink, news was brought to MacLean that twenty cows had been stolen from him the night before. 'Did you not keep insisting to me in the past,' said MacLean, 'that it was Mac Iain Ghearr who was stealing cattle everywhere ; whereas now it is clear that the man who slept along with myself was not stealing cattle last night?' And never again did MacLean believe one word of the reports of Mac Iain Ghearr's misdeeds.

Ghiarr had been listening to the dairymaid who was singing to her favourite young cow, and he replied, although she did not hear—

> "*A bhean ud thall ris an t-sìor bhleoghann*
> *Bheir mi 'n dubh 's an donn 's a' chiar uat*
> *'S dusan de na [h-]aighean ciad-laoigh.*"

And before morning he fulfilled his threat, and only left the breast-bit, or *caisean-uchd*, of each cow to indicate that they need not look for them again upon the hill. We may imagine the sorrow of the dairymaid, who neither had her *dubhag*, nor her *donnag*, nor her *ciarag*, to milk in the morning.' *Trans. Gael. Soc. Inverness*, xv., p. 162.

The Water Dog (*Dobhar-Chù*) called also the King Otter (*Rìgh nan Dobhran*), is a formidable animal, seldom seen, having a skin of magic power, worth as many guineas as are required to cover it. It goes at the head of every band of seven, some say nine, otters, and is never killed without the death of a man, woman, or dog.[1] It has a white spot below the chin on which alone it is vulnerable. A piece of its skin keeps misfortune away from the house in which it is kept, renders the soldier invulnerable in battle by arrow or sword or bullet, and placed in the banner makes the enemy turn and fly. 'An inch of it placed on the soldier's eye,' as a Lochaber informant said, 'kept him from harm or hurt or wound though bullets flew about him

---

[1] The belief recorded in *An Gàidheal* (1924, Dec.), xx., p. 44, is that finding a hoard of buried treasure always brings sorrow and misfortune, and had much the same results as killing an *odhar-bhèist* (presumably an ordinary otter, *odhar-chù* being another name for the animal), for it is never killed without the death of a man and a dog following. This hidden treasure and otters, though both valuable, brought disaster when found or killed.

like hailstones, and naked swords clashed at his breast.   When a direct aim
was taken, the gun refused fire.'

Others say the vulnerable white spot was under the King Otter's arm,
and of no larger size than a sixpence.   When the hunter took aim, he required
to hit this precise spot, or he fell a prey to the animal's dreadful jaws.   In
Raasay and the opposite mainland the magic power was said to be in a jewel
in its head, which made its possessor invulnerable and secured him good
fortune ; but in other respects the belief regarding the King Otter is the
same as elsewhere.

'The word *dobhar* (pronounced *dooar, dour*) signifying water, is obsolete in
Gaelic except in the name of this animal' ; *Superstitions*, p. 216.

'In the north it was held that an otter, while in its den, should not be
called *béisd du*[*bh*] (the black beast, its common name), but *Carnag* [= the
dweller in the cairn ?].   It would otherwise be impossible for the terriers to
drive it from its refuge' ; *ibid.*, p. 240.

The great value attached to the mythical King Otter and the belief in
the magic of its skin, probably explains the remark of the reiver to his brother
that he had got a fortune.   The reiver probably knew that some otters were
there, and guessed that their movements had been the cause of his brother's
shooting.   Otters are known to haunt caves and rocks, etc., at the water's
side.

'The mythical zoology of Sutherland contains also a white otter.   These
animals have a king, sometimes all white, sometimes dun with a white star.
He has a jewel in his forehead, and is only vulnerable in one spot on the
breast.   I do not know if it is an elective or hereditary sovereignty.'
(Campbell's English List, tale No. 50).

'The Dun Otter (Ouar Hoo).   Such an animal was killed in Assynt by
the man who told me the story.   It had a white spot on the forehead, and
one on each side of the muzzle, with one under each shoulder, and a large
white place on the breast.   It is always seventh in the hole, and said to be
the king, and that the others cater for it.   The skin is much larger than that
of the other otters, and is a profitable thing to have ; for owing to some
superstition on the part of ship captains here, they are afraid to let the skin
go out of the ship, if it has once been in it, and so any one taking a skin to
a ship to sell it may name his own price.   It is very fierce, and called in
Gaelic Ouar Hoo [Odhar Chù].   It is supposed to be invulnerable, except
in the breast, but my friend shot it in the hind quarter.'   Campbell of Islay's
English List, Nos. 50, 58.

Another story says that the reiver stole so many cattle from MacLean
that he made him his deadly enemy.   But the reiver came upon some witches
who were sticking pins into a clay doll (*corp creadha*) intended to represent
MacLean.   He scattered the witches, brought the clay doll to MacLean
whom he found at death's door, and in his presence took the pins out one
by one.   When the last pin was taken out, MacLean jumped up a hale man,
and remained ever after the warm friend of the reiver.   See *Witchcraft*, p. 47.

EACH UISGE RATHARSAIDH

BHA siod ann uair gobha ann an Ratharsaidh. Agus mar a thachair, is e cuideachd an teaghla[i]ch fhéin a bu bhuachaillean. Agus bha a nighean oidhche ag iarraidh nan caorach, agus cha tànaig i dhachaigh, agus dh'fhalbh iad a màireach dh'a h-iarraidh. Agus bha loch ann am mullach Rarsair [*sic*] air an robh an t-each-uisge a' fuireach. Agus thànaig iad a dh'ionnsaigh an loch, agus fhuair iad an cridhe 's an sgamhan aig an nighinn ann an cladach an loch. Agus bha an gobha ro dhuilich. Shuidhich e 'na inntinn fhéin gun dèanadh e rian air an each-uisge a mharbhadh. Thòisich e fhéin is a ghille air togail ceàrdaich aig an loch, agus dar a rinn iad a' cheàrdach deas, dh'fhalbh an gobha agus a ghille ann air an oidhche. Thug an gille leis molt, agus chuir e air bior e g'a ròstadh. Bha cromagan móra, dearga aige anns an teallach, agus deas nan tigeadh rud sam bith an rathad. Bha dorus na ceàrdaich ris an loch, agus chunnaig iad an loch a' dol 'na smùid dearg : agus thuirt an gobha, 'Ma thig rud sam bith oirnn, bi tapaidh.' Chunnaig iad tighinn a staigh anns an dorus a mach samhladh biorach-eich, piollach, grànda. Chuir an gobha mór agus a ghille an dà chromaig ann dearg as an teallach, agus leag e air ialltaich agus shìn e air teicheadh, agus thug e faisge air an dorus iad. [Thug e an sin a mach air an dorus iad.] Chuir an gobha mór na buinn an taice, agus thug e air ais e chun an doruis a rithist, agus chum iad ann an siod e. Dh'iarr an gobha mór air a' ghille e a dhol agus a' chromag mhór a thoirt as an teallach, agus a sàthadh ann, agus rinn an gille sin, agus chum iad ann an siod e ach gun do mharbh iad e. Agus dar a thànaig an là, cha robh aca ach dùn de mhac-samhladh salachar rionnag.

8th Augt. 1859.

THE WATER-HORSE OF RAASAY

No. 42.   [*MS. Vol. x., No. 64*]

THERE was once upon a time a certain smith in Raasay. And as it so happened, the people of the household themselves acted as herdsmen. But one night, his daughter, who had been looking for the sheep, did not come home, and they went out next day to search for her. There was a loch in the high ground of Raasay where the water-horse used to live ; when they came to it, they found the heart and lungs of the girl on the shore of the loch. The smith was deeply distressed, and in his own mind he determined he would find a way to kill the water-horse. He and his lad began building a smithy by the side of the loch, and when they had made the smithy ready, the smith and his lad went there during the night. The lad took a wether with him, and put it on a spit to roast it. In the fire he had great hooks, red-hot, and ready should anything come that way. The door of the smithy faced the loch, and they saw the loch becoming a blaze of vapour ; and the smith said, 'If anything comes upon us, be a man !' Then they saw coming in at the outer door what seemed to be a year-old horse, shaggy and ugly. The big smith and his lad fixed the two hooks in him red-hot out of the fire : the water-horse began to yell and tried to escape, and dragged them near the door. The big smith dug his heels in and dragged him back to the door again, and there they held him. The smith ordered the boy to go and fetch out the great hook from the fire and thrust it into the water-horse, and the boy did so. And they held him there until they killed him. But when day came there was nothing there but a heap of what looked like star slime.

NOTES

At the top of the first page of the MS. is written, possibly in transcriber's (Thomas Cameron's ?) hand, the words—'A story—Related by Roderick McKenzie, Strath of Gairloch, Ross-shire.'—J. F. Campbell has written by the side of these words—'Good : kelpie, 64.'

A water monster, when killed, becomes a fresh water lake in *W. H. Tales*, i., No. 4, Var. 4. Other monsters turn into turves, jelly, etc. See *ibid.*, ii., No. 37, where there is a tale about catching a 'Vough' or 'Fuath,' a terrible bogle though feminine. Her captor brought her to an inn, and called to his companions who were anxiously awaiting him, to come out and see the Vough. 'Then they came out with lights, but as the light fell upon her she dropt off, and fell to earth like the remains of a fallen star—a small lump of jelly. (These jellies are often seen on the moors ; dropt stars resembling the medusie [recte, Medusae] on the shore—Collector. They are white, do not seem to be attached to the ground, and are always attributed to the stars. They are common on moors, and I do not know what they are.—J. F. C.)'

For other notices of the dreaded water-horse, see *W. H. Tales*, i., *intro.*, lxxxvii. or lxxix., IV., p. 312 or 342, and Index, and English List at end, tales Nos. 8, 49, 93, 96, 97, 98, 99, 100, 106, 107, 174, 373, 377, 382, 383. Also Gaelic List, Nos. 293, 298 (MS. vol. xi.).

Folk-Lore Journal (1884), vol. ii. *Folk-Lore*, vii., p. 400 ; viii., p. 385 ; xxxiii., pp. 307-308. *Celtic Magazine*, iii., p. 349 ; xii., pp. 511, 572. *Celtic Review*, iii., p. 177; v., pp. 166, 251 ; x., p. 52. *Inverness Courier*, 1874, Nov. 5. *Trans. Gael. Soc. Inverness*, xiv., p. 248 ; xix., p. 41 ; xxii., p. 203 ; xxix., p. 26 ; xxxiv., p. 148. *Waifs and Strays*, iii., pp. 195, 294. Dr K. N. MacDonald, *Gesto Collection of Highland Music*, Appendix, p. 20. Rev. Dr Geo. Henderson, *Survivals*, pp. 116, 141, 161-162 and *The Celtic Dragon Myth*, xxiv. Rev. W. Gregor, *Folk-Lore of the North East of Scotland*, p. 66. Rev. J. G. Campbell, *Superstitions*, pp. 203-205. Rev. Alex. Stewart, *Twixt Ben Nevis and Glencoe*, p. 45. Dr Alex. Nicolson, *Gaelic Proverbs*, p. 306. Col. W. G. Wood-Martin, *Traces of the Elder Faiths of Ireland*, i., p. 378. *Journal Folk-Song Society*, iv., part iii., p. 162. MacDougall and Calder, *Folk Tales and Fairy Lore*, p. 308.

Some tales of the water-horse picture him as being somewhat like a hippopotamus ; *Celtic Review*, v., p. 52. [*Cf.* the story in Boswell's *Journal of a Tour to the Hebrides*, 1936 ed., p. 145.—A. M.]

SGEULA DHOMHNAILL DAOILIG

BHA duine àraidh ann o shean, d'am b'ainm Alasdair Òg, a bha fuireach ann an àite monaidh, do'm b'ainm Coilleach, ann an Siorrachd Rois : aig an robh teaghlach beag, a bha air a dhèanamh suas leis fhéin, a bhean, agus dithis chloinne. Aig am sònraichte, thànaig aon [duine] cloinne eile air, ann an am an earraich ; agus do bhrìgh 's gum b'e an t-earrach e, b'eudar dha féin a bhith tric aig obair a' bhaile. Thachair e air latha àraidh, an uair a bha e ag obair anns an raon, gun tànaig na sìdhichean a dh'ionnsaigh an taighe, agus thrus iad a bhean leò as a leabaidh-shiùbhla. An uair a thànaig Alasdair dhachaigh, cha robh sgeul aige air a mhnaoi, ach an leanabh 'na aonar air a fhàgail ; dh'aithnich e gur iad na sìdhichean a thug a bhean air falbh, maille ri breacan sgàrlaid a bha aice uimpe. Cha robh fios aige ciod a dhèanadh e air a son, agus na h-uile saothair a ghabh e air a son, cha b'fheàirrd e nì air bith.

Mu chuairt is mìos an déidh di bhith air a toirt air falbh, bha aon d'am b'ainm Dòmhnall Daoilig a' buachailleachd spréidh moch air maduinn, an uair a chunnaig e móran sluaigh a' falbh anns an athar, agus air dha amharc na bu ghéire, chunnaig e coltas giùlain eatorra, is iad 'ga thogail is 'ga leagail fa seach, leis an fhuaim seo aca—

> 'Leagamaid a' chulaidh mhagaidh,
> Is togamaid a' chulaidh mhagaidh,
> Is iomanamaid a' chulaidh mhagaidh.' [1]

---

[1] *a' chulaidh mhagaidh* in MS. It is probable that though they carried the woman through the air, the fairies' procession in this story is a reflection of some custom of mortals, in which things or persons were carried in a manner designed to mimic and ridicule some serious procession, and to deride those who had taken part in it. A similar function was *a' bhanais mhagaidh*, the mock or burlesque marriage, designed, if I remember rightly, to annoy obnoxious people who had lately married or were about to marry ; it was performed in full view of the house of the unpopular ones. *An Caoineadh Magaidh*, or The Mock Weeping, is the name of a tale given by Dr George Henderson (*The Norse Influence on Celtic Scotland*, pp. 284, 327) in which the Tiree people weep and cause their flocks and herds to weep also for the death of a boy

THE TALE OF DONALD DAOILIG

No. 43.   [*MS. Vol. x., No. 66*]

THERE was a man long ago called Alasdair Og who lived on the moor in a place called Coilleach in the county of Ross. He had a small family, composed of himself, his wife and two children. Then, one Spring, another child was born ; and since it was Spring he himself often had to be engaged on the work of the farm. One day when he was working in the open fields it happened that the fairies came to the house and swept his wife away with them out of her lying-in bed. When Alasdair came home, there was no sign of his wife ; only the child left there alone. Then he knew that it was the fairies who had taken his wife away, and with her a scarlet plaid she had been wearing. He was at a loss to know what to do for her, and despite all his efforts on her behalf he was nothing the better for it.

About a month after she had been taken away, a certain man called Donald Daoilig was herding cattle early in the morning when he saw a great number of the fairy people travelling in the air and, looking more keenly, he noticed what seemed to be a litter carried by them ; and they were lifting and dropping it alternately and chanting—

> 'Let us lower the butt of our mockery,
> And let us raise up the butt of our mockery,
> And let us drive onwards the butt of our mockery.' [1]

---

and a girl, children of a Norse Queen, whose wrath at her bereavement they desired to appease. A similar story will be found in *The Wizard's Gillie*, p. 80. See Henderson's *Survivals*, p. 101, for a notice of a tale in which calves were separated from their mothers 'in lamentation for noble Mahon.' See also 'Dubh-a-Ghiuthais,' *An Deò Gréine*, July, 1914, ix., p. 149. In *Widecombe Fair*, ch. xxx., Eden Phillpotts gives an account of a mock execution and mock-burial as practised in the Celtic County of Devon. These burlesques were also designed to annoy obnoxious neighbours. See also *Folk-Lore*, xxxiv., p. 39.

Air do Dhòmhnall amharc na bu ghéire agus tighinn na b'fhaisge dhoibh, chunnaig e coltas mnatha 'na laighe ann am breacan aca. Dh'òrdaich e le ùghdarras [1] dhoibh uile a tréigsinn. Rinn iad sin 'nan aon cheò buidhe ; [is] thug e leis a' bhean dachaigh. Bha i cho lag is gun robh i fada fann, agus mar an ceudna dìochuimhneach : cha do chuimhnich i riamh air ainm a' bhaile as an do thogadh i.

An ceann dà bhliadhna, chaidh Dòmhnall Daoilig a dh'ionn-saigh na Féille Muire-Earraich [2] a dh'Inbhir Nis, agus thug e leis breacan na mnatha. Bha Alasdair Òg air an fhéill ; dh'aithnich e breacan a mhnà. Dh'fheòraich e de Dhòmhnall c'àite an d'fhuair e am breacan, agus air dha ìnnseadh dha, dh'fhalbh e maille ris. Thug e a bhean dachaigh ; bha i slàn gu leòr 'na dhéidh sin, is teaghlach mór aice, is bha i cur deise aodaich anns a' bhliadhna 'na dhéidh sin gu Dòmhnall Daoilig air son a choibhneis agus a dhàimh do a taobh mar sin. Thànaig Alasdair Òg air aghaidh ann an teaghlach, agus mar an ceudna ann an cuid.

Recited by Catherine McRae, Dibaig, Gairloch, which she learned some time ago from John McRae. Written by Angus McRae, Dibaig.

NOTES

In his Gaelic List, Islay has given this tale the number 65, and has spelt the title differently, thus—'No. 65. Domhnull Duileag (a fairy).' In MS. Domhnall Duilaig.

[There is a Kintail version of this tale in the Carmichael MSS. It begins : *B'e Dòmhall Dùilig Dòmhall Mac Rath, Fear Aird an t-Sobhail, Loch Aillse. Tha Dùilig an Coire Luinge am bràigh Ghlinn Eilcheig.* (MS. has *Dùilig* and *Duillig*.) *I.e.* 'Donald of Dùilig was Donald Macrae, laird of Ardintoul, Lochalsh. Dùilig is in Coire Luinge in the braes of Glen Elchaig.' See also *Trans. Gael. Soc. Inverness*, iii.-iv., p. 189 : 'Oran Dhomhnuill Daoilig le a Bhean.'—A. M.]

The fairies also travel and carry people away in eddy winds. The Rev. J. G. Campbell, *Superstitions*, p. 24, says, speaking of this practice—'When "the folk" leave home in companies, they travel in eddies of wind. In this climate these eddies are among the most curious of natural phenomena. On calm summer days they go past, whirling about straws and dust, and as not another breath of air is moving at the time their cause is sufficiently puzzling. In Gaelic the eddy is known as "the people's puff of wind" (*oiteag sluaigh*), and its motion "travelling on tall grass stems" (*falbh air chuiseagan*

---

[1] *Ùghdarras*, authority, may imply the use of some magic formula or word.
[2] *Ceud-Fhéill-Muire-Earraich*, the First-Fair-of-Mary-of-Spring, 2nd February.

When Donald looked more carefully and came closer to them, he saw that they had what appeared to be a woman lying in a plaid. He ordered them all commandingly to leave her alone, and the whole lot of them went off in a puff of yellow smoke. Donald brought the woman home, but she was so weak that for a long time she was spiritless and suffered from loss of memory as well. She was never able to recall the name of the village from which she had been carried away.

At the end of two years, Donald Daoilig went to the First Fair of St Mary in the Spring at Inverness,[2] and he took the woman's plaid with him. Alasdair Og was at the fair and he recognised his wife's plaid. He asked Donald where he had got the plaid and, when Donald told him, off he went along with him. Alasdair fetched his wife home, and afterwards she was perfectly well, and had a large family. Every year after that she used to send a suit of clothes to Donald Daoilig for his kindness and affection towards her. Alasdair Og's household grew, and so did his possessions.

---

treòrach). By throwing one's left (or *toisgeal*) shoe at it, the fairies are made to drop whatever they may be taking away—men, women, children, or animals. The same result is attained by throwing one's bonnet, saying "this is yours, that's mine" (*Is leat-sa seo, is liom-sa sin*), or a naked knife, or earth from a mole-hill.

'In these eddies, people going on a journey at night have been "lifted", and spent the night careering through the skies. On returning to the earth, though they came to the house last left, they were too stupefied to recognise either the house or its inmates. Others, through fairy despite, have wandered about all night on foot, failing to reach their intended destination though quite near it, and, perhaps in the morning, finding themselves on the top of a distant hill, or in some inaccessible place to which they could never have made their way alone. Even in daylight some were carried in the Elfin eddy from one island to another, in great terror lest they should fall into the sea.' See *ibid.*, pp. 88-89, for a tale in which a married woman who had been carried away from Mull by the 'folk', is rescued from their clutches by a man from the Bridge of Awe. In his house, at a great distance from her native place, she is eventually discovered by her husband.

A man who had been taken away by the Lady of the Green Island (*Baintighearna an Eilein Uaine*) instructs his wife to throw a dirk at the next eddy wind she saw. She does so, and he drops at her feet, and she recovers him. *Ibid.*, p. 87.

Another man, whose child had been taken by the fairies, drew a furrow round the fairy hillock with the plough. He had not gone far when he heard a cry behind him, and on looking back found his child lying in the furrow. *Ibid.*, p. 84.

Another woman taken by the fairies instructs her husband to take the plough and draw a furrow with it thrice round a certain hillock sunwise. He did not do so, and never recovered her. *Ibid.*, p. 83.

A woman who had been carried away by the fairies appears to her husband in dreams and reproaches him with having failed to throw a bunch of keys at her, or between her and the door, when she was passing him. As a result of his neglecting to do so, the husband fails to recover her. *Ibid.*, p. 83.

A king, his daughter, and her attendant maidens, come in an eddy wind in a tale given in *Trans. Gael. Soc. Inverness*, xvi., p. 115.

In Islay's Collections, MS. vol. xi., No. 190, occurs another tale of the recovery of a wife by a man who strikes with his plaid at the place in the air where he hears a tremendous noise and music coming overhead. His wife drops at his feet. She tells him that the fairies had laid another female in her bed. The husband goes home, takes the other female, who was an old fairy woman, out of bed, and puts her on the fire. She leaps out of the fire and becomes a stump of oak at the threshold. Similar tale in *Superstitions*, p. 83, and in Islay's English List, No. 286. For travelling with the fairies, see also *W. H. Tales*, ii., No. 28 (Ross), p. 67 or 77. For an Irish changeling, see *Béaloideas*, iii., p. 142.

MURCHADH, MAC TIGHEARNA GHEÀRRLOCH

No. 44.   [*MS. Vol. x., No. 67b*]

Air do Mhurchadh mac Tighearna Gheàrrloch, òganach àillidh,
laoch gaisgeil, meas mór a ghabhail air nighean Mhic Ghille
Chaluim, Tighearna Ratharsaidh, boireannach ro àillidh agus
am meas ceudna aice-se air-san, dh'fhalbh e le soitheach gu a
leannan a phòsadh is a toirt dhachaigh.   Bha mac Tighearna
Thulach aige mar ghille-suirghich, òganach gaisgeil eile, a
dh'altaicheadh an dà chlaidheamh còmhla.   Bha triùir dhaoine
treubhach eile a Geàrrloch 'nan cuideachd, Coinneach mac
Ruairidh a Eàrradal, Iain mac Eachainn Chaoil a Bad a' Chrò
(le chéile de Chlann Choinnich), agus Murchadh Mór mac
Ailein Ruaidh, Dòmhnallach.

Rànaig an soitheach Ratharsaidh, ach air do mhuinntir
Ratharsaidh a thuigsinn gun robh mac Tighearna Thulach air
bòrd, thànaig cuid diubh gun dàil do'n t-soitheach, agus air
[dha] bhith teachd a nìos gu bord-uachdar an t-soithich, mharbh
iad e, gun fhaireachdainn, an dorus seòmar na luinge, air son
falachd [a bha] eadar e féin agus mac Tighearna Ratharsaidh.
An uair a chunnaig Murchadh Gheàrrloch mar a thachair,
leum e anns a' mhuir, air dha bhith ealanta air snàmh, chum
dol gu tìr do'n chaisteal, anns am biodh e tèarainte o gach
cunnart.   Ach air a fhaicinn do na boireannaich, agus a' saoilsinn
gur e mac Tighearna Thulach a bha ann, mharbh iad leis na
clachan e mun do rànaig e tìr, agus a leannan 'ga fhaicinn tre
uinneag a' chaisteil, ach gun fhios aice gur h-esan a bh'ann.
Cha d'fhuair i slàinte tuilleadh 'na dhéidh sin.

Mar seo, chaidh an dithis òganach uasal a mharbhadh gun
chomas iad féin a dhìon.   Chaidh an adhlaiceadh an sin, agus
is e ainm an àite o sin, Corran an Oighre.[1]   Thànaig an sin na
bha de bhàtaichean 'san eilean gu teachd do'n t-soitheach, agus
ma thànaig, thòisich an arabhaig a nis da rìreadh.   A' chuid

---

[1] *corran*, a taper point of land running out into the sea.

MURDOCH, THE SON OF THE
LAIRD OF GAIRLOCH

No. 44.   [*MS. Vol. x., No. 67b*]

MURDOCH the Son of the Laird of Gairloch, a handsome young man and a doughty warrior, fell passionately in love with the beautiful daughter of Mac Gille Chaluim, the Laird of Raasay ; and, she being as much in love with him, he sailed off to marry his sweetheart and bring her home. As best man he had with him another young champion, the son of the Laird of Tulloch who could wield two swords at once. Three other gallant fellows from Gairloch accompanied them : Coinneach the son of Ruairidh from Earradal, Iain the son of Eachann the Slender from Bad a' Chrò—both of the Clan MacKenzie—and Great Murdoch the son of Allan the Red, a MacDonald.

The vessel arrived at Raasay, but when the men of Raasay understood that the Laird of Tulloch's son was on board a number of them came immediately to the ship and killed the Laird of Tulloch's son without warning in the cabin door, as he was making his way from below to the ship's upper deck. This was because of a feud between himself and the Laird of Raasay's son. When Murdoch of Gairloch saw what had happened he leaped into the sea, for he was an expert swimmer, so as to get to the castle where he would be safe from all danger. But when the women of Raasay saw him they thought it was the Laird of Tulloch's son, and they stoned him to death before he reached land, with his sweetheart watching him—although she did not know that it was he—through the castle window. She never recovered health again.

Thus were the two noble youths killed without the power to defend themselves. They were buried there, and since then the name of the place has been The Corran of the Heir.[1] All the boats in the island came to attack the ship, and then the battle began in earnest. Those who were not killed were

nach do mharbhadh, bhàthadh iad.　Bha gunna air bòrd a
dhiùlt losgadh ré an latha, ach air do bhàta làn de dhaoine bhith
teachd gu taobh na luinge, thog Coinneach mac Ruairidh an
gunna a rithist, agus loisg [e] i, agus cha b'ann gun bhuaidh.　Bha
sreath dhaoine air beul a' bhàta, agus leag an urchair sìos iad,
agus thug iad fuidhe i leis na bha innte.　Chuir Coinneach
bàta eile, làn sluaigh, fuidhe le prais a bha air bòrd a thilgeadh
sìos 'na meadhon.　Cha deach aon beò as o'n triùir dhaoine treun
seo ach aon fhear, ach chuir Coinneach a chluas dheth.　Cha
deachaidh soitheach an sin o'n là sin a mach.

NOTES

Vol. x., No. 67*b*.　This is probably the tale numbered '60' in Islay's
Gaelic List, and entitled 'Historical Traditions.'

For variants, see *Celtic Magazine*, i. (1876), p. 331 ; ii., p. 192 ; xi., p. 316.

In Applecross, south of Gairloch, there is a place called *Port 'ic-Ghille-
Chaluim Rarsaidh,* the landing place of Mac Gille Chaluim of Raasay.　'There
seems to have been a skirmish here once with the Raasay men.　An Annat

drowned. On board the ship was a gun that had refused to fire all day, but when a boat full of men was coming alongside, Coinneach the son of Ruairidh picked it up again and fired it— and not without effect ! There was a line of men on the gunwale : the shot knocked them down and they sank the boat with all on board. Coinneach sank another boat, full of people, by hurling a cauldron from the ship down into her middle. Only one man escaped alive from these three champions, but Coinneach struck that one's ear off. From that day no ship went there.

man, whose son and house had been burnt by the Raasay band, is said to have performed some destructive archery practice from Sgeir na Saighid, killing a whole boat-load by himself !' Professor W. J. Watson, *Place Names of Ross and Cromarty*, p. 217 (Inverness and London, 1904). [For the historical incident on which this tale is based see 'The Genealogie of the Surname of MacKenzie since their coming into Scotland', *Highland Papers*, ii., pp. 52-54 ; *History of the Feuds and Conflicts among the Clans*, pp. 71-74.—A. M.]

EACHANN RUADH, MORAIR ROIS, RUAIRIDH SUARACHAN, MAC CAILEIN, AGUS AN RÌGH

No. 45.   [*MS. Vol. x., No. 67c*]

Phòs Eachann Ruadh nighean Mhorair Rois, agus thànaig eadar Morair Rois agus Eachann Ruadh [an dòigh air] choireigin agus is ann a chuireadh e a nighean dachaigh chuige. Agus bha am boireannach cam. Agus fhuair Eachann Ruadh gille cam, agus each cam, agus cù cam, agus chuir e dhachaigh i. Agus dar a chunnaig Morair Rois an dòigh anns an do chuir e dhachaigh i, is ann a thog e feachd seachd ceud fear agus rachadh e a sgrios Eachainn Ruaidh, agus na bha aige. Thog Eachann Ruadh seachd fichead. Ghabh Morair Rois air aghaidh, agus choinnich iad a chéile agus thòisich an cath. Agus thànaig duine ri taobh Eachainn Ruaidh ris an abradh iad [Ruairidh] Suarachan. Sheas e 'gan coimhead. Thànaig Eachann Ruadh 'na rathad, agus thuirt e, 'An ann mar sin a tha thu dèanamh, agus mi 'nam theas?' 'Ciod è gheibh mi?' ars esan. 'Gheibh thu cuid fir.' Dh'éirich e is mharbh e duine, agus shuidh e air. Thànaig Eachann Ruadh an rathad a rithist. 'O a Ruairidh! an e sin a tha thu dèanamh, 's mi 'nam theas?' 'Cha do gheall thu dhomh,' arsa Ruairidh, 'ach cuid fir, agus rinn mi cuid fir.' 'Gheibh thu cuid dithis.' Dh'éirich e, is mharbh e fear eile, agus shuidh e air. Thànaig Eachann Ruadh an rathad is thuirt e, 'An ann mar sin a tha thu dèanamh orm, a Ruairidh, 's mi 'nam theas?' 'Cha do gheall thu ach cuid dithis dhomh,' arsa Ruairidh, 'agus mharbh mi dithis.' 'Cha bhithinn a' cùnntas riut' arsa Eachann Ruadh. Dh'éirich Ruairidh agus thuirt e, 'Am fear nach biodh a' cùnntas rium, cha bhithinn a' cùnntas ris.' Is bha iad ag obair, agus chuir iad an ruaig air Morair Rois.

Thànaig na Rosaich gu taigh caillich ri taobh na h-aibhne. Dh'fhaighnich iad, 'C'àit' a bheil àth air an abhainn?' Thuirt a' chailleach, 'Aon àth an abhainn, ged a tha i dubh, chan 'eil

RED HECTOR, THE EARL OF ROSS, CONTEMPTIBLE RORY, MAC CAILEIN, AND THE KING

No. 45.   [*MS. Vol. x., No. 67c*]

RED HECTOR married the daughter of the Earl of Ross, but [somehow or other] Red Hector quarrelled with the Earl and he decided on sending his daughter home to him. Now, the woman was one-eyed ; so Red Hector found a one-eyed lad, a one-eyed horse and a one-eyed dog, and sent her home. When the Earl of Ross saw how she had been sent home, he raised a host of seven hundred men and set out to destroy Red Hector and all he had. Red Hector raised seven score men. The Earl of Ross advanced, and the two parties met and the battle began. Then a man whom people called Contemptible [Rory] came to Red Hector's side and stood looking on at them. Red Hector came to him and said, 'Is this how you act, and I hard pressed ?' 'What shall I receive ?' asked the other. 'You shall have a man's share.' So Contemptible Rory got up and killed a man, and sat on him. Red Hector came that way a second time. 'O Rory, is this how you act, and I hard pressed ?' 'You promised me only a man's share,' said Rory, 'and I have accomplished a man's share.' 'You shall have two men's share !' So Contemptible Rory got up, killed another man, and sat on him. Again Red Hector came that way and said, 'Is this how you treat me, Rory, when I am hard pressed ?' 'You promised me only two men's share,' said Rory, 'and I have killed two.' 'I shall not haggle with you,' said Red Hector. Rory got up, and said, 'He who wouldn't haggle with me, I wouldn't haggle with him.' They struggled on, and they put the Earl of Ross to flight.

The Ross men came to an old woman's house by a riverside and asked, 'Where is there a ford across the river ?' 'The whole river is one ford,' said the old woman; 'though it is black it is

i domhain.' Shìn iad-san air dol a mach, agus shìn iad air dol
leis an abhainn. Agus shìn iad air beirsinn air geugan a bha ri
taobh na h-aibhne. Bha Suarachan 'gan ruagadh, agus thànaig
e chun na h-aibhne as an déidh. Agus a h-uile duine a gheibheadh
greim air géig, theireadh Suarachan, 'O'n a bha mi leigeil a
h-uile dad leat, leigidh mi sin leat.' [Is sgaradh e a' gheug
bho'n chraoibh], is bhàth e móran mar sin. Is char an cath
seachad.

Agus shuidh Eachann Ruadh is a chuid daoine gu biadh.
Agus cha robh ann ach bonnach do na h-uile fear. Cha robh
bonnach ann do Shuarachan. Ach is ann a bheireadh a h-uile
fear dha greim as a bhonnach fhéin. Is bha gu leòr aig Suarachan.
Agus ghabh Eachann Ruadh le a sheachd fichead bochd air
Morair Rois le a sheachd ceud. Agus is ann a rinn Morair Rois
a dhol chun an Rìgh, agus fhuair e o'n Rìgh gun rachadh
breitheachd air Eachann Ruadh, is char airgead-cheann [1] a
chur as. B'eudar a dh'Eachann Ruadh teicheadh g'a dhìon
fhéin. Ach bha dà fhear dheug 'na chuideachd an còmhnaidh.

Anns an am sin, is e an Rìgh a bha tagairt màl Ghallaibh.
Agus is e Mac Cailein a bha e cur g'a thogail. Agus dar a
rànaig e Gallaibh, chan earbadh e e féin ri taigh, ach chuir e
suas bothan aodaich.[2] Dar a dh'éirich e 'sa' mhaduinn, chunnaig
e na Gallaich [3] fo an làn armachd. ''Fheara,' ars esan, 'mura
toir sinn ceann daibh, cuiridh iad a mach air a' mhuir sinn.
Ach,' ars esan, 'tha mi faicinn fir mhóir air an cùl agus dà dhuine
dheug cuide ris, agus is mò a tha iad a' cur a dh'eagal orm na
càch.' Thòisich na Gallaich [3] agus Mac Cailein air a chéile,
agus bhrist am fear mór troimh na Gallaich.[4] Agus [is ann]
le Mac Cailein a bha e, agus is e Eachann Ruadh a bha an siod.
Agus ghabh iad air na Gallaich [4] agus thog iad am màl. Rinn
Mac Cailein agus Eachann Ruadh cùnnradh. Agus dh'fhalbh
Eachann Ruadh gu Dùn Éideann cuide ri Mac Cailein. Agus
dar a rànaig Mac Cailein an Rìgh, dh'innis e dha gum faca e
Eachann Ruadh. Agus thuirt an Rìgh gum b'fheàrr leis gum
faighte greim air. Thuirt Mac Cailein, 'Ma bheir sibh dhòmh-sa

---

[1] *airgead-cinn* is also used, in which the second element in the compound is
governed in the genitive singular instead of the genitive plural.

[2] I have also heard for a tent, *taigh 's aodach*, lit. a house and clothes. ['s = *as*,
'out of,' *i.e.* 'made of'?—A. M,]

not deep.' The men began to go out into the water and were being carried away. They began to clutch at branches by the riverside. Contemptible Rory was pursuing them, and followed them as far as the river. To every man who caught hold of a branch, Rory would say, 'Since I let you have everything else, I shall let you have that too.' [And he would sever the branch from the tree], and so he drowned many. Thus the battle came to an end.

Red Hector and his men sat down to food and there was only one bannock for each man, and none at all for Contemptible Rory. But every man gave him a piece out of his own bannock and Rory had plenty. Red Hector, then, with his paltry seven score defeated the Earl of Ross with his seven hundred. So what the Earl of Ross did was to go to the King, and he succeeded in getting the King's promise that Red Hector should be seized, and a price was set on his head. Red Hector had to flee to protect himself; but there were twelve men always with him.

At that time, it was the King who claimed the Caithness tax, and he used to send Argyll to levy it. When Argyll came to Caithness, he would not trust himself to a house, but set up a tent. When he got up in the morning, he saw the men of Caithness fully armed. 'Men,' said Argyll, 'if we do not oppose them they will drive us into the sea. But,' he added, 'I see behind them a mighty man and twelve others with him, and these I fear much more than the rest.' The men of Caithness and Argyll attacked each other, but this mighty man broke through the Caithness men, and it was Argyll's side that he took ! Who was this but Red Hector. They defeated the men of Caithness and collected the tax. Argyll and Red Hector made a bargain and Red Hector went to Edinburgh with Argyll. When Argyll saw the King, he told him he had seen Red Hector. The King said that he wished he could be caught. Argyll said, 'If you grant me my wish, I will give him to you by the hand.' So the King promised to grant him what he wished. Argyll went to Red Hector and told him this and arranged a time when the King and himself

³ MS. *Galamich*.
⁴ MS. *Galamhich*.

m'iarrtas, bheir mi dhuibh air làimh e.' Gheall an Rìgh iarrtas da. Rànaig Mac Cailein Eachann Ruadh, agus dh'innis e dha : agus rinn e am suidhichte ris, anns an tachradh Mac Cailein 's an Rìgh ris. 'Agus théid thu air do ghlùn,' arsa Mac Cailein, 'agus beireas esan air làimh ort gu do thogail ; agus fairichidh e gum beir thu air làimh air ; agus gabhas tu seachad air, an taobh a bha thu dol.'

Agus rinn e sin. Agus dh'fhalbh Eachann Ruadh. Agus thuirt an Rìgh ri Mac Cailein, 'Cha do rug duine riamh orm a rinn a leithid siod ; seall tu mar a chuir e an fhuil a mach air barran mo mheur.' 'Car son nach do chum sibh e ?' arsa Mac Cailein. 'Cha robh duine anns an rìoghachd a chumadh an duine ud air làimh,' [1] [ars an Rìgh]. 'Siod Eachann Ruadh,' arsa Mac Cailein, 'agus gheall mise gun tugainn duibh air làimh e. Agus gheall sibh-se dhòmh-sa m'iarrtas.' 'Agus gheibh thu sin,' ars an Rìgh. 'A shìth do dh'Eachann Ruadh, ma thà,' arsa Mac Cailein. Agus chuir e an céill do'n Rìgh na rinn Eachann Ruadh dha ann an Gallaibh. Agus is ann a dh'fheumadh Mac Cailein Eachann Ruadh fhaighinn dachaigh air ais. Agus fhuair e sin. Agus dh'fhàs Eachann Ruadh agus an Rìgh 'nan càirdean nach do chuir duine riamh eatorra.

'Cho fad 's gun cualas cliù na h-Alba,
Fhuaireas ainm na dùthch' ud,
An am a h-uaisle dhol ri cruadal,
Bidh Eachann Ruadh air thùs diubh.'

---

[1] [Air làimh could also mean 'in prison, a hostage.' *Cf.* 7 úa na ógána[ch] ar làimh an Dún Édan, Reliquiae Celticae, ii., p. 174. A pun may be intended.—A. M.]

NOTES

MS. Vol. x., No. 67c. Not mentioned in Islay's Gaelic List. Locality, scribe, and reciter, unknown. Related tales are : Mac Iain 'Ic Sheumais, MS. vol. xi., No. 271. Domhnall Gorm Dhùn Tuilm, *The Céilidh Books,* xxvi. (Alex. MacLaren and Sons, Glasgow). Blàr Chàirinnis, *An Deò Gréine,* xvi., p. 67. Alex. Mackenzie, *The Prophecies of the Brahan Seer,* p. 63 (Stirling, 1913). *Celtic Magazine,* ii. (1877), pp. 61, 107, 432. The incidents concerning the sending home of the one-eyed lady occur in all these. The incident of a champion bargaining as to what he was to receive as his price for killing a man occurs in Sir Walter Scott's *The Fair Maid of Perth,* chap. 34 ; Nicolson's *Gaelic Proverbs,* p. 20. It will be noticed that at the beginning of the tale, might meet him. 'You will go down on your knee,' said Argyll, 'and he will take hold of you by the hand to raise you up : let him feel your grip ; then pass him by and keep on as you were.'

And Red Hector did that, and went out. Then the King said to Argyll, 'No man ever took hold of me who did anything like that—look how he forced the blood out of my finger-tips !' 'Why did you not keep hold of him ?' asked Argyll. 'There was never anyone in the kingdom who could hold that man by the hand,'[1] replied the King. 'That was Red Hector,' said Argyll, 'and I promised that I should give him to you by the hand. And you promised to grant me my request.' 'You shall get that,' said the King. 'Peace for Red Hector, then,' said Argyll. Then he related to the King what Red Hector had done for him in Caithness. So Argyll insisted that he should have Red Hector allowed home again, and he obtained his request. Red Hector and the King became such friends that no one could ever make them quarrel.

'However far Scotland's fame has travelled
There has that district's name been found ;
When Scotland's nobility go to meet danger
Red Hector will be foremost of them.'

when Red Hector requires Rory's assistance, he takes care not to call him by the epithet *Suarachan* or Contemptible.

See *Folk-Lore*, i. (1890), p. 276. 'The fairies in the Highlands are all supposed to be drowned in a place called the Ferry. They wanted to cross, and they asked an old woman if the water was deep ; she replied in Gaelic, "Although it's black, it is not deep." James G. Frazer.'

The dark answer given by the old woman in our tale about the ford is traditionally connected with the retreat of the MacDonalds after Blàr na Pàirce (*c.* 1493), when trying to cross the Conon at Moy. Suarachan figures in the same tradition. See *Highland Papers*, ii., pp. 21-24 ; *Clan Donald*, i., p. 262 ; *Ross-shire Past and Present*, pp. 84-93.

The words *Galamh*, *Galamich* [*sic*] have been rendered *Caithness, Caithness people*. But if these renderings are correct, the forms should be *Gallaibh*, and *Gallaich*.

SGEULACHD NA COMRAICH

No. 46. [*MS. Vol. x., No. 67d*]

BHA duine ann an Sgìreachd na Comraich anns na linntean a
dh'fhalbh aig an robh teaghlach cloinne, maille ri beagan cruidh
agus móran ghabhar. Thachair gun do chaill e an teaghlach
leis a' bhàs, ach aon ghille, do'm b'ainm Iain Bàn, agus mar an
ceudna chaill e a mhaoin uile gu inbhe ro bheag, air chor 's
nach robh aige rian air e féin a chumail suas, ach le beagan a
choisneadh [e] air bhith dèanamh agus a' reic sguaban fraoich.
Air dha dol air chuairt do Mhuile, agus a bhith air a thoileachadh
le feabhas an fhraoich anns an eilean sin, smuaintich e fuireach
ann. Air dha an gille a chur do Ghlaschu a reic nan sguab,
thachair e air nighinn òig uasail a cheannaich na sguaban, agus
a thairg dha, air dhi bhith air a toileachadh le a mhodh, a dhol
maille rithe féin gu bhith 'giùlain a cuid leabhraichean do'n
sgoil, air son am faigheadh e tuarasdal agus sgoil. Cha robh e
deònach air gabhail aice, gus am faigheadh e cead bho a athair,
nì a fhuair e, an déidh do'n nighinn uasail banoglach a chur
maille ris.

Bha Iain Bàn a' toileachadh a bhanmhaighstir ro mhath,
agus mar an ceudna bha e togail an fhoghlaim ro mhath, air
chor 's gun robh e ann an ùine ghoirid cho foghlaimte rithe
féin. Thànaig Iain Bàn air aghaidh cho mór ann an gliocas
agus deagh-ghean, is gun robh a bhanmhaighstir deònach air a
phòsadh, nì nach fuilingeadh a bràthair dhi a dhèanamh ; ach
is ann a dh'fhuathaich e cho mór e is gun d'fhuair e a cheangal
ri maighstir-luinge a bha dol do na h-Ìnnseachan an Ear, ag
òrdachadh dha Iain Bàn a chur a mach air a' mhuir, mun
tigeadh e dhachaigh. Chuir a bhanmhaighstir ciste dha anns
an luing agus thug i dha fàinne òir a bha aice féin. Dh'fhalbh
iad, agus fhuair Iain Bàn móran de dhroch-laimhseachadh air
an turus, gun nì de na bha 'sa' chiste fhaighinn,[1] fiù na léine.

Air dhaibh an luchd a reic, agus a bhith deas gu pilleadh

---

[1] MS. 'fhaigheal.

THE TALE OF APPLECROSS

THERE was a man in the parish of Applecross in times past who had a number of children : he also had a few cattle and many goats. It happened that he lost his family by death, all but one boy called Fair Iain ; he lost, besides, practically all his wealth and so he had no means of maintaining himself except what little he could earn making and selling heather brooms. Having gone on a visit to Mull, and being pleased with the quality of the heather in that island, he resolved to stay there. He sent the boy to Glasgow to sell the brooms, and the boy met a young girl of gentle birth who bought the brooms, and invited him, being pleased with his fine manners, to go along with her and, in return for a wage and his education, to carry her books to school. He was not willing to enter her service until he should get his father's assent—and that he received after the young lady had sent a maidservant along with him.

Fair Iain pleased his mistress very much ; moreover, he progressed so very well in learning that in a short time he was as well educated as she. He also progressed so much in wisdom and favour that his mistress wanted to marry him. But this her brother would not allow her to do ; indeed he hated Fair Iain so much that he succeeded in apprenticing him to the master of a ship that was going to the East Indies, giving the master orders to throw Fair Iain into the sea, before he came home. But his mistress provided him with a chest aboard ship, and she gave him a gold ring she had. They sailed away, and Fair Iain suffered a good deal of rough handling on the journey, nor did he get any of the contents of the chest, not even so much as a shirt.

Having sold all their cargo, and being now ready to return

dhachaigh, chaidh iad uile air tìr, ach Iain Bàn, an oidhche mun
d'fhàg iad na h-Ìnnseachan ; ach air dha a bhith leis féin anns an
luing, chunnaig e leanabh dlùth air an luing anns a' mhuir,
am beul na tràghad : dh'fhalbh e, is rug e air an leanabh, 's
thog e leis e. An ùine ghoirid, thànaig boireannach do'n luing,
is dh'iarr [i] an leanabh air. Cha robh e deònach a thoirt dhi
air ball, ach thug i searrag dha, agus thuirt i ris, nì sam bith
cruaidh a dh'fhaodadh a thighinn 'na rathad, an t-searrag a
tharraing, is bhiodh e air ball umhailte.[1] Cho-dhùin e gur
h-i a' Mhaighdean Mhara a bh'ann : thug e an leanabh dhi, is
dh'fhalbh i leis. An ceud fhear a thànaig de sgioba na luinge,
tharraing Iain Bàn an t-searrag, is bha e air ball umhailte dha,
agus bha an sgioba uile mar sin, am maighstir cho math ris a'
chuid eile.

Dh'fhàg iad na h-Ìnnseachan, agus lean iad air seòladh gus
an do rànaig iad Cordoba anns an Spàin, a b'e, aig an am sin,
àrd-bhaile na rìoghachd. Bha iad ro bhrònach anns a' bhaile
aig an am sin, do bhrìgh 's gun tug na famhairean leò triùir
nigheanan an Rìgh, is nach robh rian air an toirt uatha ; dh'innis
sgioba na luinge mu Iain Bàn, agus cumhachd na searraige.
Chuir an Rìgh fios air, agus chuir e impidh [2] air gu falbh, agus a
chuid nigheanan a thoirt bho na trì famhairean. Dh'fhalbh e,
is rànaig e an ceud fhear de na famhairean, agus dh'iarr e air
nighean an Rìgh a chur fa sgaoil air ball. Bha am famhair a'
dol a leum air, an uair a thug e tarraing air an t-searraig, agus [3]
dh'ùmhlaich am famhair e féin, agus gun dàil thànaig e le
nighean an Rìgh. Rinn an dara agus an treas famhair an nì
ceudna ; mar sin fhuair e triùir nigheanan an Rìgh a chur fa
sgaoil, agus thug e d'an athair iad. Bha an Rìgh toileach e a
dh'fhuireach maille ris féin, ach nam b'e a b'fheàrr leis falbh,
gun tugadh e nì sam bith a b'àil leis a bha anns an rìoghachd aige
dha. Cha do thagh e ach aon long bhrèagh ùr, a bha ann an
cabhlach an Rìgh, ach chuir an Rìgh móran òir is airgid innte.
Dh'fhalbh e leatha, agus dh'fhalbh maighstir na luinge eile le a
thé féin, agus an uair a rànaig iad Glaschu, thànaig a' mhaighdean
òg uasal, agus a bràthair, a dh'fhaicinn maighstir na luinge.
Bha a' mhaighdean òg uasal ro dhuilich nuair nach fhac i Iain

---

[1] See *Larminie*, pp. 224, 227, for a magic ring, which when held up between
one's self and one's enemies, blinds and kills them all.

home, they all went ashore the night before they left the Indies, all except Fair Iain. He was alone in the ship when he saw a child in the water, near the ship and close to the shore : he went out and seized hold of the child and carried it away with him. A little while afterwards, a woman came to the ship and asked him for the child. He was not willing to give her the child at once, but she gave him a phial and told him, should he meet with any difficulty, to pull out the phial and immediately his adversary would submit.[1] He concluded that she was a mermaid : so he gave her the child and she went off with it. As soon as the first man of the ship's crew returned Fair Iain pulled out the phial and instantly the man became submissive to him, and all the crew became the same, the master as much so as the rest.

They left the Indies and continued to sail until they arrived at Cordoba in Spain, which was then the capital town of the kingdom. The people of the town were in great mourning at the time because giants had stolen away the King's three daughters and there was no means of recovering them ; so the ship's crew told all about Fair Iain and the power of the phial. The King sent for him and importuned him to go and get his daughters from the three giants. Off he went, and visited the first one of the giants and told him to release the King's daughter immediately. The giant was going to spring on him, but he pulled out the phial and the giant humbled himself and brought out the King's daughter without delay. The second and third giants acted in the same way ; and thus Fair Iain got the King's three daughters released and restored them to their father. The King wished him to stay with himself ; but if he preferred to go, he would give him anything at all in his kingdom that he wanted. Fair Iain chose nothing but a fine new ship that was in the King's fleet, but the King put much gold and silver aboard her. He sailed away in the ship, and the master of the other vessel sailed away in his own ship, and when they came to Glasgow the young lady and her brother came to see the master of the vessel.

The girl was distressed when she failed to see Fair Iain on the ship, but her brother was very pleased. The master of the

[2] MS. *iompaidh.*
[3] MS. *an uair a.*

Bàn anns an luing, ach bha a bràthair ro thoilichte. Dh'òrdaich maighstir na luinge fios a chur air maighstir na luinge eile, a bha 'na chuideachdas a' tighinn dhachaigh. Thànaig Iain Bàn, agus dh'aithnich e a' mhaighdean òg uasal agus a bràthair, ach cha d'aithnich a h-aon dhiùbh-san esan. Thug e am fàinne do'n mhaighdinn leis an robh i ro thoilichte. Dh'fhalbh iad, agus phòs iad, agus bha iad toilichte òrdail tuilleadh gu latha am bàis.

Recited by Hector MacKenzie, Dibaig, Gairloch, and [he] learned it some time ago from Kenneth MacKenzie at Dibaig. Written by Angus McRae, Dibaig.

NOTES

From MS. vol. x., No. 67d. This tale is not mentioned in Islay's Gaelic List. The MS. is bound up after the one which I have called 67c. As it bears no number, I here call it 67d. In the MS. against the title, Islay has written 'Good, genuine, demi-god [?].'

For the Mermaid, see No. 102, this book.

The befriending of the hero by a heroine who was rich, and the throwing of the hero into the sea, occur in tales like No. 40, which combine the themes of the Grateful Dead and the Married Children. No. 67d seems to be but the merest outlines of something greater, and may have at one time contained

ship sent word for the master of the other ship which had
accompanied him home.   Fair Iain came and recognized the
girl and her brother, but neither of them recognized him.   He
gave the ring to the girl and she was delighted with it.   Then
they got married and ever after they were happy and agreeable
to the day of their death.

these two themes.   But this is very uncertain, in as much as it is a mermaid
and not a grateful ghost who saves the hero.

That the hero and her brother fail to recognize the hero upon his return
from foreign parts, suggests the loss of incidents which accounted for the
implied alteration in the hero's appearance.   It is also clear that a recognition
incident has been lost, and that this should have come in when the hero
gives the heroine back her ring.   As a rule, it is the hero's enemy, and only
he, who fails to recognize him.

MAR A CHAIDH CAIT AN TOISEACH
DO'N SPÀIN

No. 47. [*MS. Vol. x., No. 73*]

BHA Probhaist Dhùn Éideann agus aon de Bhàillidhean a' bhaile glé mhór aig a chéile. Bha iad fada eòlach, agus chinn an [t-]eòlas 'na chàirdeas daingeann. Aig am tòiseachaidh ar sgeulachd, bha iad glé bheairteach : chruinnich iad le chéile an cuid stòrais o cheàirde [1] no marsantachd. Cha robh smuain-eachadh aig a h-aon aca gun cuireadh bochdainn trioblaid gu bràth orra. Cha robh duine cloinne aig a' Phrobhaist. Bha dithis nighean aig a' Bhàillidh. Mu dheireadh, an aghaidh coltais, rugadh nighean do'n Phrobhaist, agus air an latha cheudna, rugadh mac do'n Bhàillidh. Bha cùisean a' dol air an adhart leis an dà theaghlach gu mìn, càirdeil, fortanach [?]. Bha na fir an còmhnaidh cuideachd, agus bha a' chuid eile de'n dà theaghlach mar aon. Latha de na làithean, bha am Probhaist agus am Bàillidh cuideachd leò féin. Thuirt am Probhaist ris a' Bhàillidh mar a leanas—'Tha mi féin is tu féin eòlach air a chéile o chionn iomadh bliadhna, is cha b'urrainn dithis bhràithrean a bhith na bu ghaolaiche air a chéile ; is tha ar teaghlaichean air an aon dòigh. Tha mise toileach a h-uile nì as urrainn mi a dhèanamh a lìonas an càirdeas seo eadar an dà theaghlach an déidh dhuinne an saoghal seo fhàgail—agus a chum na crìche seo, tha mise glé thogarrach gum pòsadh sinn do mhac-sa agus m'aon nighean, ged nach 'eil iad fhathast ach ochd bliadhna a dh'aois.' Bha am Bàillidh mar a b'àbhaist deònach air nì sam bith a dhèanamh a chitheadh a charaid iomchuidh. Chaidh a' chlann a phòsadh uaigneach— cha robh iad féin no eadhon am màthraichean gu fios fhaotainn air nì mu dheighinn gus am biodh a' chlann ochd bliadhna deug. Bha tochradh nighean a' Phrobhaiste a réir beairteis a h-athar, is thug am Bàillidh an aire nach biodh esan an déidh làimh

---

[1] *uath chuirde* [?] in MS. Obscure to me. [leg. *o cheàird na marsantachd*, 'from the trade of merchandise' ?—A. M.]

HOW CATS FIRST WENT TO SPAIN

No. 47.   [*MS. Vol. x., No. 73*]

THE Provost of Edinburgh and one of the Bailies of the town were very friendly : they had long been acquainted and acquaintance had ripened into firm friendship. At the time our story begins they were very rich, for they had both accumulated wealth in their profession or from trade.[1] It never occurred to either of them that poverty could ever trouble them. Now, the Provost had no children, but the Bailie had two daughters : at last, however, against all likelihood, a daughter was born to the Provost. On the same day a son was born to the Bailie. Both families were progressing smoothly and in a friendly, prosperous way ; the two men were always together, and the rest of the households were as one. One day the Provost and the Bailie were together and the Provost spoke to the Bailie thus : 'You and I have known each other for many a year, and no two brothers could be more attached—and so with our families. I want to do everything I can to increase this friendship between the two households after we have left this world, and to that end I am very eager that we marry your son and my only daughter, although they are yet only eight years old.' As usual, the Bailie was willing to do anything his friend should see fit. The children were married secretly—neither they nor even their mothers were to hear about it until the children were eighteen years of age. The Provost's daughter's dowry was to be according to her father's wealth, and the Bailie saw to it that he should not be behind in providing plenty for his son. The an[n] a [bhith] fàgail gu leòr aig a mhac. Chaidh na cùmhnantan a dhèanamh cho sàbhailte is a b' urrainn lagh an dèanamh, agus bha am Probhaist ri an gleidheadh gu diamhair, cùramach.

Ann am beagan bhliadhnachan 'na dhéidh seo, bha am Bàillidh cho mì-fhortanach is gun do chaill e a chuid airgid gu léir, agus ann an ùine ghoirid, bhàsaich e le briseadh-cridhe, a' fàgail a theaghlaich glé bhochd. Shaoileamaid nach biodh dìth nì sam bith air teaghlach a' Bhàillidh nach leasaicheadh am Probhaist, ach tha mi duilich gur éiginn domh a ràdh [1] gun do thionndaidh e a chùlaibh riu air fad. Agus o nach robh fios aig duine sam bith a nise ach e féin mu'n phòsadh eadar a nighean agus mac a' Bhàillidh, chuir e roimhe nach abradh e guth am feasda mu dheighinn, agus gun sealladh e mun cuairt air son cliamhain [2] bheairtich a measg a luchd-eòlais.

Mu'n am seo thachair gun deachaidh am Probhaist agus a bhean o'n bhaile, a' fàgail na h-ighinn aig an taigh. Le tuiteamas, thachair gun d'fhuair i na pàipearan mu dheighinn a pòsaidh ri mac a' Bhàillidh. Thachair mu'n am seo, gun d'fhàg mac a' Bhàillidh an sgoil aig an robh e, agus chaidh e do sgoil eile 'sa' bhaile nach robh cho cosgail. Chaidh i air ball far an robh e, agus fhuair i a mach an t-adhbhar air son e a dh'fhàgail na sgoileach [3] aig an robh e an toiseach. Chaidh i mar an ceudna a dh'fhaicinn a mhàthar, agus fhuair esan air ais do'n sgoil aig an robh e roimhe, agus aig an robh i féin 'san am. Gheall i gum pàidheadh i féin air a shon. O'n am seo, dh'fhàs i féin agus mac a' Bhàillidh glé mhór aig a chéile, ach cha d'innis i dha gun robh iad pòsda.

Latha de na lathaichean, choinnich am Probhaist e féin riu, an uair a bha iad a' sràidimeachd. Bha e làn feirge, is chaidh e dhachaigh agus dh'innis e d'a mhnaoi gun do choinnich e ri nighinn agus ri mac a' Bhàillidh cuideachd, agus gun robh e smuaineachadh gun robh iad na bu mhò aig a chéile na bu toil leis ; gun cuireadh e air falbh as an rìoghachd e. An uair a chuala a bhean seo, thòisich i ri caoineadh, a' cuimhneachadh cho fada is a bha an dà theaghlach 'nan càirdean dìleas, gus an do chuir bochdainn a' Bhàillidh stad air an càirdeas. Bha e dol a thoirt tairgse luinge agus luchd sam bith a roghnaicheadh e

[1] I am sorry to be obliged to say : the idea is modern, and would never have occurred to a shennachy of the old school.

contracts were made as secure as the law could make them, and the Provost was to keep them secretly and carefully.

A few years after this the Bailie was so unfortunate as to lose all his money, and in a short time he died of heart-break, leaving his family very poor. We might have thought that the Bailie's family would suffer no want that the Provost would not relieve, but I am sorry to have to say [1] that he turned his back on all of them. And since no one but he knew anything of the marriage between his daughter and the Bailie's son, he made up his mind never to say a word about it and to look around for a wealthy son-in-law among his acquaintances.

About this time, the Provost and his wife happened to go out of town, leaving their daughter at home. By accident she discovered the papers concerning her marriage to the Bailie's son. About the same time it happened that the Bailie's son left the school where he was and removed to another less expensive school in the town. The girl went to him straight away and found out why he had left the school he attended before. She went to see his mother as well, and the boy got back to the school where he had formerly been and where she was at the time : she herself, she promised, would pay for him. From this time, the Bailie's son and she grew very fond of each other but she never told him that they were married.

One day the Provost himself met them strolling in the street : he was enraged, and went home and told his wife that he had met their daughter and the Bailie's son together, and that he thought they were friendlier than he liked, and that he would send him out of the kingdom. When his wife heard this she began to cry, remembering how long the two families had been true friends until the Bailie's poverty had put a stop to their friendship. The Provost was going to offer the youth a ship and any cargo he cared to choose to get him off to Spain, for he was making sure that he should never return. While he was

---

[2] *mac-céille* (recte, *mac-céile*) in MS.
[3] MS. *sgoilleach*. It is rare for *sgoil* to go over to the guttural declension.

féin do'n ghille òg gus e a dhol do'n Spàin, oir bha e dèanamh
cinnteach nach pilleadh e am feasda. An uair a bha e 'ga
ìnnseadh seo do'n mhnaoi, bha an nighean 'ga éisdeachd, ach
cha robh fios aige-san air. Bha iad ochd bliadhna deug a
dh'aois 'san am seo.

Chuir nighean a' Phrobhaist na pàipearan mu'n phòsadh 'na
broilleach, agus chaidh i a choinneachadh a leannain. Chaidh
iad a staigh do thaigh-òsda, agus an déidh cuid mhath chòmh-
raidh, dh'innis i dha gun robh iad pòsda o'n a bha iad ochd
bliadhna a dh'aois, agus sheall i dha na sgrìobhaidhean mu a
dheighinn. Dh'innis i dha mar an ceudna an nì a bha am
beachd a h-athar a dhèanamh ris gu faighinn cuibht is e.
Chomhairlich i dha dèanamh mar a dh'iarradh a h-athair air.
Thuirt i ris, e thoirt luchd guail leis agus cat fireann is cat
baineann, agus gum faiceadh e ann an tìm feum nan cat agus
a' ghuail—bhiodh e seachd bliadhna air falbh, agus dh'fhanadh
ise gun phòsadh seachd bliadhna ris.

Bha am Probhaist air son faighinn cuibht is an gille òg cho
luath is a b'urrainn da. Bha e cumail a mach a measg a luchd-
eòlais gun robh e dol dh'a dhèanamh seo air son cuideachaidh
a dhèanamh le mac a sheann charaid. Anns an am cheudna,
bheireadh e suim mhath airgid air son a fhaicinn marbh. Bha
fios math aig a nighinn gu dé bu mhiann le a h-athair a dhèanamh
air a leannan nam b'urrainn da, ged a bha e cumail a mach
gum bu charaid da e.

An déidh móran dàlach, fhuair an gille òg an long deiseil,
agus le cridhe trom, muladach, dhealaich e ris an nighinn òig
shuairce a bheireadh an saoghal air son a bhith 'na chuideachd,
is gun fhios an coinnicheadh iad air an t-saoghal seo tuilleadh.
Rànaig an long an Spàin gun choinneachadh ri mì-fhortain
sam bith. Chuir Rìgh na Spàin a dh'fhiosrachadh ciod an luchd
a bha 'san luing. An uair a chuala e gum b'e gual a luchd, bha
e ro thoilichte, do bhrìgh nach robh gual r'a fhaotainn 'san
Spàin. Bha ainm cho fiadhaich de na Spàintich nach leigeadh
iad duine air falbh beò as an rìoghachd. B'e sin an [t-]adhbhar
mu'n do chuir am Probhaist an gille òg seo do'n Spàin, chum a
mharbhadh. Ach an àite a mharbhadh, is ann a chuir an Rìgh
fios air gu a thràth-nòin a ghabhail cuide ris. An uair a bha
iad 'nan suidhe aig a' bhòrd mun tànaig am biadh a staigh,

telling this to his wife, their daughter was listening to him but he did not know that. At this time, the young people were eighteen years old.

The Provost's daughter put the papers concerning the marriage in her bosom and went off to meet her sweetheart. They went into an inn, and after they had talked a good deal she told him that they had been married since they were eight years old, and she showed him the contracts. She also told him what her father meant to do to get rid of him, and she advised him to act as her father would ask. She told him to take a cargo of coal with him and a male and female cat, and eventually he would realise what the good of the cats and the coal was. Seven years he would be away, and she would wait for him without marrying for seven years.

The Provost was for getting rid of the young man as soon as he could. Among his friends he gave out that he was going to do this to help the son of his old friend ; at the same time he would have given a tidy sum of money to see him dead. The Provost's daughter knew well what her father would like to do to her sweetheart—were he able—although he professed to be his friend.

After much delay the young man got the ship ready and with a heavy, sad heart he parted with the delightful girl who would have given the world to be with him—and no knowing if they would ever meet again in this life. Without any mishap at all the ship reached Spain. The King of Spain sent to enquire what sort of cargo they had, and when he heard it was coal he was delighted because there was no coal to be had in Spain. Now the Spaniards were notorious for their fierceness, for, it was said, they never allowed a man to leave the kingdom alive. That was why the Provost sent this young lad to Spain—that he might be killed. But instead of killing him the King asked him to lunch with himself. When they were seated at the table and before the meal was served he noticed that a stout mallet had been placed in front of everyone

thug e an aire gun do chuireadh òrd math maide[1] air beulaibh
a h-uile duine a bha 'na shuidhe aig a' bhòrd. An uair a
dh'fheòraich e gu dé bu chiall do'n fhasan iongantach ud, chaidh
innseadh dha mur biodh na maidean sin aca deiseil, nach bu
leò féin am biadh a chuirte air am beulaibh, mar a chitheadh e
ann an ùine ghoirid.

Cho luath 's a chuireadh am biadh air am beulaibh, mach
a thànaig na radain 'nan ceudan, agus an sàs anns a' bhiadh
ghabh iad. Rug a h-uile fear air a' mhaide a bha ri a thaobh
gu gabhail air na radain is an cumail o'n bhiadh. Chuimhnich
e a nis air na cait. Dh'fheòraich e de'n Rìgh gu dé na bheireadh
iad do dhuine a leigeadh leò am biadh a ghabhail gun maide
a laimhseachadh. Thuirt an Rìgh nach biodh ath[2] duais sam
bith a b'urrainn da a thoirt seachad ro mhór air son duine a
dhèanadh sin. Chuir an Caiptean a dh'iarraidh an dà chait.
Aig an ath-bhiadh, chuir e cat air gach glùn : thànaig na radain
mar a b'àbhaist. Ma thànaig, thòisich na cait—sin far an robh
an obair, gus an do theich nach deachaidh a mharbhadh de na
radain.

Bha an Rìgh is na h-uaislean a bha maille ris làn iongantais
mu ghnìomh nan cat, oir chan fhac iad cat riamh roimhe.
Dh'fheòraich iad uile an creiceadh an duine-uasal na h-ain-
mhidhean neònach, comasach, a rinn a leithid de ghnìomh.
Thuirt mac a' Bhàillidh nach ceannaicheadh òr no airgead iad,
ach gun tugadh e mar ghibhte do'n Rìgh iad. Bha an Rìgh
cho toilichte de[3] dhuine a sheall e fhéin cho fialaidh mu'n
chùis, is nach robh fios aige gu dé dhèanadh e ris, no ciamar
a phàidheadh e e. Cheannaich e an luchd guail, is dh'òrdaich
e an long a luchdachadh le airgead ruadh. Thug e deise aodaich
da air a shon féin, deise air son a mhnatha, agus deiseachan air
son a dhithis pheathraichean, nach bitheadh an leithidean ri
fhaighinn ann an Albainn, agus each nach robh a leithid 'sa'
Chrìosdachd, maille ri móran de nithean luachmhor eile. Mu
dheireadh, fhuair mac a' Bhàillidh a h-uile nì ullamh air son an
Spàin fhàgail. Dhealaich e fhéin is an Rìgh 'nan càirdean dìleas,
làn thoilichte le càch a chéile, agus fhuair e e fhéin na bu
bheairtiche na bha a athair roimhe.

---

[1] MS. *mhath mhaide.*   [2] So MS. : *aon* ?   [3] So MS.

present, but when he asked what was the meaning of this strange practice he was told that unless they had these sticks handy the food set in front of them would not be theirs, as he would see very shortly.

As soon as the meal was served, out came rats in their hundreds and attacked the food. Everyone seized the mallet by his side to strike at the rats and keep them from the food. The young man now remembered the cats, and he asked the King what they would give a man who would enable them to have their food without their touching a stick. No reward that he could give, replied the King, would be too great for a man who could accomplish that. The Captain sent for the two cats and at the next meal he placed a cat on each knee. As usual, out came the rats. But if they did, so did the cats begin—it was extraordinary work, until those rats that had not been killed fled !

The King and the nobles who were with him were amazed at the cats' performance for never before had they seen a cat. They asked if the gentleman would sell these strange, resourceful brutes that had accomplished such a deed. The Bailie's son said that neither silver nor gold could purchase them but that he would present them to the King. The King was so pleased with a man who showed such generosity in the matter that he did not know what to do for him or how he should reward him. He bought the cargo of coal and ordered the ship to be laden with red money. He gave him a suit of clothes for himself, a suit for his wife and suits for his sisters, of a quality not to be found in Scotland ; and he gave him a horse that had no equal in Christendom, and many other precious things besides. At last the Bailie's son got everything ready for leaving Spain, and he and the King parted firm friends, thoroughly pleased with each other ; and the Bailie's son found himself richer than his father had been before him.

Thànaig an long gu sàbhailte gu talamh tioram Alba ; o'n
a bha na seachd bliadhna a nis air dol thairis bho'n a dh'fhàg
e Lìte, chuir e roimhe gum marcaicheadh e gu Dùn Éideann—
thug e leis an t-each is na deiseachan aodaich.   Cha robh
drochaid 'san am sin air aibhnichean Alba.   An uair a thànaig
e gu abhainn a tha os cionn Obar Dheathain, bha naoinear
dhaoine 'nan seasamh a' feitheamh gu dol thairis air.[1]   Bha
tuil mhór 'san abhainn.   Thuirt e riu iad a ghlacadh dual am
fear de earball an eich dhuibh ;[2] thug e an naoinear dhaoine
thairis.   An uair a bha e fàgail na h-aibhne, chunnaig e duin'-
uasal a' tighinn le a charbad a dh'ionnsaigh na h-aibhne, agus
a' seasamh, oir cha b'urrainn da a dhol thairis.   Phill e air ais—
cheangail e eich an duin'-uasail ri earball an eich dhuibh, agus
thug e tioram thairis air an abhainn iad.   Thachair gun robh
iad le chéile a' gabhail an aon rathaid.   Thòisich an coigreach
air labhairt glé shaor ri mac a' Bhàillidh.   A measg móran de
nithean a bhuineadh do a theaghlach agus do a shìnnsearan,
dh'innis e da gum bu mhac do Phrobhaist Obar Dheathain e,
is gun robh e dol 'san am do Dhùn Éideann gu pòsadh ri nighean
Probhaist a' bhaile sin—gum b'i an ath-oidhche oidhche a'
chòrdaidh, is o'n a bha esan a' dol gu Dùn Éideann gum biodh
e fada 'na chomain air son a chuideachd aig taigh a' Phrobhaist
an ath-oidhche.   Cha robh an ceatharnach ro bhruidhneach ris
a' choigreach o'n a thachair iad ri chéile, is faodaidh sinn a
bhith cinnteach nach robh e coltach gun tugadh an naidheachd
a chuala e móran togail do a chridhe, no fuasgladh do a theang-
aidh.   Bha e air son a bhith 'na aonar, is ghabh e air gun robh
cabhag glé mhór air, is nach b'urrainn da bhith feitheamh air
a' choigreach ged a bha iad le chéile a' falbh do Dhùn Éideann.
Dh'fheòraich an coigreach dheth c'ainm a bha air.   Fhreagair
esan, 'Is mise am math a bha, is a chaidh a dholaidh.'   'Is
neònach an t-ainm a tha ort,' thuirt am fear eile, 'chan urrainn
dòmh-sa a sgrìobhadh a sìos.'   Dh'iarr an ceatharnach a leabhar-
pòcaid gus an sgrìobhadh e a ainm féin ann ; 'na dhéidh sin
[dhealaich iad] a' gealltainn a chéile a choinneachadh ann an
Dùn Éideann.   Chaidh iad le chéile gu Dùn Éideann.   Chaidh

---

[1] [sic] ; leg. oirre.
[2] See No. 117, this book, for this method of crossing a swollen river ; and *The
Wizard's Gillie*, p. 73.

The ship came safely to dry land in Scotland and, as the seven years had now passed since he left Leith, the young man determined to ride to Edinburgh taking the horse and the dresses with him. At the time there were no bridges over the rivers of Scotland. When he came to a certain river above Aberdeen, there were nine people standing there waiting to cross, and the river was in high flood. He told them each to seize a strand of the black horse's tail,[2] and so he brought the nine over. When he was leaving the river he saw a gentleman with his carriage coming towards the river and standing there, for he was not able to get across. The Bailie's son turned back, tied the gentleman's horses to the black horse's tail and fetched them across the river. It happened that they were both taking the same road, and the stranger began to speak very freely to the Bailie's son. Among many things that related to his family and his ancestors he told him that he was the Provost of Aberdeen's son, and at that very time that he was going to Edinburgh to marry the daughter of the Provost of that town. The betrothal, he said, was on the following night, and since the young man was going to Edinburgh he would be very gratified by his presence in the company next evening. The bold fellow had not been over-talkative to the stranger since they had met and we may be certain that the news he heard was not likely to raise his heart very much or loosen his tongue. He wanted to be alone, and so he pretended that he was in a great hurry and could not wait for the stranger although they were both going to Edinburgh. The stranger asked him what his name was. 'I am the good that was and that went to waste,' he replied. 'You have a strange name,' said the other, 'I cannot write it down.' The youth asked for his pocket-book so that he might write his proper name in it ; after that [they parted], promising to meet in Edinburgh. They both went to Edinburgh.

mac a' Bhàillidh a shireadh taigh a mhàthar, am fear eile taigh
a' Phrobhaist. Fhuair mac a' Bhàillidh a mach taigh a mhàthar.
Cha d'aithnich i e. Dh'fheòraich e am faigheadh e cairtealan
maille rithe ; thuirt ise, 'Cho cruaidh is ged a dh'fheuch an
saoghal rium, is urrainn domh leabaidh a thoirt do dhuin'-
uasal sam bith fathast.' Chaidh e a chadal, is thug e òrdugh nach
ìnnseadh iad do neach sam bith gun robh esan 'san taigh. Bha
e glé fhialaidh mu airgead ; thug e ginidh seachad air son
gach nì a dh'iarr e, is cha ghabhadh e sgillinn iomlaid air ais.

Chaidh mac Probhaist Obar Dheathain dìreach gu taigh
Probhaist Dhùn Éideann. Chaidh na h-uile nì fhathast [?] leis
mar bu mhath leis—chaidh an réiteach is gach cùmhnanta eile a
bha fasanta seachad gu tlachdmhor, is iad gu bhith pòsta 'sa'
mhaduinn. Bha càirdean an lànain òig air gach taobh cruinn
aig an am seo—gu math air adhart 'san fheasgar—an uair a
bha a' chuideachd gu léir cridheil, aighearach. Chuimhnich
fear-na-bainnse air a chompanach-siubhail a gheall a bhith
maille ris 'san am. Thug e làmh air a leabhar-pòcaid gu a
ainm a leughadh, oir dhìochuimhnich e e. Ghabh a' chuideachd
gu léir iongantas mu'n ainm. An uair a leugh bean-na-bainnse
e, cha dubhairt i facal, dh'fhàg i a' chuideachd gun fhios daibh,
agus thug i taigh bantrach a' Bhàillidh oirre. Bha meas mór
aig a' bhantraich oirre, oir bha i ro mhath dhi o'n a dh'fhalbh
a mac. An uair a chaidh i a staigh, dh'fheòraich i an robh
coigreach sam bith a' fuireach leatha—thuirt a' bhantrach gun
robh, ach nach faodadh i ìnnseadh. Fhuair nighean a' Phrobhaist
solus, agus a dh'aindeoin toil na bantraich, chaidh i do sheòmar-
cadail a leannain—thuirt i ris a' bhantraich gum b'e siod a
mac. Air ball, chaidh i a laighe leis [agus] is beag nach deach
an duine bochd a mhort, le a mhnaoi, le a mhàthair, agus le a
dhithis pheathraichean còmhla 'ga phògadh 'san leabaidh. Mu
dheireadh, chaidh iad gu léir a chadal an taigh na bantraich—
anns an am cheudna, cha robh smuaineachadh aig a h-aon an
taigh a' Phrobhaist air cadal—bha a nighean air chall, is ged
a bha a h-uile clag is druma 'sa' bhaile a' bualadh air a son,
cha d'fhuaradh i. An uair a dh'éirich mac a' Bhàillidh 'sa'
mhaduinn, chuir e féin is a bhean is a dhithis pheathraichean
na deiseachan luachmhor Spàinteach orra, is chaidh iad a
ghabhail sràid. Chaidh iad caochladh uairean seachad air taigh

The Bailie's son set off to find his mother's house, the other the
house of the Provost.   The Bailie's son found his mother's house
but she failed to recognise him.   He asked if he might get lodgings
with her.   'Harshly though the world has dealt with me I am
still able to provide any gentleman with a bed,' she replied.   He
went to get some sleep, and gave orders not to tell anyone that
he was in the house.   He was very generous with his money : he
gave a guinea for everything he asked, and would not take a
penny back in change.

    The son of the Provost of Aberdeen went straight to the
Provost of Edinburgh's house.   Up to this point everything
turned out as well for him as he desired : the betrothal and all
the usual formalities passed off pleasantly, and they were to be
married in the morning.   Friends of the young couple on both
sides were assembled now—well on into the evening—and the
entire company were happy and gay.   Then the bridegroom
remembered his companion on the journey who had promised
to be with him at this time and he turned to his note-book to
read his name, for he had forgotten it.   The whole company
were astonished at the name.   But when the bride read the
name she uttered never a word, but she left the gathering unknown
to them and went straight to the house of the Bailie's widow.
The widow had a great affection for her, for she had been very
good to her ever since her son left.   When the girl went in she
asked the widow if any stranger were staying with her ; the
widow replied that there was, but that she must not reveal it.
The Provost's daughter got a light, and against the widow's
wish she entered her lover's bedroom.   She told the widow that
the man was her son.   Then straight away she got into bed with
him, and what with his wife, his mother and his two sisters all
kissing him at once in bed, the poor man was almost suffocated.
Finally all in the widow's house went to sleep, but no one in
the Provost's house was thinking of sleep at that moment : the
Provost's daughter was lost, and although every bell and drum
in the town was being beaten for her, she was not to be found.
When the Bailie's son got up in the morning, he, his wife and his
two sisters put on the costly Spanish dresses and went for a walk.
Several times they passed the Provost's house but their clothes
were so very splendid that no one recognised them.   The last

a' Phrobhaist, ach bha an deiseachan aodaich cho fìor rìomhach
is nach d'aithnich duine iad.   An uair mu dheireadh a chaidh
iad seachad, chuala mac a' Bhàillidh am Probhaist ag ràdh,
'Mur bitheadh an t-aodach a tha air a' mhnaoi-uasail ud, theirinn
gur i mo nighean féin a th'ann.'

Thionndaidh mac a' Bhàillidh air a shàil, agus thuirt e ris,
'Is i do nighean a th'ann, a bhodaich. Ged a rinn thu gnìomh
math dhòmh-sa, cha toir mi móran taing dhuit—rinn thu na
b'urrainn dhuit gus a cumail uam-sa : is i mo bhean-sa a nis i,
is tha sinn coma de nì sam bith as urrainn duit-sa a dhèanamh
ruinn.'   An uair a chunnaig an ceatharnach mac Probhaist
Obar Dheathain, ghabh e a leisgeal féin da air son an nì a
rinn e, ach dh'innis e dha gun robh iad-san pòsta an uair a bha
iad ochd bliadhna a dh'aois, agus sheall e dha sgrìobhaidhean
an athraichean.   Thuirt e ris gun robh dithis pheathraichean
aige-san cho tlachdmhor eireachdail ri nighean a' Phrobhaiste,
is gun robh esan comasach air na's motha de thochradh a thoirt
seachad na bha am Probhaist.   Bha mac Probhaist Obar
Dheathain toilichte leis na chuala e, is roghnaich e té de nigheanan
a' Bhàillidh.   Phòs iad.   Chaidh an dà bhanais a chumail 'san
aon oidhche.   Chinn teaghlach a' Bhàillidh agus a' Phrobhaiste
cho mór aig a chéile 's a bha iad riamh, is chaith am Probhaist
deireadh a làithean gu sona toilichte a measg leth-dusan de
dh'oghaichean àlainn, is cha do ghabh an nighean a riamh
aithreachas air son a bhith dìleas do mhac bochd a' Bhàillidh.
Agus a thuilleadh air sin, bha an [t-]urram aice gun robh i
'na meadhon air na ceud chait a chur do Rìoghachd na Spàine.

NOTES

MS. vol. x., No. 73.   This tale has been listed by Islay at the end of
W. H. Tales, iv., thus—

'73. How Cats went first to Spain. (Known to Urquhart.) Place,
London. Reference, Whittington.'

In the MS. of No. 73, there is no signature and no mention of either locality
(apart from the word 'London'), or of the reciter. The MS. is written in a
lady's hand.

At the end of No. 40, Islay says 'See How Cats went first to Spain.
McCraw's version.'   As No. 73 is the only tale bearing this title I at first
concluded that No. 73 must be 'McCraw's version.' But Islay gives London
as the place from which No. 73 emanated, and I have no evidence that
McCraw ever went to London. And Professor Watson has kindly pointed

time they went by, the Bailie's son heard the Provost say : 'Were it not for the clothes that lady there is wearing, I would say it is my own daughter.'

The Bailie's son turned on his heel and said : 'She is your daughter, old fellow. Although you did me a good turn I shall not give you many thanks : you did what you could to keep her from me. She's my wife now, and we do not care a straw for anything you can do to us.' When the bold fellow saw the son of the Aberdeen Provost he apologised to him for what he had done, but he explained that they two had been married ever since they were eight years of age, and showed him what their fathers had written. He had two sisters, he told him, as charming and handsome as the Provost's daughter and moreover he was able to give a larger dowry than the Provost was. The son of the Provost of Aberdeen was pleased with what he heard, and chose one of the Bailie's daughters. They married and the two weddings were celebrated on the same night. The Bailie's family and the Provost's became as intimate with each other as ever they had been, and the Provost spent the end of his days contented and happy among half a dozen lovely grandchildren ; and his daughter never regretted having been faithful to the poor son of the Bailie. Besides all that, she had the honour of having been the means of sending the first cats to the Kingdom of Spain.

out that the reciter of No. 73 has allowed his own personality to intrude, and the probability is that if he did so once, he did it always. I therefore examined all the tales recited by McCraw, and found that he did *not* allow his personality to intrude in them. The conclusion therefore is that No. 73 was not recited by McCraw. And as I cannot find that he recited any Whittington tale, I further conclude that Islay must have confused him with the reciter of No. 73. The identity of the reciter can never now be known, or the place whence he came. It must be admitted, however, that though No. 73 is miserably Anglicized (it looks like a Gaelic translation of an English translation of a Gaelic original), it elaborates the Married Children theme (see No. 40) more fully than any other.

Footnote, *mac-céille* (recte, *mac-céile*). The correct translation of 'son-in-law' is *cliamhain*. Evidently misled by a fanciful analogy with such words as *bràthair-céile* (*lit.* 'the brother of a spouse') a brother-in-law ; *athair-céile* (*lit.* 'the father of a spouse') a father-in-law, the scribe supposed that *mac-céile* would be a suitable equivalent for 'son-in-law,' forgetting for the moment the literal meaning of *céile*, and investing it with the meaning of '-in-law.' But *mac-céile* (*lit.* 'the son of a spouse') means 'a step-son,' not 'a son-in-law' ; in any case it is obsolete, the word in current use for a step-child or foster-child of either sex being *dalta*. The use of *mac-céile* suggests that the scribe was translating from English, though as indicated already, that English version had probably been made from a Gaelic original.

In No. 73, the Provost hopes that the hero will be killed by the wild Spaniards. But in more ancient versions, the belief that it was unlucky for a contracted bridegroom to go on board a boat must have been the reason that prompted the fraudulent partner to send him to sea, though this belief is never alluded to.

In No. 73, it is definitely indicated that the three dresses disguised the wearers, especially the bride. See Nos. 14, 23 (MS. vol. x., Nos. 28, 40).

FEADAN DUBH AN T-SIOSALAICH

O CHIONN fada, fada, chaidh an Siosalach Glaiseach air aiseag
do'n Eadailt a dh'fhaotainn leasan do'n sgoil-duibh. Cha robh
e thar lethbhliadhna air falbh, an uair a dh'fhàs a' Bhaintighearna
ro mhì-uireasach mu dheighinn a fir.[1] Cha d'fhuair i a h-aon
rachadh air a thòir ach an Camshronach, am pìobaire. Rànaig
esan eaglais anns an Eadailt far an robh sùil aige ris an t-Siosalach
fhaicinn. Chan fhaca e suidheachan falamh ach a h-aon,
làimh ris an dorus. Ciod a bha an seo ach cathair na
h-aoigheachd far an cuirte neach a thigeadh gu bochdainn
chum a dhèanamh suas. An am sgaoilidh do'n phobull, bha
gach neach a' cur bonn ann am boineid a' Chamshronaich ;
mu dheireadh thall, thànaig an Siosalach, is chuir esan bonn
anns a' bhoineid mar an ceudna. Dh'éirich an Camshronach
leis na bha aige, agus lean e an Siosalach, agus dh'innis e dha
gum feumadh e dol dachaigh air na h-uile cor.

Char [2] iad an sin a dh'ionnsaigh a' Mhaighstir-Sgoile,
[Maighstir na Sgoile Duibhe], agus air tuigsinn da-san gun robh
an t-airgead aca, thug esan na h-uiread brosnachaidh agus
misnich dhaibh. Thuirt e gun robh fireannach 'na laighe anns
an leabaidh còmhla ris a' Bhaintighearna, agus air son suim
àraidh, gun cuireadh esan iad [an Siosalach agus an Cam-
shronach] le chéile gu tìr an Earghlais [3] mun tigeadh an là.
Chaidh còrdadh a thiota, agus an Siosalach a chur a laighe [4]
agus an Camshronach aig a chasan, agus thug e [Am Maighstir
Sgoile] feadan da, air am feumadh iad a bhith cluich gus an
goireadh an coileach. Bha fear mu seach dhiubh a' cluich gu
fada de'n oidhche, agus thuit iad 'nan cadal, agus dhùisg iad

---

[1] *Mo dhen fhear* in the manuscript. The Chisholm of Strath Glas, or the Chisholm
of Chisholm, the Chief of Clan Chisholm. He is represented here as learning magic,
as did other chiefs who were experts in the art (see *Superstitions*, p. 286). Italy was
'the country above all others in which the Black Art was to be acquired,' *Celt. Mag.*,
i. (1876), p. 340. See also MS. vol. x., No. 30 ; xi., No. 300.

[2] Dialect for *chaidh*.

THE CHISHOLM'S BLACK CHANTER

No. 48. [*MS. Vol. x., No. 75*]

LONG ago the Chisholm of Strath Glas travelled to Italy to learn black magic. He had not been away more than six months, however, when the Lady of Strath Glas became very anxious about her husband.[1] But she could find no one to go and look for him except Cameron, the piper. Cameron arrived at a church in Italy where he expected to see the Chisholm : he could discover only one empty seat, near the door. Now this chair was none other than the chair of hospitality where a person who had come to poverty was placed, in order to set him up again. As the congregation dispersed, each person placed a coin in Cameron's bonnet ; at last the Chisholm himself came and put a coin in the bonnet too. On this Cameron got up, carrying all the money he had obtained, followed the Chisholm and told him that at all costs he must go home.

Then they went to the Master [of the School of Black Magic], and as soon as he understood that they had the money he urged and prompted them very strongly to go. He told them that there was a man in bed with the Lady of Strath Glas and that for a certain sum of money he would transport them both [the Chisholm and Cameron] to Erchless[3] before daybreak. They agreed immediately. The Chisholm was given a bed with Cameron at his feet, and the Master gave the Chisholm a chanter which they were to keep playing until cock-crow. Turn about they played it, far into the night ; then they fell asleep. They

---

[3] Erchless Castle in Strath Glas, Inverness-shire, is the seat of the Chisholm. *Earghlais* in the MS. of No. 75, and in Dwelly's *Dict.*, p. 1013. *Air-ghlais*, according to Dr Alex. Macbain, *Trans. Gael. Soc. Inverness*, xxv., p. 83. [Eirchealais is the form used by *Ailean Dall* ; 1829 ed., p. 167.—A. M.]

[4] *A chur laibh* in manuscript.

ann an coillidh Roise, fo Chaisteal Earghlais, am beul an latha.[1]
Ruith an Siosalach a dh'fhaicinn có bha maille ris a' Bhaintighearna, agus có bha an seo de rogha nam fear [2] ach leanabh gille
a rugadh a raoir ; bha an seo na h-uile nì ceart ; bha an Siosalach
air teachd, oighre air a bhreith, agus a' Bhaintighearna sàbhailt.

'Nuair a fhuair an Siosalach am feadan bho'n Eadailteach,
dh'iarr e buaidh a thoirt air, agus gun ìnnseadh e dha na h-uile
car a thigeadh air a theaghlach gu bràth, agus bha sin ceart.
Cha tànaig am bàs air Siosalach bho'n là sin nach do sgàin
am Feadan Dubh, agus rachadh cearcall airgid a chur air an
sin ; tha cóig cearcaill air 'san am seo ; agus thuit cuid dheth
le caitheamh nam meur, o'n a bha e riamh o fhuaireadh e
'na sheannsair do phìob.

Is iomadh sgeul a bha air aithris mu'n Fheadan Dubh o'n
latha sin. Mu bhliadhna nan cóig deug (1715), char taigh a'
Chamshronaich, am pìobaire, 'na theinidh, air othail [?] [3] an
fhir a bha anns an Eadailt. An uair a chuala an Siosalach seo,
ruith e do Chnoc a' Mhòid agus ghlaodh e a mach, an robh am
Feadan Dubh an làthair. 'Tha, tha,' arsa Tómas Pìobaire,
'an uair a thàr mise a mach, thug mi sgrìob air a' phìob, ach
chaidh na h-uile nì eile a chall.' 'Cè, cè [4] am Feadan Dubh,'
ars an Siosalach, agus air a fhaotainn da, is ann a leag e air seinn
agus dannsadh—

> Feadan Dubh mo shinnseanar,
>   'S maith liom a bhith 'nam làimh,
> 'S coma liom na bheil 'san teinidh,
>   Bho nach 'eil am Feadan ann.
>
> 'S coma liom na chaidh a losgadh,
>   'S coma liom na chaidh a chall,
> 'S coma liom na bheil 'san teinidh,
>   Bho nach 'eil am Feadan ann.

B'e seo toiseach na Ruidhle ainmeil dannsaidh sin, 'Feadan Dubh
an t-Siosalaich,' a dh'fheumadh a bhith air a cluich air na

---

[1] A transporting whistle occurs in other Highland tales. The incident of the
father finding his own child in its mother's bed, and supposing it to be her paramour,
occurs in MS. vol. x., No. 15.

[2] I checked the manuscript on two different occasions for these words, but the
writing is so bad that it is impossible to be certain of them ; they look like *a roobhadh
na fear*, which I have dealt with as above.

awoke in Ross Wood below Erchless Castle as day was breaking.[1] The Chisholm ran ahead to see who was with the Lady of Strath Glas, and of all the choicest who should it be but a baby boy born the night before. So all was right : the Chisholm was home again, an heir had been born, and the Lady was safe.

When the Chisholm received the chanter from the Italian he asked him to lay a spell upon it that it should tell him of everything that might ever come upon his household ; and so it was. From that day onwards, death never came to a Chisholm without the Black Chanter cracking. On such occasions a silver ring was fitted on it : it has five such rings at the present time, but some fell off through the wearing action of the fingers, for ever since it was obtained it has been used as a pipe chanter.

Many a tale has been told of the Black Chanter since that day. About the time of the 'Fifteen, piper Cameron's house was burned down when occupied by the grandson of the man who had been in Italy. When the Chisholm heard of this he ran to the Meeting Hill and shouted : 'Is the Black Chanter there ?' 'It's here ! it's here !' said Thomas the piper. 'When I escaped I snatched up the pipes. Everything else has been lost.' 'Give it to me, give me the Black Chanter,' said the Chisholm, and when he got it he suddenly started dancing and began to sing :

> Black Chanter of my great grandsire
> I rejoice that it is in my hand ;
> I care not for all that the fire got
> Since the Chanter is not there.
>
> I care not for what was burnt,
> I care not for what was lost,
> I care not for what was burnt,
> Since the chanter is not there.

This was the origin of that famous reel, 'The Chisholm's Black Chanter,' which had to be played at every meeting and feast held in Strath Glas since that day. The people then gathered to help Thomas ; and the man who did not add a stone to his

---

[3] [*air othail* should be perhaps *air ogha*, i.e. in 1715 the piper was a grandson of the piper who had been in Italy and the Chisholm was a great-grandson of the Chisholm who had been there. According to this the chief who went to Italy would be Alexander, XVII of Chisholm, who married a daughter of Mackenzie of Gairloch in 1639, *History of the Chisholms*, p. 55.—A. M.]

[4] *Cè* = 'hand me.' *Cè an t-òrd* = 'hand me the hammer.'

h-uile coinnimh agus cuilm bhiodh ann an Srath Ghlais o'n là sin. Thionail an tuath mun cuairt air Tómas, agus am fear nach cuireadh clach 'san taigh ùr, chuireadh e cabar ann. Chaidh tunna uisge-bheatha a chur as a' Chaisteal, chuir Tómas a suas a' phìob agus chluich e 'Feadan Dubh an t-Siosalaich,'

'S coma liom na chaidh a losgadh, etc.

Thug gach fear làmh air a sporan, is bha Tómas na bu bheairtiche na bha e riamh roimhe.

Goirid 'na dhéidh seo, bha banais ann an Comar, agus chuir na h-uile tuathanach muilt agus na h-uile ban-tuathanach ìm agus càise gu leòr dh'a h-ionnsaigh. Cha b'fhiach seo uile mur bitheadh Tómas agus am Feadan Dubh ann. Air dha bhith cluich le fonn air am àraidh de'n oidhche, thug am Feadan Dubh sgailc fo a mheur. Cha tugadh [1] (?) na bha air a' bhanais air cluich na b'fhaide. Thrus e a' phìob ann an lùib a' bhreacain, agus thriall e, agus air ruigheachd a' Chaisteil da, bha an Siosalach an déis a chàradh.

Tha am Feadan Dubh fhathast an làthair, agus sliochd nan Camshronach, ach is e am fear mu dheireadh a chluicheadh [air] a' phìob dhiubh, Alasdair Camshron, Pìobair-Màidsear do Réisimeid Dhiùc Gordon (92 Highlanders) ri linn cogadh na Spàine agus Waterloo. Is e esan [2]a chluich 'Johnny Cope' roimh[e],[2] an là a ghlacadh San Sebastian. An oidhche mun do thriall an t-arm Breatannach a Brussels, dhòirt Còirneal Camshron an Fhasaich Fheàrna canastair fìona a bha aig Alasdair agus aig a chompanaich, agus air siubhal dhoibh an òrdugh 'sa' mhaduinn sheinn Alasdair 'Lochaber no More, and we shall never return to Lochaber no more.' Mharcaich an Còirneal d'a ionnsaigh, agus thuirt e,[3] 'Tha thu breugach, Alasdair, tillidh sinn do Loch Abar fhathast,' agus dh'atharr-aicheadh am port.

From Alex. Fraser, of Mauld by Beauly, November 15, 1859.[4]

[1] duthadh (?) in MS.

[2]-[2] [or, "kept on playing 'Johnny Cope.'"—J. M.]

[3] Like Cato's Etruscan haruspices, Fassifern knew there was nothing in divination, or omens, and that the best way of averting an omen was simply to deny it. Cf. the proverb, Cuir manadh math air do mhanadh, 's bidh tu sona ; Nicolson, Gaelic Proverbs, p. 158 ; 'Give thine omen a lucky interpretation, and thou shalt be lucky.'

[4] [Cf. Alasdair Friseal—Fear Mhault: An Gàidheal, July 1958, pp. 62-3.—A. M.]

new house added a rafter. From the castle a tun of whisky was sent. Thomas struck up the pipes, and played 'The Chisholm's Black Chanter,'

> 'I care not for what was burnt,' etc.

And every man took out his purse, and Thomas was wealthier than he had ever been before.

A short time after this there was a wedding in Comar to which all the farmers sent wethers and all the farmers' wives plenty of butter and cheese. Still, that was nothing if Thomas and the Black Chanter were not there. But that night, at a particular moment when he was playing with zest the Black Chanter cracked under his finger, nor could the whole assembly of guests persuade him to play any longer. He wrapped up the pipes in the fold of his plaid and set off : when he arrived at the Castle, the Chisholm had been laid out for burial.

The Black Chanter still exists and Cameron's descendants are still living, but the last of them who could play the pipes was Alasdair Cameron, Pipe-Major to the Duke of Gordon's Regiment (92nd Highlanders) at the time of the Peninsular War and Waterloo. It was he[2] who had played 'Johnny Cope' when advancing,[2] the day San Sebastian was taken. The night before the British Army moved out of Brussels, Colonel Cameron of Fassifern spilt a jar of wine belonging to Alasdair and his companions. In the morning, when they were marching in line, Alasdair played 'Lochaber no More, and we shall return to Lochaber no more.' The Colonel rode up to him and said, 'You're lying, Alasdair ! We shall return to Lochaber yet' [3]—and the tune was changed.

NOTES

MS. vol. x., No. 75. In the published list, the tale is numbered 74, and called 'The Black Pipe.' Who the scribe was is unknown, but it was certainly not Hector MacLean, though the published list seems to imply that it was. Islay has written on the first page of the MS.—'Recd. Nov. 17/59. Answer to No. 179.[?] Written July 3. Answered Nov. 16/59. Beaulay 75.' These remarks are obscure to me. The MS. was badly written and badly spelt ; *ionnsaigh*, for instance, is written *uiseadh, uisidh*, etc.

[From the way in which it was bound the *Feadan Dubh* was also called *Maighdean a' Chuarain*. See Alexander MacKenzie, *The History of the Chisholms*, pp. 73-74.—A. M.]

UIRSGEUL NA NIGHINN GUN BHAISTEADH

No. 49.   [*MS. Vol. x., No. 83.2*]

BHA siod ann roimhe seo, duine bochd, agus rugadh aon nighean
da. Bha i gu maith fada gun bhaisteadh, agus dh'fhalbh e
chun a' mhinisteir air son baistidh. Thuirt am ministeir ris
gum faigheadh e baisteadh air a leithid seo de latha. Thill e
dhachaigh is bha bean-uasal chiatach a staigh roimhe 'nuair a
thànaig e. Thuirt i ris, 'An toir thu dhòmh-sa [a'] ghoisteachd,
o'n a tha thu dol a dh'fhaotainn baistidh?' 'Bheir,' ars esan.
'Chan 'eil agad,' ars ise, 'ach sùil a thoirt thar do ghualainn chlì,
'nuair a bhios tu dol a staigh do'n eaglais, is chì thu mise.'
Is ann mar seo a bha, is dh'fhalbh e an là a thuirt am ministeir
ris, a bhaisteadh a' phàisde, is nuair a bha e dol a staigh do'n
eaglais, thug e sùil thar a ghualainn chlì, is chunnaig e ise.
Chaidh i a staigh leis, is fhuair i a' ghoisteachd. Thànaig iad
dachaigh, i féin agus iad-san, is thug i cóig puinnd Shasannach
do'n phàisde an uair a bha i dealachadh ris, is cha robh fios
aca có an té a bh'ann, no có as a thànaig i, no c'àite an robh i dol.

An ceann latha is bliadhna, thànaig i a dh'amharc a' phàisde
rithist, is bha iad a' cluinntinn fuaim an t-sìoda bha oirre mun
robh i chòir a bhith aca.[1] Thànaig i a staigh, is dh'fhaighnich
i dé mar a bha am pàisde, is thuirt iad gun robh gu maith.
Chuir i a làmh 'na pòca, is thug i cóig puinnd deug Shasannach
d'a mhàthair. Dh'fhalbh i, is an ceann là is dà bhliadhna,
thànaig i rithist, is mun robh i chòir a bhith aca, bha iad a'
cluinntinn fuaim an t-sìoda. Dh'fhaighnich i dé mar a bha am
pàisde, is thuirt iad gun robh gu maith. 'Tha mise,' ars ise,
'dol dh'a toirt liom.' 'A bheil?' ars a h-athair, 'cha bu mhaith
liom sin : bidh mi gu maith duilich as a deighinn.' 'Coma
có dhiùbh, feumaidh tu a leigeil liom.' Chuir i a làmh 'na
pòca, is thug i dha cuid mhaith airgid,[2] na chum gu maith ri a

---

[1] See *Folk-Lore*, xxxiv., p. 241 ; MS. vol. x., No. 158.
[2] A claim to the person of a heroine, a claim based on the payment of moneys,
appears in *W. H. Tales*, ii., No. 18 ; MS. vol. x., No. 33.

THE STORY OF THE UNBAPTIZED GIRL

No. 49.   [*MS. Vol. x., No. 83.2*]

THERE was once a poor man to whom a daughter was born. For a good length of time she remained unbaptized, and so the man went to the minister to arrange for baptism. The minister said he should have the baptism performed on such and such a day. The man returned home and when he arrived there he found an elegant lady awaiting him in the house. 'Will you let me act as sponsor, since there is to be a christening?' asked the lady. 'Yes,' he replied. 'All you have to do,' said the lady, 'is to glance over your left shoulder as you enter the church and you will see me.' So it was. On the day the minister appointed, the man set out to have the child baptized, and as he entered the church he glanced over his left shoulder, and he saw the lady. She went inside with him, and was admitted to sponsorship. They came home, both she and they, and as she parted from the baby the lady gave it five pounds sterling. Yet they knew neither who she was nor where she came from nor where she was going.

At the end of a year and a day the lady came to see the child again ; and they could hear the rustle of her silks long before she was near them.[1] She came inside and asked how the baby was ; they replied that it was well. The lady put her hand into her pocket and gave fifteen pounds sterling to the mother. She went away, and at the end of two years and a day she came again ; and long before she was near them, they could hear the rustle of silk. She asked how the child was, and they said it was well. 'I am going to take it with me,' said she. 'Are you ?' said the father : 'I should not like that at all : I shall miss her very much.' 'Whether you do or not, you must allow me,' said she. The lady put her hand into her pocket and gave him quite a large sum of money[2]—as much as kept him comfortably

bheò e, 's thug i leatha a' chaileag far an robh i féin a' fuireachd.
Bha i 'ga h-ionnsachadh an sin air a h-uile nì a bu chòir d'a
leithid ionnsachadh.   Bhiodh i a' falbh a h-uile latha, is cha
bhiodh leis a' chaileig ach i féin a staigh.

Bha iuchair a h-uile seòmair a staigh aice, ach iuchair aon
seòmair.   Cha d'fhuair i iuchair an t-seòmair sin riamh, is cha
mhò fhuair i sealladh de na bha ann, gus an d' fhàs i 'na nighinn
mhóir, is i ag ionnsachadh snìomh.   Aon latha, dh'fhalbh a
muime o'n taigh, is dhìochuimhnich i an seòmar seo a ghlasadh.
Bha ise dèanamh rudeigin feadh an taighe, is thug i an aire
nach robh an seòmar glaiste, ach cha deach i ['n]a chòir, is
shuidh i aig a cuidheil a' snìomh, ach smaointich i rithist, gum
b' fhearra dhi éireachd, is amharc dé bha ann, o'n bha e cho
cùramach is nach fhaca i sealladh dheth riamh.   Dh'éirich i,
is dh'fhalbh i sìos,[1] a dh'amharc dé rud a bh'ann.   'Nuair a
dh'fhosgail i an dorus, is a dh'amhairc i a staigh, bha e làn de
dhaoine beaga crìona, 's iad a' dannsadh.   'Nuair a chunnaig
i iad, ghabh i an t-eagal, dhùin i an dorus, chaidh i suas, is
shuidh i a' snìomh mar a bha i roimhe.   'Nuair a thànaig a
muime dachaigh, chaidh i sìos do'n t-seòmar, is chasaid an
fheadhainn a bha a staigh rithe, gun robh an té bha a staigh ag
amharc a staigh orra.   Thànaig a muime a nìos, agus thuirt i
rithe, 'A dhalt, agus a dheagh-dhalt ! gu dé chunnaig thu ann
am sheòmar-sa ?'   'Chan fhaca mise nì sam bith ann !' ars ise.
'Innis domh gu dé chunnaig thu ann am sheòmar, air neò
marbhaidh mi thu.'   'Chan fhaca mise nì sam bith ann !' Thug
i leatha i, is chroch i air ghruaig ri craoibh i, agus bha i an
sin crochte air ghruaig car treis [agus dh'fhàg a muime an sin i].

Bha duine-uasal a' dol seachad air mharcachd.   Chunnaig
e i, is leis cho bòidheach 's a bha i, ghabh e gaol oirre.   Thùirling
e bhàrr an eich, thànaig e far an robh i ;   thug e a mach sgian-
pheann as a phòca, gheàrr e a gruag, is leig e mu sgaoil i, is
thuirt e rithe, có a chroch an siod i, is thuirt i nach robh fios
aice.   'Có as a thànaig thu ?' thuirt esan.   'Chan 'eil fhios a'm,'
ars ise.   'Cà bheil thu dol ?'   'Chan 'eil fhios a'm.'   Thug e leis
air druim an eich i, is thug e dh'a thaigh fhéin i.   Cha robh e

---

[1] Going from one end of the house to the other is 'going up' or 'going down',
or 'coming from above, coming from below' ; suas, shuas, up, refers to the inner
end of the house ; sìos, shìos, to the end nearer the door.

for the rest of his life—and she took the girl with her to where she herself lived. There she used to teach her everything that a girl should learn. Every day the lady would go away, and the girl would have no one at home but herself.

The girl had the keys of every room in the house but one. She never got the key of that room, nor did she get a glimpse of what was inside it until she had grown to be a big girl, and was learning to spin. One day, her foster-mother left home and forgot to lock this room. The girl was doing something or other about the house, and she noticed that the room was not locked ; but she did not go near it, but sat at her wheel, spinning. But then, she thought, she had better get up and see what was there, since it was kept so carefully that she had never had one look at it. She got up and walked through to see what it was. When she opened the door, the room was full of tiny little people, dancing. When she saw them, she became terrified, shut the door, returned to her wheel and sat down to spin as she had been doing before. When her foster-mother came home she went into the room, and those who were inside complained that the girl in the house had been spying on them. The foster-mother came to the girl. 'Foster-child,' said she, 'good foster-child, what did you see in my room ?' 'I saw nothing at all there,' replied the girl. 'Tell me what you saw in my room or I will kill you.' 'I saw nothing at all.' She took her away, and hanged her by the hair of her head to a tree ; and there she hung by her hair for a time, and her foster-mother left her.

A gentleman was riding by. He noticed the girl, and because of her beauty he fell in love with her. He leapt off his horse and came to her. He drew a penknife out of his pocket, cut her hair, freed her, and asked who had hanged her there. The girl replied that she did not know. 'Where did you come from ?' he asked. 'I don't know,' answered the girl. 'Where are you going ?' 'I don't know.' He carried her off with him on horseback, and he brought her to his own house. He himself was pòsda. Ghléidh e i a h-uile car gu ceann latha is bliadhna ; fhuair e ministeir, is phòs iad.

An ceann trì ràithean, bha mac aice. An oidhche a dh' asaideadh i, thànaig an aona cheòl a bu bhòidhche chualas riamh timcheall an taighe, is chaidil a h-uile duine bha staigh, ach ise. Thànaig a muime a staigh, is thuirt i rithe, 'A dhalta, agus a dheagh-dhalta ! gu dé chunnaig thu ann am sheòmar-sa ?' 'Chan fhaca mi nì sam bith ann.' Thug i a mach cuilean as a broilleach, agus sgian as a pòca ; mharbh i an cuilean, is chuir i an fhuil air beul a dalta, is air taobh na leapa, is thug i leatha am pàisde. 'Nuair a bha i a mach an dorus, ghlaodh i, 'O ! a' bhean a dh'ith am pàisde,' is dhùisg i a h-uile duine. Chunnaig iad an fhuil air a beul is air taobh na leapa, is thòisich iad air a ràdh gur e a itheadh a rinn i. Dh' fhaighnich a h-athair-céile dhi, gu dé thànaig air a' phàisde, is thuirt i nach robh fios aice. Thuirt cuid de na bha a staigh gum marbhadh iad i. Thuirt a h-athair-céile nach marbhadh ; gum faigheadh i maitheanas air an t-siubhal seo, thaobh i bhith cho bòidheach. An darna siubhal, bha a' chùis air an aon dòigh. An treas siubhal, bha a' chùis air an aon dòigh. Bha i an seo air a dìteadh gu bhith air a losgadh.

Ann am beagan làithean, an uair a bha i na b'fheàrr, chuir iad an òrdugh gealbhan air son a losgadh. Thug iad a mach i, agus cheangail iad i air son a tilgeil ann. Thog a h-athair-céile a shùilean, is chunnaig e bhean-uasal mhór a' tighinn, is dà choisiche leatha, is a h-aon air a gàirdean. 'Nì sinn moille bheag gus an tig i seo,' ars esan, 'air eagal gu bheil fios sam bith leatha.' 'Nuair a thànaig i seo air a h-adhart, dh'iarr i a leigeil mu sgaoil, nach rachadh a marbhadh, chionn gun robh na trì leanabain aice an siod. 'Bha trì daltaiche deug agam,' ars ise, ' 's cha robh a leithid seo riamh agam. Bha mise fo gheasan gus am faighinn dalta a dh' àicheadh a h-uile nì gus am bitheadh triùir chloinne aice. Bha trì deug agam, agus b' éiginn a h-uile gin a mharbhadh, ach i seo. Tha mi nis mu sgaoil, is bidh mi 'nam charaid maith dhi uile làithean a beatha.' Chaidh a togail a staigh 's a h-éideadh ann an sìodaichean. Fhuair i a leanaban fhéin 'na h-uchd, is chòrd i féin is a fear-pòsda is a h-athair-céile riamh tuilleadh.

unmarried. For a year and a day he kept her with him continuously ; then he got a minister and they were married.

At the end of nine months she bore a son. On the night she was delivered, the most beautiful music that ever had been heard came all round about the house and everyone inside fell asleep, all but she. In came her foster-mother : 'Foster-child, good foster-child,' said she, 'what did you see in my room ?' 'I saw nothing at all there.' The woman took a puppy out of her bosom and a knife from her pocket : she killed the pup and smeared its blood on her foster-child's mouth and on the bedside, and she carried off the baby. As she went out through the doorway, she called out, 'Oh ! the woman who devoured the child !' and she woke everyone up. They all saw the blood on her mouth and on the bedside, and began to say that what she had done was to eat the baby. Her father-in-law asked her what had happened to it, and she replied that she did not know. Some of those who were in the room said that they would kill her. But her father-in-law said no : that because of her beauty she should, on this occasion, be forgiven. The second time, the same thing happened, and the third time. So now she was condemned to be burnt.

In a few days, when she was better, they prepared a fire to burn her ; and having brought her out, they bound her to throw her in the fire. As he glanced up, the father-in-law noticed a great lady approaching, and with her two children walking and a third in her arms. 'We will wait a little until this woman comes,' said he, 'in case she brings some message.' When the lady had come up to them, she ordered the girl to be set at liberty and not killed ; for there, with her, she had the three babies. 'Thirteen foster-children had I,' she said, 'but never such a one as this. I was under a spell until I should get a foster-child who would deny everything until she had had three children. I had thirteen foster-children, and every one of them had to be killed except this one. I am now set free, and I will be a true friend to her all the days of her life.' Then the girl was carried inside and clothed in silks. She received her own babe to her bosom again, and she and her husband and her father-in-law lived together in concord ever after.

NOTES

MS. vol. x., No. 83 (2).

Hector MacLean, the scribe, added the following note at the end of the MS. 'We have a prohibited room in this one as well as in that of the grey horse, but its character is different. The whole tale seems to point to the importance of keeping a secret. This tale I have got also from James MacLachlan, but he cannot give the name of the person from whom he learnt it. It was from a mason who was working at Keills. James MacLachlan resides at Mulrees, Islay, a farm labourer.' By 'the grey horse' MacLean probably refers to Var. 1 or Var. 2 of No. 41 in *W. H. Tales*, ii., where a grey horse turns into a king's son or a giant, both being of the Bluebeard variety.

In his Gaelic List (*W. H. Tales*, iv.) Campbell of Islay speaks of this tale as having been 'translated.' The translation was made by himself and is bound up with the original Gaelic. But it were more accurate to speak of the translation as a transliteration. Such a method of rendering has its value, but would in many places be quite unintelligible to those who know English only. However, Campbell must have been greatly struck by the tale, as it is the only one among the hundreds in MS. vols. x., xi., and xii., that he has so dealt with. In some notes to the tale, he says—

'This is exceedingly like "The Lassie and her Godmother" (page 217, second edition Dasent [Sir George Webbe Dasent, Norse Fairy Tales]) but there are great differences and this is fitted to Highland customs and ceremonies as the other is to Norse habits. In Norway paying the fee causes the difficulty in finding the Godmother ; here there is no difficulty, but the Muime (Godmother) who offers herself and gives the usual present to the child. The sun, moon, and stars are in the Norwegian room—little tiny men in the Islay one.

'The Norse incident of the reflection in the well occurs in another Gaelic story (No. 1, Cath nan Eun) [1] but it is not here—the music which sends every one to sleep is not in the Norse version. An old queen is mother-in-law in Norway : in Islay it is a father-in-law who is the gentleman. The blood is in both, but it comes from a different source.

'The Muime turns out to be the Virgin Mary [2] in the one case, she is the enchanted lady in the other. There can be no doubt that both are derived from the same source. Now, in the *Arabian Nights*, Vol. iv., there is a story which contains a part of the incidents in this tale. The two sisters, who were jealous of their younger sister, stole her three children and she is punished, not for eating them, but for giving birth to supposed monsters [as in this book, p. 284-6]. The children are finally restored, and the mother again taken into favour.

'But the Norsk and Gaelic story [= stories], though they contain a very similar incident, are composed of other incidents which in no way resemble the remainder of the story in the *Arabian Nights*.

---

[1] Recte, No. 2, *W. H. Tales*, i.
[2] The Virgin Mary stands sponsor in another tale, Paul Sébillot, *Contes des Marins*, Paris, 1888, quoted by Alfred Nutt, *Waifs and Strays*, ii., p. 461.

'It is perfectly impossible that a farm labourer in Islay can have seen Dasent's book or can have so altered the tale. So there is nothing for it but to believe that the story is common to many lands, the property of many races who have each altered it to suit their own manners and customs so far as the ground-work of the tale would permit.

'The tip to the Nurse is a common Highland custom, when anyone goes to see a baby. It is often given to the mother.[1]

'The incident of the stolen children occurs in the Princess Belle Étoile, Madame D'Aulnoy, which [= whose tales] were translated into English in the beginning of last century. Puppies were substituted for the three children, and the rest of the French story is marvellously like that in the *Arabian Nights*—but it is unlike the Norsk and Gaelic versions.

'The Woodcutter's Child, Grimm, contains a similar incident, but the personages are all different. The gentlewoman is an angel and [the] girl [is] dumb [?]. The Twelve Wild Ducks also contains the same incident.'— Thus far Campbell of Islay.

Related Tales :—No. 20 (MS. vol. x., No. 34). The Black Lady (*Journal of Gypsy Lore Society*, July, 1907), p. 26. Patrick Kennedy's *Legendary Fictions*, p. 17. Islay's English List, No. 343, MS. vol. xiii., The Handless Maiden (summarized *W. H. Tales*, iii., last pages). William of the Tree, Dr Hyde, Beside the Fire, pp. 167, 194.[2]

---

[1] The following is reported of the Scots population of Prince Edward Island, Canada. 'When visiting a new-born baby, put a piece of silver into its hand. This will bring luck to the baby and also to the giver. Neglect of the observance means bad luck for both, but especially for the visitor' ; *Folk-Lore*, xxxii., p. 126. Giving silver to anyone who shows you a young baby for the first time, will ensure the child health and happiness ; a custom recorded for North Bedfordshire, *ibid.*, xxxvii., p. 77. See also *Folk-Lore Journal*, ii. (1884), p. 257.

See Nicolson's *Gaelic Proverbs*, pp. 233, 320 :—*Is e a leanabh fhéin as luaithe bhaisteas an sagart*, 'The priest christens his ain bairn first.' *Mullach do bhaistidh*, 'The top of your baptism' (the forehead). *Cho cinnteach ris an airgead bhaistidh*, 'As sure as the baptism money.' I forget where I saw this proverb. It refers to the fact that the priest would not baptize without first receiving his fee. See also for baptizing, this book, Vol. i., pp. 308, 389.

[2] [The story is a märchen of somewhat complicated type. The godmother claiming the child suggests that it had been promised to her (*Homecomer's Vow*). Then follows *Bluebeard* and, dovetailed into that, *Calumniated Wife*. The Norse story may be the source, though *Calumniated Wife* is good Celtic (the story of Rhiannon in the Mabinogion)—H. J. R.] [For a discussion of the Calumniated Wife theme, on Celtic soil, with further examples, see now G. Murphy, *Duanaire Finn*, iii. (Dublin, The Irish Texts Society, 1953), pp. xiv. ff.—K. H. J.]

SGEULACHD FEAR A' CHÒTA SHLIBISTICH LIATHGHLAIS

No. 50. [*MS. Vol. x., No. 84*]

BHA Fionn, le cuid eile de na Fianntan, ann an Éirinn, agus chaidh e latha do'n bheinn-sheilg, le buidheann de'n Fhéin. Mharbh iad móran fhiadh, agus shuidh iad a leigeil an sgìos ann an àite fasgach, air chùl gaoithe agus air aodann gréine. Chunnaig Fionn gun robh barrachd sìdhne aca na b' urrainn daibh a ghiùlan dhachaigh, agus thubhairt e, 'B' fheàrr liom gun robh fear giùlan eallach agam!' Thog e a shùil, agus chunnaig e coite air an tràigh, agus fear mór le còta slibisteach liathghlas a' leum aiste. Thànaig e far an robh Fionn, agus thubhairt an Rìgh ris, 'Cia an taobh as an do tharraing thusa?' ['As a h-uile h-àite anns an robh mi riamh, có dhiùbh a gheibh mi as a seo, gus nach fhaigh.' 'Agus có thu féin?'] [1] 'Is gille math mi, ag iarraidh maighstir.' 'Ciod e a' cheàird air an fheàrr thu?' ars an Rìgh. 'Giùlan eallachan,' ars an gille. 'Is tu a' cheart fhear a bha dhìth orm,' arsa Fionn. 'Mun dèan mi cùmhnant riut,' arsa Fear a' Chòta Shlibistich Liathghlais, 'is fheudar dhuit a ghealltainn dhomh gun cuir thu dhachaigh le onoir mi.'

Bha an Rìgh toileach an cùmhnant seo dhèanamh ris, a bharrachd air tuarasdal math air son a sheirbhis. Dh'iarr e an sin ròp anns an ceangladh e an t-sidheann. Bha leth-cheud fiadh ann, a bharrachd air sidheann eile. Thug iad dha ròp an déidh ròpa, ach na h-uile ròpa a gheibheadh e, an uair a theannaicheadh e iad [bhristeadh iad]. Mu dheireadh, thilg e air falbh na h-uile ròpa dhiubh, agus thug e ròp as a phòca féin, agus cheangail e an t-sidheann ann, agus dh'iarr e orra an eallach a thogail air a mhuin. Cha b' urrainn dhaibh sin a dhèanamh; ach thilg e fhéin thar a ghualainn e, agus dh'fhalbh

---

[1] The sentences between square brackets, which were taken from another tale, *Waifs and Strays*, ii., p. 32, were interpolated in order to give a reasonable amount of sequence to the conversation.

THE STORY OF THE MAN WITH THE SLOVENLY BLUE-GREY COAT

No. 50.   [*MS. Vol. x., No. 84*]

FIONN and a number of the Fiann were in Ireland. One day he went hunting with a band of them. They killed many deer and then sat down to rest themselves in a sheltered place at the back of the wind and in the sun's face. Fionn saw that they had more venison than they could carry home, and he said, 'I do wish I had a man to carry burdens.' He raised his eyes, and there he saw a boat on the beach and a great man with a slovenly blue-grey coat jumping out of it. He came to where Fionn was and the King asked, 'Where have you come from?' [From every place that I have ever been in, whether I escape from this one or not.' 'And who are you?']¹ 'I am a good servant, seeking a master.' 'What craft are you best at?' asked the King. 'Carrying burdens,' replied the lad. 'You are the very man I needed,' said Fionn. 'Before I make any bargain with you,' said the Man of the Slovenly Blue-grey Coat, 'you must promise to send me home honourably.'

The King was quite ready to agree to this condition, besides giving him good wages for his services. He then asked for a rope in which he might tie up the carcasses : there were fifty deer besides other game. They gave him rope after rope, but every rope [broke] when he tightened it. At last he threw away every one of them, and brought a rope out of his own pocket. He bound up the carcasses in it and asked them to hoist the load up on to his back for him. But that they were unable to do. He himself swung the burden over his shoulder and set off, saying that they were to hurry after him and that he would prepare their dinner for them. None of them could

e, ag ràdh iad a ghreasad 'na dhéidh, agus gun deasaicheadh e
an dìnneir dhaibh. Cha chumadh a h-aon aca ris an coiseachd,
agus an uair a rànaig e, dh'fhionn e seachd féidh, agus bhruich
agus dh'ith e iad, an uair a bha a' chuideachd fada leis gun
tighinn. Dh'fhionn e an sin tuilleadh de na féidh, mun tànaig
a' chuid eile de na daoine ; bhruich e iad, agus thug e dhaibh
an dìnneir.

Bha e mar fhiachaibh air a h-uile maduinn connadh a
ghiùlan dachaigh, a dheasachadh bìdh do na sealgairean, ach
dh'fhàgadh aige an connadh ri a ghearradh, cho maith ri
a ghiùlan. Thubhairt e ri a mhaighstir aon latha nach
leanadh e air seo a dhèanamh na b'fhaide, ach nam biodh
an connadh air a ghearradh, gun tugadh e dhachaigh e.
Thubhairt an Rìgh ris gum biodh sin air a dhèanamh dha. Na
h-uile craobh a leagadh iad, chuireadh e anns an ròpa, gus nach
b'urrainn aon de luchd-leanmhainn an Rìgh an eallach a
ghluasad, ach thog esan gun spàirn air a mhuin féin an eallach,
agus thug e dhachaigh i.

Lean e mar seo greïs, ach bha fear de luchd-coimhideachd
an Rìgh a bha fìor chrosda, agus aig an robh farmad ris, a bha
gun tàmh a' dèanamh tàir air, agus a' dèanamh culaidh-
mhagaidh dheth. Dh'fhuiling e seo gu fada le foidhidinn, ach
mu dheireadh dh'fhàs e cho mì-mhodhail ri am cuirme a bha
aca, nach robh e comasach dha éisdeachd ris na b'fhaide. B'e
ainm an duine chrosda seo, Conan. 'Mo cheann air son do
chinn,' arsa Conan ris, 'mur ruig mi mullach Bheinn Éidir air
thoiseach ort.' 'Cha chuir mise mo cheann an éirig do chinn,'
arsa Fear a' Chòta Shlibistich Liathghlais, 'ach ma chuireas
duine sam bith geall as do leth, tha mi toileach d'fheuchainn.'
'Cuiridh mise geall,' arsa Fionn, 'gum buidhinn thusa.' [1]

Dh'fhalbh [iad] còmhla, Conan cho luath ri gaoith luaith
Mhàirt, ach Fear a' Chòta [Shlibistich Liath]ghlais gu socair
a' dèanamh astair mhaith. Lean an Rìgh agus a chuideachd
iad, mar a b'urrainn dhaibh, gus an do rug iad air Fear a'
Chòta [Shlibistich Liath]ghlais, 'na shuidhe aig taobh an rathaid-
mhóir. 'Ciod e seo e,' arsa Fionn, 'atà 'gad chumail an seo ?'
'Tha,' arsa esan, 'mo bhròg sracte, agus chan urrainn mi dol

[1] *i.e.* the Man of the Cloak.

keep pace with him, and when he got to his destination and it seemed to him the rest were long in coming, he flayed seven deer, cooked them and ate them. He had skinned more deer before the others arrived ; then he cooked the deer and served the men.

Every morning it was his duty to carry firewood home in order to prepare food for the hunters, but he was left to do the cutting as well as the carrying. He said to his master one day that he would not continue to do so any longer, but that if the firewood were cut, he would carry it home. The King said that that should be done for him. Every tree that the others cut down, he would lay on the rope, until no one of the King's retainers could move the burden ; but he hoisted the burden effortlessly on to his own back, and brought it home.

For some time he continued this practice. But there was one of the King's retinue who was very cross-grained and who was jealous of him ; this person was always showing his contempt for him and making a butt of him. For a long time he bore it with patience, but at last the other became so rude during a certain feast that he could listen no longer. The name of this cross-grained fellow was Conan. 'My head against yours,' said Conan to him, 'if I do not reach the summit of the Hill of Howth before you.' 'I will not stake my head against yours,' said the Man of the Slovenly Blue-grey Coat, 'but if anyone wagers on your behalf, I am willing to compete with you.' 'I wager,' says Fionn, 'that you [1] will win.'

They set off together, Conan as fast as the swift March wind, and the Man of the Slovenly Blue-grey Coat unhurriedly making good progress. The King and his company followed them as well as they could until they overtook the Man of the Slovenly Blue-grey Coat sitting by the side of the highway. 'What is this !' said Fionn : 'What keeps you here ?' 'Why,' said he, 'my shoe is torn and I cannot go on until I mend it.' He brought a rusty awl

air m'aghaidh gus an càirich mi i.' Thug e minidh meirgeach
as a phòca, agus chàirich e a bhròg. Ghabh e, an sin, air
aghaidh a' dìreadh a' bhruthaich. Cha deach e fada, an uair
a fhuair iad e a rithist, 'na shuidhe aig taobh loch uisge. 'Ciod
air an t-saoghal atà 'gad chumail an seo a nis?' arsa Fionn;
'tha eagal orm gun caill mise mo gheall.' 'O,' ars esan, 'chì mi
lach air an loch, agus chan urrainn mi dol air m'aghaidh gus
am marbh mi i.' Dh'fheuch iad na h-uile bogha-saighead a
bha aca, ach cha b'urrainn dhaibh an lach a chuimiseachadh.
Mu dheireadh, ghabh esan mìr de chorran maol meirgeach a
bha 'na phòca, agus thilg e air an lach e, agus mharbh e i, ach
cha tugadh a h-aon de na coin air tìr i. Chuir Fear a' Chòta
[Shlibistich Liath]ghlais dheth a aodach, agus shnàmh e dh'a
h-iarraidh, agus thug e gu tìr i, agus dh'fhalbh e air aghaidh,
ach cha [b'] fhada gus an [d'] fhuair iad e 'na shuidhe a rithist.
'Ciod am buaireadh a thànaig ort a nis?' arsa an Rìgh; 'caillidh
mise, gun amharus, mo gheall.' 'Tha,' ars esan, 'an còta seo
cho fada mu mo chasan, gu bheil e ag cur mhoille mhóir [1] orm,
agus feumaidh mi a chur an giorraid mus urrainn mi dol air
m'aghaidh. Nam faighinn sgian no siosar a ghearradh e!'
Cha robh sgian no siosar aig a h-aon aca, ach rùraich e a phòca
féin, agus fhuair e siosar leis an tug e pìos de'n chòta. Ghabh
e an sin air aghaidh pìos beag, ach fhuair iad e a rithist 'na
shuidhe. 'Gun deireadh [2] ort!' ars an Rìgh; 'gun teagamh sam
bith, bidh an geall agam-sa ri a phàidheadh.' 'Chan urrainn
mi dol na's fhaide gus am faigh mi am pìos a thug mi bhàrr na
casaige fhuaigheal rithe a rithist.' Fhuair e an sin snàthad agus
snàthainn agus chuir e am pìos ris a' chòta, agus dh'fhalbh e
gu sgairteil, agus rànaig e mullach na beinne fada air thoiseach
air Conan.

Bha Conan ann am feirg mhóir, an uair a chunnaig e gun
do bhuidhinn e an geall, agus thug e builleadh dha. Thug Fear
a' Chòta Shlibistich Liathghlais do Chonan buille 'na éirig, a
thionndaidh a cheann cùl air bheulaibh. An uair a chunnaig
Fionn an coltas a bha air Conan, ghuidh e air ceann Chonain a
chur ceart, agus gun dèanadh e nì sam bith a dh'iarradh e air. 'Nì
mi sin,' ars esan, 'ma gheallas tusa dol liom, dha'm fhaicinn

---

[1] MS. *ag cur mhoille mhor orm.*
[2] [Read *dìreadh*?—A. M.]

from his pocket and he mended his shoe. Then he pressed on, breasting the hillside, but he had not gone far before they found him again, this time sitting by the side of a fresh-water loch. 'What on earth is keeping you here now?' asked Fionn. 'I fear I shall lose my bet.' 'Oh,' said he, 'I see a wild duck on the loch, and I cannot go farther until I have killed it.' They tried every bow they had, but they could not hit the duck. At last he took a fragment of a blunt, rusty sickle that was in his pocket, and he threw it at the duck and killed it; but not one of the dogs could bring it to land. The Man of the Blue-grey Coat undressed, swam out to get it, and brought it ashore. Then he went on his way, but it was not long before they found him sitting down again. 'What distraction has seized you now?' asked the King. 'I shall undoubtedly lose my bet.' 'This coat hangs down about my feet so much,' he replied; 'it hinders me very much; I must shorten it before I can go on. If only I had scissors or a knife to cut it with!' Not one of them had a knife or scissors, but he rummaged in his own pockets and found a pair of scissors with which he cut a piece off the coat. Then he went on a little, but they found him sitting down once more. 'Bad luck to you!' exclaimed the King. 'Without any doubt at all, I shall forfeit the bet.' 'I can go no farther until I get the piece that I cut off my coat sewn on to it again,' said he. He took a needle and thread then, sewed the piece on to the coat and set off vigorously, and reached the top of the mountain long before Conan.

Conan was very angry when he saw that the other had won the bet, and he hit him a blow. The Man of the Slovenly Blue-grey Coat hit Conan one in return that drove Conan's head round back to front. When Fionn saw what Conan looked like, he begged the Man of the Slovenly Blue-grey Coat to put Conan's head right, and he would do anything he asked him. 'I will do that,' said he, 'if you promise to come with me yourself and dhachaigh.' Gheall Fionn sin dha ; thug Fear a' Chòta [Shlibistich Liath]ghlais buille do Chonan air taobh eile a chinn, agus chuir e ceart e. Theirinn iad an sin a' bheinn, agus thubhairt fear ghiùlan nan eallachan ri Fionn, 'Tha toil agam a nis tilleadh dhachaigh, agus tha dùil agam gun cum thusa do ghealladh rium mo chur dhachaigh gu measail, agus gun téid thu féin liom.' 'Nach foghainn leat ma chuireas mi bàta agus sgioba maith leat ?' 'Chan fhoghainn,' ars esan ; 'cha ghabh mi na's lugha na thu féin, agus duine cho urramach agus a tha anns a' chuideachd leat, gu mo thabhairt gu h-onorach a dh'ionnsaigh mo chàirdean.'

An uair a chaidh iad do'n bhàta, bha Fear a' Chòta [Shlibistich Liath]ghlais fìor aoibheil, agus dh'innis e do'n Rìgh an t-adhbhar mu'n do dh'iarr e air dol leis, a chionn gun d'fhuair e ìnnseadh dha nach còrdadh e féin agus a aona bhràthair gus an rachadh Fionn do'n taigh aca. 'Bha,' ars esan ri Fionn, 'm' athair-sa 'na rìgh, agus air son olc éigin a rinn e, bha draoidheachd air a chur oirnne a bha ri leantainn ruinn gus an tigeadh tusa a dh'ionnsaigh ar taighe ; [1]agus smaointich ar màthair agus sinn féin air an ìnnleachd a chuir mise ann an gnìomh, gu d' thabhairt a dh'ionnsaigh ar n-àite còmhnaidh.' [1]

An déidh dhaibh seòladh astar mór, shaoil iad nach ruigeadh iad an ceann-uidhe idir. An uair a thànaig eilean bòidheach ann am fradharc, 'Sin,' arsa Fear a' Chòta [Shlibistich Liath]ghlais, 'an rìoghachd againn' ; agus an uair a rànaig iad an cladach, thànaig am màthair gu am fàilteachadh, agus thug i pòg dhaibh ag ràdh gum b'e am beatha, a chionn gun robh i cinnteach gun tugadh iad sìth a dh' ionnsaigh a teaghlaich. Dh'fhàs a mic, a bha roimhe sin borb agus garg, 'nan daoine ciùine, sèimh, dreachmhor, eireachdail, a' dèanamh na h-uile nì a b'urrainn dhaibh, cho maith ri am màthair, a thoileachadh nan aoighean anns na h-uile coibhneas a nochdadh dhaibh le pailteas bìdh [2] is dibhe, am feadh agus a dh' fhan iad, agus an uair a bha iad a' fàgail an eilein, chuir iad [leò anns a' bhàta] na h-uile seòrsa bìdh [2] agus dibhe, cho maith ri òr agus airgead, agus a' bhanrìgh làn toil-inntinn leis an dà phrionnsa, a mic.

[1-1] These words have been written twice over in the MS., suggesting that it is a fair copy of another MS.

[2] MS. *bedhidh* (representing O. Ir. disyllabic *biid*).

see me home.' And Fionn promised that. The Man of the Blue-
grey Coat hit Conan on the other side of his head, and put it
right. Then they descended the mountain and the burden-
carrier said to Fionn, 'I should like to go home now, and I expect
you to keep your promise to send me home in an honourable way
and come with me yourself.' 'Will it not be enough if I send a
boat and a good crew with you?' 'No, it will not,' said he ;
'I will not accept anyone less than you yourself and with you
someone else as high in degree as any in the company, to
convey me with due honour to my friends.'

When they got into the boat, the Man of the Slovenly Blue-
grey Coat became very affable, and told the King why he had
asked him to go with him. For it had been told him that he and
his only brother should never agree until Fionn visited their
home. 'My father was a King,' said he to Fionn, 'and because
of some wrong he did, spells were laid upon us that were to bind
us until you should visit our house. So our mother and ourselves
thought of the plan which I have carried out to bring you to
our dwelling.'

After they sailed so great a distance that they thought they
would never reach their journey's end, a beautiful island came
into view. 'There,' said the Man of the Blue-grey Coat, 'is our
kingdom.' When they reached the shore, their mother came to
greet them and kissed them, saying they were heartily welcome
since she was sure that they would bring peace to her household.
Her sons who had been fierce and rough before became mild,
gentle men of good presence ; and they, as well as their mother,
did all they could to entertain their guests and show them every
kindness, providing them with abundance of food and drink for
as long as they stayed. And when they were leaving the island,
they sent in the boat with them every kind of food and drink as
well as gold and silver. As for the queen, she was filled with
gladness at her sons, the two princes.

NOTES

MS. vol. x., No. 84. In the MS. there is no clue to reciter or provenance, but Islay's Gaelic List attributes the tale to Mrs MacTavish of Islay, and says that the story is also in Irish. For reasons too long to be set down here, and depending upon certain facts concerning Nos. 216 and 217 of Islay's English List, the probability is that No. 84 was recited by a Miss Jean MacTavish, who was then [in 1859 or 1860] above 73 years old. See No. 63 (MS. vol. x., No. 117).

Of the said story, No. 217, Islay says—'A very good story, something like the story of Murdoch M'Brian,' No. 38 of *W. H. Tales*, ii. The Man of the Slovenly Blue-grey Coat appears in these ; in *Trans. Gael. Soc. Inverness*, xxv., pp. 185, 247 ; in *Silva Gadelica*, ii., p. 325 ; and by a different name in *Waifs and Strays*, iii., p. 27.

For Conan, see *Waifs and Strays*, iii., p. 41 ; iv., p. 73 ; Nicolson's *Gaelic Proverbs*, pp. 53, 75, 96, 329. For magic servants hired by Fionn, see *Waifs and Strays*, ii., pp. 443, 445 ; iii., pp. 17, 56 ; 'Sealg Bheinn Eidir,' *An Gàidheal*, iv. (1875), p. 81 (reprinted with translation by MacLaren and Sons, Glasgow); Islay's MS. vol. xi., No. 216.

The incident of knocking some one's head round so that it is back foremost, and of knocking it again so that it resumes its proper position, occurs in Islay's MS. vol. xi., No. 216 ; *Folk Tales and Fairy Lore*, p. 222 ; *Superstitions*, p. 162.

DOMHNALL DONA, MAC NA BANTRAICH

No. 51.   [*MS. Vol. x., No. 85*]

BHA ann roimhe seo bantrach aig an robh aon mhac nach robh ro ghlic. Bha iad an déidh an cuid barra a chur cruinn, ach thànaig gaoth mhór a leag na mulain, agus a sgap an t-arbhar. Thuirt a mhàthair aon latha ri Dòmhnall—'B' fheàrr liom gun rachadh tu a dh'iarraidh pàidheadh nam mulan air a' ghaoith.' 'Théid,' arsa Dòmhnall, agus air falbh a ghabh e. Rànaig e taigh leth-an-rathaid, agus stad e ré na h-oidhche an sin, agus dh'fhalbh e air a thurus anns a' mhaduinn. Rànaig e taigh na gaoithe, agus chuir e a làmh air toll an doruis. 'Có sin a' cur stopadh air m'anail?' ars a' ghaoth. 'Tha mise, Dòmhnall Dona, Mac na Bantraich, ag iarraidh pàidheadh mo chuid mhulan air a' ghaoith.' 'Thig a staigh,' ars a' ghaoth, 'agus bheir mi sin duit anns a' mhaduinn.' Chaidh e a staigh a chur seachad na h-oidhche, agus an uair a dh'éirich e anns a' mhaduinn thuirt a' ghaoth ris, 'Bheir mise dhuit brà, a mheileas duit aon seòrsa mine a dh'iarras tu, ma their thu "Meil, meil, a bhrà !"'

Thug e leis a' bhrà gu taigh leth-an-rathaid, agus dh'fhaigh-nich iad dheth ciod am pàidheadh a fhuair e air son nam mulan. Dh'innis e dhoibh ciod a thuirt a' ghaoth ris, agus an uair a chaidil e, thug iad air falbh a' bhrà, agus chuir iad té eile 'na h-àite. Dh'fhalbh esan 'sa' mhaduinn, agus rànaig e a mhàthair. Dh'innis e mar a chaidh dha. Dh'iarr e air a' bhrà meileadh, ach cha mheileadh i blas. Thuirt a mhàthair ris air an latha màireach, 'Is fheàrr dhuit falbh a rithist, a dh'ìnnseadh do'n ghaoith nach 'eil math sam bith anns a' bhrà.' Dh'fhalbh e air a thurus, agus dh'fhan e ann an taigh leth-an-rathaid, agus bha e an ath-oidhche ann an taigh na gaoithe. Chuir e làmh air toll an doruis, agus ghlaodh a' ghaoth ris, 'Có sin a' cur stopadh air m'anail?' 'Tha mise, Dòmhnall Dona, Mac na Bantraich, ag iarraidh pàidheadh mo chuid mhulan air a' ghaoith.' 'Thig air t'aghaidh,' ars a' ghaoth, 'agus gheibh thu a màireach e.' Dh'fhan e an oidhche sin, agus air an là màireach

GOOD-FOR-NOTHING DONALD,
SON OF THE WIDOW

No. 51. [*MS. Vol. x., No. 85*]

THERE was once a widow who had one son who was not very
wise. They had gathered in their crops, when there came a great
wind which knocked down the ricks and scattered the corn.
One day his mother said to Donald, 'I wish you would go and
ask the wind to pay for the ricks.' 'Yes : I will go,' said Donald,
and away he went. He came to a half-way house and there he
stopped for the night ; in the morning he set off on his journey.
He came to the Wind's house and placed his hand on the hole
in the door. 'Who's that stopping my breath ?' asked the Wind.
'It is I, Good-for-Nothing Donald, Son of the Widow, seeking
payment for my ricks from the wind.' 'Come in,' replied the
Wind, 'and I shall give you that in the morning.' He went
inside to spend the night there, and when he got up in the
morning the Wind said to him, 'I will give you a quern which
will grind any sort of meal you wish if you say, "Grind, quern,
grind !" '

He took the quern away with him, and came to the half-way
house where they asked him what payment he had got for the
hay-ricks. He told them what the wind had said to him. But
when he was asleep, they removed the quern and put another
in its place. In the morning Donald left and came home to his
mother and told how he had fared. He asked the quern to grind,
but it would not grind a thing. Next day, his mother said to him,
'You had better go again, and tell the wind that the quern is
useless.' Donald set off on his journey, stayed at the half-way
house, and the next night he was at the Wind's house. He laid
his hand on the hole in the door and the Wind shouted at him,
'Who's that stopping my breath?' 'It is I, Good-for-Nothing
Donald, Son of the Widow seeking payment for my ricks from
the wind.' 'Come forward,' said the Wind, 'and you shall get
that tomorrow.' That night he stayed there, and next day the
Wind gave him a filly, telling him that when he said to her,

thug a' ghaoth dha loth, ag ìnnseadh dha, an uair a theireadh e rithe, 'Crath, crath, a loth !' gun crathadh i peic òir air an dara taobh, agus peic airgid air an taobh eile.

Thug e leis an loth, agus rànaig e taigh leth-an-rathaid. Dh'fharraid iad deth ciod a bha e dol a dhèanamh ris an loth, agus dh'innis e dhoibh. Ach an uair a chaidil esan, thuirt iad ris an loth, 'Crath, crath, a loth !' agus chrath i peic òir air an dara taobh agus peic airgid air an taobh eile. Ach cha robh fios aig Dòmhnall bochd air a sin, agus ghléidh iad an loth cho math ris a' bhrà, agus thug iad loth eile dha 'na h-àite. Thug e an loth a dh'ionnsaigh a mhàthar, ach an uair a dh'iarr e air an loth crathadh, cha chrathadh i dad. Thuirt a' mhàthair ris an treas uair, 'Feumaidh tu falbh a rithist, a dh'iarraidh pàidheadh nam mulan air a' ghaoith.'

Dh'fhalbh e, agus rànaig e taigh leth-an-rathaid, agus an ath-oidhche taigh na gaoithe. An uair a chuir e a làmh air toll an doruis, ghlaodh a' ghaoth, 'Có sin a' cur stopadh air m'anail ?' 'Tha mise, Dòmhnall Dona, Mac na Bantraich, ag iarraidh pàidheadh mo chuid mhulan air a' ghaoith.' 'Thig a staigh is fan an nochd, agus bheir mise dhuit a màireach pàidheadh nam mulan.' Dh'fhan e an oidhche sin, agus air an là màireach thug a ghaoth dha ploc agus iall, ag ràdh ris, 'Ceanglaidh an iall agus buailidh am ploc gus an iarr thusa orra sgur. Thug iad uait a' bhrà agus an loth a thug mise dhuit, ach gheibh thu air an ais iad.'

Dh'fhalbh e leis an éill agus leis a' phloc gu taigh leth-an-rathaid, agus dh'innis e dhoibh ciod a thuirt a' ghaoth ris a ràdh ris an éill agus ris a' phloc. An uair a chaidil esan, shaoil iad gum faigheadh iad nì-éigin math an uair a ghlaodhadh iad, 'Ceangail, a iall !—buail, a phluic !' Ach is ann a thòisich an iall ri ceangal, agus am ploc ri bualadh, gus an robh na h-uile h-aon 'san taigh a' glaodhaich 'Mort!' agus a' guidhe air Dòmhnall stad a chur orra, agus gun tugadh iad dha a' bhrà agus an loth. Fhuair e iad le chéile, agus thug e air an éill sgur a [1] cheangal, agus air a' phloc sgur a bhualadh. Chaidh e dhachaigh a dh'ionnsaigh a mhàthar leis a' bhrà a mheileadh mar am miann min, agus an loth a chrathadh dhoibh òr agus airgead mar a dh'fheumadh iad.

[1] = de.

'Shake, filly, shake !', she would shower down a peck of gold on one side and a peck of silver on the other.

He took the filly away with him and came to the half-way house. There they asked him what he was going to do with the filly, and Donald told them. But when he had gone to sleep, they said to the filly, 'Shake, filly, shake !' ; and she showered down a peck of gold on one side and a peck of silver on the other. But poor Donald knew nothing about that, and they kept the filly as well as the quern, and gave him another filly in its place. He brought the filly to his mother, but when he told the filly to shake, she would not shower down anything. For the third time his mother said to him, 'You must go again and ask payment for the hay-ricks from the wind.'

Off he went, reached the half-way house, and next night he came to the Wind's house. When he laid his hand on the hole in the door, the Wind shouted, 'Who's that stopping my breath ?' 'It is I, Good-for-Nothing Donald, Son of the Widow, seeking payment for my ricks from the wind.' 'Come in and stay here tonight : tomorrow I will pay you for the hay-ricks.' That night he stayed there, and next day the wind gave him a bludgeon and a thong and told him, 'The thong will bind and the bludgeon will strike until you yourself tell them to stop. They have stolen the quern and the filly I gave you, but you shall get them back again.'

Donald went off with the thong and the bludgeon to the half-way house, and divulged what the wind had told him to say to the thong and the bludgeon. When he had gone to sleep, the people of the house, expecting to get something good, shouted, 'Bind, thong ! strike, bludgeon !' But what happened was that the thong began to bind and the bludgeon to strike until everyone in the house was yelling, 'Murder !' and begging Donald to make them stop and they would give him back the quern and the filly. He got them both, and he made the thong stop binding and the bludgeon stop striking. Then he went home to his mother with the quern that would grind meal as they wanted, and the filly that would shower down gold and silver for them as they had need.

NOTES

From MS. vol. x., No. 85.

List of Variants :—MS. vol. ix., No. 227 ; MS. vol. x., Nos. 65, 115 ;
MS. vol. xi., Nos. 177, 183, 309 ; English List, Nos. 63, 307, 359.

Hector MacLean, who transcribed No. 85, added the following :—'The
title of the foregoing tale in Islay is "Domhnull nach robh glic" [*i.e.* Donald
who was not wise].   In Lorne, where I heard it in my youth more than
sixty years since, it has the title I have given it.   Lizzie Campbell, from whom
I got the Peata Bàn [*i.e.* the White Pet, *W. H. Tales*, i., No. 11, Notes] gave
me also what follows of "Domhnull nach robh glic".   On a future occasion,
I will, if you wish it, give you some further account of Domhnull Dona, as
it is told in Lorne.'   Hector does not say who it was from whom he got No. 85.
Very possibly it is a tale which he himself knew and had known from childhood.

DÒMHNALL NACH ROBH GLIC

No. 52.   *[MS. Vol. x., No. 86]*

Bu bhantrach bhochd màthair Dhòmhnaill, agus cha robh duine cloinne aice ach esan. Chuir i latha do'n choillidh e a dh'iarraidh cual chonnaidh. An uair a thill e, thuirt e ri a mhàthair, 'A mhàthair ! fhuair mi snàthad mhór an diugh.' 'Ciod e rinn thu rithe ?' ars a mhàthair. 'Chuir mi 'sa' chual chonnaidh i,' ars esan. 'Och, a Dhòmhnaill,' ars ise, 'bu chòir dhuit a cur an sàs ann ad mhuilchinn.'

An ath-latha a chaidh e do'n choillidh, fhuair e caora. 'A mhàthair !' ars esan, 'fhuair mi caora an diugh.' 'Ciod a rinn thu rithe ?' ars a mhàthair. 'Shàth mi a h-adharc ann am mhuilchinn,' ars esan. 'Nach b'e sin na smuaintean,' ars ise. 'Is ann a bu chòir dhuit a casan a cheangal, agus a tilgeil thar do ghualainn.' An ath-latha a chaidh e a dh'iarraidh connaidh, thachair each air. Rug e air, agus cheangail e a chasan, agus thilg thar a ghualainn e [ach bhrist an ròpa, agus dh'fhalbh an t-each.[1]] 'A mhàthair !' ars esan, 'fhuair mi each an diugh.' 'Ciod a rinn thu ris ?' ars a mhàthair. 'Cheangail mi a cheithir chasan, agus chuir mi thar mo ghualainn e, ach bhris an ròpa agus dh'fhalbh e.' 'Och !' ars a mhàthair, 'am bi thu gu bràth glic ? Car son nach do ghlac thu air a mhuing e, agus leum air a mhuin, agus a mharcachd dhachaigh ?'

Chuir a mhàthair e latha eile a dh'iarraidh cual chonnaidh, agus chunnaig e tarbh, agus leum e air a mhuin ; ach cha do thaitinn a eallach ris an tarbh, agus ruith e air falbh, a' leum cho àrd agus nach robh e fada a' tilgeil Dhòmhnaill gu làr. Bha nighean rìgh ag amharc air, agus ghàir i gu cridheil. Bha Dòmhnall fo gheasaibh, agus bha e ri leantainn mar sin gus an tugadh e gàire air nighinn òig le a ghòraich, agus ge bè té a ghàireadh, b'fheudar dhi a phòsadh. Thug iad air a' bhana-phrionnsa bhochd a phòsadh.

'Na dhéidh sin, chaidh i féin agus a màthair-chéile a mach

---

[1] MS. very uncertain here.

DONALD WHO WAS NOT WISE

No. 52.   [MS. Vol. x., No. 86]

DONALD'S mother was a poor widow and she had no children but himself. One day she sent him to the woods to bring home a load of firewood. When he came back he said : 'Mother, I found a big needle today.' 'What did you do with it ?' asked his mother. 'I placed it in the bundle of firewood,' said he. 'Oh, Donald,' said his mother, 'you should have stuck it in your sleeve.'

The next day he went to the woods he found a sheep. 'Mother,' said he, 'I found a sheep today.' 'What did you do with her ?' asked his mother. 'I thrust her horn into my sleeve,' said he. 'What an idea !' said his mother. 'Why, what you should have done was to tie her feet and throw her over your shoulder.' The next time he went for firewood he met a horse. He caught it, tied its feet and threw it over his shoulder, [but the rope broke and the horse got away]. 'Mother,' said he, 'I found a horse today.' 'What did you do with it ?' asked his mother. 'I tied its four legs and threw it over my shoulder, but the rope broke and it got away.' 'Oh ! will you never become wise ?' said his mother. 'Why did you not seize it by its mane, jump on its back and ride it home ?'

On another occasion his mother sent him for firewood and he saw a bull, and leaped on his back ; but the bull was not pleased with his burden, and he ran off and jumped so high that he was not long throwing Donald to the ground. A King's daughter was looking on, and she laughed heartily. Now Donald had been bewitched and was to remain in that condition until he should make a young girl laugh at his folly ; and whoever laughed would have to marry him. So they made the poor princess marry him.

One day, some time afterwards, she and her mother-in-law

latha a' spaisdearachd, agus dh'fhàg iad Dòmhnall a' còcaireachd trì geòidh a bha gu an ròstadh aig an teinidh, aon do Dhòmhnall, aon do a bhean, agus aon do a mhàthair. Thànaig bana-choimhearsnach a staigh, agus an uair a chunnaig i na geòidh 'gan ròstadh, dh'iarr i pìos de dh'fhear dhiubh. Thug e dhi pìos de ghèadh a mhàthar. Smuainich e an sin nach bitheadh an coire ro mhór ged a ghabhadh e féin feuchainn deth, ach an uair a dh'fheuch e a bhlas, cha b'urrainn da stad gus an d'ith e air fad e. Dh'ith e an sin gèadh a mhnà agus a ghèadh féin.[1] Dh'iarr a bhana-choimhearsnach an sin feuchainn de bhrot a bha air an teinidh. Thuirt i gum biodh e math, nam biodh peabar ann. Bha cù beag aig a mhàthair air an robh Peabar mar ainm, agus chuir e Peabar anns a' phoit bhrot. Thòisich e an sin air smuaineachadh ciod an leisgeal a ghabhadh e ri a mhàthair air son nan gèadh, agus chuimhnich e gun robh gèadh air ghur, agus chuir e le a iteach mar a bha e ris an teinidh e, agus chaidh e féin a ghur nan uighean. Thànaig a bhean agus a mhàthair a dh'ionnsaigh an doruis ag iarraidh a fhosgladh. Ach ghlaodh e gun robh e a' gur nan uighean, agus [nach] b'urrainn da éirigh. Ach ghlaodh iad gum feumadh e a fhosgladh. Dh'éirich e, agus bhris e na h-uighean a' feuchainn ri tighinn a mach as a' chliabh anns an robh an gèadh air ghur. Shalaich e a aodach, agus bha dragh aig a bhean agus aig a mhàthair 'ga ghlanadh.

[1] *agus* [*gèadh*] *a mhàthar*, 'and his mother's [goose]' in MS., which does not make sense.

NOTES

Vol. x., No. 86. In his Gaelic List, Islay refers to this with the words 'Very old. Grimm.' *Gèadh*, a goose, is referred to in this tale with a masculine pronoun.

were out walking, and they left Donald to cook three geese which were to be roasted at the fire : one for Donald, one for his wife and one for his mother. A neighbour came in, and when she noticed the geese being roasted she asked for a bit of one of them. Donald gave her a piece of his mother's goose. Then it occurred to him it would be no great harm if he himself sampled it ; but having tasted the goose, he was unable to stop until he had eaten the whole of it. Then he ate his wife's goose and his own. The neighbour woman thereupon asked for a taste of the broth on the fire, and said it would be good if only it had pepper added. Now, Donald's mother had a little dog called Pepper, and Donald put Pepper into the pot of broth. Then he began to wonder what excuse he should offer his mother about the geese, when he remembered that there was a goose sitting on eggs. He set it up in front of the fire with its feathers on, just as it was, and went and sat on the eggs himself. His wife and his mother came to the door, asking to have it opened. But he shouted that he was brooding on the eggs and could not get up. But they shouted back that he would have to open the door. Then he did get up, but he broke the eggs, trying to come out of the creel where the goose had been brooding. He soiled his clothes, and his wife and his mother had a good deal of trouble cleaning him.

MAC AN RÌGH AGUS FEAR A'
BHRATAIN UAINE

No. 53.

BHA o chionn tìm fhada ann an tìr fad as, Rìgh agus Banrìghinn, agus bha mac aca. Dh'eug a' Bhanrìghinn, agus fhuair an Rìgh muime-chìche air son a mhic, agus dh'altraim i e. An ceann beagan bhliadhnachan, smaointich an Rìgh air pòsadh a rithist, agus chuir e mac na ceud Bhanrìghinn còmhla ri càirdean eile a bh'aige, gus a bhith air a thogail leò, agus a mhuime-chìche a ghabhail cùraim dheth.

Phòs an Rìgh bean eile, agus bha mac aice, agus bha i ro mhórdhalach uime, agus an uair a bha e suas agus a thànaig e gu ionad ionnsachadh fhaotainn, fhuair iad fear gu ionnsachadh da mar bu chòir da am bogha-saighead oibreachadh agus claidheamharachd, agus mar a chuireadh e saighdearan ann an òrdugh, agus bha a' Bhanrìghinn ro thoileach mar a bha a mac a' tighinn air aghaidh. Ach bha an Rìgh anns a' bheinn-sheilg latha, agus bha a' Bhanrìghinn ag amharc air cho math is a bha a mac air a' bhogha-saighead, agus thànaig Cailleach nan Cearc an rathad, agus thuirt i ris a' Bhanrìghinn, 'Ge mór an obair a tha ort le d' mhac, chan e a gheibh an rìoghachd 'na dhéidh sin uile ; tha mac eile aig an Rìgh ged nach 'eil fhios agad air ; agus is e esan a gheibh an rìoghachd.' Agus dh'fharraid a' Bhanrìghinn, 'An robh an Rìgh pòsda mun d'fhuair e mise ?' agus fhreagair Cailleach nan Cearc, 'Bha, agus mac aige.' Dh'fharraid a' Bhanrìghinn, 'C'àite am bheil e ?' agus deir Cailleach nan Cearc, 'Ach air son làn na gusgaige [1] duibhe de shùgh na bracha agus bonnach eòrna, chan innis mi sin duit.' Theann a' Bhanrìghinn mun cuairt, agus dh'fhalbh i a staigh do'n taigh, agus chaidh i a laighe.

An uair a thànaig an Rìgh dachaigh as a' bheinn-sheilg, bha a' Bhanrìghinn gu tinn teth, 'na laighe air an leabaidh, agus

---

[1] *gusgaice* (?) in MS. [Cf. *Orain le Iain Lom MacDhomhnaill*, p. 46 : '*G òl mo ghuscaig 's mi 'm shìneadh air fàradh.*—A. M.]

THE KING'S SON AND THE MAN
OF THE GREEN CLOAK

No. 53.   [*MS. Vol. x., No. 97*]

A LONG time ago, there lived in a far country a King and Queen
who had a son. The Queen died, and the King got a foster-
mother for his son and she nursed him. After a few years the
King thought that he would marry again, and he sent the son
of the first Queen to some friends of his own to be brought up
with them, and he sent the foster-mother to look after him.

The King married another wife and she had a son. She
was very proud of him, and when he was getting big and had
come to the age for being instructed they found a man to teach
him how to use a bow and a sword, and how to drill soldiers,
and the Queen was very pleased with the progress her son was
making. But one day, when the King was on the hunting-hill
and the Queen was watching her son and observing how expert
with the bow he was, the Hen-Wife came that way and said to
the Queen : 'Despite the fuss you're making with your son, it
isn't he who will have the kingdom after all ; the King has
another son, although you do not know it : it's he who will have
the kingdom.' And the Queen asked : 'Was the King married
before he married me ?' 'Yes, he was,' said the Hen-Wife,
'and he had a son.' 'Where is he ?' asked the Queen. 'Except
in return for a black noggin full of whisky and a barley bannock,
I will not tell you that,' said the Hen-Wife. The Queen turned
on her heel, walked into the house and went to bed.

When the King came home from the hunting-hill, the Queen
was lying in bed, ill and feverish. The King came to her and
asked her what was the matter with her, but never a word did

thànaig an Rìgh far an robh i, agus dh'fharraid e dhith gu dé
bha oirre, ach cha dubhairt i diog.   Thuirt an Rìgh, 'Innis
domh, agus ma tha nì air bith as urrainn dòmh-sa a dhèanamh
air do shon, nì mi e.' 'Tha aon achanaich agam r'a iarraidh ort,
a Rìgh, agus is math liom a fhaotainn uait.'   'Gheibh thu sin.'
'Tha mac eile agad-sa : ach cha d'innis thu dhòmh-sa mu a
thimcheall, agus bu mhath liom fhaicinn.'   Cha robh an Rìgh
ro thoilichte, ach o'n a gheall e, cha b'urrainn da i dhiùltadh.

Chaidh fios a chur air, agus thànaig e, agus an uair a chunnaig
a' Bhanrìghinn e, thaitinn e rithe gu ro mhath : ach an uair a
fhuair ise do'n taigh e, dh' iarr i gun cuireadh e a làmh ri còir
na rìoghachd gur e a mac-se a gheibheadh a bhith 'na oighre,
agus bha a athair cuideachd 'ga iarraidh air, ach dh'iarr e
beagan làithean gu smaointeachadh air.   Fhuair e sin.   Chaidh
e far an robh athair a mhuime-chìche, o'n a bha e 'na sheanghal
eòlach, agus dh' iarr e comhairle air.   Agus thuirt an Seanghal
ris, 'Ma bheir thusa seachad do chòir, is urrainn daibh do chur
as an rìoghachd, agus mur dèan thu sin, chan 'eil fhios nach
marbh iad thu.   Agus is e mo chomhairle dhuit, thu fhéin a
dh'fhàgail na rìoghachd, agus thu a dhol a dh'iarraidh an
fhortain rathad eile, gus gum faigh thu fios bàs t'athar, air neò
do bhràthar ; agus an sin is urrainn duit an rìoghachd agairt
no a leigeil dhìot, mar a shanntaicheas tu.'   Cha tug e suas a
chòir, ach dh'fhalbh e a dh' iarraidh an fhortain.   Thug e leis
gille agus bogha-saighead agus dòrlach math airgid, agus
dh'fhalbh iad.

Thànaig sneachd trom air, là a bha 'n sin.   Thilg Mac an
Rìgh fitheach, agus an uair a chunnaig e e 'na laighe a' sileadh
fala air an t-sneachd, thug e bòid, a' bhean a bhiodh aige-san
gum biodh a falt cho dubh ri iteagan an fhithich, agus a
gruaidhean cho dearg ris an fhuil a bha a' tighinn as, agus a
craiceann cho geal ris an t-sneachd a bha air an làr.[1]

An ceann tìme, chinn airgead Mac an Rìgh gann, agus
b'éiginn da a ghille a leigeil uaidh, agus falbh leis fhéin.   Là a
bha 'n siod, chunnaig e féin fear agus brat uaine air a' tighinn

---

[1] Similar incident, *W. H. Tales*, iii., p. 215 or 201 ; Carmichael's *Deirdre*, p. 37 ;
Waifs and Strays, iii., p. 289 ; ii., p. 431.   *W. H. Tales*, i., No. 2, Var. 8, *Nighean
Dubh Gheal Dearg*, The Black White Red Lass, is probably another instance.   See
also *ibid.*, iv., p. 255 or 279.   *Cf.* also the episode in the Welsh tale of Peredur the

she say. 'Tell me,' said the King, 'and if there is anything at all that I can do you for you, I will do it.' 'I have one request to make of your Majesty and I hope you will grant it.' 'You shall have it,' said he. 'You have another son, but you didn't tell me about him, and I should like to see him.' The King was none too pleased, but since he had promised he could not refuse her.

The son was sent for and he came, and when the Queen saw him she was very pleased with him ; but when she got him to the house she requested that he should sign the charter of succession to the effect that it should be her son who would become heir. His father also urged him to do this, but the son asked for a few days to think it over, and he got that. He went to his foster-mother's father because he was a sage Counsellor and he asked his advice. The Counsellor said to him : 'If you resign your rights, they can banish you from the kingdom ; and if you do not, it is possible that they will kill you. My advice to you is to leave the country and go to seek your fortune in some other quarter, until you get news of your father's death or else of your brother's death, and then you can either claim the kingdom or relinquish it, as you choose.' So he did not give up his rights, but went off to seek his fortune. He took a lad and a bow and arrows with him and a good deal of money, and off they went.

One day it snowed heavily. The King's Son shot a raven, and when he saw it lying on the snow dripping blood, he made a vow that the wife he would have should have hair as black as the raven's feathers, cheeks as red as the raven's flowing blood, and skin as white as the snow on the ground.[1]

After a time the Prince's money became scarce, and he was forced to part with his lad and go on alone. One day he saw in the distance a man wearing a green cloak coming after him·

---

son of Evrawc : 'And Peredur stood, and compared the blackness of the raven and the whiteness of the snow and the redness of the blood to the hair (etc.) of the lady that best he loved.' Lady Guest's version.

as a dhéidh fada air ais. Ach ge b'fhad air ais, cha b'fhada gus
an robh e air adhart, agus thuirt e ris, 'An gabh thu gille?'
Thuirt Mac an Rìgh, 'Cha ghabh, cha do rinn mi ach an gille
a bh'agam a chur bhuam.' 'Nan gabhadh tu mise, bhithinn cho
math ri m' rùm.' 'Cha ghabh, chan 'eil cumail gille agam.'
'Chan iarr mise mar dhuais ach darna leth na sholaireas mi
fhéin.' 'Nach iarr?' 'Chan iarr,' arsa Fear a' Bhratain Uaine.
'Ma thà, tha thu coibhneil,' agus dh'fhalbh iad còmhla.

An uair a bha an oidhche a' tighinn, thuirt Mac an Rìgh
ri Fear a' Bhratain Uaine, 'An saoil thusa c'àite am bi sinn an
nochd?' Thuirt Fear a' Bhratain Uaine, 'Na biodh eagal ort.'
Chunnaig iad solus crìon fad air astar, ach ge b'fhada uath e,
cha b'fhada dhaibh-san 'ga ruigheachd. An uair a rànaig Fear
a' Bhratain Uaine an dorus, chòmhdaich e e fhéin gu buileach
leis a' bhratan uaine, agus an uair a chòmhdaicheadh e gu
buileach, chan fhaiceadh iad-san e, agus chaidh e a staigh.
Bha an sin na poiteachan air sìor-ghoil, agus na coireachan air
sàr-ghoil, agus bonnaich 'gan tionndadh air greidil, agus biorain
a' tionndadh leò fhéin. Thànaig e a mach, agus thuirt e ri
Mac an Rìgh, 'Gheibh sinn aoigheachd an seo,' agus bhuail iad
aig an dorus, agus thànaig nighean bhrèagha a mach, agus bha
a craiceann cho geal ris an t-sneachd, ach bha a falt bàn, agus
a gruaidhean bàn, ach bha i ro bhrèagh; agus dh' iarr i a
staigh iad. Chaidh iad a staigh, agus fhuair iad oidhche an sin
gu subhach, agus an ath-là, an uair a bha Mac an Rìgh agus
Fear a' Bhratain Uaine leò fhéin, thuirt Fear a' Bhratain Uaine,
'Nach fialaidh muinntir an taighe seo!' Agus thuirt Mac an
Rìgh, 'Seadh, tha mi air son an nighean bhrèagha ud iarraidh
air son bean.' 'Chan i siod an té mun do bhòidich thu.'

Air dhaibh tràth eile fhaighinn, ghabh iad an cead de
mhuinntir an taighe, agus dh'fhalbh iad air an slighe. Agus
an uair a bha an oidhche a' tighinn, thuirt Mac an Rìgh ri
Fear a' Bhratain Uaine, 'C'àite am bi sinn an nochd?' 'Na
biodh eagal ort; gheibh na h-eòin fhéin àite tàimh, agus gheibh
sinne àite cuideachd.' Air dhaibh gabhail air an aghaidh,
chunnaig iad solus, etc.[1], agus is e a bha an sin taigh-mór a
bha aig duine a bha an àrd-inbhe. Chòmhdaich Fear a' Bhratain

---

[1] *etc.*; so in MS.

But though he was a long way behind, the man soon approached and said : 'Will you have a servant ?' 'No,' said the King's Son, 'I will not : I have only just sent away the lad I had.' 'If you were to employ me, I'd be as good as my keep.' 'No, I haven't the means to employ a servant.' 'I shan't ask any wages beyond half of what I myself procure.' 'Will you not ?' 'No, I will not,' said the Man of the Green Cloak. 'Why, you *are* kind !' And off they went together.

When night was coming on, the King's Son said to the Man of the Green Cloak : 'Where do you suppose we shall be tonight ?' 'Have no fear,' said the Man of the Green Cloak. A long way off, they saw a feeble light, but distant though it was, they were not long in reaching it. When he reached the door, the Man of the Green Cloak clothed himself entirely with the green cloak, and when he was completely covered the inmates could not see him, and he entered there. There there were pots ever boiling, cauldrons boiling hard, bannocks being turned on the girdle and spits turning by themselves. Out he came again and said to the King's Son : 'We shall receive hospitality here,' and so they knocked at the door. A beautiful girl came out ; her skin was as white as snow, but her hair was fair and her cheeks were pale. Still, she was very beautiful ; and she asked them in. They went in, and spent a cheerful night there, and the next day when the King's Son and the Man of the Green Cloak were alone, the Man of the Green Cloak said : 'Are not the people of this house hospitable ?' 'Yes,' said the King's Son, 'and I want to ask that beautiful girl to be my wife.' 'She is not the one you made your vow about.'

After having had another meal, they took their leave of the people of the house, and went off on their journey. When the night was coming, the King's Son said to the Man of the Green Cloak : 'Where shall we be tonight ?' 'Have no fear : even the birds find a resting place, and we shall find a place too.' When they had pressed on, they saw a light, etc., and there was a mansion belonging to a man of high rank. The Man of the Green Cloak covered himself with the cloak and went inside,

Uaine e fhéin leis a' bhratan uaine, agus chaidh e a staigh, agus
an uair a thuig e gu dé an seòrsa sluaigh iad, thànaig e a mach
agus thuirt e ri Mac an Rìgh, 'Gheibh sinn a bhith an seo an
nochd.' Bhuail iad aig an dorus, agus chaidh a fhosgladh, agus
thànaig nighean bhrèagh a mach a chur fàilte orra, agus 'gan
iarraidh a staigh, agus bha a craiceann cho geal ris an t-sneachda,
agus a gruaidhean cho dearg ris an fhuil, agus a falt bàn. Chaidh
iad a staigh leatha, agus bha an sin na poiteachan air sìor-ghoil,
is na coireachan air sàr-ghoil, bonnaich 'gan tionndadh air
greidil, agus biorain a' cur char diùbh leò fhéin, agus fhuair
iad an deagh ghabhail aca an sin ; is an uair a chaidh iad a
laighe, thuirt Fear a' Bhratain Uaine ri Mac an Rìgh gum b'e
iad seo sliochd rìgh an tìr fad as, agus thuirt Mac an Rìgh gun
robh a mhiann air an nighean bhrèagha ud a bhith aige air son
mnaoi :—'Chan e sin an té mun tug thu na bòidean fhathast,'
thubhairt Fear a' Bhratain Uaine.

An ath-là, fhuair iad deagh bhiatachd, agus dh'fhalbh iad
air an slighe, agus an uair a bha an oidhche a' tighinn, deir
Mac an Rìgh, 'C'àite am bi sinn an nochd ?' agus thuirt Fear a'
Bhratain Uaine, 'O ! a chailleach ! is ann ort a tha an t-eagal
roimh an àite tha air thoiseach oirnn,' [1] agus ghabh iad air an
aghaidh, agus an ceanna ghreis, chunnaig iad solus crìon ann
an coillidh, is e fada uatha, ach ge b'fhada uatha, cha b'fhada
dhaibh-san 'ga ruigheachd. An uair a rànaig iad e, bhuail iad
aig an dorus, agus is e famhair mór a dh'fhosgail an dorus agus
thuirt e riutha, 'An tànaig sibh, a dhaoine ?' agus thuirt iad-san,
'Thànaig.' Agus thuirt esan, 'Cha robh 'san fhàisneachd ach
sibh. Thigibh, agus gun leig mi fhaicinn duibh c'àite am bheil
sibh gu dol.' Chaidh iad leis agus sheòl e iad a dh'ionnsaigh
àite far an robh solus mór greis uapa.[2] Thug e oidhche mhaith
leò, agus chuir [3] iad-san air an aghaidh, agus an uair a bha iad-
san teann air an àite, choinnich Cailleach nan Cearc iad, agus
thuirt i, 'An tànaig sibh, a shuirghichean ? Cha robh 'san
fhàisneachd ach sibh ; tha dìreach dà stob anns a' chladh r'an
lìonadh, agus is iad na cinn agaibh-se a lìonas iad.' 'Cha mhath
do sgeul,' arsa Fear a' Bhratain Uaine. 'Tha siod 'san

---

[1] Green Cloak knew of the dangers before them.
[2] The giant is the heroine's lover. He shows the heroes the way to her house.
[3] [*chuir* = *char* (= *chaidh*) ?—A. M.]

and when he understood what sort of people lived there, he came out and said to the King's Son : 'We shall be allowed to stay here tonight.' They knocked at the door ; it was opened and a beautiful girl came out to welcome them and ask them in, and her skin was as white as snow, her cheeks as red as blood, and her hair was fair. They went inside with her, and there there were pots ever boiling, cauldrons boiling hard, bannocks being turned on a girdle, and spits turning by themselves. They were very hospitably treated there. When they went to bed, the Man of the Green Cloak said to the King's Son that these people were the descendants of the King of the Far-Away-Country, and the Prince said that it was his desire to have that beautiful girl for a wife. 'That is still not the one you made your vow about,' said the Man of the Green Cloak.

Next day they were well entertained, and away they went on their journey, and when night was coming on, the King's Son said : 'Where shall we be tonight ?' 'Oh, you old woman ! You are terribly afraid of the place that is ahead of us,' [1] said the Man of the Green Cloak, and they kept on. After a while, they saw a faint light in a wood a long way from them, but far away though it was, they were not long in reaching it. When they arrived, they knocked at the door, and it was a great giant who opened the door, and he said to them, 'Have you come, men ?' 'We have,' said they. 'You are the very ones mentioned in the prophecy. Come and I will show you where you are to go.' They accompanied him and he guided them to where a great light was to be seen some distance away from them. [2] Then he bade them good night. They held onwards ; and when they were close to the place the Hen-Wife met them, and she said : 'Have you come, you suitors ? You were the very ones mentioned in the prophecy : there are just two stakes in the graveyard to be crowned (*lit.* filled) and it is your heads that shall crown them.' 'Your news is not good,' said the Man of the Green Cloak. 'That is in the prophecy,' she answered ; 'there were twenty stakes in fhàisneachd,' arsa ise ; 'bha fichead stob anns a' chladh r'an lìonadh,[1] agus tha ochd deug ann, agus an uair a bhitheas an dà cheann agaibh-se ann, bidh an sin an fhichead ann,' agus thionndaidh i a cùl riu, is dh'fhàg i iad. Agus chaidh iad-san air an aghaidh, agus rànaig iad an taigh-mór, agus bhuail iad air an dorus, agus chaidh a fhosgladh, agus thànaig nighean bhrèagh a mach. Agus bha a falt cho dubh ris an fhitheach, agus a gruaidhean cho dearg ris an fhuil, agus a' chuid eile de a craiceann cho geal ris an t-sneachd, agus i ro bhrèagha ; agus chuir i fàilt orra gu suilbhearra, agus dh'iarr i a staigh iad. Agus bha an sin poitean a' sìor-ghoil, agus coireachan a' sàr-ghoil, is bonnaich 'gan tionndadh air greidil, is biorain a' cur dhiubh fhéin nan car, agus fhuair iad an deagh bhiatachd an sin. Chaidh an cur a laighe 'san aon seòmar, ach leabaidh an t-aon aca, agus thuirt Mac an Rìgh ri Fear a' Bhratain Uaine, 'Is e an nighean ud an té mun do bhòidich mi i bhith agam air son bean.' Agus thuirt Fear a' Bhratain Uaine, 'Ma bhitheas tu tapaidh, is i.'

An ath-latha, an uair a dh'éirich iad 'sa' mhaduinn chaidh iad a mach a ghabhail sràid, agus chaidh nighean an duine mhóir [2] leò a chumail conaltraidh riutha, agus dh' fhàg Fear a' Bhratain Uaine Mac an Rìgh agus an cailin brèagh gu bhith a' cainnt eadar iad fhéin. Dh'iarr Mac an Rìgh i air son bean, agus thill iad a staigh do'n taigh-mhór a dhèanamh a' chùmh-nanta, agus dh'innis i da, a h-uile fear a dh'iarradh ise gum feumadh iad a ceud trì achanaighean a dh'iarradh i fhaotainn di, air neò gun rachadh na cinn a chur dhiùbh, agus an cur air na stuib a bha gun lìonadh 'sa' chladh ; gun robh ochd deug ann a cheana, is nam bitheadh na cinn aca-san ann, gum bitheadh fichead ann. Air an oidhche, an uair a bha iad aig am biadh, leig i fhaicinn daibh an spàin a bh' aice aig a suipeir. Thuirt i riu, 'Mur bi an spàin seo a th' agam-sa [agaibh dhòmh-sa] aig mo thràth-maduinn a màireach, is e na cinn agaibh a thèid a chur air na stuib anns a' chladh.' Agus deir Fear a' Bhratain Uaine, 'An toir thu dhuinn i r'a gleidheadh ?' 'Cha toir, no do dhuine bhuineadh do ur daoine.' 'Agus an innis thu dhuinn c'àite an cuir thu i ?' 'Chan innis, no do dhuine bhuineas do ur daoine.' Agus thuirt Fear a' Bhratain Uaine,

---

[1] The head-crowned spikes, see *Waifs and Strays*, ii., p. 453.

the graveyard to be crowned.[1] Eighteen are crowned already, and when your two heads are there, then there will be a complete score' ; and she turned her back on them and left them. They kept on, and came to a mansion, and knocked at the door. It was opened, and a beautiful girl came out, and her hair was as black as the raven, her cheeks as red as blood, and the rest of her skin as white as snow, and very beautiful was she ; and she welcomed them very cheerfully and asked them in. And there there were pots ever boiling, and cauldrons boiling hard, bannocks being turned on a girdle, and spits turning by themselves, and they were well fed there. They were put to bed in one room, but they had separate beds ; and the King's Son said to the Man with the Green Cloak, 'That girl is the one I vowed to have for a wife.' And the Man with the Green Cloak answered, 'Yes, if you are plucky.'

The next day, when they rose in the morning, they went out for a walk, and the great man's[2] daughter went with them to chat with them ; and the Man of the Green Cloak left the King's Son with the lovely girl to talk together alone. The King's Son asked her to be his wife, and they returned to the mansion to draw up the contract ; and she told him that every one who sought her hand must procure for her the first three things that she required of them, otherwise, their heads were to be cut off and placed on the stakes that had not been crowned and that stood in the graveyard ; that eighteen of the stakes had been crowned already, and that if their heads were there also, there would be twenty. In the evening, when they were at their meal, she showed them the spoon which she had at supper. Said she, 'Unless you get this spoon of mine for me at my breakfast tomorrow, it is your heads that will be set upon the stakes in the graveyard.' The Man of the Green Cloak said, 'Will you give it to us to keep?' 'No, nor to any man related to your kin.' 'Will you tell us where you are going to put it?' 'No, nor to any man related to your kin.' And the Man of the Green Cloak said, 'It will be very difficult for us to

[2] The heroine's father.

'Is duilich dhuinn a faotainn, mur bi fios againn c'àite am bi i, no c'àite an téid sinn 'ga h-iarraidh.' Thuirt ise, 'Faiceadh sibh-se da sin.' An uair a chaidh an cur a laighe, bha leabaidh aig gach aon aca dhaibh fhéin.

Chuir Fear a' Bhratain Uaine toll tora troimh a' chlàraidh, is gum faiceadh e gu dé bhiodh Mór a' dèanamh (b'e Mór a h-ainm), is chunnaig e i 'ga sgeadachadh fhéin gu brèagha, agus an spàin làimh rithe ; agus chuir esan a bhratan uaine air, agus chaidh e, is sheas e aig cùl an doruis, is an uair a bha ise deas, chaidh i a mach, agus Fear a' Bhratain Uaine aig a cùlaibh. Fhuair i an fhalaire, agus leum i air a druim ; leum esan air a cùlaibh, is an uair a b'àirde esan, a b'ìsle ise, is an uair a b'ìsle esan, a b'àirde ise,[1] agus an fhalaire 'na leum-ruith gus an do rànaig iad taigh an fhamhair. Thànaig ise a nuas, agus chaidh i a staigh, is thànaig esan a nuas is chaidh e a staigh, is sheas e aig cùl an doruis. Thuirt am famhair rithe, 'An do rànaig na daoine ud thu ?' Thuirt ise, 'Rànaig.' Thuirt esan, 'Gu dé an fhàilte chuir iad ort ? An do chuir iad an gnothach an céill ?' 'Chuir,' ars ise ; 'is e an ceud achanaich a chuir mi mu'n coinnimh, iad a dh'fhaotainn na spàine seo dòmh-sa 'sa' mhaduinn a màireach.' Thug i do'n fhamhair i, agus [thuirt i], 'Gléidh dhòmh-sa i.' Thuirt am famhair, 'Cuiridh sinn anns a' chiste i, far am b' àbhaist di bhith.' Thànaig Fear a' Bhratain Uaine, agus sheas e ri taobh na ciste, agus thànaig iad-san cuideachd, agus dh'fhosgail iad brod na ciste ; is [an uair] a bha iad a' tilgeil na spàine anns a' chist, thilg Fear a' Bhratain Uaine plathadh de'n bhratan uaine mu'n sùilean, sgioblaich e leis an spàin, agus dh' fhàg e stràbh 'na [h-]àite, agus chaidh e a rithist agus sheas e aig cùl an doruis gun robh ise deas gu falbh. Agus an uair a phòg is a chniadaich iad a chéile, dh'fhalbh ise gu dol dachaigh, agus chaidh Fear a' Bhratain Uaine a mach aig a cùlaibh ; agus an uair a leum ise air an fhalaire, leum esan air a cùlaibh, is an uair a b'àirde ise a b'ìsle esan, agus an uair a b'ìsle ise a b'àirde esan, gus an do rànaig iad an taigh-mór, agus chuir iad stad air an fhalaire, agus ghrad-leum Fear a'

---

[1] For other examples of these curious expressions, see *W. H. Tales*, i., Nos. 13, and 17, Var. 4 ; *Waifs and Strays*, iv., p. 233 ; *Trans. Gael. Soc. Inverness*, xvii., pp. 61, 67 ; *Norse Influence*, p. 289 ; *Larminie*, p. 52.

find it, if we don't know where it is, or where to go to look for it.'
'It is for you to see to that,' said she. When they were put to
bed, there was a bed for each of them.

The Man of the Green Cloak bored a hole through the partition
with an auger, so that he might see what Mór was doing (Mór
was her name), and he saw that she was dressing herself most
beautifully, and that the spoon was lying beside her ; so he put
on his green cloak, and went and stood behind the door, and
when she was ready she went out, and the Man of the Green Cloak
was just behind her. She got a palfrey and vaulted on to its back,
and he sprang up behind her ; and when he was highest she
was lowest, and when he was lowest she was highest,[1] and all
the while the palfrey galloped furiously on until they reached
the giant's house. She dismounted and went in, and he also
dismounted and went in, and stood behind the door. The giant
asked her, 'Have those men visited you ?' 'They have,' said she.
'How did they greet you ?' he asked. 'Did they declare their
errand ?' 'Yes, they did,' she replied ; 'and the first task I
asked them to perform was to get this spoon for me tomorrow
morning.' She gave the spoon to the giant. 'Keep it for me,'
[she said]. 'We will put it in the chest, where it used to be,'
said the giant. The Man of the Green Cloak approached the
chest, and stood beside it, and then they came too and opened
the lid. [And when] they were throwing the spoon into the
chest, the Man of the Green Cloak flashed his green cloak before
their eyes, snatched up the spoon, and left a straw in its place.
Then he stood behind the door again until she was ready to go,
and when she and the giant had kissed and caressed each other,
she made to go, and the Man of the Green Cloak went out after
her, and when she jumped on the palfrey's back, he leaped up
behind her ; and when she was highest he was lowest, and when
she was lowest he was highest, until they arrived at the mansion.
There they stopped the palfrey, and quickly the Man of the Green
Cloak jumped off. While she was giving the palfrey to the groom,

Bhratain Uaine gu làr. An tìm a bha ise a' toirt an fhalaire [*sic*] do'n fhear a bha freasdal di, chaidh Fear a' Bhratain Uaine a staigh do'n cheàrn far an robh a leabaidh fhéin agus leabaidh Mhic an Rìgh.

Bha Mac an Rìgh a' rubadh a bhoisean, agus a' suathadh a dhòrn, agus thuirt Fear a' Bhratain Uaine ris, 'Gu dé a tha ort, a Mhic an Rìgh ?' agus thuirt Mac an Rìgh, 'O ! nach 'eil gun téid ar marbhadh a màireach chionn [1] nach urrainn duinn an spàin fhaotainn ?' Thuirt Fear a' Bhratain Uaine, 'Tha an spàin agam-sa.' 'A bheil ?' 'Tha,' thuirt Fear a' Bhratain Uaine, agus thug e an spàin do Mhac an Rìgh. Thuirt e ri Mac an Rìgh e a leigeadh leatha móran a ràdh mun tugadh e di an spàin.

An ath-latha, dh'éirich ise air thoiseach orra-san, agus thuirt i riu iad a dh'éirigh. Thuirt iad-san nach robh móran cabhaig ann : agus thuirt ise iad a dh'éirigh agus gum faigheadh i a biadh a ghabhail, air neò gun rachadh na cinn a thoirt diùbh anns an leabaidh. Dh'éirich iad, agus chaidh iad do'n t-seòmar far an robh an clàr-bìdh, agus dh'iarr ise an spàin fhaotainn di. Thuirt Mac an Rìgh, 'An tug thu dhuinn i ?' Thuirt ise, 'Cha tug, no do dhuine bhuineas do 'r daoine.' 'Agus an d'innis thu dhuinn c'àite an do chuir thu seachad i, ma thà ?' arsa Mac an Rìgh. 'Cha d'innis, no do dhuine a bhuineas do 'r daoine,' arsa ise. Agus thuirt Mac an Rìgh, 'Nach duilich dhuinn a faotainn, ma tà !' Agus thuirt ise, 'A nuas an claidheamh nach d'fhàg fuidheall riamh a dh'aona bheum,' [2] agus thilg Mac an Rìgh an spàin air a' chlàr. Thog ise an spàin, agus sheall i oirre, agus chunnaig i gum b' i a spàin fhéin a bh'ann, agus a h-ainm oirre, is air fad, is ghabh i ioghnadh dheth.

Agus an ath-oidhche an uair a bha i aig a tràth-feasgair, leig i fhaicinn daibh an sgian a bha aice aig a tràth-feasgair, agus thuirt i riu, 'Faicibh an sgian seo a tha agam-sa aig mo thràth-feasgair an nochd ; mur faigh sibh-se dhòmh-sa i gu bhith agam aig mo thràth-maduinn a màireach, théid na cinn a chur dhìbh, agus an cur air na stuib a tha 'sa' chladh.' Thuirt Fear a' Bhratain Uaine, 'Thoir thusa dhuinn i r'a gleidheadh air do

---

[1] MS. *chun.*

[2] *Lit.* the sword which with a single stroke never left remains. In other words, a sword of Sharpness. See Nicolson's *Gaelic Proverbs,* p. 95.

the Man of the Green Cloak went in to the place where he and the King's Son had their beds.

The King's Son was rubbing his palms together and wringing his hands. 'What is worrying you, son of the King?' said the Man of the Green Cloak to him, and the King's Son said, 'Oh! what but that we shall be killed tomorrow, because we cannot find the spoon?' 'I have the spoon,' said the Man of the Green Cloak. 'Have you?' 'Yes,' said the Man of the Green Cloak, and he gave the spoon to the King's Son, and told him to let the girl talk freely before giving her the spoon.

The next day she was up before they were. She told them to rise. They replied that there was no great hurry. But she told them to get up so that she might have her food, or else that they should be beheaded in bed. They rose and went to the room where the dining table was, and she asked to have the spoon produced for her. 'Did you give it to us?' asked the King's Son. 'No, nor to any man related to your kin,' she replied. 'And did you tell us where you put it away then?' 'No,' said she, 'neither did I tell anyone related to your kin.' 'How very difficult it must be for us to find it then!' said the King's Son. Then she said, 'Bring down the sword whose single stroke never left a remnant!' [2] And the King's Son threw the spoon on the table. She picked up the spoon, looked at it, and saw it was her own spoon, with her name on it and all, and she was amazed.

Next evening when she was at supper, she showed them the knife she used for supper, and said to them, 'Look at this knife which I have at my supper tonight; unless you get it for me so that I may have it at breakfast tomorrow morning, your heads shall be cut off and set on the stakes in the graveyard.' 'Then give it to us to keep for you,' said the Man of the Green Cloak.

shon.' 'Cha toir, no do dhuine bhuineas do 'r daoine.' Chaidh
an cur a laighe.

Bha Fear a' Bhratain Uaine a' sealltainn troimh an toll a
chuir e 'sa' chlàraidh, agus chunnaig e i 'ga sgeadachadh fhéin
gu maiseach agus an sgian aice air ciste làimh rithe.   Chuir
esan am bratan uaine air, agus chaidh chun cùl an doruis, agus
sheas an sin gus gun deach i a mach ; lean e i, gus an do rànaig
i far an robh a fear-freasdail leis an fhalaire, agus an uair a leum
ise an àirde, leum esan air a cùlaibh, agus an uair a b'àirde
esan a b'ìsle ise, is an uair a b'ìsle esan a b'àirde ise, agus an
fhalaire 'na leum-ruith, gus an do rànaig iad taigh an fhamhair.

An uair a chuir i stad air an fhalaire, leum Fear a' Bhratain
Uaine gu làr agus chaidh e a steach do thaigh an fhamhair,
agus sheas e aig cùl an doruis, agus chaidh ise a staigh do'n
cheàrn far an robh am famhair, agus dh'fharraid am famhair
dith gu dé mar a thànaig i air a h-aghaidh leis na daoine ud ?
Thuirt ise, 'Thànaig, gun tug thusa seachad daibh an spàin.'
'Cha tug ; tha i fhathast anns a' chiste far an d'fhàg sinn i.'
Chaidh iad, agus sheall iad, agus cha robh an sin ach stràbh
'na h-àite, agus ghabh iad ioghnadh.   Thuirt am famhair,
'Cuiridh sinn na seachd glasan air an sgian an nochd.'   Ach
an uair a bha iad a' cur na sgeine 'sa' chiste, thànaig Fear a'
Bhratain Uaine agus thilg e platha[dh] de'n bhratan uaine
mu'n sùilean, agus bheir [sic] e air an sgian eadar an làmhan
agus a' chiste,[1] [agus dh'fhàg e stràbh 'na [h-]àite] agus thug
e leis i fo'n bhratan uaine, agus chaidh e, agus sheas e aig cùl
an doruis far an robh e roimhe.   An uair a phòg agus a chniadaich
iad a chéile, thug Mór beannachd leis an fhamhair, agus dh'fhalbh
i gu dol dachaigh.   Chaidh Fear a' Bhratain Uaine a mach aig
a cùl, agus an uair a leum ise air a falaire, leum esan an àird
aig a cùlaibh, agus chuir i an fhalaire 'na leum-ruith ; agus an
uair a b'àirde ise b'ìsle Fear a' Bhratain Uaine, agus an uair a
b'ìsle ise b'àirde esan, gus an do rànaig iad an taigh-mór.

An uair a chuir i stad air an fhalaire, leum Fear a' Bhratain
Uaine gu làr, agus an tìm a bha ise a' toirt an fhalaire [sic] do
a fear-freasdail, chaidh esan a staigh far an robh a leabaidh

---

[1] As the knife fell through the air, he caught it midway between its starting point
and its destination.

'I will not, nor will I give it to anyone who belongs to your kin.'
They were put to bed.

The Man of the Green Cloak looked through the hole he
had made in the partition, and saw her arraying herself most
elegantly. On a chest by her side she had the knife. He put
on his green cloak, and went behind the door, and stood there
until she had gone out ; he followed her till she came to where
her groom was waiting with the palfrey, and when she sprang up
on its back, he sprang up behind her ; and when he was highest
she was lowest, and when he was lowest she was highest, while
the palfrey galloped on all the way until they came to the giant's
house.

When she stopped the palfrey, the Man of the Green Cloak
jumped down, went into the giant's house, and stood behind the
door. She went in where the giant was, and the giant asked her
how she had got on with those men. 'This is the way I got on !'
she answered : 'You gave the spoon away to them.' 'I did not ;
it is still in the chest where we left it.' They went and looked,
but there was only a straw in its place, and they were amazed.
'We will put the seven locks on the knife tonight,' said the giant.
But when they were putting the knife in the chest, the Man of
the Green Cloak came and waved the green cloak before their
eyes for a twinkling, caught the knife between the chest and their
hands,[1] [left in its place a straw], and took the knife with him
under the green cloak, and stood behind the door where he had
been before. When they had kissed and caressed each other,
Mór said goodbye to the giant, and set off home. The Man of
the Green Cloak went out at her heels, and when she sprang
on to her palfrey, he sprang up behind her. She set the palfrey
off galloping, and when she was highest the Man of the Green
Cloak was lowest, and when she was lowest he was highest, until
they came to the mansion.

When she stopped the palfrey, the Man of the Green Cloak
alighted, and while she was giving the palfrey to her groom he
went in to where his own bed and that of the King's Son were. But

fhéin, agus leabaidh Mhic an Rìgh, agus is ann a fhuair e Mac
an Rìgh a' rubadh a bhoisean agus a' suathadh a dhòrn. Thuirt
Fear a' Bhratain Uaine, 'Gu dé tha ort, a Mhic an Rìgh?'
'O! tha, gun téid na cinn a chur dhìnn a màireach, chionn[1]
nach urrainn duinne an sgian fhaotainn.' 'Tha an sgian agam-
sa.' 'O! a bheil? Is maith gun d'fhuair thu i.' Thug Fear
a' Bhratain Uaine an sgian da agus fhuair Mac an Rìgh an
cadal an sin.

An ath-latha, dh'éirich Mór air thoiseach orra-san agus thuirt
i riutha iad a dh'éirigh. Thuirt iad-san, 'Chan 'eil móran cabhaig
oirnn.' Thuirt ise iad a dh'éirigh an ceart-uair, agus gum
faigheadh i a greim-maduinn a ghabhail. Deir Mac an Rìgh,
'Chan 'eil adhbhar cabhaig ann.' Thuirt ise, mur éireadh iad,
gun rachadh na cinn a chur dhiùbh anns na leapaichean.
Dh'éirich iad an sin, agus chaidh iad suas do'n cheàrn far an
robh Mór agus a h-athair. Dh'iarr i an sgian orra; thuirt Mac
an Rìgh, 'An tug thu dhuinne an sgian r'a gleidheadh?' 'Cha
tug, no do dhuine a bhuineadh do ur daoine.' 'An tug thu
dhuinne fios c'àite an do chuir thu i?' 'Cha tug, no do dhuine
bhuineadh dhuibh.' 'Nach cruaidh duilich dhuinne a faotainn,
an nì nach [deach] earbsadh ruinn.' 'Cuiribh a làthair an sgian,
mun téid na cinn a thoirt dhìbh:' agus ghlaodh i a nuas an
claidheamh buaidh nach d'fhàg fuidheall riamh a dh'aona
bheum, agus thilg Mac an Rìgh an sgian air a' chlàr-bhìdh.
Thog Mór an sgian, agus sheall i oirre, is b'e dìreach a sgian
fhéin a bh'ann, agus ghabh i móran ioghnaidh dheth.

An uair a thànaig an oidhche agus a bha i aig a tràth-feasgair,
thuirt i riu, 'Is e a th'agaibh ri a fhaotainn domh 'sa' mhaduinn
a màireach, am beul mu dheireadh a phògas mise an nochd,
agus mur faigh sibh dhomh e, théid na cinn agaibh a chur
dhìbh, agus an cur air na stuib a tha gun lìonadh anns a' chladh.'
Thuirt Fear a' Bhratain Uaine, 'Is an innis thu dhuinn
có e?' 'Chan innis no do dhuine bhuineas do ur daoine.' ''S
nach duilich dhuinn a fhaotainn mur bi fios againn có e?'
'Faiceadh sibh-se da sin.' An uair a chaidh Fear a' Bhratain
Uaine agus Mac an Rìgh a laighe, sheall Fear a' Bhratain Uaine
troimh an toll a bha 'sa' chlàraidh, agus chunnaig e Mór 'ga

---

[1] MS. *chun.*

he found the King's Son rubbing his palms and wringing his hands. 'What worries you, Son of the King ?' asked the Man of the Green Cloak. 'Oh ! that our heads will be cut off tomorrow because we cannot find the knife.' 'I have the knife,' said the Man of the Green Cloak. 'Oh ! Have you ? I'm glad you got it.' The Man of the Green Cloak gave him the knife, and then the King's Son was able to sleep.

The next day, Mór rose before they did. She told them they must rise. 'We are in no great hurry,' said they. She replied that they were to get up that instant, so that she might have her morning meal. 'There is no cause for haste,' said the King's Son. She replied that if they did not rise, they would be beheaded in their beds. So then they got up, and went to where Mór and her father were. She asked them for the knife ; and the King's Son said, 'Did you give the knife to us to keep ?' 'I did not, nor to anyone belonging to your kin.' 'Did you tell us where you put it ?' 'I did not, nor did I tell anyone belonging to you.' 'How very hard and difficult it must be for us to find a thing that was not entrusted to us !' 'Produce the knife, or else off come your heads' ; and she called out to bring down the Sword of Virtue whose single stroke never left a remnant. Then the King's Son threw the knife on the dining table. Mór picked up the knife and looked at it, and it was indeed her own knife, and she was amazed at it.

When night came, and she was at her evening meal, she said to them, 'What you have to get for me tomorrow is the last mouth I shall kiss tonight, and unless you get it for me, your heads shall be cut off and set upon the vacant stakes in the graveyard.' 'Will you tell us who he is ?' asked the Man of the Green Cloak. 'I will not, nor will I tell anyone who belongs to your kin.' 'But how hard it must be for us to find him if we do not know who he is !' 'You see to that,' said she. When the Man of the Green Cloak and the King's Son went to bed, the Man of the Green Cloak looked through the hole in the partition, and saw Mór getting herself ready. He went and

dèanamh fhéin deas. Chaidh e, agus ghoid e leis an claidheamh
buaidh, agus thug e leis e, agus chuir e a staigh e fo'n bhratan
uaine, ach cha deach e aig cùlaibh Móir an uair sin, air eagal is
gum faigheadh i a mach e, ach is ann a bha e a' caitheamh
falacha talmhanda oirre.[1] Dh'fhalbh e, agus bha e aig taigh
an fhamhair air thoiseach oirre, agus chaidh e agus sheas e
aig cùl an doruis, mar a [2] b'àbhaist da bhith.

An uair a thànaig ise, chuir i fhéin agus am famhair fàilte air
a chéile, agus dh'fharraid am famhair dith, gu dé mar a thànaig
i air a h-adhart leis na daoine ud : agus a deir ise ris an fhamhair,
'Thànaig, gun tug thusa daibh an sgian.' 'Cha tug ; tha i
fhathast anns a' chiste far an d'fhàg sinn i.' 'Chan 'eil : bha i
aca, agus thug iad domh i an diugh 'sa' mhaduinn.' Agus deir
am famhair, 'Seallaidh sinn.' Sheall iad, agus cha robh an sin
ach stràbh a bha ann an grunnd na ciste. Ghabh am famhair
iongantas deth. Thachais e a cheann, agus thuirt e, 'Gu dé
a chuir thu mu'n coinnimh r'a dhèanamh a rithist ?' 'Chuir
gum faigheadh iad dhòmh-sa 'sa' mhaduinn a màireach am beul
mu dheireadh a phògainn-sa an nochd.' Thuirt am famhair,
'Chan fhaigh iad sin,' agus phòg e i, agus an uair a bha iad
sgìth a' pògadh agus a' cniadachadh a chéile, dh'fhalbh ise gu
dol dachaigh. Chaidh i a mach, agus leum i an àird air an
fhalaire, agus chuir i an fhalaire 'na deannruith dachaigh.

Agus [chaidh] am famhair gu taobh an teine gu garadh
chùl-chas a dhèanamh air fhéin mun rachadh e a laighe, agus
thànaig am fear beag [3] agus e còmhdaichte le a bhratan uaine,
gus gun robh e aig cùl an fhamhair, agus ghabh e an claidheamh
buaidh agus bhuail e am famhair leis ann an cùl na h-amhaich,
agus chuir e an ceann deth. Thug e leis e, agus rinn e suaibealadh
ghlanaidh air, agus rug e air falt air a' cheann anns an darna
làimh agus an claidheamh 'san làimh eile ; agus chaidh e a
dh'ionnsaigh an taigh-mhóir leò, agus chaidh e a staigh far an
robh a leabaidh fhéin, agus far an robh Mac an Rìgh 'na laighe.

---

[1] *Lit.* he played the game of land-hiding with her, or administered or dealt
out land-hiding against her. The idea is very like that implied in *stalking*, as in
stalking a deer. *Falach-cuain*, ocean-hiding, means *marooning*, and also *outsailing*, as
when one boat gets ahead of another. But a person furnished with a cloak of
invisibility need not have feared being seen. Perhaps the real reason of Green
Cloak's action has been lost.

stole the Sword of Virtue, and taking it with him, put it under his green cloak. But he did not mount behind Mór on that occasion, in case she should discover him, but he took advantage of all the natural features of the country to hide himself from her.[1] Off he went, and he was at the giant's house before she was, and then he stood at the back of the door as he had done before.

When she arrived, she and the giant greeted each other, and the giant asked her how she had got on with those men. 'This is the way I got on,' she replied : 'you gave them the knife !' 'I did not ; it is still in the chest where we left it.' 'It is not : they had it, and they gave it to me this morning.' 'We will look,' said the giant. They looked, and there was nothing but a straw at the bottom of the chest. The giant was astonished at it. He scratched his head and said, 'What have you set them to do next ?' 'This—that they should bring me tomorrow morning the last mouth that I should kiss tonight.' 'They will not get that,' said the giant, and he kissed her ; and when they were tired of kissing and caressing each other she set out to go home. She went out of the house, sprang up on the palfrey, and urged it homewards at a headlong gallop.

The giant [went] to the fireside to warm the backs of his legs before going to bed, and the little man,[3] covered up in his green cloak, crept up behind the giant. Then he took the Sword of Virtue and struck the giant with it on the nape of his neck and cut off his head. He took the head with him and gave it a rough wash ; then, gripping it by the hair in the one hand and seizing the sword in the other, he carried them off to the mansion, and went in where his own bed was and where the King's Son was sleeping. He stowed away the giant's head, and replaced the Sword of Virtue where he had found it. Then he went back to

[2] [? read *far am*, 'where he used to be'—A. M.]
[3] The only place where Green Cloak is called little. The fact suggests a pygmy or fairy origin for him. [Perhaps 'little' only as compared to the giant ; so Herakles is 'short' in his adventure with Antaios, Pindar, Isthm., 4, 57.—H. J. R.]

Thaisg e an ceann aig an fhamhair, agus chaidh e agus thaisg e an claidheamh buaidh far an d'fhuair e e, agus thill e far an robh a leabaidh agus chaidh e a laighe, agus chaidil e, agus bha Mac an Rìgh a' rubadh a bhoisean, is a' suathadh a dhòrnaibh, agus b'ioghnadh leis cho sunndach 's a bha am fear eile a' cadal.

An ath-latha, dh'éirich Mór, agus thànaig i far an robh iad 'nan laighe, agus bha an claidheamh buaidh aice ri a cruachan. Thuirt i riu, 'Éiribh, éiribh.' Dh'éirich iad agus chaidh iad do'n t-seòmar, agus bha ceann an fhamhair 'ga ghleidheadh am falach fo'n bhratan uaine aig Fear a' Bhratain Uaine. Chuir Mór an claidheamh buaidh air a' chlàr, agus thuirt i riu, 'Faighibh dhòmh-sa an seo am beul mu dheireadh a phòg mi a raoir.' Chuir Fear a' Bhratain Uaine ceann an fhamhair air a' chlàr air muin a' chlaidheimh : agus thuirt a h-athair, 'O ! an e sin am beul mu dheireadh a bha i a' pògadh ?' agus thuirt Fear a' Bhratain Uaine, 'Is e sin fhéin am beul mu dheireadh a bha ise pògadh.' Thuirt a h-athair, 'Ma thà, cha do shaoil mi fhéin gum pògadh mo nighean gu bràth a leithid sin de bheul.' Thuit ise 'na brag air a' bhòrd. Thuirt Fear a' Bhratain Uaine ri Mac an Rìgh, 'Tog do bhean : tha i glé choisinnde agad a nis.' Thog Mac an Rìgh i, agus ghabh i gaol air an sin, o'n[1] a dh' fhuasgail e na h-achanaighean[2] dith agus gun robh am famhair marbh.

Is e am famhair a bha cur draoidheachd oirre, gum biodh gaol aice air famhair, agus nach bitheadh air a h-aon air bith eile, a chionn gun robh móran stòrais aig a h-athair, agus bha am famhair ro thoileach a faotainn agus stòras a h-athar leatha : ach cha b'urrainn da a faotainn gus gun rachadh an toiseach fichead fear a mharbhadh air a son, agus na cinn aca a chur diùbh agus an cur air na stuib a bha anns a' chladh. Chaidh ochd deug de dhaoine a mharbhadh, agus na cinn a chur diùbh, agus an cur [air] na stuib a bha anns a' chladh. Agus nan rachadh na cinn aig Mac an Rìgh agus Fear a' Bhratain Uaine a chur ann, bhiodh an fhichead ann, ach bha Fear a' Bhratain Uaine tuilleadh is seòlta air son an fhamhair. Bha am famhair

---

[1] *chun* in MS. Read, perhaps, *chionn gun d'fhuasgail.*

[2] *na h-achanaighean,* the exceedingly urgent bonds, obligations, *i.e.* 'spells, charms.' Later on, in the same paragraph, *na h-achanaighean* is used again in a context that

his bed, got into bed and fell asleep while the King's Son was rubbing his palms and wringing his hands, and thinking how extraordinary it was that the other should be sleeping so happily.

Next day Mór arose and came to where they lay, and at her hip was girded on the Sword of Virtue. 'Get up ! Get up !' said she to them. They got up and went to the room, the Man of the Green Cloak keeping the giant's head hidden beneath his green cloak. Mór laid the Sword of Virtue on the table and said to them, 'Bring me here the last mouth that I kissed last night.' The Man of the Green Cloak placed the giant's head on the table on top of the sword. Her father cried, 'Oh ! is that the last mouth she was kissing ?' and the Man of the Green Cloak answered, 'It is that very same, that is the last mouth she was kissing.' 'Well, well,' said her father, 'I did not think that my daughter would ever kiss such a mouth as that.' She collapsed on the floor with a thud. The Man of the Green Cloak said to the King's Son, 'Lift up your wife : you have well earned her.' The King's Son lifted her up, and then and there she fell in love with him, because he had freed her from the spells,[2] and because the giant was dead.

It was the giant who had bewitched her, so that she might love a giant and no one else. He had done so because her father was a very rich man, and the giant greatly desired to win her, and with her her father's riches : but he could not win her until twenty men had been killed for her sake and their heads taken off and set on the stakes in the graveyard. Eighteen men had been killed, and their heads cut off and set on the stakes in the graveyard. And if the heads of the King's Son and of the Man of the Green Cloak had been placed there, there would have been a full score, but the Man of the Green Cloak had been too clever for the giant. The giant was to have won her in marriage when the head of the Man of the Green Cloak and that of the

suggests that in more ancient versions, Mór had categorically bespelled the heroes to their tasks in the good old-fashioned Highland way.

gus a faighinn ri a pòsadh an uair a rachadh na cinn aig Fear a'
Bhratain Uaine agus Mac an Rìgh a chur air na stuib, agus is
e an t-seòltachd aig an fhamhair a thug dhi a bhith ag iarraidh
nan achanaighean orra, is gun rachadh na cinn a chur bhàrr
nan daoine. Ach chaidh an ceann a chur dheth fhéin mu
dheireadh. Bha a h-athair a' smaointeachadh gum b'e fear ann
an inbhe anabarrach àrd a bha i gu fhaotainn aig cho stalbharach[1]
is a bha i : agus cha robh a h-athair idir toileach gun rachadh
na daoine a bha 'tadhal air a nighinn a chur gu bàs, ach chaidh
siod a dhèanamh gun fhios da. An uair a thuig e mar a bha,
thug e duais do Fhear a' Bhratain Uaine air son e bhith cho
tapaidh, agus bha e ro thoileach a nighean a bhith aig Mac
an Rìgh, agus an ceann beagan làithean, chaidh am pòsadh a
dhèanamh, agus bha banais aca a mhair ré seachdain.

An uair a chaidh am pòsadh a chur seachad agus a bha
gnothaichean an òrdugh, thuirt Fear a' Bhratain Uaine ri Mac
an Rìgh, 'A bheil fios agad có mi ?' Thuirt Mac an Rìgh nach
robh. Thuirt Fear a' Bhratain Uaine, 'Is mise [an] gille a
chuir do mhuime-chìche as do dhéidh gu d' thoirt as na cunnartan
anns an robh thu gu dol, ach a nis, o'n (?) [2] a fhuair mi do thoirt
as gach cunnart, faodaidh mi nis a dhol dachaigh do m' dhùthaich
fhéin.' Cha robh Mac an Rìgh toileach dealachadh ris, ach
chan fhuireadh e. Thug Mac an Rìgh da le gean-math beagan
airgid. Ghabh Fear a' Bhratain Uaine a chead de Mhac an
Rìgh agus d'a bhean nuadh-phòsta, agus chaidh e dhachaigh
d'a dhùthaich fhéin.

An uair a rànaig e dachaigh, chaidh e far an robh an té
chuir air falbh e, agus dh'innis e di mar a thachair, agus chuir
i a dh'ionnsaigh an Rìgh, agus dh' innis i da gun d'fhuair i
sgeul air a mhac a bhith ann an tìr eile, agus e pòsta air nighinn
urramaich, agus móran stòrais aice. Bha an Rìgh ro thoileach
sgeul fhaotainn air a mhac, oir bha an Rìgh a' bristeadh a
chridhe le duilichinn air son a mhic, oir bha am mac a b'òige
air dol gu an-strògh air an rìoghachd. Bha a' Bhanrìghinn air
fàs caoin-shuarach mu'n Rìgh nam faigheadh i a mac féin
ceart, agus bha an Rìgh ro thoileach nam faigheadh e a mhac
a bu shine dachaigh. B'àil leis Fear a' Bhratain Uaine a chur

---

[1] *stalbharach*, over-trimmed, over-behaved ? The word is not in the dictionary.
[2] MS. *chun*. Read *chionn gun d'fhuair* ?

King's Son had been set on the stakes, and it was the giant's cunning that had caused her to lay upon them those urgent demands of hers, in order that they might be beheaded. But in the end it was the giant's own head that was cut off. Her father had supposed that it was a man in some very high position she was to marry, so pompous and important was she : her father was in no way willing that the men who came to visit his daughter should be put to death, but it was done without his knowledge. When he understood how matters were, he rewarded the Man of the Green Cloak for his bravery and resource; and he was very pleased that the King's Son should have his daughter, and at the end of a few days the marriage was celebrated, and they had a wedding that lasted a week.

When the wedding was over and everything was in order, the Man of the Green Cloak said to the King's Son, 'Do you know who I am ?' The King's Son said he did not. The Man of the Green Cloak said, 'I am the lad whom your foster-mother sent after you to keep you from the dangers into which you were to go, but now, seeing that I have brought you safely out of every danger, I may go home to my own country.' The King's Son was not willing to part with him, but he would not stay. So with great good will he gave him a little money. Then the Man of the Green Cloak took his leave of the King's Son and his newly-wedded wife, and went to his own country.

When he got home, he went to see her who had sent him on his journey, and told her what had happened. She sent word to the King and told him she had news of his son's being in another country, that he was married to a girl of rank, and had much wealth. The King was delighted to have news of his son, because he was breaking his heart with grief on his account and because the younger son was ruining the kingdom with extravagance. As to the Queen, she would have become utterly indifferent about the King had she been able to have her own son settled, but the King would have been very glad if only he could have had his elder son at home. He wished to send the Man of the Green

air falbh g'a iarraidh, ach dh'fharraid Fear a' Bhratain Uaine
de a bhana-mhaighstir agus dh'iarr i air dol, agus chuir an
Rìgh Fear a' Bhratain Uaine a dh'iarraidh a mhic a bu shine,
agus nan tigeadh e dhachaigh gum faigheadh e an rìoghachd,
agus gun cuireadh a athair an seilbh e, an uair a thigeadh e.

Dh'fhalbh Fear a' Bhratain Uaine dh'a iarraidh, agus an
uair a rànaig e, thuirt e ris, 'Thànaig mi le teachdaireachd do
d'ionnsaigh, thu a dhol dachaigh far am bheil t'athair, agus
cuiridh e thu an seilbh anns an rìoghachd.' Rinn Mac an
Rìgh agus a athair-céile suas mar a dhèanadh iad, mur bitheadh
gnothaichean mar a b'àil leò an uair a ruigeadh e taigh a athar.
Thug e beannachd le a athair-céile, is thug e leis a bhean, agus
chaidh e do thìr a athar, a dh'fhaotainn seilbh 'san rìoghachd,
agus an uair a rànaig e, rinn a athair gàirdeachas mór ri a mhac
fhaicinn agus thaitinn bean a mhic ris an Rìgh gu ro mhaith,
agus chuir an Rìgh a mhac an seilbh anns an rìoghachd : ach
bha farmad mór aig a mhuime agus a leth-bhràthair ris an
Rìgh Òg, agus r'a mhnaoi. Bha iad a los, nam faigheadh iad
dòigh air, cur as da.

Ach 'san toiseach, is ann a dh'fhalbh am bràthair òg a
dh'iarraidh an fhortain, ach cha deachaidh leis. Thànaig e air
ais an ceann trì bliadhna, agus rinn a bhràthair ceannard-airm
deth. Rinn e Fear a' Bhratain Uaine 'na fhear-riaghlaidh ann
an taigh an Rìgh. Ach bha a mhuime toileach an Rìgh Òg
a phuinseanachadh, agus chuir i puinsean ann am biadh an
Rìgh. Ach bha coin aig Fear a' Bhratain Uaine, agus bha e
feuchainn gach bìdh ris na coin, agus fhuair e a mach i, agus
chaidh a cur air fògradh do dhùthaich athair-céile an Rìgh.

Bha eagal air Fear a' Bhratain Uaine roimh leth-bhràthair an
Rìgh. Fhuair e toll a chur 'san ùrlar anns an rathad a bha a
dh'ionnsaigh leabaidh an Rìgh, agus dà bhrod air, a' carachadh
air bannan 'san teis-mheadhon, agus an dithisd a' fosgladh le
leathad ri chéile 'sa' mheadhon. Bha crann orra 'san latha 'gan
gleidheadh dùinte agus aodach tharta.[1] Chuir e a leithid eile
mu choinneamh a leabaidh fhéin. Bha, le leth-bhràthair an
Rìgh [Òig], nam biodh an Rìgh [Òg] marbh, gum faigheadh e
fhéin an rìoghachd, agus fhuair e fear eile leis, agus chaidh

---

[1] *MacTalla*, a Gaelic newspaper of Cape Breton, mentioned a similar trap used
by Scotch colonists in Canada for catching bears.

Cloak away to fetch him, and the Man of the Green Cloak asked his mistress, and she told him to go. So the King sent the Man of the Green Cloak to seek his elder son, and to tell him that if he came home he should have the kingdom, and that his father would put him in possession of it when he did come.

So the Man of the Green Cloak went off to seek him, and when he came to him, he said, 'I have come with a message for you, that you should go home to your father, and he will put you in possession of the kingdom.' The King's Son and his father-in-law planned together how they should act, if, upon coming to his father's house, the King's Son found that matters were not as they might wish. Bidding his father-in-law goodbye, and taking his wife with him, he went to his own father's country to get possession of the kingdom. When he got there, his father rejoiced greatly at seeing his son, and was delighted with his son's wife. He put his son in possession of the kingdom ; but his stepmother and his half-brother were very envious of the Young King and his wife, and were bent on killing him, if they could find a way.

At first, the younger brother set out to seek his fortune, but he did not succeed. He came back at the end of three years, and his brother made him a general in the army. He made the Man of the Green Cloak steward of the royal household. But his stepmother wished to poison the Young King, and she put poison in his food. But the Man of the Green Cloak had some dogs, and he tried all the food on the dogs, and so he found her out, and she was banished to the country of the King's father-in-law.

The Man of the Green Cloak was afraid of the King's half-brother. So he had a hole made in the floor on the way towards the King's bed, with two lids over it which moved on hinges, both opening downwards together in the middle. There was a bar across them which kept them shut during the day, and a cloth was laid over them. In front of his own bed he put a similar trap.[1] The [Young] King's half-brother thought that if the [Young] King were dead he should get the kingdom. He got another man to join him, and in the night they went to kill iad a mharbhadh an Rìgh agus Fear a' Bhratain Uaine 'san oidhche. Ach thuit iad anns na tuill a bha air thoiseach orra, agus chaidh an glacadh an ath-latha, agus an cur air fògradh do thìr athair-céile an Rìgh, agus nan rachadh an cur na b'fhaide as, bu mhiosa dhaibh, agus nan tigeadh iad air ais, chan fhaigheadh iad a bhith beò.

NOTES

MS. vol. x., No. 97. There is no signature at the end of this story, nor is any locality mentioned. But in his Gaelic List, Islay gives John Dewar, labourer, as the reciter, the locality as Glendaruail, and refers to the tale as 'good.' The MS. is certainly in Dewar's hand, and the idiom is very much Anglicized. Dewar's written Gaelic differed greatly from the Gaelic he spoke, says Islay, MS. vol. viii., No. 204. Still his stories are very complete and exhaustive, seldom lacking in detail or balance.

In No. 97, the second Queen, incited by the Hen-Wife, requests the hero, her stepson, to sign away his rights to the kingdom. The King sides with his second spouse. But the stepson thereupon goes to the *Seanghal eòlach*,[1]

[1] This character appears in *W. H. Tales*, i., No. 1 ; ii., No. 38 ; MS. vol. xi., No. 177 ; *An Gàidheal* (1875), iv., p. 84. He is probably the same as the Irish character, An Seann Dall Glic, 'The Old Blind Wise One,' *Oireachtas Proceedings* (1899), p. 149 ; Dr Douglas Hyde, *Beside the Fire*, p. 190. Nowadays, *Seanghal* is a word for a wise-acre [but originally *seneschal* ? Cf. *seann mhaor eòlach.*—A. M.]

the King and the Man of the Green Cloak.   But they fell into
the holes placed in their way, and were caught next day, and
were banished to the land of the King's father-in-law.   Had they
been sent farther away, it would have been worse for them, and
had they come back, they would not have been allowed to live.

the wise, knowing, and experienced Councillor or Soothsayer, for assistance
and advice.   The Seanghal happened to be the father of the hero's foster-
mother.   As is well-known, the tie of fosterage among the Gael was stronger
by far than that of any other relationship.   And so, the foster-mother being
bound by that tie to do all she could for her foster-son, sends him an
auxiliary.

[Though long, the story is incomplete.   Green Cloak stipulates that he
shall have for wages half of what he gets.   By analogy with similar stories,
he should test the prince's honesty by asking for half of Mór.—H. J. R.]
[The Man of the Greek Cloak represents the 'Grateful Dead Man,' but this
motif has become lost.   See Aarne and Thompson, *The Types of the Folktale*,
no. 507A ;   and *Scottish Gaelic Studies*, vi., p. 109.—K. H. J.]

Parallels :—*Celtic Magazine*, xiii., p. 20 ;   *Myths and Folk-Lore of Ireland*,
p. 187 (Jeremiah Curtin) ;   *Béaloideas*, i., p. 167 ;   *Scottish Gaelic Studies*, vi.,
p. 98 ;   *The Grateful Dead*, pp. 62-64 (G. F. Gerould, The Folk-Lore Society,
1907, Nutt, London).

A' MHAIGHDEAN MHARA

No. 54.   [*MS. Vol. x., No. 102*]

BHA tuathanach ann a roimhe seo, do'm b'ainm Otram, is bha e falbh troimh choillidh ri taobh mara, is chunnaig e (mar a bha leis) seachd ròin a' teachd gu cladach, is chaidh e am falach orra. Thànaig iad gu tìr, agus is e a bh'ann seachd maighdeanan mara. Chuir iad diùbh na cochuill-éisg, agus is e a bha annta seachd nigheanan briagh. Chaidh iad gu an nigheadh féin anns a' mhuir, is chaidh Otram, is ghoid e leis an aon bu mhotha de na cochuill, is chuir e am falach e. An uair a thànaig na maighdeanan air an ais a dh'ionnsaigh nan cochull, fhuair gach aon a cochull féin, ach an té bu mhotha dhiubh. Dh'iarr ise a cochull féin gus an robh i sgìth. Dh'fhalbh càch a mach air a' chuan, is dh'fhuirich ise leatha fhéin, is i a' caoineadh is a' caoidh, 'na suidhe air aon de chlachan a' chladaich, is i rùisgte. Thànaig Otram far an robh i, is chuir e a bhreacan mu a timcheall, agus thug e leis dachaigh i. Fhuair e aodach dhi, is dh'ionnsaich i obair a dhèanamh, agus bha i grunndail, gnìomhach. Phòs Otram i, is rinn i clann ris.

Fada 'na dhéidh sin, an am an Earraich, bha Otram a mach a' treabhadh, agus bha a bhean a mach ag amharc mun cuairt air gnothaichean, agus an uair a thànaig i a staigh, thuirt i ri a mac, 'Nach ioghnadh leat nach 'eil t'athair a' cur mu dheighinn a' mhulain arbhair sin a bhualadh, is gum bi feum aige air an t-sìol gu goirid?' Agus thuirt a mac, 'Tha rud bòidheach aig m'athair 'ga ghleidheadh anns a' mhulan sin, is chan fhaca mi riamh nì cho bòidheach ris.' Agus dh'fharraid ise gu dé bu chumadh, is gu dé bu dath dha. Agus dh'innis am balach an cumadh mar a b'fheàrr a b'urrainn da, is gun robh dath uaine air. Chaidh ise a staigh do'n ghàrradh far an robh am mulan, agus sgap i am mulan as a chéile. Ruith am balach, is dh'innis e d'a athair mar a thachair, is thànaig Otram gu luath a dh'fhaicinn na mnà aige mum fàgadh i e. Ach bha an cochull-éisg oirre mun tànaig e. Dh'iarr e oirre fuireach leis,

THE MERMAID

No. 54.   [*MS. Vol. x., No. 102*]

THERE was once a farmer called Otram, and one day he was passing through a wood near the sea when he saw, as he thought, seven seals moving towards the shore. He hid from them, and they came to land, and what were they but seven mermaids. They put off their fish skins and became seven beautiful young women ; and now they set about washing themselves in the sea. Then Otram went and stole away the biggest of the skins and hid it. When the maidens came back to where the fish skins were, each of them found her own, all except the biggest maiden. She searched for her skin until she was exhausted. The others went off out to sea, but she remained there all alone, weeping and lamenting, seated on one of the stones of the shore, and naked. Otram came up to her and put his plaid round her and took her home with him. He found clothes for her, and she learned to do housework, and she was thrifty and industrious. Otram married her and she bore him children.

Long after that, one spring-time, Otram was out ploughing and his wife was out too, looking after things. When she came in, she said to her son, 'Isn't it strange that your father is doing nothing about threshing that cornstack when very soon he will need the seed ? ' Her son replied, 'My father keeps a pretty thing in that stack : I have never seen anything so pretty.' She asked him what shape the thing had, and what colour ; and the boy described its shape as best he could and said it was green in colour. She went into the garden where the stack was and scattered it all to pieces. The boy ran and told his father what had happened, and Otram hurried back to see his wife before she left him. But before he arrived, she had the fish skin on. He asked her to stay with him, but she would not. So he asked

ach chan fhuiricheadh.   Agus dh'iarr e oirre i a thoirt comhairle
air mum fàgadh i e, agus thuirt i ris e a threabhadh, 'Aire chaol
gheur dhoimhne [1] is a cùl fòipe,[2] agus fras-chuir an sìol ged a
robh a' ghaoth 'na aghaidh ;

> is olc air mhath gum bi an t-sìon,
> cuir an sìol 'sa' Mhàirt,
> 's an uair thig tlus na gréine air,
> fàsaidh e an àird.'

Agus is e seòrsa na Maighdinn Mhara o'n tànaig clann ——

JOHN DEWAR.

[1] Dial. for *dhomhain.*
[2] *ar* (= tillage) here fem.

NOTES

MS. vol. x., No. 102.   John Dewar, the scribe, does not say whether the
story was one which he knew personally, and had written from memory, or
whether he had lately heard it recited by some other person.   He appended a
few proverbs, none of which are relevant, and all of which have been published
in Sheriff Nicolson's *Gaelic Proverbs.*

Otram, the name of the hero in No. 102, may be a form of MacCodrum.[1]
The clan of this name were traditionally supposed to have derived their
descent from seals (see *Uist Bards,* vi. ;   Nicolson's *Gaelic Proverbs,* p. 150 ;
Norse Influence, p. 260).[2]   For a monster descended from a seal, and for other
instances of seal-descent, see No. 8 (MS. vol. x., No. 18) ;   Islay's English
List, Nos. 250, 251.   But the last sentence in No. 102 witnesses to the belief
that some people or clan were descended from a mermaid, and does not
mention seals in this connection.   In the case of No. 102, and in a parallel
in *Celtic Magazine,* xi., p. 566, I suspect that two tales have been partly fused,
one of a seal-maiden, and one of a sea-maiden.   For seals and sea-maidens,
see *Rosg Gàidhlig,* pp. 23-25, 28.   There is a Skye tradition that all fair-haired
people are the descendants of mermaids.   See *Folk-Lore,* xxxiii., pp. 308-310,
for this and for a mermaid tale like No. 102.   For Irish tales of sea-people,
see *Folk-Lore,* xxxii., p. 114.

No. 102 is the only tale known to me which makes the mermaid the
authoress of the proverbs about sowing seed in the *Màrt,* and to do so even

[1] *MacCodrum* is from Norse *Goðormr.*   [I have recorded the same story in North
Uist, where the reciter definitely mentioned the Clan MacCodrum.—K. H. J.]

[2] [See also W. Matheson, *The Songs of John MacCodrum,* xxxiv.-xliv. ; David
Thomson, *The People of the Sea,* pp. 157-168.—A. M.]

her to give him some counsel before she left him, and she counselled him to plough 'A furrow narrow, clean-cut, deep with the back of the sod beneath and scatter the seed though the wind were unfavourable ; and good or bad the weather, sow the seed in March, and when the sun's warmth comes upon it it will grow up.'

And it is from the Mermaid's kind that the Clan ——— are descended.

JOHN DEWAR.

if the wind were so strong that one could scarcely throw a stone one's nail's breadth against it ; see No. 30 (MS. vol. x., No. 55). No. 102 therefore makes the mermaid a benefactress of the human race. A captive mermaid appears as a benefactress to mortals in another tale (see *Folk-Lore*, viii., p. 384) where she advises people to clean well the fish they were going to eat, adding that there were many little beasts in the sea, the reference being to the animalculæ which it was desirable to scour off the skin of the fish before eating it.

In No. 46 (MS. vol. x., No. 67*d*) a mermaid befriends the hero who encounters her at the shore. But to encounter her at sea was a presage of drowning : see *Folk-Lore*, viii., p. 385. To encounter a witch at sea in the shape of a rat sailing in a sieve, to see the water-horse, and to see a phantom deer under certain conditions, were portents of drowning and storms. Mermaids might come ashore and commit depredations in the country. *Trans. Gael. Soc. Inverness*, xv., p. 295. To drink water from the Mermaiden's Well was fatal to any member of the House of Ravenswood (Sir Walter Scott, 'The Bride of Lammermoor.') In other tales sea-maidens have flocks of sea-cattle. *W. H. Tales*, iii., p. 412, No. 86 *n.* ; *Celtic Review*, v., p. 54 ; *Folk-Lore*, viii., p. 384 ; *Superstitions*, pp. 136, 199, 201.

Very different from No. 102 is the story called 'The Sea-Maiden,' *W. H. Tales*, i., No. 4. Islay gave summaries there of several variants, some of which have been dealt with by the Rev. Geo. Henderson, *The Celtic Dragon Myth*, pp. 149, 155. See also Islay's English List, Nos. 70, 110, 113, 124, 346, and his Index, *W. H. Tales*, iv., arts. merman, Sea-Maiden ; *Waifs and Strays*, iii., p. 146.

MAC AN T-SEÒLADAIR

BHA seann seòladair anns an Eilean Sgitheanach, agus bha baile fearainn aige, agus cha robh aige ach an aon mhac. Cheannaich e soitheach do a mhac, air chor is gum biodh e dèanamh rud dha fhéin. Bha a mhac 'na dhuine cosgail, [air] chor is gach nì a dhèanadh e air falbh, chosgadh e air tìr e. Ged a bha e cosgail, bha boireannach as a dhéidh ag agairt pòsaidh, agus smaointich e o nach b'urrainn da a cur seachad gun creiceadh e an soitheach, is gun gabhadh e an t-saighdearachd is gum biodh e réidh is i. Reic e an soitheach, is ghabh e an t-saigh-dearachd, agus is e an tuarasdal a bha aige, sia sgillinnean 'san latha. Cha robh an t-saighdearachd a' còrdadh ris, agus smaointich e gun teicheadh e as an arm ; agus gun rachadh e air bòrd air soitheach, far am biodh e diongalt as a lòn. Theich e, agus rinn e fasdadh ri maighstir aon-chrannaich.[1] Thug e trì turuis air an aon-chrannach seo gu Sasainn.

Air an treas turus, bha e ag òl ann an taigh-òsda ann an Sasainn, agus thuit e ann an cuideachd maighstir-luinge. 'A Ghille Mhóir,' thuirt maighstir na luinge, 'mur am bithinn deònach t'fhasdadh—[2] agus ma nì thu fasdadh rium, bheir mi dhuit deagh thuarasdal.' Rinn e fasdadh ri maighstir na luinge. Chaidh e dhachaigh do'n t-soitheach anns an robh e roimhe, agus dh'innis e mar a thachair da fhìn. 'Ma thà,' arsa maighstir an aon-chrannaich, 'is tu duine as duiliche liom dealachadh ris ris an do dhealaich mi riamh.' 'Chan 'eil cothrom air,' ars esan ; 'thuit e a mach.' 'O'n a tha mi eòlach air maighstir na luinge, ruigidh mi e, agus fiachaidh mi am faigh mi as thu fhathast, ma bhitheas tu deònach,' arsa maighstir an aon-chrannaich. 'Tha mise buileach deònach.' Rànaig sgiobair an aon-chrannaich maighstir na luinge.[3] 'Dh'fhasdaidh thu fear de mo ghillean,' arsa maighstir an aon-chrannaich ri maighstir

---

[1] *sloop* in MS.
[2] = 'if I would not like to engage thee, I'm a Dutchman' ; =aposiopesis.

THE SAILOR'S SON

No. 55.   [*MS. Vol. x., No. 104*]

IN the Isle of Skye there was an old sailor who owned a farm.
He had only one son, and he bought a ship for him so that he
might do something for himself. The son was an extravagant
man : whatever he made on his trips, he spent ashore. But
extravagant though he was, there was a woman after him,
importuning him to marry her ; and since he could not shake
her off, he resolved to sell the ship, take to soldiering and be rid
of her. He sold the ship and took to soldiering, and the wages
he had were sixpence a day. But soldiering did not agree with
him, and he determined to desert from the army and go aboard
some vessel where he would be sure of his food. So he deserted
and signed on with the master of a sloop. On this sloop he made
three voyages to England.

On the third voyage, when he was drinking in a tavern in
England, he fell in with the captain of a sailing ship. 'What
wouldn't I give to sign you on, big fellow !' said the captain of
the sailing ship, 'and if you will sign on, I'll give you good wages.'
So he signed on with the captain of the sailing ship. Then he
returned to the vessel he had been on before and told what had
happened. 'Well, it is harder for me to part with you,' said the
master of the sloop, 'than with anyone I ever parted with.'
'That can't be helped,' replied the other, 'it happened so.' 'I
know this ship's captain,' said the master of the sloop, 'and I
will go and see him, and if you are willing, I will try and get you
out of this yet.' 'I am perfectly willing,' replied the other. So
the master of the sloop went to the ship's captain. 'You've taken
on one of my boys,' said the master of the sloop to the ship's
captain. 'I have,' replied the captain. 'Would you be willing

---

³ *caibhtinn na luinge*, in MS.

na luinge. 'Dh'fhasdaidh,' arsa maighstir na luinge. 'Am bitheadh tu deònach am fasdadh a leigeil air ais ?' arsa maighstir an aon-chrannaich ; 'nam bitheadh tu deònach a leigeil air ais, bheirinn-sa tuarasdal da cho math riut fhìn.' 'Dé bheireadh tu dha seachad air an tuarasdal ?' arsa maighstir na luinge. 'Bheirinn deise dha,' arsa maighstir an aon-chrannaich. 'Ma tà, saoilidh mi gur suarach orm fhéin tuarasdal agus deise a thoirt da, seach ort-sa. O'n a tha teisteas gille cho math agad air, cha dealaich mi idir ris,' arsa maighstir na luinge. 'Chan 'eil cothrom air. Tha math eile air ; chan 'eil aon acarsaid do'n téid thu, nach cum e sealg riut,' arsa maighstir an aon-chrannaich.

Ghabh e cuideachd ri maighstir na luinge, agus sheòl iad do na h-Ìnnsean. An uair a rànai iad na h-Ìnnsean, thug e gunna leis a shealgaireachd, agus bha e cumail seilge ris an luing. An uair a bha an luchd aca air bòrd, thill iad dachaigh do Shasainn. An ceud latha an déidh dhaibh tighinn, fhuair e gunna agus breacan sealgair, agus dh'fhalbh e a shealgaireachd. Bha ceòragaich uisge ann. Bha e tighinn seachad air bad coille, agus gu dé chuala e ach an aon ghearan a bu bhochdainne a chuala e riamh. Sheall e a staigh, agus gu dé chunnaig e ach boireannach chun a bhith marbh, 'na sìneadh an sin. Smaointich e aige fhéin an toiseach nach bitheadh gnothach ri boireannach gu bràth aige ; ach ghabh e de dhuilchinn, leis cho bochd 's a bha staid a' bhoireannaich seo, is nach b'urrainn da gabhail seachad oirre. Chaidh e far an robh i, agus chuir e am breacan uimpe, agus thog e leis air a mhuin i. Rànaig e taigh-òsda. Bhuail e anns an dorusd. Thànaig bean-an-taighe a nuas far an robh e. Dh'iarr e seòmar a dhèanamh ullamh air son a' bhoireannaich. Rinn bean-an-taighe seòmar ullamh gun dàil.

Chuir e a staigh ann am boireannach, agus dh'iarr e gach aire [1] a dh'fheumadh i a thoirt di, gus an rachadh i am feobhas, agus gun dìoladh esan air a shon. Thuirt e ri bean an taigh-òsda, ged a rachadh i am feobhas, gun a leigeil air falbh, gus an tilleadh esan bhàrr an ath-turuis. Sheòl esan, agus cha robh e fad air falbh, an uair a dh'fhàs ise gu math. Chum bean an taigh-òsda i gus an do thill esan air ais. An uair a thill esan air

---

[1] MS. *taire.*

to forego the agreement?' asked the master of the sloop; 'if you were, I would give him quite as good wages as you.' 'What would you give him in addition to wages?' asked the captain. I'd give him a suit of clothes,' replied the master of the sloop. Ah, well,' said the ship's captain, 'I feel it would be very much easier for me to give him a wage and a suit of clothes than for you. And since you make him out to be such a good fellow, I shan't part with him at all.' 'Then that can't be helped,' replied the master of the sloop. 'He has another good quality. You will never anchor anywhere but he will keep you in game.'

The lad went off with the captain of the ship, and they sailed to the Indies. When they arrived in the Indies, he took a gun with him to hunt, and he kept the ship in game. When they had the ship loaded, they returned home to England. The first day after their return, the young man got a gun and a hunter's plaid and went off hunting. There was a drizzling mist, and he was passing a clump of trees when he heard the most pitiable moaning he had ever listened to. He looked in and what did he see but a woman, almost dead, lying there. His first thought was that he would never have anything to do with any woman; but he was so moved at the pitiful state this woman was in that he could not pass by. He went up to her and wrapped his plaid about her, and carried her off on his back. He came to an inn and knocked at the door. The woman of the house came down to him. He asked to have a room made ready for the woman, and the woman of the house prepared a room without delay.

He put the woman in the room, and requested that she should be given every attention she needed until she recovered, and said that he would pay for it. He told the woman of the inn not to let the woman go away—even if she got better—until he returned from his next voyage. He sailed away, but he was not long absent when the woman recovered. The woman of the inn kept her there until he returned; when he did, he went to the inn

ais, chaidh e do'n taigh-òsda far an robh i. Bha e air ais is air
aghaidh eadar an taigh-òsda agus an soitheach gus an robh an
soitheach deiseil a dh'fhalbh air an ath-turus. An uair a bha e
deiseil a dh'fhalbh, thuirt e rithe-se, am bitheadh i deònach a
phòsadh. Thuirt ise gum bitheadh i deònach a phòsadh seach
duine air an t-saoghal air fad. Is ann mar sin a bha. Fhuair
iad pearsa-eaglais, is phòs iad, is air Moire fhìn ! bha ise glé
thoilichte dhe seo.

An latha mun do sheòl an long, có bha tighinn a dh'ionnsaigh a' cheidhe, ach am fear do 'm beanadh i. An uair
a bha e tighinn a nuas, chunnaig e boireannach a' coimhead
a mach air uinneig. Laom a dhà shùil,[1] agus thill e dhachaigh.
Ghabh e a staigh, agus chuir e a làmh fo a leithcheann.
Dh'fhaighnich a bhean dheth, gu dé bha air. Thuirt e gun
robh na leòr ; gum faca e coltas a nighinn a' coimhead a mach
air uinneig far an robh e. Thuirt a bhean nach b'i a bh'ann.
Thuirt esan gun robh i anabarrach coltach rithe. 'Nam b'i
bhitheadh ann,' ars a bhean, 'gu dé chumadh i ?' Dh'iarr e
air a bhean falbh còmhla ris, is gum faiceadh iad, có aca b'i no
nach b'i a bh'ann. Dh'fhalbh a bhean leis, agus rànaig iad an
t-àite 'san robh ise. An uair a chaidh iad seachad air an taigh-
òsda, chunnaig iad boireannach a' coimhead a mach air uinneig.
Cho luath 's a chunnaig a màthair i, dh'aithnich i i. Ghabh i
a staigh do'n taigh-òsda, is dh'iarr i a staigh far an robh i.
'Chan fhaod mise do leigeil a staigh,' arsa bean an taigh-òsda.
An uair a chunnaig an nighean a màthair, dh'fhosgail i an dorusd,
is thànaig i 'na coinnimh, is chuir i a dà làimh mu a h-amhaich,
is bha a màthair is a h-athair toilichte gun d'fhuair iad i, is
aighearach gum biodh i leò dhachaigh. 'Dé dh'éirich dhuit, a
nighean ?' ars a h-athair is a màthair rithe. 'Bha mi anns a'
choillidh còmhla ri nigheanan eile, is bhuail greim mi. Dh'fhuirich
mi air deireadh air càch, is cha do leig mi dad orm riu, an
dùil gun rachainn na b'fheàrr. Dh'fhalbh iad-san agus is ann
na bu mhiosa chaidh mise, is cha b'urrainn mi dol na b'fhaide,
is cha robh agam ach mi fhìn a leigeil 'nam shìneadh ann an
siod, is mur an tigeadh gille coibhneil an rathad, agus mo

---

[1] Note in MS. by H. MacLean, the scribe :—'*Laom a dhà shùil*—His two eyes
filled with tears.' *Laom* is commonly applied to corn in the case of its lodging. I
have never heard it used in this sense before. *Laom an coirce*, the oats has [*sic*] lodged,

where she was. He kept going to and fro between the ship and the inn until the ship was ready to sail on the next voyage. When the young man was ready for going away, he asked the woman if she would marry him. She replied that she would marry him sooner than any man in the whole world. So it was. They got a cleric and married ; and by Mary herself, she was delighted at this !

The day before the ship sailed, who came to the quay but the ship's owner. As he was coming down, he saw a woman looking out of a window. His eyes filled with tears ; he returned home and went indoors and leaned his head on his hand. His wife asked him what was wrong with him. He replied that there was enough wrong with him, that he had seen in a place he visited what seemed to be his daughter looking out of a window. His wife said it was not she ; he replied that it was extremely like her. 'If it were she,' said his wife, 'what would keep her there ?' He asked his wife to go with him so that they might see whether it was their daughter or not. So his wife went with him and they came to the place where she was ; and when they were passing the inn, they saw a woman looking out of a window. Immediately they saw her, the mother recognised her. She went straight into the inn and asked to get in where she was. 'I cannot let you in,' said the woman of the inn. But when the girl saw her mother, she opened the door and went to meet her and flung her two arms round her neck. Her father and mother were delighted at having found her and joyous at the thought of having her home with them. 'What happened to you, daughter ?' asked her father and mother. 'I was in the woods with other girls when a sudden pain gripped me. I lagged behind the others, but I did not give any sign to them, thinking that I'd get better. They went away, but I got worse until I could go no farther, and I had nothing for it but to lay myself down there ; and were it not that a kind young man came that way and carried me off, I should certainly have died. He brought me to this house and ordered that every attention

---

falling to the ground for want of strength to support itself. The most literal meaning of the above phrase is I think (is), 'His two eyes gave way to tears' [*sic*].

thogail leis, cha robh ach gun robh mi marbh. Thug e mi
do'n taigh seo, agus dh'iarr e a h-uile aire [1] a dh'fheumainn a
thoirt domh, is phàidh e air son gach nì, agus tha e fhìn agus
mise an déidh pòsaidh. Tha e 'na sheòladair air a leithid seo de
luing, agus tha e ri seòladh gun dàil.' 'Tha e coltach,' thuirt a
h-athair, 'nach ann a h-uile rathad a bha leithid a' ghille sin
r'a fhaotainn.'

Chaidh a h-athair dachaigh. Sgrìobh e litir chun sgiobair
na luinge, agus chuir e [d']a ionnsaigh [i], agus chuir e rud
'na cuideachd. Fhuair an sgiobair an litir, agus bha e air
iarraidh air anns an litir gun obair sam bith iarraidh air a'
ghille air bòrd, agus bha trì cheud punnd Sasannach [a dh']ionn-
saigh a' ghille còmhla ris an litir. Dh'innis an caibhtinn da gun
[robh] trì cheud punnd Sasannach [d']a ionnsaigh an siod o'n
fhear leis am bu leis an long, agus cead fuireachd 'na thàmh
air bòrd. 'Sin rud nach dèan mi. Gabhaidh mi an t-airgead,
ach fuireachd 'nam thàmh, cha dèan mi,' ars esan. 'Do thoil
fhìn,' ars an sgiobair. Fhuair e an trì cheud punnd Sasannach.

An uair a rànaig iad thall, chaidh esan a shealgaireachd mar
a b'àbhaist da. Chaidh e do'n bhaile-mhór, agus cheannaich e
trì deiseachan mnatha leis an trì cheud punnd Sasannach. An
uair a thànaig e, thuirt an caibhtinn ris, 'Dé cheannaich thu?'
'Cheannaich mi trì deiseachan mnatha,' ars esan. 'Bheir mi
dhuit ceud gu leth punnd Sasannach an t-aon orra, ma gheibh
mi iad,' ars an sgiobair. 'Chan fhaigh—chan fhaigh neach iad,
ach an neach do'n do cheannaich mi iad.'

An uair a bha an luchd aca air bòrd, sheòl iad air an ais gu
ruige Sasainn. An uair a rànaig iad, có thànaig a nuas air bòrd
air an luing ach am fear leis am bu leis i. Bha e bruidhinn ris a'
chaibhtinn mu'n t-seòladair. Thuirt an caibhtinn nach fhaca
e [a] leithid de ghille riamh. 'Cheannaich e,' ars an caibhtinn,
'trì deiseachan mnatha leis an trì cheud punnd Sasannach,
agus bha mise a' tairgse ceud gu leth an t-aon da orra, is cha
tugadh e dhomh iad. Thuirt e nach fhaigheadh neach iad,
ach an t-aon do'n [2] do cheannaich e iad.' 'Is ann as fheàrr
dhomh feuchainn ris,' arsa fear an t-soithich, 'feuch an creic e
rium fhìn iad.' 'Faodaidh sibh a fheuchainn, ach tha mi làn
chinnteach nach creic,' ars an caibhtinn. 'C'à'm bheil e?'

---

[1] MS. *taire*.   [2] MS. *air son an.*

I needed be given me—and he paid for everything. He and I have got married. He is a sailor on a certain ship and he has to sail straight away.' 'It appears,' said her father, 'that it wasn't everywhere that such a young man was to be found !'

The father returned home, and wrote a letter to the captain of the ship and sent it to him, and sent something with it. The captain received the letter, and in the letter he was requested not to ask the youth to do any work on board ; and along with the letter was a sum of three hundred pounds sterling for the boy himself. The captain told him that [there were] three hundred pounds sterling there for him from the ship's owner and leave to remain idle on board ship. 'I shall not do that,' said the young man. 'I will take the money, but to remain idle that I will not do.' 'As you wish,' said the captain, and the youth got the three hundred pounds.

When they arrived overseas, he went hunting as was his custom. He went to the city and bought three ladies' dresses with the three hundred pounds. When he returned, the captain asked him, 'What did you buy ?' 'I bought three ladies' dresses,' he replied. 'I'll give you a hundred and fifty pounds each for them if I may have them,' said the captain. 'You shall not have them—no one shall have them but the one I bought them for.'

After getting the cargo on board, they sailed back to England. When they arrived, who came on board the ship but the owner, and he began to talk to the captain about the sailor. The captain said that he had never met a lad like him. 'He bought three ladies' dresses with the three hundred pounds,' said the captain, and 'although I offered him a hundred and fifty pounds each for them, he wouldn't give them to me. He said no one should have them but the one he bought them for.' 'Then I had better have a try at him,' said the owner, 'and see if he will sell them to me.' 'You may try him, but I am perfectly certain he won't sell,' replied the captain. 'Where is he ?' asked the owner. 'There he is, down there,' said the captain. The owner arsa fear an t-soithich. 'Siod e shìos,' ars an caibhtinn. Chaidh e far an robh e. 'Tha trì deiseachan briagha mnatha agad ?' arsa fear na luinge. 'Tha,' ars an seòladair. 'Bheir mi dhuit dà cheud an t-aon orra,' arsa fear na luinge. 'Ged a bheireadh sibh dà cheud an t-aon orra, chan fhaigh sibh iad,' ars an seòladair. 'Is ann as fheàrr dhuit dol a ghabhail sràid tacan [còmhla] rium fhìn,' arsa fear na luinge.

Chaidh iad air tìr, agus ghabh iad sràid a suas. An uair a rànaig iad an taigh-òsda, leum an seòladair a staigh, agus dh'fhaighnich e an robh am boireannach a dh'fhàg esan an siod ann. Thuirt iad ris nach robh. Goirid 'na dhéidh seo, thànaig ise is a màthair. An uair a chunnaig a màthair esan, cha bu mhotha an tlachd a bha aig a mhnaoi dheth na bha aice fhìn. Rinneadh banais an seo do'n t-seòladair agus do nighean fear na luinge, is bha aighear is toil-inntinn mhór aca. Thuirt a athair-céile ris-san, gum faodadh e falbh a nis 'na mhaighstir air an luing e fhìn. Thuirt esan nach falbhadh—gum b'olc an airidh a toirt o'n fhear aig an robh i, ach gum falbhadh e 'na mhaighstir air an luchd. Dh'fhalbh e 'na mhaighstir air an luchd leis an sgiobair, agus is e trì turuis a thug e air falbh, is dh'fhan e aig an taigh tuilleadh as a dhéidh sin, is bha na leòr aige, is bha e fhìn is a bhean gu sona toilichte còmhla.

NOTES

Vol. x., No. 104. The scribe was Hector MacLean.

At the beginning of the MS. Campbell has written—'The Sailor's Son, which I heard repeated by Patrick Smith almost in the very words in which it is written.—It is without any supernatural occurrences. A sailor finds a sick woman in a wood whom he rescues and marries and he becomes a rich man. It is well told and I know nothing quite like it.' The incident of Campbell's hearing Patrick Smith recite the story probably took place a little while after the story had been written down. See MS. vol. xiii., No. 339.

went over to him. 'You have three fine ladies' dresses,' said the owner. 'Yes, I have,' said the sailor. 'I'll give you two hundred pounds each for them,' said the owner. 'Even if you gave two hundred pounds each for them, you should not have them,' said the sailor. 'Well, then, you had better come and walk with me for a while,' said the owner of the ship.

They went ashore and took a walk inland. When they reached the inn, the sailor rushed inside and asked if the woman he had left with them was still there. They told him that she was not. But very soon she and her mother appeared, and when her mother saw the sailor she was no less delighted with him than his wife was. Then a wedding was made for the sailor and the shipowner's daughter, and there was much gaiety and happiness. His father-in-law said he might now sail as ship's master himself, but he refused and said it would be an ill turn to take her from the man who had her, but that he would sail as supercargo. So he went as supercargo with the captain. Three voyages he made in all : after that he stayed at home for good. He had wealth enough, and he and his wife were happy and contented together.

At the end of the MS. Campbell has written—'Mac an t'Seòladair. From Patrick Smith, South Boisdale, South Uist, August or July 1859.— Hector MacLean, smith, heard it often recited by Neill MacDonald, South Boisdale, Angus Smith, ditto, and numerous others.'

The three ladies' dresses occur in No. 73.

Domestic folk-tales, and tales without supernatural occurrences, are rare in the Highlands.

AM MARSANDA A CHUIR AN T-SŪIL
A MAC AN DUINE EILE

No. 56.   [*MS. Vol. x., No. 105*]

BHA Marsanda mór beairteach ann, agus chaidh e do bhaile,
agus dùil aige ri soithichean a bha aige air muir. Chaidh e a
staigh do bhad coille, agus bha e spioladh chnothan.[1] Cha
robh e fada spioladh nan cnò, an uair a thànaig fear far an robh
e, 's a thuirt e ris, 'Tha mi dol 'gad chur gu bàs.' 'Car son?'
ars esan. 'Chuir thu an t-sùil as mo mhac,' ars an t-Òlach seo.[2]
'Dé mar a chuir mise an t-sùil as?' ars am Marsanda. 'Bhuail
thu plaosg cnotha air mo mhac 'san t-sùil,' ars am fear seo.
'Ma bhuail, is ann gun fhios domh,' ars am Marsanda. 'Biodh
sin is a roghainn da,' ars an t-Òlach seo, 'cuiridh mise gu bàs
thu.' 'Is olc an gnothach sin,' ars am Marsanda. 'Siod mar
bhitheas,' ars esan. 'Tha móran ainbhfhiach orm, agus tha
móran ainbhfhiach a mach agam, agus chan urrainn domh aona
chuid mo chuid fhìn a thogail, no na tha orm a phàidheadh
ann an deifir ; ach ma gheibh mi dàil gus an dèan mi sin, bheir
mi dhuit-sa gealladh do choinneachadh ann an seo, am sam
bith a chì thu iomchuidh, an déidh dhomh cùisean a shocrachadh,'
ars am Marsanda. 'Bheir mi dàil bliadhna dhuit, agus cuimh-
nich gun coinnich thu mise air a' chnoc seo thall ann an ceann
bliadhna,' ars am fear eile.

Chaidh am Marsanda dachaigh gu trom-inntinneach, dubh-
bhrònach, agus dh'innis e d'a theaghlach mar a bha chùis.
Bha e pàidheadh gach ainbhfhiach a bha air, agus a' cruinneachadh gach ainbhfhiach a bha aige a mach, agus is ann mar
sin a bha gus an tànaig ceann na bliadhna. An uair a thànaig
ceann na bliadhna, tha sibh a' faicinn, b'éiginn da dol a choinneachadh an fhir a bha dol 'ga chur gu bàs. Dh'fhalbh e, agus
rànaig e an t-àite, agus shuidh e air a' chnoc a' feitheamh an
fhir eile. Cha robh e fad a' feitheamh an uair a thànaig an

---

[1] *spioladh* = breaking the husks to get at kernel.
[2] *Òlach*, a champion, a giant. The word has several other meanings, but in
these tales it is used of some weird, mysterious, supernatural character. In this tale,

THE MERCHANT WHO PUT OUT THE EYE
OF THE OTHER MAN'S SON

No. 56.   *[MS. Vol. x., No. 105]*

THERE was once a great, wealthy merchant who had gone to
a town because he was expecting ships that he had at sea. He
entered a copse and began to shell nuts. He had not been
shelling the nuts for long when a man approached him and said to
him, 'I am going to put you to death.' 'Why?' said he. 'Because
you have put out my son's eye,' replied the ogre.[2] 'How did I
put his eye out?' asked the merchant. 'You hit my son in the
eye with a nutshell,' said the other. 'If I did, it was unwittingly,'
said the merchant. 'Be that as it may,' answered this ogre, 'I
shall put you to death.' 'That is a dreadful thing to do,' said
the merchant. 'That is what will happen,' replied the ogre. 'But
I owe much money, and I have also much money out on loan,'
said the merchant, 'and I can neither collect my own goods
nor pay up what I owe in a hurry ; but if I may have some respite
until I have done so, I will promise to meet you here after I have
settled my affairs, at any time you see fit.' 'I will give you a
year's respite,' said the ogre, 'but remember to meet me on
yonder hill at the end of a year.'

The merchant went home heavy-hearted and very dejected, and
told his family how things stood. He began paying all the debts
he owed, and collecting all the monies he had out on loan, and
so things went on until the end of the year came. When the
end of the year came, you see, he was obliged to go and meet
the one who was going to put him to death. He set out, and
having arrived at the place, sat down on the hill to await the
other. He had not been waiting long when the ogre came.
'It's you,' said the ogre to the merchant. 'Yes,' said the merchant.

it seems to be a substitute for the jinnee of the *Arabian Nights*. But in MS. vol. xiii.,
Islay says that 'the Genii [*sic*] was Faich [= Fathach, a giant],' which implies that
when Patrick Smith recited the story to Islay, he used the word *fathach* not *òlach*.

t-Òlach. 'Tha thu ann,' ars an t-Òlach seo ris a' Mharsanda.
'Tha,' ars am Marsanda. 'Chum thu do ghealladh,' ars esan
ris a' Mharsanda. 'Chum,' ars am Marsanda. 'Cha b'fhuilear
dhuit,' ars esan.

Is ann mar seo a bha, is cha robh tuilleadh ri bhith ann ach
am Marsanda a chur gu bàs. Anns an am 'san robh an t-Òlach
uamhasach a' dol a chur a' Mharsanda gu bàs, gu dé chunnaig
iad a' dol seachad ach fear agus dà chù as a dhéidh ; agus tha
sibh a' faicinn, an uair a chunnaig e iad, ghabh e suas gus a'
chnoc far an robh iad. 'Gu dé an rud a tha sibh a' dèanamh an
seo ?' ars am fear a bha an dà chù as a dhéidh ris a' Mharsanda
agus ris an fhear eile. Dh'innis iad sin da. 'Nach olc an rud a
tha thu dol a dhèanamh ?' ars am fear a bha an dà chù as a
dhéidh ris an fhear a bha dol a mharbhadh a' Mharsanda.
'Bidh an treas cuid d'a anam maithte, ma dh'ìnnseas tu sgeul
gun fhacal bréige innte,' thuirt am fear a bha dol a mharbhadh
a' Mharsanda ris an fhear a bha an dà chù as a dhéidh. 'Is mi
nì sin,' arsa fear an dà choin.

'Bu mhac marsanda mise, agus bha dithis bhràithrean agam.
Dh'fhàg m'athair as a dhéidh sia ceud punnd Sasannach.
Dh'fhaighnich mo bhràithrean dhìom fhìn gu dé dhèanamaid—
is mise bu shine. Is e 'n rud a bh' ann, gun do chuir iad-san
rompa gum falbhadh iad feuch dé 'm fortan a thigeadh orra ;
agus an ceann là is bliadhna, bha sinn r'a chéile [choinneachadh]
aig taigh-seinnse a bha 'san àite. Is ann mar sin a bha. An
ceann là is bliadhna, chaidh mise do'n taigh-sheinnse, is cha
robh gin de mo bhràithrean romham. Eadar sin is beul na
h-oidhche, chunnaig mi mo bhràithrean a' tighinn. Rinn mi
toileachas-inntinn mór an uair a chunnaig mi tighinn iad.
Dh'òrdaich mi suipear a chur air dòigh. Thànaig iad, is bha
sinn ro thoilichte a chéile choinneachadh. Ghabh sinn ar
suipear, is an déidh ar suipear a ghabhail, shuidh sinn ag òl
fad na h-oidhche. Anns a' mhaduinn, an uair a dh'iarr mi
sealltainn dé bha aca, cha robh aca na phàidheadh an suipear.
Bha sia ceud agam-sa. Dh'fhalbh mi an seo, agus thug mi dà
cheud am fear dhaibh, agus gheall sinn d'a chéile gu'n coinn-
icheamaid a chéile 'sa' cheart àite an ath-bhliadhna.

'An ath-bhliadhna, choinnich sinn a chéile anns an àite
cheudna, is bha iad-san cho falamh is a bha iad roimhid.

'You have kept your promise,' said he to the merchant. 'Yes,' said the merchant. 'It's as well for you,' said he.

Thus it was, and without more ado he was going to put the merchant to death. But just when this terrible ogre was going to kill the merchant, what did they see going past but a man with two dogs following him ; and, you see, when he observed them he came to the hill where they were. 'What are you doing here ?' enquired the man with the two dogs of the merchant and the other. They told him. 'What a wicked thing you are going to do !' said the man with the two dogs to the one who was about to kill the merchant. 'A third part of his life shall be redeemed if you will tell a story without an untrue word in it,' said he who was going to kill the merchant to the man with the two dogs. 'Yes ; I'll certainly do that,' said the man with the two dogs.

'I was a merchant's son, and I had two brothers. My father left behind him six hundred pounds sterling. I was the eldest, and so my brothers asked me what we should do. The upshot was that they resolved to travel and see what fortune might come their way ; and at the end of a year and a day we were [to meet] each other again at an inn in the place. So things stood. At the end of a year and a day I went to the inn, but neither of my brothers was there before me. Between then and evening I saw my brothers approaching, and I was greatly delighted when I saw them coming, and I ordered supper to be prepared. They arrived, and very glad we were to meet again. We had supper, and after taking our supper we sat drinking all night long. In the morning, when I desired to see how much they had, they had not as much as would pay for their supper. Now I had six hundred pounds. And so I went and gave them two hundred each, and we promised to meet each other at the same place the next year.

' The next year accordingly we met each other at the same place, but they were as empty-handed as they had been before.

Chunnaig mi nach robh mo bhràithrean glic gu leòr air son feum a dhèanamh mar siod. Dh'iarr mi orra ceàird ionnsachadh air an dèanadh iad am beòshlainte. Thuirt iad gun dèanadh iad seo. Chaidh fear a dh'ionnsachadh a bhith 'na shaor, agus fear eile a dh'ionnsachadh a bhith 'na ghobha, agus bha ceangal trì bliadhna orra. Chaidh mi fhìn air falbh le màileid, agus bha mi air falbh mar seo fad trì bliadhna. Ann an ceann trì bliadhna thànaig mi, agus bha iad-san ullamh, ionnsaichte, an uair sin. Dh'fhaighnich mo bhràithrean dìom an uair a thànaig mi dé dhèanadh iad an sin, o'n a bha ceàird ionnsaichte aca. "Am fear a tha 'na shaor, gheibh e saoir, agus am fear a tha 'na ghobha, gheibh e goibhnean, agus bheir mise cuideachadh dhuibh [gu soitheach a thogail]," arsa mise. Dh'fhalbh mise gu marsandachd, agus thòisich iad-san air togail an t-soithich. An uair a thill mise, bha an soitheach ullamh. Dh'fhaighnich mo bhràithrean dìom dé dhèanamaid ris an luing a nis, gun robh i ullamh. Dh'iarr mi orra a leithid de luchd a chur innte. Luchdaich sinn i. An uair a bha i luchdaichte, sheòl sinn do na h-Ìnnsean.

'An uair a rànaig sinn na h-Ìnnsean, ghabh mi air tìr feuch dé chithinn. Chunnaig mi taigh brèagha romham, is air Moire fhìn, ghabh mi a staigh. Choinnich caile ruadh mi aig an dorus, is chuir i a staigh mi. Chuir i biadh mu m' choinnimh, agus tha sibh a' faicinn, ghabh mi am biadh. Shuidh mi treis a' seanchas rithe. An uair a bha mi treis a' seanchas rithe, thuirt mi gum falbhainn. Thuirt ise, "Chan. fhalbh ; fan gu[s an] déidh am suipearach." Is ann mar sin a bha ; dh'fhan mise. An déidh am suipearach, thug mi làmh air falbh, is thuirt i rium, "Is fhearra dhuit fantail an nochd," is tha sibh a' faicinn, o'n bha e anmoch, dh'fhan mi. Rinneadh leabaidh deas dhomh, is chaidh mi a laighe, is chaidil mi.

'An uair a bha mi treis 'nam chadal, dh'fhairich mi duine air mo chùl. Cha do charaich mi fad na h-oidhche. An uair a chunnaig e an latha tighinn, cha do dh'fharraid e nì sam bith, is dh'fhalbh e uam. Lean mi sìos e, is dé a bh'ann [ach] boireann-ach breagha.[1] "Seadh, dé mar a dh'éirich dhuit ?" ars ise.

---

[1] This passage originally stood, 'Lean mi sias e, 's *chunnaic mi e 'tionndadh 'na bhoireannach briagha*,' the words in italics having been afterwards run through, and the words '*s de 'bh'ann* being substituted on the other side of the MS. The

I saw that my brothers were not wise enough to be of any use in that way. I told them to learn a trade at which they might make a living, and they said they would. One of them went to learn carpentry, and the other to learn to be a blacksmith, and they were apprenticed for three years. For my part I went off with a pack, and I was travelling about in that way for three years. In three years' time I came back, and they were then trained and finished craftsmen. My brothers asked me when I came what they should do now, seeing that they had learned their trades. "Let the one who is a carpenter get other carpenters, and let the one who is a blacksmith get other blacksmiths, and I will give you help [to build a ship,]" said I. I went back to my business as a merchant, and they began to build the ship. When I returned, the ship was ready. My brothers asked me what we were to do with the ship now that she was ready. I told them to put such and such a cargo in her. We loaded her, and when she was loaded we sailed to the Indies.

'When we arrived at the Indies, I went ashore to find out what I could see. I saw a beautiful house in front of me, and by Mary herself, I went inside. I met a red-haired girl at the door, and she invited me in. She set food before me, so you see, I took the food. I sat talking to her for a while. When I had been talking to her for a while, I said I would go. "No ; you must not go," said she ; "stay till after supper-time." And so it happened ; I stayed. After supper, I made to go, but she said to me, "You had better stay tonight," and as it was late, you see, I stayed. A bed was made ready for me, and I went to bed and slept.

'When I had been asleep for a while, I [awoke and] noticed that there was some one else behind me in the bed. I never moved the whole night. When the other observed that day was coming, he asked no question, but went away and left me. I followed him down the stairs, and who was it but a beautiful

original sentence meant 'I followed him down the stairs, and *saw him turning into a beautiful woman.*' See *Waifs and Strays*, ii., pp. 310, 480.

"Dh'éirich gu math," arsa mise. Thill mi suas, is chaidil mi. An uair a dhùisg mi, bha mo bhiadh deas. Dh'fhuirich mi an latha sin. Bha mi air son falbh 'san fheasgar. "Fan an nochd," ars a' chaile ruadh. Dh'fhan mi an oidhche sin, is chaidh mi a laighe. Is ann mar sin a bha. Mun robh mi fada 'nam laighe, thànaig a' cheart bhoireannach agus laigh i còmhla rium. Cha do charaich mi an oidhche seo na's motha na a' cheud oidhche. An uair a bha an latha tighinn, dh'fhairich mi i falbh uam. Moire fhìn, lean mi i. "Seadh, dé mar a dh'éirich dhuit ?" ars ise. "Dh'éirich gu math," arsa mise. Thill mi agus chaidh mi a laighe, is chaidil mi. An uair a dhùisg mi, dh'éirich mi. Dh'fhan mi an latha sin. An uair a thànaig am feasgar, bha mi air son falbh. "Fan an nochd," ars an nighean ruadh. Dh'fhan mi. Chàirich i an leabaidh cheudna dhomh, is chaidh mi a laighe. An uair a chaidil mi treis, dh'fhairich mi neach a' tighinn a laighe còmhla rium. Cha do charaich mi fad na h-oidhche. An uair a bha an latha tighinn, dh'fhairich mi ise a' falbh uam. Dh'éirich mi agus lean mi i. "Seadh, dé mar a dh'éirich dhuit a raoir ?" ars ise. "Dh'éirich gu math," arsa mise. "Tha mise nis cuibhte de na geasan," ars ise. Chaidh mi a laighe mar a bha mi roimhe.

'An uair a dh'éirich mi, chaidh mi sìos. Bha boireannach brèagha, tlachdmhor, romham an sin. Chuir i am biadh air dòigh, agus shuidh i liom. "Is boireannach mise a bha fo gheasan agus fo dhraoidheachd, is tha mi nis air m'fhuasgladh uapa.[1] Tha sràid thaighean agam ann an Sasainn. Ma phòsas tusa mi, cha bhi a dh'fhear dìolain no pòsda am feasd agam ach thu, is théid mi leat do Shasainn." "Pòsaidh," arsa mise. "Bidh mi falbh còmhla riut, ma tà," ars ise. Dh'fhalbh mise chun na luinge, is chaidh ise liom, is tha sibh a' faicinn, ghabh sinn air bòrd. Is ann mar sin a bha, is an uair a bha an luchd air bòrd, sheòl sinn dachaigh [agus mo bhràithrean còmhla ruinn].

'Dh'amais eilean oirnn air an t-slighe, is thuirt ise rium fhìn, am bithinn deònach dol air tìr air an eilean a shealgaireachd. Thuirt mise gum bitheadh. Chaidh mi air tìr, agus ghabh mi mun cuairt air cnoc, agus air Moire fhìn, an uair a sheall mi uam, bha an long air falbh, is dh'fhàg iad mise air an eilean.

---

[1] Similar motif in *W. H. Tales*, i., No. 10, Vars. 1 and 2.

woman. "How did you fare [last night]?" asked she. "I
fared well," said I. I returned upstairs, and slept. When I
awoke, there was my food, ready. I stayed there that day. In
the evening, I was for going. "Stay tonight," said the red-haired
girl. So I stayed that night, and went to bed. That is how it was.
I had not been long in bed when the same woman came and lay
down along with me. I did not move this night any more than
I did on the first night. When the day was drawing near, I
became aware that she was leaving me. By Mary herself, I
followed her. "Well, how did you fare?" said she. "I fared
well," I answered. I returned and went to bed and slept.
When I awoke, I got up. I stayed there that day. When evening came, I was for going. "Stay tonight," said the red-haired
girl; so I stayed. She made up the same bed for me and I
went to bed. When I had slept for a while, I felt some one
coming into bed with me. All night long I did not move. When
day was coming, I noticed that she was leaving me. I arose and
followed her. "Well, how did you fare last night?" said she.
"I fared well," I replied. "I am now free from enchantment,"
said the woman. I went back to bed as before.

'When I arose, I went down. I found a beautiful, charming
woman there before me. She got food ready and sat there with
me. "I am a woman who was under the power of spells and
enchantment, but now I have been released from them," [1]
said she. "I have a street of houses in England. If you will
marry me, I will never have lover or husband but you, and I will
go to England with you." "Yes, I will marry you," I answered.
"Then I will go with you," said she. I went off to the ship and
she went with me, and so you see, we went on board. That is
what happened, and so when the cargo was on board, we sailed
home, [my brothers being with us].

'On the way we chanced to come to an island, and she asked
me if I would like to go ashore in the island and hunt. I replied
that I would. I went ashore, and went round a hill, but by
Mary herself, when I looked around the ship had gone, leaving
me there on the island. That was what happened; there was

Is ann mar sin a bha ; cha robh agam ach fuireachd ann an siod ; is sheòl iad-san dhachaigh do Shasainn. Is e mo bhràithrean a rinn seo orm, is dùil aca gum biodh a h-uile rud aca fhìn. An uair a rànaig iad Sasainn, rug ise air mo bhràithrean, agus spàrr i ann am prìosan iad. Thill i an long air falbh dha'm iarraidh-sa. Chunnaig mise an long a' tighinn, is tha sibh a' faicinn, bha mi glé thoilichte. Chaidh mi air bòrd air an luing, agus rànaig mi Sasainn.

'An déidh dhomh ruigheachd, phòs mi fhìn agus am boireannach. Bha sinn latha a' gabhail sràide, is thachair dhuinn dol seachad air a' phrìosan. A' dol seachad air a' phrìosan, có chunnaig mi a staigh an sin ach mo dhà bhràthair. Ghabh mi duilichinn an uair a chunnaig mi an siod iad. "Is oil leat do dhithis bhràithrean a bhith anns a' phrìosan." "Seadh," arsa mise. "Is math a thoill iad e," ars ise. "Nam biodh tu cho math 's an leigeil a mach," arsa mise. "Bithidh," ars ise. Chaidh i far an robh mo bhràithrean, is tharraing i slat a h-uchd, is bhuail i orra i, is rinn i dà chù dhiubh, agus siod iad a' falbh as mo dhéidh.'

'Shàbhail thu an treas cuid d'a anam,' ars am fear a bha dol a mharbhadh a' mharsanda, 'ach coma leat, cuiridh mi gu bàs e.' 'Nach co math dhuit a leigeil beò,' thuirt am fear a dh'innis an sgeul. Anns an am seo, chunnaig iad fear eile dol seachad, agus cù as a dhéidh. Ghabh e far an robh iad. Dh'fhaighnich e dhiubh gu dé bha iad a' dèanamh an siod. Dh'innis iad sin da. 'Ma dh'ìnnseas tu sgeul gun fhacal bréige innte, sàbhailidh tu an treas cuid d'a anam,' ars am fear a bha dol a mharbhadh a' mharsanda. 'Nì mi sin,' ars am fear a thànaig.

'Bha mise mi fhìn ann am mhac marsanda. Thug m'athair dhomh ochd ceud punnd Sasannach air son rud a dhèanamh dhomh fhìn. Cheannaich mi bathar, agus rinn mi feum leis an airgead. Cha robh duine cloinne ann ach mi fhìn. Ann an ceann trì bliadhna as a dhéidh seo, dh'iarr m'athair orm pòsadh. Bha boireannach a dhìth oirnn, agus cha robh e faicinn gin a bu fhreagarraich' orm [na nighean coimhearsnaich]. Thug e a staigh i, is bhruidhinn e rithe. An uair a chunnaig mise i, bha mi toileach gu leòr am boireannach a phòsadh. Thog e taigh dhuinn, is an uair a bha an taigh iomchuidh, phòs mi i.

nothing for me to do but stay there, while they sailed home to England. It was my brothers who played this trick on me, thinking that everything would now be theirs. But when they got to England, the woman seized my brothers and thrust them into prison. She made the ship go back to fetch me. I saw the ship returning, and you see, I was delighted. I went on board, and arrived in England.

'When I got there, the woman and I married. One day we were taking a walk, and we happened to pass the prison. When going past the prison, whom did I see inside but my two brothers. I was very sorry when I saw them there. "It grieves you that your two brothers should be in prison." "Yes, it does," said I. "They well deserved it," she replied. "Would you be so kind as to let them out?" I asked. "Yes," she said. She went over where my brothers were, drew a wand from her bosom, struck them with it and made two dogs of them, and there they are following me.'

'You have saved a third part of his life,' said he who was going to kill the merchant, 'but never mind, I shall put him to death.' 'Would it not be as well for you to let him live?' asked the man who had told the story. At this moment, they saw another man going past, and a dog following him. He came up to them and asked them what they were doing there, and they told him. 'If you will tell a tale without an untrue word in it, you shall save a third part of his life,' said he who was going to kill the merchant. 'I will do so then,' said the newcomer.

'I was a merchant's son myself. My father gave me eight hundred pounds sterling that I might make something for myself. I purchased merchandise and made good use of the money. There were no other children except myself. After this, at the end of three years, my father asked me to marry. We were looking for a wife, and he could see none more suitable for me than [a neighbour's daughter]. He brought her into the house and spoke to her. When I saw her, I was quite willing to marry the woman. He built a house for us, and when the house was ready, I married her.

'Beagan ùine an déidh dhuinn pòsadh, chaidh mi do'n bhàthaich, agus chunnaig mi bó mhaol dhonn, agus damh maol dubh an sin. Bha iongantas orm diùbh. Thuirt mi ris a' mhnaoi gum bithinn 'na comain nan ìnnseadh i dhomh gu dé na beathaichean a bha 'n siod. "Ma tà, mionnaich thusa dhòmh-sa nach innis thu gu bràth gu dé a' bhó mhaol dhonn no gu dé an damh maol dubh a tha an sin, agus ìnnsidh mi dhuit sin." Mhionnaich mi siod, agus dh'innis i dhomh e. "Tha an [sin]," ars ise, "bean-dìolain agus mac dìolain duine-uasail."

'Bha féill gu bhith anns an teaghlach. "Falbh," ars ise ris a' bhuachaille, "agus thoir dhachaigh a' bhó mhaol dhonn, agus gum marbhte i air son na féille." Thugadh dhachaigh a' bhó mhaol dhonn, agus mharbhadh i. Dh'iarr i an damh maol dubh a thoirt dachaigh, is gum marbhte e. Thug iad dachaigh an damh maol dubh. Cheangail iad a chasan gus an fhuil a leigeil as. Có thànaig dachaigh 'san am ach mi fhìn. Chuala mi mar a bha, is chaidh mi mach do'n bhàthaich. Chunnaig mi an damh maol dubh ceangailte. "Thug mi mionnan duit nach ìnnsinn gu bràth gu dé bh'anns na beathaichean, ach a nis, o'n mharbh thu a' bhó, faodaidh mi ìnnseadh mar a thogras mi. Bu bhean-dìolain duine-uasail a bha anns a' bhó, agus is e a mhac an damh maol dubh," arsa mise. Thug mi orra fhuasgladh. Is ann mar sin a bha. Cha robh cothrom air.

'Chaidh mi far an robh seann duine bha 'san àite. Dh'innis mi dha mar a dh'éirich dhomh. "Siod an rud a nì thu," ars esan, "cumaidh tu trì oidhchean 'na dùisg i,[1] is air a' cheathramh oidhche, leigidh tu cadal di, is an uair a chaidleas i, gheibh thu an iuchair, is fosglaidh tu a' bhàthach, agus gheibh thu ciste luaidhe innte ; fosglaidh tu a' chiste luaidhe, agus gheibh thu trì slatan innte, agus bheir thu leat na slatan, agus an uair a dhùisgeas i, buailidh tu an t-slat [2] oirre 'san aodann, agus creutair sam bith air an smuainich thu an sin, bidh ise air a tionndadh ann." Is ann mar sin a bha.

'Chum mi 'na dùisg trì oidhchean i, is air a' cheathramh oidhche leig mi cadal di. An uair a chaidil i, fhuair mi iuchair na bàthaich, is dh'fhosgail mi i, is fhuair mi ciste luaidhe 'na

---

[1] Similar stratagem in *Larminie*, p. 16.

[2] 'wand' : the singular is used here. Three other wands of witchcraft occur later

'A short time after we were married, I happened to go to the byre, and I saw a brown polled cow and a black polled ox there. They caused me some surprise. I told my wife that I should be obliged to her if she would tell me what animals they were. "Well then, swear to me that you will never reveal what the brown polled cow is, or what the black polled ox is, and I will tell you." So I swore, and she told me. "Those," she said, "are the mistress and the illegitimate son of a gentleman."

'A festival was due in the household. "Go and bring home the brown polled cow, so that she may be killed for the festival," said she to the herdsman. The brown polled cow was fetched home accordingly and killed. Then she ordered the black polled ox to be brought home, so that he also might be killed. They brought the black polled ox home. They tied his feet in order to slaughter him. Who should come home at that moment but myself. I heard what was going on, and out I went to the byre. I saw the black polled ox bound. "I gave you my oath that I would never tell what those beasts were, but now, since you have killed the cow, I may tell what I please. The cow was the mistress of a gentleman, and the black polled ox is the son," said I. I made them loose him. So the matter stood: there was no help for it.

'I visited an old man who lived in the place, and I told him what had happened to me. "This is what you must do," said he, "you must keep her awake for three nights ; [1] and on the fourth night you shall let her go to sleep, and when she is asleep you shall get the key, open the byre, and there you will find a leaden chest ; open the leaden chest, and in it you will find three wands ; take them with you, and when she awakes, strike her in the face with the wand,[2] and whatever creature you think of at the moment, that shall she be turned into." So things were.

'So I kept her awake for three nights, and on the fourth I let her sleep. When she slept, I got the key of the byre and opened it and found a leaden chest inside. I opened the leaden

on in the story, and the use of each is described. Three wands of magic and mastery grow on one tree in a tale in *Larminie*, p. 18.

broinn.   Dh'fhosgail mi a' chiste luaidhe, tha sibh a' faicinn,
agus fhuair mi trì slatan innte.   Thug mi liom iad.   An uair
a dhùisg i, bhuail mi a h-aon de na slatan oirre 'san aodann,
agus có air a smuaintich mi ach air galla choin.   Bha i air
a dèanamh 'na galla choin a thiotamh ; agus seo i as mo
dhéidh.'   'Shàbhail thu an treas cuid d'a anam,' ars am fear a
bha dol a mharbhadh a' mharsanda, 'ach marbhaidh mise e.'
'Is fhearra dhuit a leigeil beò,' ars am fear a bha a' ghalla as a
dhéidh.

Aig a' cheart am seo, chunnaig iad fear a' tighinn, agus cù
as a dhéidh.   Thànaig e far an robh iad.   'Gu dé tha sibh a'
dèanamh an seo ?' ars esan.   Dh'innis iad sin da.   'Ma dh'ìnnseas
tu sgeul gun facal bréige innte, sàbhailidh tu an treas cuid d'a
anam,' ars am fear a bha dol a mharbhadh a' mharsanda.   'Nì
mi sin,' ars esan.   'Cha bu mhac marsanda mise ach mac iasgair,
is bha mi fhìn a' leantainn na ceàird a bha aig m'athair.   Bha
mi mach ag iasgach, agus lìon agam 'ga tharraing.   An am
togail an lìn, mhothaich mi cudthrom mór air, is cha b'urrainn
mi a thoirt a staigh do'n bhàta.   Cheangail mi ri deireadh a'
bhàta e.   Thug mi gu tràigh e, agus gu dé an rud a bh' ann
ach coire cupair agus bòrd air a cheann.   Thug mi am bòrd
bhàrr a' choire, agus thànaig smùid uaine agus ceò bàn as.   An
uair a bha an smùid treis a' falbh as, gu dé thànaig a mach fo'n
smùid ach fireannach mór.   "Tha mise a' dol 'gad chur gu bàs,"
ars esan rium fhìn.   "Car son ?" arsa mise.   "Chionn gun do
leig thu as a' choire mi," ars esan.   "Có thusa bha 'sa' choire ?"
arsa mise.   "Is mise an droch spiorad," ars esan.   "Dé chuir
'sa' choire thu ?" arsa mise.   "Feadhainn a chuir ann le caran
mi, is mhionnaich mise duine a leigeadh as mi a chur gu bàs,"
ars esan.   Chaidh e 'na smùid anns an iarmailt.   Dh'iarr mi
air dol air ais anns a' choire, is gum faicinn gu dé mar a bha e
'ga chumail.   Thill e air ais.   An uair a chunnaig mise deireadh
na smùid a' dol anns a' choire, ghléidh mi am bòrd air a cheann.
"Tha thu nis mar a bha thu roimhid," arsa mise.   "Leig as mi,
agus bheir mi thu gu h-àite am faigh thu iasg, agus falbh [1] cuide
rium," ars esan.   Leig mi as e, agus dh'fhalbh mi cuide ris, agus
rànaig sinn sloc dubh monaidh.   Dh' iarr e orm an t-slat a chur

---

[1] MS. *thalla*, and pronounced so in dialect.

chest, you see, and found three wands in it and I took them with me. When she awoke, I struck her in the face with one of the wands, and of what beast did I think but a bitch. Instantly she was turned into one ; and here she is, following me.' 'You have saved a third part of his life,' said he who was going to kill the merchant, 'but I am going to kill him.' 'You had better let him live,' said the man who had the bitch following him.

At this very moment, they saw a man coming, and a dog following him. He approached them. 'What are you doing here ?' he asked ; and they told him. 'If you will tell a tale without an untrue word in it, you shall save a third part of his life,' said the one who was going to kill the merchant. 'I will do that,' said he. 'I was no merchant's son but the son of a fisherman, and I followed my father's trade. One day, I was out fishing, and drawing a net. When I was hauling the net in, I noticed that it was very heavy, and I could not pull it into the boat. So I tied it to the boat's stern and I brought it ashore, and what was it but a copper cauldron with a lid on the top. I took the lid off the cauldron, and out came green vapour and white smoke. When the vapour had been coming out for a little, what emerged from beneath it but a huge man. "I am going to put you to death," said he to me. "Why ?" I asked. "Because you let me out of the cauldron," he replied. "And who are you who were in the cauldron ?" said I. "I am the evil spirit," he answered. "What put you into the cauldron ?" I asked. "Some people put me into it by trickery, and I swore that I would put to death any man who let me out," said he. He then became a cloud of vapour and floated up in the air. I asked him to go back into the cauldron so that I might see how it had been able to hold him. Back he went. When I saw the last of the vapour going into the cauldron, I clapped the lid on again. "Now you are just as you were before," said I. "Let me out, and I will take you to a place where you shall get fish, so come with me," said he. I let him out, and went off with him and we came to a black pit in the moor. He asked me to cast ; I did so,

a mach. Chuir mi a mach an t-slat, agus mharbh mi trì bric
bhriagh. "Chan fhaigh thu gin ach siod, agus gheibh thu siod
a h-uile latha," ars esan. Thug mi liom iad, agus rànaig mi am
baile.

'Cha robh duine ann a bheireadh airgead domh air son nan
trì breac. Rànaig mi taigh-seinnse, is fhuair mi airgead air an
son, is chuir iad na bric air teinidh. Bhuail mi air òl. An uair
a thànaig goil air na bric, có thànaig a staigh ach Bean a' Chaol-
chòt' Uaine.[1] "Tha sibh an sin, a ghràisg, agus mise 'gur
n-iarraidh," ars ise ris na bric. Leum na bric as a' choire 'na
sgùird, is a mach a bha i. Thànaig iad 'gam thòrachd fhìn a
thaobh mar a thachair, is ag iarraidh orm na dh'òl mi a
phàidheadh, air neò gun cuireadh iad do'n phrìosan mi. Thuirt
fear de na bha a staigh nach b'urrainn iad, is thuirt fear eile a
leithid eile. Is ann mar sin a bha. Thuirt mi riutha iad a chur
duine còmhla rium, 's gum faiceadh iad far an d'fhuair mi na
bric. Chuir iad duine còmhla rium, agus tha sibh a' faicinn,
fhuair mi trì bric eile. Thill mi leò do'n taigh-sheinnse, agus
chaidh mi do'n chidsin g'am faicinn air teinidh. An uair a
thànaig goil orra, thànaig Bean a' Chaol-chòt' Uaine, agus rinn
i air an turus seo mar a rinn i roimhid. Chaidh mi an treas
siubhal a dh'iasgach, agus fhuair mi trì bric eile is thill mi gus
an taigh-sheinnse. Air Moire fhìn, chuir fear an tigh-sheinnse
dusan glas air na dorsan, agus dhùin e a h-uile h-àite. Bha
fosgladh aig cloich nach do mhothaich e dha. Thànaig Bean
a' Chaol-chòt' Uaine a staigh air an toll. "Tha sibh an sin, a
ghràisg, agus mise 'gur n-iarraidh," ars ise ris na bric. Leum
na bric 'na h-uchd, agus siod a mach a bha i, agus siod a mach
mise as a déidh.

'An uair a bha mi chun a bhith còmhla rithe, chunnaig mi
caisteal mór dubh thall mu mo choinnimh. An siod an uair a
bha mi gu bhith aig a' chaisteal, chuala mi duine as mo dhéidh.
Thill mi, agus gu dé ach faicear duine [agus a cheann] ann an
ceap.[2] "O till ! na bi an déidh an droch bhoireannaich sin ;
cuiridh i gu bàs thu," ars esan. "Gu dé am boireannach a

---

[1] A name for the fairy woman in several Highland tales. See No. 22 (MS.
vol. x., No. 37).
[2] *Ceap*, see Notes.

and caught three fine trout. "Not another fish shall you catch but those, but you shall catch as many every day," said he. I took the fish with me, and went to a town.

'There was no one there who would give me money for the three trout. I arrived at an inn, and they gave me some money for the trout and put them on the fire. I began drinking. When the trout began to boil, who came in but the Dame of the Fine Green Kirtle.[1] "So that's where you are, you rabble, and I looking for you," said she to the trout. The trout leapt out of the cauldron into her lap, and off she went with them. As a result of what had happened, the people of the house came after me and demanded that I should pay for what I had drunk, or else that they would throw me into prison. One of the people who happened to be in the house said they could not put me into prison, and another said the same. So things were. I asked them to send some one with me that they might see where I had caught the trout. They sent some one with me accordingly, and so you see, I caught three more trout. I went back to the inn with them, and went to the kitchen to see them put on the fire. When they began to boil, the Dame of the Fine Green Kirtle came, and as she had done before, so she did on this occasion. For the third time I went to fish, caught three more trout, and returned to the inn. By Mary herself, the man of the inn put a dozen locks on the doors and closed up every chink. But there was a stone which could be moved to make an opening, and which he did not notice. The Dame of the Fine Green Kirtle came in through the gap. "There you are, you rabble, and I searching for you," said she to the trout. The trout leapt into her lap, and out she rushed, and out I rushed after her.

'When I had nearly caught up with her, I saw a great black castle in the distance before me. Then, when I had nearly reached the castle, I heard somebody coming after me. I turned back, and what should I see but a man [with his head] in a *ceap*.[2] "Oh, don't pursue that wicked woman, she will put you to death!" said he. "What woman is she?" said I.

th'ann ?" arsa mise. "Siod a' bhean agam-sa," ars esan. "Bu liom fhìn[......] fo'n chaisteal sin.[1] Bha mi fada gun phòsadh, is chomhairlich iad domh am boireannach sin a phòsadh, agus phòs mi i. Chan itheadh i biadh, ach le pluc prìne airgid. Bha i toirt deoch-chadail domh anns an oidhche, agus thuitinn ann am shuain. Oidhche bha'n sin, dhòirt mi an deoch taobh na leapach, agus leig mi orm gun robh mi am chadal. Dh'éirich i, agus dh'fhalbh i sìos gu h-uaimh a tha aig a' chladach. Bha ciuthach [2] a' fuireach anns an uaimh. Lean mi fhìn i. Bha i fhìn agus an ciuthach an sin is corp aca, is dh'ith iad an leòr dheth. Dh'fhalbh mi an siod dachaigh, is thànaig ise dachaigh as mo dhéidh. An uair a shuidh i aig a biadh 'sa' mhaduinn, chan itheadh i sgath ach le pluc prìne [3] airgid. Dh'innis mi dhi gu dé chunnaig mi i dèanamh. Chuir i draoidheachd [4] orm, agus dhùisg mi anns a' cheap an seo. Ma théid thu sìos do'n uaimh, na gabh sgath bìdh mur an innis i a h-uile dìomhaireachd dhuit."

'Rànaig mi an uaimh. Fhuair mi claidheamh meirgeach fo'n leabaidh. Mharbh mi an ciuthach, is shlaod mi sìos air ùrlar na h-uamha e. Thànaig ise. Thuirt i rium an gabhainn biadh. Thuirt mi nach gabhadh gus an ìnnseadh i a h-uile dìomhaireachd dhomh.[5] "Gu dé na trì slatan a tha an siod ?" arsa mise. "Tha an siod," ars ise, "trì slatan, agus nì a h-aon diubh carragh cloiche dhìot ; nì an té ud duine mar a bha e roimhid ; agus nì an té ud eile creutair sam bith air an smuainich thu de'n aon [6] air am buailear i." An uair a chuala mi seo, air Moire fhìn, rug mi air an t-slat, agus bhuail mi an clàr an aodainn i, agus rinn mi galla dhith. Thill mi far an robh am fear a bha 'sa' cheap, agus bhuail mi an t-slat eile air, agus bha e mar a bha e roimhid, agus sin agaibh Bean a' Chaol-chòt' Uaine as mo dhéidh 'na galla coin.' 'Shàbhail thu an treas cuid d'a anam, is tha e nis mu sgaoil,' thuirt am fear a chuireadh an t-sùil as a mhac. Fhuair am marsanda mu sgaoil, is tha

[1] Bo leom fhin fo'n chaisteal sin in MS. Some word or sentence has been omitted from MS.

[2] MS. 'ciuch [= ciuthach] a savage or wild kind of person residing in caves or wild places.' Note in MS. See Notes.

[3] MS. frìn. (frìne in Uist).

[4] MS. draochd.

"That is my wife," said he. "Mine was the . . . . [?] under that castle.[1]   I was for a long time unmarried, and people advised me to marry that woman, and I married her. She would eat no food, save what she ate with a silver pin's head. She used to give me a sleeping draught every night, and I used to fall sound asleep. However, one [night I spilt the drink by the bedside, and pretended to be asleep. Up she got, and went out to a cave down by the shore. In the cave lived a Savage.[2] I followed her. There they were, she and the Savage, and they had a corpse there, of which they ate their fill. Then I went off home, and she came home after me. In the morning when she sat down to take food, she would not eat a thing save what she ate with the head of a silver pin. I told her what I had seen her doing. So she bewitched me, and I awoke in this *ceap*. If you go down to the cave, do not take any food unless she tells you all her secrets."

'I went to the cave. I found a rusty sword under the bed. I killed the Savage and dragged him over the floor of the cave. Then she came. She asked if I would take any food. I said I would not take anything unless she told me all her secrets.[5] "What three wands are those ?" I asked. "Those three wands," said she, "are such that one of them will make a pillar of stone of you ; this other one will restore a man as he was before ; and this other one again will turn any one who is struck with it into any animal you think of." When I heard this, by Mary herself, I snatched up the wand, struck her right in the face with it, and turned her into a bitch. I then went back to the man in the *ceap*, struck him with the other wand, and he was restored and became what he had been before, and there following me you have the Dame of the Fine Green Kirtle turned into a bitch.' 'You have saved a third part of his life, and he is now free,' said the one whose son's eye had been put out. The merchant was

---

[5] The refusal by a guest to accept hospitality until the host has complied with his commands occurs in other tales. See p. 166. It was a sure method of bringing pressure upon the host, and of compelling him to do what otherwise he would never have done.

[6] MS. *de'n t-aon*.

mi cinnteach gun robh e glé thoilichte.   Thug e móran buidh-
eachais do'n fheadhainn a choisinn [bea]tha dha, is dhealaich e
riutha, is dhealaich iad-san ris.   Thill e dhachaigh, is bha a
bhean is a chlann glé thoilichte fhaicinn.

> From Patrick Smith, South Boisdale, South Uist, who heard it often
> recited by Neil Macdonald, also a tenant, who died about twelve
> years ago at an advanced age.   Heard it also often from Angus
> Smith, South Boisdale, and from numerous others.   It was
> common when reciter was young.

(Signed)   HECTOR MACLEAN.   July or August /59.

NOTES

MS. vol. x., No. 105.   Islay wrote the following on the flyleaf of this
tale—
   'The Merchant—I heard this also and it is almost word for word the
same except that the man [the Òlach] was called a Fa[tha]ch.   I think it is
clearly a résumé of several stories from the *Arabian Nights*, but the very
same incidents are woven into a Breton tale in Le Foyer Breton.—Smith
[the Reciter] speaks only Gaelic, he is 60 and cannot read, he told me he
had learned the story from old men like himself many years ago, but still it
may be the *Arabian Nights*.   See MacLean's letter about this date.
   R[eceive]d Dec. 22/[18]59 at Birmingham.'
   MacLean's letter, dated 17th December 1859, is bound up in MS. vol. xiv.
He says he found in the *Arabian Nights* numerous incidents very much the
same as some he had collected in the Highlands—that No. 105 is very much
the same, but that there are incidents in it not in the *Arabian Nights*—the
style of thought of language, he considered, were peculiarly Highland—that
it may have been modified by the Arabian tale, yet however close the
resemblance, No. 105 may be entirely original.—From MacLean's opinion
I differ totally, No. 105 being both in thought and language peculiarly unlike
the old Highland tales.—However, the following extract from Islay's Journal,
No. 334 of his English List (MS. vol. xiii.) refers to his meeting with Patrick
Smith, when he heard him recite Nos. 104, 105 :—
   'Called in on an old man who was famous for stories (Peter [= Patrick]
Smith).   Hector MacLean has been at him—he has written three.   The
first he repeated was clearly the *Arabian Nights*.   The Genie was Faich
[= *Fathach*, though MacLean has written *Òlach*, suggesting that Patrick
Smith's reciting varied slightly in detail]—another creature was Keogh
[= *Ciuthach*].   But the story was that of the merchant that throws nuts.
Three men come and save his life.   The one was the story of the Fisherman.
The other of the man whose wife and son were turned into a cow and calf.
The Man [Patrick Smith] can neither read nor write—he knows nothing but
Gaelic, and he says he learnt the story from another like himself some thirty-
five years ago in this Island.   I cannot understand how this got here, but

released, and I am certain he was very glad. He gave many
thanks to those who had saved his life for him, and he parted
from them, and they parted from him. He returned home,
and his wife and children were very pleased to see him.

there is no doubt it is the *Arabian Nights* [1] and nothing else. In this there
was none of the old language, it was narrative and dialogue. . . . He
[Patrick Smith] said he could recite very many stories. Those who were
there said [he could recite] five or six every winter's night, he could not tell
how many he knew, he said he could not remember [the names of] them all
or count them, but when he began, others came into his mind. I feel quite
sure that the stories of that man's mind would fill a large volume.' In *W. H.
Tales*, i., No. 7, Notes, Islay says he heard in 1859 Patrick Smith in South
Uist and other men recite stories in alternate prose and verse.

Ceap. See a very different tale in which the word *ceap* occurs, *W. H.
Tales*, iii. (1862), p. 21 :—

'6. Ceap may have been substituted for *Currachd*, a cap, which was the
old Gaelic name for all head-dresses, male or female.—H. M'L[ean].'
Campbell comments on this as follows—

'I have no doubt that the man who told the story meant a cap, and I
have so translated the word, but the Gaelic word means a trap or gin, and
many things besides. [It also means the punishment called the stocks.]
An old man who told me a story [No. 105] exceedingly like 'The Fisherman'
in the *Arabian Nights*, introduced the character who resembled the young
King of the Black Isles, not as a man half marble, but as a man with his head
in a *ceap*, and on being interrogated, explained that this was a kind of head-
dress used for punishment or torture, in which the head of the victim was
fastened. Such head-dresses, made of rusty iron, may be seen in museums,
and *ceap* may have meant something like a helmet, whose machinery bears
some resemblance to a rat-trap.' [2]

[1] [*The Merchant and the Jinnee + The Fisherman.*—H. J. R.] [These *Arabian Nights*
tales would have become known in the Highlands in a chapbook version ; the
present tale is too close to the *Arabian Nights*, and too little assimilated to the Gaelic
story-telling tradition, to have had a long history as an oral folk-tale in the Highlands.
—K. H. J.]

[2] [The *ceap* in the present tale is apparently a portable pillory or cangue.—
K. H. J.]

Ciuthach. The incidents concerning the ghoul also occur in No. 21 (MS. vol. x., No. 35), where the monster is called a *cù rùta*, a dog for herding rams. In No. 105, the ghoul is called by a native word, *ciuthach.* But it is contrary to the natural history of a *ciuthach* to dig up corpses and eat them. The explanation of the use of the word *ciuthach* probably is, that the character of *ghoul* being unknown in Gaelic lore, reciters substituted for it whatever native word they thought came nearest to it in meaning or sound, indifferent to or unconscious of the fact that they were casting unwarrantable aspersions on their own native supernaturals. The only justification they had for so treating the *ciuthach* was the belief, prevalent in the Long Island (or Outer Hebrides) that he and his kind were regarded as naked wild men dwelling in caves ; cf. *W. H. Tales,* iii., p. 55 or 65, footnote. But see Professor W. J. Watson's masterly monograph on the Ciuthach, *Celtic Review* (1914), ix., p. 193, and see also *ibid.,* p. 344, viii., p. 265 : and see David MacRitchie, *The Savages of Gaelic Tradition.* Professor Watson thinks that the *Ciuthach* was originally a hero, a hero of the Picts.

In making the Dame of the Fine Green Kirtle the confederate of the ghoul, the reciter did another injustice to one of his own supernaturals. For the Dame of the Fine Green Kirtle, is, in all the tales I remember, a friendly character, and above suspicion. See No. 22 (MS. vol. x., No. 37).

FIACHAIRE GOBHA

No. 57.

BHA Gualadair ann an Albainn uair, is thànaig Fiachaire Gobha far an robh e ; is dh'iarr e a mhac bliadhna air is gun tugadh e sgoil da ; agus thug e leis e, agus thug e bliadhna sgoil da, is an ceann bliadhna thill e air ais leis. Dh'iarr e bliadhna eile dheth, is fhuair e siod. Thug e leis e, is thug e bliadhna eile sgoil da, agus an ceann na bliadhna, thill e air ais leis. Dh'iarr e a rithist e, agus air an turus seo [cha] d' ainmich e ùine, is thug an Gualadair da e. Ruith a' bhliadhna, is cha do thill Fiachaire Gobha le a mhac chun a' Ghualadair.

Dé smuainich e, ach o nach do gheall e tighinn leis, nach tigeadh e am feasd leis. Ghabh e air falbh, is thug e an latha sin air falbh fad an latha. An am an fheasgair, rànaig e taigh boireannaich. Dh'innis e dhi dé bha dhìth air. Thuirt i ris gun robh loch dlùth, is gun robh a mhac air an taobh eile de'n loch, is gun robh boireannaich a null is a nall air an loch ann an riochd ealachan, is e a dh'fheuchainn am faigheadh e cochull a ghoid air té dhiubh. Rànaig e taobh an locha, is ghoid e leis a h-aon de na cochullan, is thug an cochull a null e. Choinnich a h-aon e, is dh'fheòraich e dheth c'àite an robh Fiachaire Gobha fuireachd. Leig am fear seo fhaicinn da an taigh. 'Nis, iarraidh e ort dol a staigh : tha e a staigh agus cnòcaid [1] dhearg mu a cheann,' ars am fear seo ris : 'tha do mhac 'sa' bheinn-sheilge, agus thig e 'na fhaoileann, agus dà fhaoileann deug as a dhéidh. An uair a thig iad, nì esan trì chalamain deug diubh, is bheir e a staigh iad, is bheir e leis clàrsach, is tòisichidh e air seinn, is tòisichidh na trì chalamain deug air dannsadh. Tha ite gheal ann am bun sgéith do mhic-sa. An uair a chì thu an calaman

---

[1] I have been told that a *cnòcaid* was a head-dress shaped like a nightcap, hanging down at the back, and finished with a tassel or knob, and that in former times, aged men wore these in the kirk, when feeling cold in the head.

FIACHAIRE THE SMITH

No. 57.   [*MS. Vol. x., No. 107*]

THERE was once a Collier in Scotland, and Fiachaire the Smith visited him and asked him to hand his son over to him for a year, saying that he would educate him [in magic]. He took him away, gave him a year's instruction, and at the end of the year returned with him. He asked to have him for another year, and was granted that. He took the boy away, gave him another year's instruction, and at the end of the year he brought him back. Then he asked to have him again, and the Collier gave him his son, but this time Fiachaire did not mention any period. The year ran out and Fiachaire did not bring the Collier back his son.

What did the Collier conclude but this : that since Fiachaire had not promised to bring him back he would never return him. So the Collier set out and all that day he spent travelling. In the evening he came to the house of a certain woman, and told her what he wanted. She said to him that there was a loch nearby, that his son was on the other side of the loch, and that there were certain women who went to and fro across the loch in the form of swans, and that he should try and see if he could steal her swan cloak from one of them. He went to the loch-side and stole away one of the swan cloaks, and the cloak bore him across. There he met a man whom he asked where Fiachaire the Smith lived. The man pointed Fiachaire's house out to him. 'Now,' said this man to him, 'he will ask you to go in : he himself is inside wearing a red hood.[1] Your son is away hunting in the mountain ; he will come back in the form of a seagull, followed by twelve other seagulls. When they come, Fiachaire will turn them into thirteen pigeons and bring them into the house. Then he will fetch a harp and begin to play, and the thirteen

seo a' tighinn mun cuairt, beir thusa air.　Abair mur am bi nì
eile agad an àite do mhic, gum bi seo agad.　Iarraidh e ort an
calaman a leigeil as, is abair thusa nach leig.　Gabh a mach as
an taigh an sin, is an calaman agad.'

Ghabh an Gualadair gu taigh Fhiachaire Ghobha.　Dh' iarr
e air dol a staigh.　Bha e 'na shuidhe an sin, agus cnòcaid dhearg
mu a cheann.　Thànaig trì faoileannan deug chun an taighe ;
is chaidh esan a mach, is rinn e trì chalamain deug diubh, is
thug e a staigh iad.　Thug e leis clàrsach, is thòisich e air a
seinn, is thòisich na trì chalamain deug air dannsadh.[1]　Bha
an Gualadair a' sealltainn feuch am faiceadh e am fear a bha
an ite gheal am bun a sgéith : agus an uair a chunnaig e e, is
a thànaig e mun cuairt, rug e air.　'Mur am bi nì eile agam air
son mo mhic, bidh seo agam,' thuirt an Gualadair.　'Leig as
an calaman,' arsa Fiachaire Gobha.　'Cha leig,' ars an Gualadair.
Ghabh an Gualadair a mach, is an calaman leis.　An uair a bha
iad treis air falbh, ghèarr an calaman leum, is chaidh e 'na dhuine,
is dh'aithnich an Gualadair a mhac.　'Tha thu 'gad shàrachadh,'
thuirt a mhac ris a' Ghualadair.　'Chan 'eil,' ars an Gualadair.
Ghabh iad gu lùchairt Rìgh na Spàine.　Chaidh iad gu ruig
sabhal, is dh'fhuirich iad an sin.　'A nis,' ars a mhac ris a'
Ghualadair, 'bidh leigeadh[2] chon an seo a màireach.　Bidh
mise ann am chù agad-sa, agus buidhnidh mi, agus gheibh thusa
an t-airgead-gill.　Bidh mise ann am chù agad-sa air lomhainn,
agus thig Fiachaire Gobha mun cuairt, agus bheir e dhuit
ceud punnd Sasannach orm.　Thoir thusa dha mi, ach gléidh
an lomhainn, o chionn, bidh mise anns an lomhainn.'
　An là-'r-na-mhàireach, bha an leigeadh chon ann, is chaidh
esan 'na chù as déidh a athar, agus is e a bhuidhinn.　Thànaig
Fiachaire Gobha far an robh an Gualadair, is thairg e dha ceud
punnd Sasannach air a' chù.　Thug an Gualadair da an cù,
agus ghléidh e an lomhainn.　An uair a dh'fhalbh Fiachaire
Gobha leis a' chù, leum an lomhainn 'na dhuine.　'Bidh leigeadh
each ann a màireach,' thuirt a mhac ris a' Ghualadair ; 'bidh

---

[1] MS. *damhsadh*.

[2] *ligeadh*, in MS. and a note, 'Ligeadh, a race, *lit.* a letting,' *i.e.* a letting slip
(from the leash) (recte, *leigeadh*).　Now simply means 'send away,' *e.g.* after sheep.

pigeons will begin dancing. At the base of your son's wing there is a white feather. When you see this pigeon coming round, you seize it. Say that if you cannot get anything else in place of your son, at least you will have this. Fiachaire will order you to let the bird go, but you say that you will not. Then get out of the house and take the pigeon with you.'

The Collier went off to the house of Fiachaire the Smith. Fiachaire asked him to come in, and there he was sitting with a red hood on his head. Thirteen seagulls came to the house. Fiachaire went out and turned them into thirteen pigeons and brought them inside. Then he fetched a harp and began playing it, and the thirteen pigeons began to dance. The Collier was looking to see which of the pigeons had a white feather at the base of his wing ; and when he did see it and it came round to him, he caught it. 'If I cannot have anything else for my son, I will have this,' said the Collier. 'Let the pigeon go,' said Fiachaire the Smith. 'I will not,' said the Collier. And out he went, taking the pigeon with him. When they had gone some distance the pigeon gave a leap and became a man, and the Collier recognised his own son. 'You are worn out,' said his son to the Collier. 'No,' said the Collier, 'I am not.' They journeyed to the palace of the King of Spain. They went to a barn and there they stayed. 'Now,' said his son to the Collier, 'there will be a dog-race here tomorrow. I shall be your dog, and I shall win, and you will get the stakes. You shall have me as your dog on a leash, and Fiachaire the Smith will come round and give you one hundred pounds sterling for me. You hand me over to him but keep the leash, because I shall be in the leash.'

Next day the dog-race took place and the Collier's son followed his father in the shape of a dog, and it was he who won. Fiachaire the Smith came to the Collier and offered him one hundred pounds sterling for the dog. The Collier gave him the dog but kept the leash. When Fiachaire the Smith had gone off with the dog, the leash all at once became a man. 'Tomorrow there will be a horse-race,' said his son to the Collier ; 'I shall be a

mise ann am each, is bidh ubhal òir an ceann na sréine. Buidhnidh mi an geall. Thig Fiachaire Gobha, agus tairgidh e ceud
punnd Sasannach orm. Thoir dha mi, ach thoir an ubhal òir
a ceann na sréine.'

An là-'r-na-mhàireach, bha an leigeadh each ann. Chaidh
mac a' Ghualadair 'na each, agus bhuidhinn e an geall. Thànaig
Fiachaire Gobha far an robh e, agus thairg e ceud punnd
Sasannach do'n Ghualadair air an each. Thug an Gualadair
an ubhal òir a ceann na sréine, is thug e dha an t-each, is fhuair
e ceud punnd Sasannach. Thilg e an ubhal òir air an làr, is
leum an ubhal òir 'na duine.[1] 'Nis,' thuirt a mhac ris a'
Ghualadair, 'bidh leigeadh sheabhag ann a màireach. Bidh
mise ann am sheabhag agus cnòcaid dhearg mu m' cheann.
Buidhnidh mi an geall. Tairgidh Fiachaire Gobha ceud punnd
Sasannach orm ; is thoir thusa dha mi, ach gléidh a' chnòcaid,
chionn, bidh mise anns a' chnòcaid.'

An là-'r-na-mhàireach, bha leigeadh sheabhag ann, is chaidh
mac a' Ghualadair 'na sheabhag, is bhuidhinn e an geall.
Thànaig Fiachaire Gobha far an robh an Gualadair, agus thairg
e dha ceud punnd Sasannach air an t-seabhag. Thug an
Gualadair da e, ach cha do chuimhnich e a' chnòcaid a thoirt
bhàrr a chinn. Ghabh Fiachaire air falbh leis, agus rinn e
gearran bacach, bàn dheth.[2] Chuir e a staigh air stàbull e,
agus cheangail e ann an siod e. Bha nighean aig Fiachaire
Gobha, is bha i fhéin is an gille òg a' leannanachd ri chéile
roimhid. Thàinig i a staigh do'n stàbull, 's thuirt esan rithe,
'Nam bitheadh cuimhne agad-sa air a' mhaith a bha, bheireadh
tu chugam-sa na [3] leòr de'n uisge.' An uair a chuala i siod,
dh'fhosgail i an dorusd, is thug i chun an uillt e. Bhuail e air
òl anns an allt, is bhuail ise air a tharraing air ais ; is mar a
bu mhò a thàirneadh ise a cheann, is ann a bu mhò a chuireadh
i fodha 'san allt e.[4] Dé chunnaig i ach trì faoileannan deug a'
tighinn, is b'eudar di am bristeadh a ghabhail, is esan fhàgail

[1] The understanding is that the hero had transferred his personality from the
horse to the apple. Dashing the apple on the ground may be a method of disenchanting it.
[2] A lame white gelding, or a lame white horse, is a magical animal in several
tales.
[3] MS. has *na leòir*.

horse, and at the end of the reins will be a golden apple. I shall win the stakes. Then Fiachaire the Smith will come and offer one hundred pounds sterling for me. Give me to him, but take the golden apple off the end of the reins.'

The horse-race was held the following day. The Collier's son became a horse, and won the stakes. Fiachaire the Smith came to the Collier and offered him one hundred pounds sterling for the horse. The Collier took the golden apple off the end of the reins, gave Fiachaire the horse, and received one hundred pounds sterling. He flung the golden apple on the ground and the golden apple leapt up, a man.[1] 'Now,' said his son to the Collier, 'tomorrow there will be a hawk-race. I shall be a hawk with a red hood on my head and I shall win the stakes. Fiachaire the Smith will offer one hundred pounds sterling for me ; so hand me over to him, but keep the hood because I shall be in the hood.'

Next day there was a hawk-race, and the Collier's son became a hawk and won the stakes. Fiachaire the Smith came to the Collier and offered him one hundred pounds sterling for the hawk. The Collier handed the hawk over to him, but forgot to take the hood off his head. Fiachaire went off with the hawk and turned him into a lame white gelding.[2] He put him into a stable, and there he tied him up. Fiachaire the Smith had a daughter, and she and the young fellow had been sweethearting together before then. She came into the stable and he said to her, 'If only you remembered the good times that have been, you would bring me plenty of water.' When she heard that she opened the door and took him down to the burn. He began to drink at the burn, and she began to pull him back ; but the more she pulled his head, the more she pushed it under the water.[4] What did she see but thirteen seagulls coming, and she was obliged to accept defeat and leave him at the burn. He went and leaped out into the burn in the shape of a trout. The seagulls

[4] This may mean that the hero's magic checkmated that of Fiachaire's daughter, so that she did the reverse of what she wished to do. In other versions, the hero gradually wriggles out of the halter, thereby releasing himself from the magic power of the thing. The power of a magic bridle appears in *W. H. Tales*, ii., p. 60 or 70. In the MS. the daughter sees twelve seagulls coming, but the latter part of the tale shows that she must have seen thirteen.

aig an allt. Dh'fhalbh esan, is gheàrr e leum a mach 'san allt 'na bhreac. Chaidh na faoileannan 'nan trì balgairean [1] deug as a dhéidh. Bhuail iad air stopadh an uillt is air a thraoghadh. Chaidh esan 'na choileach lacha-riabhach [2] anns na speuran. Chaidh iad-san as a dhéidh 'nan trì seabhagan deug. Chaidh esan a staigh an sin air simileir Rìgh na Spàin, is chaidh e 'na fhàinne daoimean mu mheur Nighean Rìgh na Spàin. 'Nis,' ars am fàinne ri Nighean Rìgh na Spàin, 'thig Fiachaire air mo shon-sa, agus iarraidh e ort am fàinne [r'] a cheannach, 's abraidh e riut gun toir e ceud punnd Sasannach duit, ma bheir thu dha e ; is abair thusa nach toir, an trusdar a dh'fhàgail t'aodainn, is gun a bhith ag iarraidh an fhàinne agad-sa. Abraidh esan, an uair sin, gun dèan e àilleagan [3] mu d' mheur 'san latha, agus suirghiche 'san fheasgar. Beir thusa, an uair sin, orm-sa, agus tilg a meadhon an t-simileir mi.'

Thànaig Fiachaire Gobha far an robh Nighean Rìgh na Spàin, is thuirt e rithe, 'Dé ghabhas tu air an fhàinne sin mu do mheur ? An gabh thu ceud punnd Sasannach air ?' 'Fàg m' aodann, a thrusdair, is na bi ag iarraidh an fhàinne agam-sa,' arsa Nighean Rìgh na Spàin. 'Nì e àilleagan maith mu do mheur 'san latha, agus suirghiche 'san fheasgar,' thuirt Fiachaire Gobha ri Nighean Rìgh na Spàin. Rug ise an seo air an fhàinne, agus thilg i ann a meadhon an t-simileir e. Chaidh Fiachaire Gobha 's a chompanaich 'nan trì builg-shéididh dheug, is thòisich iad air séideadh an teine. Bha tòrr bracha a staigh, is chaidh esan 'na spiligean eòrna anns an tòrr bhracha. Chaidh iad-san 'nan trì chalamain deug, is bhuail iad air itheadh na bracha. Chaidh esan 'na mhadadh-ruadh, is thug e na trì chinn deug diubh. Phòs e fhéin agus Nighean Rìgh na Spàin, is bha iad fada beò ann an deagh bheatha is toil-inntinn còmhla. Thug e d'a athair na chum gu maith e fad a shaoghail.

From Donald MacFie, Iochdar, South Uist, who says he learnt it in his boyhood from John MacDonald, Aird a' Mhachair, who was an old man at the time.

---

[1] '*balgaire*, an otter.' Note in MS.
[2] '*coileach lacha riabhach*, a grey drake.' Note in MS. *Am Faclair*, however, gives *lacha riabhach* as meaning a *mallard*.
[3] '*àilleagan*, a jewel.' Note in MS.

turned into thirteen otters and gave him chase. They began to dam the burn and drain it. Then he became a mallard drake flying away in the skies. Away they flew after him as thirteen hawks. He then went down the King of Spain's chimney and became a diamond ring on the finger of the King of Spain's Daughter. 'Now,' said the ring to the King of Spain's Daughter, 'Fiachaire will come to get me, and he will ask you to let him buy the ring, and he will tell you that he will give you one hundred pounds sterling if you give it to him ; but you say that you will not give it to him, that the rascal is to leave your presence, and not to ask for your ring. Then he will say that during the day it will make you a jewel on your finger, and a suitor in the evening. Then you seize me and pitch me into the middle of the fireplace.'

Fiachaire the Smith came where the King of Spain's daughter was, and said to her, 'What will you take for that ring on your finger ? Will you take one hundred pounds sterling for it ?' 'Leave my presence, rascal, and don't ask for my ring,' said the King of Spain's Daughter. 'It will make you a fine jewel on your finger during the day, and a suitor in the evening,' said Fiachaire the Smith to the King of Spain's Daughter. Thereupon she seized the ring and threw it into the middle of the fireplace. Fiachaire the Smith and his companions became thirteen pairs of bellows and they began blowing up the fire. But there was a heap of malt in the house, and the Collier's son became a grain of barley in the heap of malt. They became thirteen pigeons and began to eat the malt. He became a fox, and snapped their thirteen heads off. He and the King of Spain's Daughter married, and they lived long and prosperously and were happy together. He gave his father as much as kept him well off all his life.

NOTES

MS. vol. x., No. 107. On the flyleaf of the MS. of this tale, Islay has written, 'Fiachaire Gobha—Gaelic Index 107—Printer's Index—From Malcolm MacLean, Lochmaddy, North Uist, who learned it from his grandfather, Hugh MacLean, a very old man. He was in his prime and living at Lochmaddy in 1765. [Scribe] Hector MacLean. Aug[ust] 11, 1859. See the Collier in my Journal.'

But at the end of the tale, the scribe says that he got it from Donald MacFie of Iochdar, South Uist. The scribe is probably right, for he would have appended the reciter's name to the tale while in his presence and before he ceased writing. It may be then that Islay has confused Donald MacFie with Malcolm MacLean. But it may also be that Islay himself heard the tale recited by Malcolm MacLean, though Hector heard it from Donald MacFie.

Parallels :—No. 16 (MS. vol. x., No. 30) ; Islay's English List, No. 348 ; *Béaloideas*, viii., pp. 3 ff., 85 ff. And see *Scottish Gaelic Studies*, iii., p. 181.

FEAR GHEUSDO

THACHAIR do dh'Fhear Gheusdo anns an Eilean Sgitheanach
gun tànaig e aon uair a choimhead caraid ann am Beinne Bhadhla
an Uibhist, e fhéin agus a ghille le bàta. Chaidh iad a staigh
troimh sheòlaid ris an canadh iad Seòlaid Rubha Eubhadh.
Chaidh iad air tìr an Àirigh a' Phuill an Eubhal. Dh'fhalbh
iad 'nan cois air son dol gu ruige Beinne Bhadhla. Thànaig an
t-sìde gu h-olc orra le cur agus le cathadh air an rathad. An
uair a rànaig iad àite cumhang air an rathad ris an canar A'
Chlaigeann, eadar Beinne Bhadhla is Uibhist, chunnaig iad
solus rompa, agus rinn iad dìreach air, agus an uair a bha iad
aig an t-solus, bha sin fosgailte rompa, agus chaidh iad a staigh
ann.

Bha siod làn de dhaoine, 's bha seann duine liath 'na shuidhe
an taobh shuas de'n teine. Bha e a' coimhead nan coigreach,
's gun fhios aige gu dé chuir an rathad idir iad. Thuirt e ris
an fheadhainn a bha a staigh còmhla ris dol agus tràth-oidhche
fhaotainn do'n choigreach 's d'a ghille. Dh'fhalbh an fheadhainn
a bha còmhla ris a' bhodach air son tràth-oidhche fhaotainn do
na coigrich ; 's cha d'fhàg iad a staigh ach am bodach le Fear
Gheusdo 's le a ghille.

Thànaig iad dachaigh. 'Am bheil tràth-oidhche agaibh do
na coigrich ?' thuirt am bodach riutha. 'Chan 'eil dad againn,'
ars iad-san ; 'shiubhail sinn Leódhas, agus Barraidh, agus
Uibhist a' Chinn a Deas agus Tuath, 's chan fhaca sinn creutair
nach robh air a bheannachadh, 's cha b'urrainn duinn dad a
dhèanamh dheth.' 'Ud !' thuirt am bodach, 'chan 'eil sin gu
math ; falbhaibh fhathast agus faighibh tràth-oidhche do'n
choigreach.' Dh'fhalbh iad, 's ma dh'fhalbh, cha robh iad fada
gun tighinn agus mart brèagha buidhe aca. Arsa gille Fir
Gheusdo r'a mhaighstir, 'O Dhia ! nach fhaic sibh a' Phrìseag ?' [1]

---

[1] The gillie is terrified, and well he may be ; for he recognizes one of his master's
cows, and knows it could have never been brought there in the time, but by some
uncanny agency.

THE LAIRD OF GESTO

No. 58.   [*MS. Vol. x., No. 107a*]

THE Laird of Gesto in Skye once happened to go on a visit to a friend in Benbecula in Uist. He went by boat, he and his attendant ; and, passing through a channel known as Eubhadh Point Channel, landed at Àirigh a' Phuill in Eubhal. They set out on foot for Benbecula. On the way they met with foul weather, and driving snow came down on them. When they reached a defile called A' Chlaigeann, on the road between Benbecula and Uist, they saw a light and made straight for it, and when they arrived at it, there was a house there. It was open for them and they went inside.

The place was full of people, and there was an old grey man sitting at the farther side of the fire. He kept gazing at the strangers, puzzled at what could have sent them that way. He ordered those who were in the house with him to go and get supper for the stranger and his lad, and off they went to look for supper for the newcomers, leaving no one indoors except the old man with the Laird of Gesto and his lad.

The others returned home. 'Have you brought any supper with you for the strangers?' asked the old man. 'We haven't a thing,' they replied ; 'we travelled Lewis and Barra and Uist North and South, but not a creature did we see that had not been blessed, and we could do nothing.' 'Bah !' said the old man, 'that's not very good. Go away again, and find supper for the strangers.' Off they went, but this time they were not long in returning, and with them they had a fine tawny cow. 'God ! look at Prìseag !' exclaimed the Laird of Gesto's lad to his master.[1] His master nudged him and told him to keep quiet.

Phut a mhaighstir e, agus thuirt e ris fuireach sàmhach.
Dh'fhaighnich an seann duine dhiùbh, 'C'à'n d'fhuair sibh seo?'
agus thuirt iad-san ris, 'Thànaig sinn gu ruig Geusdo, 's bha a'
bhanchag a' bleoghan a' chruidh. Thog bó a cas, 's bhuail i
an cuman, agus dhòirt i e. Dh'éirich a' bhanchag 'na seasamh,
's thog i a' bhuarach, 's bhuail i a' bhó leatha, agus thuirt i—
"Na na bhlighear agus na na bhuailichear gu bràthach tuilleadh
thu, agus gum b'e droch chòmhdhail a dh'éireas duit." An
uair a chuala sinn seo, ghrad bha sinn aice, agus thug sinn leinn
i.' Bhruich iad a' bhó agus dh'ith iad i, 's fhuair Fear Gheusdo
a leòr dhith.

Cho luath 's a thànaig an latha, chuir Fear Gheusdo air,
agus thog e fhéin agus a ghille orra gu ruig Geusdo. An uair
a rànaig e am baile, cha robh duine a staigh nach robh gus a
bhith marbh : fhuair e a mach gu dé bha orra. Fhuair iad a'
bhó marbh, agus dh'ith iad i. Shaoil iad-san gur h-i a' bhó
a bha aca. Chuir e fios air a' bhanchaig.[1] Dh'fhaighnich e dhith
gu dé thànaig eadar i fhéin agus a' Phrìseag a raoir. Thuirt ise
nach tànaig dad. Thuirt esan rithe, 'Nach dubhairt thu an
uair a dhòirt i an cuman ort, "Na na bhlighear agus na na
bhuailichear gu bràthach tuilleadh thu, agus gum b'e droch
chòmhdhail a dh'éireas duit?"' Dh'aidich i gun robh siod
ceart. Thuirt e riutha an uair sin, gun d'ith iad am bodach-
sìdh ann an àite a' mhairt. Dh'innis fear-an-taighe [Fear
Gheusdo?] mar a bha, agus leighis e na h-uile duine, agus
phàidh e a' bhanchag, agus thug e a cead di.[2]

From Malcolm MacLean, Lochmaddy, who learnt it from his grandfather, Hugh MacLean, who was a very old man when reciter learnt
it. The old man was in his prime and living at Lochmaddy in
1765. Written down at Lochmaddy, August 11th, 1859.

NOTES

Claigeann, skull : scalp ; best field of arable land on a farm ; *Faclair
Gàidhlig*. *Claigeannach*, head-stall of a halter : best arable land of a district ;
ibid.

A' Bhuarach. The cow-fetter, or cow-shackle, or cow-spancel, which was
placed on a cow's hindlegs while being milked to prevent her from kicking.
The important part played by this homely article in the tale of 'Fear Gheusdo'
makes some notice of it desirable. Though of common and everyday use,
it was of extremely ominous character.

The old man asked the others, 'Where did you get this one?'
They replied, 'We came to Gesto and found the dairymaid
milking the cows. One of the cows raised her hoof, kicked the
milk-pail, and spilt the milk. The dairymaid got on her feet and
picked up the spancel, and struck the cow with it, saying, "May
you nevermore be milked nor driven to the fold, and may it be
an evil fate that befalls you!" When we heard this, we pounced
on her and carried her off with us.' Then they cooked the cow
and ate her, and the Laird of Gesto got as much as he wanted of
her.

As soon as it was day, the Laird dressed, and he and his lad
started off for Gesto. When the Laird arrived home, all within
were on the point of death. Gesto discovered what was wrong
with them—they had found the cow dead, and had eaten it, under
the impression that it was the real cow. He sent for the dairymaid and asked her what had come between herself and Prìseag the
night before. The dairymaid replied that nothing had happened.
'Did you not say,' said the Laird, 'when she upset your milk-pail
for you, "May you nevermore be milked nor driven to the fold,
and may it be an evil fate that befalls you"?' Then she admitted
that that was so. At this, the Laird told them that they had
eaten the old fairy man instead of the cow. So he gave them the
whole story, and healed all of them, but the dairymaid he paid
and dismissed.

[1] *Dh' fheòraich e air son na banachaig*, in MS.
[2] *Phaigh e dheth a' bhanachaig*, in MS.

'*Eadar a' bhadhbh 's a' bhuarach*, "twixt the vixen and the cow-fetter,"
"betwixt the Devil and the deep sea." It was a superstitious fancy that if a
man got struck by the "buarach," he would thenceforth be childless.' Nicolson,
p. 171.[1] Other creatures were also supposed to wield the *buarach* as a weapon.
Thus the fairy-woman was credited with having nine cow-fetters (nine being
a number of intensity) and these figure in almost every bespelling run, when

[1] [This power was also attributed to the *cuigeal*, distaff.—A. M.]

characters bespell or conjure one another to carry out some task or go on some quest, 'by crosses and by spells and by the nine cow-fetters of the busily-roaming, misleading fairy woman,' *mar chroisean 's mar gheasan, 's mar naoi buaraichean mnatha-sìdhe, siùbhlaiche, seachranaiche.*

There is a tale in the *Gàidheal*, ii., 371, in which the gigantic 'Cailleach Beinn a' Bhric' comes to the door of a hunter's hut in the gloaming, and tells him that when he sees her next day milking her herd of deer, he is to mark and afterwards to pursue whichever hind she strikes with the *buarach* for being refractory at milking time, for the hind so struck is doomed to become the prey of the hunter. In the similar case of Murdoch of Gàig, the hunter sees the fairies strike a hind and say, 'may a dart from Murdoch's quiver pierce your side before night,' the hind so cursed falling in due course a victim to the hunter's skill. *Trans. Gael. Soc. Inverness*, xvi., 261.

But it is a dairymaid, an ordinary mortal, who figures in 'Fear Gheusdo,' and who strikes her cow with the *buarach*, and *curses* it, the animal being at once rendered liable to attack by fairies ; in fact, it almost seems as if the fairies were provoked to attack it, though they had been quite unable to touch animals that had been blessed. In the *Celtic Review*, v., 58, appeared (in English) a very interesting tale, similar in some incidents to 'Fear Gheusdo,' in which cows are rendered immune to fairy attack by *blessing*, charming and shackling. In legends preserved by the Rev. J. G. Campbell, a blow from the *buarach* seems enough to secure immunity (*Superstitions*, p. 230), and the reverend gentleman further says that 'after milking a cow, the dairymaid should strike it *deiseal* with the shackle, saying "out and home" (*mach 's dachaigh*). This secures its safe return.' See also *ibid.*, p. 82. But in these cases there is no cursing, and the shackle must have been made of *lonaid chaorrainn 's gaoisid stallain*, 'rowan-tree withe, and stallion's hair,' according to A. R. Forbes, who adds that the *buarach* 'should be carefully looked after and preserved from any others getting at it '; *Gaelic Names of Beasts*, p. 97. The use of these materials in the manufacture of the shackle clearly indicates a desire to get rid of its ancient harmfulness, for the rowan-tree was sovereign against evil, as all know, and a stallion afforded such complete protection that while on the back of one a man might ride to a meeting of witches, yet return unscathed.

In this story, 'Fear Gheusdo,' the Laird and his servant partake of the flesh of a real cow called 'Prìseag,' the Laird's own property, which the fairies had transported through the air across the sea in order that they might have something to set before their guest, the laws of hospitality being as binding in fairyland as in any part of Scotland. There are indeed several stories in which a mortal compels magicians or bogles to execute his commands by simply refusing their offer of hospitality until his wishes have been carried out, for rather than that their mortal guest should go away without tasting food, the unearthly hosts will comply with any request.

The fairies had searched far and wide for food, but as every creature and beast had been blessed, they were unable to touch anything. (They are equally unable in another tale in *Superstitions*, p. 82, when on a very similar expedition for a very similar purpose, to touch one cow because a dairymaid had struck it with the *buarach*, and unable to touch a second, because its knee was resting on a tuft of *bruchorcan*, dirk grass, *juncus squarrosus*.) But in 'Fear Gheusdo,' when on foray for the second time, the fairies take away the cow Prìseag that the dairymaid had struck *and cursed*, and leave behind them in its stead what seemed indeed to be the carcase of the cow, but was in reality the body of an *old* fairy.

The Laird's people, presently finding what they take to be the dead Prìseag, cook and eat it, and fall ill, the usual result of eating changeling or fairy animals. But the Laird and his servant, who had eaten the flesh of a real cow, take no harm, and even though they eat it in fairyland they suffer no detention there.

Upon reaching home, and finding all his people ill, the Laird, remembering the tale he had heard in the fairy *brugh*, questions his dairymaid, and she confesses to striking the cow with the *buarach*, and cursing it. He pays her off, and heals his own people, telling them that they had eaten *the* old *bodach-sìdh* or fairy man. The definite article '*the*' is frequently used in the Gaelic idiom to introduce a fresh character or person, and at first sight it might seem to have been so used here, and that *the bodach-sìdh* is a fresh character, for how could the Laird's people, who were in Skye and on one side of the Minch, how could they have eaten an old *bodach* while Gesto himself was talking to him in the fairy *brugh* in Benbecula on the other side of the Minch ? But then a divisible personality is not unknown in Gaelic mythology, and characters sometimes become two, or even three different persons or creatures, with a corresponding ability to appear in two or more different places at once, so that one and the same old *bodach-sìdh* might appear both in Benbecula and Skye at the same time. Similarly in ' Rìgh Éireann 's a dhà mhac,' *Celtic Review*, vi., p. 371, the '*creutair grànda*' appears as three red-haired women on the first occasion, and as two women on another ; and in the well-known tale of 'Dùn-Bhuilg,' the fairies are able, though locked out of the house, to pound and kick the head of the sleeping goodman, who is inside the house, which they could only have done on the supposition of a divisible personality. And in the case of 'Luran,' a farmer, a man who had suffered severely from fairy depredations, the poor fellow actually sees himself helping the fairies drive his own cows away to the fairy knoll, so that divisibility was possible even for mortals.

Luran's case is very much in point, for after beholding himself help the fairies drive his own cow into the fairy *brugh*, he there sees an old elf, a tailor with a needle in the right lapel of his coat, who is forcibly caught hold of by the other elves, stuffed into the hide of the cow that Luran had seen his second self chasing, and then sewn up.

Next morning, this very cow is found lying at the foot of the fairy knoll, and Luran prophesies that a needle will be found in its right shoulder ; on this proving to be the case, he allows none of the flesh to be eaten, but throws it out of the house. For full details of this curious legend, see *Superstitions*, p. 52, *et seq.*, also *Trans. Gael. Soc. Inverness*, xxvi., p. 271.

Possibly, in older versions of our tale, Gesto would have beheld the other fairies sew the old *bodach* up in Prìseag's hide, before they transported him to Skye. In any case it seems essential to attribute divisibility of personality to the *bodach*, and that one of these personalities was taken everywhere that night by the other fairies when foraging for food. Then, when on their second foray, they changed it into an appearance of the cow that the dairymaid had cursed, and left it in the animal's place.

When an elf-smitten beast (*beathach a chaidh a ghonadh*) dies, it should not be eaten : its flesh is not flesh but a stock of alder-wood, an aged elf or some trashy substitute. If the dead animal be rolled down a hill, it will disappear altogether. In the case of a bull that had been killed by falling over a precipice, a nail was driven into the carcase to keep the fairies away, *ibid.*, pp. 33, 47, 93.

It is always old superannuated individuals of their race whom the fairies, who have very much the same customs as other races, hand over to mortals in the shape of changeling babies, changeling wives, or as in the case of 'Fear Gheusdo,' changeling cows. See an article, *Folk-Lore*, i., p. 197, by Sir G. L. Gomme who takes for his text a tale from the Gaelic contributed by J. F. Campbell himself to the *Ethnological Society's Journal*, ii., p. 336, 1869-70, the Gaelic original of which tale I have not yet found.

The fairies think that in sending or leaving their old people amongst mortals, they do away with them, kill them in short ; for the world of mortals is to the fairies what the other world is to us mortals, and that the fairies actually regarded mortals as ghosts appears clearly enough from the fact that in one tale a mortal woman is actually addressed by a fairy as having come from the land of the dead, and in a second, when the Glaistig and its bantling see a man hiding behind the door, they call him in one version a *logaid*, and in another a *tamhasg*, both of which words mean a ghost or bogle. See *Superstitions*, pp. 58, 177 ; *Celtic Review*, July 1908, p. 63 ; and *Folk Tales and Fairy Lore*, p. 263.

It would be quite in keeping with this that Cailleach Beinn a' Bhric should threaten refractory deer with the hunter, who, being an ordinary mortal, was, to the fairies as well as to the whole world of *sìdh*, a ghost ; and to the deer, a dreaded enemy.—Mortal mothers used to threaten their children with the strange bogle, 'MacGlumaig nam Mias, o Liath Tarruing Shìoda, Burrach Mór' ; *Witchcraft*, p. 187 ; *Trans. Gael. Soc. Inverness*, xv., Sgoil nan Eun, note.

LOCH AILLSE

Bha Loch Aillse 'na àite cho fiadhaich, air chor is gun robh móran eachdraidh mu thimcheall. Is e smaointich Mac Leòid Dhùn Bheagain agus Iain Garbh Mac Gille Chaluim Rathar-saidh [1] gun rachadh iad ann feuch gu dé an dòigh a bha aig na daoine a bha ann. Dh'fhalbh iad fhéin is an cuid ghillean ; chaidh iad air tìr : agus cha do thachair àite riu ach monaidhean fiadhaich. Bha iad a' siubhal air feadh nam monaidhean fada, agus cha robh taigh a' tachairt riu. Dhealaich Mac Leòid is a ghillean ri Iain Garbh. Mu dheireadh, chunnaig Iain Garbh solus. Bha bothag bheag ann an sin : ghabh iad [Iain Garbh agus a ghille] a steach—bha seann duine a staigh innte ; dh'iarr iad cuid na h-oidhche [agus an oidhche a] chur seachad innte. 'Ma thà,' ars an seann duine, 'is e tha an seo àite fiadhaich anns am bheil robairean ; cha bhi e glic dhuibh fantainn ann, ach gheibh sibh biadh, agus falbhaidh sibh mun tig iad.' Ghabh iad biadh. 'Ma tà,' ars Iain Garbh, 'cha charaich mi as a seo an nochd, ge bè air bith mar a bhitheas : cuiridh sinn suas anns an t-seòmar as faide air falbh 'san taigh, is chan fhaigh iad sinn gu tig an là.' Rinn an seann duine seo.[2]

Cha robh iad fada an sin an uair a thànaig na robairean. Bha a h-uile fear dhiubh is gruaim air le acras. Dh'iarr iad an sin am biadh a chur a nall. [Thug iad sùil agus chunnaig iad Iain Garbh is a ghille, agus chuir iad rompa gum biodh spòrs aca orra]. 'Nuair a bha iad ag itheadh, a h-uile cnàimh [3] a lomadh iad, gheibheadh Iain Garbh sgailc dheth mu'n aodann

---

[1] Mac Gille Chaluim is the patronymic of MacLeod of Raasay. Iain Garbh, or Stout John, was one of the chiefs of this house. He was a famous champion, and the hero of many stories. [He was drowned in 1671.—A. M.]

[2] If this means that the old man accommodated them by showing them into some inner room, it is contradicted by the statement about the robbers throwing bones at them, which proves that Iain Garbh and his gillie were not hidden, and therefore not in any inner room when the robbers came. It is possible, however, that they had gone into the inner room, and coming out incautiously, were noticed by the robbers.

LOCH ALSH

Loch Alsh was a very wild place, so much so that many stories
were attached to it. Accordingly, MacLeod of Dunvegan and
Iain Garbh Mac Gille Chaluim of Raasay [1] determined to go
there themselves and see what sort of life the people there led.
They set out, they and their attendants, and landed there ; but
they found nothing but wild moorland. For a long time they
traversed the moors, and not a house did they meet with. Finally
MacLeod and his followers parted from Iain Garbh. At last
Iain Garbh saw a light. There, there was a little bothy, and [Iain
Garbh and his lad] went straight in. Inside was an old man.
They asked if they could have hospitality for the night there.
'Well,' said the old man, 'this is a lawless place where robbers
live ; it will not be wise for you to stay here, but you shall have
food, and you will go before they come.' They had a meal.
'Now,' said Iain Garbh, 'I will not stir from here tonight, no
matter what happens. We will put up in the farthest away
room in the house, and they will never find us.' This the old
man did. [2]

They were not long there when the robbers came in, every
one of them grim-faced with hunger, and they ordered food to
be brought. [They glanced around, and saw Iain Garbh and
his lad, and they decided to have some amusement at their
expense.] Every bone [3] the robbers picked while they were
eating, Iain Garbh would get a knock in the face from it when

---

[3] *creabh* (?) in MS. 'This is somewhat similar to what happened to the *Fear
Claon Ruadh's* Nephews in Connal Gualpenach's story and afterwards to the robbers
themselves. The only difference being that Iain Garbh was not killed.' Footnote
in MS. by D. Torrie, the scribe. He does not seem to have sent any versions of
Connal (or Conall) Gulban (or Gualpenach—the word is very variously spelt)
and the incidents he refers to do not occur in the versions given in *W. H. Tales*,
iii., No. 76. They do occur in No. 17 (MS. vol. x., No. 31).

'nuair a thilgeadh iad uatha e. [Chaidh Iain Garbh is a ghille
sìos gu seòmar eile]. Dh'iarr Iain Garbh air a ghille a léine
chur dheth gu solus a dhèanamh, agus e air preas fhaicinn làn
de gheir (tallow). Rinn an gille seo, agus rinn iad coinnlean
glas' air, ann am mionaid. Las iad a h-aon dhiubh, is chunnaig
iad preas làn de airm. Thug Iain Garbh claidheamh d'a ionnsaigh. Cha robh iad fada mar sin, 'nuair a thànaig fear de na
robairean a dh'ionnsaigh an doruis, is e ag éigheach air càch
tighinn a nuas, is gum faigheadh iad spòrs orra. Le seo, chaidh
e a staigh far an robh Iain Garbh, ach bha an ceann de'n robair
ann am mionaid. Thànaig fear eile a nuas, feuch gu dé dh'éirich
dha ; rinneadh air an fhear sin mar an ceudna, gus an do
mharbhadh am fear mu dheireadh dhiubh. Thànaig e féin agus
a ghille a nuas[1], agus an uair a chunnaig an seann duine an
coltas bha air le a chlaidheamh, dh'fhalbh e gu teicheadh.
Dh'éigh Iain Garbh ris tilleadh, agus gun eagal a bhith air
roimhe-san. Thuirt an seann duine ris, 'O ! bu tu am mac
sona gu do bhreith ;[2] is iomadh fear thànaig an seo riamh nach
do dh'fhalbh as ; is mór a bha iad siod a' dèanamh de olc, ged
nach do thachair duine treun riutha chuir as daibh gu seo. Tha
móran anns an taigh seo de ionmhas an t-saoghail : bhitheas[3]
tusa gu maith air fad as beò thu, agus do shliochd 'nad dhéidh :
thoir leat dhachaigh gach nì a th' ann.'

Dh'fhalbh Iain Garbh gu ruig Ratharsaidh. Phill e air ais
gu Loch Aillse a rithist, agus a chuid sheirbhiseach maille ris.
Thug iad leò gach nì a bh' ann. Ged a bha Iain Garbh Mac
Gille Chaluim ann an cothrom riamh, is ann a bha am pailteas
'na theaghlach an uair a thill iad, agus bha sin a' leantainn
riutha am fad 's a bha riamhag[4] [?] dhiubh ann. Chum e an
seann duine 'na theaghlach fhad 's a bha e beò, agus aran duine-
uasail aige. Phill Mac Leòid is a ghille dhachaigh, agus chan
fhac iad nì sam bith a b'fhiach bhith ag aithne as [?] do bhrìgh
nach do ghabh iad misneach gu Iain Garbh a leantainn.

[1] Sentence repeated in MS.

[2] [*Bu tu am mac sona gu do bhreith :* Perhaps we should read *'ga do bhreith*. *Cf*. the
proverb : *Chan 'eil air an duine shona ach a bhreith* (in Nicolson's *Gaelic Proverbs*, p. 112 :
Chan 'eil do dhuine sona ach a bhreith, 's bidh duine dona 'na lom-ruith). *Cf*. the Welsh
proverb : *ny reit y detwyd namyn y eni*, ' the fortunate needs but to be born ' (Jackson,
Early Welsh Gnomic Poems, p. 53). See O'Rahilly, *Miscellany of Irish Proverbs*,
no. 345.—A. M.]

they threw it from them.   [Iain Garbh and his lad went down
to another room.]   Iain Garbh noticed a press full of tallow
there, and asked his lad to put off his shirt to make lights.   The
lad did that, and they made grey candles of the tallow in a moment.
They lit one of them, and they saw a cupboard full of weapons.
Iain Garbh picked a sword for himself.   They had not been
long thus, when one of the robbers came to the door, shouting
to the rest to come along and amuse themselves with the men.
With this, he went in where Iain Garbh was, but the robber's
head was off him in a flash.   Another one came down to see
what had happened to the first ; the same thing was done to him,
and so on until the last one of them was killed.   Then Iain Garbh
and his lad came out, and when the old man saw how fierce he
looked with his sword, he made to fly.   Iain Garbh shouted to
him to come back and not to be afraid of him.   The old man said
to him, 'Oh, lucky son to bear ! many a man has come here who
never left ; the evil that these men were doing was great, but
not till now did they meet a mighty man who destroyed them.
There is very much wealth in this house : you will be able to
live well on it all your life, and your descendants after you.   Take
everything there is home with you.'

Iain Garbh went off to Raasay, and returned to Loch Alsh
again with his retainers.   Everything there was they carried
off with them.   Although Iain Garbh Mac Gille Chaluim had
always been well-to-do, it was when they returned that abundance
reigned in his household !   And that abundance followed them
as long as a scion of them remained.   He kept the old man in
his household all his days, living a gentleman's life.   MacLeod
and his lad went back home, nor did they see anything worth
acquainting themselves with, because they had not had courage
enough to follow Iain Garbh.

---

³ So MS. [read *bitheas* or *bios*.—A. M.]
⁴ MS. *riabhag*.

NOTES

MS. vol. x., No. 111. The scribe was D. Torrie.

See *W. H. Tales*, iv., Gaelic List, at end of book, where the tale is dated 19th January 1860, and the reciter is described as a pauper and bedridden. She was probably failing, and this may account for the confusion noticeable in the tale, and also for the strange remark at the end to the effect that MacLeod of Dunvegan had not had courage enough to follow Iain Garbh. Whereas in separating from Iain Garbh and thereby depriving himself of his assistance MacLeod of Dunvegan, it is clear, showed as much courage as Iain Garbh did.

The same pauper woman recited Nos. 112, 113 (= Nos. 60 and 61 of this book).

a bha thusa ro fheumail dhuinn fad an rathaid.' Chuir e a
mach am bàta, agus chuireadh gu tìr i. Bha i an sin, is gun i
faicinn neach a dh'aithnicheadh i. Sheall i, agus chunnaig i
nighean ag imeachd a nall g'a [h-]ionnsaigh. Thuirt i rithe,
'Cha chreid mi nach ban-choigreach thusa an seo mar an
ceudna.' 'Ma tà, seadh,' ars an té eile. 'Is ann an dé a thànaig
mi an seo.' 'Ma tà, is ann an diugh a thànaig mise.' 'Gu dé
a nì sinn, ma tà ?' [ars an té eile]. Thuirt an nighean Sgitheanach
rithe, 'Leanamaid a chéile fad 's as beò sinn ; is ma gheibh sinn
cosnadh anns an aon àite, gheibh sinn e, ach mur faigh ach a
h-aon againn e 'san aon àite, cha ghabh sinn e.'

Air dhaibh bhith air an t-seanchas seo, thànaig coslas urra
mhóir far an robh iad. Dh'fhaighnich e dhith-se an gabhadh i
seirbhis aige. Thuirt i ris, 'Ma gheibh sinn le chéile e.' Thuirt
esan an uair sin, 'Chan 'eil feum agam ach air aonan.' Chunnaig
an Caiptean an t-urra mór [1] is na nigheanan a' bruidhinn, is
thànaig e far an robh iad, agus dh'fhaighnich e gu dé bha orra.
Dh'innis i dha. [Dh'innis an Caiptean da an sin cho math 's a
bha an nighean Sgitheanach.] Thuirt an [t-]urra mór [1] an
uair sin, gun gabhadh e le chéile iad. Thug e do'n nighinn
Sgitheanaich gad iuchraichean. 'Falbh,' ars esan, 'is ruig an
caisteal sin shuas, is tòisich air obair ; cha bhi ban-mhaighstir
ort ach thu fhéin.' Rinn i sin. Thug e litir do'n nighinn eile,
agus dh'iarr e oirre dol do'n taigh bha goirid do'n chaisteal,
agus gum pilleadh iad a rithist far an robh [an] nighean
[Sgitheanach] 'sa' chaisteal. [Dh'fhalbh ise leis an litir do'n
taigh a dh'ainmich e, agus dh'fhalbh esan a rathad féin. Ma
dh'fhalbh, cha robh iad a' pilleadh do'n chaisteal.] Bha i [an
nighean Sgitheanach] an sin a' gabhail fadachd dhiubh.
Dh'fhalbh i a dh'ionnsaigh an taighe sin, agus sheall i aig
uinneig, agus gu dé chunnaig i ach esan 'ga tràigheadh air fuil.
Shìn i a mach do'n chaisteal, agus dh'fhosgail i ciste, agus bha
té eile 'na broinn sin, làn òir is airgid. Bha neapaiginn mór
mu a h-amhaich. Cheangail i a' chist ann, is dh'fhalbh i.
Dh'éigh i do'n Chaiptean bàta chur a nall. Rinn e sin. Dh'innis
i dha mar a thachair. 'Ma tà,' ars esan, 'thig e, is bidh sinne
agus thusa an sàs.' 'Ma tà,' ars am mate, 'bheir sinn an car as.

---

[1] *leg.* an urra mhór ?

she was set ashore. There she was, not seeing anyone she knew. But she looked around and saw a girl walking over towards her. The Skye girl said to her, 'I think you are a stranger here too.' 'Yes ; so I am,' replied the other. 'It was only yesterday that I came here.' 'Well, it was today I came.' 'What shall we do, then ?' asked the other girl. 'Let us keep together so long as we live,' replied the Skye girl, 'and if we both find employment in the same place, we will take it ; but if only one of us can get employment in any place, we will not take it.'

While they were engaged in this conversation, a man who seemed to be an important personage approached them. He asked the Skye girl if she would take service with him, and she replied, 'Yes ; if both of us can have it together.' Then he said, 'I require only one person.' The captain saw the gentleman and the girls talking, and he came up to them and asked them what the matter was. The Skye girl told him. [Then the captain told the great man how good the Skye girl was.] The great man said then that he would take them both, and gave the Skye girl a bunch of keys. 'Go to the castle up there,' said he, 'and begin work. You will have no mistress over you but yourself.' She did as he said. He gave the other girl a letter and told her to go to the house near the castle ; that later they would return to the castle, where the [Skye] girl was. [The girl went off with the letter to the house he had named, and he went his own way. But though he did, there was no sign of them returning to the castle.] Then [the Skye girl] began to tire of waiting for them, so she went to that house and looked through a window. What did she see but the man bleeding the girl to death. Back to the castle she ran, and opened a casket ; inside there was another casket full of gold and silver. She had a large handkerchief round her neck, and she tied the casket up in it and went off. She shouted to the captain to send a boat over, and he did so. She told him what had happened. 'Well,' he said, 'the man will come, and then we and you will be arrested.' 'Why,' said the mate, 'we will outwit him ! [We] will put her in the crow's nest and the

Cuiridh [sinn] i do'n chrannaig, agus a' chist maille rithe. Cùrainnichidh sinn i leis na siùil, agus ceanglaidh sinn i le buill, is chan fhaigh e i.' Rinneadh seo.

Có thigeadh ach an t-urra mór, agus maor maille ris. 'Faighibh dhòmh-sa an té thug sibh an seo, is a chreach mise,' [ars an t-urra mór]. Thuirt am mate ris, 'Ma tà, ma rinn thusa nì olc air na nigheanan sin, fuilingidh tu air a shon.' Shiubhail e an soitheach, is cha d'fhuair e i, ach thuirt e gun tigeadh e a rithist. Dh'fhalbh iad-san, agus sheòl iad gu ceàrn eile de'n àite. Fhuair iad luchd an sin, agus sheòl iad do Lunnainn, agus as a sin gu Grianaig. An uair a bha iad a' dealachadh, thuirt an Caiptean, 'Nis, tha pailteas agad le do thapachd fhéin ; bi glic, agus dèan feum maith leis.' Arsa ise, 'Tha roinn mhaith agam ri thoirt dhuibh fhéin.' 'Cha ghabh mi sgillinn dheth,' ars esan.

Chaidh i gu tìr agus có chunnaig i air an t-sràid ach mac an duine-uasail bha dèanamh suas rithe. Ghabh i seachad air, agus dh'aithnich i e, agus dh'aithnich esan ise. Air dhi tilleadh air ais, thuirt e rithe, 'An tu a th'ann?' 'Is mi,' ars ise. 'Ma tà,' ars esan, 'cha do thaobh mise ri mo chuideachd o'n a dh'fhalbh thu, agus ma bhitheas tusa nise deònach, pòsaidh sinn.' Rinn iad sin. Ghabh iad taigh ann an Grianaig.

Beagan 'na dhéidh sin, chunnaig iad gun robh oighreachd ri a reic ann an Cinn-tìre. 'Fhalbh,' ars ise, 'agus cuir tairgse as an staid.'[1] Rinn esan gàire. 'Chan ann le làimh fhalaimh dh'fheumainn-sa sin a dhèanamh.' 'Falbh thusa,' ars ise, agus i toirt dha sporain làn airgid, 'agus bheir dìnneir do na h-uaislean bhitheas ann nach d'fhuair iad riamh a leithid, agus bithidh mi féin [ann] mu dheireadh na dìnneireach.' Dh'fhalbh [e]. Thuit an staid air, air an treas tairgse. Thug e dìnneir dhaibh. Rànaig ise, is dh'innis e dhi gun robh an staid aige, ach gu dé mar a phàidhteadh e ! 'Tiugainn thusa,' ars ise, 'far am bheil am fear aig an robh i.' Rànaig iad, agus phàidh i a h-uile sgillinn dhith, is ghabh iad còir air an oighreachd. Ghabh iad còmh-naidh ann, agus tha meanglan de na thànaig uaithe gabhail còmhnaidh ann an Cinn-tìre chun an là an diugh.

From the recitation of Mary Morrison or Widow Samuel McDonald, Aird, Benbecula. A pensioner's widow. Very old and confined to bed. Previously spoken of as a pauper.

casket with her. We will cover her with the sails and tie her up with ropes, and he will never find her.' This was done.

Who should now come but the great man, and with him a sheriff-officer. 'Find me the woman you brought here and who robbed me,' [said the great man.] 'Well, if you've done anything wrong to those girls,' said the mate to him, 'you shall suffer for it.' He went over the ship and could not find the girl ; but he said he would come again. They went and sailed to another part of the country. There they took a cargo on board and sailed for London, and from there to Greenock. When they were parting, the captain said, 'Now, you are well provided for through your own courage ; be wise and make good use of it.' 'I must give a good share to yourself,' said the girl. 'I will not take a penny of it,' said he.

She went ashore, and whom did she see in the street but the gentleman's son who had been making love to her. She passed him, but she recognised him and he recognised her. She turned back, and he said to her, 'Is it you ?' 'Yes, it is I,' she replied. 'Well,' said he, 'I have not been near my people since you left, and if you consent, we will get married.' They did that, and they took a house in Greenock.

Shortly afterwards, they saw that there was an estate for sale in Kintyre. 'Go and make an offer for the estate,' said the girl. He laughed. 'It is not empty-handed I could do that !' 'You go on,' said she, handing him a purse full of money, 'and give a dinner to the gentry who will be there, such a dinner as they have never had before, and I myself will be there towards the end.' Off he went. At the third bid the estate fell to him, and he gave the gentry a dinner. The girl arrived, and he told her that he now had the estate, but how was it to be paid for ? 'Come with me to the man who owned it,' said she. They went to the house of that man, and the girl paid every penny of the price, and they took possession of the estate. There they settled down, and to this very day a branch of those who descended from her are still in Kintyre.

---

[1] So MS.

NOTES

MS. vol. x., No. 112. For the reciter, see Notes to No. 59 of this book. One of the few domestic tales, without supernatural occurrences. The befriending of the heroine by the captain and mate is paralleled in No. 7 (MS. vol. x., No. 16).

AN NIGHEAN AGUS NA MÈIRLICH

BHA tuathanach ann aig an robh móran beairteis agus bha
nighean aige, agus dh'fhalbh i a dh'amharc chaorach. Rug
ceò mór oirre, agus chaidh i iomrall. Thànaig an oidhche, agus
cha robh fios aice gu dé a dhèanadh i. Bha i falbh gus am
faca i solus. Rànaig i e, agus chaidh i a staigh do'n taigh. Cha
robh duine beò ann, ach dh'aithnich i gun robh daoine ri tighinn.
Chunnaig i fear [marbh] an ceann shìos an taighe. Chaidh i
sìos ann, agus dh'fholaich i i féin, agus gu dé thachair rithe ach
duine mór agus claidheamh ri a thaobh. [Thug e dhi e, agus
dh'fhalbh e.] Thog i an claidheamh 'na làimh. Cha robh i
fad an sin an uair a thànaig dà fhear dheug de robairean, agus
mart aca. Mharbh iad i : bhruich iad cuid dith, agus thòisich
iad ri a h-itheadh. Bha i doirbh [a] cur as a chéile, agus na
sgeanan gann. 'Falbh,' arsa fear dhiubh, 'agus thoir chugad
an claidheamh sin shìos.' Chaidh e sìos, ach sgar ise an ceann
deth. Chaidh fear eile sìos, feuch gu dé bha 'ga chumail. Rinn
i an dòigh cheudna air. Chaidh iad o fhear gu fear a sìos, gus
an do mharbhadh uile iad, ach am maighstir.[1] Chaidh esan
a sìos feuch gu dé dh'éirich dhaibh, agus bhuail i e, ach cha do
mharbh i e. Shìn e a mach, agus e air a ghoirteachadh gu mór.
Thug e taigh a athar air, agus bha ceithir bliadhna deug o'n
a bha e roimh ann. Rinn iad toileachadh mór ris, ged a bha
nàire orra air son a cheàird. Thug an nighean taigh a h-athar
fhéin oirre.

Bha esan [an robair] glé thinn. Bha luchd-léigh a' tighinn
g'a fhaicinn. Thuirt [duine] d[h]iu[bh] ris nach rachadh e am
feobhas gus am faigheadh e cridhe agus grùthan na maighdinn
a bhuail e, oir dh'aithnich e gur [e] buille fhuair e. [Ach cha
robh fios aig duine có a' mhaighdean a bhuail e.] 'Ma tà,'
arsa a chomhalta, agus e a staigh, 'falbhaidh mise, agus bithidh

---

[1] Similar incidents in Nos. 13, 59 (MS. vol. x., Nos. 26, 111) ; *Béaloideas,* ii.
(1930), p. 351.

THE GIRL AND THE ROBBERS

No. 61.   [*MS. Vol. x., No. 113*]

THERE was once a very rich farmer who had a daughter, and she went out to look after sheep. A great mist overtook her, and she lost her way. Night came, and she did not know what to do. She kept going on until she saw a light ; she came to it and entered the house. There was not a living person there, but she could see that people were coming. In the farther end of the house she saw a [dead] man. She went down there and hid herself, and what did she meet with there but a big man with a sword by his side. [He gave her the sword, and went away], and the girl picked it up in her hand. She was not there long when there came twelve robbers with a cow. They killed the cow, and cooked part of it and began to eat it. As there were so few knives, the cow was difficult to cut up. 'Go and fetch yourself that sword down there,' said one of them. He went down, but the girl lopped off his head. Another one went down to see what was keeping the first one and she did the same to him. And so, one after another they went down until all of them except the leader had been killed.[1] The leader himself went down to see what had happened to them ; she struck him, but did not kill him, and he ran away severely wounded and made for his father's house. It was fourteen years since he had last been there. They were overjoyed to see him, although they felt ashamed on account of his profession. The girl went to her own father's house.

The robber lay very ill, with doctors attending him. One of them told him that he would not recover until he obtained the heart and liver of the girl who had struck him, for the doctor realised that he had had a blow. [But no one knew who the girl was who had given him the blow.] 'Well,' said his foster-brother, who was in the house at the time, 'I will go about and

mi faighneachdainn de gach neach, anns an teagamh gun
tachair i rium, is gun innis i mar a rinn i. [Bidh fios agam, an
sin, gur h-i a tha agam.]' Dh'fhalbh e, agus thachair dha dol a
steach do thaigh athair na h-ighinne. Thòisich iad air sgeulachdan. 'Ma tà,' ars ise, 'is e rinn an treuntas mi féin.' Dh'innis i
mar a rinn i. 'Ma tà,' ars esan, 'cha phòs mi aon gu bràth ach
thu o'n a bha thu cho tapaidh.' [1] Dh'aontaich cuideachd an
taighe ris a seo, agus phòs iad.

Dh'fhalbh iad an sin gu dachaigh a' ghille, agus e ag ìnnseadh
gun robh móran beairteis aige. Air an rathad, chunnaig ise
craobh ùbhlan, agus dh'iarr i tighinn bhàrr muin an eich gus
am faigheadh [i] beagan dhiubh. 'Is beag a leigeas tu leas ;
is pailt anns a' ghàrradh agam féin iad.' Ghabh iad air aghaidh ;
rànaig iad taigh cailleach nan cearc, is chaidh iad a steach.
Chaidh esan a dh'ionnsaigh an taigh-chòmhnaidh. 'Ma tà,' ars
a' chailleach, 'is tusa ceann mìthealach,[2] mas e do chridhe agus
do ghrùthan [3] a tha gu mac fir a' bhaile seo a leigheas.' Dh'aithnich an nighean gu dé bha gu tachairt. Shìn i air falbh, agus
rànaig i a' chraobh ùbhlan. Bha i a' ruighinn air pàirt dhiubh,
agus có thigeadh ach am fear a phòs i. 'Gu dé chuir an seo thu ?'
ars esan. 'Tha mi ag iarraidh nan ùbhlan,' ars ise. 'Dèan
cabhag, ma tà,' ars esan, 'agus gum bitheamaid a' tilleadh
dhachaigh.' 'Tha gad gu h-àrd ann an siod : thoir dhomh
an claidheamh sin agad, agus gun leagainn iad.' Thug e dhi
e, ach chuir ise [4] an ceann deth 'san spot. Thug i dheth an
t-eudach a bha air, agus chuir i uimpe féin e, agus dh'fhalbh i.
Smuaintich i nach rachadh i chòir taigh a h-athar, mum
faigheadh iad i. Rànaig i taigh gobha, agus ghabh i muinntireas
aige.

Bha i còrdadh riutha gu maith, ach gu dé rinn nighean a'
ghobha ach gaol a ghabhail oirre. Thuirt i ri a h-athair nach
biodh i beò, mur am pòsadh an gille ud i. Bhruidhinn an gobha
ris, ach dh'innis i do'n nighinn mar a bha i ; ach air a shon

---

[1] Somewhat similar incidents in No. 13 (MS. vol. x., No. 26) and MS. vol. xi.,
No. 172.

[2] = mi-shealbhach.

[3] For the heart, liver, etc., see No. 15 (MS. vol. x., No. 29) ; *Béaloideas*, ii., p. 280.

[4] In MS. *esan*, he. This confusion is almost certainly due to the fact that the
reciter is anticipating the next incident in which the heroine dons male attire, in

keep asking everybody on the chance that I shall meet her, and that she will divulge what she did. [Then I'll know it is she.'] He went off, and it happened that he visited the girl's father's house. They began to tell stories. 'Why,' said the girl, 'I myself did a daring deed once !' And she told what she had done. 'Then,' said he, 'I will never marry anyone but you, since you were so fearless.' [1] The people of the house agreed to this, and they got married.

Then they went off to the young man's home, for he had been telling that he was very wealthy. On the way, they saw an apple tree and she wanted to dismount from her horse, to pick a few of the apples. 'You need not trouble yourself,' said he, 'there are plenty in my own garden.' They kept on ; and coming to the house of the hen-wife, they went in. The man went on towards the dwelling-house. 'You certainly are an ill-starred person,' said the old wife, 'if it is your heart and your liver [3] that are going to cure the son of the laird of this place.' The girl realised what was going to happen. Away she ran, and came to the apple tree. She was pulling some of them when who should come up but the man who had married her. 'What sent you here ?' he asked. 'I want the apples,' said she. 'Hurry up then,' said he, 'that we may return home.' 'There's a bunch of them high up there ; give me that sword of yours to cut them down.'[5] He gave it her, and she took his head off there and then. She stripped off his clothes, dressed herself in them, and made off. She decided not to go near her father's house in case her enemies should find her, and she went to a smith's house, and took service with him.

She was getting on very well with the people there, but what did the smith's daughter do but fall in love with her : she told her father that she could not live if that boy did not marry her. The smith spoke to 'him' ; so she told the girl what she really

order to pass herself off as a man. The masculine pronoun seems to be used in sentences in which persons ignorant of her sex are mentioned (except once, p. 188). For similar use of pronouns, see MS. vol. xi., No. 327, where one heroine marries another. See also List of Tales, No. 83 (1).

[5] For the trick of setting a person to gather apples, see No. 15 (MS. vol. x., No. 29) ; *Folk-Lore*, xxxvi., p. 166.

sin, phòs iad. Bha nighean a' ghobha gu toilichte leis a' phòsadh, ach bha a màthair fad an aghaidh a' phòsaidh, agus i daonnan a' faighinn coire dha. Bha i a' gabhail amharais mu a thimcheall, agus a' ceasnachadh na h-ighinne, ach chan ìnnseadh i sìon dhi. Leis a' ghràin a bha aice air an fhear a phòs a h-ighean, bha i deònach droch lìon a chur m'a thimcheall. Is e a rinn i, dh'fhalbh i agus dh'innis i do'n Bhan-uachdaran bha air an fhearann mu thimcheall na h-ighinne agus a pòsaidh ; gur e a bha ann, boireannach ; [is e sin a] bha i a' dèanamh [dheth], agus nach robh fhios nach ann a dhèanadh i olc air cuideigin. 'Coma leat,' ars a' Bhan-uachdaran, 'nì mise dòigh.' Chuir i dh'a iarraidh. 'Gu dé ur gnothach rium-sa ?' ars esan. 'Fanaidh tu an nochd, is ìnnsidh mi duit a màireach e,' ars ise. Bha a companach [fear a' bhaile] a' tighinn [dhachaigh] ; an uair a thànaig e dhachaigh, is e a dh'innis i dha, gun robh [am] fear [a] phòs nighean a' ghobha a staigh a raoir, agus gun tànaig e a steach d'a seòmar air feadh na h-oidhche. Theab an t-Uachd-aran boil a ghabhail leis an tàmailt. Dh'òrdaich e teine mór a thogail, agus a losgadh. Bha nighean a' ghobha gu tùrsach an uair a bha i gu bhith air a cur anns an teinidh. Thuirt i ris an Uachdaran bruidhinn ris. Rinn e sin, agus dh'innis e dha mar a bha gach nì, agus mar a dh'éirich dhi. An uair a chunnaig an duine-uasal seo cho olc is a bha a bhean, loisg e i 'san teinidh, agus [bean a' ghobha] màthair na h-ighinne. Phòs esan an nighean a bha an seo, agus thug e air a' ghille-frithealaidh aige nighean a' ghobha a phòsadh, agus bha iad uile cho sona. An déidh gach nì, chuir e fios gu a cuideachd mar a thachair dhi, ach cha robh fios ciamar a dh'éirich do'n robair.

(Mary Morrison, or Widow Samuel McDonald, Aird, Benbecula.)

NOTES

The scribe was D. Torrie. For the reciter, see Notes to No. 59 of this book.

The object of the plot may have been to create a dilemma for the heroine —either be condemned for her alleged crime, or admit that she was a woman was ; in spite of that, however, they married. The smith's daughter was quite pleased with the marriage, but her mother was much against it, and she was always finding fault with 'him'. She was getting suspicious about 'him', and questioning her daughter, but her daughter would not tell her anything. Because of her loathing for the 'man' her daughter married, the mother wanted to trap 'him' in an evil snare. What she did was to go and tell the laird's wife about her daughter and about the marriage ; that the husband was a woman—[at least that was what] she made [of it], and that there was no knowing but that she would do somebody some mischief.

'Never you mind,' said the laird's wife, 'I will devise a plan.' The laird's wife sent for 'him'. 'What is your business with me ?' 'he' asked. 'You shall stay here tonight, and tomorrow I will tell you,' she replied. Now her husband, the laird of the place, was coming home ; when he did, what his wife told him was that [the] man [who] had married the smith's daughter had been in the house the night before, and that during the night he had come into her bedroom. The laird nearly went mad with the disgrace of the thing. He ordered a big fire to be kindled and to have 'him' burnt. The smith's daughter was very miserable when the girl was about to be put into the fire, and she asked the laird to speak to 'him'. The laird did so, and 'he' told him how things were, and what had happened to her. When the gentleman saw how wicked his wife was, he burned her in the fire and the smith's wife as well, the girl's mother. Then he married this young woman, and he made his serving-boy marry the smith's daughter, and they were all so happy. When everything was over, the laird sent word to the girl's people, telling them how she had fared, but no one knew what happened to the robber.

in order to clear herself. If the smith's wife did not suspect that she was a woman, what was it that she wished to find out from her daughter and that her daughter refused to tell her ?

NA TRI SAIGHDEARAN

No. 62.   [*MS. Vol. x., No. 116*]

(Glaschu, sèathamh deug de Iuli, aon mhìle ochd ceud
agus dà fhichead 's a naoi deug.)

BHA siod ann uair, an taobh tuath na h-Alba, saighdear, agus
is e a b'ainm dha, Iain ; agus latha de na lathaichean smuainich
e teicheadh, agus mar seo a bha. Theich Iain, agus bha e
gabhail roimhe có dhiùbh astar là no dhà mus tànaig an tòir
air. Ach chaidh Iain ionndrainn, agus chuireadh as a dhéidh,
agus fhuair an dithis dhaoine a dh'fhalbh òrdugh cia fhad a
bha iad gu fuireach, có dhiùbh gheibheadh iad Iain gus nach
fhaigheadh. Bha aca-san ri bhith air ais anns an am a dh'òrd-
aicheadh dhaibh, air neadh bha iad féin gus a bhith air am
peanasachadh cho math ri Iain, ged a bhiodh e aca, ma bha e
thairis air an tìm a fhuair iad. Bha seo gu math, is cha robh
gu h-olc. Chaidh na daoine ro fhada air adhart mus d'fhuair
iad Iain agus nach b'urrainn daibh a bhith air ais ann an sìde.[1]
Ghlac iad Iain, [ach] cha robh fios aca gu dé dhèanadh iad,
ach thuirt Iain riutha, 'Nis,' ars esan, 'innsidh mise dhuibh gu
dé nì sibh. Tha sibh a nis là air dheireadh air na h-òrduigh,
agus ma théid sibh air ais gheibh sibh a cheart uiread de pheanas
is a gheibh mise, agus is e as fheàrr dhuibh falbh còmhla rium-sa,
agus chan eagal duinn.'

Mar seo bha. Dh'fhalbh an triùir cuideachd, Iain agus an
Sergeant agus an Corporal : (chan 'eil Gàidhlig agam orra
sin ceart).[2] Ach coma, bha iad a' gabhail air adhart gus an
tànaig iad a dh'ionnsaigh seann chaisteil mhóir ann am monadh,
agus cha robh taigh eile, cù, no duine mar uidhe mhìltean do'n
taigh seo. Ghabh iad a staigh, ach cha robh duine beò ann a
chuireadh dragh orra. 'Gabhaidh sinn fois na h-oidhche ann
an seo,' ars Iain. Bha eagal air an dithis eile fuireach, ach coma,

---

[1] The Gaelic is wrong here. It should have been either *cho fada*, or, *cha b'urrainn*.
For *sìde* read *tìde* ?
[2] Comment by the reciter.

THE THREE SOLDIERS

No. 62.   [*MS. Vol. x., No. 116*]

(Glasgow, the seventeenth of July, 1849.)

ONCE upon a time there was a soldier in the North of Scotland called Iain. One day he made up his mind to desert, and so he did. Iain fled, and had completed at least a day's journey and perhaps two before he was pursued. But, having been missed, Iain was pursued and the two men who went after him received orders as to how long they were to stay away—whether they found Iain or not. They were to be back in the time allowed them, or else they were to be punished as well as Iain, even if they had caught him, if they were over the time allotted to them. This was all very well. But the men had travelled so very far before they found Iain that they were unable to be back in time ; and when they caught him, they did not know what to do. So Iain said to them, 'I will tell you what to do. You are now a day late beyond the time allowed, and if you go back, you will be punished quite as much as I ; so you had better go with me instead, and we'll be all right.'

That was what they did. The three of them went off together, Iain and the Sergeant and the Corporal (I have no proper Gaelic words for these).[2] Anyway, they pressed on till they came to a huge old castle on the moors, and there was neither house nor dog nor man within miles of it. They went straight in, but there was not a single person there to trouble them. 'We will rest here for the night,' said Iain. The other two were afraid to stay, but nevertheless they did stay. Next day Iain said, 'We will get dh'fhuirich iad, agus an ath-là thuirt Iain, 'Nì sinn dòigh air teinidh, agus théid fear againn a dh'iasgach agus fear a shealg, agus fanaidh fear aig an taigh a dheasachadh an tràth-nòin.' B'e an tràth-nòin a bha gus a bhith aca caob de fheòil a fhuair iad dòigh air choireigin, agus bha an Sergeant gus a ròstadh air chionn chàich.

Mar seo bha. Dh'fhalbh Iain is an Corporal, agus an uair a bha an Sergeant a' ròstadh na feòla, thànaig bodach[1] beag ruadh a staigh, agus ars esan, 'Is brèagha am fàileadh a tha agad, a dhuine ; an toir thu dhòmh-sa pàirt de'n ròsta ?' 'Cha toir bìdeag,' ars an Sergeant. Chaidh am Bodach suas air a tharsaing, agus bhuail e an Sergeant ann an toll na cluaise, agus dh'fhalbh e leis an ròsta. An uair a dh'éirich an Sergeant as a' phaisean, cha robh sgeul air an ròst. Cha robh fios aige ciod a dhèanadh e an uair a thigeadh na fir eile dhachaigh. Coma, thànaig na fir, is cha robh smod aig an t-Sergeant dhaibh. Thòisich iad air a chàineadh an uair a dh'innis e dhaibh mar a dh'éirich dha. 'Dìth-bìdh ort,' ars iad-san, 'a leig an tràthnòin leis a' bhodach ghrànda.' 'Theagamh,' ars esan, 'gun dèan e a leithid cheudna oirbh-se fhathast.' Bha seo gu math, is cha robh gu h-olc.

A màireach dh'fhan an Corporal aig an taigh, agus b'e an t-samhail cheudna dha-san. An uair a bha an ròsta gus a bhith deas, thànaig am Bodach Ruadh a staigh. 'Fiu, fomha, fomhagraich,' ars am Bodach Ruadh, 'tha mi faighinn[2] fàile an fhiadhbheathaich. An toir thu dhomh fhéin pàirt de'n ròsta ?' 'Ma tà, cha toir bìdeag,' ars an Corporal. Char[3] am Bodach suas air a tharsaing, bhuail e an Corporal ann an toll na cluaise, agus leag e e, agus dh'fhalbh e leis an ròsta. B'e an dòigh cheudna an uair a thànaig na daoine eile dhachaigh. Cha robh tràthnòin aig a' Chorporal air an cinn.[4] 'Nach duirt mi riut,' ars an Sergeant, 'gun dèanadh e a leithid cheudna ort-sa is a rinn e orm-sa ?' 'Dìth-bìdh oirbh le chéile, mar dhaoine tapaidh, an uair a leig sibh an tràth-nòin leis a' bhodach ghrànda,' ars Iain. 'Stad thusa,' ars iad-san, 'nì e a leithid cheudna ort-sa a màireach.' 'Ma nì, chì sinn,' ars Iain.

Coma, dh'fhuirich Iain an ath-latha, agus an uair a bha an

---

[1] *bodach*, besides meaning an old man, means also a goblin, spectre. In these tales it usually connotes something unearthly, impossible to render in English.

a fire going somehow, and one of us shall go fishing, another shall go hunting, and the third can stay at home and cook the evening meal.' The meal they were to have was a chunk of meat which they had found in some manner, and the Sergeant was to roast it and have it ready for the others.

So it was. Iain and the Corporal went off, but while the Sergeant was roasting the meat, a little, red-haired old man [1] came in. 'What a fine smell you have here, my good man,' said he. 'Will you give me a piece of the roast?' 'Not a bite,' replied the Sergeant. The old man edged up to the Sergeant and struck him in the ear and made off with the roast. When the Sergeant recovered consciousness there was no sign of the roast, and he did not know what to do when the others came home. However, the men came, and not a bit did the Sergeant have for them; and when he told them what had befallen him, they began to miscall him. 'Bad luck to you,' said they, 'to let the disagreeable old man go off with the dinner!' 'Perhaps he will do the same to you yet,' replied the Sergeant. This was all very well.

Next day, the Corporal stayed at home, and the same thing happened to him. When the roast was almost ready, in came the red-haired old man. 'Fee, fie, fo fum,' said the red-haired old man, 'I smell a wild animal's flesh. Will you give me a piece of the roast?' 'No, not a bite,' replied the Corporal. The old man edged up to him, struck him in the ear, knocked him down, and made off with the roast. So things were just the same when the others came home—the Corporal had no dinner for them. 'Didn't I tell you,' said the Sergeant, 'that he would do the same to you as he did to me?' 'Bad luck to you both for smart fellows, to let the disagreeable old man go off with the dinner!' said Iain. 'You wait,' said they, 'he'll do the same to you tomorrow.' 'We shall see,' said Iain.

Anyway, Iain stayed at home next day, and when the evening

---

[2] *feibbin* (?) in MS. [3] So MS., for *chaidh*. [4] So MS., for *cionn*.

tràth-nòin ris an teinidh, thànaig am Bodach Ruadh a staigh, agus thuirt e ri Iain mar a thuirt e ris an t-Sergeant an ceud là, 'Is brèagha am fàileadh a tha agad, a dhuine chòir ; an toir thu dhomh pàirt de'n ròsta ?' 'Ma tà, is mi bheir,' ars Iain, 'teann a nuas.' Bha stob de dh'iarann dearg aig Iain anns an teinidh a' feitheamh air a' Bhodach. Thòisich an dithis air còmhradh tacan, ach mus d'fhuair am Bodach sìde air Iain a bhualadh, thug e tarraing air a' ph[l]ocan iarainn a bha aige 'san teinidh, agus spàrr e siod an sùil a' Bhodaich. Dh'éirich am Bodach a mach leis a' bhior 'na shùil agus Iain 'na dhéidh, agus e ag éigheach, 'Diathad mo dhuidh ! diathad mo dhuidh !' [1] Ach lean Iain am Bodach gus am faca e c'àite an deach e. Rànaig am Bodach tolm gorm cnuic, agus dh'fhosgail an cnoc agus chaidh am Bodach a sìos a fianais, ach chum Iain beachd air an àite, agus thill e dhachaigh a dhèanamh deas an tràth-nòin do na seòid a bha air falbh. An uair a thànaig iad-san, ghabh iad iongantas mór an ròsta bhith air an cinn. Dh'fhèoraich iad de Iain am faca e am Bodach Ruadh an diugh ; thuirt gum faca, agus gun tug e dha a chòir de'n tràth-nòin. Dh'innis Iain mar a rinn e, agus mas e siod am Bodach grànda a bha toirt uapa a' bhìdh, nach mór a b'fhiach iad. Thuirt Iain riutha bhith sgiobalta, is an tràth-nòin a ghabhail, gus am falbhadh iad an déidh a' Bhodaich.

Fhuair iad cliabh, agus clag, agus na b'urrainn daibh de ròpan a thional, agus dh'fhalbh iad a dh'ionnsaigh an tuill anns an deach am Bodach a sìos. Cheangail Iain an clag ris a' chliabh, agus chuir iad an Sergeant anns a' chliabh, agus leig iad a sìos e. Cha b'fhada char [= chaidh] e sìos, dar a bhuail e an clag. Tharraing na fir a bha urad. 'Ciod a chunnaig thu an siod ?' ars Iain. 'Ach ! chan fhaca dad ach toll dubh, grànda, agus bha mi gabhail eagail.' 'Thud ! ud ! mo nàire ort féin !' ars Iain. Coma, char an Corporal 'sa' chliabh, agus char esan beagan na b'fhaide sìos na an Sergeant, agus bhuail e an clag. Tharraing na fir a bha urad. 'Gu dé chunnaig thu an siod ?'

---

[1] MS. *diathad mo dhuidh*. As the writing and spelling of the MS. were very poor, it is not certain whether these words are spelt correctly or what they mean. If *dìot*, a meal of food is meant, *mo dhuidh* probably means 'of my disaster,' and is possibly a corruption of *mo dhubhaidh*, 'of my blackening.' Context would appear to warrant such a translation. *Dubh* is used in Gaelic to mean disaster or misfortune. *Cf.*

meal was at the fire in came the red-haired old man, and he said to Iain as he had said the first day to the Sergeant, 'What a fine smell you have here, good man ; will you give me a piece of the roast ?' 'Why, surely,' replied Iain, 'come along.' Iain had a red-hot iron spit in the fire, ready waiting for the old man. The two began to talk for a little, but before the old man had time to strike, Iain drew out the iron spit he had in the fire and thrust it into the old man's eye. The old man leapt out with the spit in his eye, and Iain after him, the old man shouting, 'Dinner of my woe ! Dinner of my woe !' But Iain followed the old man till he saw where he went. The old man came to a little green knoll ; the hill opened and he disappeared ; but Iain took note of the place and returned home to prepare dinner for the lads who were away. When they came home, they were very much surprised that the roast was there awaiting them. They asked Iain if he had seen the red-haired old man that day ; he said that he had, and that he had given him his fair share of the meal. Then he told them what he had done, and said that if this was the disagreeable old man who took the food from them, they were not worth much. He ordered them to look sharp and eat their meal, so that they might go after the old man.

They got a basket and a bell and as much rope as they could gather, and set off for the hole down which the old man had gone. Iain tied the bell to the basket ; they put the Sergeant into the basket and let him down. He had not gone far down when he struck the bell and the men who were above hauled him up. 'What did you see there ?' asked Iain. 'Oh, I saw nothing but a hideous black hole, and I was becoming frightened.' 'Shame on you !' said Iain. But then the Corporal got into the basket ; he went down a little farther than the Sergeant ; then he struck the bell, and the men above hauled. 'What did you see there ?' asked Iain. 'Oh, I saw nothing but a hideous black

expression *Mhic na duibhe* which is very common. So with *black* in English, *e.g.* Black Friday, etc. Or read *mo dhunaidh* ? or *mo dhuaidh* ? For a supernatural who comes up from underground and fights mortals for their dinner, see *Folk-Lore*, xxxiv., p. 363.

ars Iain. 'Ach ! chan fhaca mise ach toll dubh, grànda, agus
bha mi gabhail eagail.' 'Dìth-bìdh oirbh le chéile,' ars Iain,
'leigibh mi féin ann.' Leig iad Iain a sìos gus an do theirig na
ròpan daibh, is chan fhaigheadh Iain na b'fhaide. Bhuail e an
clag agus tharraing na fir. Thànaig Iain. 'Car son nach do
leig sibh sìos na b'fhaide mi ?' ars esan. 'Theirig na ròpan,'
ars iad-san. 'Bithibh a' falbh agus faighibh tuilleadh.' Dh'fhalbh
iad agus fhuair iad tuilleadh ann an àiteigin, agus thànaig iad
do [*sic*] Iain. Chaidh Iain anns a' chliabh a rithist, agus rànaig
e shìos, agus dar a rànaig, is e a bha aige an saoghal bu bhrèagha
chunnaig duine riamh.

Thug e sùil thar a ghualainn, agus chunnaig e feannag air
cnoc os a chionn. Thuirt an fheannag, 'Iain bhochd ! Iain
bhochd ! cha tànaig duine riamh an seo a chaidh air ais.' 'Tha
a chead aige,' [1] ars Iain. An ath-shùil a thug e, bha an fheannag
'na pònaidh beag eich 'na seasamh làimh ris, agus mharcaich
e am pònaidh, agus thug am pònaidh e a dh'ionnsaigh caisteil
a bha air a dhèanamh le copar. Agus bha boireannach anns
a' chaisteal cho brèagha is a chunnaig e riamh, agus ghabh e
tlachd mór dhith, agus ise dheth. Ach coma có dhiùbh, thànaig
e a dh'ionnsaigh a' phònaidh an dara h-uair, agus thug am
pònaidh e do chaisteal a bha air a dhèanamh le h-airgead, agus
bha boireannach an seo a bha na bu bhrèagha na an té a bha
'sa' chaisteal chopair gu fada. Agus seo an té a dh'fheumadh
a bhith aig Iain. Ach coma, bha Iain 'na bhalach glé sgiobalta,
glan, le a chòta beag dearg air.[2] Cha mhór a chunnaig iad riamh
a bha coltach ris, agus ghabh a h-uile té tlachd de fhear a'
chòta ruaidh : ach thànaig e a rithist a dh'ionnsaigh a' phònaidh
agus thug e e do chaisteal a bha air a dhèanamh le h-òr, ach is
ann an seo a bha an òigh àlainn, chan fhaca duine riamh
boireannach cho brèagha rithe seo. Seo a nise an té a
dh'fheumadh a bhith aig Iain, agus rinn e suas ris na h-uile
h-aonan de na boireannaich gu falbh leis, ach bha an té bu
bhrèagha gu bhith aige fhéin, 's cha b'fhuilear dha air son a
thuruis.

Ach bha am Bodach Ruadh fhathast gun fhaotainn. Cha

---

[1] *Lit.* he (it) has his (its) permission, *i.e.* let things be as they please. The phrase
also means 'serves him right !'

[2] The scarlet coat. The ladies who now begin to appear always refer to the hero,

hole, and I was becoming frightened.' 'Bad luck to you both !' said Iain, 'let me get in myself.' They lowered him down till they came to the end of the ropes and he could get no farther. He struck the bell, and the men above hauled, and he came up. 'Why didn't you let me down farther?' said he. 'The ropes came to an end,' replied the men. 'Off with you, and get some more !' Off they went, found more rope somewhere, and came back to Iain. He got into the basket again, and went down to the bottom. When he got down, what did he find there but the most beautiful world that man ever saw.

On glancing over his shoulder he saw a crow on a hill above him. 'Poor Iain ! poor Iain !' said the crow. 'No man ever came here who went back again.' 'What do I care !' said Iain.[1] But the next glance he gave, the crow was a little pony standing beside him. Off he rode on the pony, and the pony brought him to a castle built of copper. In the castle was a woman as beautiful as he had ever seen, and he took a great liking to her, and she to him. However, he came to where the pony was a second time, and the pony carried him to a castle built of silver ; and here there was a woman who was far more beautiful than the one in the copper castle. And she was now the one that Iain must have. Iain was a fine, smart lad in his little red coat ;[2] people had seldom seen his equal, and every woman took a liking to the man of the red coat. But he went to the pony again, and the pony carried him to a castle built of gold. In this castle lived a lovely maiden—no man had ever seen one so lovely. She was now the one that Iain must have. He arranged with all three women to go with him, but the most beautiful one was to be for himself, nor was that more than a fit reward for his journey.

But the red-haired old man was still undiscovered, and there

later on in the story, when he provides them with the crowns, as *fear a' chòta ruaidh*, 'the man with the red coat' ; *dearg* and *ruadh* are different shades of red, but both are applied to the red coats formerly characteristic of the British Army.

robh fios c'àite an robh e ri bhith air fhaotainn, ach chaidh
e a dh'ionnsaigh a' phònaidh, agus mharcaich e a rithist e,
agus thug e e troimh àite brèagh, ro bhrèagh a làthair,[1] agus a'
dol seachad aig taobh sràid no rathaid air choireigin, chunnaig
e am Bodach Ruadh, agus leig am Bodach an glaodh as—
'Diathad mo dhuidh ! diathad mo dhuidh !'[2] 'Nach d'fhuair mi
nise thu ?' ars Iain. 'O ! fhuair,' ars am Bodach Ruadh, 'ach,'
ars esan ri Iain, 'innsidh mise dhuit gu dé nì sinn. Théid thusa
trì làithean 'gad fhalach, agus théid mise trì làithean eile, agus
ma gheibh mise thusa anns na trì làithean sin, faodaidh mi do
mharbhadh, ach ma gheibh thusa mise, faodaidh tu mise a
mharbhadh.'[3]

Mar seo a bha. Chaidh Iain dh'a fhalach an toiseach, agus
thànaig e a dh'ionnsaigh a' phònaidh, agus dh'innis e dha an
cùnnradh a bha eadar e fhéin agus am Bodach Ruadh, agus
có e am Bodach Ruadh ach rìgh an àite air fad, agus an lagh
a rinn e fhéin, cha b'urrainn da a bristeadh [sic]. Ach dh'fheòraich
Iain de'n phònaidh, c'àite an rachadh e dh'a fhalach. 'Feuch,'
ars esan, 'am bheil fiacail fuasgailte 'nam charbad ?' 'Tha,'
ars Iain, 'aonan ann.' 'Spìon as i, agus leum fhéin 'na h-àite.'
Rinn Iain siod, 's cha d'fhuair am Bodach Ruadh an oidhche
sin e. An ath-oidhche, thànaig Iain do'n [sic] phònaidh. 'C'àite
an téid mi an nochd ?' ars esan. 'Feuch,' ars ise,[4] 'am bheil
tarraing fuasgailte 'nam chrudh ?' 'Tha aonan ann,' ars Iain.
'Spìon as i, agus leum fhéin 'na h-àite.' Rinn Iain sin, is cha
d'fhuair am Bodach Ruadh an oidhche sin e. 'Diathad mo
dhuidh, diathad mo dhuidh !' ars am Bodach. 'Cha d'fhuair
thu an diugh mi,' ars Iain. 'Cha d'fhuair,' ars esan, 'ach gheibh
mi an nochd thu.' 'Feuch ris,' arsa Iain. Thànaig e do'n [sic]
phònaidh. 'C'àite an téid mi an nochd ?' 'Feuch am bheil
gaoisdean liath 'nam fheaman ?' 'Tha aonan ann,' ars Iain.
'Spìon as e, agus leum fhéin 'na àite.' Rinn Iain sin. 'S cha
d'fhuair am Bodach Ruadh an oidhche sin e.

A nise, bha Iain deas de a fhalach, ach bha am Bodach
Ruadh ri tòiseachadh. Dh'fhalbh am Bodach Ruadh dh'a

---

[1] This is probably intended to be 'a leabhara', 'by the Book.'
[2] See p. 194.
[3] At this point, they probably bespell each other to the duel in the good old-
fashioned Gaelic way.

was no knowing where he was to be found. So Iain came to the pony and mounted him again, and the pony brought him through a beautiful place, very splendid indeed it was ; and when he was going along at the side of some street or road, he saw the red-haired old man. The old man gave a loud cry : 'Dinner of my woe ! Dinner of my woe !' [2] 'I've found you now, have I not,' said Iain. 'Yes, you have,' said the old man. 'But,' said he to Iain, 'I'll tell you what we shall do. You shall go and hide for three days, and if I find you during these three days, I may kill you ; but if you find me, you may kill me.' [3]

That is what they did. Iain was the first to go and hide, and he came to where the pony was and told the pony of the bargain between himself and the red-haired old man. Now, who should the red-haired old man be but the king of the whole place, and the law that he made himself, he could not break. Iain asked the pony where he should go to hide himself. 'See if there's a tooth loose in my jaw,' said the pony. 'Yes,' said Iain, 'there is one.' 'Tug it out and jump into its place yourself.' Iain did this, and the red-haired old man did not find him that night. The following night, Iain went to the pony. 'Where shall I go tonight ?' he asked. 'See if there's a nail loose in my shoe,' said she. 'Yes,' said Iain, 'there is one.' 'Tug it out and jump into its place yourself.' Iain did this, and the red-haired old man did not find him that night. 'Dinner of my woe ! Dinner of my woe !' said the old man. 'You didn't find me today,' said Iain. 'No,' replied the other, 'but I'll find you tonight.' 'Try it !' said Iain, and went to the pony. 'Where shall I go tonight ?' ' See if there's a grey hair in my tail.' 'There is one there,' said Iain. 'Tug it out and jump into its place yourself.' Iain did so, and the red-haired old man did not find him that night.

Iain had finished his part of the hiding now, and the red-haired old man was to begin. He went off to hide himself, and

---

⁴ *ise* (= she, herself) here, the mind of the reciter anticipating the assumption of hoodie shape.

fhalach, ach cha robh fios aig Iain c'àite am faigheadh e e.
Thànaig e a dh'ionnsaigh a' phònaidh. 'Saoil thu,' ars Iain,
'c'àite am bheil am Bodach Ruadh an nochd?' 'Ìnnsidh mise
sin dhuit,' ars Anna.[1] Bha am pònaidh a nise 'na fheannaig[2]
a rithist. 'Théid thu suas a dh'ionnsaigh loch a tha os cionn
cùirtibh an rìgh, agus chì thu trì tunnagan a' snàmh air an loch,
agus bheir thu leat slat agus cuiridh tu na tunnagan air tìr ;
agus buailidh tu slat air té dhiubh agus beiridh i ugh, agus
togaidh tusa an t-ugh agus buailidh tu e ri cloich, agus tha am
Bodach Ruadh ann an sin.'

Mar seo a bha. Rinn Iain mar a dh'iarr an fheannag air,
agus fhuair e mar a thuirt i. Agus dar a bha Iain dol a bhristeadh
an uighe, 'Och ! mi fhéin a th'ann ! mi fhéin a th'ann !' ars
am Bodach Ruadh. 'Dìth-bìdh ort, a bhodaich ghràinde, ciod
e a thug an seo thu ? Nach robh mi an dùil gum faighinn an
t-ugh ud d'a itheadh ? Fhuair mi nis thu,' ars Iain. 'Fhuair,'
ars esan, 'ach feuch am faigh thu a rithist mi. Diathad mo
dhuidh !' ars am Bodach Ruadh an dara uair. Chaidh e dh'a
fhalach.

Thànaig Iain do'n [sic] fheannaig. 'Saoil thu c'àite am bheil
e an diugh ?' ars Iain. 'Ma tà, ìnnsidh mise sin duit,' ars Anna ;
'théid thu suas do phàirc bhrèagh a tha os cionn taigh an rìgh,
agus chì thu craobh ann an sin air am bheil ùbhlan, agus bheir
thu crathadh air a' chraoibh, agus tuitidh ubhal dhith agus
togaidh tu e, agus nì thu dà leth dheth leis an sgian, agus tha
am Bodach Ruadh ann an sin.' Rinn Iain mar a dh'iarr Anna
air, agus dar a bha e dol a ghearradh an ubhail, leig am Bodach
Ruadh a' ghrad éigh as, 'Mi féin a th'ann ! mi féin a th'ann !'
'O ! dìth-bìdh ort, a Bhodaich ghràinde ! ciod e thug an seo
thu ? Nach robh mi an dùil gum faighinn an t-ubhal ud dh'a
itheadh ? Fhuair mi nis thu,' ars Iain. 'O ! fhuair,' ars am

---

[1] *anna*, in MS. at this place.

[2] *fheannaig*, in MS. at this place, one and the same creature being spoken of as
a hoodie-crow, a pony, or Anna, without any explanation of the change of name or
change of character. A hoodie-crow in Gaelic is *feannag*. When the article is
prefixed, we have *an fheannag*. As the *fh*, or 'aspirated' *f*, is silent, and has no effect
on the other letters, the word sounds almost exactly like *Annag*, or 'little Annie.'
The scribe was very uncertain in the spelling of the MS., and it is quite possible that
he imagined that *Anna* was the proper way of spelling the 'aspirated' *fheannag*. After

Iain did not know where he should find him. So he came to the pony. 'Where do you suppose the red-haired old man will be tonight?' asked Iain. 'I'll tell you that,' said Anna. The pony was now a crow again.[2] 'You shall go up towards the loch above the King's courts, and there you will see three ducks swimming. Take a rod with you and drive the ducks ashore; you shall strike one of them with a rod, and it will lay an egg. You shall pick up the egg, and knock it against a stone, and there the red-haired old man will be.'

So it turned out. Iain did as the crow asked him, and found that things happened as she had said. When Iain was going to break the egg: 'Oh, it is I! it is I!' cried the red-haired old man. 'Bad luck to you, ugly old man, what brought you here?' said Iain. 'Did I not expect to have that egg to eat! But I have found you now,' said he. 'Yes, you have found me,' said the old man, 'but try if you can find me again.' Then said the old man a second time, 'Dinner of my woe!' He went to hide himself.

Iain went to the crow. 'Where do you suppose he is today?' asked Iain. 'Well, I'll tell you that,' said Anna; 'you must go up to the fine park above the King's house, and there you will see a tree with apples on it. Shake the tree and an apple will fall. Pick up the apple and cut it in two halves with a knife, and there will the red-haired old man be.' Iain did as Anna asked him, and when he was about to cut the apple the old man gave a sudden shout, 'It is I! it is I!' 'Oh, bad luck to you, ugly old man; what brought you here?' said Iain. 'Did I not expect to have that apple to eat! But I have found you now,' said he. 'Yes, you have found me,' replied the old man, 'but try if you can find me tonight.' This was the last time the old

---

careful examination of the MS. I could not be sure whether the scribe, in writing *Anna* with a capital *A*, did so because of his ignorance of the rules of spelling, or because he wanted to convey that Anna was the name of the hoodie. Islay notes elsewhere that one of his collectors thought that the name of another Anna, Anna Diucalas, had something to do with raven black hair. *W. H. Tales*, iii., p. 217 *n.*

In other tales, a carrying eagle brings the hero up from the underground regions, or takes him across the ocean. See Nos. 15, 24 (MS. vol. x., Nos. 29, 44).

Bodach, 'ach feuch am faigh thu an nochd mi.' B'e seo an turus mu dheireadh do'n Bhodach bhith fo gheasan,[1] ach bha aige ri dol dh'a fhalach aon uair eile.

Rànaig Iain Anna. 'Saoil thu,' ars Iain, 'c'àite am bi e an nochd?' 'Ma tà, ìnnsidh mise sin duit,' ars Anna, 'tha cuirm mhór gus a bhith an nochd ann an taigh an rìgh, agus tha na h-uile fear de uaislibh [2] an àite gus a bhith ann cuideachd, agus cuiridh mi fhéin deise ort, agus cha bhi na's fheàrr na i aig a' chuirm, agus cuiridh mi fàinne òir air do mheur, agus nì thusa suas ri nighean an rìgh, agus bidh thu a' gealltainn a pòsadh, agus bidh fàinne brèagh oirre fhéin, agus their thusa rithe, "Thoir dhomh fhéin feuchainn de'n fhàinne sin, agus cuiridh mi làimh ri m'fhear fhéin e, agus dar a phòsas sinn, gheibh thu le chéile iad," agus dar a gheibh thu e, théid thu a mach, agus cuiridh tu am fàinne eadar dhà chloich mar gum bitheadh tu dol d'a bhristeadh, agus tha am Bodach Ruadh an sin.'

Rinneadh mar a thuirt Anna ; sgeadaich i Iain coltach ri tighearna-fearainn, agus dh'fhalbh e a shuirghe air Nighean an Rìgh. Fhuair e am fàinne [bho Nighean an Rìgh, mar a chomhairlich an fheannag da] agus chaidh e a mach leis, agus chuir e eadar dhà chloich e, agus dar a thog e a' chlach eile gus a bhristeadh, leig am bodach a' ghrad éighe, 'Mi féin a th'ann ! Mi féin a th'ann !' 'Dìth-bìdh ort, a bhodaich ghràinde ! Ciod e thug an seo thu ? Nach robh mi an dùil gum faighinn am fàinne gus a thoirt do m' bhean, dar a phòsas sinn ?' 'Och ! och !' ars am Bodach Ruadh, 'diathad mo dhuidh ! diathad mo dhuidh !' 'A nis,' ars Iain, 'tha comas agam-sa do mharbhadh mu dheireadh.' 'Och, tha,' ars am Bodach, 'ach nì thu na's fheàrr na sin. Leig liom mo bheatha, agus gheibh thu gu ruig leth mo rìoghachd ; is mise rìgh an àite seo, agus tha mi nise uaithe [3] sheachd bliadhna fuidh gheasan, ach tha mi gu bhith réidh is iad a màireach, agus nì mi duine sona dhìot-sa ri do bheò, ma leigeas tu mo bheatha liom. Bheir mi dhuit mo nighean, agus leth na rìoghachd.' An uair a chunnaig Iain seo, bha e coma dha fhéin is dh'a rìoghachd, ach fhuair e suim mhath airgid air son beatha a' Bhodaich.[4]

---

[1] A definite indication that the Bodach and Iain must have bespelled each other in the usual Gaelic manner to have this curious game at hide-and-seek, the stakes to be the life of the loser.

man had to act under spells,[1] but he still had to go and hide himself once more.

Iain went to Anna. 'Where do you think he will be tonight?' 'Well, I'll tell you,' said Anna : 'there is going to be a great feast tonight in the King's house, and all the nobles of the place are to be there together. Now, I will dress you in a suit, and a better one will not be seen at the banquet ; I will put a ring of gold on your finger, and you shall pay court to the King's daughter. She will be wearing a fine ring too. You must say to her, " Let me have that ring for a while, and I will wear it beside my own ; and when we marry, you shall have them both." But when you get the ring, go outside and put the ring between two stones as though you were going to break it. You will find the red-haired old man in the ring.'

What Anna said was done. She arrayed Iain like a landed laird, and off he went to court the daughter of the King. He got the ring [from the King's daughter as the crow had advised him], and taking it outside with him, placed it between two stones to break it. But when he raised the other stone to do so, the old man gave a sudden shout, 'It is I ! it is I !' 'Bad luck to you, ugly old man ; what has brought you here ?' asked Iain. 'Did I not expect to have that ring to give my wife when we marry ?' 'Alas,' said the red-haired old man, 'Dinner of my woe ! Dinner of my woe !' 'Now,' said Iain, 'at last it is in my power to kill you.' 'Alas, that is so,' said the old man, 'but you shall do better than that. Grant me my life, and you shall have up to half of my kingdom. I am the king of this place, and for seven years have I been enchanted, but tomorrow I am free, and I will make a happy man of you as long as you live, if you will spare my life. I will give you my daughter and half of the kingdom.' When Iain saw how things were, he was quite indifferent to the old man and his kingdom, but he got a good sum of money for the old man's life. [4]

---

[1] *na h-uile do dhusleibh*, in MS.

[3] So in MS.

[4] The Bodach, by far the most interesting character, drops out of the story here, together with his rejected daughter.

Ach bha rudeigin ann an sùil Iain chòir fad na h-ùine le [1] chunnaig e na boireannaich anns na caisteil. Bha e nis air falbh air tòir nam boireannach air son an toirt leis do chàch, agus bha an té bu bhrèagha gu bhith aige féin. [Fhuair e na boireannaich.] Thànaig Iain a nise a dh'ionnsaigh an tuill leis an triùir bhoireannach, agus creid thusa gun robh gu leòr aca leò.[2] Bha iad uile toileach tighinn còmhla ris, agus an t-àite fhàgail. Chuir e an té a bha anns a' chaisteal chopair anns a' chliabh an toiseach, agus bhuail e an clag. Tharraing na fir a bha urad, is bha a shìde aca le dh'fhalbh Iain. Dar a chunnaig iad am boireannach brèagha a bha an seo, is ann a bhitheadh iad aig a chéile a dh'fheuchainn có aige bhitheadh i. 'O,' ars ise, 'leigibh a sìos ; tha té na's brèagha na mise gun tighinn fhathast.' Leig iad a sìos an cliabh, agus tharraing iad a rithist, agus ma bha an té eile brèagha, is i an té seo bu ro bhrèagha. Chaidh na fir [am badaibh] a chéile a rithist, air son na té bu bhrèagha. 'O,' ars ise, 'leigibh a sìos, tha té na's brèagha na mise gun tighinn fhathast.' Leig iad a nise a sìos a rithist. Chuir Iain an té aige fhéin air falbh mu dheireadh, agus dar a rànaig ise siod far am bitheadh an t-sabaid a dh'fheuchainn có aige bhitheadh an té bu bhrèagha na càch uile, ach cha ghabhadh ise gnothach ri duine dhiubh gus an tigeadh Iain. 'Leigibh a nise,' ars ise, 'a sìos air a shon fhéin.'

* * * * *

[Chunnaig Anna agus Iain an cliabh an seo a nuas dh'an ionnsaigh a' cheathramh uair.] 'A nise,' ars Anna, 'cha tug mi droch chomhairle a riamh ort, agus gabh mo chomhairle an trò seo, agus cuir clachan anns a' chliabh, oir chì thusa nach téid e ro fhada dar a thig a h-uile dad a th'ann a nuas cearta còmhla mu do chlaigeann.' Mar seo a bha. Ghabh Iain comhairle na feannaig. Bhuail e an clag. Tharraing na fir, is dar a bha iad mun cuairt agus leth an tuill, leig iad as na h-uile damnug [so in MS.][3] a bha ann. Thànaig an cliabh, is

---

[1] le = o, bho, since. Used in this sense twice in this tale, and four times in *An Gàidheal*, i. (1872), pp. 178, 295, twice on p. 229. A rare usage, and probably marks the reciter as a native of West Ross-shire, though he says he got the tale from a Skye man.

But the bold fellow had something else in his mind's eye ever since he had seen the women in the castles. He now started off to find the women, in order to take them with him for the others, the most beautiful one to belong to himself. [He found the women], and came to the hole with them ; and you may be sure they had treasure enough with them.[2] They were all willing to come along with him and leave the place. The first woman he put into the basket was the one who had been in the copper castle. Then he struck the bell. The men who were above hauled on the rope—and high time, too, they thought, so long had Iain been away. But when they saw the lovely woman who now appeared, they must fight to see who should have her. 'Oh, let down the basket again,' said she ; 'there is one more beautiful than I yet to come.' They let down the basket and again they hauled. And if the first woman was beautiful, this one was outstandingly so ! Again the men attacked each other to see who should win the more beautiful woman. 'Oh, let down the basket again,' said she ; 'there is one more beautiful than I yet to come.' So now again they lowered away the basket. Iain sent his own woman off last, and when she arrived at the top, what a fight there was then to decide which of them should have the most beautiful of all ; but she would have nothing to do with either of them, but would wait till Iain came. 'Lower the basket for *him* now,' she said.

*   *   *   *   *

[Then Anna and Iain saw the basket coming down to them for the fourth time.] 'Now,' said Anna, 'I have never given you bad counsel, so take my advice on this occasion. Put stones in the basket, and you will see that it will not go up very far before everything in it will come down about your ears, all together.' And so it was. Iain took the crow's advice. He struck the bell. The men hauled, but when they had hauled the basket about half-way up the hole, they let go every damned thing there was. Down came the basket, the stones, the ropes

---

[2] Probably treasure of copper, silver, and gold, from their respective castles.
[3] i.e. *damnadh*.

na clachan, is na ruip, is na h-uile mollochdainn [so in MS.]
a bha ann, an ceann a chéile. Bha iad-san an dùil gun robh
Iain bochd marbh, agus dh'fhalbh iad leis na boireannaich.
'Nach duirt mi riut,' arsa Anna, 'gur ann mar siod a bhitheadh !
Nam bitheadh tusa an siod, bha thu marbh.' 'Bha,' ars Iain.
'Cionnas a nise a gheibh thu as a seo ? Thuirt mi riut, nach
tànaig duine riamh an seo a chaidh air ais, ma gheibh thusa air
ais. Ach,' ars ise, 'ceannaich dhòmh-sa punnd tombaca,[1] agus
thig air chùl mo dhà sgéith fhéin, agus feuchaidh mi ri do chur
a suas, agus cuiridh tu caob is caob 'nam bheul air an rathad.'
   Mar seo a bha. Chaidh Iain air chùl sgiathan na feannaig,
agus comharradh leat gun robh an t-astar fada, cha robh aig
Iain de'n phunnd tombaca ach aona chriomag mus do rànaig
iad shuas, agus chuir e an caob mu dheireadh 'na beul mus faca
iad solus an là. Ach coma có dhiùbh, rànaig iad sàbhailte. Ach
cha robh sgeula ri fhaicinn air càch. Coma, ghabh Iain agus
Anna beannachd le chéile, agus thuirt i ris, 'Chan 'eil àite an
gairm thu orm ri do bheò, nach freagair mi thu.' Dh'fhalbh
Iain agus Anna an rathaid[ean] fhéin. Bha Iain a' gabhail
roimhe gus an do rànaig e a dh'ionnsaigh baile-mhóir, ach chan
'eil fhios agam c'ainm a bha air a' bhaile, ach coma, chuala
e mu thimcheall nam boireannach, gun robh iad pòsda, agus
ro mhaith dheth, ach an té a bha 'sa' chaisteal òir, cha ghabhadh
i duine sam bith gus an toireadh i dùil de Iain a thighinn, ach
bha càch pòsda aig na saighdearan.[2]
   Ach latha de na làithean, smuainich an té a bha anns a'
chaisteal chopair gum feumadh i crùn copair mar a bha aice
anns a' chaisteal chopair fhaighinn, agus chuir i fios a dh'ionnsaigh a' ghobha-chopair, mur am bitheadh e deas aige mu dhà
uair dheug a màireach, gun cailleadh e an ceann. Cha robh
fios aig a' ghobha gu dé a dhèanadh e : cha b'urrainn da a
dhèanamh cho luath, agus bha e fo'n chaothaich. Chuala Iain
seo, agus chaidh e far an robh an gobha, agus thuirt e ris gun
dèanadh esan e, nan tugadh e dha cóig ceud not. Bheireadh an
gobhainn dha a chuid uile, mun cailleadh e a cheann. 'Thoir

---

[1] To the reciter, tobacco was probably a very precious thing. In *W. H. Tales*,
iii., No. 57 also, the hero rewards the carrying-raven with tobacco.
[2] It will be noticed that after coming up from below and getting safely above-
ground once more, Iain does not immediately reveal himself. He was biding his

and every cursed thing there was, all together. The men up above, thinking that poor Iain was dead, went off with the women. 'Didn't I tell you,' said Anna, 'that that was what would happen. Had you been there, you would have been dead.' 'So I would,' replied Iain. 'How will you get out of here now?' she asked. 'I told you that no man ever came here who returned, that is if you do return. But,' she added, 'buy me a pound of tobacco,[1] and come up behind my own two wings, and I will try to carry you up; and on the way, you must put the tobacco chunk by chunk in my mouth.'

So it was. Iain got up behind the crow's wings, and to show you that the journey was long, Iain had only one morsel left of the pound of tobacco when they reached the top; he placed the last chunk in her mouth just before they saw the light of day. Nevertheless, arrive they did, and that safely. But there was no sign of the others. However, Iain and Anna said goodbye to each other; then she said to him, 'You will never call me anywhere as long as you live but I will answer you.' Iain and Anna parted and went their own ways, and Iain pressed on until he came to a big town, but I do not know what the name of the town was. There he got news of the women, that they were married and very well off, all except the one who had been in the castle of gold: she would accept no man until she should give up all hope of Iain's return. The other women were married to the soldiers.[2]

But one day the woman who had been in the castle of copper resolved that she must get a copper crown such as she had had in the castle, and she sent word to the coppersmith that unless it were ready about twelve noon the next day, he should lose his head. The smith did not know what to do: he was unable to make it in so short a time, and he was beside himself. Iain heard about this, and off he went to the smith and said that he would make the crown if the smith would give him five hundred pounds. The smith was willing to give him all he had rather than lose his head. 'Give me a locked room, bellows and

time, until an opportunity should occur for winning the most beautiful lady, she of the golden castle.

dhòmh-sa rùm glaiste, agus balg agus òrd, is na cuireadh neach
air bith dragh orm, gus an toilich mi fhéin.' [1] Fhuair Iain seo,
agus shuidh e agus thuirt e, 'O Anna ! c'àite am bheil thu,
oir tha mi ann an seo ?' [Thànaig Anna, an fheannag.] 'Ciod
e tha uait ?' 'O,' ars esan, 'nach fheuch an tugadh tu leat an
crùn a bha aig an té a bha 'sa' chaisteal chopair ?' 'Ma thà,
thug,' ars ise, 'agus seo dhuit e.' Thànaig Iain chun a' ghobha
leis a' chrùn, agus bha e cho toilichte agus ged a bu leis oighreachd.
Fhuair Iain a chóig ceud not, agus taing. Dar a rànaig an crùn
a' bhean-uasal, 'O !' ars ise, 'tha fear a' chòta ruaidh beò
fhathast. Feumaidh mise fhaicinn.'

Chaidh fios a chur air Iain, agus fhuaradh a mach far an robh
e fuireach, agus chaidh carbad agus ceithir eich a dh'iarraidh
Iain. Cha robh Iain toileach a dhol ann, ach bha fhios aige
gum freagradh Anna e. Chaidh Iain anns a' charbad, agus
leig e an éigh air Anna. 'O, Anna, c'àite am bheil thu ?' 'Tha
mi ann an seo.[2] Ciod e tha uait ?' 'O,' ars esan, 'nach feuch
an toir [thu] mise as a seo, agus gun lìon thu làn chlach e.' 'Nì
mise sin,' ars Anna. [Thug i Iain as, agus lìon i an carbad làn
chlach. An uair a rànaig an carbad,] bha na h-uile [fear] a'
feitheamh gus an tigeadh na h-uaislean a mach as a' charbad,
ach dar a dh'fhosgail am fear-frithealaidh an dorus, thànaig an
smùd chlach a nuas mu a cheann, agus theab iad a mharbhadh.[3]
Bha a' chùis an seo na bu mhiosa na bha i riamh, na h-eich làn
fallais a' tarraing nan clach an àite an duin'-uasail. Biodh siod
aca ! Bha siod gu maith, cha robh gu h-olc.

Smuainich an té a bha anns a' chaisteal airgid, gum faigheadh
i fhéin crùn mar a bha aice roimhe, agus chuir i fios chun a'
ghobha-[airgid] gum feumadh e bhith deas aig dà uair dheug a
màireach, air neadh gun cailleadh e an ceann. A dhèanamh
mo sgeòil na's giorra, b'e an dòigh cheudna do'n ghobha-airgid.
Dìreach mar a rinn Iain roimhe, rinn e an turus a bha seo, ach
dar a fhuair a' bhean-uasal an crùn, 'O !' ars ise, 'tha fear a'
chòta ruaidh beò fhathast, feumaidh mise fhaicinn.'

[1] 'Gregory the armourer, and every good hammerman, locks himself in when
he is about some masterpiece of craft' ; Sir Walter Scott, *The Abbot*, Chap. XIV.
Compare *W. H. Tales*, ii., No. 30, Var. 2, 'There would be a covering on the smithy
windows when he would be mending such things.' So also *ibid.*, iii., p. 26, 'Lock me
into the smithy.' See also *Waifs and Strays*, iv., where, the night he made Mac-a[n]-
Luin[n], Fionn's famous claymore, the smith shuts himself into his smithy.

a hammer, and let no one disturb me until I myself wish,' [1] said Iain. Having got these, Iain sat down and said, 'Oh Anna, where are you, for I am here?' [Anna, the crow, appeared.] 'What do you want?' 'Oh,' said he, 'will you try and fetch the crown that the woman who was in the copper castle had.' 'Well then,' said she, 'I have brought it with me, and here it is for you.' Iain went off to the smith with the crown, and the smith was as pleased as if he owned an estate. Iain received his five hundred pounds and thanks as well. When the crown came to the lady's hand she said, 'Oh, the man of the red coat is still alive. I must see him.'

Iain was sent for; they discovered where he was staying, and a carriage and four horses were sent to fetch him. Iain did not want to go there, but he knew that Anna would answer him. So he got into the carriage, and called to Anna. 'Oh Anna, where are you?' 'Here I am.[2] What do you want?' 'Oh,' said he, 'will you take me out of this, and fill the carriage full of stones.' 'Certainly,' said Anna, [and she took Iain out of the carriage, and filled it full of stones. When it arrived at its destination] everybody there was waiting for a gentleman to come out of it, but when an attendant opened the door, a shower of stones came down about his head and nearly killed him.[3] Things were now worse than ever. The horses were bathed in sweat through hauling a load of stones instead of a gentleman. Well! let them be so. That was all capital. But now the woman who had been in the castle of silver determined that she must have a crown as she had had before, and she sent word to the silversmith that a crown must be ready at twelve o'clock the next day, otherwise he should lose his head. To make my story shorter, the same thing happened to the silversmith. Just as Iain had done before, so he did on this occasion, but when the lady received the crown, she said, 'Oh, the man of the red coat is still alive. I must see him.'

---

[2] *Tha mi ann an so.* MS. is always uncertain as to whether it is the hero or the hoodie who utters these words.

[3] Same incident in *The Celtic Dragon Myth*, p. 75 ; *W. H. Tales*, i., No. 16.

Mar seo a bha. Chaidh carbad eile a dh'iarraidh Iain, agus air an rathad, leig e an éigh air Anna. 'Anna, c'àite am bheil thu?' 'Tha mi ann an seo. Ciod e tha uait?' 'O ! nach fheuch an toir thu mise as a seo agus gun lìon thu làn eabair e.' 'Ma tà, bheir,' arsa Anna '[agus lìonaidh mi an carbad làn eabair].' Bha na h-eich gu math blàth, leis a' chudthrom a bha 'san duin'-uasal. [Rànaig na h-eich agus an carbad taigh na té a bha 'sa' chaisteal airgid]. Bha iad uile a' feitheamh gus an tigeadh . . . [?] [1] na h-uaislean a mach, ach dar a chaidh an dorus fhosgladh, is ann a thànaig an steall eabair a nuas mu cheann agus mu ghuaillibh an duine [a dh'fhosgail e]. Cha robh fios aige air an t-saoghal co as a thànaig e.

Ach coma, smuainich an té aig an robh an caisteal òir,[2] gum feumadh i fhéin crùn fhaighinn mar a bha aice anns a' chaisteal òir roimhe, agus chuir i fios a dh'ionnsaigh an òir-cheàird gum feumadh e bhith aice 'san aon sìde ri càch, air neadh gun cailleadh e an ceann. [Air] an aon dòigh ri càch, rinn Iain e, ach is e Anna thug leatha e, ach dar a fhuair am boireannach brèagh, uasal, an crùn, 'O !' ars ise, 'tha fear a' chòta ruaidh beò fhathast. [Feumaidh mise fhaicinn].'

Cha chreideadh i nach e an crùn a bha aice roimhe a bh'ann. Dh'fheòraich i mu thimcheall gille a' ghobha, agus fhuair i a mach e. Chaidh fios a chur air Iain, agus is e a bha toilichte.[3] Thànaig an carbad a dh'iarraidh Iain, agus an uair a bha e a staigh ann, leig Iain an éigh air Anna. 'C'àite am bheil thu, Anna?' 'Tha mi ann an seo. Ciod e tha uait?' 'O ! nach fheuch an cuir thu orm a nise an deise a chuir [thu] orm an oidhche a char mi a shuirghe air Nighean an Rìgh [anns an t-Saoghal fo Thalamh].' 'Ma tà, cuiridh,' ars Anna. 'A nise, cha chuir thu feum orm-sa tuilleadh ri do bheò. Tha thu air an rathad a nise a dh'ionnsaigh do shonais shaoghalta. Beann-achd leat, Iain bhochd, chan fhaic thu mise tuilleadh, cha ruig thu leas.'

Ach mar seo a bha. Rànaig Iain an caisteal, agus ge bè

---

[1] MS. illegible here.

[2] The other ladies are only said to have been *in* the castles, not to have owned them.

[3] In *W. H. Tales*, i., No. 16, the hero 'will not come till he is taken by the hand by the King's own confidential servant.' Compare Campbell's words, *ibid.*, iv.,

And so it was. Another carriage went to fetch Iain ; and on the way he shouted for Anna. 'Anna ; where are you ?' 'Here I am ; what do you want ?' 'Oh ! do try and take me out of this and fill it full of mud.' 'Well then, I will take you out,' said Anna, ' [and I will fill the carriage full of mud].' The horses became pretty warm, because the gentleman was so heavy. [Finally, horses and carriage all arrived at the house of the woman of the silver castle.] The people of the house were all waiting till . . . . . [?] the gentleman should come out of the carriage, but when the door was opened, down came a cataract of mud about the head and shoulders of the man [who opened it]. Where on earth it came from, he could not tell.

But now, the woman who had owned the castle of gold [2] determined that she must have a crown as she had before when she lived in the golden castle ; so she sent word to the goldsmith that she must have it in the same time as the others had theirs, or else he should lose his head. Iain made it in the same way as he had made the others, for Anna brought it with her, and when the beautiful lady got the crown she said, 'Oh, the man of the red coat is still alive. [I must see him].'

She would not believe that it was not the crown she had before. She enquired about the smith's lad, and found him out. Iain was sent for, and very pleased he was.[3] The carriage went to fetch Iain, and when he was inside it he shouted for Anna. 'Where are you, Anna ?' 'Here I am. What do you want ?' 'Oh ! do clothe me in the suit you put on me the night I went to court the King's Daughter [in the Underground World].' 'Why, certainly,' said Anna ; 'and now you will no longer need me, not for the rest of your life. You are now on the way to your worldly happiness. Farewell, poor Iain, you will see me no more ; you will not need to.'

And so it happened. Iain arrived at the castle, and whoever

p. 256, 'the warrior who comes to a trial of arms disguised, who borrows money and clothes from a craftsman, wins, and will not come for his reward ; who resists force by force, but comes at last for fair words.' In No. 116 also, fair words were probably used on the last occasion Iain was sent for. A wilder example of this trait of character occurs in *Waifs and Strays*, ii., p. 83.

rinn an t-aoibhneas ri fhaicinn, b'e a sheann leannan. Chaidh a' chuirm air dòigh. Fhuaradh am ministeir, agus chaidh am pòsadh air adhart gun dàil, agus fhuair Iain agus a ghaol còmhla aon uair eile, air dòigh agus nach do dhealaich iad bho chéile air an taobh seo de'n bhàs, agus dh'fhàg mise iad le chéile cho sona 's a bha an là cho fad, agus ma bha càch gu maith air an dòigh, bha iad-san na's seachd feàrr.

Fhuair mi an sgeulachd seo bho Alasdair Mac Neacail as an Eilean Sgitheanach. Tha e fhéin gu maith sean, agus bha i seo aig a shean-athair, agus chan 'eil fhios cia fhad roimhe sin.

Is mise, Coinneach Mac Coinnich, ann an Glaschu.

KENNETH MACKENZIE, Glasgow.
Glasgow, 30th July 1859, finished.

NOTES

MS. vol. x., No. 116. The scribe was Hector Urquhart.

The MS. of No. 116 was entitled 'An Saighdear,' *i.e.* 'The Soldier.' But in his Gaelic List, Islay calls it 'Na trì Saigdairean [= Saighdearan],' *i.e.* 'The Three Soldiers,' a more accurate title, and therefore adopted here.

In the following group, the first three tales are partly similar to No. 116, and all have much in common.

Group I. The Three Crowns; A. P. Graves, *The Irish Fairy Book.* The King of Lochlin's Three Daughters; *W. H. Tales,* i., No. 16. A sailor and others; *ibid.,* iv., English List, No. 360. The Rider of Grianaig; *ibid.,* iii., No. 57. The copper, silver, and golden castles also appear in an un-related tale, *W. H. Tales,* i., No. 4, Var. 6. See also *Béaloideas,* iv., p. 423.

It is necessary to distinguish the above groups of three-soldiers-three-castles-and-three-crowns stories, from a second group of three-soldier stories, similar in title or in opening [1] to the first group, but quite different in plot and incident. This second group contains the following tales—Group II. The Three Soldiers, *W. H. Tales,* i., No. 10, Var. 1. The Soldier, *op. cit.,* i., No. 10, Var. 2 (= MS. vol. x., No. 61). The Soldier, *op. cit.,* i., No. 10, Var. 3 (= MS. vol. viii., No. 38).

Examination of the MSS. of Nos. 61 and 38 show that they are Vars. 2 and 3 of No. 10, *W. H. Tales.* i. But Islay speaks of a fourth Variant of No. 10, and it is certain that he is thinking of No. 116 from the fact that in his Gaelic List he refers all three tales, Nos. 61, 38 and 116 to No. 10. That he half realized that he erred in classing No. 116 as a Variant of No. 10, is clear from his Notes to No. 10, where he says—

'4. I have another story from a Ross-shire man now in Glasgow

[1] It is to be noted that this opening is entirely modern. It must therefore have superseded something primitive.

else was glad to see him, certainly his old sweetheart was. The feast was prepared, a minister was found and the marriage took place without delay, and Iain and his love were united once more in such a way that they never parted from each other on this side of death. I left them together as happy as the day was long, and if the others were happily settled, Iain and his wife were seven times better off.

I got this story from Alexander Nicolson from the Isle of Skye. He himself is very old, and this story was known to his grandfather, and there is no knowing how long before that.

I am Kenneth MacKenzie, in Glasgow.

KENNETH MACKENZIE, Glasgow.
Glasgow, 30th July, 1859, finished.

which begins in the same manner [as No. 10] but the incidents are very different.'

The incidents of No. 116 are indeed different from No. 10, and the plot is still more so. 'The Tale of the Soldier,' *W. H. Tales*, ii., No. 42, is not related to any of the foregoing in either group.

Islay must have had a high opinion of No. 116, or he would not have written on the flyleaf of the MS. the lengthy summary of it that follows here :—

'116. Saighdear. From Kenneth MacKenzie, Glasgow, 28th July, '59, who says he learned it from Alexander MacNicol from the Isle of Skye who was pretty old at the time—who learnt it from his grandfather, and he does not know how much older it is. A soldier, Ia[i]n, deserts—a corporal and sergeant follow and desert also.—They go to an old castle somewhere. Two get out, one to fish, one to hunt, the third stays to prepare dinner—a little red Bodach Ruagh comes in and says words, asks for food and is refused, floors the man and bolts—so with the sergeant [recte, the corporal]. John sticks a red hot poker into him and he runs into a green hill.—Ropes are got and a creel and a bell. The two go down, take fright, ring, and are hauled up. John goes to the bottom, finds a hoodie [crow] who becomes a ponie and carries him to a castle of copper, one of silver and one of gold. Then he finds the old Bodach, and they have a game at hide-and-seek. John goes in place of a tooth, a nail, and a grey hair in the horse [= pony] and is not found. The Bodach into an egg in a duck, an apple on a tree, a ring on the Queen's [recte, King's] daughter's hand, and is found ; gives money for his life. John goes back. The others carry off the ladies of the castle[s] and throw down the rope. The Hoodie carries him up by the help of some tobacco. Then come the incidents of the crowns.' Thus far Campbell of Islay.

Though it is not so said, the hero probably refuses point-blank to marry the Bodach's daughter, as he does in *W. H. Tales*, i., No. 10, Var. 1 (and probably in Vars. 2 and 3) ; *ibid.*, iii., p. 419 or 438 ; Gaelic List, No. 328 (pub. *Scottish Gaelic Studies*, i., p. 187).

A series of competitions almost exactly similar to 'the game at hide-and-seek' occur in an Irish tale (*Imtheachta an Oireachtais*, 1899, p. 137. The Gaelic League, Dublin). There, the enemy and the hero conjure each other to the competition with what seems to be a fragment of some ancient be-spelling run, and the enemy, when defeated, evinces disgust just as he does in our story. The 'hide-and-seek' incidents occur in 'Farmer Weathersky.'

It is remarkable that the hero does not appear to take any revenge on the corporal and sergeant. They would scarcely have dropped out of the story if there had been any incident of revenge. The reason may be that they had married the other two ladies (p. 206), whose happiness the hero did not wish to spoil.

[*Cf.* the tale *Eachtra Iollainn Airmdheirg* (also called *Tóraigheacht Fhiacail Ríogh Gréag* and *Sgéal Úcaire na Seachtmhaine*). Aarne-Thompson, No. 301. R. Flower, *Catalogue of Irish Manuscripts in the British Museum*, ii., 360 ; *Béaloideaʿs* viii., pp. 97-99, and xii., p. 125 ; Ó Duilearga, *Leabhar Sheáin Í Chonaill*, pp. 417, 466-467. References given by Gerard Murphy, *The Ossianic Lore and Romantic Tales of Mediæval Ireland* (1955), p. 44, *n.*—A. M.]

SGEULACHD MU THEAGHLACH RÌGH

No. 63.   *[MS. Vol. x., No. 117]*

BHA Rìgh ann roimhe seo, aig an robh triùir mhac agus aon nighean. Shiubhail an Rìgh, agus cha d'fhàg e a bheag de stòras aig a theaghlach. Thug fuamhair air falbh an nighean ; is cha robh fios aig a màthair no aig a bràithrean c'àite an tug e i. Thuirt am fear a bu shine de na mic aon latha ri a mhàthair, 'Tha bliadhna an diugh o'n a chaidh mo phiuthar a thoirt air falbh ; falbhaidh mise a dh'iarraidh m'fhortain agus dh'fheuch an tachair i orm.' 'Dèan, ma tà,' ars a mhàthair, 'ach chan fhaod thu falbh gus am fuin mise bonnach agus am marbh mi coileach a bhios agad air an astar.' Dh'fhuin i am bonnach agus mharbh i an coileach ; [rinn i dà leth de gach aon diubh,] agus thuirt i ris, 'Có dhiùbh as fheàrr leat a' bhloigh mhór agus mo mhollachd, no a' bhloigh bheag agus mo bheannachd ?' 'Tha mi coma, có dhiùbh a gheibh mi do mhollachd no do bheannachd, ach biodh leth mhór a' bhonnaich agus a' choilich agam,' ars esan. Thug a mhàthair dha iad le chéile, agus dh'fhalbh e air a thurus.

Choisich e fad an latha ; ach an uair a bha am feasgar a' teannadh air, bha e ag amharc am faiceadh e taigh anns an cuireadh e seachad an oidhche. Mu dheireadh, chunnaig e dùbhradh mór air thoiseach air. Ghabh e air aghaidh gus am faca e gur taigh a bh'ann. Chaidh e a staigh ; agus chunnaig e aig ceann shuas an taighe seana chailleach a' tochras snàth òir bhàrr eachan airgid.[1] 'Is dalma thu a thànaig an seo,' ars ise. 'Tha mi cho dalma sin,' ars esan. Cha tug i leabaidh dha, ach dh'fhan e fad na h-oidhche ; ach dh'fhuin i bonnach dha an uair a bha e falbh anns a' mhaduinn, agus rinn i 'na dhà leth e, agus thuirt i ris, 'Có dhiùbh a ghabhas tu a' bhloigh mhór agus mo mhollachd, no a' bhloigh bheag agus mo bheannachd ?' 'Tha mi suarach mu do bheannachd no mu do mhollachd ; ach is i a' bhloigh mhór de'n bhonnach a bhios agam.' Thug i dha sin, agus dh'fhalbh e air a thurus.

A TALE ABOUT A KING'S FAMILY

No. 63.   [*MS. Vol. x., No. 117*]

THERE was once a King who had three sons and one daughter. The King died and left his family with little estate. A giant carried off the daughter, and neither her mother nor her brothers knew where he had taken her. One day the eldest son said to his mother : 'It is a year today since my sister was carried off : I will go and seek my fortune and see if I may come across her.' 'Yes, do,' said his mother, 'but you must not go until I bake a bannock and kill a cock which you will have on the journey.' She baked the bannock and killed the cock [made two halves of each of them], and said to him : 'Which do you prefer : the big piece with my curse or the little piece with my blessing ?' 'I don't care,' said he, 'whether I get your curse or your blessing ; but let me have the big half of the bannock and of the cock.' His mother gave them both to him and he set out on his journey.

He walked all day long, but when evening was closing in on him he began to look around whether he could see a house where he might spend the night. At last he saw a great dark mass in front of him ; he pressed on until he saw that it was a house. He went inside, and saw at the inner end of the house an old woman winding gold thread from a silver winding-horse.[1] 'You are a bold fellow who have come here,' said she. 'I am as bold as that,' he replied. She gave him no bed, but he stayed there all night. When he was leaving in the morning, however, she baked him a bannock and made two halves of it and said : 'Which will you have : the big piece with my curse or the little piece with my blessing ?' 'I don't care a straw for your blessing or your curse, but the big piece of the bannock is what I'll have.' She gave him that and off he went on his journey.

---

[1] An old woman similarly engaged occurs in No. 170, Islay's English List.

Ghabh e air aghaidh fad an latha, agus an uair a bha an oidhche a' tuiteam, chunnaig e uamh, agus chaidh e staigh innte. Có a thachair air ach a phiuthar a thug am fuamhair leis a' bhliadhna roimhe sin. 'Ciod air an t-saoghal a thug an seo thu an nochd?' ars ise : 'thig am fuamhair dachaigh gun dàil, agus marbhaidh e thu.' 'Ma mharbhas,' ars esan, 'chan fhaigh mi bàs ach aon uair, agus fanaidh mi gus an tig e.' Chuir i e am falach ann am preas, ach cho luath 'sa thànaig am fuamhair a staigh, ghlaodh e, 'O huagaich ! O hoagaich ! tha boladh an fharbhalaich a staigh—c'àite am bheil an coigreach, no có e?' 'Is e mo bhràthair e,' ars ise, 'agus chuir mi 'sa' phreas e.' Thug e air tighinn a mach as a' phreas, agus dh'fharraid e dheth an robh e 'na bhuachaille math. Thuirt e ris gun robh. Thuirt e ri a mhnaoi, 'Dèan leabaidh dha.' Rinn i sin, agus anns a' mhaduinn chuir am fuamhair a mach trì bà maola as a' bhàthaich, agus dh'iarr e air a' ghille gun e dhealachadh riu gus an tugadh e dhachaigh iad 'san fheasgar. Cha deach e fada leis na bà an uair a chunnaig e craobh agus aon ubhal mhaiseach [1] air a' mheanglan a b'àirde dhith. Chuir e roimhe gum faigheadh e an t-ubhal.[1] Streap e do'n chraoibh, ach an uair a rànaig e a bàrr, chunnaig e an t-ubhal air a' mheanglan a b'ìsle. Theirinn e, ach bha an t-ubhal a rithist mar gum biodh e ann am bàrr na craoibhe. Chuir e an latha seachad a' strìth ris an ubhal fhaotainn, ach aig laighe na gréine, chaidh na bà seachad air ag geumnaich. Lean e iad dachaigh, agus chuir e a staigh do'n bhàthaich iad. Dh'òrdaich am fuamhair d'a mhnaoi am bleoghan, agus bhleoghainn i trì pinntean fola aig gach bó.[2] An uair a chunnaig am fuamhair an fhuil, thuirt e, 'Is math a' bhuachailleachd seo ;' agus ann am feirg mhóir, rug e air shlacan-draoidheachd, agus bhuail e an gille air a cheann, agus dh'fhàs e 'na charra cloiche.

*   *   *   *   *   *

An uair nach robh a choltas air a' mhac a bu shine gun tilleadh e, thuirt an dara mac ri a mhàthair, 'Tha dà bhliadhna an diugh bho'n a dh'fhalbh mo phiuthar, agus bliadhna o'n a dh'fhalbh mo bhràthair ; falbhaidh mise dh'fheuch am faigh

---

[1] Note change of gender. *Cf.* p. 187.

[2] In No. 216 of Islay's English List, which is a version of this one, she gets one

All day long he kept going, and when night was falling he saw a cave and went inside. Who met him but his sister whom the giant had carried off the year before. 'What in the world brought you here tonight?' she asked ; 'the giant will come home presently and he will kill you.' 'If he does,' said he, 'I can die but once, and I will stay until he comes.' She hid him away in a cupboard, but as soon as the giant came in he roared : 'Ho ! ho ! the smell of a strange person is about the house ! Where is the stranger or who is he ?' 'He is my brother,' said the girl, 'and I put him in the cupboard.' The giant made him come out of the cupboard, and inquired if he was a good cowherd. He said he was. 'Make him a bed,' said the giant to his wife. She did so and in the morning the giant drove three polled cows out of the byre and told the boy not to leave them until he brought them home in the evening. He had not gone far with the cows when he saw a tree, and on its highest branch one beautiful apple. He determined to get that apple. He climbed up into the tree but when he reached the top he saw the apple on the lowest branch. He went down, but again the apple seemed to be at the top of the tree. He spent the whole day trying to get the apple, but at sundown the cows walked past him lowing. He followed them home and put them into the byre. The giant ordered his wife to milk them, and she milked three pints of blood from each cow.[2] When the giant saw the blood he said, 'A pretty kind of herding this is !', and in great fury he seized his magic wand and hit the boy on the head, and he became a pillar of stone.

When there seemed no likelihood of the eldest son's return, the second son said to his mother : 'It is two years today since my sister went away and one year since my brother left. I will go and see if I can find them.' 'You must not go,' said his mother,

pint of milk and three pints of blood from each cow. The wizard wand appears in No. 216, as an 'enchanting maul.'

mi iad.' 'Chan fhaod thu falbh,' ars a mhàthair, 'gus am fuin
mise bonnach, agus am marbh mi coileach a bhios agad air an
astar.' Dheasaich i bonnach, agus mharbh i coileach. Rinn
i dà leth [de gach aon] dhiùbh, agus thuirt i ris, 'Có aca ghabhas
tu, a' bhloigh mhór agus mo mhollachd, no a' bhloigh bheag
agus mo bheannachd ?' 'Tha mi coma có aca a gheibh mi, do
mhollachd no do bheannachd, ach bidh a' bhloigh mhór de'n
bhonnach agus de'n choileach agam.' Thug i da an dà chuid,
agus dh'fhalbh e, agus an uair a bha an oidhche a' tighinn air,
chunnaig e taigh fada uaidhe, ach cha robh e fada 'ga ruigheachd.
Chaidh e a staigh, agus chunnaig e cailleach le aon fhiacail an
dorus a beòil. Chaidh e gu ceann uachdrach an taighe, agus
an uair a chunnaig i a dhalmachd, thuirt i, 'Cha dèan thusa
feum fathast.' An uair a bha e falbh 'sa' mhaduinn, dheasaich
i bonnach dha, agus rinn i dà leth dheth. Dh'fharraid i dheth
có dhiùbh a ghabhadh e an leth mhór agus a mollachd, no an
leth bheag agus a beannachd. Thuirt e gun robh e coingeis
có aca gheibheadh e, a mollachd no a beannachd, ach gun
gabhadh e a' bhloigh mhór de'n bhonnach. Thug i dha sin,
agus dh'fhalbh e. Anns an anmoch, chunnaig e uamh agus
smùid aiste. Chaidh e a staigh do'n uaimh, agus fhuair e a
phiuthar 'na suidhe innte, a' gàireachdaich an darna greis, agus
a' caoineadh a' ghreis eile. An uair a chuimhnich i mar a
dh'éirich do a bhràthair a bu shine, 'Chan 'eil math dhòmh-sa,'
ars ise, 'feuchainn ri t'fholach bho m'fhear, oir gu cinnteach gheibh
e thu.' An uair a thànaig am fuamhair dachaigh, dh'fharraid
e có an coigreach a bha a staigh. 'Och, a rìgh !' ars ise, 'tha
fear de mo bhràithrean.' Leig am fuamhair da fuireachd 'san
oidhche, agus dh'fhaighnich e dheth anns a' mhaduinn, 'A
bheil thu 'nad bhuachaille math ?' 'Tha,' ars an gille. Chuir
am fuamhair a mach trì bà maola, ruadha, as a' bhàthaich, agus
thuirt e ris, 'Na dealaich ris na bà gus an toir thu sàbhailt air
an ais do m' ionnsaigh iad 'san fheasgar.' Cha deach e fada
air falbh an uair a chunnaig e a' chraobh leis an ubhal mhaiseach
anns a' mheanglan a b'àirde dhith. Streap e an àird gu bàrr
na craoibhe, ach an uair a bha e aig mullach na craoibhe,
chunnaig e an t-ubhal air a' mheanglan a b'ìsle dhith. Coltach
ri a bhràthair, chosd e an latha, a' strìth ris an ubhal fhaotainn,
ach dh'fhairtlich air fhaotainn, agus air tighinn an fheasgair,

'until I bake a bannock and kill a cock which you will have on the journey.' She prepared a bannock and killed a cock. [Each of them] she halved, and she said to him : 'Which will you have : the big piece with my curse or the little piece with my blessing ?' 'I don't care which of them I get,' said he, 'your curse or your blessing, but I will have the big piece of the bannock and the cock.' She gave him both and he set out ; and when night was coming upon him he saw a house a long way off, but he was not long in reaching it. He went inside and saw a woman with one tooth in the front of her mouth. He went up to the farthest end of the house, and when she observed his boldness she said, 'Nor will even you succeed.' In the morning when he was leaving she prepared him a bannock, and made two halves of it. She asked him whether he would take the big portion and her curse or the little portion and her blessing. He said he was indifferent as to which he should get—her curse or her blessing ; but he would take the big portion of the bannock. She gave him that and off he went. At nightfall he saw a cave with smoke billowing from it. He went into the cave, and there he found his sister sitting laughing and weeping by turns. When she thought of what had happened to her eldest brother she said, 'It is useless for me to try to hide you from my husband, for he will certainly find you.' When the giant came home he asked who the stranger in the house was. 'Alas,' said she, 'it is one of my brothers.' The giant allowed him to stay there for the night and in the morning he asked him : 'Are you a good cow-herd ?' 'Yes I am,' said the youth. The giant drove three red polled cows out of the byre and said to him : 'Do not part from the cows until you bring them back safely to me in the evening.' He had not gone far when he saw the tree with the beautiful apple on its highest branch. He climbed up to the top of the tree, but when he was at the top he saw the apple on the tree's lowest branch. Like his brother, he spent the day trying to get the apple, but he failed ; and when evening was come the cows went past him, lowing, and he followed them. The giant ordered his wife to milk the cows, and she got three pints of blood from each of them. When

chaidh na bà seachad air a' geumnaich, agus lean e iad. Dh'iarr
am fuamhair air a bhean am bleoghan, agus fhuair i trì pinntean
fala aig gach bó. An uair a chunnaig am fuamhair an fhuil,
rug e air an t-slacan-draoidheachd, agus bhuail e ceann a'
ghille leis, agus dh'fhàg e 'na charra cloiche e làimh ri a bhràthair.

*   *   *   *   *

An uair a chunnaig am fear a b'òige de mhic an Rìgh nach
robh a choltas air aon de'n teaghlach tilleadh, thuirt e ri a
mhàthair, 'Tha trì bliadhna bho'n a thug am fuamhair air falbh
mo phiuthar, agus dà bhliadhna bho'n a dh'fhalbh mo bhràthair
a bu shine, agus bliadhna bho'n a dh'fhalbh mo dhara bràthair
'gan iarraidh. Leanaidh mise iad a dh'fheuch am faigh mi
iad.' 'Dèan,' ars a mhàthair, 'ach chan fhalbh thu gus an
deasaich mise bonnach agus am marbh mi coileach a bhios
agad air an astar.' Mharbh i an coileach agus dh'fhuin i am
bonnach, agus rinn i dà leth [de gach aon] dhiùbh, agus thuirt
i ris, 'Có aca as fheàrr leat—an leth mhór is mo mhollachd, no
an leth bheag is mo bheannachd?' 'Nìor leig am Maitheas
gum biodh do mhollachd agam-sa; thoir dhomh an leth bheag
is do bheannachd.' Fhuair e sin, agus dh'fhalbh e. Chunnaig
e 'san fheasgar taigh fada bhuaidh, is ge b'fhada bhuaidh, cha
b'fhada 'ga ruigheachd. Chaidh e a staigh, agus shuidh e gu
h-iriseal aig an dorus, agus chunnaig e bean mhór 'na suidhe
aig ceann uachdrach an taighe. Thuirt i ris, 'Is ìosal a shuidh
thu, òganaich—thig a nìos agus suidh làimh rium—tha fios
agam air adhbhar do thuruis na's fheàrr na agad féin.' Rinn i
an sin bùrn blàth d'a chasan, agus leabaidh bhog d'a leasan;
chuir i a' chluasag shìoda fo a cheann, agus brat sìoda thairis
air, agus thuirt i ris gum biodh i conadal ris anns a' mhaduinn.
[Anns a' mhaduinn] an uair a bha e dèanamh deas air son falbh,
dh'fhuin i bonnach dha, agus rinn i dà bhloigh dheth, agus
dh'fharraid i ris, 'Có dhiùbh a ghabhadh tu—a' bhloigh mhór
is mo mhollachd, no a' bhloigh bheag is mo bheannachd?'
'Is fheàrr liom,' ars esan, 'a' bhloigh bheag agus do bheannachd.'
Thairg i breacan da; ach thuirt e nach robh feum aige air.
'Bidh feum agad air,' ars ise, 'agus biodh do shùil daonnan air
an speur, agus ma chì thu nì sam bith nach còrd riut, tarraing
do bhreacan teann umad, agus na toir feairt air, ach biodh do
ghnàth do shùil an àird.'

the giant saw the blood he seized the magic wand and struck the boy's head with it and left him a pillar of stone beside his brother.

When the youngest of the King's sons saw that there seemed no likelihood of any of the family coming back he said to his mother : 'It is three years since the giant carried away my sister, and two years since my eldest brother went off, and there is a year gone since my second brother went to look for them. I will follow them to see if I can find them.' 'Do,' said his mother, 'but you shall not go until I prepare a bannock and kill a cock which you will have on the journey.' She killed the cock and baked the bannock, and halved [each] of them, and said to him : 'Which would you prefer—the big half and my curse or the little half and my blessing ?' 'Providence forbid that I should have your curse ; give me the little half !' He got that, and away he went. In the evening he saw a house a long way off, but far away though it was he was not long in reaching it. He went in and sat down humbly at the door, and he saw a big woman sitting at the inner end of the house. She said to him : 'You have taken a lowly seat, young man : come farther in and sit by me. I know the reason for your journey better than you do yourself.' Then she made him warm water for his feet and a soft bed for his thighs ; she put a silken pillow under his head, and a silken coverlet over him, and said that she would talk to him in the morning. [In the morning] when he was making ready to go she baked a bannock for him, made two portions of it and asked him : 'Which would you prefer : the big portion and my curse, or the little portion and my blessing.' 'I prefer,' said he, 'the little portion and your blessing.' She offered him a tartan plaid, but he said he had no need of it. 'Need it you will,' said she ; 'and always keep your gaze on the sky, and if you see anything that does not please you, draw your plaid close about you and take no heed of it, but keep looking up all the time.'

Ghabh e air aghaidh gus an do rànaig e an uamh anns an
robh a phiuthar agus am fuamhair a chòmhnaidh. An uair a
chunnaig a phiuthar e, chaoin i an darna greis agus ghàir i a'
ghreis eile, agus thuirt i nach robh math sam bith dhi feuchainn
ri a fhalach bho'n fhuamhair, oir gur cinnteach gum faigheadh
e a mach e. Thànaig am fuamhair agus thuirt e, 'Có e an
coigreach a tha agad an nochd?' 'Och,' ars ise, 'tha am fear
as òige de mo bhràithrean.' Leig am fuamhair leis fuireach an
oidhche sin, agus anns a' mhaduinn mar a b'àbhaist chuir e
na trì bà maola, ruadha, a mach as a' bhàthaich, agus thuirt e
ris a' ghille, 'Lean na bà sin, agus na dealaich riu gus an toir
thu air an ais iad 'san fheasgar.' Dh'fhalbh e leò, agus chaidh
e seachad air a' chraoibh leis an ubhal mhaiseach, agus tharraing
e a bhreacan teann mun cuairt air, agus dh'amhairc e an àird
ris an speur, agus lean e na bà mar a dh'iarr am fuamhair air.
Ghabh iad air aghaidh troimh phàirc anns an robh feur àlainn.
Shaoil e gum fanadh na bà a dh'itheadh, ach cha d'fhan.
Chunnaig e trì bà ag ionaltradh anns a' phàirc, caol ann am
feòil, ged a bha am feur cho math aca. Chaidh na bà maola
[ruadha] troimh phàirc eile anns an robh feur seacta, lom, ach
bha trì bà ag ionaltradh innte cho reamhar ri ròin.[1] Chaidh
na bà maola, ruadha air an aghaidh, agus an gille 'gan leantainn,
gus am faca e teine mór air thoiseach orra air an rathad-mhór.
Cha robh fios aig a' ghille gu dé dhèanadh e an uair a chunnaig
e gun robh an rathad-mór a' dol troimh an teinidh. Thionndaidh
aon de na bà, agus thuirt i ris, 'Na biodh eagal ort,' ars ise,
'gabh greim de m'earball-sa, agus bheir mise sàbhailt troimh
an teinidh thu.' Rinn e sin, agus chaidh iad troimh an teinidh
gun dochann. Chunnaig e an sin muileann, agus an rathad-
mór a' dol troimh a mheadhon. Labhair a' bhó ris a rithist,
agus thuirt i ris, 'An uair a théid thu troimh a' mhuilinn, na
dèan moille.' Ghabh na bà air an aghaidh an toiseach, agus lean
esan iad. An uair a chaidh iad troimh a' mhuilinn, dh'amhairc
e as a dhéidh, agus chunnaig e taobh a' mhuilinn gu h-iomlan
làn de ghloineachan, làn de dh'uisge a bha sruthadh asta; bha
na h-uile gloine crochte le snàthainn, agus na h-uile gloine a
bhiodh falamh, bha an snàthainn air a ghearradh le aon de

---

[1] *Cho reamhar ris an ròn,* 'As fat as a seal.' Nicolson's *Gaelic Proverbs,* p. 143.

He pressed on until he arrived at the cave where his sister and the giant were living. When his sister saw him she wept and laughed by turns and said it was useless for her to try and hide him from the giant for he would surely find him out. The giant came and asked : 'Who is the stranger you have with you tonight?' 'Alas, he is my youngest brother,' she replied. The giant allowed him to stay that night, and in the morning, as usual, he drove the three red polled cows out of the byre and said to the boy : 'Follow those cows and do not part from them until you bring them back in the evening.' He went off with them, and he passed the tree with the beautiful apple. He pulled the plaid tightly round him and looked up to the skies and followed the cows as the giant had asked him to do. They went on through a park where there was excellent grass. He expected that the cows would stay to eat, but they did not. In the park he noticed three cows grazing, lean in flesh although they had such good grass. The red polled cows passed through another park where the grass was withered and bare, but grazing there were three cows as fat as seals. The red polled cows went straight on with the boy following them until he saw on the road in front of them a great fire. The boy did not know what to do when he saw that the road lay through the fire. One of the cows turned round and said to him : 'Have no fear,' said she : 'get a grip of my tail and I will take you safely through the fire.' He did so, and they went through the fire uninjured. Then he saw a mill, and through the middle of it ran the road. The cow spoke to him again, and said : 'Make no delay when you go through the mill !' The cows went on ahead, and he followed them. When they got through the mill he looked behind him and saw the whole side of the mill full of glasses filled with water which was streaming from them ; every glass was hanging by a thread, and when it became empty the thread was cut by one of a number of people who were sitting watching the glasses with scissors in their hands.

mhóran dhaoine a bha 'nan suidhe 'gam faire le siosar 'nan làimh. An uair a chaidh iad seachad troimh a' mhuilinn, dh'iarr na bà air an leanachd, agus thill iad 'san fheasgar do'n bhàthaich.

Chuir am fuamhair a staigh iad, agus thug e air a bhean am bleoghan, agus fhuair i ceithir pinntean bainne aig gach té dhiubh. 'Is tu am buachaille as fheàrr a fhuair mi riamh,' ars am fuamhair ; 'am bu mhath leat a nis fios fhaotainn ciod as ciall do gach nì a chunnaig thu an diugh?' 'Bhiodh sin tait-neach liom,' ars an gille. 'Ma tà,' ars am fuamhair, 'b'e an t-ubhal a chunnaig thu anns a' chraoibh samhla an droch spioraid a bha 'gad bhuaireadh dearmad a dhèanamh air an obair a ghabh thu os làimh a dhèanamh. Bha a' phàirc leis an fheur mhath agus leis na bà caola 'nan samhladh do dhaoine beairteach an t-saoghail seo, aig am bheil na h-uile nì a dh'fhaodas sòlas a thoirt doibh, ach a tha neo-thoilichte leò, agus tha iad caol le mì-thoil-inntinn. Tha na bà reamhra a chunnaig thu anns a' phàirc sheacta, lom, 'nan samhladh do bhochdan an t-sluaigh a tha toilichte le an staid, agus a' trusadh sult, o nach 'eil nithean an t-saoghail seo a' cur iomagain orra. Tha an teine a chunnaig thu, agus roimh an robh eagal cho mór ort, 'na shamhladh do thrioblaidean agus do dheuchainnean an t-saoghail seo ; ach le bhith gabhail dìreach agus gu neo-sgàthach trompa le greim de earball na bà, fhuair thu seachad gun deireas. Tha na gloineachan làn uisge a chunnaig thu an déidh dol troimh a' mhuilinn 'nan samhladh do'n chinne dhaoine aig am bheil am beatha air a ghearradh, agus a tha tuiteam gu làr an uair a tha an gloine air ruith a mach. Bha mise fo gheasaibh agus ri leantainn mar sin gus am faighinn buachaille cosmhail riut. Tha mi nis air mo shaoradh, agus seo dhuit-sa uisge a dhòirteas tu air do dhà bhràthair g'an toirt beò, agus air do phiuthair, agus gun tilleadh sibh dhachaigh a dh'ionnsaigh bhur màthar ; agus bheir mise dhuibh de dh'òr agus de dh'airgead na chumas socair sibh am feadh a bhios sibh beò.' Thill iad an sin dachaigh, agus bha am màthair làn gàirdeachais, agus bha iad sona fad an làithibh còmhla.

The above tale was got [Jan. 19, 1860] from Miss Jean McTavish, now seventy-three years of age, who heard it in her youth from an old tailor, in the Island of Mull, Argyleshire. See Notes to No. 50 (MS. vol. x., No. 84).

When they were through and past the mill the cows told him to follow them, and in the evening they returned home to the byre.

The giant put them into the byre and made his wife milk them, and she got four pints of milk from each of them. 'You are the best herd I have ever had,' said the giant : 'would you like now to know the meaning of all that you saw today ?' 'Very much,' said the boy. 'Well, then,' said the giant, 'the apple you saw in the tree was a symbol of the evil spirit that was tempting you to neglect the work you had undertaken to do. The park with the good grass and the lean cows were symbols of the rich men of this world who have everything that can give them pleasure but are dissatisfied with that, and are lean with discontent. The fat cows you saw in the bare withered park are symbols of the poor people, those who are happy with their lot, and who become fat because the things of this world cause them no anxiety. The fire you saw, and which you dreaded so much, is a symbol of the troubles and trials of this world ; but going on fearlessly straight through them by keeping hold of the cow's tail, you got past them unscathed. The glasses full of water which you saw after passing through the mill are symbols of the human race, whose lives are cut off and who fall to the ground when their glass has run out. I was bewitched, and fated to continue so till I should get a cow-herd like you. Now I am freed. Here is some water for you : sprinkle it on your two brothers to bring them to life, and on your sister that you may all return home to your mother. I will give you as much gold and silver as will keep you comfortably as long as you live.' Then they returned home, and their mother was full of joy, and they were happy together all their days.

NOTES

MS. vol. x., No. 117.—No. 216 in Islay's English List is very similar. For a version that is much more Highland, see Index, No. 1b, of which Islay says (*W. H. Tales*, i., introduction, p. xx. or xii.), 'Dr MacLeod, the best of living Gaelic scholars, printed one old tale, somewhat altered, with a moral added, in his "Leabhar nan Cnoc," in 1834,' etc.—The moralizing and symbolism suggest a mediæval source.

There is yet another version which I hope to find in MS. vol. xviii. in which the hero has to fight three slim-waisted giants. There is no mention of either moralizing or cattle.   Somewhat similar is a Breton tale which the late Dr E. S. Hartland calls 'a traditional Pilgrim's Progress, which is known from Brittany to Transylvania, from Iceland to Sicily'; *The Science of Fairy Tales*, pp. 190-192 (London, 1891).

[For this story, Aarne-Thompson no. 471, see Stith Thompson, *The Folktale* (New York, 1946), p. 148.—K. H. J.]

[See also Thompson, *Motif-Index*, J. 229-3.—H. J. R.]

MAC A' CHÌOBAIR

 [*MS. Vol. x., No. 118*]

BHA mac cìobair de mhuinntir an Àth Leathann ann, agus bha e 'na ghille anabarrach glic, agus 'na ghille measail a réir a chumhachd. Bha bràthair athar da 'na mharsanta ann am Peairt. Bha esan 'na sgoilear maith, is chuir bràthair a athar fios air air son e bhith 'na ghille-bùth aige. Chaidh e chun bhràthair a athar. Bha e dèanamh gnothaich glé mheasail, beusach fad trì bliadhna. Ann an ceann trì bliadhna, dh'fhàs e na b'aotromaiche, is bha e air son a bhith ann an sgoil-dannsa. Chaidh e do sgoil-dannsa, agus bha e trì bliadhna ag ionnsachadh dannsa. Cha b'urrainn duine sam bith coire fhaotainn d'a dhannsa an ceann trì bliadhna.

Thànaig long a staigh do'n acarsaid, is bha esan a' sealltainn gun tàmh air an dealbh a bha air a toiseach. Ghabh e gaol air an dealbh ; agus chaidh e a dh'ionnsaigh an sgiobair feuch am faigheadh e leis an luing, ge bè taobh a rachadh i. Dheònaich an sgiobair sin da. Chaidh e chun a' bhùth a dh'ionnsaigh bhràthair a athar, agus dh'innis e dha gun do ghabh e gaol air an dealbh a bha air toiseach an t-soithich, is gun robh e falbh leatha gus am faiceadh e an té do'n do thàirneadh an dealbh. Is e cóig ceud punnd Sasannach a bha aige de dh' airgead, agus leig bràthair a athar leis dà dheise aodaich, a bharrachd air na bha aige fhéin. Dh' fhalbh e 's chaidh e air bòrd.

Sheòl iad air an là-'r-na-mhàireach an déidh dha dol air bòrd. An uair a bha iad a' seòladh cùnntas làithean air falbh, dh'fharraid an sgiobair dheth cia fhad an ruigeadh e. Ach dh'innis esan gur h-ann a bha e 'na ghille-bùth ann am Peairt ; agus an oidhche a thànaig esan agus a shoitheach a staigh, gun do ghabh e gaol air an dealbh a bha air toiseach an t-soithich, is nach robh e ri fois a ghabhail gu bràth gus am faiceadh e 'n té do'n do thàirneadh e. Thuirt an sgiobair ris, 'Nam biodh fhios agam air sin an am fàgail, cha do leig mi air bòrd thu. Dé a' cheàird air an fheàrr thu ?' 'Is ann air sgoil agus air dannsa

THE SHEPHERD'S SON

No. 64.   *[MS. Vol. x., No. 118]*

THERE was once a shepherd's son from Broadford, a very sensible boy and respected for his ability. He had a paternal uncle who was a merchant in Perth, and the boy being a good scholar his uncle sent for him to become his shop boy. So he went to his uncle's, and for three years he worked worthily and honourably. At the end of three years he became more frivolous, and wished to join a dancing school. He went to a dancing school and he spent three years learning dancing. No one could find a flaw in his dancing at the end of three years.

A ship came into the harbour and the boy was constantly gazing at the figure on its bows. He fell in love with the figurehead, and he went to the captain to find out if he could sail on the ship wherever she might be going, and the captain granted him his wish. He went to his uncle's shop and told his uncle that he had fallen in love with the figure on the vessel's bows, and that he was going to sail with the vessel until he saw the woman from whom the figurehead had been modelled. Five hundred pounds sterling was all the money he had, and his uncle let him have two suits of clothes to take away with him besides what he had of his own. So he set off and went on board.

The next day after he embarked they sailed. After they had been sailing for several days, the captain asked him how far he wanted to go. But the youth told him that in actual fact he had been a shop boy in Perth, and that the night the captain and his ship had come in he fell in love with the figure on the bows and that he would never have any rest until he saw the woman from whom it was modelled. 'Had I known that at the time of leaving,' said the captain to him, 'I would not have allowed you on board. What trade do you know best ?' 'I am best as a scholar and a dancer,' replied the Shepherd's Son.

as fheàrr mi,' thuirt Mac a' Chìobair. 'Tha i siod 'na boireannach
cho anabarrach uaibhreach is nach fhiach leatha tighinn a
ghabhail a bìdh còmhla ri a h-athair no ri a màthair,' thuirt an
sgiobair. 'Dé th' agad de dh'airgead?' 'Cóig ceud punnd
Sasannach,' arsa Mac a' Chìobair. 'Ma bhios na h-ochd luingeas
a th' aig a h-athair a staigh an uair a ruigeas sinn, bidh bàil
ann an oidhche sin,' thuirt an sgiobair ri Mac a' Chìobair.

An uair a nochd iad ris a' phort, chunnaig iad na h-ochd
luingeas a staigh. Rinn iad-san r'a chéile mar a dhèanadh iad,
nan tigte dh'an iarraidh. An uair a rànaig iad tìr, chuir an
caiptean a h-uile sìon air bòrd air dòigh. Chuir e leth-dusan
coinneal air bòrd, agus móran leabhraichean. Chaidh an
sgiobair gu tìr an uair sin, 's choinnich e fear na luinge ; is leis
an toileachas-inntinn a bha aig fear na luinge ris an sgiobair,
rinn iad bàil mór a chur air a bhonn. Chruinnicheadh daoine-
móra agus mnathan-uaisle an àite, agus chaidh am bàil a chur
air adhart ; agus cha b'fhiach le nighean fir nan luingeas dol
do'n bhàil. An uair a bha am bàil a' dol air aghaidh, dh'innis
an caiptean gu'n robh duine-uasal mór de mhuinntir Albann
aige air bòrd, agus gun robh e smuainteachadh gun còrdadh a
leithid seo de chuideachd ris gu math, agus gum bu ghlé
mhath leis a bhith 'nam measg ; agus labhair fear nan luingeas
an sin, agus thuirt e gum biodh e glé dheònach air a leithid
siod de dhuine-uasal fhaotainn do'n chuideachd. Thuirt
sgiobair an t-soithich an uair sin, nach robh fios aige, ged a
labhair e mar siod, am b' fhiach leis an duine-[uasal] tighinn
do'n chuideachd—(Mac a' Chìobair !) Thuirt fear nan luingeas
gun robh e smuainteachadh gum faodadh duine sam bith tighinn
do'n chuideachd a bha an siod, is gum bu chòir dol dh'a iarraidh.
Dh'fhalbh iad le chéile, an caiptean agus fear nan luingeas,
chun an t-soithich. An uair a chaidh an caiptean sìos, rinn e
modhannan, is rinn fear nan luingeas mar an ceudna. Dh'fhaighnich fear nan luingeas dheth, ann am modhalachd, an rachadh
e do'n chuideachd cuide riu ; agus dheònaich esan gun rachadh,
is thuirt e gum biodh e glé thoilichte falbh leò. Bha [an] dithis
[agus fear dhiubh] fo gach achlais aige an uair a rànaig e ;
agus rànaig iad far an robh a' chuideachd cruinn, agus thug iad
a' chathair a b'fheàrr a bha staigh dha air son suidhe oirre.
(Sin agaibh Mac a' Chìobair a nis !)

'That woman is so very haughty that she will not even condescend
to have her meals with her father or her mother,' said the captain.
'How much money have you ?' 'Five hundred pounds sterling,'
said the Shepherd's Son. 'If her father's eight ships are in port
when we arrive,' said the captain to the Shepherd's Son, 'there
will be a ball that night.'

When they hove in sight of the port, they saw the eight ships
lying there.   Together they arranged what to do if anyone
came to fetch them.   When they moored, the captain put everything on board in order : on a table he set out half a dozen
candles and a great number of books.   Then he went ashore
and met the owner of the vessel, who was so delighted to see
the captain that they made plans to hold a big ball.   The great
men and the ladies of the place were assembled, and the ball
was opened ; but the shipowner's daughter did not deign to
appear.   When the ball was under way, the captain remarked
that he had an important gentleman from Scotland on board
and he thought that he would very much enjoy such a company as
this, and that he would like very much to be amongst them.
Whereupon the shipowner spoke and said that he would be
very glad to have such a gentleman brought into their company.
The captain thereupon said that although he had spoken as he
had, he was not sure whether the gentleman would condescend
to join the company. (The Shepherd's Son !) The shipowner
replied that he thought any person might well join such a
company, and that the proper thing was to send and ask him.
Off they went to the ship together, the captain and the owner.
Upon going below, the captain paid his respects and the owner
did likewise, and with great courtesy the latter asked him if he
would like to join the guests with them ; and the Shepherd's
Son agreed to go and said that he would be very pleased to
accompany them.   By the time he arrived, they each had an
arm of his, and they proceeded to where the guests were
assembled and gave him the best chair in the house to sit on.
(There's the Shepherd's Son for you now.)

Thuirt an sgiobair ris an dannsadh e ruidhle leis, is thuirt esan gun dannsadh. Dhanns e an ruidhle leis, is ma dhanns, chan fhac iad a leithid a' seasamh air ùrlar 'san àite sin riamh ; is mun robh e réidh is an ruidhle, cha robh bean-uasal a staigh nach do thuit ann an gaol air. (An Gàidheal glan ! nam biodh féile-beag air !) Bha 'n darna té putadh na té eile, feuch có bu dlùithe shuidheadh air. Chaidh brath a mach a dh'ionnsaigh nam mnathan-uaisle móra gun robh Albannach urramach an déidh tighinn do'n bhaile, agus nach fhac iad duine riamh cho brèagh ris a' seasamh air ùrlar. Thug an sgiobair mu-near a chur a dhannsa a rithist, 's thànaig ise g'a choimhead. Mun robh an ruidhle leathach, thuit i ann an trom ghaol air. (Nach bu mhath Mac a' Chìobair ! Nam biodh am féile-beag air !) Thug fear nan luingeas mu-near am bàil a sgaoileadh, agus an duine a chumail nan gabhadh e cumail. Aig cho mór 's a bha e 'ga shealltainn fhéin, cha robh e deònach fuireachd. Laigh iad air mu dheireadh 'ga chuireadh, gus an do dh'fhan e an oidhche ud ; agus an té bha cóig bliadhna gun suidhe le a h-athair is le a màthair aig biadh, shuidh i leotha. An là-'r-na-mhàireach, an uair a dh'éirich e, thug e trì cheud punnd Sasannach do'n té a ghlan na brògan aige. Bhuail e staigh aca uile gu léir gum bu duine anabarrach comasach e. Bhruidhinn ise r'a h-athair air son gum pòsadh e i ; agus bhruidhinn a h-athair ris-san air son gum pòsadh e i, is gum faigheadh e a h-uile nì a bh' aige-san de'n t-saoghal. Thuirt esan gun robh na leòr de mhnathan-uaisle is de bheairteas anns an àite as an tànaig e. Bhataich[1] iad air. Dhiùlt e dhaibh anns an am, gus an dèanadh e turus-cuain eile. Agus an uair a dh'fhalbh an soitheach an là-'r-na-mhàireach, cha deach ise a staigh fo dhruim taighe fad 's a bha an soitheach 'na fianais.

Dh'innis e do'n sgiobair mar a bha eatorra, agus bha 'n sgiobair ro thoilichte an sin. Thug an sgiobair da trì cheud punnd Sasannach air son nan trì cheud a thug e do'n té a ghlan a bhrògan ; agus is e sia seachdainean a bha iad gun tilleadh chun a' phuirt cheudna. An uair a nochd e ris a' phort, dh'aithnich ise a' tighinn e ; is le barrachd toileachas-inntinn a dhèanamh ris an t-soitheach a' tighinn, chuir iad brat-ùrlair

---

[1] *Bhataich*, urged strongly, as if with sticks.

The captain asked him if he would dance a reel with him, and he said he would. He danced the reel with him, and if he did !—never before had they seen anyone like him take the floor there. Before he had finished the reel there was not a lady in the house who had not fallen in love with him. (Splendid Gael ! If he'd been wearing the kilt !) The women were jostling each other to see who could sit nearest him. Word went out to all the great ladies that a Scotsman of high rank had come to town and that never had they seen so handsome a man take the floor. The captain contrived to send him to dance again, and the owner's daughter came to observe him. Before the reel was half way through, she had fallen deeply in love with him. (Wasn't the Shepherd's Son good ! If only he had been wearing the kilt !) The owner considered bringing the ball to an end, and having the man kept there if he could be kept. But the Shepherd's Son now felt so important that he did not care about staying. But at last they pressed him so much with their invitations that he stayed that night ; and she who had not sat at table with her father and mother for five years sat with them. Next day when he got up he gave three hundred pounds to the girl who cleaned his shoes. It struck them all very forcibly that he must be a very wealthy man, and the girl spoke to her father to get him to marry her. Her father spoke to the Shepherd's Son to get him to do so, and that he would receive all his worldly wealth. The Shepherd's Son replied that there were plenty of ladies and plenty of wealth where he came from. They urged him very strongly but he refused them for the time being—until he should have made another voyage. When the ship sailed the following day the owner's daughter did not as much as go indoors while it remained in sight.

The Shepherd's Son told the captain how things stood between himself and the girl, and the captain was delighted, and gave him three hundred pounds in place of the three hundred he had given the girl who cleaned his shoes. Six weeks passed before they returned to that port. When they came in sight, the girl knew it was he who was coming, and to make a greater show of welcome at the ship's arrival they laid a carpet from the house eadar an taigh agus an ceidhe. Air an rathad eadar an taigh agus an ceidhe, bhuail a h-athair agus a màthair air air son a pòsadh ; agus cha robh dàil ri bhith ann ach e a phòsadh na nighinn air ball. An uair a bha am pòsadh dèanta, chaidh a h-athair agus esan, is thug e a roghainn do 'n chaiptean de na h-ochd soithichean, is ghabh e an soitheach a bha aige roimhid air son a roghainn. Bha toil-inntinn is greadhnachas is càirdeas eatorra ; is chaidh a h-uile nì seachad le toileachas-inntinn.

Written down [by Hector MacLean] from the recitation of Kenneth Boyd, Carinish, North Uist, at Lochmaddy Inn, on 11th August 1859. Reciter says he heard it often recited by some old men, but does not remember their names.

NOTES

Vol. x., No. 118. Scribe, Hector MacLean.
For journeying in search of a heroine, see No. 7 (MS. vol. x., No. 16).

to the quay. On the way from the quay to the house, her father and mother urged the young man to marry her ; there was to be no delay, but he must marry her forthwith. When the wedding had been celebrated, the girl's father and the young man went to the captain and gave him leave to choose whichever ship of the eight he liked best. The captain chose the one he had had before. Happiness and gaiety and friendship reigned amongst them all and everything passed off delightfully.

AN CAT GLAS

BHA Rìgh ann roimhe seo, is phòs e, is rug a' Bhanrìghinn mac dha. Bhàsaich a' Bhanrìghinn, is phòs e Banrìghinn eile. Rug an dara Banrìghinn mac eile dha, is bha an dà mhac a' fàs suas còmhla. Bhiodh an Rìgh a h-uile là dol do'n bheinn-sheilg, is am mac a bu shine còmhla ris. Thuirt an Iochlach Ùrlair [1] ris a' Bhanrìghinn gur h-i bha gòrach nach fhaigheadh rathad air a' mhac a bu shine a chur a dhìth, gur h-e a ghleidheadh oighreachd a athar uile gu léir, agus nach biodh mìr dhìth aig a mac-se. 'Cuir thusa,' ars ise, 'an rud seo anns a' chupan aige an uair a thig e dhachaigh, agus marbhaidh e e.'

Agus có bha 'gan cluinntinn ach a bhràthair a b'òige ; agus an uair a chuala e a athair agus a bhràthair a' tighinn, ruith e 'nan coinnimh. Thuirt an gille òg ri a bhràthair gun e a dh'òl na deoch a bheireadh a mhàthair-san da ; 'chionn,' ars esan, 'dh'iarr an Iochlach Ùrlair air mo mhàthair rud a chur ann gu thus' a mharbhadh ; ach na h-innis thusa, mum marbh mo mhàthair mise.' An uair a shuidh iad, dh'fhalbh an gille le a chupan fhéin, is thug e do'n chù bheag a bha staigh e ; agus fhuair an cù beag bàs mun d'òl e e. Cha dubhairt e facal is cha d'innis e dad ; is bha an Rìgh duilich, an uair a fhuair an cù beag bàs.

An là-'r-na-mhàireach, dh'fhalbh an Rìgh is a mhac do'n bheinn-sheilg. An uair a dh'fhalbh iad, thànaig an Iochlach Ùrlair far an robh a' Bhanrìghinn. 'Cha d'rinn siod feum,' ars ise, 'ach cuir air theachdaireachd do m' ionnsaigh-sa e, is cuiridh mi bior nimhe ann.' Bha an gille [a b'òige] 'gan cluinntinn ; agus shìn e an coinnimh a athar is a bhràthar an uair a chunnaig e tighinn iad ; agus dh'innis e dhaibh a h-uile facal a bha eadar a mhàthair agus an Iochlach Ùrlair. 'Ma chuireas mo

---

[1] The *Iochlach Urlair* is a domestic witch, see this book, vol. i., Appendix 2, pp. 492 ff. The younger half-brother in a tale in *Celtic Review*, vi., p. 364, and in *W. H. Tales*, No. 22, protects his elder half-brother in the same way as in this tale.

THE GRAY CAT

No. 65.   [*MS. Vol. x., No. 121*]

THERE was a King once, and he married, and his Queen bore him a son. The Queen died, and he married another Queen. The second Queen bore him another son and the two boys were growing up together. Every day the King went to the hunting hill, and his eldest son with him. The Iochlach Ùrlair [1] said to the Queen that she was truly foolish not to find a way of getting rid of the elder son, seeing that it was he who would inherit all his father's estate, whereas her own son would not have a scrap of it. 'You put this stuff in his cup when he comes home,' said she, 'and it will kill him.'

But who was listening to them but the younger brother, and when he heard his father and his brother coming he ran to meet them. The young boy told his brother not to take the drink his mother would give him. 'Because,' he said, 'the Iochlach Ùrlair told my mother to put something in it to kill you. But don't you tell, for fear my mother kills me.' When they sat down the youth took his own cup and gave it to the little dog that was in the house. The little dog died before he had finished drinking it. Not a word did the youth say, nor did he tell a thing, and the King was distressed when the little dog died.

Next day the King and his son went off to the hunting hill. After they had gone, the Iochlach Ùrlair came to the Queen. 'That was no use,' said she, 'but send him to me on an errand, and I will thrust a poisoned pin into him.' The [younger] boy was listening to them, and he ran to meet his father and brother when he saw them coming, and he told them every word that had passed between his mother and the Iochlach Ùrlair. 'If my mother sends you on an errand, don't go,' said the boy to his

mhàthair air teachdaireachd thu, na teirig ann,' ars esan ri a
bhràthair.   An là-'r-na-mhàireach, an uair a dh'éirich iad 's
a ghabh iad an tràth-maidne, dh'iarr a' Bhanrìghinn air dol air
theachdaireachd chun na h-Iochlach Ùrlair.   An uair a chaidh
e a mach, thuirt e ris a' bhràthair a b'òige, 'Bidh mise a' falbh,
is biodh an oighreachd agad fhéin, o'n as ann gu cothrom a
thoirt duit a tha iad ag iarraidh mis' a mharbhadh.'

Bha a bhràthair ro dhuilich air son e bhith falbh.   'Théid
mis' a staigh, feuch am faigh mi airgead a ghoid air mo mhàthair
a bheir mi do d'ionnsaigh, air eagal thu bhith falbh falamh,'
thuirt am bràthair a b'òige.   'Cha ghabh mi airgead nach
fhaighinn air dòigh cheart ; chan urrainn e feum a dhèanamh
dhomh.   Is fheàrr liom falbh ann am freasdal an fhortain, o
nach fhaighinn gu ceart e,' thuirt am bràthair a bu shine.
Dh'fhalbh an dà bhràthair le chéile, agus rànaig iad tulach gorm
treis o'n taigh.   Thòisich iad air caoineadh còmhla.   Ghabh
iad an cead dhe chéile.   Dh'fhuirich am fear a b'òige is a bheul
fodha air a' chnoc, a' caoineadh fad an latha.   Chaidh am fear
a bu shine gu taigh oide aig an Rìgh.   Am beul na h-oidhche
rànaig e taigh an oide.   Cha robh a staigh ach a mhuime, is
droch theine aice air.   'Fàilt' ort, a mhic as sine an Rìgh ;
b'fhurasda aithneachadh gur h-ann mar sin a bhitheadh mu
dheireadh.'   Dheasaich i biadh dha.   Chuir i uisge blàth air a
chasan, is chuir i a chadal e.   Chuir i sràbh-suaine fo a cheann
is fo a chasan.[1]

Chaidil e gun dùsgadh gus an tànaig an là, agus an uair a
dh'éirich e, dheasaich i a thràth-maidne.   Thug i paidhir bhròg
dha, is thuirt i ris, 'Bheir na brògan thu go dorus beòil na h-uamha
gus am bheil thu dol ; agus an uair a ruigeas tu dorus na h-uamha,
cuiridh tu an aghaidh air an eòl is an cùl air an aineol, agus
ruigidh iad mise an seo.[2]   Seo agad deich tasdain fhichead airgid ;
is e sin na bheil agam.   Bheir thu leat iad.   Agus an uair a

---

[1] This sentence may mean that there were two slumber-straws, one for the head
and one for the feet.   If there were only one, it must have been a very long one.
In *Trans. Gael. Soc. Inverness*, xxv., p. 249, occurs a *sràbh-suain* or slumber-straw
which is placed beneath the head, and a *rann suain*, or slumber verse (?) which is
placed beneath the feet.   In other tales, the magical apparatus for inducing sleep
is a pin.   In others, a poisonous prickle, or an apple, or a pear.   See No. 24 (MS.
vol. x., No. 44).   In No. 25 (MS. vol. x., No. 47), the hero's mother's sister puts a
Humming Harp of Harmony at his bed-head to make him sleep the better.   The

brother. The following day, after they had got up and had their breakfast, the Queen asked the youth to go on an errand to the Iochlach Ùrlair. When he went outside, he said to his brother, 'I will go away altogether, and you have the inheritance since it's to give you a clear field that they want to kill me.'

His brother was very grieved that the other was leaving. 'I will go in,' he said, 'to see if I can steal any money from my mother to bring you, for fear you are setting out with nothing.' 'I will not accept money that I could not get lawfully : it cannot do me any good,' said the elder brother ; 'I would rather go away trusting to Fortune since I cannot obtain it in an honourable way.' The two brothers set off together, and a little way from the house they came to a green hillock. Here both of them began to weep, and then they took leave of each other. The younger remained face-downwards on the hillock and wept all day long. The elder brother went to the house of one of the King's foster-fathers, and arrived at nightfall. There was no one at home but his foster-mother, and she had a poor fire burning. 'Welcome, elder son of the King,' said she, 'it was easy to see that this is what it would come to at last.' She prepared a meal for him ; she washed his feet with warm water and put him to bed ; and she placed a slumber-straw under his head and his feet.[1]

He slept without waking until daybreak and when he got up she made his breakfast. She gave him a pair of shoes and said to him: 'The shoes will bring you to the door of the cave where you are going. When you come to the door you will make the shoes face the way they know with their back to the way they do not know, and they will come to me here.[2] Here are thirty silver shillings for you ; it is all I have ; take it with you. When you

sleeping bag mentioned in the following proverb was probably also at one time something magical ; *Chuir iad am balgan suain fo 'cheann* (They put the sleeping bag under his head). Applied, says Macintosh, to a person who sleeps too much, in allusion to the bag or cocoon in which the caterpillar sleeps (Nicolson's *Gaelic Proverbs*, p. 145). A 'hop pillow,' or pillow full of hops, is still used in English country places for inducing sleep.

[2] The usual method of returning magic brogues to their owner. See *An Gàidheal*, iv. (1875), p. 305 : expressed differently, No. 22 (MS. vol. x., No. 37).

ruigeas tu an uaimh is a théid thu a staigh, chì thu cat mór glas a staigh, agus ma nì an cat gàire riut, dèan dà ghàire rithe.' [1] Thuirt e ri a mhuime gun dèanadh e siod, is ghabh e a chead dith ; is dh'fhalbh e. Thug na brògan gu dorus beul na h-uamha e. An uair a rànaig e, chuir e an aghaidh air an eòl is an cùl air an aineol, is dh'fhalbh iad air an ais dachaigh.

Chaidh e staigh do'n uaimh, is chunnaig e cat mór glas a staigh an sin. Rinn an Cat gàire ris, agus rinn esan dà ghàire ris a' chat. 'Fàilt' ort fhéin, a Mhic as sine an Rìgh,' ars an Cat, 'is iomadh mac rìgh agus ridire thànaig air an astar seo nach do thill dachaigh, agus tha eagal orm nach tusa as fheàrr a shàbhaileas. Tha fuamhair mór a' fuireach an seo is tha e tighinn dachaigh a h-uile h-oidhche ; is ged nach tig a staigh ach eun adhair, aithnichidh e e an uair a thig e ; ach nì mise mo dhìcheall riut, air a shon sin.' Thog an Cat leac mhór bhàrr sluic a bha an taobh shìos de'n teinidh ; agus chuir i an sin e goirid o'n am a bhiodh am fuamhair a' tighinn dachaigh, agus chuir i an leac air beul an tuill, is dh'fhàg i an sin e.

Cha b'fhada bha iad mar sin, an uair a chuala iad a' ghleadh-raich sin a' tighinn, is an talamh a' dol air chrith ! Có bha 'n seo ach Fuamhair Mór nan cóig ceann, is nan cóig meall, is nan cóig muineal—gad fhìor-iasg anns an darna làimh, is gad chailleacha marbha anns an làimh eile ! [2] 'Imh ! amh ! amhragaich ! tha fàileadh an fharbhalaich a staigh !' ars am Fuamhair. 'Chan 'eil ann ach eun beag a thànaig a staigh ; is mharbh mise e, is loisg mi anns an teinidh e,' ars an Cat Glas. 'Chan 'eil fhios agam nach e sin fhéin a th'ann,' ars am Fuamhair. 'Greas air an iasg sin a bhruich dhòmh-sa.' Bhruich i an t-iasg da, is chaidh e a laighe air beinge. Cha robh srann a dhèanadh e nach saoilte gun leagadh e an taigh. Anns a' mhaduinn, an là-'r-na-mhàireach, ghabh e a' chuid eile de'n iasg, is dh'fhalbh e. An uair a dh'fhalbh am fuamhair, leig an Cat Glas Mac an Rìgh a mach as an t-sloc. Dh'fhaighnich e de'n Chat an robh biadh sam bith ann a dh'itheadh e. Thuirt an Cat nach robh

---

[1] A cat who helps a hero against a giant occurs in *W. H. Tales*, ii., No. 41, Var. 2.

[2] *gad fhìor-iasg*, a withy of salmon. The word *fìor-iasg* is applied to the salmon as the king of fishes : similarly *fìor-eun* means an eagle. *Gad chailleacha marbha*, lit. 'a withy of dead old women.' A note in the MS. runs 'cailleacha marbha, a kind of fish according to reciter.' The fish is probably the black sea bream, *sparus*

reach the cave and go in, you will see a great gray cat inside, and if the cat laughs at you, laugh back at her twice.'[1] He told his foster-mother that he would do so ; and taking his leave of her, he set off. The shoes brought him right up to the mouth of the cave, and when he arrived he made them face the way they knew with their back to the way they did not know, and they returned home.

He entered the cave and saw a great gray cat there. The cat laughed at him, and he laughed twice at the cat. 'Welcome to you, elder son of the King,' said the cat. 'Many a king's son and knight's son have come on this journey and have not returned home, and I fear that you will fare no better than they did. There is a great giant living here : every night he comes home, and though only a bird of the air enters, the giant notices it when he comes. But I will do my utmost for you, nevertheless.' The cat raised a great stone slab from off a pit on the far side of the fire, and a short time before the hour at which the giant used to come home she put him down into it, and placed the slab on the mouth of the pit and left him there.

They were not long thus when they heard a hubbub approaching and felt the earth quivering. Who was this but the Great Giant of Five Heads and Five Humps and Five Necks, with a withy of salmon in one hand and a withy of dead 'Old Women' in the other.[2] 'Ho ! ho ! ho ! the smell of a stranger is about the place !' said the giant. 'It is only a little bird that came in, and I killed it and burnt it in the fire,' said the Gray Cat. 'Perhaps that's all it is,' said the giant. 'Hurry up and cook that fish for me.' She cooked the fish for him and he went to sleep on a bench. Not a snore he gave but seemed it would knock the house down. Next morning he ate the rest of the fish, and went off. When he had gone, the Gray Cat let the King's Son out of the pit. He asked the cat if there was any food there he might eat. There was not a bite, replied the cat, except some nasty fish. 'Not far from us is a town, and anything we need can be got there,' she said. 'Here is some money,' said the King's

vetula, sparus lineata, called in some English books on fishes, *old wife*. See Nos. 25, 67 (MS. vol. x., Nos. 47, 126). The 'dead carlins' which a giant brings home attached to his shoe-ties in *W. H. Tales*, i., No. 6, were probably a brace of black sea bream. For giants with seven or five heads, humps and necks, see *ibid.*, i., No. 4, Var. 2 ; *Celtic Dragon Myth*, xiv., No. 4 ; Islay's MS. vol. viii., No. 170.

blas ach iasg mosach a bha 'n siod. 'Tha baile-mór goirid uainn ;
agus gheibhear rud sam bith a dh'fheumas sinn ann,' ars ise.
'Tha airgead an seo,' arsa Mac an Rìgh. Thug e rud de'n
airgead do'n Chat, agus dh'fhalbh i do'n bhaile-mhór, is cheannaich i fìon is aran.[1]

A neas [2] a bha an Cat Glas air falbh, smaointich esan gun
rachadh e air feadh na h-uamha, feuch gu dé chitheadh e.
Chunnaig e dorus an sin, agus e glaiste. Sheall e a staigh air
toll na h-iuchrach. Chunnaig e a h-uile mìr de'n ùrlar còmhdaichte le carraghan dubha.[3] Chaidh e gu dorus eile. Sheall
e a staigh air toll na h-iuchrach. Fad 's a bu léir dha, bha e
faicinn ghunnan, is chlaidheamhnan, is aodaichean dhaoin'-
uaisle. Chaidh e chun doruis eile ; is chunnaig e bean-uasal
òg àlainn, nach fhaca e riamh na bu bhrèagha, is i air a sgeadachadh
ann an aodach geal. Bheireadh i treis air caoineadh, is treis
eile air cìreadh a cinn. An uair a chunnaig e na trì àitean, agus
a thànaig an Cat leis na nitheannan a cheannaich i, ghabh e a
bhiadh. 'Is e an dòigh a nì sinn, ma bhitheas sinn a' gabhail
bìdh mar seo gu ceann seachdain gus am bi sinn làidir, làimh
a thoirt air an Fhuamhair mhór a mharbhadh an uair a bhios
e 'na chadal,' thuirt an Cat Glas ri Mac an Rìgh. 'Glé mhath,'
arsa Mac an Rìgh. Lean iad air an obair seo gus an do theirig
na deich tasdain fhichead. A h-uile latha, an uair a bhiodh
an Cat air falbh, bheireadh esan an seòmar an robh a' bhean-
uasal air ; is bhiodh e a' coimhead a steach troimh tholl na
glaise gus an tilleadh an Cat. A h-uile h-oidhche, an uair a
thigeadh am Fuamhair dhachaigh, bhiodh e cho fiadhaich ris
a' Chat, is a' coiteachadh oirre gun robh farbhalach a staigh.

Chuir iad rompa, oidhche bha an sin, gun cuireadh iad
ceann-crìche air. Thuit e 'na chadal trom. An uair a chaidil
e, chuir an Cat Glas teine mór air, agus chuir i dà bhior-ròstaidh
'san teinidh. Bha srann aig an Fhuamhair a bha toirt crith air
an uaimh. An uair a bha na biorain iarainn geal, thog i an
leac bhàrr Mac an Rìgh, agus leig i a mach e. Dh'éirich e, agus
thug e fear de na biorain as an teinidh ; is spàrr e troimh uchd

---

[1] Wine and wheaten bread occur in *W. H. Tales,* ii., No. 51.

[2] *A neas,* 'while,' probably from *an fheith's* ; *feith,* 'to wait,' is used as a noun in
the expression *feith romh'n bhàs* ; *an fheith's a dh'fhan e* [=] *an fhad's a dh'fhan e* (note
in MS.). [But *A neas* is more probably for *an fheadh is,* = 'while.']

Son, and he gave the cat part of the silver. Off she went to the town and bought wine and bread.[1]

While the cat was away he decided to explore the cave to see what he could find. He saw a door, and it was locked. He peeped in through the keyhole and saw that every inch of the floor was covered with black pillar-stones.[3] Then he went to another door and looked in through the keyhole. As far as he could see, he made out guns and swords and gentlemen's clothing. He went to another door ; there he saw a beautiful young lady— a lovelier he had never seen—and she was dressed in white. She would spend some time weeping, and then she would comb her hair for a while. When he had inspected the three rooms and the cat had returned with what she had bought, he had a meal. 'If we keep on taking food in this way for a week until we become strong,' said the Gray Cat to the King's Son, 'this is what we will do : we will have a try at killing the Great Giant when he is sleeping.' 'Very good,' replied the King's Son. They continued to act in this way until the thirty shillings had gone. Every day when the cat was gone he would make for the room where the lady was, and he would spend the time looking through the keyhole until the cat returned. Every night when the giant came home he used to be very savage to the cat, insisting that there was a stranger in the house.

One night they determined to put an end to him. The giant had fallen into a heavy slumber, and, when he was sound asleep, the Gray Cat put on a great fire and put two roasting spits in the fire. The giant's snores were making the cave tremble. When the iron spits were white-hot the Gray Cat lifted the stone slab off the pit and let the King's Son out. He rose up, took one of the spits out of the fire, and thrust it through the giant's

---

[3] *carrannan dugha* in the MS. at this place—*carraghan dubha* in other places. Similar pillar-stones occur in *Waifs and Strays*, ii., p. 371.

an Fhuamhair e. Thug an Cat Glas am bioran eile as, agus am beagan a b'urrainn di fhéin a dhèanamh, spàrr i troimh àite eile dheth e. A mach thug am Fuamhair ag éigheach 's a' rànaich. Gu dé ach theirigidh [*sic*] e tarsaing 'san dorus, is chum na biorain an siod e. Rug Mac an Rìgh air claidheamh an Fhuamhair, is thuirt e ris, 'Tha bàs os do chionn ; gu dé t'fhuasgladh ?' 'Is mór sin,' ars am Fuamhair ; 'tha tronnc làn òir is airgid ann an seòmar de na bheil 'san uaimh.' 'Is liom féin sin ; tha am bàs os do chionn, gu dé t'fhuasgladh?' arsa Mac an Rìgh. 'Tha seòmar agam làn de charraghan dubha ; is chan 'eil an sin ach clann rìghrean, is ridirean, is dhiùcannan air an cur fo gheasaibh. Tha slacan-draoidheachd anns an t-seòmar, agus an uair a bhuaileas tu buille de'n t-slacan a tha an sin orra, théid iad mar a bha iad roimhe. Tha seòmar eile ann, làn de'n cuid aodaich agus de'n cuid armaibh. Mar a nì an slacan feum do chàch, nì e feum do'n Chat Ghlas. Is nighean rìgh air a cur fo gheasaibh i, is ghlac mise i. Bha mi glé mhath dhi, ged as olc an taing a thug i dhomh air a' cheann mu dheireadh. Tha rud na's fheàrr na sin uile gu léir agam— tha nighean rìgh an àite seo fhéin agam. Bha i mach a' snàmh, agus ghlac mise i. Tha mi cinnteach gur h-ann agad fhéin a bhios i sin.' Ged a dh'innis e a h-uile dad a bha an sin da, thug e na cinn deth leis a' chlaidheamh.

Is e an ceud rud a rinn e an déis a mharbhadh dol do'n t-seòmar far an robh a' bhean-uasal, is a leigeil a mach. Chaidh iad an sin do'n t-seòmar an robh na carraghan dubha [agus an slacan-draoidheachd]. Fhuair e an slacan-draoidheachd, is thug e a' cheud bhuille do'n Chat deth. Dh'fhàs i an sin 'na boireannach brèagha, àlainn, mu ochd bliadhna deug a dh'aois. Bhuail e an sin air bualadh nan carraghan ; is leumadh mac rìgh is mac ridire is mac diùc a suas, gus an robh an seòmar làn de na bha an sin de sheòid. Dh'éid [*sic*] iad iad fhéin le an aodach fhéin anns an t-seòmar eile. Roinneadh an t-òr 's an t-airgead uile gu léir orra, is fhuair an Cat Glas a deagh roinn de na bh'ann. Phòs esan agus nighean an rìgh, agus phòs an Cat Glas agus fear de na ridirean a bha 'san t-seòmar. An uair a bha na bainnsean is a h-uile rud seachad, smaointich e gun rachadh e dhachaigh far an robh a athair. Thug e a bhean leis, agus bha rìomhadh gu leòr còmhla riu.

＊　　　＊　　　＊　　　＊　　　＊

chest. The Gray Cat took out the other spit and, with what little strength she had, thrust it through another part of him. The giant rushed out shouting and crying. But what does he do but go through the door sideways and there the spits held him. The King's Son seized the giant's sword and said : 'Death is over your head ! What is your ransom ?' 'No little one,' replied the giant. 'There is a trunk full of gold and silver in one of the rooms in the cave.' 'That's mine !' said the King's Son. 'Death is over your head ! What is your ransom ?' 'I have a room full of black pillar-stones ; they are none other than the children of kings and knights and dukes bound by enchantment. There is a magic wand in the room, and if you strike them with that wand they will resume their former shape. There is another room full of their clothes and weapons. What the wand will do for the others it will do for the Gray Cat. She is a king's daughter who was bewitched, and I caught her. I was very good to her though ill has she repaid me in the end. But I have one possession better than all that—I have the daughter of the king of this very place. She was out swimming, and I caught her. I suppose you yourself will have that one.' Although the giant told him all that, the King's Son took off his heads with the sword.

The first thing he did after killing him was to go to the room where the lady was and let her out. Then they went to the room where the black pillar-stones [and the magic wand] were. He found the wand and gave the cat the first stroke with it. At once she became a fine, beautiful woman, about eighteen years old. Then he began striking the pillar-stones, and a king's son would leap up and a knight's son and a duke's son until the room was full of all those fine fellows. They dressed themselves in their own clothes in the other room. Then all the gold and silver was divided among them and the Gray Cat got her own good share of what was there. The young man and the King's daughter married, and the Gray Cat married one of the knights who had been in the room. When the weddings and everything else were over the King's Son thought he would go home where his father was. He took his wife with him, and along with them went treasure enough.

An uair a dh'fhalbh e a taigh a athar, dh'ionndrainn a athair
e.   Bha iad ro bhrònach as a dhéidh.   Bhiodh a bhràthair a
h-uile là a' dol gus an tulach far an do dhealaich e ris, dh'a
chaoineadh ; is cha robh fios aig duine dé bha tighinn ris.
Bha e cnàmh is a' dol as.   Chuir a athair roimhe gun leanadh
e e, is gum biodh fios aige c'à'n robh e dol.   Lean e e a dh'ionnsaigh an tulaich, agus fhuair e an sin e, agus a bheul fodha, agus
e a' caoineadh.   'Feumaidh tu ìnnseadh dhòmh-sa gu dé tha
tighinn riut,' ars a athair.   Cha robh e deònach a ìnnseadh,
ach chuir a athair roimhe nach leigeadh e as e gus an ìnnseadh
e e.   'Tha eagal orm ma dh'ìnnseas mi e, gu marbh thu mo
mhàthair,' ars esan ; 'seo an tulach air an do dhealaich mo
bhràthair gaolach rium-sa.   Chaidh e do thaigh m'oide an oidhche
sin, is chan 'eil tuilleadh lorg agam-sa air.'   Chaidh an Rìgh
do thaigh a oide, feuch am faigheadh e a mach o a mhuime gu
dé dh'éirich dha.   Cha robh dad aig a' mhuime ri ìnnseadh
dha, ach gun d'fhalbh e.   Thill e dhachaigh an sin, agus chuir
e an Iochlach Ùrlair gu bàs.   Leis an nàire ghabh a' Bhanrìghinn,
laigh i, is cha robh i fada beò.

*   *   *   *   *

An uair a choinnich esan is a athair is a bhràthair a chéile,
bha toil-inntinn na leòr orra.   Dh'fhàg e an rìoghachd aig a
bhràthair ; bha gu leòr aige-san dha fhéin.   Thill e fhéin agus
a bhean air an ais d'an rìoghachd, an uair a chuir iad treis
ùine seachad le a athair.   Cha robh mac no nighean a nis
aig a athair, ach am mac a b'òige, is phòs e.

NOTES

MS. vol. x., No. 121.   From B. MacAskill, Island of Berneray, who
learnt it in her youth from Christie MacAskill, a native of Eigg.   Collector,
Hector MacLean.

After the King's Son left his father's house, his father yearned for him, and everyone was very sorrowful because of his going. Every day his brother used to go to the hillock where he had parted from him to lament him ; nor did anyone know what was ailing him. He was getting thin and wasting away. His father determined to follow him to find out where he was going. He followed him to the hillock and found him there, lying on his face weeping. 'You must tell me what's the matter with you,' said his father. The boy did not want to tell, but his father determined not to let him go until he had told. 'I'm afraid you will kill my mother if I tell,' said he. 'This is the hillock on which my darling brother parted from me. That night he went to my foster-father's house, and beyond that I have no trace of him.' The King went to his foster-father's house to see if he could find out from his foster-mother what had happened to the youth. The foster-mother had nothing to tell him but that he had gone away. Then the King returned home and put the Iochlach Ùrlair to death. The Queen was so seized with shame that she took to her bed and did not live long.

When the King's Son and his father and brother met there was joy in plenty. The King's Son left the kingdom to his brother—he had abundance for himself. After he and his wife had spent some time with his father, they returned to their own kingdom. The king had now neither son nor daughter, except the younger son, and he married.

For a helping foster-father and foster-mother, see No. 53 (MS. vol. x., No. 97). For helping a princess in a cave, and thrusting a red-hot spike into a giant's eye, see *Waifs and Strays*, ii., p. 265.

AN TRIÙIR A CHAIDH A DH'IARRAIDH
FIOS AN ÀNRAIDH

No. 66.   *[MS. Vol. x., No. 123]*

BHA Triùir Chlann Rìgh [Bana-phrionnsachan] ann an siod roimhe seo, 's cha robh an athair no am màthair beò, 's bha iad a' fuireach ann an taigh leò fhéin. Thuirt an té bu shine ri càch, 'Cha stad mi 's chan fhois mi a choidhche gus am faigh mi Fios an Ànraidh.' 'Ma tà,' ars a piuthair mheadhonach, 'nì mi féin an cleas ceudna, 's cha stad mi fhéin gus am faigh mi Fios an Ànraidh.' Thuirt an té a b'òige, 'Chan fhan mise liom fhéin an déidh dhuibh-se falbh ; ach chan ann a dh'iarraidh Fios an Ànraidh a théid mi, air a shon sin.'

Dh'fhalbh iad, 's bha iad an sin a' falbh gus an robh dubhadh a' tighinn air am bonnaibh agus tolladh air am brògan. Thuit an oidhche an sin ; 's chunnaig iad solus fada uatha ; 's ge b'fhada uatha, cha b'fhada 'ga ruigheachd. Chaidh iad a staigh an sin, 's bha seann duine a staigh leis fhéin, 's teine beag biorach aige a' cur smàil. 'Fàilt oirbh fhéin, a Thriùir Chlann an Rìgh ; b'uaibhreach dhuibh falbh as bhur taigh fhéin,' ars an seann duine. 'A Nighean as sine an Rìgh, éirich, agus deasaich ar tràth-feasgair,' ars an seann duine. Rinn i siod. 'A dhà Nighean as òige an Rìgh, theirigibh a bhuain luachrach [1] a bhios fodhainn anns na leapaichean,' ars an seann duine. Dh'fhalbh iad an seo, agus bhuain iad luachair, an dithis nighean, an té mheadhonach agus an té òg. Thill iad dachaigh leis an luachair, 's bha an dorus dùinte, 's chan fhaigheadh iad a staigh !

Cha robh cothrom aca ach fuireach air chùl na còmhla a' caoineadh an sin. Dh'fhuirich iad an sin gus an tànaig an là, 's an uair a shoillsich an là dh'fhalbh iad. Bha iad a' falbh fad finn finn foinneach an latha gus an tànaig an oidhche. Chunnaig iad an solus fada uatha, 's ge b'fhada uatha, cha b'fhada 'ga ruigheachd. Chaidh iad a staigh, 's bha seann duine an sin, 's teine beag biorach aige, a' cur smàil.

---

[1] *Trì coilceadha na Féinne, bàrr gheal chrann, cóinneach, agus ùr-luachair* ; 'The three Fenian bedstuffs, fresh tree-tops, moss, and fresh rushes.' Nicolson, *Gaelic Proverbs,* 389.

THE THREE WHO WENT TO DISCOVER
WHAT HARDSHIP MEANT

No. 66.   *[MS. Vol. x., No. 123]*

THERE were once three princesses whose father and mother
were dead and who lived in a house by themselves. The eldest
said to the others, 'I will never rest nor remain quiet until I
get to know what Hardship is.' 'Well, then,' said the next
sister, 'I will do the same myself, for neither will I rest until I
find out what Hardship is.' The youngest sister said, 'I will
not stay here by myself after you have gone, but, despite that,
it isn't to find out what Hardship is that makes me go.'

They set off, and kept travelling until the soles of their feet
began to get black and their shoes full of holes. Then night
fell, and they saw a light far away from them ; but far away
though it was, they were not long in reaching it. They entered
the place where the light was, and there was an old man by
himself, with a little, smouldering, conical fire. 'Welcome,
three children of the King : it was daring of you to leave your
own house,' said the old man. 'You, eldest daughter of the King,
get up and prepare our supper.' She did that. 'You two younger
daughters of the King, go and pull rushes to place underneath
us in our beds,' said the old man. Thereupon the two girls, the
middle one and the youngest, went out and gathered rushes.
When they returned with them, the door was shut and they
could not get in.

They had no choice but to wait outside the door, and there
they remained crying. They stayed until the day came, and
when it dawned, they went away. They were travelling all the
live-long day until night came. They saw a light far away from
them, but far away though it was, they did not take long to
reach it. They entered the place where the light was, and there
was an old man with a little, smouldering, conical fire.

'Fàilt oirbh fhéin, a dhithis Nighean an Rìgh ; b'uaibhreach dhuibh tighinn an seo,' ars an seann duine. 'A Nighean mheadhonach an Rìgh, éirich 's deasaich ar tràth-feasgair.' Dheasaich i an tràth-feasgair 's ghabh iad i. 'A Nighean as òige an Rìgh, falbh a bhuain luachrach a théid fodhainn anns na leapaichean.' Dh'fhalbh i, 's bhuain i an luachair, 's thill i leatha, 's thànaig i chun an doruis, 's bha an dorus dùinte, 's chan fhaigheadh i a staigh na's mò na gheibheadh a brògan. Bha i a' caoineadh air chùl na còmhla fad na h-oidhche.

An uair a thànaig an là, 's a bu léir dhi, dh'fhalbh i. Bha i a' falbh fad an latha, 's feasgar an sin thànaig i a dh'ionnsaigh taighe, 's cha robh a staigh ach fear agus bean, is iad 'nan leabaidh leis an aois. 'Fàilt ort fhéin, a Nighean an Rìgh ; tha thu làn sgìos agus mìothlachd, ach ma nì thu féin an rud a dh'iarras mise ort, tachraidh gu math dhuit,' ars a' bhean a bha a staigh an sin. Thug i biadh dhi, 's chuir i uisge blàth air a làmhan 's air a casan, 's chuir i a laighe i. Chaidil i gus an tànaig an là. An uair a ghabh i a dìot-maidne, thug an t-seana-bhean oirre an sin falbh. 'Bidh thu nis a' falbh, 's tha taigh mór, geal, gun a bhith fad as a seo, 's théid thu a staigh an sin.' Dh'fhalbh i an sin, 's cha robh i fada a' falbh, an uair a thachair an taigh geal oirre. Cha do thachair duine beò oirre, 's fhuair i na dorsan fosgailte ,'s ghabh i a staigh roimpe. Ghabh i suas do sheòmar brèagha a bha an sin. Bha teine mór brèagha anns an t-seòmar. Shuidh i a staigh ann, 's cha robh i a' faicinn duine. An uair a thànaig am a' bhìdh, bha am bòrd air a chòmhdachadh leis a h-uile biadh is deoch a smuaintichte. Ghabh i na dh'fheumadh i de na bha air a' bhòrd. An uair a thànaig an oidhche, lasadh na coinnlean, 's cha robh seòmar a bha a staigh gun solus. Bha i an seo a' gabhail misnich. Chaidh i suas an staighir, 's bha a h-uile h-àite air a lasadh. Bha seòmar fosgailte roimpe an sin, is coinneal 's coinnleir air a' bhòrd, 's teine brèagha 'san t-simileir. Leabaidh bhrèagh an sin air a dèanamh sìos deiseil air son dol a laighe innte. An uair a bha i treis an sin, 's a ghabh i a tràth-feasgair, smuaintich i air dol a chadal. Chaidh i a laighe.

An uair a bha i an sin 'na laighe, 's i dol a thuiteam 'na cadal, dh'fhairich i cudthrom mór, mór, air a muin ! Chuir i a làmh a mach, 's gu dé bha an sin ach Colainn gun Cheann, agus bhuail e air iarraidh a dhol fo'n aodach còmhla rithe. A

'Welcome, two daughters of the King, it was daring of you to come here,' said the old man. 'You, second daughter of the King, get up and prepare our supper.' She prepared supper, and they ate it. 'Youngest daughter of the King, go and pull rushes to be placed underneath us in our beds,' said the old man. She went off and gathered the rushes, and returned with them. But when she came to the door it was shut, and she could no more get in than her shoes could. All night she remained outside the door, crying.

When day came and she could see, she went away. She kept going all day, and in the evening she came to a house where there was no one but a man and a woman, both bedridden with age. 'Welcome, daughter of the King,' said the woman who was there, 'you are disconsolate and full of weariness, but if you do what I order, things will go well with you.' She gave her food and warm water for her hands and feet, and sent her to bed, where she slept until day came. When she had had her breakfast, the old woman made her leave. 'You must go now,' she said, 'and there is a big, white house not far from here, which you will enter.' The girl left then, and had not been going for long when she came to the white house. She did not meet a living soul, but she found the doors open and went straight in. There was a beautiful room there to which she made her way ; there was a fine big fire in the room, and the girl sat down there, still seeing nobody about. When mealtime came, the table was covered with every imaginable kind of food and drink, and she took as much as she needed of what was on the table. Candles were lit when night fell, nor was there a single room in the house without light. The girl began to take courage ; she went upstairs, and every place was lit up. There was a room open before her there, a candle and candlestick on the table, and a bright fire on the hearth. A beautiful bed was ready and made down, all prepared for sleeping in. When the girl had been there for some time and had had her supper, she thought of going to sleep, and went to bed.

While she was lying there and about to fall asleep, she felt a very great weight on top of her. She put out her hand, and what should it be but a Headless Body who began to ask if it might come under the clothes with her. In spite of all her efforts, it

dh'aindeoin 's na rinn i, chaidh e fo'n aodach ; ach cho luath
's a fhuair e fo'n aodach, dh'fhàs e 'na aon òganach a b'àille
chunnacas o thùs an domhain gu deireadh na dìle ! Dh'innis
e dhi gum b'e féin mac rìgh a bha aig a mhuime air a chur fo
gheasaibh, agus gum biodh e fo na geasaibh ud am feasd, gus
an tachradh a leithid-se ris. An là-'r-na-mhàireach, thuirt e
rithe, 'Ged a chluinneas tu an taobh a tha fodha de'n taigh a'
dol os a chionn, na fosgail an dorus.'

An uair a dh'éirich ise, bha ciste làn de na h-aodaichean a
bu bhrèagha mu a coinnimh. Cha bu luaithe dh'fhalbh esan,
na thòisich a' ghleadhraich sin sìos is suas feadh an taighe. Bha
iad ag iarraidh oirre-se an dorus fhosgladh, 's chan fhosgladh i e.
An uair a thànaig an oidhche 's a chaidh i a laighe, thànaig an
cudthrom air a muin. Cha luaithe a bha e 'na laighe fo'n aodach
còmhla rithe, na bu e an t-òganach a bu bhrèagha 's a b'àille o
thùs domhain gu deireadh na dìle ! An uair a dh'fhalbh esan
an là-'r-na-mhàireach, thuirt e rithe, 'Cuiridh iad an diugh
barrachd dragh ort 's a chuir iad riamh, ach na fosgail thusa
an dorus air na chunnaig thu riamh.'

Lean iad sia làithean mar seo. Bha ise a' faotainn na h-aon
trioblaid o'n fheadhainn a bha ag éigheach 'san dorus, 's ag
iarraidh a staigh. An uair a thigeadh esan dachaigh, bhiodh
e cho toilichte ise bhith cho daingeann riu. 'Nis,' ars esan, air
maduinn an t-siathamh latha, 'is e an diugh an là mu dheireadh,
's tha mise cuibhte 's a' gheasachd leis an latha an diugh ; agus
bheir mi thusa liom, agus is tu mo bhean-sa.' Có thànaig
an latha seo ach a peathraichean chun an doruis. Thòisich
iad air glaodhaich, 'A phiuthair ghràdhach, nach fosgail thu
an dorus, 's gum faiceamaid aon sealladh dhìot. Mura leig
thu a staigh sinn, cuir a mach bàrr do mheòir air an dorus,
's gun tugamaid pòg dhi.' Chuir ise a mach bàrr a meòir
air toll na h-iuchrach, 's ghrad chuir iad am bior nimhe 'na
meur, 's thuit i sìos marbh air chùl na còmhla. An uair a thànaig
esan [am prionnsa] dachaigh, 's a fhuair e marbh i, cha robh
fios aige gu dé dhèanadh e ris fhéin. Fhuair e ciste bhrèagha
a dhèanamh dhi, 's a cur anns a' chiste, 's i làn de spìosraidh
mun cuairt oirre. Thug e dhachaigh i, 's ghlais e ann an seòmar
i, 's cha robh e a' leigeil duine a staigh do'n t-seòmar ach e fhéin.
Phòs e té eile.

came under the clothes ; but as soon as it got there, it became the most exquisite youth ever seen from the beginning of the world to the end of doom. He told her that he was a king's son bewitched by his stepmother and fated to continue thus until he should meet someone like her. The next morning he said to her, 'Although you should hear the house being turned upside down, do not open the door.'

When she got up, there was a chest full of the most beautiful clothes in front of her. No sooner had the youth gone than a tremendous din began which raged up and down throughout the house. They (the unseen creatures) were demanding that she should open the door, but she would not open it. When night came and she had gone to bed, the weight came upon her again. No sooner was it lying under the clothes with her than it became the most exquisite and most handsome youth ever seen from the beginning of the world to the end of doom. Next day when the youth left, he said to her, 'They will give you more trouble than ever today, but do not on any account open the door.'

They kept this up for six days, and the girl continued to suffer the same annoyance from those who shouted at the door, demanding admittance. Every time he came home, the young man was always very pleased with her for being so resolute against them. 'Now,' said he, on the morning of the sixth day, 'this is the last day, and by the end of it I shall be free from the spell. Then I will take you with me, and you shall be my wife.' But that day, who should come to the door but her sisters. They began to call, 'Darling sister, will you not open the door and let us have one glimpse of you ? If you won't let us in, put the tip of your finger out through the doorway, so that we may kiss it.' The girl put the tip of her finger out through the keyhole. In an instant they put a poisoned pin into it, and she fell down dead behind the door. When the youth returned home and found her dead, he was beside himself. He had a beautiful coffin made for her, full of spices round her body, and had her placed in it. He took her [to his] home and locked her in a room, and in that room he allowed nobody but himself. Then he married another woman.

Cha robh seòmar a staigh nach robh i a' faotainn na h-iuchrach, ach cha tug e iuchair an t-seòmair ud do dhuine a chunnaig e riamh. Bhiodh e a h-uile là a' dol do'n bheinnsheilg ; agus bhiodh a bhean 'ga choinneachadh an uair a bha e dol a thighinn dachaigh. Dh'fhalbh i an siod là, agus ghoid i an iuchair as a phòca, agus dh'ionndrainn esan an iuchair mun tànaig e dhachaigh. Gu dé rinn ise ach dol a staigh do'n t-seòmar an uair a dh'fhalbh esan. Dh'fhosgail i a' chiste, 's chunnaig i am boireannach àlainn sin anns a' chiste, marbh ! Dh'fheuch i a h-uile bìdeag dhith o a ceann gu a casan, gach meur 's gach làmh 's gach cas aice. Faighear am bior nimhe 'na meur, agus thug i as e, agus chuir i teine mór anns an t-seòmar, agus thug i am boireannach as a' chiste, agus chuir i 'na suidhe mu choinnimh an teine i, [agus is ann mar sin a thug i beò i]. An uair a chunnaig i an rìgh a' tighinn dachaigh, chaidh i 'na choinnimh, ach leis an fheirg a bha aige rithe, cha bhruidhneadh e rithe, thaobh gun do ghoid i an iuchair as a phòca. Ghabh e seachad, 's cha chanadh e facal rithe. Thug i air a dhol a staigh an seo. Thug i a staigh e do'n t-seòmar anns an robh ise. An uair a chunnaig e beò i, cho brèagha, slàn 's a bha i riamh, cha mhór nach do thuit e fhéin marbh leis an t-sòlas. Rug e oirre air dhà làimh. Ghabh iad am biadh còmhla air an fheasgar sin le mór aoibhneas.

An là-'r-na-mhàireach, an uair a bha a h-uile greadhnachas a bh'ann seachad, thuirt an té mu dheireadh, iad-san [an rìgh agus a cheud bhean] a bhith còmhla, o'n as ise a bha pòsd' air an toiseach, agus gum falbhadh ise. Dh'fhalbh i, agus phòs i fear a bha gaol aice air roimhe, 's bha iad mar gum biodh peathraichean agus bràithrean ann.

NOTES

From B. MacAskill, Island of Berneray, who learnt it in her youth from Ann McDonald, Uig, Lewis.

J. F. Campbell makes the following reference to our story, No. 123, 'A woman who has no fear'; *W. H. Tales*, iv., p. 408. The opening is a little like No. 119, 'Cù Bàn an t-Sléibhe'; of which there is another version,

There was not a room in the house but she had the key to it—but he did not give the key to that room to anyone he ever saw. Every day he used to go to the hunting-hill, and his wife used to meet him when he was about to come home. But one day she went and stole the key out of his pocket, and before he came home, he noticed it was missing. What did his wife do but enter the room when he had gone. She opened the coffin, and there she saw that beautiful woman, dead. She felt every part of her from head to foot, every one of her fingers and each of her hands and feet. She found the poisoned pin in her finger and drew it out ; then she made a great fire in the room and took the woman out of the coffin, and placed her sitting opposite the fire [and thus she brought her to life again]. When she saw the King coming home, she went to meet him ; but he was so angry with her for having taken the key out of his pocket that he would not speak to her. He went straight past her, and would not say a word. But she induced him to enter, and brought him into the room where the girl was. When he saw her alive and as lovely and healthy as ever, he himself almost fell dead with joy. He seized her by her hands. That evening, they all dined together in great happiness.

Next day, when all the celebration was over, his second wife said that they [the King and his first wife] were now to live together, since it was she who had been first married to him, and that she herself should go away. So she went away and married a man whom she had loved before, and they were all like sisters and brothers.

Zeitschrift f. Celtische Phil., i., p. 146 ; Tarbh Mór na h-Iorbhaig, *Celtic Review*, v., p. 259 ; and 'The Roan Bull of Oranges,' *Folk-Lore*, iv. For the heroine's sisters determine to find out Fios an Ànraidh. The heroine accompanies them but not with the same purpose. Thus far does our story slightly resemble the openings in those above-mentioned, but the after events are quite unique.

CLANN AN RÌGH FO GHEASAIBH

No. 67.   [*MS. Vol. x., No. 126*]

BHA uaireigin ann an tìr fad as, Rìgh agus Banrìghinn, agus bha aca trì mic agus nighean, agus mun robh an nighean ach òg, dh'fhàs a' Bhanrìghinn tinn, agus ghabh i am bàs d'a h-ionnsaigh féin, agus chuir i fios air té as am b'urrainn i earbsa a chur, gus i bhith 'na muime-chìche aig an nighinn. Thànaig an té a bha a' Bhanrìghinn ag iarraidh, a ghabhail cùraim de'n nighinn. Thuirt a' Bhanrìghinn ris a' bhanaltram, 'Mas e is gun tig bàs aithghearr[1] orm-sa, tha mi a' cur mar chomraich ort-sa, gun gabh thu cùram de mo nighinn is gun toir thu foghlam di,' is gheall a' mhuime-chìche gun dèanadh i sin. An ceann beagan làithean, fhuair a' Bhanrìghinn bàs, agus bha an nighean air chùram a muime-chìche.

An ceann beagan bhliadhnachan, smaointich an Rìgh air pòsadh a rithist, agus chuir e a thrì mic is a nighean, agus luchd-freasdail a ghleidheadh an gnothaichean an òrdugh dhaibh, a staigh do dh'àite d'am b'ainm an Lùchairt Éibhinn, 'Air chùl na gaoithe 's ri aodann gréine, le an dìol deoch 's an leòr de bhiadh, far am faiceadh iad gach neach 's chan fhaiceadh a h-aon idir iad.' Agus bha trian de'n bhiadh, is trian de'n deoch, is trian de gach nì a bha air a thoirt do thaigh an Rìgh, 'ga chur a staigh an sin 'nan ionnsaigh a h-uile latha, agus bha a muime-chìche còmhla ris an nighinn a' toirt foghlaim di.

Phòs an Rìgh bean eile, agus ri tìm bha aice trì mic, agus bha farmad mór aig a' Bhanrìghinn dheireannaich ri clann na ceud mhnà a bha aig an Rìgh, agus aig ceann na h-uibhir de bhliadhnachan, an uair a bha a clann fhéin a' fàs suas, bha i ro thoileach nam faigheadh i dòigh air clann na ceud Bhanrìghinn a chur as an rathad. Dh'innis i a sgeul do Chailleach nan Cearc. Thuirt Cailleach nan Cearc, gu cinnteach gum bu mhór an anstruigh a bhith gleidheadh suas dà theaghlach. Thuirt a' Bhanrìghinn gun tugadh i ceannach air iad a bhith

---

[1] MS. *athghiorra.*

THE KING'S CHILDREN UNDER ENCHANTMENTS

No. 67.   [*MS. Vol. x., No. 126*]

ONCE upon a time and in a far country, there was a King and a Queen. They had three sons and a daughter, but while the daughter was still very young the Queen became ill, and realised that she was going to die ; and so she sent for a certain woman on whom she could rely, that she might become wet-nurse for the girl. The woman the Queen wished for arrived, to take charge of the child. The Queen said to the nurse, 'If it happens that I die soon, I solemnly enjoin you to take charge of my daughter and educate her,' and the nurse promised that she would. At the end of a few days the Queen died, and the girl became the charge of her nurse.

At the end of a few years the King thought of marrying again. So he sent his three sons and his daughter, with attendants to keep their affairs in order for them, to a place called the Palace of Delight, 'At the back of the wind and facing the sun, with plenty food and drink, where they could see every one and none could see them.' And a third of the food and a third of the drink and a third of everything that was brought into the King's own house was sent in there to them every day. And the nurse was there with the girl, and was instructing her.

The King married another wife, and in course of time she had three sons, and this second queen was very jealous of the children of the King's first wife ; and at the end of a number of years, when her own children were growing up, she became very eager to devise some method of having the children of the first Queen put out of the way. She told the Hen-Wife what was in her mind, and the Hen-Wife said that to keep two households going was certainly a very wasteful business. The Queen replied that she would pay well to have the children put out of the way.

as an rathad. Dh'innis Cailleach nan Cearc gun robh draoidheachd aig an Eachalair Ùrlair,[1] is gum b'urrainn di-se an cur
air dòigh nach cuireadh iad tuilleadh dragha oirre. Chuir a'
Bhanrìghinn fios air an Eachalair. Thànaig i. Dh'innis a'
Bhanrìghinn do'n Eachalair Ùrlair gu dé bha i 'g iarraidh. 'Chan
urrainn domh nì air bith a dhèanamh orra, am fad 's a bhiodh
iad a staigh 'san Lùchairt Éibhinn : ach nam faighinn a mach
iad, dh'fheuchainn gu dé a ghabhadh dèanamh.' Rinn iad
cùmhnant ri chéile. 'Na dhéidh sin, a' cheud uair a fhuair a'
Bhanrìghinn tìm air a bhith cainnt ris an Rìgh, ghabh i fàth
air, ag ràdh, 'Tha clann na ceud mhnà a bh' agad anns an
Lùchairt Éibhinn, air chùl gaoithe 's ri aodann gréine, le'n
dìol deoch 's an leòr de bhiadh, far am faic iad-san na h-uile
duine 's chan fhaic duine idir iad. B'fheàrr liom fhéin gun robh
iad a mach còmhla ri mo chloinn fhéin ; oir, am fad 's a bhiodh
iad a staigh 'san Lùchairt Éibhinn, chan fhaigh an dà chloinn
fàs eòlach air a chéile. Bidh mise cho maith do'n cheud chloinn
a tha aig an Rìgh 's a bhithinn do mo chloinn fhéin ; agus
rachadh rian na b'fheàrr a dhèanamh air gach biadh is deoch,
agus air gach nì eile, a tha mu thaigh an Rìgh. Tha trian de
gach nì a tha tighinn do'n taigh-mhór air a chur a staigh do'n
Lùchairt Éibhinn, agus is beag nach fóghnadh sin do'n dà
theaghlach ; agus gum bitheadh an dà theaghlach mar aon.'
Bha leis an Rìgh gun robh sin ceart, is ghéill e do'n mhiodal aice.
Chaidh a' chlann a thoirt a mach as an Lùchairt Éibhinn, far
an robh iad air chùl gaoithe, etc., agus an uair a fhuair am muime
a mach iad, ghabh i oirre gun robh i ro phrìseil umpa, ré tìm
bhig an toiseach ; gus gum b'éiginn do'n Rìgh dol air thurus
fad as.

An uair a bha an Rìgh air falbh, thòisich clann na Banrìghinn mu dheireadh air a bhith peasanach air clann na ceud
Bhanrìghinn. Thug a h-aon de'n fheadhainn bu shine sgailc
do a h-aon de na bràithrean a b'òige ; ghabh a' Bhanrìghinn
fearg ri a dalta, agus thog i oirre, agus chaidh i do thaigh na
h-Eachalair Ùrlair, agus chasaid i a dalta, agus thuirt [i] gum
b'fheàrr leatha gun robh clann na ceud Bhanrìghinn a bha aig

---

[1] Variously spelt in this MS. as *eachlair-*, *eachalair-*, *eachlaraiche-ùlair*, or *-ùrlair*.
Of the various forms, the spelling *eachlaraiche* appears in all the grammatical cases.
See vol. i., pp. 492-499, and vol. ii., p. 238.

The Hen-Wife then told her that the Eachlair-Ùrlair had magic powers, and that she could deal with the children so that they would trouble the Queen no more. Thereupon the Queen sent for the Eachlair. The Eachlair came, and the Queen told her what she wanted. 'I cannot do a thing to them, as long as they are in the Palace of Delight ; but if I could get them out of that place, I would see what could be done.' And they agreed on it together. Later on, the first time the Queen got a chance of speaking to the King, she seized her opportunity and said, 'Your children by your first wife live in the Palace of Delight, at the back of the wind and facing the sun, with plenty of food and drink, where they can see every one, and none can see them. I wish they were out with my own children ; for as long as they remain in the Palace of Delight the two families cannot become acquainted with each other. I will be as good to the first children of the King as I would be to my own children ; and the food and drink and every other thing connected with the King's house would be much better managed. A third of everything that comes to the royal residence is sent in to the Palace of Delight, and that amount alone would almost suffice for the two households ; and thus the two households might be as one.' It seemed to the King that that was quite right, and so he yielded to her blandishments. The children were therefore fetched away from the Palace of Delight, where they had been at the back of the wind, etc., and when their stepmother had got them away, she pretended for a little while at first that she was very fond of them ; until it happened that the King had to go on a long journey.

When the King had gone, the children of the second Queen began to treat the children of the first Queen slightingly. One of the elder children gave one of the younger brothers a slap ; the Queen was angered with her step-child, and set off for the house of the Eachlair Ùrlair, and there she complained of her step-child and said that she wished that the children of the King's first Queen were somewhere where she would neither see them an Rìgh far nach faiceadh i iad, agus far nach cluinneadh i iomradh orra. 'Air son duais bhig,' [1] thuirt an Eachalair Ùrlair, 'chuirinn as an rathad iad, far nach dèanadh iad tuilleadh dragha ort.' Rinn a' Bhanrìghinn agus an Eachalair Ùrlair cùmhnant. 'An uair a bhios tusa dol a chìreadh cinn do chloinne, cuir do dhaltachan aon an déidh aoin, a dh'iarraidh na cìre-mìne, is cuiridh mise gach aon mar a thig ris a' bheinn a measg nam fiadh.'

An ath-latha, thòisich a' Bhanrìghinn air cìreadh cinn na cloinne agus dh'iarr i air an aon bu shine de chloinn na ceud Bhanrìghinn e a dhol sìos do thaigh na h-Eachlaraiche Ùrlair, is a' chìr-mhìn a thoirt a nìos. Chaidh e ann, agus an uair a rànaig e an taigh, dh'iarr an Eachalair Ùrlair air tighinn a staigh, agus thuirt i ris, 'An tànaig thu, a ghaoil? Mur bhith bior 'nam chois, cnàimh 'nam leis,[2] 's cath-chlair [3] mo leanaibh bhig 'nam uchd, dh'éirinn is ghabhainn duit le pògan !' 'Do leisgeal gabham a bhean bhochd,' ars esan, 'is ann a chuir [mo] mhuime a nuas mi a dh'iarraidh na cìre-mìne.' 'Seo a' chìr aig roinn mo choise, is tog fhéin leat i.' Ach an uair a chrom esan e fhéin, a thogail na cìre, bhuail ise e thar mullach a chinn leis an t-slacan-draoidheachd aice. Bha an uinneag fosgailte, is leum esan a mach air an uinneig, is chuir e a mach trì brùchdan de fhuil a chridhe, agus chaidh e ann an riochd féidh, is dh'fhalbh e fiadhaich do'n bheinn.

An uair nach robh e tighinn, dh'iarr a' Bhanrìghinn air an ath-mhac aig an Rìgh e a dhol sìos do thaigh na h-Eachalair Ùrlair, is a' chìr-mhìn a thoirt a nìos. Agus chaidh e ann. An uair a rànaig e, dh'iarr an Eachalair air e a thighinn a staigh, is thànaig e. Thuirt i ris, 'An tànaig thu, a ghaoil? Mur bhith bior 'nam chois, cnàimh 'nam leis, agus cath-chliar [3] mo leanaibh bhig 'nam uchd, dh'éirinn is ghabhainn duit le pògan.' 'Do leisgeal gabhte,[4] a bhean bhochd,' ars esan, 'is ann a chuir mo mhuime mi a nuas a dh'iarraidh na cìre-mìne.' Agus thuirt

[1] The terms required by the witch for her services are not mentioned in this tale, as in others. See p. 88.

[2] I have heard my father say to a child who wanted him to fall in with some childish whim, and go through impossible gymnastics—'I cannot do it just now— I have a bone in my leg.' My father may have heard the expression from my grandfather, who was a Gaelic-speaking man. See also *Superstitions*, p. 282.

nor hear anything about them. 'For a little reward,' [1] said the Eachlair Ùrlair, 'I would put them out of the way and send them where they would no longer trouble you.' Then the Queen and the Eachlair Ùrlair made an agreement. 'When you are going to comb your children's hair, send your step-children, one after the other, to fetch the fine comb ; and as each one comes, I will send him away to the hills among the deer.'

The next day the Queen began combing the children's hair, and she asked the eldest of the first Queen's children to go down to the house of the Eachlair Ùrlair and bring back the fine comb. He went off, and when he came to the house the Eachlair Ùrlair asked him to come in, and said to him, 'Have you come, my love ? Were it not for the thorn in my foot, the bone in my thigh,[2] and the . . . . struggling [?] [3] of my little baby in my lap, I would rise and cover you with kisses !' 'I accept your apologies, poor woman,' said he, 'but the fact is that [my] stepmother sent me here to fetch the fine comb.' 'Here is the comb at the tip of my foot ; pick it up yourself and take it with you.' But when he bent down to pick up the comb she struck him over the top of his head with her magic wand. The window was standing open, and he sprang out through it and vomited three belches of his heart's blood ; then he changed into the shape of a deer and away he went, a wild creature to the hills.

When there was no sign of his coming, the Queen asked the next son of the King to go down to the house of the Eachlair Ùrlair and bring back the fine comb. And he went. When he got there the Eachlair asked him to come in, and he did so. She said to him, 'Have you come, my love ? Were it not for the thorn in my foot, the bone in my thigh, and the . . . . struggling [?] of my little baby in my lap, I would rise, and cover you with kisses !' 'You are excused, poor woman,' said he, 'but the fact is that my stepmother sent me here to fetch the

---

[3] *cath-chliar* in MS. For *cath-làthair*, 'battlefield'?

[4] *gabh-te* in MS. : *gabham* on p. 266. In any given tale, the wording of three similar incidents ought to correspond closely. But Dewar usually deviated from this rule.

ise, 'Seo i aig roinn mo choise, is tog fhéin leat i.' Agus an uair
a chrom esan e fhéin a thogail na cìre, bhuail ise e thar mullach
a chinn leis an t-slacan-draoidheachd aice, is leum esan a mach
air an uinneig, is chinn e coltach ri fiadh, is dh'fhalbh e is chuir
e a mach trì brùchdan de fhuil a chridhe,[1] is dh'fhalbh e ris a'
bheinn cho fiadhaich ri fiadh.

Dh'iarr a' Bhanrìghinn air an treas mac a bha aig an Rìgh
a dhol a sìos do thaigh na h-Eachlair Ùrlair, a dh'iarraidh na
cìre-mìne, is chaidh e sìos, is an uair a chaidh e a staigh, thuirt
i ris, 'An tànaig thu, a ghaoil? Mur bhith bior 'nam chois,
cnàimh 'nam leis, agus cath-chliar [2] mo leanaibh bhig 'nam uchd,
dh'éirinn is ghabhainn duit le pògan.' 'Tha mi gabhail do
leisgeal, a bhean bhochd,' ars esan, 'is ann a chuir mo mhuime
mi a nuas a dh'iarraidh na cìre-mìne.' Agus thuirt an Eachlaraiche, 'Seo i aig roinn mo choise, is tog fhéin leat i,' agus an
uair a chrom esan a thogail na cìre, thug an Eachlair Ùrlair
buille dha thairis air mullach a chinn leis an t-slacan-draoidheachd aice, agus leum esan a mach air an uinneig, is chuir e
a mach trì brùchdan de fhuil a chridhe, is bha e ann an riochd
féidh, agus dh'fhalbh e ris a' bheinn cho fiadhaich ri fiadh.

Agus an sin dh'iarr a' Bhanrìghinn air Nighean na ceud
Banrìghinn, i a dhol sìos chun an taighe aig an Eachalair, agus
i a thoirt an àird na cìre-mìne d'a h-ionnsaigh. Dh'fhalbh i.
Choinnich a muime-chìche oirre, agus dh'fharraid di, c'àite
an robh i a' dol. Dh'innis an Nighean di, gun robh i dol a
dh'ionnsaigh taigh na h-Eachalair Ùrlair a dh'iarraidh na cìre-
mìne, agus thuirt a muime-chìche rithe, i a dh'fhaotainn na
cìr-réidhtich,[3] agus i a thoirt na cìr-réidhtich sìos 'na [h-]ionn-
saigh, agus mun togadh i a' chìr-mhìn, i a thairgseadh na cìre-
réidhtich do'n Eachalair Ùrlair, agus mur gabhadh an Each-
laraich a' chìr uaipe, i 'ga tilgeadh oirre. Phill Nighean an
Rìgh, is thug i leatha a' chìr-réidhtich, is chaidh i do thaigh
na h-Eachlaraiche. Thuirt an Eachalaraiche rithe mar a thuirt
i ri a bràithrean, 'An tànaig thu, a ghaoil? Mur bhith bior
'nam chois, cnàimh 'nam leis, is cath-chliar [2] mo leanaibh bhig

---

[1] The Glaistig of Lianachan does the same when discomfited ; *Superstitions*, p. 171.
In version 3 of MS. vol. x., No. 159, the Three Green Dogs do the same when struck
with a red-hot griddle. See p. 281.

[2] So in MS.

fine comb.' And she said, 'Here it is at the tip of my foot, pick it up yourself.' But when he stooped to pick up the comb, she struck him over the top of his head with her magic wand, and out he sprang through the window, and became like a deer, and he went and vomited three belches of his heart's blood,[1] and away he went to the hills as wild as any deer.

The Queen then asked the third son of the King to go down to the house of the Eachlair Ùrlair and bring back the fine comb ; and he went, and when he went in, she said to him, 'Have you come, my love ? Were it not for the thorn in my foot, the bone in my thigh, and the . . . . struggling [?] of my little baby in my lap, I would rise and cover you with kisses !' 'I accept your apologies, poor woman,' said he, 'but the fact is that my stepmother sent me here to fetch the fine comb.' And the Eachlair said, 'Here it is at the tip of my foot ; pick it up yourself.' But when he stooped to pick up the comb, the Eachlair Ùrlair struck him over the top of his head with her magic wand and he sprang out of the window, and vomited three belches of his heart's blood, and he was in the shape of a deer and away he went to the hills as wild as any deer.

Then the Queen asked the Daughter of the first Queen to go down to the house of the Eachlair and bring her up the fine comb. She started off, but her nurse met her and asked her where she was going. The Daughter told her that she was going to the house of the Eachlair Ùrlair to fetch the fine comb. Her nurse told her to get the unravelling comb first [3] and to take that down to the Eachlair, and to offer the unravelling comb to the Eachlair Ùrlair before picking up the fine comb, and if the Eachlair would not take the comb from her, to throw it at her. The King's Daughter turned back, fetched the unravelling comb, and went to the Eachlair's house. The Eachlair addressed her as she had addressed her brothers. 'Have you come, my love ? Were it not for the thorn in my foot, the bone in my thigh, and the . . . . struggling [?] of my little baby in my lap, I would arise and cover you with kisses !' 'I accept your apologies, [poor

---

[3] The unravelling or disentangling comb. This may have been used before the fine comb, but I have no information about the matter. The hair-combing seems to have constituted an important function, and the combs themselves are clearly full of magic. See *infra*, p. 266 and MS. vol. x., No. 159.

'nam uchd, dh'éirinn is ghabhainn duit le pògan !' 'Do leisgeal gabham, [a bhean bhochd],' ars an nighean, 'is ann a chuir mo mhuime mi a dh'iarraidh na cìre-mìne.' 'Sin i aig roinn mo choise, is tog fhéin leat i.' 'Seo dhuit-sa a' chìr seo an toiseach,' thuirt Nighean an Rìgh. 'Thoir thusa leat an dà chìr,' thuirt an Eachlaraiche. Thilg Nighean an Rìgh a' chìr-réidhtich air an Eachalair Ùrlair, is bhuail i anns an t-sùil i, agus thuit an Eachlaraiche mar gum bitheadh i marbh, agus thug Nighean an Rìgh leatha a' chìr-[mhìn?], agus chaidh i a dh'ionnsaigh na Banrìghinn leatha.[1]

Dh'iarr a muime-chìche air Nighean an Rìgh, i a dhol a sìos far an robh taigh na h-Eachalair Ùrlair, a sheall am faiceadh i a bràithrean. Thuirt a muime-chìche rithe gum faca i a bràithrean aon an déidh aoin diubh a' dol do thaigh na h-Eachlaraiche, agus nach fhaca i a h-aon diubh tighinn air an ais. Chaidh an Nighean a sìos, is chan fhaca i gin diubh, agus dh'innis i sin do a muime-chìche. Thuirt a muime-chìche rithe gum bu chòire dhaibh dol a dh'ionnsaigh an fhiosaiche a dh'fheuchainn an ìnnseadh esan daibh gu dé thànaig ri ceud mhic an Rìgh. Chaidh Nighean an Rìgh agus a muime-chìche a dh'ionnsaigh an fhiosaiche, a sheall am faigheadh iad fios gu dé thànaig ri Mic an Rìgh, agus dh'innis am fiosaiche dhaibh gun do chuir an Eachlaraiche Ùrlair iad an riochd féidh, is gun d'fhalbh iad fiadhaich ris a' bheinn, is gun do chuir iad, gach aon diubh, trì brùchdan de fhuil an cridhe a mach mu choinnimh uinneag na h-Eachalair Ùrlair, is gum bu chòir do am piuthar sin a thogail, agus fuil gach aoin diubh a chur air leth ann am bréid, agus a ghleidheadh gus am faiceadh i iad, agus a thoirt daibh ri òl, agus an sin gum b'urrainn daibh féin an uireasan ìnnseadh.[2]

---

[1] This should surely read 'to her foster-mother.' It will be observed that the foster-mother foresaw that the witch would refuse to accept the unravelling comb. But no reason is given for her refusal. Whether such a comb was made of some material supposed to defeat all magic, or whether some virtue, sovereign against witchcraft, resided in its shape or make, or whether the giving of it in return for the fine comb, constituted a counteracting tit-for-tat, is not said. But it is clear that the witch had an objection to taking it. And later the brothers inform the heroine that after she had struck the witch with the comb, they recovered their human sense.

In a series of taboos which the Rev. A. Macdonald tabulated for the Isle of Eriskay and its neighbourhood, occurs the following—'It is not right to throw a comb to a person : do not throw a comb but at thine enemy' ; *Survivals*, p. 293.

woman,]' said the daughter, 'but the fact is that my stepmother has sent me here to fetch the fine comb.' 'There it is at the tip of my foot, so pick it up yourself.' 'First you take this comb here,' said the King's Daughter. 'No, you take both combs yourself,' said the Eachlair. The King's Daughter hurled the unravelling comb at the Eachlair Ùrlair ; she hit her in the eye with it, and the Eachlair fell down as if dead. The King's Daughter took the [fine?] comb away and went off to the Queen [1] with it.

Her nurse asked the King's Daughter to return to the house of the Eachlair Ùrlair to try if she could see her brothers. Her nurse told her that she had seen her brothers go down to the Eachlair's house one after another, and she had not seen any of them come back. So the King's Daughter went there but failed to see any of them, and she told her nurse so. Her nurse replied that they had better go to the seer to find out if he could tell them what had happened to the King's first sons. The King's Daughter and her nurse went to the seer to see if they could learn what had happened to the King's Sons ; and the seer told him that the Eachlair Ùrlair had turned them into deer shape, and that they had gone off to the hills as wild creatures, and that each of them had vomited three belches of his heart's blood opposite the Eachlair Ùrlair's window, and that their sister ought to gather up in separate kerchiefs the blood of each and preserve it until she should see them, and then give it to them to drink, and that then they would be able to tell what their needs were.[2]

'It is not right to count the number of teeth in a comb. It means that you are numbering the days of your life' ; *ibid.*, p. 294. To leave a coarse comb behind one when travelling is disastrous ; *W. H. Tales*, i., No. 3. Giving a comb as a present procures magical help ; *Trans. Gael. Soc. Inverness*, xvi., p. 120.

[2] The recovery of some part or emanation of the body that a person had been deprived of in the course of suffering enchantment, is an important part of dis-enchantment. The seer's advice seems to mean that upon the recovery of the blood, the brothers would also recover the power of human speech, which they would have lost upon being turned into deer. Subsequent events make it probable that the brothers received the blood in due course, and that thereupon, their heads, till then cervine, became human (except for the antlers which remained attached to, or going from, their heads), and that it was this improvement, presumably, which appro-priately preceded their recovery of speech. Probably, too, the seer, in more ancient versions, informed the heroine to this effect, though the fact has dropped out of this version.

Chaidh Nighean an Rìgh agus a muime-chìche a dh'ionn-saigh na h-Eachlaraiche. Sheall iad aig taobh a mach na h-uinneige, agus chunnaig iad fuil nan cridheachan aig Clann an Rìgh ; agus thog am piuthar an fhuil, agus ghléidh i fuil gach aon diubh air leth ann am bréid. Chaidh i fhéin agus a muime-chìche air an ais a dh'ionnsaigh an fhiosaiche, a dh'fhaotainn tuilleadh sgeòil air Mic an Rìgh, agus dh'innis am fiosaiche daibh, gun deach a' Chlann aig an Rìgh do bheinn d'am b'ainm a' Bheinn Àrd ; [1] gun robh creag àrd aig ìochdar na beinne, agus gun robh famhair ann ris an canadh iad 'Famhair nan Seachd Bliadhna,' agus gun robh fàradh aig an Fhamhair, is gun cuireadh e am fàradh ris a' chreig uair anns na seachd bliadhna, agus an uair a gheibheadh na bha gu h-àrd a' sireadh a nuas tighinn a nuas, agus na bha gu h-ìosal a' sireadh an àird dol an àird, gun tugadh am famhair air falbh am fàradh, agus nach fhaigheadh a h-aon air bith dol an àird no a nuas gu ceann seachd bliadhna tuilleadh.

* * * * *

An uair a thànaig an Rìgh dachaigh is a thuig e mar a thachair d'a chuid Mhac, chaill e trian d'a thùr, is trian d'a choiseachd, is trian de a fhradharc,[2] agus dh'fhalbh e air feadh nam fàsaichean a dh'iarraidh a chuid Mhac.[3] Cha robh fios aig an Nighean c'àite an deach e. Bha i ro aonarach, is i gun athair, gun mhàthair, gun phiuthar, gun bhràthair a dhèanadh cainnt rithe. Bha a muime is a leth-bhràithrean a' tàir oirre, agus coma ged a dhèanadh iad cron oirre. Chaidh i fhéin 's a muime-chìche a rithist a dh'ionnsaigh an fhiosaiche a dh'iarraidh

---

[1] On the previous occasion, the seer had spoken as if the brothers had taken to hills in general, in accordance with the habit of the wild deer. Now he speaks of a particular hill. His words do not necessarily mean that the brothers had arrived at the hill, but may merely mean that they had begun the journey thither.

[2] See No. 25 (MS. vol. x., No. 47).

[3] The brothers later inform their sister that their father, the King, met them in the wilderness, and that thenceforward they were human in shape, except for their heads, which continued cervine and antlered. The meeting of father and sons ought to occur here. As the wilderness appears to be situated in the ordinary terra firma of mortals, it is to be presumed that when they met him the brothers had not yet made the ascent to the upper country. This seems to be confirmed by the statement of the second giant, who meets the heroine on terra firma, apparently

The King's Daughter and her nurse went to the house of the Eachlair. They looked around outside the window, and saw the heart's blood of the King's Children ; and their sister gathered it all up, and preserved the blood of each in a separate kerchief. Then she and her nurse went back to the seer, to get further information about the King's Sons, and the seer told them that the King's Children had gone to a mountain called the High Mountain ; [1] that there was a high rock at the foot of the mountain and that a giant lived there who was called 'The Giant of the Seven Years,' and that he had a ladder which he used to set up against the rock once in seven years, and that when those who were above and wished to get down had got down, and when those who were below and wished to get up had got up, the giant would take away the ladder. And then no one at all who wished to go up or down could do so till the end of another seven years.

*　　*　　*　　*

When the King came home and understood what had happened to his sons, he lost a third of his reason, a third of his walking powers, and a third of his powers of sight,[2] and he set off to wander through the wilderness to seek for his sons.[3] But where he had gone, his Daughter did not know. She was now very lonely, with neither father nor mother, sister nor brother, to talk to her. Her stepmother and her half-brothers treated her insultingly and would not scruple to do her harm. Once more she and her nurse went to the seer to ask his advice, and they

a few days later, and tells her that her brothers had passed by him three days before. All this seems to fit, and we may perhaps surmise that after meeting their father, the brothers, being now equipped with human hands and feet, as is implied later on (p. 280), arrived at the High or Great Rock, and ascended it by means of the ladder, ere the Giant who owned the ladder took it away. They had no pegs, or any other means of ascent. The story, unfortunately, does not say anywhere anything about their ascent ; that they did ascend, however, is to be inferred from the fact that the sister meets them after she has ascended. Neither does the story give the slightest hint of any reason the brothers had for going to the upper country, or whether they expected that so doing would benefit them, or whether they were forced to go there by magic.

comhairle air, agus fhuair iad a chomhairle,[1] agus chuir
a muime-chìche mar chroisean 's mar gheasan air Nighean an
Rìgh nach robh i gu pòsadh no gus tàladh ri fear air bith gus
am faigheadh i a bràithrean air an ais a rithist gu an riochd
fhéin.   Rinn an Nighean aig an Rìgh i fhéin deas, agus thug a
muime-chìche a beannachd dhi, is dh'fhalbh i a dh'iarraidh a
bràithrean.

Latha dhi air feadh nam monaidhnean, thànaig ceò air,
agus cha robh fhios aice c'àite an robh i dol, agus aig dorchadh
nan tràth aig toiseach oidhche thànaig i air taigh air a thughadh
le fraoch.   Chuir i a làmh ris an dorus, is dh'fhosgail an dorus
air thoiseach oirre agus chaidh i a staigh.   Bha smùchan de
theinidh beag air,[2] is cha leasaicheadh e, is cha rachadh e as,
ach dìreach mar a bha e, air son a h-aoin air bith ach an t-aon
a chuir air e.   Shuidh ise sìos ri taobh an teine gus an tànaig an
oidhche.   Is e famhair a thànaig chun taobh a mach an doruis,
agus ghlaodh e, 'Hì ! hó ! hù ! huagaich ! tha mi mothachainn
fàileadh an fharbhalaich[3] a staigh.'   'Sìth biodh eadarainn,'
arsa Nighean an Rìgh.   'Is e sìth a th'ann,' thuirt am Famhair.
Thànaig e a staigh, agus leasaich e suas an teine, is leig e air
làr sidheann a bha aige, is dh'iarr e oirre biadh a dhèanamh
deas.   Dh'fhuin i bonnaich, agus chuir i iad dh'an gréidheadh
ris an teinidh gus gun robh iad deas, is ròiste ; is bhruich i cuid
de'n t-sidhinn, is rinn i eanbhruich, is chuir i an clàr-bìdh
còmhdaichte air a bheulaibh, is ghabh i féin a cuid 'sa' chùil.
Dh'ith am Famhair a chuid a dh'aon teum, is dh'òl e a dheoch
a dh'aon sùpaig.

Agus an uair a ghabh Nighean an Rìgh a suipear, thuirt am
Famhair rithe, 'Greas agus dèan mo leabaidh, is rach féin a
laigh air thoiseach orm ; is fad o nach robh bean ann am

---

[1] The advice probably was that the foster-mother should indeed bespell the heroine
(see Counter-be-spelling, vol. i., Appendix iv., p. 504), but not to the effect specified.
For the heroine marries *before* releasing her brothers, about three years before, which
proves that the foster-mother's commands have been wrongly reported ; the spells
she probably laid upon the heroine were, that she was not to marry until she had
met her brothers, and had ascertained from them how to disenchant them.   It is also
probable that in more ancient versions the foster-mother gave the heroine long and
detailed instructions for her guidance, told her of the giants she was to meet, and
directed her to plead the pressure of vows and spells as a reason! for not consorting
with any one of them, and as an inducement to them to make her the pegs she
wanted for the purpose of ascending to the overhead country.   If this conjecture

got it.[1] And her nurse bound the King's Daughter with crosses
and with spells that she should neither marry nor flirt with any
man until she had restored her brothers to their own proper
forms. So the King's Daughter made ready, her nurse gave
her her blessing, and away she went to seek her brothers.

One day when she was wandering about the moors, a mist
came down and she could not tell where she was going; but
with the darkening of the hours at the beginning of night she
came to a house thatched with heather. She put her hand to
the door and the door opened before her, and she went inside.
There was a half-smothered little fire going,[2] but it could neither
be roused up nor would it go out; it just remained as it was no
matter what anybody might do, except the person who had
kindled it. She sat down by the side of the fire until night fell.
Who should come to the outside of the door but a giant, and he
shouted, 'Fee, fie, fo, fum! I smell a stranger in the house.'
'Peace between us!' said the King's Daughter. 'Peace it is,'
said the Giant. In he came and roused up the fire, laid down
on the floor some venison he had with him, and asked her to
prepare a meal. She kneaded some bannocks and set them
to bake at the fire until they were ready and toasted; she boiled
part of the venison, made soup and laid the table before the
Giant, but she took her own food in the corner. The Giant
swallowed his food at one bite and drank off his drink at one
draught.

When the King's Daughter had had her supper, the Giant
said to her, 'Hurry up and make my bed, and go yourself and lie
down there before I come; it is long since I last had a woman

be correct, it implies that by this time the heroine knew she would not arrive at
the rock until after the Giant of the Seven Years had taken his ladder away, when
she should be too late to avail herself of that means of ascent.

   [2] For another magic fire of different character, see No. 66 (MS. vol. x., No. 123).
In No. 126, the fire refuses to burn faster or slower. Presumably the giant who
kindled it was the magician who had bespelled it. Heroes in several tales ask the
magicians who had bespelled them to rescind their spells, but they never ask any
other magician to do so. This suggests the existence of a belief that he who pronounced
any particular spell was the only person capable of abrogating or annulling it.
Superstitions, p. 283.
   [3] *na heiribiele* in MS., presumably intended for *an fharbhalaich*, the stranger.

leabaidh a roimhe a' feitheamh riut.' Agus thuirt ise, 'Tha
bòidean [agus croisean] agus geasan orm-sa nach téid mi a
laighe le fear air bith ach an aon fhear sin a dhèanadh dhomh
air luirgnean chailleachan marbha sè fichead dealg de fhiodh,
is iad cho cruaidh, geur, righinn is gun rachadh iad a staigh ann
an aodann cruaidh creige cho furasda is a rachadh iad a staigh
ann an talamh bog creadha.' [1] Agus thuirt am Famhair, 'Mur
'eil de dh'fhuireachd ort ach sin, chan fhad is fuireachd e.' [2]
Agus ghlac e a thuagh 'na làimh is leum e an àird air an fharadh.
Chaidh ise a chadal. Is bha am Famhair air an fharadh a'
dèanamh nan dealgan gu maduinn. Agus an uair a thànaig an
ath-latha, rinn ise biadh deas air a son féin agus air son an
Fhamhair. Ghabh ise a biadh. Thànaig am Famhair a nuas
bhàrr an fharaidh, is thug e dhi dà fhichead dealg a bha cho
cruaidh, righinn, 's cho geur is gun rachadh iad a staigh ann
an aodann cruaidh creige cho furasda is a rachadh iad a staigh
ann an talamh bog creadha.

Thug i leatha iad, is dh'fhalbh i air a turus ; agus bha i fad
an latha sin a' fàrsan air feadh na beinne, gun aon air bith
fhaicinn fad an latha gus an tànaig an oidhche. Aig beul na
h-oidhche chunnaig i taigh beag, is e air a thughadh leis na
béin aig beathaichean fiadhaich. Chaidh i d'a ionnsaigh, is
chuir i a làmh ris an dorus, is dh'fhosgail an dorus roimpe, is
chaidh i a staigh. Bha smùchan de ghealbhan beag air, agus
cha leasaicheadh e is cha rachadh e as, [ach dìreach mar a bha
e, air son a h-aoin air bith] ach air son an aoin a chuir air e.
Shuidh i air cathair ri taobh a' ghealbhain. Agus aig an oidhche
thànaig [an dara] Famhair chun an taighe, agus ghlaodh e,
'Hì ! hó ! hù ! huagaich ! tha mi mothachainn fàileadh an
fharbhalaich a staigh.' Agus ghlaodh ise, 'Sìth biodh eadarainn.'
Is thuirt esan, 'Is e sìth a th'ann.' Thànaig am Famhair a
staigh, is bha sidheann aige ; leig e an t-sidheann air làr, is

[1] For a remarkable parallel to these incidents, see *Béaloideas*, ii., p. 111. *Cailleach
mharbh*, 'dead carline,' is the Gaelic name of the black sea bream, called in parts
of England 'old wife,' because its head resembled that of an old woman. But the
word *luirgnean*, 'legs,' shows that the reciter thought he was speaking of a woman,
not a fish. How wooden pegs could be made of legs, or what was the process of
manufacture are points that remain obscure. It is clear that the heroine knows
she will be too late to avail herself of the ladder belonging to the Giant of the Seven
Years.

in my bed, because of waiting for you.'   And she said, 'I am
bound by vows [and crosses] and spells not to go to bed with
any man but with him who will make me out of the shanks of
dead hags six score wooden pegs, which must be so hard and sharp
and tough that they will pierce the hard face of a rock as easily
as they would go into soft clayey earth.' [1]   And the Giant said, 'If
that is all you are waiting for, it shall not be a long wait.' [2]
And he seized his axe in his hand and sprang up on to the loft.
She went to sleep, and the Giant was in the loft till morning
making the pegs.   When the next day came, she prepared food
for herself and for the Giant.   She ate her own food.   The Giant
came down from the loft and gave her two score pegs, which
were so hard and tough and sharp that they would pierce the
hard face of a rock as easily as they would go into the soft clayey
earth.

She took them with her and set off on her journey ; and all
that day she was wandering about over the mountain, without
seeing any one all day, till night came on.   When night was
falling, she saw a little house thatched with the skins of wild
animals.   She went up to it and put her hand to the door.   It
opened before her, and she went in.   There was a little half-
smothered fire there, but it could neither be roused up nor
would it go out, [but it remained just as it was no matter what
anybody might do] except the person who had kindled it.   She
sat down on a chair at the side of the fire.   At night time [a
second] Giant came to the house, and shouted, 'Fee, fie, fo, fum !
I smell a stranger in the house.'   'Peace between us !' cried she.
'Peace it is,' replied the Giant.   He came in, and he was carrying
venison ;   he laid the venison on the floor and asked her to
prepare food.   She kneaded some bannocks and set them to

[2] The Giant's words seem to imply that he hoped to make the complete number
of pegs himself, and thereby win the heroine for his bride.   He is, however, apparently
contented with making only a third of the requisite number.   The next giant is
equally lukewarm.   And the third, though he congratulates the heroine upon getting
her full complement of pegs, appears to suffer no dissatisfaction at losing her.

dh'iarr am Famhair oirre biadh a dhèanamh deas. Dh'fhuin i bonnaich, agus chuir i dh'an gréidheadh ris an teine iad, is bhruich i pàirt [de'n] t-sidhinn, is rinn i eanbhruich, is chuir i an clàr-bìdh còmhdaichte air beulaibh an Fhamhair, is ghabh i féin a cuid 'sa' chùil. Dh'itheadh am Famhair a chuid a dh'aon teum, is dh'òl e a dheoch a dh'aon sùpaig, agus dh'fharraid e de Nighean an Rìgh cia as di, agus ciod fàth a turuis. Dh'innis Nighean an Rìgh do'n Fhamhair cia as a thànaig i, is gun robh i a' dol a dh'iarraidh a bràithrean, agus mar a chaidh an cur ann an riochd féidh leis an Eachlair Ùrlair. Dh'innis am Famhair di gun deach iad seachad o chionn trì làithean, is an taobh a chaidh iad.

An uair a fhuair iad sgeul o a chéile, thuirt am Famhair, 'Tha tìm dol gu tàmh—éirich, fharbhalaich,[1] is dèan mo leabaidh, is rach féin a laighe air thoiseach orm ; is fada bho nach robh bean air mo leabaidh a roimhe a' feitheamh riut.' Is thuirt ise, 'Tha bòidean is croisean is geasan orm-sa nach tàlaidh is nach téid mi le h-aon air bith gus gum faighinn fear a dhèanadh dhomh [air luirgnean chailleacha marbha] sè fichead dealg de fhiodh cruaidh, is iad cho cruaidh, geur, righinn is gun rachadh iad a staigh ann an aodann cruaidh creige cho furasda is a rachadh iad a staigh ann an talamh bog creadha.' Agus thuirt am Famhair, 'Mur ['eil] de dh'fhuireachd ort ach sin, chan fhad is fuireachd e' ; agus thug e làmh air a thuaigh is leum e an àird air an fharadh. Is chaidil Nighean an Rìgh. Is bha am Famhair air an fharadh gu latha a' dèanamh nan dealgan. Agus dh'éirich ise anns a' mhaduinn, is rinn ise biadh is deoch di féin is do'n Fhamhair. Thànaig am Famhair a nuas bhàrr an fharaidh. Chòmhdaich ise an clàr-bìdh do'n Fhamhair, is ghabh i féin a cuid 'sa' chùil.

Is thug i leatha na dealgan a rinn am Famhair. Bha dà fhichead ann is dh'fhalbh i leotha air feadh a' mhonaidh leatha féin. Thànaig ceò air, is bha Nighean an Rìgh air faondradh air feadh a' mhonaidh, is aig beul na h-oidhche thànaig i air taigh beag is e air a thughadh le itean eun. Is chuir i a làmh ris an dorus, is dh'fhosgail an dorus roimpe, is chaidh i a staigh. Bha teine beag air, is cha leasaicheadh e is cha rachadh e as,

---

[1] *eiripile*, in MS.

bake at the fire ; she boiled some of the venison and made soup, and she laid the table and set it before the Giant, but she herself ate her food in the corner. The Giant swallowed his food at one bite and drank off his drink at one draught, and then he asked the King's Daughter where she had come from and what was the object of her journey. The King's Daughter told the Giant where she had come from, and that she was going to look for her brothers, and how they had been put into the form of deer by the Eachlair Ùrlair. The Giant told her that they had passed by three days before, and also the direction in which they had gone.

When they had listened to each other's news, the Giant said, 'It is time to go to rest—get up, stranger, and make my bed, and go yourself and lie there before I come ; it is long since I last had a woman on my bed because of waiting for you.' And she said, 'I am bound by vows and crosses and spells neither to flirt nor consort with any man until I find one who makes me, [out of the shanks of dead hags,] six score pegs of hard wood, and all of them so hard and sharp and tough that they will pierce the hard face of a rock as easily as they would go into soft clayey earth.' And the Giant said, 'If that is all you are waiting for, it shall not be a long wait,' and he laid hold of his axe and sprang up on to the loft. Then the King's Daughter went to sleep. The Giant was in the loft till dawn, making the pegs. In the morning she got up, and she made food and drink for herself and the Giant. The Giant came down from the loft. She laid the table for him, and she ate her own food in the corner.

Then she went off with the pegs that the Giant had made. There were two score of them, and she walked with them over the moors by herself. Mist came on, and the King's Daughter went astray among the moors, but when night was falling she came to a little house thatched with birds' feathers. She put her hand to the door, and it opened before her, and she went inside. There was a little fire there, but it could neither be

ach [dìreach mar a bha e, air son a h-aoin air bith ach] air son
an aoin a chuir air e. Agus aig an oidhche, thànaig [an treas]
Famhair, agus ghlaodh e, 'Hì! hó! hù! huagaich! tha mi
mothachainn fàileadh an fharbhalaich a staigh.' Agus ghlaodh
Nighean an Rìgh, 'Sìth biodh eadarainn.' Agus thuirt am
Famhair, 'Is e sìth a th'ann.' Agus thànaig am Famhair a
staigh, is leig e an t-sidheann air làr. Agus dh'fharraid am
Famhair cia as a bha i, agus ciod fàth a turuis. Dh'innis i dha
mar a thachair do a bràithrean, agus mar a bha i dol dh'an
iarraidh, agus dh'innis am Famhair di gun deach iad seachad
air-san aon latha anns a' bheinn-sheilg ; gun deach iad gu
Beinn Àird aig cùl na Creige Móire, is gun seòladh esan i a
màireach an taobh a b'aithghiorra gu dol d'an ionnsaigh. Agus
rinn Nighean an Rìgh deas bonnaich is sidheann is eanbhruich,
is chuir i air beulaibh an Fhamhair clàr-bìdh còmhdaichte, is
dh'ith i fhéin a cuid 'sa' chùil ; agus dh'ith am Famhair a bhiadh
a dh'aon teum, is dh'òl e a dheoch a dh'aon sùpaig.

Agus thuirt e ri Nighean an Rìgh, 'Greas is dèan mo leabaidh,
is rach féin a laighe air thoiseach orm : is fada bho nach robh
bean ann am leabaidh a roimhe a' feitheamh riut.' Agus thuirt
Nighean an Rìgh, 'Tha mar chroisean is mar gheasan is mar
bhòidean orm-sa nach tàlaidh mi [is nach téid mi] ri fear air
bith ach am fear a dhèanadh dhomh air luirgnean chailleacha
marbha sè fichead de dhealgan de dh'fhiodh, is iad cho cruaidh,
cho geur, is cho righinn, is gun téid iad a staigh ann an aodann
creige cruaidh [sic] cho furasda is a ghabhadh an cur a staigh
ann an talamh bog creadha.' Agus thuirt am Famhair, 'Mur
'eil de dh'fhuireachd ort ach sin, chan fhad is fuireachd e.'
Thog e an tuagh 'na làimh, is leum e an àird air an fharadh, is
fhuair e fiodh cruaidh is luirgnean chailleacha marbha, is
thòisich e air dèanamh nan dealgan. Chaidh ise a chadal ;
ach bha am Famhair ag obair air dèanamh nan dealgan gu
latha ; agus tràth thànaig an latha thànaig e a nuas bhàrr an
fharaidh, thug e a nuas leis dà fhichead dealg, is thug e do Nighean
an Rìgh iad, is bha aice an sin sè fichead dealg. Thug i taing
do'n Fhamhair, agus thuirt am Famhair,

'A tha agad a nis sè fichead stob,
Is cha diùlt iad cruaidh no bog,

roused up nor would it go out, [but remained just as it was no matter what anybody might do,] except the person who had kindled it.   At night, [the third] Giant came, and he shouted, 'Fee, fie, fo, fum ! I smell a stranger in the house.'   The King's Daughter cried, 'Peace between us !'   'Peace it is,' said the Giant. Then he came in, and laid the venison on the floor.   And the Giant asked where she came from and what was the object of her journey.   She told him what had happened to her brothers, and how she was going to look for them, and the Giant told her that they had passed him one day in the hunting hill ;   that they had gone to High Mountain at the back of the Big Rock, and that tomorrow he would show her the shortest way of getting to them.   Then the King's Daughter prepared bannocks and venison and soup, and laid the table before the Giant, but she ate her own food in the corner.   The Giant swallowed his food at one mouthful and drank off his drink at one draught.

Then he said to the King's Daughter, 'Hurry up and make my bed, and go yourself to bed before I do : it is long since I last had a woman in my bed because of waiting for you.'   And the King's Daughter replied, 'I am bound by crosses and spells and vows neither to flirt [nor consort] with any man except one who makes me, out of the shanks of dead hags, six score pegs of wood, and all of them so hard, so sharp and so tough, that they will pierce the face of a hard rock as easily as they can be driven into soft clayey earth.'   And the Giant said, 'If that is all you are waiting for, it shall not be a long wait.'   He snatched up his axe in his hand, and sprang up on to the loft, got some hard wood and the shanks of dead hags, and began to make the pegs.   She went to sleep, but the Giant was at work making the pegs till day came ;   and when day came he climbed down from the loft, brought two score pegs down with him, and gave them to the King's Daughter, and now she had the six score pegs.   She thanked the Giant, and he replied,

'Six score pegs have you now,
They will not jib at hard or soft ;

Is iad gu cruaidh, righinn, geur,
Gu dol ann an creig mar ann an cré,
Is bu mhaith gun dèanadh iad dhuit stàth,
Gu dol gu mullach na creige àird,
Is gum bu slàn a théid thu stàn,
Is a rithist thig thu a bhàn.'

Thog i oirre, agus chaidh am Famhair leatha mar iùil, is ghiùlain e na stuib air a son am fad is a chaidh e. Leig e fhaicinn di taigh, is dh'iarr e oirre bhith an sin mun tigeadh an oidhche, agus i a dh'fhantainn 'san taigh sin ré na h-oidhche, is gun leigeadh fear an taighe sin fhaicinn di an rathad a dh'ionnsaigh na Creige Àirde. Leig i a sgìos tacan beag, dh'éirich i a rithist, is chaidh i a dh'ionnsaigh an taighe ; is an uair a rànaig i, dh'fharraid am Famhair a bha anns an taigh sin dith, cia as a bha i, is ciod fàth a turuis. Dh'innis i dha mar a thachair do a bràithrean leis an Eachlaraiche, is mar a bha i a' falbh air an luirg. Ghléidh am Famhair an sin i fad na h-oidhche, is an ath-latha leig e fhaicinn di a' Chreag Mhór aig beulaibh na Beinn Àird, is ghiùlain e na dealgan air a son.

Tràth rànaig iad a' Chreag, thuirt am Famhair rithe, 'Is e seo an t-àite far an àbhaist do'n Fhamhair am fàradh a chur suas ris a' chreig, ach bidh e teann air seachd bliadhna mun tig e dh'a chur suas a rithist, agus is truagh liom do chor, ma bhitheas tu an seo ré na tìme sin.' Thug i taing do'n Fhamhair air son a shuairceis ; is ghabh i na stuib agus stobadh i aon 'sa' chreig, is rachadh i an àird ceum ; is stobadh i a h-aon eile ann, is mar sin, gus an robh i an àird thar mullach na creige. Dh'fhalbh i air a h-aghaidh air aodann na Beinne, ach bha a h-uile fiadh a bha i a' faicinn a' teicheadh uaipe. Thànaig i a dh'ionnsaigh àite far an robh bùthan ri taobh sruthain. Chaidh i a staigh ; leig i a sgìos dhith tacan beag, is chaidil i. An uair a dhùisg i, bha an t-anmoch ann, is bha na féidh air gabhail gu tàmh. Chaidh i a measg nam fiadh, ach cha d'fhuair i a bràithrean. An ath-latha chaidh i a staigh do bhùthan beag a thachair oirre, is bha fiadh an sin a rinn cainnt rithe, is a dh'innis c'àite an robh a bràithrean, is bha i 'sa' bhùthan sin fad na h-oidhche.

An ath-latha chaidh i do'n àite far an robh fiughair aice a

> Hard and tough and sharp are they,
> To pierce rock as they will clay.
> And may they serve your purpose well,
> To scale the tall rock ;
> And may you go up safely,
> And safely again come down.'

Away she went, and the Giant went along with her as a guide and carried the pegs for her as far as he went. He pointed out a house to her and told her to get there before night fell, and to stay in that house for the night, and that the man of that house would show her the road to the High Rock. She rested herself for a little, then got up again and made for the house ; and when she got there, the Giant who was in that house asked her where she came from and what was the purpose of her journey. She told him what had happened to her brothers through the Eachlair, and how she was searching for them. The Giant made her stay there for the night, and next day he pointed out to her the Great Rock in front of High Mountain, and he carried the pegs for her.

When they came to the Rock the Giant said to her, 'This is the place where the Giant is accustomed to set the ladder up against the rock, but it will be close on seven years before he comes to put it up again, and I pity you if you are to be here for all that time.' She thanked the Giant for his kindness ; and she took the pegs and began sticking them into the rock. When she had stuck in one, she would go up a step ; then she would stick in another, and so on till she was right up on the top of the rock. She pressed on over the face of the Mountain, but every deer she saw fled from her. She came to a place where there was a little hut by the side of a stream. In she went ; she rested herself there for a little, and she fell asleep. When she awoke it was late, and the deer had gone to rest. She went out among the deer, but she did not find her brothers. Next day, she went into a little hut she came to, and there was a deer there who spoke to her and told her where her brothers were, and she stayed in that hut all night.

The day after that, she went to the place where she had hoped

bràithrean fhaicinn.[1] Thànaig i air bùthan beag is e ri taobh
sruthain ; is chuir i a làmh ris an dorus, is dh'fhosgail an dorus
roimpe, is chaidh i a staigh, is fhuair i air bòrd a bha an sin
buileann arain, agus cuman làn fìona. Dh'ith i pàirt de'n aran,
is dh'òl i balgam de'n fhìon, agus chaidh i am falach fo mheasair-
nigheachain a bha a staigh, is dh'fhuirich i an sin. Agus an
uair a bha i an sin ré greis, thànaig triùir fhear a staigh, 's bha
cròic féidh air na cinn aca, is thuirt am fear bu mhò dhiubh,
'Ma tha mo phiuthar mhór beò fhathast, is i thug an teum mu
dheireadh as a' bhuilinn seo' ;[2] agus thuirt an ath-fhear, 'Ma
tha mo phiuthar mhór beò fhathast, is i a thug am balgam mu
dheireadh as an fhìon seo' ; agus thuirt an treas fear, 'Ma tha
mo phiuthar mhór beò fhathast, tha i a staigh fo'n mheasair-
nigheachain seo', agus thog iad a' mheasair-nigheachain is fhuair
iad ise ann a sin. Chaoin i gu goirt, air dhi a bràithrean fhaicinn
is cròic féidh air ceann gach fir dhiubh.[3] Dh'innis iad di gun
robh iad-san gu h-iomlan an riochd féidh an toiseach, gus an
do bhuail am piuthar an Eachlaraiche Ùrlair leis a' chìr-
[réidhtich], ach 'na dhéidh sin, gun robh fios aca ciod a bha iad
a' dèanamh. Gun do choinnich an athair orra anns an fhàsach,
is gun d'fhuair e [iad] le feartan buadhach a fhuair e o fhamhair
a rinn còmhnadh ris : is 'na dhéidh sin, gun robh iad an riochd
dhaoine, ach cinn agus cròic féidh a bhith orra.[4] Gum faigheadh

---

[1] *far an robh i a smuaintiche ri a brathairean fhaicinn*, in MS.

[2] Similar incident in No. 267 *a*, MS. vol. xi., and *Waifs and Strays*, ii., p. 353.
She had probably left the blood of each brother outside the hut or in it.

[3] Note that the heroine finds her brothers on the third night of her wanderings
in the upper country.

[4] The brothers inform the heroine that after meeting with their father, they
recovered human shape except as regards their heads, which continued cervine
and crowned with antlers. Perhaps the friendly giant had accommodated their
father with some magical potion or other nostrum, which had counteracted the
Eachlair's enchantments to the extent indicated. However that may be, when they
enter the hut where they find their sister, the brothers are able to speak, and the
only remaining brute characteristics are the antlers. This probably implies that
in accordance with the seer's instructions (p. 266), the heroine had supplied her
brothers with the blood, after which, so the seer had said, they would be able to
describe their needs. Perhaps then, we may suppose, that the heroine had left the
blood outside or inside the hut for them, that they found it there, recognized it as
their own (as happens in other tales) and drank it outside the hut ; that thereupon
their heads, except for the antlers, became human, and that this further measure
of disenchantment was appropriately accompanied by a corresponding ability for
speech (see note, p. 267). Unfortunately, the brothers fail to refer to this improve-

to see her brothers. She came on a little hut by the side of a stream ; she put her hand on the door, and it opened before her ; she went inside and found on a table there a loaf of bread and a jar full of wine. She ate some of the bread and drank a mouthful of the wine, and then she hid under a washing-tub that was in the house, and there she waited. When she had been there for a while, three men came in, upon whose heads there were deer's antlers, and the biggest of them said, 'If my big sister is still alive, it was she who took the last bite out of this loaf.' [2] The next one said, 'If my big sister is still alive, it is she who took the last mouthful of this wine.' And the third one said, 'If my big sister is still alive, she is under this washing-tub' ; and they lifted up the washing-tub and found her there. She wept bitterly when she saw her brothers with deer's antlers on their heads.[3] They told her that at first they had been completely in deer form until their sister struck the Eachlair Ùrlair with the [unravelling] comb, but that after that they knew what they were doing. They said that their father had met them in the wilderness, having found them by means of powerful charms he obtained from a giant who had helped him ; and that after that, they had human form except for their deer's heads and antlers.[4] They would recover their own shapes, they said, if they could find some woman who would make them shirts of

ment in their condition. And most unaccountably, the story fails to say anywhere that the sister restored their blood to her brothers, but it is clear that the paragraph before the previous one is the point in the story where she ought to do so. At any rate, the restoration of some such incidents as those suggested here, though the precise form of them cannot of course be guaranteed, would harmonize other details of the story. It may, however, be pointed out that the recovery of some lost part of, or emanation from, the body, usually has a restorative, not to say, an enchantment-breaking effect. See No. 29, *Folk-Lore*, xxxvi., p. 170, and *W. H. Tales*, iii., p. 418 or 436. An interesting example occurs in the *Celtic Monthly* version of No. 159 (this book, p. 356) where three sons of a king are changed into hounds. An enemy strikes the animals with a red-hot griddle, whereupon while still in brute-shape, they vomit blood and depart. The blow with the griddle had apparently a disenchanting effect, for they next appear in the story as three young men. But though their humanity had been recovered, their health had not ; they are represented as being so dangerously ill, that all hope had been given up unless they could recover the blood they had lost while in hound-shape. When this is presented to them, they become quite well again. In the foregoing case, the blood is vomited while in animal shape, and administered while in human shape. But in No. 126, the blood is vomited (as far as can be guessed) while in human form, and is to be administered when the heads of the recipients are in animal form.

iad a rithist do'n riochd fhéin, nam faigheadh iad té a dhèanadh
dhaibh léintean air an dèanamh air canach an t-sléibhe.¹ Ghabh
ise fos làimh sin a dhèanamh, is thug i beannachd leò, is dh'fhalbh i.

Rànaig i a muime-chìche, is dh'innis i di gu dé bha i dol a
dhèanamh. Dh'innis a muime-chìche do'n fhiosaiche.² Thuirt
esan gum feumadh i na léintean a dhèanamh gun ghean, gun
ghuth, gun ghàire, is gum b'e a chomhairle-san di a dhol do'n
fhàsach far nach biodh gin a chuireadh buaireadh oirre. Thug
i taing dha, is beannachd leis, is dh'innis i do a h-athair c'àite
an robh i dol. Dh'fhalbh i, is chaidh i do'n fhàsach, is bha i
an sin is i leatha fhéin, is i a' trusadh a' chanaichean.³

*　　*　　*　　*　　*

Agus aon latha, thànaig trì rìghrean a bha sealg seachad oirre, is
an uair a chunnaig iad i, chuir iad stad air na h-eich aca, is
thòisich iad air bruidhinn rithe. Ach cha dubhairt ise diog,
is cha do ghabh i oirre gun robh i 'gan cluinntinn. Dh'fhalbh
iad an latha sin, ach thànaig iad an rathad latha eile, is chaidh
aon seachad, ach stad dithis, is rinn iad cainnt rithe, ach cha
dubhairt ise diog, is cha do ghabh i oirre gun robh i 'gan cluinntinn. Dh'fhalbh iad an latha sin cuideachd, is thànaig latha eile.
Chaidh dithis dhiubh seachad, ach sheas an treas fear dhiubh
a dhèanamh cainnte rithe, agus bhruidhinn e rithe. Ach chan
abradh ise diog, is cha ghabhadh i oirre gun robh i 'ga chluinntinn no 'ga fhaicinn. Ghabh esan gaol mór oirre aig cho
bòidheach 's a bha i, is thug e leis i air a chùlaibh air muin an
eich agus thug e leis dachaigh i, agus phòs e i air son a bòidhchid.

Bha i ann an taigh-mór an Rìgh, is bha am pailteas de luchd-
freasdail aice, ach chan abradh i diog, ach sméideadh le a làimh
'nuair a bhiodh nì air bith a dhìth oirre, agus chìr is shnìomhaich
i an canaichean. Ri tìm cheart, dh'fhàs i torrach, is an uair a
bha tìm a h-asaid dlùth a làimh, bha aig an Rìgh ri dol air
astar mu phàirt de ghnothach na rìoghachd. Dh'fhàg e an dà
chuid luchd-freasdail is luchd-frithealaidh gu feitheamh oirre.

---

¹ *cain-chean* in MS. at this place—*trusadh a chainechean* in MS. in another place.
For the *canach* down, see *More West Highland Tales*, i., p. 369.

² Had the foster-mother and the seer climbed up the peg-ladder to the upper
country, or did the heroine go down to them? The last supposition seems more
likely, as after this, the heroine, in order to gather the down goes to the wilderness,
a place which seems to belong to the ordinary mortal terrain. The fact that she
tells her father of her intentions also suggests that in order to see him she had

bog-cotton down.[1] She undertook to do this, and bidding them good-bye, she left them.

She now went to see her nurse and told her what she was going to do, and her nurse told the seer.[2] He said that she would have to make the shirts without mirth, without speaking, without laughter, and that his advice to her was to go to the wilderness where there would be no one to disturb her. She thanked him, took her leave of him, and told her father where she was going. She set out and went to the wilderness, and there she was all alone, gathering bog-cotton down.

*   *   *   *

One day three kings who were hunting came by, and when they saw her they halted their horses and began to talk to her. But she said never a word, nor did she even show that she heard them. That day they went away but they came by another day, and while one passed on, two of them stopped and talked to her, but never a word did she say, nor did she show that she heard them. That day also they went away, but they came again on another day. Two of them passed on, but the third stood still to talk to her, and addressed her. But she would not say a word, nor even show that she heard or saw him. He fell deeply in love with her because she was so beautiful, and he took her up behind him on the horse's back and carried her home and married her on account of her beauty. She was now in the King's palace and had plenty of attendants, but not a word would she say, only beckoning with her hand when she wanted anything ; and she combed and spun the bog-cotton down. In due time she became pregnant, and when the time of her delivery was near at hand, the King had to go on a journey concerning some affairs of the kingdom. He left both attendants and watchers to wait upon her. But one night, when the women were all round about the Queen, the most melodious music ever heard

descended to common earth, as there is no mention of her father's ascending to the upper country. But the question whether these and other happenings took place in the upper or lower sphere remains uncertain. It is to be hoped that some other tale will turn up that will resolve the matter.

[3] *a' chanaichean* : I do not know whether this is a permissible spelling. In MS. *a chainechean*, which may be an attempt to make the word collective. Read *a' chanaich ann* ? 'gathering the bog-cotton there.' But cf. *infra*, p. 284.

Agus aon de na h-oidhchean, tràth bha na mnathan mun cuairt air a' Bhanrìghinn, thànaig an aon cheòl bu bhinne chualas a riamh [mun cuairt an taighe], agus thuit a h-uile h-aon de na mnathan 'nan cadal, is tràth dhùisg iad, chunnaig iad gun do rugadh an leanabh is gun robh e air a thoirt air falbh, is cha robh fios aca ciod a dhèanadh iad. Ach smaointich an té aig an robh cùram a' ghnothaich, gun dèanadh ise dòigh, is air eagal 's gum marbhadh an Rìgh iad, is e mar a rinn iad, fhuair iad greim air piseag chait, is mharbh iad a' phiseag, agus chuir iad an fhuil is an gaorr mu bheul is mu fhiaclan na Banrìghinn.[1] An uair a thànaig an Rìgh dhachaigh, is a dh'fharraid e gu dé mar a bha gnothaichean, thuirt a' bhean-ghlùin, 'Marbhaisg air a' Bhanrìghinn mhosaich, dhona, dhòlaich ! Cha b'ionann i is a' Bhanrìghinn shona, shòlach ![2] Cha robh aice ach piseag chait, is cha bu luaithe a rug i a' phiseag, na dh'ith i fhéin a rithist i.' Thuirt an Rìgh, 'Tha a' cheud choire gus a leigeadh leatha.'

An uair a dh'éirich a' Bhanrìghinn, thòisich i is shnìomh i an canaichean le cuigeil is dealgan : is tràth a bha e snìomhte, thòisich i air deilbh eige, agus a chion beairt, b'éiginn di féin loinn a dhèanamh, agus an snàth a chur air, agus figheadh le bhith togail nan snàithnean le snàthaid, is rinn i dà eige mun robh i torrach a rithist. Tràth thuig an Rìgh mar a bha i, chuir e i a staigh do'n taigh, is mnathan a thoirt an aire oirre ; bha na dorsan glaiste, is dh'fhalbh an Rìgh e féin bho 'n taigh. Bha na mnathan a' suidhe suas leatha anns an oidhche a thoirt an aire oirre. Is bha an oidhche ann, is thànaig an aon cheòl a bu bhinne a chuala iad riamh, is thuit a h-uile h-aon diubh 'nan cadal, is an uair a dhùisg iad, bha a' Bhanrìghinn air a h-asaid, is an duine cloinne air a thoirt air falbh. Bha eagal orra an uair a thigeadh an Rìgh dhachaigh gum marbhadh e iad, is fhuair iad greim air cuilean coin, is mharbh iad e, is chuir iad an fhuil is an gaorr mu bheul is mu fhiaclan na Banrìghinn. An uair a thànaig an Rìgh dhachaigh, is a dh'fharraid e ciod e mar a bha a' Bhanrìgh, thuirt a' bhean-ghlùin,

---

[1] Similar incident in *Béaloideas*, ii., p. 400.

[2] This sentence certainly does not fit here, as it implies that the King had been married before. It must have been brought in from other stories, for it is always said of a second or stepmother Queen, as in *W. H. Tales*, ii., No. 46 (notes after

came round the house, and every one of the women fell asleep ; and when they awoke they saw that the child had been born and had been taken away, and they did not know what to do. But the woman who had the responsibility of the matter, fearing that the King would kill them all, thought that she would contrive something ; and so what they did was this [1]—they got hold of a little kitten, killed it, and rubbed its blood and gore over the mouth and the teeth of the Queen. When the King came home, and asked how things were, the midwife said, 'Death take this vile, wretched, ruinous Queen ! How different from the happy, prosperous Queen ! [2] She brought forth only a kitten, and no sooner had she done so than she ate it.' The King said, 'She is to be forgiven for the first offence.'

When the Queen rose from her bed, she began work, and span the bog-cotton down with distaff and spindle. When it was spun, she began to set up the web, and for want of a loom, she had to make a device herself, and to put the thread on it, and weave by picking up the threads with a needle, and she made two webs before she became pregnant again. When the King understood what her condition was, he had her sent inside the house with women to look after her ; the doors were locked but the King himself left home. During the night the women were sitting up with her to keep a watch over her. And night fell, and there came the most melodious music ever heard and every one of them fell asleep ; and when they awoke the Queen had been delivered and the child taken away. They feared that when the King came home, he would kill them, and so they got hold of a puppy dog and killed it, and rubbed the blood and gore all over the mouth and teeth of the Queen. When the King came home and asked how the Queen was, the midwife said, 'Death take this vile, wretched, ruinous Queen ! How different

Var. 4), where Islay has unfortunately translated 'O ! bad straddling Queen.' *Dhòlaich*, 'wretched, destructive,' sounds very like *ghobhlaich*, 'straddling' ; both words are dative singular feminine forms.

'Marbhaisg air a' Bhanrìghinn mhosaich, dhona, dhòlaich ! Cha b'ionann i is a' Bhanrìghinn shona, shòlach. Cha robh aice ach cuilean mosach coin, is cha bu luaithe a rug i e, na dh'ith i féin a rithist e.' Thuirt an Rìgh, 'Leigear a' choire seo leatha fhathast.' Dh'iarr na mnathan gun rachadh a losgadh, ach cha leigeadh an Rìgh sin a bhith.

An uair a dh'éirich i, thòisich i air a h-obair, agus rinn i eige eile, agus an sin thòisich i air dèanamh nan léintean, agus bha iad gu inbhe bhig dèante mun d'fhàs i torrach a rithist. Tràth bha a tìm aig làimh, chaidh a cur a staigh do thaigh, agus am pailteas de gach nì a dh'fheumadh iad agus gu leòr de luchd-fritheil is de luchd-freasdail, agus dh'iarr an Rìgh orra an aire shònraichte a thoirt oirre, is dh'fhuirich e féin aig an taigh an uair sin. Ach an oidhche a bha fiughair aca i bhith aig làimh, bha iad dlùth m'a timcheall, ach mar a b'àbhaist thànaig an ceòl, is chuir an ceòl a chadal iad. Is tràth dhùisg iad, bha am pàisde air a thoirt air falbh. Is tràth chunnaig iad gun robh a' Bhanrìgh air a h-asaid, is an leanabh air a thoirt air falbh, chaidh a h-aon diubh is fhuair i uircean muice. Is mharbh iad an t-uircean, is chuir iad an fhuil [is an gaorr] mu bheul agus mu fhiaclan na Banrìgh, agus chuir iad fios air an Rìgh, is an uair a thànaig e, leig iad fhaicinn da mar a bha an fhuil [is an gaorr] mu fhiaclan is mu bhilean na Banrìgh, is thuirt a' bhean-ghlùin, 'Nach fhaic thu do Bhanrìghinn dhona, dhòlach ; cha b'ionann is a' Bhanrìghinn a bhiodh gu sona, sòlach ! Tha thu féin, a Rìgh, a' faicinn. Cha robh aice ach uircean muice, is cha bu luaithe a rug i e na dh'ith i féin a rithist e. Cha bu chòir dàil a thoirt di, ach a losgadh.' 'Tha dùil agam fhéin,' thuirt an Rìgh, 'gu bheil i glé fhada agam a' breith chat, is chon, is mhuc, is 'gan itheadh a rithist.'

Rinn na h-uaislean coinneamh mu dheighinn na Banrìghinn : is thug iad a mach breith gun robh a' Bhanrìghinn gus a bhith air a losgadh. Chaidh tulach mór connaidh a thrusadh, is teine chur ris, gus a' Bhanrìghinn a losgadh air ; chaidh a toirt a mach. Tràth bha iad a' dol dh'a cur air an teinidh, chuala iad glaodh, is thuirt an Rìgh, 'Stadamaid, a sheall gu dé as brìgh do'n ghlaodh seo.' Agus bha aon de na léintean dèante aig a' Bhanrìghinn, is rinn i gàire, is chaidh an teine as. Thòisich iad, she is from the happy prosperous Queen ! She brought forth only a puppy dog, and no sooner had she done so than she ate it.' 'The offence is to be forgiven her this time also,' replied the King. The women wanted to have her burned, but the King would not allow that.

When she rose from her bed she began at her work again, and she made another web, and then she began to make the shirts, and they were within a little of being finished before she became pregnant again. When her time was near at hand, she was put into a house, with ample sufficiency of everything that might be needed, and plenty of attendants and guardians, and the King ordered them to watch over her with particular care, and on that occasion he himself remained at home. But the night they expected that her hour was near, and when they were all in close attendance upon her, the music came as usual and put them to sleep. And when they awoke, the child had been taken away. When they saw that the Queen had been delivered, and that the child had been taken away, one of them went and procured a little pig. They killed the little pig and rubbed its blood [and gore] over the mouth and teeth of the Queen ; then they sent word for the King, and when he came, they showed him how the blood [and the gore] were on the teeth and lips of the Queen, and the midwife said, 'Look at your vile, wretched Queen ; she is utterly unlike the Queen who was so happy and prosperous. You can see for yourself, your Majesty. She brought forth only a little pig, and no sooner had she done so than she ate it. No respite should be allowed her. She ought to be burnt.' 'I do feel myself,' said the King, 'that she has been with me long enough bringing forth cats and dogs and pigs and then eating them.'

The nobles held a meeting about the Queen, and they sentenced her to be burnt. A great pile of faggots was gathered and set alight in order to burn the Queen upon it ; and she was brought out. But when they were going to put her on the fire, they heard a shout, and the King said, 'Let us wait and see what is the meaning of that shout.' The Queen had finished making one of the shirts, and she laughed, and out went the fire. They began and kindled the fire again, and said to the King that she 's bheothaich iad an teine a rithist, is thuirt iad ris an Rìgh gum bu chòir a cur air, nach robh brìgh air bith aig a' ghlaodh ud. Agus [anns an fhacal] bha léine eile dèante aice, is rinn i lachadh mór ghàire. Tràth bha iad a' dol dh'a cur air an teinidh, chuala iad glaodh mór eile. 'Stadamaid beagan fhathast, a sheall gu dé as brìgh do'n ghlaodh seo,' ars an Rìgh. Stad iad tacan beag, is chan fhac iad nì air bith ; agus thòisich pàirt de na h-uaislean agus na mnathan air a ràdh ris an Rìgh nach b'fhiach da bhith a' toirt tuilleadh dàlach di ; gum b'fheàrr a tilgeadh 'san teinidh. Ach an uair a bha iad a' dol dh'a cur ann, chuala iad [an treas] glaodh.[1] Sheall iad, is chunnaig iad trì marcaichean, is iad a' marcachd an cùrsa [?] [2] gu dian, agus [ri linn sin,] bha an treas léine dèante aig a' Bhanrìghinn, is rinn i lachanaich de ghàireachd-aich. Thànaig na marcaichean air an aghaidh.

'Faiceamaid,' ars an Rìgh, 'ciod iad na marcaichean seo a thànaig oirnn.' Thuirt na mnathan gum b' iongnadh leò féin gun robh an Rìgh a' toirt na h-uibhir dàil di, is i cho dona. Chaidh na marcaichean dìreach an taobh a bha a' Bhanrìghinn, agus bha cròic féidh air gach fear dhiubh, is ghabh an sluagh gu léir iongnadh a bhith 'gam faicinn. Bha, aig an fhear bu mhò, tuaiream aois dà bhliadhna de phàisde aig a bheulaibh air muin an eich, is aig an ath-fhear, aois aona bhliadhna de phàisde, is aig an treas fear leanabh-cìche air a bheulaibh. [Ach bha na marcaichean a' sìor-dhèanamh dìreach air a' Bhanrìghinn, is bu ghoirid a' mhoill daibh a ruigsinn, is an uair a rànaig,] thug i na léintean daibh, is thug iad-san di-se a' chlann ; is chuir na fir orra, gach aon diubh, a léine fhéin air ; thuit a' chròic bhàrr nan cinn aca, is bha iad mar dhaoine eile, agus iad ro bhrèagh. Agus thuirt a' Bhanrìghinn ris an fhear bu mhò dhiubh, 'Gu meal thu do léine, a bhràthair mhóir !' Agus thuirt esan, 'Gu meal thusa do shlàinte, a phiuthar !' Thuirt i, 'Gu meal thusa do léine, a bhràthair mheadhonaich !' Agus thuirt esan, 'Gu meal thusa do shlàinte, a phiuthar !' Thuirt i, 'Gu meal thusa do léine, a bhràthair [as] òige !' Agus thuirt esan, 'Gu meal thusa do shlàinte, a phiuthar !' Thuirt na trì

---

[1] The shouts are probably given by the brothers, who had been living in the upper country all this time, and who presumably descend thence at the appropriate moment to rescue their sister. But this supposition is merely conjecture, and by no means certain.

ought to be put on top of it, and that that shout had no meaning whatever. But [even as they spoke the word] she had finished making another shirt, and she gave a loud shout of laughter. When they were going to put her on the fire, they heard another great cry. 'Let us wait a little while yet and see what is the meaning of that shout,' said the King. They waited a little while, but they saw nothing at all ; and some of the nobles and the women began to say to the King that it was not proper to allow her any further respite ; that it were best to throw her on the fire. But when they were going to put her on, they heard [the third] shout.[1] They looked, and saw three horsemen riding hard, and [at the moment of their coming] the Queen had finished making the third shirt, and then indeed she laughed loudly and long. On came the horsemen.

'Let us see,' said the King, 'what riders these are who have thus approached us.' The women said that they were surprised at the King for allowing the Queen so long a respite, seeing how wicked she was. The horsemen made straight in the direction of the Queen, and on the head of each of them there were deer's antlers, and the people were amazed at seeing them. Now, in front of the biggest horseman, and mounted on his horse, was a child about two years old. The next horseman had a child about one year old, and the third horseman had a suckling babe in front of him. [But they continued to make straight for the Queen, and short was the time they took in coming to her, and when they had come up] she gave them the shirts and they gave her the children ; and each of the riders put on his own shirt. The antlers fell off their heads, and they became as other men, and very handsome they were. And the Queen said to the biggest of them, 'May you enjoy your shirt, big brother !' And he said, 'May you enjoy health, sister !' She said, 'May you enjoy your shirt, second brother !' And he replied : 'May you enjoy health, sister !' She said, 'May you enjoy your shirt, youngest brother !' 'May you enjoy health, sister !' said he. Then the three brothers said :

---

[2] ? *cùrsairean* 'coursers' [or *cùrsain* ?—A. M.]

bràithrean, 'Guma slàn do d' chloinn, a phiuthar !' agus thuirt
ise, 'Guma slàn duibh, a thriùir bhràithrean !'

An sin thànaig an Rìgh far an robh iad, agus thuirt a'
Bhanrìghinn ris, 'Seo dhuit do thriùir mhac,' agus dh'innis a'
Bhanrìghinn da mar a thachair, agus an reuson mar nach
faodadh i cainnt a dhèanamh gus gum bitheadh na léintean
dèante : is gum b'e na trì fir a thànaig, a trì bràithrean. Chuir
an Rìgh agus a bhràithrean-céile fàilte air a chéile, agus dh'òrdaich
an Rìgh na mnathan a bha los a' Bhanrìghinn a losgadh, iad
fhéin a bhith air an cur air an teinidh a chaidh a chur air air
son na Banrìghinn a losgadh ; chaidh an tilgeil air an teinidh
agus ghlaodh iad-san air [? son] maitheanas, is ghuidh a' Bhanrìghinn air an son is chaidh an leigeil as. Rinn an Rìgh cuirm
mhór air son na Banrìghinn agus a bràithrean : is rinn iad
gàirdeachas mór bho'n a fhuair iad buaidh air draoidheachd na
h-Eachlaraiche Ùrlair.

An uair a bha sin seachad, thug na trì bràithrean beannachd
le am piuthair, is leis an Rìgh, is dh'fhalbh iad dachaigh, do an
dùthaich fhéin. Choinnich an athair iad, agus fhuair e a rithist
an trian a bha dhìth air de a thùr, de a choiseachd, is de a
fhradharc. Chaidh an seann Rìgh is a Mhic dachaigh do'n
dùthaich fhéin, is cha b'fhad a bha iad aig an taigh gus an
deach greim fhaotainn air an Eachlaraiche Ùrlair agus a losgadh.
Cha d'fhuair a' Bhanrìghinn mu dheireadh aig an Rìgh a chead
gnothach a ghabhail ri nì sam bith, ach clann na ceud Bhanrìghinn a' cumail smàdaidh oirre, is cha robh diog aice ri ràdh
a ghabhail a leisgeal fhéin, is an déidh bàs an t-seann Rìgh, cha
robh móran meas oirre, is chaidh crìoch air an sgeul le sin.

JOHN DEWAR.

NOTES

MS. vol. x., No. 126. On the flyleaf of the MS., Islay has written 'Clan[n]
an Rìgh fo Gheasaibh. John Dewar. Version of the Wild Ducks, Cannach
Shirts &c: seems very good.' John Dewar was from Gleanndaruail, Cowal,
Argyllshire. Whether he wrote the story from his own personal recollection,
or took it down from another person's telling, does not appear.
As usual and as Islay himself observed (MS. vol. viii., No. 204 ; *W. H.
Tales*, ii., No. 46, Notes) of other stories by Dewar, this one is spoilt by Dewar's
attempts to Anglicize. The innumerable repetitions of *agus*, 'and,' and the
almost total absence of full-stops, as in other tales written by Dewar, necessitated

'Sound and healthy may your children be, sister!' and she replied : 'May health be yours, my three brothers!'

The King went up to where they stood, and the Queen said to him, 'Here are your three sons for you,' and she told him what had happened and the reason why she might not speak till the three shirts had been made. The three men who had come, she said, were her brothers. The King and his brothers-in-law greeted each other, and the King ordered that the women who had wanted to have the Queen burnt should themselves be put on the fire that had been built to burn the Queen ; and on to the fire they were thrown, but they cried for mercy, and the Queen also begged for them, and so they were let go. The King made a great banquet for the Queen and her brothers ; and they exulted greatly at having overcome the witchcraft of the Eachlair Ùrlair.

When that was over, the three brothers bade their sister and the King farewell and set off home to their own country. Their father met them, and he recovered the third of his reason, the third of his walking powers, and the third of his powers of sight that had been wanting to him. The Old King and his Sons went home to their own country, and had not been long at home before the Eachlair Ùrlair was caught and burnt. The King's last wife was not permitted to take a part in anything at all ; instead of that, the children of the first Queen kept her in subjection and she had not a word to say by way of excuse for herself. And after the Old King's death she got little respect, and with that the story comes to an end.

JOHN DEWAR.

slight alterations in many places, but the sense has not been altered in the least. In an interleaved copy of his *W. H. Tales,* i., after p. cxxxv., Islay says—'Dewar's spoken Gaelic is not the same as his written Gaelic. The last loses datives and the initial changes here and there. . . . Dewar's stories written out omit incidents which he tells, and change the form of diction and change from dialogue to narrative.' And Hector MacLean in a letter bound up in vol. ii. between pp. 194, 195, says 'Does Dewar belong to a district where Gaelic is on the decline because I observe that the genitive and dative cases are wanting while the reciters in the Long Island are like the man who spoke prose all his life without knowing it and in many respects rival our ministers, many of whom speak worse Gaelic than the most illiterate.'

Though the idiom and diction of No. 126 are wretched in the extreme, it is a much fuller and far more important and complicated story than No. 22 (MS. vol. x., No. 37), which is related to it. But it differs from it in framework, and in many other ways, and there are various points that are obscure. Why, for instance, was it necessary for the brothers to journey to the mysterious upper country? Were they forced to it by magic? Did so doing benefit them? If so, in what way? Again, the heroine is instructed to gather up her brothers' blood, and to deliver it again to them later. The incident of her gathering it up is recorded, but how or when she delivered it to them, is not recorded. I have suggested in a footnote where this gap in the story may be filled in (p. 280). Again, the incident of the foster-mother's be-spelling of the heroine (p. 270), is probably wrongly recorded, and greatly curtailed. But it is clear that before setting out after her brothers, the heroine knew that she would be too late to avail herself of the ladder which the Giant of the Seven Years would set up against the Great Rock.

There are also other gaps in the story. We are not told how the brothers ascend to the upper country. But we may perhaps suppose that after meeting the Old King, their father, in the wilderness (a place which the present little piece of reconstruction would locate in the ordinary world of mortals) the brothers (as suggested in a note on p. 268) being now restored to human shape (with the exception of their still cervine and antlered heads) would have been able to climb the Giant's ladder with hands and feet like ordinary people. Nothing being said as to their providing themselves with magic pegs, the conclusion is that the ladder was the only method of ascent of which they could avail themselves. It is to be assumed that before setting out on this errand, they knew that they could get there in time, and before the Giant took the ladder away. It is clear that they arrived in the upper country before their sister did.

Then again, though the heroine's ascent is duly recorded, there is not a hint as to how or when she descended, or whether she ever descended at all. We can only infer that she did descend from the fact that soon after parting with her brothers in the upper country, she visits, first the seer and then her father, who are not said to have ascended.

We read nothing as to the how or the when of the brothers' descent from the upper country. Did they come down by means of the pegs which their sister may have left sticking in the rock? Presumably, their descent was made at the end of the tale, and just in time to save their sister. But if (as in No. 37, vol. i, p. 366), the brothers were the persons who stole the children, newly born in the lower world, how did they manage it, if they were still in the upper world? Had they each a divisible personality capable of being present in two places at once, as other characters have (see 'Fear Gheusdo,' p. 167)?

The tale is also obscure in the matter of time. Nine days at least elapse between the metamorphosing of the brothers by the witch and the finding of them by the heroine, but it is quite possible to suppose that the interval was much longer.

The six giants who figure in the tale are all friendly. Three of them are induced by the heroine to make the magic wooden pegs that are to enable her to ascend the Great Hill or High Rock to the upper country. The fourth Giant directs the heroine to the Great or High Rock, and gives her, as do the first three, a night's quarters. The fifth Giant is he of the Seven Years, who possesses the ladder. The sixth Giant enables the King to find his stag-sons by means of some kind of magic, whether material or not does not appear. The fact that after meeting their father the sons recover human form (except as to their heads, which remained cervine and antlered) suggests that it was this last Giant who possessed the power of counteracting the influence of the witch's spells to this extent, and that he may have given the father the necessary magic apparatus for the purpose, or may have directed him how to act.

The mysterious upper country, situated at the top of a high rock, occurs also in 'the Rider of Greenock,' *W. H. Tales*, iii., No. 58. In that tale, three heroines are carried thither by giants, and the hero who would follow them is hauled up in a creel or basket. Who they are who haul him up does not transpire. He returns on the back of a magic steed 'to which [steed] sea and shore are alike.' Very little is told us of this mysterious upper country, neither is any reason given as to why it was necessary for the brothers to go there. The giant, who, once in seven years, plants a ladder against the rock, to enable people to descend from, or ascend to, the upper country, does not occur in any other story known to me.

SGEUL BHLOINIGEIN BHIG

BHA uaireigin bean ann, agus bha mac aice do'm b'ainm
Bloinigein, agus thog iad taigh dhoibh féin, ach cha robh iad
ach tìm gun a bhith fada anns an taigh gus an do shiubhail a'
bhean, agus bha Bloinigein anns an taigh, agus e leis fhéin.
Chaidh e a mach, là bha 'n sin, agus thug e sùil a sìos agus sùil a
suas, agus sùil an àird, agus sùil le leathad, agus chunnaig e
cailleach mhór a' tighinn, agus bha fiacail mhór a mach air dorus a
beòil a dhèanadh lorg dhi, agus i anabarrach bucail mu'n uchd.
Theich Bloinigein a staigh, agus chaidh a' chailleach a staigh as a
dhéidh, agus sheall i air feadh an taighe, agus chan fhaca i e ;
agus ghlaodh i, 'A bheil thu a staigh, a Bhloinigein ?' Agus
cha dubhairt Bloinigein diog. 'Ma tha thu a staigh, a Bhloinigein,
thig an seo is gheibh thu aran is càise.' Thànaig Bloinigein far
an robh a' chailleach, agus rug a' chailleach air Bloinigein, agus
chuir i 'na poca e, agus dh'fhalbh i leis. Bha i dol troimh
choillidh, agus choinnich tom smeur oirre, agus thòisich i air
trusadh nan smeur, agus leig i dhith am poca, agus shnàgain
Bloinigein a mach as a' phoca [gun fhios di] agus lìon e am poca
le clachan, agus dh'fhalbh e dhachaigh. Tràth thruis a' chailleach
na smeuran, thànaig i agus thog i air a druim am poca, agus
tràth mhothaich i cudthrom nan clach, thuirt i, 'Is math trom
thu, a Bhloinigein' ; agus an uair a rànaig i dachaigh leis, bha
an nighean aice agus gealbhan math aice ris a' choire, is an
t-uisge air a ghoil, agus thuirt a' chailleach, 'Tha gealbhan
math agad air, agus tha Bloinigein math reamhar ; gheibh sinn
tràth-feasgair math dheth an nochd.' Thug i am brod bhàrr
a' choire, agus thaom i na bha de chlachan anns a' phoca anns
a' choire, agus chaidh am màs as a' choire, agus chaidh casan
na caillich agus casan a h-ighinn a sgàldadh. 'Cha dèan thu
seo orm-sa tuilleadh, a Bhloinigein,' thuirt a' chailleach, agus
dh'fhuirich i aig an taigh gus an do leighis a casan.
    Tràth bha a casan leighiste, chaidh i a rithist a dh'iarraidh

THE STORY OF LITTLE BLOINIGEIN

No. 68.   *[MS. Vol. x., No. 150]*

THERE was once a woman who had a son whose name was Bloinigein. They built a house for themselves, but had not been in it for very long when the woman died, and Bloinigein was left in the house all by himself. One day he went out and was gazing about, first one way and then another, first up the slope and then down the slope, and he saw a great hag coming towards him. She had a huge tooth sticking out of the front of her mouth, big enough to make her a staff, and she was very bulky of chest. Bloinigein fled indoors, and the hag went in after him ; she looked about all over the house but she could not see him. So she shouted : 'Are you in, Bloinigein ?' But Bloinigein said never a word. 'If you are in, Bloinigein, come here and you shall have bread and cheese.' Bloinigein came to the hag, and the hag seized him and thrust him into her sack and went off with him. She was passing through a wood when she chanced upon a bramble bush, and began to gather the blackberries ; she laid down the sack, but unknown to her, Bloinigein crawled out of the sack, filled it up with stones, and made off home. When the hag had finished gathering the berries, she came and hoisted the sack up on her back, and when she noticed the weight of the stones she said : 'You're pretty heavy, Bloinigein !' By the time she reached home with it her daughter had a good fire going under the cauldron, and the water boiling. Then the hag said : 'You have a good fire lit, and Bloinigein is good and fat ; we shall make a hearty supper off him tonight.' She took the lid off the cauldron and tipped all the stones that were in the bag into it, and the bottom of the cauldron fell out, and the hag's feet and her daughter's feet were scalded. 'You shall not do this to me again, Bloinigein,' said the hag, and she stayed at home until her feet healed.

When her feet were healed she went off again to get Bloinigein.

Bhloinigein. Bha Bloinigein a mach, is thug e sùil a suas, agus
sùil a sìos, agus sùil an àird, agus sùil le leathad, agus chunnaig
e cailleach mhór a' tighinn, agus bha fiacail mhór a mach air
dorus a beòil a dhèanadh lorg dhi fo a h-uchd. Theich Bloinigein
a staigh, agus chaidh e an sin air an fharadh am falach. Thànaig
a' chailleach a staigh, agus thug i séideadh mór do'n ghrìosaich,
agus sguaib i a' ghrìosach air feadh an taighe. Thuirt Bloinigein,
'Thud ! a chailleach ! ged a sgar thu mo ghrìosach, na loisg
mo thaigh !' 'A bheil thusa an sin, a Bhloinigein ?' 'Tha,'
thuirt esan. 'Thig a nuas,' thuirt ise. 'Cha tig.' 'Thig a nuas,
agus gum faic mi thu : is toigh liom thu, agus bu toigh liom do
sheòrsa.' 'Tha eagal orm nach 'eil agad ach miodal.' 'Chan e
miodal a tha mi dèanamh : bu toigh liom na daoine a thànaig
romhad, agus is toigh liom thu fhéin air an sgàth.' Thànaig
Bloinigein a nuas far an robh a' chailleach, agus rug a' chailleach
air, agus spàrr i 'na poca e, agus dh'fhalbh i leis. Agus tràth
rànaig i dachaigh leis, spàrr i anns a' choire e ann a measg uisge,
agus chuir i am brod air a' choire gu dlùth, daingeann,
agus chuir i an coire air an t-slabhraidh os cionn an teine.
Dh'fhàg i a h-ighean a' cumail gealbhain air ris a' choire, agus
chaidh i fhéin do'n choillidh a dh'iarraidh connaidh. Theireadh
Bloinigein, 'Is ann as brèagha a bhith an seo a measg a' bhùirn
bhlàith ; is mór an t-aighear agus an sòlas a bhith an seo a
measg a' bhùirn bhlàith :' agus theireadh nighean na caillich,
'An leig thu mise ann ?' Agus theireadh Bloinigein, 'Tha an
t-àite seo ro thaitneach liom fhéin, agus is anabarrach tlusail
an t-àite seo : chan iarrainn na b'fheàrr na bhith ann.' [1] Agus
mu dheireadh thog nighean na caillich am brod bhàrr a' choire,
agus thuirt i ri Bloinigein, 'Thig a mach, a thrusdair ; agus
leig liom-sa mo char fhéin fhaotainn anns an àite sin : thuirt mo
mhàthair mun deach i a mach gun robh sinn ri greis mu seach
fhaotainn ann.' Thànaig Bloinigein a mach, agus thuirt e,
'Chan fhaigh thu ach tacan beag dheth.' Chaidh nighean
na caillich a staigh do'n choire, agus thuirt Bloinigein, 'Crùbain
a sìos, agus cuiridh mise am brod air, is gu mothaich thu cho
gasda is a tha e.' Chrùbain ise sìos, agus chuir Bloinigein am
brod air a' choire gu dlùth, diongalta. Agus chuir e gealbhan

---

[1] Similar stratagem recorded in 'Na trì baintrichean,' *W. H. Tales*, ii., No. 39 ;
in 'Maol a' Chliobain,' *ibid.*, i., No. 17.

Bloinigein was outside, and he gazed first in one direction and then in another—up the slope and down the slope—and he saw a great hag coming. She had a huge tooth sticking out of her mouth, big enough to make her a staff to lean on. Bloinigein fled indoors and up to the loft to hide. The hag came in to the house, gave a great puff to the embers, and drove them all over the house. 'Hey, old hag !' Bloinigein cried, 'although you have scattered my embers, do not burn down my house !' 'Are you there, Bloinigein ?' 'Yes, I am,' he replied. 'Come down,' said she. 'I will not.' 'Come down so that I'll see you ; I am fond of you and I was fond of your kindred.' 'I fear you are only flattering.' 'I am not flattering at all ; I was fond of your ancestors, and I am fond of you for their sake.' Bloinigein came down where the hag was, and the hag seized him, thrust him into her sack, and went off with him. When she reached home with him she pushed him into the cauldron, into the water, fixed the lid on firmly and hung the cauldron on the chain above the fire. She left her daughter keeping up a fire to heat the cauldron, and she herself went into the forest to get firewood. Bloinigein would say, 'How nice it is to be here in the warm water ; it is most pleasant and delightful to be here surrounded by warm water '; and the hag's daughter would say, 'Will you let me come in ?' And Bloinigein would reply, 'It's too pleasant ; it's a most comfortable place ; I could wish for nothing better than to be here,' [1] until at last the hag's daughter lifted the lid off the cauldron and said to Bloinigein : 'Come out, you wretch, and let me have my turn there—my mother said before she went out that we were to have turn about in it.' Bloinigein came out, saying, 'You'll only have a short time in it.' The hag's daughter got into the cauldron and Bloinigein said : 'Crouch down, and I will put the lid on so that you'll feel how delightful it is.' She crouched down and Bloinigein put the lid on the cauldron tightly and firmly. He got a good fire going against the cauldron until the water was boiling, and though the hag's daughter screamed and screamed Bloinigein would not let her out, but kept saying :

math air ris a' choire gus an robh an coire a' goil, agus ged a ghlaodhadh is ged a ghlaodhadh nighean na caillich, cha leigeadh Bloinigein a mach i, ach theireadh e rithe, 'Cha d'fhuair thu do char [fhéin] anns an àite sin fhathast, mar a thuirt do mhàthair.'

An uair a bha an inghean marbh, thug Bloinigein sùil a mach air toll a bha anns an taigh, is chunnaig e a' chailleach a' tighinn, agus theich e is chaidh e am falach aig cùl a' mhuidhe. Thànaig a' chailleach a steach, agus cual mhór chonnaidh oirre, agus leig i sìos a h-eallach, agus chuir i gealbhan math air ris a' choire, ach is beag fios a bha aice gur h-i a h-ighean fhéin a bha i bruicheadh. Tràth bha leatha gun robh Bloinigein bruich, thug i an coire bhàrr an teine, agus chaidh i a dh'iarraidh a h-ighinne. Agus a h-ighean cha b'urrainn di fhaotainn ; agus ghlaodhadh is ghlaodhadh i ri a h-ighinn, ach ged a ghlaodhadh i gu seo fhathast, cha fhreagradh a h-ighean i. Agus tràth thog a' chailleach a h-ighean as a' choire, agus a chunnaig i gum b'i a h-ighean fhéin a chaidh a bhruicheadh, bha i ro dhuilich, agus bha fearg mhór oirre ri Bloinigein, agus i a' toirt bhòidean gun glacadh ise e fhathast, agus gun tugadh i air dìol air son mar a dh'éirich do'n nighinn aice. Ach bha Bloinigein aig cùl a' mhuidhe, agus e 'ga cluinntinn : agus fhuair e fairche, agus chaidh e a rithist am falach ann an cùil aig cùl a' mhuidhe. Agus fhuair i cuman, agus rànaig i am muidhe, 's thug i spìonadh a mach air a' chnag, agus bha i leigeadh an sgathaich do'n chuman. Thànaig Bloinigein air a cùlaibh, agus bhuail e leis an fhairche i anns a' cheann, agus leag e i, agus ghnog e an eanchainn aiste, is mharbh e i, agus dh'fhalbh e dachaigh, agus thuirt e,

> 'Cha d'fhuair mise an siod
> Ach crioman ime air éibhleig,
> 'S deur bainne an cròileig,[1]
> 'S deoch an cupan gun tonn,[2]
> 'S an crioman arain nach robh ann,
> 'S fhuair mi cead dol dachaigh.'

JOHN DEWAR.

---

[1] [craidhleig, croidhleig ?—A. M.]

[2] MS. has tònn, i.e. tòn, 'bottom' ? Cf. Tobar gun tonn, a well without water (or

'You have not had your turn there yet as your mother said you should !'

When the girl was dead, Bloinigein looked out through a hole in the house and saw the old hag coming, and he fled and hid at the back of the churn.   The hag came in carrying a great bundle of firewood, and she laid down her burden and made a big fire under the cauldron, but little did she know that it was her own daughter she was boiling.   When she thought that Bloinigein was boiled, she took the cauldron off the fire and went to look for her daughter.   But her daughter she could not find ; she shouted and shouted to her, but though she were to shout until now her daughter would not answer her.   And when she lifted her daughter out of the cauldron and saw it was her own daughter that had been boiled, she was overcome with sorrow and enraged against Bloinigein.   She vowed that she would catch him yet and make him pay for what had happened to her daughter.   But Bloinigein was at the back of the churn, listening to her, and he got a mallet, and hid himself again in a corner behind the churn.   The hag got a milk pail, came to the churn and jerked out the stopper, and began to let the dregs of the milk fall into the pail.   Bloinigein stole up behind her and hit her on the head with the mallet and knocked her down ; he dashed out her brains and killed her, and went off home, saying—

> 'I got nothing there
> But a little bite of butter on an ember,
> A little drop of milk in a creel,
> A drink from a cup that had no bottom,[2]
> A little mouthful of bread that was not there,
> And then I was allowed home.'

liquid or wave).   The beginning of a riddle about a thimble.   *W. H. Tales*, ii., No. 50 (40).

NOTES

MS. vol. x., No. 150. John Dewar, the scribe, probably came from Cowal, Argyllshire. In Dewar's hand is written, at the end of the MS., 'I heard this tale from my mother as far back as 1810.'

On the flyleaf, Islay has written :—'150. Sgeul Bhloineagan [sic] bhig. Recd., Feb. 18/60. John Dewar, who learned it from his mother as far back as 1810. Like Buttercup—Norse tales—Good, original, to be given.'

Blonag, 'fat, suet, lard'; *bloinigeach*, 'plump, soft, fat'; *bloinigein*, 'plump, fat child.'

The only other tale known to me in which Bloinigein appears, is the Maol a' Mhoibean version of Maol a' Chliobain, *W. H. Tales*, i., No. 17, Var. 3. Campbell adds :—'This Bloinigain [sic] plays a great part in another story, sent by Dewar [No. 150] ; and his name may perhaps mean "fatty" ; *Blonag*, fat, suet, lard ; *Bloinigean-Garaidh* is spinnage [sic].'

A similar story will be found in J. E. Hanauer's *Folklore of the Holy Land*, p. 217.

For a similar nonsense ending, see *W. H. Tales*, i., No. 17c, Var. 1 ; English List, No. 172 : *An Gàidheal*, v. (1876), p. 261 ; *Waifs and Strays*, iii., p. 285 ; *Folk Tales and Fairy Lore*, p. 321.

MIC A' MHUILLEIR LÒNANAICH [1]

Bha uaireigin muillear ann, agus shiubhail a' cheud bhean a
bha aige, agus phòs am muillear bean eile, ach dh'fhàg a' cheud
bhean trì mic, agus bha a' bhean mu dheireadh a bha aig a'
mhuillear ro dhona ri clann na ceud mhnà a bha aig a' mhuillear.
Agus thuirt am mac bu shine rithe, 'Tha mi dol a dh'iarraidh
an fhortain : fuin bonnach dhomh, is théid mise do'n choillidh
a dh'fhaotainn bata.' Agus dh'fhalbh e, agus dh'fhuin ise aran,
agus thànaig esan air ais tràth fhuair e bata a bha a' taitinn ris.
An uair a bha e deas gu falbh, ghabh a mhuime bonnach agus
rinn i dà bhloigh deth, agus thuirt i ri mac a' mhuilleir, 'Có
dhiùbh as fheàrr leat-sa a' bhloigh mhór is mallachd, no a'
bhloigh bheag le beannachd ?' Agus thuirt esan, 'Thoir dhomh
a' bhloigh mhór,' agus thug i dha e. Agus thug e leis bata, trì
choin, is poca, is dh'fhalbh e. Agus an déidh meadhon latha,
shuidh e a dh'ithe a' bhloigh bhonnaich a bha aige, agus an
uair a bha e ag ithe a' bhloigh bhonnaich, thànaig fitheach
bhos a cheann, agus ghlaodh e, 'Pàirt ! pàirt ! pàirt !' Agus
thuirt esan, 'Bi falbh, a bheathaich ghràinde, tha a' chriomag
seo glé bheag dhomh fhéin.' Agus dh'itealaich am fitheach air
falbh.

Agus chaidh mac a' mhuilleir air aghaidh, agus aig beul na
h-oidhche rànaig e taigh, agus bha an taigh gu tughte, slomain-
ichte, is chaidh e a staigh, is bha an taigh gu math an òrdugh,
agus an t-ùrlar air a sguabadh, agus bha teine math air. Agus
shuidh mac a' mhuilleir ri taobh an teine, agus thànaig cailleach
mhór a staigh, agus shuidh i aig ceann eile an taighe. Agus
thuirt mac a' mhuilleir rithe, 'Thig a nìos, a chailleach, is gu
faighear do chonaltradh.' Agus thuirt ise, 'Chan 'eil a bheag
de do chonaltradh-sa a dhìth orm.' Agus thuirt e a rithist rithe,
'Suidh a nìos, a chailleach, is gum faighear pàirt chainnte bhuait.'

---

[1] Possibly, 'of Lonan' ; there is a place-name *Lònan*, near Muckairn, *Celtic Review*,
viii., p. 333.

THE SONS OF THE LONAN MILLER

No. 69.   [*MS. Vol. x., No. 151*]

THERE was once a miller whose first wife died, and he married
again. But his first wife had left three sons, and the last wife was
very unkind to the children of the first. The eldest son said to
his stepmother, 'I am going to seek my fortune : bake a bannock
for me and I will go to the wood to get a staff.' He went off,
and she baked bread, and when he had found a staff that pleased
him, he returned. When he was ready to go, his stepmother
took a bannock and broke it into two pieces and said to him,
'Which do you prefer, the big piece with a curse or the little
piece with a blessing ?' 'Give me the big piece,' said he, and
she gave it him. Then he set off, taking with him his staff, three
hounds, and a sack. After mid-day he sat down to eat his piece
of bannock, and while he was eating the piece of bannock a
raven came overhead and called, 'A share ! a share ! a share !'
But he said, 'Be off, you ugly creature, this tiny bit is all too
small for myself.' And the raven flew away.

The miller's son pressed on and at nightfall he came to a
house. The house was well thatched, and the thatch well secured.
He went inside, and the house was in good order, the floor swept
and a good fire going. So the miller's son sat down by the fireside, and in came a great hag and seated herself at the other
end of the house. 'Come nearer, old hag, and chat with me,'
said the miller's son to her. 'I have no wish for any of your
chat,' said she. And he said to her again, 'Sit farther in, old
hag, and let me have a little talk with you.' 'I have no wish
for any talk with you,' she replied. Then he said, 'Come farther

Agus thuirt ise, 'Chan 'eil a bheag de do chainnt a dhìth orm.'
Agus thuirt esan, 'Thig a nìos, a chailleach, agus gum faigh thu
pàirt de àile an teine,' is thuirt ise, 'Tha mi gabhail eagail roimh
na coin agad.'   Is thuirt esan, 'Cha bhean na coin dhuit.'   Agus
thuirt i, 'Ma cheanglas tu iad, thig mi a nìos.'   Agus thuirt esan,
'Ceanglaidh.'   Agus thug i a gartain bhàrr a casan, is thug i
dha iad.   Is thuirt i ris, 'Seo dhuit crèapuill [1] a chuireas tu mu
na h-amhaichean aca.'   Agus cheangail e na gartain ri
amhaichean nan con, agus cheangail e iad ri post a bha a staigh.
Agus thànaig i gu taobh an teine, agus shuidh i ri taobh an teine,
agus thòisich i ri at, is thuirt esan, 'Ciod e an t-at a tha ort?'
Agus thuirt ise, 'Tha mo chiteagan [is mo thopagan] ag éirigh
ris an teine.'   Agus dh'at i gus an robh i ro mhór, is thuirt e
rithe, 'Ciod e an t-at a tha ort, a chailleach?'   Is thuirt ise,
'Tha at a ruigeas tusa gu bun do shlugain, a mhic a' mhuilleir
Lònanaich.   Có dhiùbh as fheàrr leat gleac cruaidh còmhnard,
no gleac bog ùrlair?'   Is thuirt esan, 'Gleac bog ùrlair.' [2]   Is
leag i e, is ghlaodh esan air a choin, is thuirt ise, 'Teann, a
chrèapulla!' agus gheàrr na gartain na cinn bhàrr nan con.
Agus thànaig a' chailleach far an robh e,[3] agus thòisich iad air
gleac, agus chinn an t-ùrlar bog, agus thuit esan.   Agus fhuair
i greim air an t-slacan-draoidheachd aice,[4] agus bhuail i e thairis
air mullach a' chinn leis an t-slacan-draoidheachd, agus rinneadh
clach chruaidh dheth, agus chuir i aig cùl an teine e.

    Agus thuirt an darna mac aig a' mhuillear ri a mhuime,
'Tha mise dol a dh'iarraidh an fhortain.   Tha mi fhéin a' dol
do'n choillidh a dh'iarraidh bata, agus fuin thusa bonnach
dhomh agus biodh e deas an uair a thig mi.'   Agus chaidh e do'n
choillidh agus fhuair e bata, is thànaig e dhachaigh leis.   Agus
dh'fhuin a mhuime aran, is bha e deas tràth thànaig e dhachaigh,
agus thuirt a mhuime ris, 'Có dhiùbh as fhearra leat bloigh
mhór le mallachd no bloigh bheag le beannachd?'   Agus thuirt
esan, 'Thoir dhòmh-sa am bonnach mór,' agus thug i dha e.
Agus ghabh e a bhata, is a phoca, agus thug e leis a choin, agus

---

[1] *creaball* in MS. This is the word used by both witch and raven (later on in
the story). This may be intended to imply that the witch belonged to a remote
and therefore more mysterious part of the country where a different dialect was
spoken, for in the body of the tale, the word *gartan* is used. *cnèbilte* (Norse, *kné-belti* ?).
[2] This paragraph is written twice over.   *Ùrlair* : I was once told that this word

in, old hag, that you may get some of the warmth of the fire ';
and she said, 'I am afraid of your dogs.' 'The dogs will not
touch you,' said he. 'If you will tie them up, I will come farther
in,' said the hag. 'I will tie them up,' he said. Then she took
her garters off her legs and gave them to him, and said, 'Here
are garters for you to put round their necks.' So he tied the
garters to the dogs' necks and fastened them to a post that was
in the house. The hag came to the fireside then and sat there,
and she began to swell. 'What are you swelling for ?' he exclaimed.
And she answered, 'It is only my duds [and my tufts] standing
out with the warmth of the fire.' She swelled till she was huge,
and he asked, 'What are you swelling for, old hag ?' She answered,
'A swelling that will reach you right to the bottom of your gullet,
son of the Lonan miller ! Which do you prefer, a hard struggle
on the level ground or a soft struggle on the floor ?' 'A soft
struggle on the floor,' [2] said he. Then she felled him and he
shouted to his dogs and she said, 'Tighten, garters !' and the
garters sheared the heads off the dogs. Then the old hag came
up to him [3] and they began to struggle. The floor became soft
and he fell. She got hold of her magic wand and she struck
him over the top of his head with it, and he was turned into a
hard stone which she set up at the back of the fire.

The miller's second son said to his stepmother, 'I am going
to seek my fortune. I shall go to the wood to find a staff, so
bake me a bannock and have it ready when I come.' He went
to the woods and got a staff, and came home with it. His stepmother baked bread, and it was ready when he came home,
and his stepmother said to him, 'Which do you prefer, a big
piece with a curse or a little piece with a blessing ?' 'Give me
the big piece,' said he, and she gave it him. He took up his
staff and his sack, and he took his dogs with him, said goodbye
to his acquaintances, and went off. When he became hungry

[here] ought to be *ùmhla*, or cowhouse, where a fall while wrestling would be softer,
owing to the presence of straw, etc. In some versions, the witch grows so tall that
her head touches the roof.

[3] A certain amount of confusion by the scribe here. See Notes.

[4] *aic* in MS.

thug e beannachd le a luchd-eòlais agus dh'fhalbh e. Agus an uair a dh'fhàs e acrach, shuidh e a dh'ithe a' bhonnaich, agus thànaig fitheach os a cheann, agus thuirt e, 'Pàirt! pàirt! pàirt!' Is thuirt esan, 'Bi falbh, a bheathaich mhosaich, tha a' chriomag bheag bhonnaich seo beag gu leòr domh féin.' Agus dh'fhalbh am fitheach, agus dh'éirich mac a' mhuilleir, agus chaidh e an taobh ceudna a chaidh a bhràthair, agus aig dorchadh nan tràth, rànaig e a' cheart taigh anns an robh a bhràthair, ach cha robh fios aige [air] nì air bith de na thachair.

Bha an taigh ann an òrdugh math, an t-ùrlar sguaibte, agus teine math air, agus shuidh mac a' mhuilleir sìos ri taobh an teine. Agus aig ceann ùine bheag, thànaig cailleach mhór a staigh, agus shuidh i aig ceann eile an taighe. Agus thuirt mac a' mhuilleir rithe, 'Suidh a nìos, is gum faighear do chonaltradh.' Agus thuirt ise, 'Chan 'eil a bheag de do chonaltradh a dhìth orm.' Agus thuirt e rithe, 'Thig a nìos, is gum faighear cainnt a dhèanamh riut.' Is thuirt ise, 'Chan 'eil a bheag de do chainnt a dhìth orm.' Agus thuirt esan, 'Thig a nìos, a chailleach, agus gum faigh thu pàirt de àile an teine,' is thuirt ise, 'Tha mi gabhail eagail roimh na coin agad.' Is thuirt esan, 'Cha bhean na coin dhuit.' Agus thuirt i, 'Ma cheanglas tu iad, thig mi a nìos.' Agus thuirt esan, 'Ceanglaidh.' Is thug i a gartain bhàrr a casan, is thug i dha iad, is thuirt i ris, 'Seo dhuit crèapuill a chuireas tu mu na h-amhaichean aca,' agus cheangail e na gartain ri amhaichean nan con, agus cheangail e iad ri post a bha a staigh, agus thànaig i gu taobh an teine, agus shuidh i ri taobh an teine. Agus thòisich i ri at, agus thuirt esan, 'Ciod e an t-at a tha ort?' Agus thuirt ise, 'Tha mo chiteagan [is mo thopagan] ag éirigh ris an teine.' Agus dh'at i gus an robh i ro mhór, agus thuirt e rithe, 'Ciod e an t-at a tha ort, a chailleach?' Is thuirt ise, 'Tha at a ruigeas tusa gu bun do shlugain, a mhic a' mhuilleir Lònanaich—có dhiùbh as fheàrr leat gleac cruaidh còmhnard no gleac bog ùrlair?' [Is thuirt esan, 'Gleac bog ùrlair,'] is leag i e. Is ghlaodh esan air a choin, is thuirt ise, 'Teann, a chrèapulla!' Agus gheàrr na gartain na cinn bhàrr nan con. Agus thòisich iad air gleac, agus de na caran a bh'ann, chinn an t-ùrlar bog agus thuit esan, agus fhuair i greim air an t-slacan-draoidheachd aice,[1] agus bhuail i thar mullach a' chinn

---

[1] *aic* in MS.

he sat down to eat the bannock, and a raven flew over him and said, 'A share ! a share ! a share !' But he said, 'Be off, nasty creature, this little bit of a bannock is all too small for myself'; and the raven went away. The miller's son got up and went in the same direction that his brother had gone, and at the darkening of the hours he arrived at the very same house that his brother was in, but he knew nothing of anything that had happened.

The house was in good order, the floor swept and a good fire on, and the miller's son sat down by the fireside. After a little while, a great hag came in and sat down at the other end of the house. 'Sit farther in and chat with me,' said the miller's son to her. 'I have no wish for any of your chat,' replied the hag. 'Come farther in, so that I may talk to you,' said the miller's son. 'I have no wish for any talk with you,' said she. 'Come farther in, old hag,' said the miller's son, 'that you may get some of the warmth of the fire.' 'I am afraid of your dogs,' said the hag. The miller's son answered, 'The dogs will not touch you.' 'If you will tie them up, I will come in,' she said. 'I will tie them up,' said he. Then the hag took her garters off her legs and gave them to him, and said to him, 'Here are garters for you to put round their necks'; and he tied the garters to the dogs' necks and fastened them to a post that was in the house, and the hag came to the fireside and sat there. Then she began to swell, and he exclaimed, 'What are you swelling for ?' 'It is only my duds [and my tufts] standing out with the warmth of the fire,' she answered. And she swelled till she was huge, and he asked, 'What are you swelling for, old hag ?' And the hag replied, 'It is a swelling that will reach you right to the very bottom of your gullet, son of the Lònan miller ! Which do you prefer, a hard struggle on the level ground or a soft struggle on the floor ?' ['A soft struggle on the floor,' he replied,] and she felled him. Then he shouted to his dogs, and she said, 'Tighten, garters !' The garters sheared the heads off the dogs. They began to fight, and with all the wrestling the floor became soft and he fell ; then she seized her magic wand and struck him e, agus dh'fhàs e 'na chloich chruaidh, agus chuir i suas aig ceann an teine e.

Agus thuirt am mac a b'òige a bha aig a' mhuillear Lònanach ri a mhuime, 'Tha mise cuideachd a' dol a dh'iarraidh an fhortain, mar a rinn mo dhà bhràthair eile.   Fuin bonnach domh, is théid mise do'n choillidh a dh'fhaotainn bata,' agus dh'fhalbh e, agus dh'fhuin ise aran, is an uair a thànaig esan dachaigh bha an t-aran deas.   Agus rinn ise dà bhloigh de a h-aon de na bonnaich, agus dh'fharraid i deth, có dhiùbh a b'fheàrr leis a' bhloigh mhór le a mallachd, no a' bhloigh bheag le a beannachd.   Agus thuirt esan gum bu mhath leis-san beann-achd le a chuid ged nach biodh ach dà ghreim ann, agus thug i dha a' bhloigh bheag.   Agus ghabh e a bhata 'na làimh, is thug e leis a phoca is a thrì choin, agus dh'fhalbh e, agus tràth bha e acrach, shuidh e a dh'ithe a' bhloigh bhonnaich, agus thànaig fitheach os a cheann, agus thuirt e, 'Pàirt ! pàirt ! pàirt !'   Agus thuirt mac a' mhuilleir, 'Thig a nuas, a bheathaich bhochd, agus gheibh thu pàirt, ged nach biodh ach dà ghreim ann.'   Agus thànaig am fitheach a nuas, agus fhuair am fitheach a chuid de'n bhonnach a bha aig mac òg a' mhuilleir.   Agus an uair a dh'ith iad an cuid, thuirt am fitheach ri mac a' mhuilleir, 'An uair a ruigeas tusa far a bheil thu gu bhith an nochd, mas e is gun tig cailleach a staigh far am bi thu, agus gun tairg i dhuit crèapu[i]ll a cheangal nan con agad, ceangail [ceann nan gartan ri post a tha a staigh, agus ceangail] stiallan brisg [1] ri ceann [2] gartain na cailliche, agus ceangail an stiallan ri amhaich[ean] nan con.   Agus ma dh'fharraideas i dìot có dhiùbh as feàrr leat gleac cruaidh còmhnard, no gleac bog ùrlair, iarr thusa gleac cruaidh còmhnard.'   Agus leum am fitheach air a sgiathan agus dh'fhalbh e.   Agus chaidh mac òg a' mhuilleir air aghaidh a dh'ionnsaigh an taighe far an robh a bhràithrean.   Ach cha robh fios aige mar a thachair doibh-san.

Agus an uair a rànaig e, fhuair e an taigh ann an òrdugh math, agus an t-ùrlar sguaibte agus teine math air, agus shuidh esan ri taobh an teine.   Agus eadar sin is ceann greis, thànaig

---

[1] Variously given in MS. as *stiullan brisg, an streang bhrisg, na sreanganan.*

[2] *ri a cheann*, in MS.   A subsequent paragraph shows that this should read *ri ceann gartain na cailliche.*

over the top of his head, and he was turned into a hard stone, and she set him up at the back of the fire.

The youngest son of the Lònan miller said to his stepmother, 'I am going to seek my fortune too, as my two brothers did. Bake me a bannock, and I will go to the wood to get a staff,' and off he went. The stepmother baked bread, and when he came home the bread was ready. She broke one of the bannocks into two pieces and asked him whether he would prefer the big piece with her curse or the little piece with her blessing. He said that he would prefer a blessing with his food though there were only two mouthfuls of it, and she gave him the little piece. Then he took his staff in his hand, his sack and his three dogs with him, and he set off. When he became hungry, he sat down to eat the piece of bannock, and a raven came over above him and said, 'A share ! a share ! a share !' 'Come down, poor creature, and you shall have a share though there were but two mouthfuls of it,' answered the miller's son. The raven came down and got his share of the bannock that the miller's young son had. When they had eaten their food, the raven said to the miller's son, 'When you reach the place where you are going to be tonight, if an old hag happens to come in and offers you a garter to tie up your dogs with, tie [the ends of the garters to a post that is in the house, and tie] a rotten cord to the ends of the hag's garters ; then tie the cord to the dogs' necks. And if she asks you whether you prefer a hard struggle on the level ground or a soft struggle on the floor, choose a hard struggle on the level ground.' The raven sprang aloft on his wings and was gone, and the miller's young son pressed on to the house where his brothers were, but he did not know what had happened to them.

When he arrived, he found the house in good order, the floor swept and a good fire on, and he sat down by the side of the fire. Shortly afterwards, a great hag came in and sat down at the

cailleach mhór a staigh, agus shuidh i aig a' cheann a b'fhaide
air falbh de'n taigh, agus thuirt mac òg a' mhuilleir ris a'
chaillich, 'Thig a nìos, is gum faighear pàirt de do chainnt.'
Agus thuirt ise, 'Chan 'eil a bheag de do chainnt a dhìth orm.'
Agus thuirt esan, 'Thig a nìos, is gum faighear pàirt de do
chonaltradh.'   Agus thuirt ise, 'Tha mi gabhail eagail roimh
na coin.'   Agus thuirt esan, 'Cha bhean na coin duit.'   Agus
thuirt ise, 'Nan ceangladh tu do choin, thiginn a nìos a
dh'fhaotainn pàirt de àile a' ghealbhain.'   Agus thuirt esan gun
ceangladh.   Agus thuirt i ris, 'Bheir mi dhuit crèapuill gu an
ceangal, ma thà,' agus dh'fhuasgail i a gartain bhàrr a casan,
agus thug i dha iad.   Agus cheangail esan ceann nan gartan
ri post a bha a staigh, agus cheangail e na sreanganan brisg [1]
ri ceann gartain na cailliche, agus car dhiùbh mu amhaichean
nan con.

   Agus thànaig a' chailleach agus shuidh i aig taobh an teine,
agus thòisich a' chailleach air cinntinn na bu mhò [2] is na bu
mhò, is thuirt mac a' mhuilleir rithe, 'Ùbh ! ùbh ! a chailleach,
is mór thu !'   Is thuirt ise, 'Tha mo chiteagan [is m' atagan]
ag éirigh ris an teine.'   Agus eadar sin is ceann tacain, bha a'
chailleach ag at agus a' cinntinn na bu mhò, agus thuirt mac
a' mhuilleir, 'Ùbh ! ùbh ! is mór thu, a chailleach !'   Is thuirt
ise, 'Chan 'eil ann ach mo chiteagan [3] [is m' atagan] ag éirigh
le blàs an teine.'   Agus dh'at a' chailleach gu meud mhór, agus
thuirt esan, 'Ciod e an t-at a tha ort, a chailleach ?'   Agus thuirt
ise, 'Tha at a ruigeas tusa gu bun do shlugain, a mhic a' mhuilleir
Lònanaich,' agus dh'éirich i agus thuirt i ris, 'Có dhiùbh as
fheàrr leat gleac cruaidh còmhnard, no gleac bog ùrlair ?'   Agus
thuirt esan, 'Is fheàrr liom-sa gleac cruaidh còmhnard,' is e ag
éirigh.   Agus 'na chéile shàs iad, agus bha spàirn chruaidh eatorra,
ach bha a choltas air mac a' mhuilleir gum fairtlicheadh e oirre,
agus ghlaodh i, 'Teann ! teann ! a chrèapulla !' agus dh'fhàs i
'na cat mór. [4]   Agus ghlaodh mac a' mhuilleir air a choin, agus
thànaig iad is shàs iad anns a' chat, agus bha iad 'ga leadairt
anns an eabar, agus chinn i 'na caillich a rithist.   Agus thuirt i,

---

[1] *an streang bhrisg*, in MS., = 'the rotten cord,' singular here.
[2] *mhomha* in MS.
[3] Glossed in footnote in MS. as 'duds or raggs.'   In other versions, *m' iteagan*
or *m' atagan* or *mo thopagan*, 'my feathers, my swellings, my tufts.'

far end of the house. 'Come farther in, so that I may talk to you,' said the miller's young son to the hag. 'I have no wish for any of your talk,' replied the hag. 'Come nearer, so that I may chat a little with you,' said he. 'I am afraid of your dogs,' replied the hag. And he said, 'The dogs will not touch you.' 'If you would tie up your dogs,' said the hag, 'I would come farther in to get a little of the warmth of the fire.' He said he would tie them up. Then the hag said to him, 'I will give you a garter to tie them up with, then,' and she unbound her garters from off her legs and gave them to him. But he tied the end of the garters to a post in the house, and he fastened the rotten cords to the ends of the hag's garters and looped them round the dogs' necks.

Then the hag came and sat at the fireside, and she began to grow bigger and bigger, and the miller's son said to her, 'Tut ! tut ! old hag, how big you are !' And she answered, 'My duds [and my tufts] are standing out with the warmth of the fire.' In no time at all the hag was swelling out and growing bigger, and the miller's son said, 'Tut ! tut ! how big you are, old hag !' 'It is only my duds [and my tufts] standing out with the warmth of the fire,' said she. The hag swelled to a tremendous size, and he exclaimed, 'What is this swelling, old hag ?' Then she answered, 'It is a swelling that will reach you right to the very bottom of your gullet, son of the Lònan miller !' And she got up and said to him, 'Which do you prefer, a hard struggle on the level ground or a soft struggle on the floor ?' 'I prefer a hard struggle on the level ground,' he replied, getting up. They leapt at each other, and desperate was their struggle, and it looked as if the miller's son would prove too much for her. 'Tighten, tighten, garters !' she cried, and became a great cat.[4] Then the miller's son shouted to his dogs, and they came and fastened on the cat, mauling it in the mud, when she turned into a hag again. 'Call off your dogs, fellow, stop the dogs !' said

[4] In several versions it is in cat-shape that she first appears at the door of the bothy, and she does not change into a witch till later in the story.

'Caisg do choin, a bhalaich ! stad na coin !' Ach chum mac
òg a' mhuilleir sìos i, agus thuirt e rithe, 'Tha do bhàs air do
mhuin, a chailleach !' Is thuirt ise, 'Cha bhàs domh e. Gheibh
thu mo shlacan-draoidheachd, agus ma bhuaileas tu an dà
chloich a tha aig cùl an teine, is e do bhràithrean a tha ann, is
gheibh thu air an ais a rithist iad.' Agus thuirt esan, 'Is liom
féin sin a roimhe is 'na dhéidh—tha do bhàs air do mhuin, a
chailleach ! c'àite a bheil t'éirig ?' Is thuirt ise, 'Cha bhàs
domh e. Gheibh [thu] mo chiste òir is mo chiste airgid a tha
am falach fo 'n lic-theine, is leig liom éirigh.' Is thuirt esan,
'Is liom féin sin a roimhe is 'na dhéidh—tha do bhàs air do
mhuin, a chailleach !' Is thuirt ise, 'Cha bhàs [domh] e. Gheibh
thu mo chlaidheamh geal soluis a bha aig m'athair, is leig liom
éirigh.' Is thuirt esan, 'Is liom féin sin a roimhe is 'na dhéidh,
agus tha do bhàs air do mhuin, a chailleach !' Agus thuirt ise,
'Chan 'eil tuilleadh agam-sa a bheirinn dhuit.' Agus an uair
a thuig e nach robh tuilleadh aice, mharbh e i.

Agus fhuair e an slacan-draoidheachd a bha aice, agus
bhuail e na clachan a bha aig ceann [1] an teine, agus fhuair e
[a] d[h]à bhràthair a bha 'nan clachan ceann an teine air an
ais do an riochd fhéin a rithist. Agus fhuair e an claidheamh
geal soluis a bha aig a' chaillich, agus chuir e as an teine, agus
thog e an leac a bha fo'n teinidh, is fhuair e a' chiste òir is a'
chiste airgid a bha aig a' chaillich. Agus [2] sheall iad, agus
chunnaig iad gun do gheàrr gartain na caillich an dà chuid na
puist agus na sreanganan [2] [brisge.] Agus dh'fhalbh e
dhachaigh, agus a dhà bhràthair 'nan gillean aige. Bha fear
diùbh a' giùlan na ciste òir agus fear eile a' giùlan na ciste airgid,
agus e fhéin is an claidheamh geal soluis aige, agus e anabarrach
aighearach.

This tale was got from John Crawford, fisherman, Lochlong Head,
    Arrochar.

---

[1] Up to now, they were at the back of the fire.
[2-2] This is placed in a note at the foot of the last page of the MS. Up to now,
only one post had been mentioned.

she. But the miller's young son held her down and said to her, 'Your death is upon you, old hag !' 'No,' said the hag, 'it is not death for me. You shall have my magic wand, and if you strike the two stones that are at the back of the fire you will find that they are your brothers, and you will have them restored to you again.' 'So much is my own in any case,' said he. 'Your death is upon you, old hag ; where is your ransom ?' 'It is not death for me,' said the hag ; 'you shall have my chest of gold and my chest of silver which are hidden under the hearth-stone, so let me get up.' 'So much is my own in any case,' said he. 'Your death is upon you, old hag.' And she said, 'No, it is not death [for me] ; you shall have my bright sword of light which was my father's, so let me get up.' And he answered, 'So much is my own in any case, and your death is upon you, old hag !' 'I have nothing more I could give you,' said she. When he understood that she had nothing more, he killed her.

He got her magic wand and he struck the stones that were at the head of the fire,[1] and restored his two brothers, who had been stones at the head of the fire, to their own forms again. He found the bright sword of light that the hag had, and he put out the fire and lifted the flagstone that was under the fire, and found the hag's chest of gold and chest of silver. Then they looked and saw that the hag's garters had sheared both through the posts and the rotten cords. The miller's son went home with his two brothers attending him as servants ; one of them carried the chest of gold and one of them carried the chest of silver, and he himself had the bright sword of light, and he was very gay.

NOTES

MS. vol. x., No. 151. On the flyleaf Islay has written—'Recd. Feby 18, [18]60 [from] John Dewar who got it from John Crawford, fisherman, Loch Long, Arrochar. A mixture of Dr MacLeod's Seann Sgeulachd, Mrs MacTavish, Sgeulachd mu Theaghlach Rìgh [see No. 63, MS. vol. x., No. 117], the witch in the Lady of the Lake, & in Grant Stewart and in the Sutherland Collection & elsewhere. Not very good. To be referred to or abstracted or used in some way. Need not be given entire ; contains some curious words and phrases.'

After writing the story out, the scribe John Dewar must have remembered that he had omitted certain incidents. He therefore wrote them on the back of p. 539 of his MS., and indicated that they ought to appear twice in the story. But he failed to notice that some of these incidents duplicated and partly contradicted what he had already written. How he actually intended the tale to run can never now be known. To do one's best with it was all that was possible. I had originally intended fusing this tale with the last one in this book, and with Nos. 178 and 255, in MS. vol. xi. : but finally decided to let each stand alone, though there is a good deal of repetition.

The growing larger and larger on the part of the witch was such a frequent incident in old Highland tales that it passed into a proverb—*Tha thu ag at, mar a bha a' chailleach* ; *Sgeulaiche nan Caol*, p. 112. The proverb means literally, 'you are swelling, as the witch did,' *i.e.* you are boasting, vapouring.

The witch's garters. Any article of dress or of personal possession, and any part of the body or emanation therefrom, were, by the well-known laws of sympathetic magic, supposed to be endued with a considerable amount of the owner's essence, and to be able to act on his behalf if called upon. Thus by binding one's garter round the neck of a female dog before a fight with a bogle, one could ensure her faithfulness during the fight.[1] Sympathetic connection between other things, and their owners or wearers, is to be understood in other tales. See 'bridle-shaking,' *Waifs and Strays*, ii., p. 462, and this book, No. 57 (MS. vol. x., No. 107).

The wild, eerie theme of a witch attacking a hunter, when he, accompanied only by his dogs, is passing the night in some lonely hunting bothy, remote from human help or human habitations, is the subject of many tales. In its simplest form, the witch is either killed, or else is driven away, to appear no more, as in the following versions—*Trans. Gael. Soc. Inverness*, v., p. 22 ; xxv., pp. 186, 260. *Imtheachta an Oireachtais*, 1899, p. 149 (The Gaelic League, Dublin). *Folk Tales and Fairy Lore*, pp. 226, 230, 237, 243 (MacDougall and Calder). *Celtic Magazine*, xii., p. 514. *Scottish Celtic Review*, pp. 262-273. J. G. Campbell, *Superstitions*, pp. 122-125. *Béaloideas*, i., pp. 315, 387 ; ii., p. 363. This book, No. 77 (MS. vol. x., No. 169).

But this theme is also found joined to the theme of the subsequent pursuit of the witch by black hell-hounds belonging to a black man, who is the Fiend, and who follows on a black horse. The hounds overtake the witch before she can reach consecrated ground or sanctuary, and the last scene in the story shows the Fiend returning with her body, a ghastly burden, lying across his saddle-bow, and a black hound hanging to it on either side of the horse. In some versions, the incident of finding the witch in her bed, horribly mangled by dogs, occurs, but without the incidents of the pursuit. In some versions again all the above incidents occur. In the following versions some or all of these incidents appear :—*An Gàidheal*, i., p. 228 (1873). Dundee Highland Society's *Celtic Annual*, 1913, p. 31. *Trans. Gael. Soc. Inverness*, xxv., p. 145. Grant Stewart's *Lectures on the Mountains*, ii. Islay's MS. vol. xi., No. 178 (in MS. 180) ; No. 255. Ditto, English List, No. 279.

Similar or related stories are :—J. G. Campbell, *Witchcraft*, p. 38. Col. Wood-Martin, *Traces of the Elder Faiths of Ireland*, ii., pp. 124, 125 *n.* *Inverness*

---

[1] *Zeits. Celt. Phil.*, i., p. 336 ; *Sgeulaiche nan Caol*, p. 201 ; Rev. J. G. Campbell, *Witchcraft*, p. 185. In another and very different tale, the chain of Fionn's hound, Bran, was as good a protection to Fionn as the faithful animal itself was ; *Waifs and Strays*, iii., pp. 18, 20.

Courier, 1874, 9th April, p. 3.   Dr Douglas Hyde, *Legends of Saints and Sinners*, p. 187.   *Béaloideas*, i., pp. 315, 387 ; ii., p. 365 ; iv., p. 434.   *Highland News*, 8th February 1902, p. 2.   *Folk-Lore*, i., p. 310.   *Trans. Gael. Soc. Inverness*, xxx., pp. 139-140.   *Survivals*, p. 105.   The great number of variants shows that the popular mind was much impressed by this story.

AN DÀ MHARSANTA

No. 70.   *[MS. Vol. x., No. 154]*

Bha dithis ann an Lìte uaireigin de 'n t-saoghal, is bha iad air dèanamh suas gu h-anabarrach, agus iad a' cumail bhùthannan móra. An uair a chunnaig iad gun robh rud aca, fhuair iad is phòs iad boireannaich. Rugadh clann daibh. Rugadh nighean do'n dara fear, agus gille do'n fhear eile. An uair a bhaisteadh iad, phòs iad ri chéile iad. Is e Uilleam a bha air a' bhalach. An déidh seo a dhèanamh, bhàsaich athair a' ghille, agus bha a bhean 'na bantraich an seo. Bha am fear eile deònach air a bhith criomadh o'n bhantraich a cuid, air alt is gun gleidheadh e dha fhéin na bh' ann. Thuirt am fear eile ris a' bhantraich gum b'fhearra dhi stiùireadh a h-uile rud a bh' ann a thoirt da fhéin, is gun tugadh e foghlam do 'n bhalach. Leig ise a h-uile rud a bh' ann aige fhéin, is bha e fhéin ag obair air a' ghille thogail suas, agus e còmhla ri a chloinn fhéin. An uair a bha iad air tighinn air an adhart an aois, bha an gille air son dèanamh suas ris an nighinn. Bha a h-athair deònach air son a' ghille chur air falbh. 'Ma dh'fhalbhas tusa,' ars an nighean ris, 'fanaidh mise cùnntas bhliadhnaichean gun phòsadh, gus an till thu.'

Dh'fhalbh e an siod, is thugar am muir air. Bha e seòladh an siod, cho fad air falbh, is gun do thuit da uaireigin a dhol do'n Tuirc; agus chomh luath 's a thànaig an soitheach gu tìr, chaidh e an sin air tìr. Bha e falbh, is gu dé chunnaig e ach feadhainn a' falbh, agus corp leò, agus maidean aca 'ga bhualadh. Dh'fhaighnich esan gu dé bu chiall da siod, no gu dé an t-adhbhar a bha aca, an déidh da bàs fhaotainn, siod a dhèanamh air. Dh'innis iad gun robh fiachan aca air an duine, is gur e siod mar a bha iad a' toirt fiach nam fiachan a chorp, o nach pàidheadh e iad mun rachadh e a null. Dh'fhaighnich e an siod an gabhadh iad pàidheadh nam fiachan agus an corp a leigeil adhlacadh; agus thuirt iad gun gabhadh; agus thug e fa-near an corp a chur fo 'n talamh, is phàidh e na fiachan air a shon.

THE TWO MERCHANTS

ONCE upon a time there were two men of Leith who had prospered exceedingly as merchants in a large way of business. When they saw that they had some wealth, they found women and married them. Children were born to them : a girl to one and a boy to the other. When the children had been baptised, they had them married to each other. William was the boy's name. After this event, the boy's father died and the wife became a widow. The other man wanted to nibble away her property from the widow so as to have everything for himself. So he told her that she had better give him the management of the whole property, and that he would educate the lad. Accordingly, she turned everything over to him, and he on his part applied himself to the lad's education, bringing him up among his own children. When they had come on well in years, the youth wanted to court the girl. Her father thereupon wanted to send him away. 'If you go away,' said the girl to him, 'I will remain without marrying for a number of years, awaiting your return.'

Then William went off to sea. He sailed so far away that on one occasion he reached Turkey, and as soon as the ship came to land he went ashore. He was wandering about, and what did he see but a group of people who were carrying a corpse as they went along, and beating it with sticks. He asked what this meant or what was their motive for so treating a man after he was dead. They told him that the man had owed them money and that this was how they exacted the worth of the debts from his body, since he would not pay them before he passed over. William then asked whether they would accept payment of the debts in return for releasing the body and allowing it to be buried ; and they replied that they would ; so he paid the man's debts for him and had the body buried.

Thill e chun an t-soithich, agus sheòl iad as an Tuirc air son tighinn dachaigh. Bha iad a' falbh is a' seòladh, agus fada goirid ge'n robh iad air falbh, gu dé an rud a thànaig iad ach a dh'ionnsaigh eilein, agus bhristeadh an soitheach air an eilean, is chaidh a h-uile duine riamh a bha innte a bhàthadh ach e fhéin 'na ònrachd, is gun duine ri fhaotainn air an eilean. Bhuail e an siod air falbh feadh an eilein, agus thachair toll ris, agus chaidh e a staigh ann. Dh'fhadaidh e teine a staigh ann, agus smuaintich e gun gabhadh e tàmh ann, agus chunnaig e an dùbhradh mór ud a' tighinn do dhorus an tuill, agus gu dé rud a bha an sin ach leómhann mór, is gun chreutair 'san eilean ach e fhéin. An uair a chunnaig an leómhann an teine a dh'uidh-eamaich e 'san toll—am beothach fiadhaich sin, dh'fhàs e cho caomh ris ; agus thigeadh e a h-uile là, agus dà ghad eun leis, gad da-san agus gad da fhéin. Bhuail esan air am bruich, agus bha e bruich rud do'n leómhann, agus bha a' chùis a' còrdadh ris an leómhann gu h-anabarrach math. Bha smuainteachadh aige air a' bhoireannach ged a bha e 'san eilean, is air am na leannanachd a bhith dol seachad. Bhiodh e an siod a' siubhal feadh an eilein, a chur dheth a' mhulaid, ged a bha an deagh chompanach leis, is e 'ga chumail glé mhath, is e a' còrdadh ris gu math.

Bha e an siod latha de na làithean, agus latha brèagh ann, is a bheul fodha air cnoc. Is ann a chunnaig e an siod duine mór, mar gum faiceadh e mu a choinnimh air gob rubha air an eilean e, is gun dòigh air duine air [bith] a bhith ann. Choisich e a null far an robh an duine, agus dh'fheòraich e có an duine e, no cia as a thànaig e, no dé mar a thànaig e an siod ; agus thuirt e ris, gun d'fhuair esan, an oidhche [1] sin, cothrom air tighinn ann—nam bu chuimhne leis fhéin an uair a bha e 'san Ana-Crìosdachd agus an uair a dh'fhuasgail e an corp, [gum b'esan a bha anns a' chorp, an samhladh a bha bruidhinn ris,]— gun d'fhuair esan cothrom, an oidhche ud, tighinn d'a ionnsaigh ; gun robh adhbhar a mhnà is a leannain an oidhche ud a' dol a réiteach ; is gun giùlaineadh esan e a dh'ionnsaigh nan crìochan sin an oidhche ud, nan dèanadh e mar a dh'iarradh esan air. 'Beir thusa air amhaich orm-sa, is na beannaich is na

---

[1] *Oidhche*, 'night,' repeated lower down, should surely be *latha*, 'day,' unless we are to suppose some sentence or event omitted.

He returned to the ship, and they sailed away from Turkey with the intention of coming home. They were sailing on and on, but whether long or short the distance, what did they come to but an island, and there the ship was wrecked. Every man on board was drowned except the youth, nor was there anyone to be found on the island. Presently he began to wander about, and finding a cave, he went inside. He kindled a fire and thought of resting there, when he saw a great dark shape approaching the mouth of the cave, and what was there but a huge lion— and no other soul on the island but himself! When the lion saw the fire the youth had prepared in the cave, that fierce beast became as gentle as could be towards him. Every day it would come, bringing with it two strings of birds, one for the youth and one for itself; and the youth began to cook them, and cooked some for the lion too, and the arrangement suited the lion extraordinarily well. Although he was left on the island, his thoughts were on the girl and how the time for courtship was passing. Then he would wander about the island to drive away the melancholy that seized him, despite the fact that he had such a good comrade who kept him well supplied and whom he very much liked.

But one day, and a beautiful day it was too, he was lying face downwards on a hillock, when he saw an immense man standing, as it seemed, on the point of a headland in the island, opposite him. Yet no man could possibly be there. He walked over to where the person was, and asked him who he was or where he had come from, or how he had got there; and the other replied that that very night he had got an opportunity of coming. Did he remember, asked the man, when he was in the land of the infidel and redeemed a certain dead body. That body was his— the body of the spectre that was speaking to him—and that night [1] he had had an opportunity of coming to him; for the youth's sweetheart and prospective wife was that night to be betrothed. But if he did as the spectre asked him, he would carry him to those parts that same night. 'Hold me round the

mallaich gus an ruig thu.' ¹ Bhuail an leómhann an seo air
caoineadh, an uair a mhothaich e esan a' falbh ; agus thuirt
an samhladh a bha bruidhinn ris, gun tugadh esan an leómhann
air adhart a rithist, as a dhéidh fhéin ; agus dh'fhalbh e leis-san
an seo, agus leig e as e aig ceann a' bhothain bhochd a bha aig
a mhàthair ; agus thuirt e ris fuireach an siod, agus nach bu
mhór an ùine dha bhith an siod gus an tigeadh esan leis an
leómhann ; agus bha e 'na sheasamh gus am faca e iad-san a'
tighinn, is mar gum bitheadh e toilichte air son iad-san a
thighinn, thòisich e air toirt taing.² Thilg esan bhàrr a mhuin
an leómhann, agus bhristeadh a chas, [agus ghabh an samhladh
a' ghaoth dha fhéin.] Agus bha am baile cho trang agus
nighean a' mharsanta mhóir sin a' dol a phòsadh. An uair a
chunnaig iad esan a' falbh leis an leómhann, bha iad a' gabhail
eagail. [Chruinnich freiceadan a' bhaile is lean iad iad is gun
fios aig a' ghille gun robh iad ann, is mun d'fhuair e sealltainn
chuige no bhuaidhe, thilg iad an leómhann le saighdean. Bu
chruaidh leis a' ghille, is gum b'eadh, dealachadh ri a chompanach dìleas a rinn an gnìomh bha càirdeil, ach chunnaig e
nach robh a àrach air. B'eudar closach an leómhainn fhàgail an
siod, agus togail air as ùr.] ³

Chaidh e do thaigh a mhàthar, agus cha d'aithnich a
mhàthair e. Cha robh trusgan sam bith air nach robh an
déidh falbh. An uair a fhuair e e fhéin a ghlanadh, is a chur
air dòigh, dh'fhaighnich e de a mhàthair am faigheadh e fuireach
an siod an oidhche ud. Fhuair e cead fuireach, is chaidh e a
laighe ; is bha ise an taigh na bainnse ud thall. [Chaidh a
mhàthair a null, agus] bhuail iad air gabhail naidheachd o a
mhàthair, an robh fios aice gu dé an duine a bh'ann. Thuirt
ise nach robh, ach gun robh a chainnt glé chosmhail ri cainnt an
àite fhéin. Thuirt bean-na-bainnse gum bu chòir di fhéin dol

¹ Lest the Sacred Name be uttered in the blessing or cursing. When Michael
Scott (*Waifs and Strays*, v., p. 50) rode through the air on a *glaistig*, or *loth-mharcachd*
(riding filly), his weird steed tried to entrap him into repeating some saying containing the Sacred Name. But her efforts were vain, her rider was too wise. Had
he complied, she would have vanished from under him, and he would have been
dashed to the ground or would have fallen into the sea. In the case of a witch who
was carrying through the air in her apron a boulder from the Isle of Man for the
Cumming's castle, her apron string breaks and the boulder falls to the ground the
instant an astonished beholder says, 'God bless me' ; *Trans. Gael. Soc. Inverness,*

neck and neither bless nor curse till you arrive,' [1] said the spectre. At this point, the lion began to mourn when it realised that the young man was leaving ; but the spectre that was speaking to him said that he would fetch the lion along next. Then he went off with the youth and dropped him at the end of the poor hut that belonged to his mother ; there the spectre told him to wait, and that it would not be long until he returned with the lion. So there the youth stood until he saw them coming ; and then, apparently because he was pleased at their coming, he began to give thanks.[2] The spectre hurled the lion off his back, and its leg was broken, [and the spectre vanished into thin air.] Now all the town was in a bustle, as the great merchant's daughter was about to marry. But when people saw the youth going about with the lion they were frightened. [The town guard mustered and followed them, without the youth's being aware of their presence, and before he could as much as glance, they shot the lion with arrows. It was hard for the youth, and little wonder, to part with his faithful friend who had acted so affectionately ; but he recognised that there was no help for it. So he just had to leave the lion's carcass there and set off afresh.] [3]

The youth went to his mother's house, but his mother did not recognise him, for he had not a stitch of clothes on that had not gone to rags. When he got himself washed and dressed, he asked his mother if he might stay there that night, and having obtained permission to stay, he went to bed. The girl was in the house across the way, where the wedding was to be. [His mother went over there, and] the people there began to interrogate his mother, whether she knew who the man was. She replied that she did not know, but that his speech was very like the speech of their own place. The bride now said that she ought

---

xv., p. 290. In the *Arabian Nights*, in like manner, when a hero who is being rowed home by a brass elephant-headed boatman begins to praise Allah, boatman and boat sink out of sight, leaving the hero floundering in the water.

[2] It is, of course, to God that the hero gives thanks. This he must have done aloud. The mere uttering of the Sacred Name constitutes an act of prayer, which immediately banishes all evil spirits and breaks all spells.

[3] The sentences between square brackets have been interpolated to account for the fact that the spectre and the lion are suddenly dropped out of the story, the narrator or the scribe having apparently forgotten all about them.

a null, a choimhead có an duine a bh'ann ; agus rudeigin
amharais aice gum faodadh e bhith gur e an gille a bh'ann, an
déidh tilleadh. Chaidh ise a null, is thug ise air maighdinn-
choimhideachd a bha còmhla rithe coinneal a lasadh. Bha e
leigeil air gun robh e 'na chadal. Dh'fhalbh i is rug i air, is
dh'aithnich i làithreach bonn e ; agus thuirt i ris e a dh'éirigh,
is e 'ga ghlanadh fhéin. Dh'éirich e an seo, agus ghlan e e
fhéin, is an seo leig ise fhaicinn gur h-i fhéin a bh'ann ; is thuirt
i ris ged a bha e mar a bha e, gun cuireadh ise air dòigh e glé
mhath. Thuirt esan nach b'urrainn e seasamh riu, a thilleadh
an fhir a thànaig air aghaidh. Thuirt ise gum fóghnadh ise dha,
gun robh a misneach na b'fheàrr an dràsd ; gun robh i feadh
nan litrichean aig a h-athair, is gun d'fhuair i litir-phòsta ann.
Dh'fhalbh i còmhla ris gu bùth, is cheannaich i trusgan, is
chòmhdaich i gu h-anabarrach pongail e, is thug i dòrlach airgid
dha cuideachd, air son e fhéin a sheasamh an àite sam bith.

* * * * *

Bha bean-na-bainnse air chall, is chan fhaigheadh an
fheadhainn a thànaig greim oirre. Thug i leatha [e] an là-
'r-na-mhàireach a dh'ionnsaigh uinneagan taigh a h-athar.
Thànaig a h-athair a mach gus a grad mharbhadh, chionn i a
dh'fhalbh leis an duine seo, is gun fhios có a bh'ann. An uair
a thànaig a h-athair air a' chuthach mar seo, is iad 'ga chumail
air ais, thug ise an litir-[phòsta] a mach as a pòca, is sheall i
dhaibh i. Cha robh dad aca an sin ach gun robh i pòsta, is
gum bitheadh a h-uile rud aca. Chaidh iad an seo chun a'
chaisteil. Agus rinneadh a leithid de bhanais anns a' chaisteal,
nach cualas a h-àicheadh de bhanais riamh. Cha d'fhàg e
gin de na seann daoine a bha ann an uair a bha e 'na bhalach
gun an cur air an daoraich le fìon.

From Joanna MacCrimmon, Caolas na Sgeire, Berneray, a native of
Skye and descendant of the celebrated piper of the same name.
Father, grandfather and uncles pipers. Learnt this tale from her
grand-uncle, Angus MacCrimmon, about 24 years ago. He was
well past 60 years of age at the time.

to go over herself, to see who this man might be ; she had a slight suspicion that perhaps it was the young man who had returned. So she went over, and she made a waiting-woman who was with her light a candle. The youth pretended to be asleep ; she went and seized him, recognised him at once, and told him to get up and wash himself. At this, he got up and washed himself, and then the girl disclosed that it was she. And she told him that poor though his circumstances were, she would see him well provided for. The youth replied that he could not face the people for the purpose of sending away the man who had come forward [*i.e.* the suitor.] The girl said that she would support him ; that her courage was firmer now ; that she had been through her father's papers, and that she had found a marriage bond among them. Off she went with him to a shop, and bought clothes, and had him dressed very neatly ; she gave him a supply of money too, that he might be able to maintain his position anywhere.

The bride was missing, and those who came to look for her could not find her. Next day she took the young man to the windows of her father's house. Her father came out to make a sudden end of her because of her going off with this man, when there was no knowing who he was. When the girl's father came out enraged in this way, and those present holding him back, she brought the [marriage] contract out of her pocket and showed it to them. They were then confronted with the fact that the girl was married and that the two of them should have everything. Thereupon they went to the castle, and such a wedding was celebrated there that none ever heard of any that surpassed it. Not a single one of the old men who were in the place when he was a boy did the youth fail to make drunk with wine.

NOTES

MS. vol. x., No. 154.

On the flyleaf of the MS., Campbell has written :—'154. An dà Mharsanda. Feby/60. Joanna MacCrimmon, Berneray, Aug., 59. Hector MacLean (transcriber). A man and a lion in a desert island and a dead man who helps them out—Queer.'

For parallels, see No. 40, Notes. For other tales in which lions appear, see *W. H. Tales*, i., No. 4, Var. 2 ; iii., pp. 261, 355, or 276, 373 ; Islay's Gaelic List, Nos. 120, 260, 304. No. 120 was published by Dr Geo. Henderson, *The Celtic Dragon Myth*, p. 149.

AN EAGLAIS UAMHALT

No. 71.   [*MS. Vol. x., No. 156*]

BHA Rìgh [Lochlainn] ann roimhe seo, is bha e pòsta, is rugadh
aon mhac da. Bhàsaich a bhean, agus phòs e té eile. Bha a
mhuime dèanamh droch cheann ris a' ghille. Thuirt e gun
robh e brath falbh a dh'iarraidh an fhortain, tachradh [1] maith
no olc ris. Bha e trì làithean is trì oidhchean a' falbh ; agus air
dha bhith falbh am beul na h-oidhche an treas oidhche, chunnaig
e taigh. Chaidh e a staigh do'n taigh, is cha robh a staigh ach
seana bhean is seann duine. Bha iad cho cianail, is dh'fhaighnich
e ciod e bha orra mar siod. 'Tha Mac Rìgh Éireann a' dol
[t]roimh an Eaglais Uamhalt [an nochd féin],' ars iad-san, 'is
cha robh duine riamh a chaidh ann a thànaig beò aiste.' 'Coma
leat sin,' ars an gille, 'tha mi fhéin a' brath air a dhol ann
còmhla ris.' [Fhuair iad an seo Mac Rìgh Éireann, agus]
chaidh iad [an dà mhac rìgh] do'n Eaglais Uamhalt, is bha iad
treis a staigh innte. Cha b'fhad a bha iad a staigh, an uair a
dh'fhairich iad an Eaglais a' dol air chrith, agus am Fuamhair
Mór sin ag éirigh ['sa' mheadhon]. 'A Mhic Rìgh Éireann, is
a Mhic Rìgh Lochlainn, is fhad a bha mo chorc bheag mheirgeach a' feitheamh oirbh,' ars am Fuamhair Mór. 'Ma tà,'
arsa Mac Rìgh Lochlainn, 'dà thrian de'n eagal ort fhéin is
aon trian orm-sa dheth.' Bha cuilean beag còmhla ri Mac
Rìgh Lochlainn. 'Sthig e, sthig e,[2] a mheasain bhig dhuinn—
bad de a chridhe, 's de a ghrùthan, 's de a àirnean,' arsa Mac
Rìgh Lochlainn ris a' chuilean. Dh'fhalbh an cuilean, is chaidh
e a staigh 'na chorp, is thug e sin as. Dh'fhalbh am Fuamhair
a' sgreadail 's a' sgiamhail, is dh'fhairich iad an taigh a' dol
air chrith fòpa.[3] 'Seadh ! seadh !' arsa Mac Rìgh Lochlainn,
'dé siod ?' 'Tha,' arsa Mac Rìgh Éireann, 'bean mo bhràthar-sa
dol a staigh dh'a rùm.' 'Ùbh ! ùbh ! nach i tha mórdhalach,'

---

[1] *nan tachradh* in MS.

[2] *Stuig* means to urge on (as dogs), to instigate. *Sthig e !* the aspirate may be
due to some fancy of the scribe. *Sig e !* is also used, and is evidently what is intended.

[3] MS. *focha.*

THE EERIE CHURCH

No. 71.   [*MS. Vol. x., No. 156*]

ONCE upon a time there was a King of Norway who was married, and to whom one son was born. His wife died and he married another woman, who treated the boy badly. So the boy said that he had a good mind to go off and seek his fortune, come good or ill. Three days and three nights he travelled ; but at nightfall on the third night, as he travelled on, he saw a house. He went in, and there was no one there but an old woman and an old man. They were so sad that he asked what was troubling them so much. '[This very night] the King of Ireland's son is to go through the Eerie Church,' they replied, 'and no man ever went there who came out alive.' 'Never mind that,' said the boy, 'I mean to go there along with him.' [They fetched the King of Ireland's son then] and [the two King's sons] went to the Eerie Church, and there they waited a little while. But they had not been long inside when they felt the church begin to tremble, and saw rising up [in the middle] a great giant. 'Son of the King of Ireland, and Son of the King of Norway, long has my little rusty knife been waiting for you,' said the Great Giant. 'So, then,' said the King of Norway's son, 'two-thirds of your terror be on yourself, and only one-third on me !' Now, the King of Norway's son had a little pup with him. 'At him, at him, little brown lap-dog : a piece of his heart, a piece of his liver and a piece of his kidneys,' said the King of Norway's son to the puppy. Away went the pup, dashed into the Giant's body, and tore those parts out of him. The Giant went off screeching and screaming, and they felt the building begin to tremble beneath them. 'Well now,' said the King of Norway's son, 'what's that ?' 'Why, that is my brother's wife going into her room,' replied the King of Ireland's son. 'Dear me, what

arsa Mac Rìgh Lochlainn ; 'b'fheàrr liom gun robh mi aig
uinneag a seòmair.' An uair a rànaig iad an uinneag, bha i a
staigh 'na seasamh 'san rùm. Ciod e chunnaig iad ach am
Fuamhair a' tighinn a staigh far an robh i. 'A bhiast ! a
bhiast !' arsa ise ris an Fhuamhair, 'car son nach tug thu aon
leòr as an fhear a bha mi beathachadh fad na bliadhna ?' Chaidh
am Fuamhair a mach as an taigh is thug e dhachaigh each mór
glas. Mharbh iad an t-each, is bhruich iad e ann an coire.
An uair a dh'ith iad e, rinn ise peàrd de chlòimhe,¹ agus chuir
i am Fuamhair am broinn na peàirde, is chuir i ann an toll 'sa'
bhalla e.

*   *   *   *   *

Chaidh na gillean dhachaigh anns a' mhaduinn, is cha
deach duine riamh dachaigh as an Eaglais [Uamhalt] rompa.
An ath-oidhche, bha Nighean Rìgh Éireann ri dol ann, is bha
a h-uile duine bha 'sa' bhaile fo leann-dubh is fo mhìothlachd
air a son. 'Coma leat,' arsa Mac Rìgh Lochlainn, 'théid mise
còmhla rithe, is mas bàs dì-se e, is bàs dòmh-sa e.' Bha an
Nighean gus a bhith marbh, agus laigse air muin laigse a'
tighinn oirre. An uair a chaidh iad a staigh do'n Eaglais,
dh'fhairich iad an Eaglais a' dol air chrith, is dé chunnaig iad
ach dà thonn ag éirigh a meadhon na h-Eaglais, 's am Fuamhair
Mór ag éirigh a meadhon nan tonn ! 'Aha ! a Nighean Rìgh
Éireann, 's a Mhic Rìgh Lochlainn, is fhad a bha mo chorc
bheag mheirgeach an toll am balla feitheamh oirbh,' ars am
Fuamhair Mór. 'Ma tà,' arsa Mac Rìgh Lochlainn, 'dà thrian
de'n eagal sin ort fhéin, is aon trian oirnne. Sthig e ! sthig e !
a mheasain bhig dhuinn ! bad de a chridhe, is bad de a ghrùthan,
is bad de a àirnean !' Dh'fhalbh am measan, is chaidh e 'na
chorp, is thug e sin as. Dh'fhalbh am Fuamhair ag éigheach
is a' sgreadail an uair a rinn am measan seo air. Dh'fhairich
iad an Eaglais a' dol air chrith fòpa.² 'Seadh ! seadh !' arsa
Mac Rìgh Lochlainn, 'dé siod ?' 'Tha,' arsa Nighean Rìgh
Éireann, 'bean mo bhràthar-sa dol a staigh dh'a rùm.' 'Ùbh !
ùbh !' arsa Mac Rìgh Lochlainn, 'nach i tha anabharrach !
B'fheàrr liom gun tugadh tu gu uinneag a seòmair mi.' Chaidh

---

¹ *Peàirt de chlòimhe,* 'a portion of wool combed or carded,' says a note in the
MS. [The word intended seems to be *peàrd, peurd*].
² MS. *fòcha.*

a grand person she must be,' said the King of Norway's son ;
'I wish I were at the window of her room.' When they arrived
at the window, she was standing in the room. What did they
see but the Giant coming into the room where she was. 'Oh,
you wretch ! you wretch !' said she to the Giant : 'Why didn't
you bring me one fill from the man I have been feeding all the
year long ?' The Giant went out of the house and brought
back a big gray horse. They killed the horse, and boiled it in
a cauldron. When they had eaten it, the woman made a roll
of carded wool, placed the Giant inside the roll, and put it into
a hole in the wall.

*   *   *   *

In the morning the boys returned home ; and before that,
no man had ever returned from the [Eerie] Church. The next
night it was the King of Ireland's daughter who had to go there,
and every person in the town was mournful and dejected for
her sake. 'Never mind,' said the King of Norway's son, 'I will
go with her myself, and if it's death for her, it will be death for
me too.' The Princess was almost dead with fear, and fit after
fit of faintness came upon her. When they had entered the
church, they felt the building begin to tremble, and what did
they see but two waves heaving up in the middle of the Church,
and a great giant rising up between the waves. 'Aha, Daughter
of the King of Ireland and Son of the King of Norway, long has
my little rusty knife been waiting in a hole in the wall for you,'
said the Great Giant. 'So, then,' said the King of Norway's
son, 'two-thirds of that terror be upon yourself, and only one-
third upon us. At him, at him, little brown lap-dog ! A piece
of his heart, a piece of his liver, and a piece of his kidneys !' Off
went the lap-dog, into the Giant's body, and tore those parts out.
The Giant fled shouting and screaming, after the lap-dog had
treated him so. They felt the church trembling beneath them.
'Well now, what's that ?' said the King of Norway's son. 'Why,
that is my brother's wife going into her room,' replied the King of
Ireland's daughter. 'Dear me, what a grand person she must be,'
said the King of Norway's son ;   'I wish you would take me to the

e gu uinneag a seòmair, is bha ise 'na seasamh air làr. Cha b'fhad a bha iad-san aig an uinneig, an uair a chunnaig iad am Fuamhair a' nochdadh. 'A bhiast! a bhiast! gabh a mach as an taigh, is nach tug thu chugam-sa mo leòr de'n té a bha mi beathachadh o'n a thànaig a' bhliadhna,' ars ise. Dh'fhalbh am Fuamhair, is thug e a staigh each mór ruadh. Mharbh iad an t-each, is dh'ith iad e. Chàrd ise peàrd chlòimhe, is chuir i am Fuamhair am broinn na peàirde, is chuir i ann an toll anns a' bhalla e.

* * * * *

An uair a thànaig an latha, an là-'r-na-mhàireach, chaidh Mac Rìgh Lochlainn is Nighean Rìgh Éireann dachaigh, is rinneadh gàirdeachas ro mhór an uair a thànaig iad. Chruinnich am baile air son bean Mhic Rìgh Éireann a chur ri theinidh. Rinn iad teine mór, is chuir iad ann i, is loisg iad i. Phòs Mac Rìgh Lochlainn agus Nighean Rìgh Éireann a chéile an uair sin. Rinn iad banais mhór, aighearach, shunndach, agus fhuair esan leth na rìoghachd air son a sàbhaladh.

NOTES

MS. vol. x., No. 156. Scribe—Hector MacLean.

On the flyleaf of the MS., Islay says—'An Eaglais Uamhalt. Margaret MacKinnon, Rusgary, Berneray. August, 1859. [Received?] February, 1860. A little dog which gets inside a giant, and a King's sister [recte, daughter-in-law] who is leagued with a giant. Compare with Dewar's Three Dogs.'

There is certainly a definite amount of parallelism between No. 156, and No. 159, to which Islay is referring when he speaks of 'Dewar's Three Dogs.' Thus in No. 156, (a) a dog fights on the hero's side against another hero's sister-in-law, (b) the latter is the enemy, and (c) she is leagued with

window of her room.' He went to the window of her room, and
there she was, standing on the floor. They had not been long at
the window when they saw the Giant appearing. 'Oh, you wretch!
you wretch! get out of this house,' cried she, 'seeing that you
have not brought me my fill of the woman I have been feeding
since the year began.' The Giant went away, and brought in
a big red horse. They killed the horse, and ate it. The woman
carded a roll of wool, placed the Giant inside the roll, and put
him in a hole in the wall.

*   *   *   *

When the next day came, the King of Norway's son and the
daughter of the King of Ireland returned home, and great was
the rejoicing when they came. The whole town assembled to
burn the wife of the King of Ireland's son. They made a great
fire, put her in it, and burnt her. Then the King of Norway's
son and the King of Ireland's daughter married. They made a
great, gay, happy wedding, and for saving her life he received
half the kingdom.

two giants. And in No. 159, (a) dogs fight on the hero's side against his sister,
(b) who is the enemy, and (c) who is leagued with a giant.

A 'Poison Maiden' leagued with a giant occurs in No. 53 (MS. vol. x.,
No. 97), and in *Larminie*, p. 155.

The manner of attack practised by the little pup is common to that of
other animals in Gaelic story. See *W. H. Tales*, iii., p. 356 or 375 ; *Waifs
and Strays*, iv., pp. 84, 180-181, 195.

[*Cf.* the saying 'Caithris na h-eaglais uamhalta,' *Journal of Celtic Studies*,
i., p. 110.—A. M.]

EÓGHANN AGUS ALASDAIR

BHA dithis ann, agus bha iad dèonach air dol a mach 'nan ceatharnaich-choille. Chaidh iad an siod do cheàrdaich gobha, agus rinn iad dà chlaidheamh innte ; agus dh'fheumte sgrìobhadh air claidheamh an darna fir gum bu esan aon làmh theòma [1] na Crìosdachd, is air claidheamh an fhir eile, gum bu esan an làmh eile dhiubh. Dh'fhalbh iad an sin air son rud a chothachadh dhaibh fhéin, agus bha iad a' falbh treis gus an do thachair iad a dh'ionnsaigh baile-mhóir an sin ; agus air treis dhaibh a bhith an sin, bha daoine a' mothachainn do na claidheamhan, agus a' leughadh an rud a bha sgrìobhte orra. Agus gu dé [ach] bha fuamhairean ann an gleann, agus iad a' dèanamh móran call air daoine, agus air spréidh ; agus is e an nì a bha ann, gun duirt iad gum bruidhneadh iad riutha seo air son dol a chòmhrag nam fuamhairean, o'n a bha a leithid seo de bheachd aca orra féin, is a leithid seo sgrìobhte air an claidheamhan. Cheannaich urra mhór a bha ann iad gu math air son gun rachadh iad a chòmhrag nam fuamhairean, agus gheall e do dh'Eóghann gum faigheadh e a nighean ri a pòsadh.

Dh'fhalbh iad an sin, agus fhuair iad a h-uile sìon a dh'iarr iad air son fóghnachdainn do na fuamhairean. An uair a rànaig iad far an robh na fuamhairean, bhiodh iad a' dearcadh orra, is theicheadh iad an sin, is cha rachadh 'nan còir. Gu dé thànaig an sin ach [seann] duine [2] far an robh iad, is dh'fhaigh-nich e dhiùbh gu dé an rud a bha iad a' dèanamh an siod, agus dh'innis iad gu saor an ceart rud a bha iad a' dèanamh ann. 'O ! a chiall !' ars esan, 'Nach sibh a bha amaideach a' smuain-teachadh gun cuireadh sibh fhéin ris na fuamhairean. Ach innsidh mise duibh an rud a nì sibh, mas e is gur math leibh an gnothach a chinneachdainn leibh. Bidh iad a' toirt dachaigh

---

[1] *Lit.* the one expert-heroic hand of Christendom. Cf. *Ceud làmh-fheuma na Féinne*, the first need-hand (or support) of the Fenians, a title applied to a Fenian hero. Two champions baptize themselves with new names in Islay's MS. vol. xi., No. 224.

EWAN AND ALASDAIR

No. 72.   [*MS. Vol. x., No. 158*]

THERE were once a couple of men who wanted to set out as
freebooters. Accordingly they went to the forge of a smith,
and had two swords made there. On the sword of one it had
to be written that his was one of the two champion hands of
Christendom,[1] and on the other's sword that his was the other.
They then set out to win themselves something, and they travelled
for a while until they came to a big town ; and when they had
been there for a while, people began to notice the swords and
read what was written on them. Now what should there be in
a certain glen but giants, and they were doing much damage
to men and cattle ; and so what happened was that they [the
people of the place] said that they would speak to these men to
go and fight the giants, seeing that such was their opinion of
themselves and that such was written on their swords. A certain
great man there bribed them well to go and fight the giants,
and he promised Ewan that he should have his daughter in
marriage.

Then they went and got everything needed for overcoming
the giants. But when they had come where the giants were,
they would spy on them and then run away. They would
not go near them. At that point who came up to them but an
[old] man,[2] who asked them what it was they were doing there,
and they told him freely just what they were doing. 'Oh, dear !'
said he, 'how silly of you to suppose that you could tackle the
giants yourselves. But I will tell you what you must do, if you
want to succeed. Every week the giants take a cow home ;
they never shut the door of the cave where they live. If you
could manage to get in through the door of the cave and hide

---

[2] Possibly a ghost, or other supernatural. He is afterwards referred to as a
bodach or old man, a word applied to many weird creatures.

mairt anns an t-seachdain ; is cha bhi iad a' dùnadh dorus na
h-uamha anns am bheil iad idir ; agus nam biodh sibh-se is
gum faigheadh sibh a staigh air an dorus an oidhche a bhios
iad a' cùnntas, agus dol an cùil, agus an uair a chì sibh an teas
a' chùnntais iad, nam buaileadh sibh clach air fear aca,
dh'fhaoidte gun dèanadh iad fhéin an gnothach, is gum faigheadh
sibh a mach gu dé bhiodh eatorra.   Chan innis mise m'ainm
duibh, is dòch gun coinnich mi fhathast sibh ; ach is dòch gun
téid an gnothach leibh ; agus ma théid iad thar a chéile, tuitidh
iad bonn ri bonn,[1] is chan 'eil ach na cinn a chur dhiùbh ; ach
is doirbhe an cumail dhiùbh an déidh an cur dhiùbh, ach
cumaibh o na colainnean iad gus an reòdh an fhuil.   Dealaichidh
mise ruibh an dràsd.'

Dh'fhalbh iad-san, agus bha iad a' faire orra gus am faca
iad mart aca 'ga toirt dachaigh.   Dh'fhalbh iad an sin, agus
bha iad a' fuireach goirid o'n uamha.   [Agus an uair a chunnaig
iad an t-am, chaidh iad a staigh air dorus na h-uamha air am
màgan, agus chaidh gach fear dhiùbh ann an cùil leis fhéin.]
An uair a chunnaig na fuamhairean am mart air dòigh, is a
thòisich iad air cùnntas, bha beagan a' tighinn eatorra, is bhuail
iad air cruaidh-dheasbaireachd mu'n rud a bha tighinn eatorra ;
agus dh'fhalbh am fear a bha 'sa' chùil, an uair a chuala e a
h-aon diùbh ag ràdh gum bu cho math leis a bhith marbh agus
e a dhèanamh siod air, tharraing e clach is bhuail e air an
fhuamhair eile an clàr an aodainn i.   Dh'éirich na fuamhairean
air a chéile.   Ghrad bhuail am fuamhair a bhuaileadh am
fuamhair eile, agus bha iad ag obair air a chéile gus an do
thuit iad bonn ri bonn.   Ghabh Eóghann chun fir, is Alasdair
chun fir eile, is chuir iad na cinn diùbh ; is bha iad a' cumail
nan ceann o na colainnean gus an d'fhuaraich an fhuil.   Cheangail iad na cinn, agus thug iad leò iad, is na fhuair iad de
dh'ionndas anns an uaimh, thug iad leò e.

Dh'fhalbh iad dachaigh leis na cinn a dh'ionnsaigh an urra
mhóir [2] a bha an sin.   An uair a rànaig iad an duine mór, fhuair
iad an seo cliù, gun robh iad 'nan daoine foghainteach, gum
b'fhìor an rud a bha air a sgrìobhadh air an claidheamhan ;

---

[1] [*bonn ri bonn*, lit. 'sole to sole ', cf. *The Songs of Duncan Bàn Macintyre*, 5830 *n* ;
Duanaire Finn, Glossary, s.v. ; T.B.C.[2] 1996, *co torchratar bond fri bond.*—A. M.]

[2] *urra* is masculine here : feminine previously.

in a corner on the night that they are reckoning up accounts ; and when you see that they are wrangling hotly, if you could hit one of them with a stone, perhaps they themselves would do the job, and you would be able to discover what they had been quarrelling about. I will not tell you my name ; perhaps I shall meet you again ; but it is probable that you will succeed. If the giants fall out with each other, they will drop down side by side,[1] and then there is nothing to do but to cut off their heads ; but it is more difficult to keep the heads apart from their bodies after they have been cut off. But keep them apart until the blood freezes. I will leave you now.'

Off they went, and they watched until they saw that the giants had got a cow and were taking it home. Then they went and waited a little distance from the cave. [And when they saw their opportunity, they crept in on all fours through the door of the cave, and each of them went into a corner by himself.] When the giants had seen to the cow and got it ready, and had begun to go into accounts, there was a slight disagreement between them and they began to dispute fiercely about it ; and the man who was hiding in a corner, when he heard one of them say that he would as soon be dead as that the other should treat him as he had, hurled a stone and hit the second giant right in the face with it. The giants sprang at each other. The giant who had been hit instantly struck the other, and they belaboured each other until they fell down side by side. Ewan went over to one of them and Alasdair went over to the other, and they cut off their heads ; and they kept the heads from the bodies until the blood got cold. They tied the heads up and took them away with them, and all the treasure they found in the cave they carried away.

They went home with the heads to the great man, and when they came to him they became renowned as being doughty fellows ; what was written on their swords was true, people said, and they should get the girl—but there was no knowing

is gum faigheadh iad an nighean, ach nach robh fios có am fear
aca a gheibheadh i. Ach thuirt an Rìgh gun dèanadh esan siod
a riarachadh glé mhath ; gun robh dà nighinn aige-san ; agus
gun robh torc-nimhe air a' ghleann ; agus nam marbhadh iad
an torc, gum faigheadh iad té an t-aon. Dh'fhalbh iad, is fhuair
iad na leòr de gach nì dh'fheumadh iad leò ; is bha barail mhath
aig a h-uile duine orra, gum biodh iad furachail, feuch am
faiceadh iad an torc ; ach bha eagal na leòr orra-san, gun
cailleadh iad am beatha. Thachair an [seann] duine a bha an
siod orra glé ghoirid o'n àite 'san do thachair e orra roimhid.
'Tha sibh fo eagal nach cinn bhur gnothach leibh, ged a ghabh
sibh os làimh tighinn ann,' ars esan ; 'ma nì sibh mar a dh'iarras
mise oirbh, dh'fhaoidte gun tuiteadh an torc leibh fhathast.
Théid sibh glé theann air a màireach, agus an uair a mhoth-
aicheas e dhuibh, falbhaidh [e] as bhur déidh, agus tha craobh
mhór an siod, agus nì sibh air a' chraoibh, agus théid sibh a
mullach na craoibhe. Agus thig esan a dh'ionnsaigh na craoibhe,
is cuiridh e a' chraobh air chrith cho cruaidh, a' cruaidh-spàirn
rithe gus am bi e air a shàrachadh. Tuiteadh an dara fear
agaibh air a mhuin, agus beireadh e air dhà chluais air, agus
biodh am fear eile falbh as a dhéidh, agus gabhaidh [sibh]
dhachaigh dìreach chun a' bhaile.' 'O ! cha dèan sinne sin
gu bràth,' ars iad-san. 'Gu dé an rud a nì sibh ma mharbhas
e sibh ?' ars am bodach ; 'mur dèan sibh siod, cha bhi stuth
agaibh air son na rinn sibh a cheana, is cha bhi meas agaibh
air a shon. Ach théid mise an urras gun dèan sibh an gnothach
mar siod, is chan iarrainn oirbh e, mur am bithinn cinnteach
gun cinneadh e leibh. Chan 'eil agaibh ach cuimhneachadh
orm-sa oidhche nam bainnsean.' Dh' fhalbh iad-san, agus
dhealaich am bodach riutha.

Chum iad air an ádhart gus an àite a dh'ainmich an duine
dhaibh. An là-'r-na-mhàireach, thànaig iad dlùth air an torc.
An uair a mhothaich esan daibh, dh'fhalbh e as an déidh.
Smuaintich iad-san mar a thuirt am bodach riu, is chum iad
air a' chraoibh, is dhìrich iad anns a' chraoibh, agus rànaig
esan a' chraobh an seo, is am Moire fhéin ! b'fheàrr leotha-san
na nì sam bith a bhi cuibht is e. Bhuail esan air sàbhadh na
craoibhe, is bha iad-san a' greimeachadh ris a' chraoibh. An
seo, an uair a smuaintich iad air cainnt an t-seann duine, is a

which of them was to have her. The King said, however, that he would settle that nicely ; that he had two daughters ; that there was a venomous boar in the glen ; and that if they would kill the boar, they should have a daughter each. The men went and got plenty of everything that they needed to take with them. Everybody had a good opinion of them, that they would be on the alert and would try to see the boar ; but the men themselves were frightened enough that they would lose their lives. But the [old] man mentioned earlier met them a very short distance from the place where he had met them before. 'You fear that you will not succeed in your business, though you undertook to attempt it,' said he, 'but if you do as I tell you, perhaps the boar will be killed by you yet. Tomorrow you must get close up to him, and when he notices you, he will go after you. There is a great tree there, and you must make for that tree and climb up into the topmost part of it. The boar will come up to the tree and he will make it shake fiercely, struggling hard with it until he is exhausted. Then let one of you drop on his back and seize him by the ears, and let the other follow after, and make for home, straight to the town.' 'O ! we shall never do that,' said they. 'And what will you do if he kills you ?' said the old man ; 'unless you do that, all that you have done before will go for nothing, nor will you be respected for it. But I guarantee that you will accomplish the task that way, and I would not have asked you to do it were I not certain that you would succeed. All you have to do is to remember me on the night of the weddings.' They set off, and the old man parted from them.

They pressed onward to the place he mentioned. Next day, they got quite close up to the boar. When the boar became aware of them, he went after them. They recollected what the old man had said to them, and they made for the tree and climbed up into it. And then the boar came up to the tree, and by Mary herself ! they would have preferred being quit of him to anything. The boar began to saw through the tree, and they were holding on to it tightly. At this point, they thought of the words of the old man, and so when the boar was getting

bha an torc a' teannadh riu, is e a' snìomh na craoibhe gus an
robh i chun tighinn gu talamh,[1] thuit fear aca air a mhuin, có
dhiùbh is ann a dheòin no a dh'aindeoin, agus rug e air dhà
chluais air. Dh'fhalbh an torc is an darna fear air a mhuin, is
am fear eile as a dhéidh, agus lean iad dachaigh, 's an uair a
chunnaig muinntir an àite iad a' tighinn dachaigh leis an torc
beò, dh'aithnich iad a nis gum bu cheatharnaich iad có dhiùbh.
Mharbh iad an torc, an uair a bha e air toirt thairis. Phòs iad
fhéin agus nigheanan an Rìgh, agus rinneadh banais shunndach
dhaibh.

> From Donald MacKillop, Rusgary, Berneray, who learnt it from Angus
> McLeod, ditto. McLeod died about two years ago at a very
> advanced age, ninety years or over ; MacKillop cannot be under
> sixty.

[1] See No. 73, for the incident of pigs tearing down a tree. Cats tear down a
tree in which a hero has taken refuge in *W. H. Tales*, i., p. 108 or 110. To save
himself from being dragged down a river by a bogle, a man clings to a tree, the
last root of which is breaking when the crow of a cock saves him ; *ibid.*, ii., p. 83
or 93. To dream of black pigs boring or tunnelling their way under the key-stone
of the house where the dreamer is, is a presage of being besieged there ; Alexander
MacDonald, *Story and Song from Loch Ness-side*, p. 278 (Inverness, 1914).

NOTES

MS. vol. x., No. 158. Scribe, Hector MacLean.

In his Gaelic List, Islay speaks of this tale as 'certainly old.' On the
flyleaf of the MS. he has written 'Eoghan agus Alasdair. Donald MacKillop,
Berneray—Aug[ust 18]59. I.P.T. [?] Feb[ruar]y [18]60. The Valiant
Tailor, Grimm. Mr MacLauchlan's Boar in the oak tree. Compare 125.'[1]

In his Gaelic List, he writes of No. 125 thus :—'125. Bodach na craoibhe
móire [= the old man of the great tree]. Donald MacLean, Edinburgh.
Mr MacLauchlan. Returned. A mystical old man found in a vast tree—
let out by king's son—adventures—horse, boar, unicorn.' It is to this latter
tale, No. 125, that Islay is probably referring, when he says (*W. H. Tales*,
i., *intro.* xcii. or lxxiv.), 'So oak trees are mythical. Whenever a man is to be
burned for some evil deed, and men [recte, women] are always going to be
roasted, faggots of "grey", probably green oak, are fetched. There is a curious
story which the Rev. Mr MacLauchlan took down from the recitation of an
old man in Edinburgh, in which a mythical old man is shut up in an oak
tree, which grows in the court of the King's palace ; and when the king's
son lets his ball roll into a split in the tree by chance, the old man tells the

[1] A valiant tailor and giants appear in 'The Tailor and the Three Beasts,'
Dr D. Hyde, *Beside the Fire*, pp. 1, 175. A valiant but insignificant looking man
defeats giants, *Waifs and Strays*, iv., p. 242.

nearer and nearer to them and twisting the tree till it was about to fall to earth,[1] one of them, whether intentionally or not, dropped on the boar's back and seized him by his ears. Away went the boar, one of the men on his back and the other following him, and in this way they held homewards. And when the people of the place saw them coming home with the boar alive, they knew then that they were champions for a certainty. They and the King's daughters got married, and a merry wedding was made for them.

boy to fetch an axe and he will give him the ball, and so he gets out, and endows the Prince with power and valour. He [the Prince] sets out on his journey with a red-headed cook, who personates him, and he goes to lodge with a swine-herd ; but by the help of the old man of the great tree, Bodach na cr[a]oibhe moire, he overcomes a boar, a bull, and a stallion, and marries the king's daughter, and the red-headed [2] cook is burnt.'

The following (MS. No. 330), is to be found at the end of the MS. vol. xi., occurring just before No. 353. It is clearly a close translation from Gaelic, but is unfortunately only a fragment. It may be part of a tale related to Nos. 125 and 158.

'There was a great tree in the town of the King of Eirinn, and it was of great age. The King of Eirinn wished that it should be cut, but he was not finding any men who would take in hand the work of cutting it. At last, he found two who said that [they] would begin upon her (the tree). They took with them their set of axes, and they betook themselves to the tree. They spent a day and a year before the one heard the strokes of the other, working at her. On the one side of the tree stood one of the men, and he saw that they were making a hole in her, that there was "còs" [= a hollow], in the inside. He made the width of the mouth of a milking pail of a hole in her. He peeped in to see if he could see anything within ; what should he see there but a big, big Bodach, and a purse dangling at each hair in his beard. The man leaped back, and he ran to his comrade. They went and they peeped at him together. They ran to the king, and the king came himself to the tree.'

Here the MS. ends. I transcribed it in 1911, and checked it again in May 1924, but though I searched, could not find any more of it. The number 330 has also been given to 'Bàs Choirreil,' MS. vol. viii.

In MS. vol. xi., No. 224, occurs a cauldron so large that the workmen making it did not hear each other's strokes for a year.

[2] A red-haired cook is the enemy in many tales ; he usually impersonates the hero, and tries to get for himself the credit due to the hero. See *The Celtic Dragon Myth*, xlvii.

TRÌ COIN NAN SREANG UAINE

No. 73.   [*MS. Vol. x., No. 159*]

BHA uaireigin Rìgh agus Banrìgh ann, agus bha mac is nighean
aca. Shiubhail a' Bhanrìgh, agus aig ceann na h-uibhir de
bhliadhnaibh, phòs an Rìgh té eile, is bha a' bhean mu dheireadh
ro dhona ri clann na ceud mnatha.[1] Smaointich iad-san gun
rachadh iad a dh'iarraidh an fhortain, agus thug Mac an Rìgh
leis a bhogha is a dhòrlach, agus thug Nighean an Rìgh leatha
trì uirceanan maola, buidhe a bha aice. Agus dh'fhalbh an
dithis còmhla. Agus air dhoibh a bhith dol troimh mhonadh,
thànaig iad a dh'ionnsaigh bothain àirigh, agus chaidh iad a
staigh ann, agus dh'fhuirich iad an sin car tamaill, is bha esan
a' dèanamh seilge, is bha ise a' fanail dlùth air a' bhothan ; is
dhèanadh i deas an t-sidheann, is bheireadh i an aire air na
h-uirceanan.

Dh'éirich esan moch maduinn a bha an sin, is chaidh e a
mach, agus chunnaig e fear a' tighinn rathad an taighe, agus
bha cù brèagha aige, agus sreang uaine mu a mhuineal. Thuirt
Mac an Rìgh ris, 'Is brèagha an cù sin a th'agad !' 'Seadh !
An ceannaich thu e ?' 'Chan 'eil dad agam a bheirinn duit air
a shon.' Thuirt am fear eile, is e cumail a mheòir ris na h-
uirceanan, 'Thoir [dhomh] aon de na h-uirceanan sin.' 'Chan
fhaod mi : is le mo phiuthair iad.' 'Théid mi fhéin an urras
air do phiuthair.' Agus chreic Mac an Rìgh aon de uirceanan
a pheathar air son a' choin. Chaidh e a staigh leis a' chù, agus
thuirt e ri a phiuthair, 'Nach brèagha an cù a fhuair mi an seo !'
Agus thuirt ise, 'Seadh. Gu dé thug thu air a' chù sin ?' 'Thug
aon de na h-uirceanan agad-sa.' 'Na h-uirc is na h-ùraindean
ort ! Cha bu chòir dhuit m'uircean-sa a thoirt seachad, cha
b'e do chuid a bh'ann.' Agus thuirt esan, 'Gheibh mi a fhiach
le sealgaireachd.' Agus chaidh e a shealg an latha sin, agus
rinn an cù gu ro mhath.

Dh'éirich e moch an ath-latha, agus chunnaig e am fear

[1] MS. bhean.

THE THREE HOUNDS WITH THE GREEN STRINGS

No. 73.   *[MS. Vol. x., No. 159]*

THERE were once a King and a Queen who had a son and a daughter. The Queen died, and at the end of a number of years the King married another wife ; but this last wife was very unkind to the children of the first. The children determined to go and seek their fortune ; the King's Son took with him his bow and quiver, and the King's Daughter took with her three tawny-yellow crop-eared little pigs that she had. And off they went together, the two of them. As they were going across a moor, they came to a sheiling and went inside, and there they lived for a time. He used to go hunting while she stayed at home or near the bothy, preparing the venison and attending to the little pigs.

Early one morning he got up, and going out, saw a man coming towards the house, who had with him a fine hound with a green string about its neck. 'A fine hound you have there !' said the King's Son to him. 'Yes ! will you buy it ?' I have nothing to give you for it.' But the other, pointing to the young pigs, said, 'Give [me] one of those little pigs.' 'I can't do that : they are my sister's.' 'I will vouch for it that your sister will not mind.' And so the King's Son bartered one of his sister's little pigs for the hound. He went into the house with the hound and said to his sister, 'Is this not a fine hound that I have got here !' 'Yes,' she said ; 'what did you give for that hound ?' 'One of those little pigs of yours,' said he. 'Wild pigs and monsters come at you ! You had no right to give my little pig away ; it was none of yours.' 'I shall recover its value by hunting,' he replied. That day he went hunting, and the hound did exceedingly well.

Next day he rose early and saw the same man he had seen

ceudna a chunnaig e an latha roimhe, agus bha cù eile aige,
agus sreang uaine mu a mhuineal. Thuirt Mac an Rìgh ris,
'Is brèagha an cù sin a tha agad !' 'Seadh ! An ceannaich
thu e ?' 'Chan 'eil stuth agam gu a thoirt air a shon.' 'Nach
toir thu dhomh a h-aon eile de na h-uirceanan ?' 'Chan fhaod
mi ; is le mo phiuthair iad.' 'Théid mi fhéin an urras air do
phiuthair.' Agus thug Mac an Rìgh a h-aon eile de uirceanan
a pheathar air son coin eile. [Chaidh e a staigh leis a' chù,
agus thuirt e ri a phiuthar, 'Nach brèagha an cù a fhuair mi an
seo !' Agus thuirt ise, 'Seadh. Gu dé thug thu air a' chù sin ?'
'Thug a h-aon de na h-uirceanan agad-sa.'] 'Na h-uirc is na
h-ùraindean ort ; creachaidh tu mi le bhith toirt seachad mo
chuid mar sin : fàgaidh tu falamh mi.' Agus thuirt esan,
'Chan eagal a ceannaich duit, is mi féin leat ; gheibh sinn sealg
na's fheàrr.' Chaidh e ris a' bheinn an latha sin, is rinn an
dà chù sealg mhath dha ; is tràth thànaig e dhachaigh, mhol
e na coin !

Air dha éirigh moch a màireach, chunnaig e am fear ceudna
tighinn, agus cù eile aige, agus sreang uaine mu a mhuineal.
'An ceannaich thu an cù seo ?' ['Chan 'eil dad agam a bheirinn
duit air a shon.' 'Nach toir thu dhomh a h-aon eile de na
h-uirceanan ?' 'Chan fhaod mi ; is le mo phiuthair iad.'
'Théid mi fhéin an urras air do phiuthair.' Agus thug Mac an
Rìgh a h-aon eile de uirceanan a pheathar air son coin eile.
Chaidh e a staigh leis a' chù, agus thuirt e ri a phiuthair, 'Nach
brèagha an cù a fhuair mi an seo !' Agus thuirt ise, 'Seadh.
Gu dé thug thu air a' chù sin ?' 'Thug a h-aon de na h-uirceanan
agad-sa.'] 'Na h-uirc is na h-ùraindean ort ! Tha thu air mo
chreachadh a nise !' 'Chan eagal duit : bidh mi féin daonnan
còmhla riut : agus gheibh mi gu leòr de sheilg leis na trì coin a
bhith agam.' Chaidh e a shealg an latha sin, agus fhuair e gu
leòr de shidheann ann an tiota. Thànaig e dhachaigh, is dh'innis
e do a phiuthair an t-sealg mhór a rinn e ann an ùine cho goirid ;
ach b'fheàrr le a phiuthair a trì uirceanan a bhith aice.

An ath-mhaduinn, chaidh e a mach, agus chunnaig e am
fear ceudna a rithist ; agus thuirt e ri Mac an Rìgh, ma bha e
gabhail aithreachais gum faigheadh e na h-uirceanan air an
ais air son nan con a rithist. Thuirt Mac an Rìgh nach robh e
gabhail an aithreachais. Thuirt am fear eile, 'Cha mhisde thu

the day before, and with him he had another hound with a green string round its neck. 'A fine hound you have there !' said the King's Son to him. 'Yes ! will you buy it ?' 'I have nothing to give you for it.' 'Will you not give me another one of the little pigs ?' 'I can't do that ; they are my sister's.' 'I will vouch for your sister.' And so the King's Son gave another of his sister's little pigs away in exchange for another hound. [He went into the house with the hound and said to his sister, 'Is this not a fine hound that I have got ?' 'Yes,' said she ; 'what did you give for that hound ?' 'One of those little pigs of yours.'] 'Wild pigs and monsters come at you ! You will ruin me, giving away my belongings in that fashion ; you'll leave me destitute.' But he replied, 'There is no fear of not being able to buy it back, since I am with you ; we shall get better hunting.' That day he went to the hill and the hounds hunted well for him ; and how he praised them, when he came home !

Next day, having risen early, he saw the same man coming, and with him still another hound with a green string about its neck. 'Will you buy this hound ?' ['I have nothing to give you for it.' 'Will you not give me another one of the little pigs ?' 'I can't do that : they are my sister's.' 'I will vouch for your sister.' And so the King's Son bartered another of his sister's little pigs for another hound. On entering the house with the hound, he said to his sister, 'See what a fine hound I have got here !' 'Yes,' she said, 'what did you give for it ?' 'Why, one of those little pigs of yours.'] 'Wild pigs and monsters come at you ! Now you have ruined me !' 'Don't worry, I shall always be with you ; and I shall get plenty of game through having the three hounds.' He went hunting that day, and in a very short time he got plenty of venison. When he came home, he told his sister what a great hunting he had had, and in how short a time ; but his sister would rather have had her three little pigs.

The next morning he went out and saw the same man again ; and the man said to the King's Son, that if he regretted the bargain, he should have the little pigs back again in exchange for the hounds. The King's Son said that he had no regrets. Then said the other, 'You will be none the worse of knowing fios a bhith agad air na h-ainmeannan aca.' [1] 'Cha mhisde,' thuirt Mac an Rìgh. Thuirt am fear eile, 'Is e ainm a' cheud choin a fhuair thu, Fios : bithidh fios aige daonnan c'àite am bi an t-sidheann, agus bheir e dhuit rabhadh, ma bhitheas cunnart dlùth dhuit. Is e ainm an ath-choin a fhuair thu bhuam, Luath ; beiridh e air gach sidhinn ris an téid e, is nam bitheadh tu ann an gàbhadh, is e an ceud aon a thigeadh a dhèanamh cobhair ort. Is e ainm an fhir mu dheireadh a fhuair thu, Trom ; tha e làidir, agus math a chum caonnaig, nan tachradh dhuit a bhith an éiginn.' Dhealaich iad mar sin. Thug Mac agus Nighean an Rìgh greis anns a' bhothan àirigh, is iad a' tighinn beò air sidhinn.

Là bha an siod, is e tighinn dachaigh as a' bheinn-sheilge, rinn e suidhe air meallan buidhe a bha os cionn an taighe. Leig Fios osna mhór as. 'Gu dé fàth t'osna, a Fhios ?' 'Tha Famhair air ceannach nan uirceanan a bha aig do phiuthair, agus tha e toileach nam faigheadh e na coin agad-sa. Mur toir thu aire air do phiuthair, bheir am Famhair leis i.' 'Ciod e an dòigh air a gleidheadh ?' Thuirt Fios nach b'aithne dha dòigh air bhith a b'fheàrr na na h-uile nì a bhiodh feumail di a bhith aice làimh rithe, oir 's nach ruigeadh i a leas dol o'n taigh. An ath-latha, mun deach Mac an Rìgh do'n bheinn-sheilg, dh'fhàg e a h-uile nì bhiodh feumail do a phiuthair làimh rithe, agus thug e òrdugh dhi, i a ghleidheadh [2] a cinn cìrte is an taigh sguaibte, agus i a shealltainn nach leigeadh i ma-thìr [3] an gealbhan, agus b'e sin na bha aice ri dhèanamh. Dh'fhalbh e ris a' bheinn, agus an tìm a bha ise a' cìreadh a cinn is a' sguabadh an taighe, leig i ma-thìr an gealbhan ; agus dh'fhalbh i cho luath 's a b'urrainn di, a shealltainn am faigheadh i beothachadh a' ghealbhain an àite air bith eile.

Air dhi a bhith dol tre chreagan, choinnich famhair oirre, is e 'na chadal ; bha éibhleag theine aige, agus, an uair a bhiodh e a' cur a mach a analach, shéideadh e an éibhleag a mach seachd slatan uaidh, agus an uair a bhiodh e a' tarraing a staigh a analach, bheireadh e a staigh gu taobh a bheòil i. Sheas

---

[1] Telling the hero the names of the hounds was equivalent to giving him magic powers over them. The green strings (in other versions, leashes) probably had a similar effect.

[2] From what is known of superstitions regarding the combing of the hair, and

their names.' [1] 'That is true,' said the King's Son. Then said the other, 'The name of the hound you had first is Knowledge ; for he will always know where the quarry is, and besides he will give you warning if danger is near you. The name of the next hound you had from me is Swift ; he will catch any quarry to which he gives chase, and if you were in any peril, he would be the first to come to your rescue. The name of the last hound you got is Weighty ; he is strong, and good in a tussle, if you happened to be in distress.' And thus they parted. For a while the King's Son and Daughter stayed in the sheiling-hut and lived on venison.

One day as he was coming home from the hunting-hill, he sat down on a sunny little hillock that was above the house. Knowledge sighed heavily. 'Why do you sigh, Knowledge ?' 'A Giant has bought the little pigs your sister had and he would like to get your hounds too. Unless you look after your sister, the Giant will steal her away.' 'How can she be kept safe ?' Knowledge replied that he knew of no better way than to let her have everything she might want placed conveniently near her, so that she should not need to leave the house. Next day, before the King's Son went to the hunting-hill, he left everything his sister might want within reach and handy, and he ordered her to keep her hair combed [2] and the house swept, and to see that she did not let the fire out, and that was all she had to do. He set out for the hill, but while his sister was combing her hair and sweeping the house, she let the fire go out. Away she went as quickly as ever she could, to see if she could find anywhere at all something to kindle the fire with.

While she was passing through a place strewn with rocks, she came across a sleeping giant. He had a fiery ember, and when he breathed out, he would blow the ember seven yards from him, and when he breathed in, he would suck the ember back to his mouth. For a while the King's Daughter stood

from other versions, the orders the hero would most probably have given, would have been, *not* to comb her hair while he was out.

[3] *ma-thìr* : so in MS. A footnote referring to it, says, 'not to let the fire out' : compare, *leig mu làr*, to let down or let drop on the ground.

Nighean an Rìgh tacan beag a' sealltainn air, ach mu dheireadh thug i leatha an éibhleag, is ruith i air falbh leatha. Dhùisg am Famhair, agus mhothaich e gun robh an éibhleag air a toirt air falbh. Dh'éirich e, is ruith e as a déidh, agus fhuair e greim oirre, an uair a bha i dol a staigh air an dorus. Chaidh e a staigh leatha, agus dh'iarr ise cead an éibhleag a ghleidheadh, gu dé air bith a bheireadh i dha air a son. Is e sin a bha am Famhair ag iarraidh ; dh'innis e dhi gun do cheannaich e na trì uirceanan a bha aice, is gum faigheadh i fhéin air an ais a rithist iad, is gun dìonadh iad bho gach cunnart i, agus gun cuireadh iad as do a bràthair, agus gum faigheadh iad na trì coin, is gum biodh iad sona dheth. Rinn iad suas e, 's chuir am Famhair gath-nimhe os cionn an doruis, agus tràth bhiodh a bràthair gu tighinn a staigh, bha an gath gu tuiteam air, is gu a mharbhadh. Rinn iad toll sìos anns an uaimh, agus chaidh am Famhair sìos anns an toll, is chòmhdaich ise thairis air.

An uair a bha a bràthair a' tighinn dachaigh as a' bheinn-sheilge, shuidh e air torran buidhe a bha os cionn an taighe. Rinn Fios osna mhór. 'Gu dé fàth t'osna, a Fhios ?' 'Tha, gun do leig do phiuthar ma-thìr an gealbhan, agus tràth bha i dol a dh'iarraidh gealbhain, choinnich am Famhair oirre, is e séideadh éibhleig theine bhuaidh is dh'a ionnsaigh le a anail ; is thug ise leatha an éibhleag, is lean am Famhair i, is fhuair e greim oirre aig an dorus, agus thànaig iad gu cainnt ri chéile, agus tha iad air dèanamh cùmhnant ri chéile, is tha iad a los thusa a mharbhadh. Tha am Famhair air gath-nimhe a chur os cionn an doruis, a tha gu tuiteam ort, mas tu a théid a staigh air an dorus an toiseach.' 'Gu dé a nì sinn, ma thà ?' 'Nì, Luath a chur a staigh an toiseach, agus ma théid e a staigh cho luath is as urrainn e, bidh e seachad mum bi ùine aig a' ghath tuiteam, agus cha téid ach bàrr an earbaill a thoirt dheth. Tha am Fuamhair ann an toll fo'n uaimh aig taobh an teine, is an uair a thig thusa a staigh, cuir air an coire sidhinn is tràth bhios e deas, thoir as cnàimh, is tilg d'ar n-ionnsaigh e, agus nì sinn caonnag mu'n chnàimh, dòirtidh sinn an coire, a sheall[tainn] an téid againn air an Fhamhair a sgàldadh gu bàs.'

Chaidh Luath a chur a staigh an toiseach. Thuit an gath-nimhe, agus bha Luath seachad uile ach bàrr an earbaill, is looking at him, but at last she took the ember and ran off with it. The Giant woke up and noticed that the ember had been taken away. Up he got and ran after her, and caught hold of her just as she was going in at the door. He went inside with her, and she asked if she might keep the ember, no matter what she would have to give him in exchange for it. That was just what the Giant wanted ; he told her he had bought the three little pigs she used to have, and that she might have them back again, and that they would protect her from every danger ; that they would kill her brother, and that they would then get the three hounds, and be happy. They hatched the plot together, and the Giant placed a poisoned dart above the door, so that when her brother should be coming in the dart was to fall on him and kill him. And down underneath the cave they made a hole, and the Giant went down into the hole, and she covered him over.

*   *   *   *

When her brother was coming home from the hunting-hill, he sat down on the sunny little hillock above the house. Knowledge sighed heavily. 'Why do you sigh, Knowledge ?' 'Why, because your sister has let the fire out, and when she went to get something to kindle it with, she came across a Giant who was blowing a fiery ember to and fro with his breath ; she took the ember away with her, but the Giant followed her, and caught hold of her at the door. And they began to talk to each other, and they have made an agreement between them, and intend to kill you. The Giant has placed a poisoned dart above the door, which is to fall on you if you are the first to enter.' 'What then shall we do ?' 'We shall do this : we shall send Swift in first, and if he goes in as fast as he can, he will have gone past before the dart has time to fall, and so only the tip of his tail will be taken off. The Giant is in a hole under the cave, at the side where the fire is. When you go in, put on the cauldron for the venison, and when it is ready, take out a bone, and throw it to us ; then we will fight for the bone, and upset the cauldron ; and we'll see if we can manage to scald the Giant to death.'

So Swift was sent in first. The poisoned dart did fall, but Swift had already got completely past, all but the tip of his tail, thug an gath-nimhe bàrr an earbaill dheth. Chaidh an gath seachd slatan anns an talamh. Thànaig Mac an Rìgh is a dhà chù a staigh. Chuir e an coire sidhinn air an teinidh. An uair a bha an t-sidheann deas, thug e bhàrr an teine i, is thug e as cnàimh, is thilg e siod a dh'ionnsaigh nan con. Rinn na coin caonnag mu'n chnàimh, dhòirt iad an coire, agus leig am Famhair raoic as. Dh'fharraid Mac an Rìgh de a phiuthair, 'Gu dé an raoic a tha an sin?' Thuirt ise, 'Tha an talamh a' fosgladh leis a' bhùrn ghoileach a dhol air.'

An ath-latha, chaidh Mac an Rìgh 's a chuid chon do'n bheinn-sheilg. Thànaig am Famhair a nìos as an toll, agus chuir Nighean an Rìgh an òrdugh e, agus chuir am Famhair an gath-nimhe os cionn an doruis, mar a bha e roimhe. An uair a bha Mac an Rìgh a' tighinn dachaigh, chaidh am Famhair sìos a rithist do'n toll a bha anns an uaimh, agus chòmhdaich ise os a chionn. An uair a bha Mac an Rìgh a' tighinn a nuas as a' bheinn, rinn e suidhe air torran buidhe a bha am bràigh an taighe. Leig Fios osna mhór. 'Gu dé fàth t'osna, a Fhios?' 'Tha,' arsa Fios, 'chan 'eil am Famhair marbh fhathast; tha e air a' ghath-nimhe a chur os cionn an doruis mar a rinn e roimhe, is tha e féin ann an toll fo'n ùrlar aig taobh clì an teine.' 'Gu dé mar a nì sinn?' 'Nì, mar a rinn sinn roimhe,' arsa Fios; 'Luath a chur a staigh an toiseach, 's cha dèan e ach crioman beag de bhàrr a earbaill a chall le tuiteam a' ghath-nimhe, is théid sinne a staigh ri a shàil, is cuir thusa air an coire sidhinn, agus tràth bhios an t-sidheann deas, thoir thusa dheth an coire, is leag sìos os cionn an Fhamhair e, is thoir cnàimh as a' choire, is tilg d'ar n-ionnsaigh-ne e, is nì sinne caonnag mu'n chnàimh, agus dòirtidh sinn an coire air an Fhamhair a dh'fheuchainn am marbh sinn e.'

[Chaidh Luath a chur a staigh an toiseach, agus ruith e cho luath is a b'urrainn da; thuit an gath-nimhe, ach bha Luath seachad, is cha do rinn an gath-nimhe ach bàrr an earbaill a thoirt deth. Chaidh Mac an Rìgh is a dhà chù eile a staigh ri a shàil. Cha do ghabh e air gun robh fios aige air nì sam bith mu dheighinn an Fhamhair a bhith a staigh, agus chuir e an coire sidhinn air an teine, agus an uair a bha an t-sidheann deas, thug e dheth an coire, is leag e air an làr e dìreach os cionn far an robh am Famhair.] Thug e cnàimh as a' choire, agus and the poisoned dart took off the tip. The dart itself sank seven yards into the earth. Then in came the King's Son and his two hounds. He put the cauldron for the venison on the fire. When the venison was ready, he took it off the fire and took out a bone which he threw to the hounds. The hounds fought over the bone and upset the cauldron, and the Giant gave a roar. The King's Son asked his sister, 'What was that roar?' 'The earth is opening because of the boiling water falling on it,' said she.

The next day when the King's Son and his hounds had gone to the hunting-hill, the Giant came up out of the hole, and after the King's Daughter had attended to him, he placed the poisoned dart above the door as it had been before. When the King's Son was coming home, the Giant went down again into the hole in the cave, and she covered him over. When he was coming down from the hill, the King's Son seated himself on the sunny hillock above the house. Knowledge sighed heavily. 'What makes you sigh, Knowledge?' 'Why,' said Knowledge, 'the Giant is not dead yet; he has put the poisoned dart above the door, as he did before, and he himself is in a hole under the floor, at the left side of the fire.' 'What shall we do?' 'We'll do as we did before,' said Knowledge; 'we'll send Swift in first; he will only lose a very little piece of the tip of his tail when the poisoned dart falls. We'll go in at his heels, and you put on the cauldron for the venison and when the venison is ready, take off the cauldron, and set it down just above the place where the Giant is. Then take out a bone and throw it to us. We will fight for the bone and upset the cauldron over the Giant, and see if we can kill him.'

[So Swift was sent in first, and in he ran as swiftly as he could; the poisoned dart fell, but Swift had already got past, and so the poisoned dart did nothing but take off the tip of his tail. In at Swift's heels went the King's Son with his other two hounds. He did not let on that he knew anything about the Giant's being in the place, but he put the cauldron for the venison on the fire, and when the venison was ready, he took off the cauldron and set it on the ground just over where the Giant was.] Then, taking a bone out of the cauldron, he threw it to the hounds,

thilg e an cnàimh a dh'ionnsaigh nan con, agus thòisich na coin
air caonnaig mu'n chnàimh, agus dhòirt iad an coire de bhùrn
goileach air an Fhamhair. Leig am Famhair beuc as. Dh'fhaighnich Mac an Rìgh de a phiuthar, 'Gu dé am beuc a bha an
siod ?' Thuirt ise, nach robh ach an talamh a' fosgladh leis a'
bhùrn ghoileach a thaomadh air ; is cha robh air sin ach sin
féin 'san am sin.

An ath-latha, tràth dh'fhalbh Mac an Rìgh do'n bheinn,
thug a phiuthar a nìos am Famhair, agus chuir i an òrdugh e,
le plàsdan a chur air na h-uile àite a chaidh a sgàldadh. Chuir
am Famhair an gath-nimhe os cionn an doruis a rithist, gu
tuiteam air a' cheud aon a thigeadh a staigh. Chaidh e a sìos
do'n toll a rithist. Tràth rànaig Mac an Rìgh an torran buidhe,
[rinn e suidhe an sin, agus] leig Fios osna mhór as. 'Gu dé
fàth t'osna, a Fhios ?' ['Tha,' arsa Fios, 'chan 'eil am Famhair
marbh fhathast ; tha e air a' ghath-nimhe a chur os cionn an
doruis mar a rinn e roimhe, is tha e féin ann an toll fo'n ùrlar
aig taobh clì an teine.' 'Gu dé mar a nì sinn ?' 'Nì, mar a rinn
sinn roimhe, le Luath a chur a staigh an toiseach, agus ma théid
e a staigh cho luath is as urrainn e, bidh e seachad mum bi
ùine aig a' ghath tuiteam, agus cha téid ach bàrr an earbaill a
thoirt dheth. An uair a thig thusa a staigh, cuir air an coire
sidhinn, is tràth bhios e deas, thoir as cnàimh, is tilg d'ar n-ionnsaigh e, agus nì sinn caonnag mu'n chnàimh, 's dòirtidh sinn an
coire, a shealltainn an téid againn air an Fhamhair a sgàldadh
gu bàs.'

Chaidh Luath a chur a staigh an toiseach, agus ruith e cho
luath 's a b'urrainn da : thuit an gath-nimhe, ach bha Luath
seachad uile ach bàrr an earbaill, is thug an gath-nimhe bàrr an
earbaill dheth. Chaidh Mac an Rìgh is a dhà chù eile a staigh
ri a shàil. Cha do ghabh e air gun robh a bheag a dh'fhios aige
mu dheighinn an Fhamhair a bhith a staigh, agus chuir e an
coire sidhinn air an teinidh, agus an uair a bha an t-sidheann
deas, thug e dheth an coire, is leag e air an làr e dìreach os cionn
far an robh am Famhair.] Thug Mac an Rìgh cnàimh as a'
choire, is thilg e a dh'ionnsaigh nan con e : thòisich na coin
air caonnaig mu'n chnàimh ; dhòirt iad an coire, is cha duirt
am Famhair diog an uair sin ; chaidh a sgàldadh gu bàs. Chuir
piuthar Mac an Rìgh gruaim oirre, ach cha duirt i diog.

and instantly the hounds began to fight over it ; and they upset
the cauldron of boiling water on the Giant. The Giant gave a
roar. The King's Son asked his sister, 'What was that roar ?'
'It was only the earth opening because of the boiling water
being poured on it,' she replied ; and for the time being the
matter was left at that.

The next day, when the King's Son had gone to the hill,
his sister fetched up the Giant and attended to him by putting
plasters on every spot that had been scalded. Again the Giant
put the poisoned dart above the door, to fall upon the first one
to come in. Then he went down into the hole again. When
the King's Son arrived at the sunny hillock, [he sat down there.]
Knowledge sighed heavily. 'Why do you sigh, Knowledge ?'
['Why,' answered Knowledge, 'the Giant is not dead yet ; he
has put the poisoned dart above the door as he did before, and
he himself is in a hole under the floor at the left side of the fire.'
'What shall we do ?' 'We'll do as we did before, by sending
Swift in first ; and if he goes in as fast as he can, he will be past
before the dart has time to fall, and only the tip of his tail will
be taken off. And when you come in, put on the cauldron
for the venison, and when it is ready, take out a bone and throw
it to us ; we will fight for the bone and upset the cauldron ;
and we'll see if we can manage to scald the Giant to death.'

So Swift was sent in first, and in he ran as quickly as he could ;
the poisoned dart fell, but Swift had already got past, all but the
tip of his tail, and the poisoned dart took off the tip. The King's
Son and his two other hounds went in at Swift's heel. The King's
Son gave no hint that he knew anything about the Giant's being
there, but he put the cauldron for the venison on the fire, and
when the venison was ready, he took the cauldron off and set
it on the ground just over the place where the Giant was.]
Then taking a bone out of the cauldron he threw it to the hounds.
The hounds began to fight over the bone ; they upset the cauldron,
but this time the Giant made no sound—he was scalded to death.
The sister of the King's Son scowled, but she said not a word.

Agus aig ceann na h-uibhir de thìm, bha Mac an Rìgh a'
sealg [agus a chuid chon leis] agus thànaig ceò air, agus chaill
Mac an Rìgh a rathad, agus bha e air seacharan air feadh nam
beann, agus chaidh e fada air falbh mun d' amais e air taigh
sam bith, ach mu dheireadh, dh' amais e air taigh duin'-uasail :
rànaig e an dorus. Thànaig nighean bhrèagh a mach, agus thug
i a staigh e, agus dh'fhuirich e car tamaill 'san àite sin, is phòs e
nighean an duin'-uasail sin.

An ceann tìm, smaointich e air dol a dh'fhaicinn a pheathar,
a sheall[tainn] an robh i beò fhathast ; agus bha e dol a dh'fhàgail
nan con aig an taigh còmhla ri a bhean. Thug a bhean da trì
ùbhlan, ag ràdh ris, 'Mas e is gun tigeadh cunnart sam bith ort,
tilg ubhal as do dhéidh, agus glaodh, "Monadh is lochan 'nam
dhéidh, is rathad réidh romham "; agus ma thig tuilleadh
cunnairt ort, tilg ubhal eile agus glaodh, "Drisean is droigheann
'nam dhéidh, is rathad réidh romham "; agus ma thig tuilleadh
cunnairt ort, tilg an treas ubhal air do chùlaibh, is glaodh,
"Coille is monadh as mo dhéidh, is rathad réidh romham." '
Dh'fhalbh e, 's thug e leis na trì ùbhlan.

An uair a rànaig e am meallan buidhe a bha am bràigh an
taighe, ghlaodh e, 'A bheil thu a staigh, a phiuthar ?' ach cha
do fhreagair i e. Ghlaodh e a rithist ach cha tug i freagairt,
agus ghlaodh e an treas uair, agus thànaig i a mach is trì uirceanan-nimhe aice a fhuair i bho'n Fhamhair. Stuig i na trì
uirceanan-nimhe ann, agus theich esan, agus thilg e ubhal as a
dhéidh, agus ghlaodh e, 'Monadh is lochan as mo dhéidh, is
rathad réidh romham,' agus chinn sin 'na mhonadh is 'na lochan
nach b'urrainn do na h-uirceanan dol troimhe. Tràth rànaig
na h-uirceanan sin, thuirt a h-aon diubh, 'Nam bitheadh agam-sa
mo thaoman mór, mo thaoman meadhonach, is mo thaoman
beag, cha b'fhada gus an dèanainn rathad troimhe seo.' Thuirt
a h-aon eile, 'Falbh dh'an iarraidh.' Chaidh e, agus fhuair e
iad, agus thaom iad an loch ann an tiota. Shìn iad as a dhéidh
a rithist, agus tràth bha iad a' tighinn teann air, thilg e ubhal
eile as a dhéidh, agus ghlaodh e, 'Drisean is droigheann as mo
dhéidh, is rathad réidh romham,' agus chinn as a dhéidh cho
dlùth le drisean is le droigheann is nach robh dòigh aig na h-
uirceanan air iad fhéin fhorcadh troimhe. Thuirt a h-aon diubh,

After a certain length of time, the King's Son was one day out hunting [with his hounds] when a mist came upon him, and he lost his way. He wandered about the hills, lost, and he travelled a long distance before he hit upon any house at all; but at last he came to one, the house of a gentleman, and he went up to the door. A handsome young woman came out and fetched him in, and he stayed some time in that place, and married the daughter of that gentleman.

In course of time, he thought he would go and see his sister and find out whether she was still alive; but he was going to leave his hounds at home along with his wife. His wife gave him three apples, and said to him, 'If any danger happens to come upon you, throw an apple behind you and shout, "Moorland and lakes behind me, and before me a clear road"; and if further danger comes upon you, throw another apple and shout, "Briers and thorns behind me, and before me a clear road"; and if yet more danger comes upon you, throw the third apple behind you, and shout, "Forest and moorland behind me, and before me a clear road."' Off he went, taking the three apples with him.

When he arrived at the sunny hillock above the house, he called out, 'Are you in, sister?' but she did not answer him. He called again but she gave no answer; then he called the third time, and she came out with three venomous little pigs she had got from the Giant. She set the three venomous little beasts at him, and he fled, but he threw an apple behind him and shouted, 'Moorland and lakes behind me, and before me a clear road,' and there grew up there a moorland and lakes through which the pigs could not go. But when the little beasts had come up to it, one of them said, 'If I had with me my big baler, my middling baler, and my little baler I'd not be long in making a road through this.' 'Go and fetch them,' said another pig. So off he went and got them, and they baled out the lake in a trice. Again they set off after him, but when they were coming very close to him, he threw another apple behind him and shouted, 'Briers and thorns behind me, and before me a clear road'; and the country behind grew so thick with briers and thorns that the little beasts had no means of thrusting themselves through. One of them spoke and said, 'If only I had with me my big

'Nam bitheadh agam-sa mo chlaidheamh mór, mo chlaidheamh
meadhonach, is mo chlaidheamh beag, cha b'fhada gus an
dèanainn rathad trompa seo.' 'Falbh dh'an iarraidh.' Dh'fhalbh
e is fhuair e iad, agus gheàrr iad rathad troimh na drisean is an
droigheann, agus shìn iad as a dhéidh a rithist ; agus an uair a
bha iad a' tighinn dlùth air, thilg e an treas ubhal as a dhéidh,
agus ghlaodh e, 'Monadh is coille as mo dhéidh, is rathad réidh
romham,' agus dh'fhàs monadh agus coille as a dhéidh nach
b'urrainn do na h-uirceanan iad féin fhorcadh troimhe, aig cho
dlùth thiugh is a bha na craobhan ri chéile.   Thuirt a h-aon
diubh, 'Nam bitheadh agam-sa mo thuagh mhór, is mo thuagh
bheag, is mo thuagh mheadhonach, cha b'fhada gus an dèanainn-
sa rathad troimhe seo.' 'Is fheàrr dhuit dol dh'an iarraidh, ma
tà,' thuirt a h-aon eile ; agus dh'fhalbh an [t-]aon sin, agus
fhuair e na tuaghan agus thòisich iad, agus gheàrr iad rathad
troimh 'n choillidh, agus shìn iad as déidh Mac an Rìgh a rithist.
Is tràth bha iad a' tighinn teann air, streap esan an àird ann
an craoibh dharaich.   Is tràth rànaig na h-uirceanan a' chraobh,
thòisich iad air a cur as a bun.[1]   Rinn esan fead, is chuala Fios
e, is thuirt e, 'Tha ar maighstir ann an cunnart,' agus ruith na
trì coin a dhèanamh còmhnaidh ri am maighstir.   Is e Luath
a thànaig an toiseach, agus thòisich na trì uirceanan air agus
cha mhór nach do mharbh iad e.   Ach b'e an ath-chù a thànaig,
Trom ; thòisich na trì uirceanan air-san ; chum Trom riutha,
gus mu dheireadh an tànaig Fios ; agus mharbh na trì coin na
trì uirceanan.

Chaidh Mac an Rìgh dhachaigh, 's bha e an oidhche sin
còmhla ri a bLean, agus chaidh e an ath-latha a dh'fhaicinn a
pheathar.   Tràth rànaig e an torran buidhe a bha am bràigh
an taighe, ghlaodh e, 'Am bheil thu a staigh, a phiuthar?'
Thànaig i a mach, agus thuirt i, 'Tha.' Dh'fharraid e dhith
an sin an robh i toileach dol leis a nise ; agus thuirt i gun robh.
Dh'fhalbh i leis, is rànaig iad an taigh 'san robh e fhéin is a bhean
a' gabhail còmhnaidh.   B'e Mac an Rìgh fear-an-taighe, is b'e
a bhean bean-an-taighe, agus bha piuthar fear-an-taighe mar
gum bitheadh bean-mhuinntir ann, agus is i bha dèanamh nan
leapaichean.

[1] See this book, p. 366.

sword, my middling sword, and my little sword, I'd not be long in driving a road through this.' 'Go and fetch them.' He went off and got them, and they cut a road through the briers and thorns, and they rushed after him again. When they were closing upon him, he threw the third apple behind him, and shouted, 'Moorland and forest behind me, and before me a clear road'; and there sprang up behind him such a moorland and forest that the little pigs were not able to thrust themselves through it, the trees were so close together and so thickly placed. One of the pigs said, 'If I had my big axe with me, my little axe, and my middling axe, I'd not be long in making a road through this.' 'You had better go and fetch them then,' said another ; and the first one went off and got the axes, and they hacked a road through the forest, and away they rushed again after the King's Son. As they were closing upon him, he climbed high up into an oak tree. When they arrived at the tree, the little pigs began to dig it up by the roots.[1] The King's Son whistled, and Knowledge heard the whistle and said, 'Our master is in danger'; and the three hounds ran to succour their master. Swift was the first to arrive ; and the three pigs set upon him and nearly killed him. But the next hound that came was Weighty ; the three little pigs set upon him, but Weighty kept them at bay until at last Knowledge came ; and then the three hounds killed the three little pigs.

The King's Son came home and he spent that night with his wife. The next day he went to see his sister. When he came to the sunny hillock above the house, he shouted, 'Are you in, sister ?' She came out, and said, 'Yes, I am.' He asked her then if she was now willing to go with him ; and she said she was. She went off with him, and they arrived at the house where he and his wife lived. The King's Son was head of the house and his wife mistress of the house, and the sister was there as if she were a servant, and it was she who used to make the beds.

Ach is ann a bha gath-nimhe aice a fhuair i bho'n Fhamhair ; agus oidhche a bha an sin, an uair a rinn i an leabaidh, chuir i an gath-nimhe fo cheann a bràthar anns a' chluasaig, agus tràth chaidh esan a laighe, chaidh an gath-nimhe ann a cheann. Chaidh e seachad 'na anfhainne mar gum bitheadh e marbh, agus bha e mar sin ré trì làithean, agus thìodhlaic iad e. Ach bha na trì coin aige os cionn na h-uaighe far an robh e tìodhlaicte is iad a' sgrìobadh. Thànaig a' bhean aige, agus thuirt i riutha, 'Gu dé ruigeas sibh a leas a bhith sgrìobadh ann a sin ? Tha esan marbh, is chan urrainn duinn a thoirt beò a rithist.' Ach thuirt Fios, 'Nan tugadh sibh-se an ùir dheth, dh'fheuchainn-sa ri a thoirt beò.' Chaidh an sin an ùir a thogail dheth, agus thug Fios an gath-nimhe a cùl a chinn, agus thànaig e beò a rithist.[1] Chaidh e dhachaigh, is chuir e air gealbhan mór de ghlas-daraich, agus an uair a ghabh an gealbhan gu math, thilg e a phiuthar air an teinidh. Agus thuirt am fear a dh'innis an sgeul dhomh, gun d'fhàg e am fear is a bhean agus na coin gu mùirneach, prìseil,[2] beadarrach aig a chéile.

From John Crawford, fisherman, Lochlonghead, Arrochar.

John Dewar.

[1] Similar incident in No. 66 ; MS. vol. x., No. 123. The poison dart is probably own brother to the sleeping pin. See No. 24 (MS. vol. x., No. 44).

[2] MS. *prìosail*.

NOTES

MS. vol. x., No. 159. On the title page of the MS. Islay wrote, '159. John Dewar. Recd. from Mr Robertson, Feb. 29/60.' On the flyleaf, Islay wrote the following summary :—

'A stepmother, two stepchildren—to seek their fortune—Brother and sister live in a cottage with three little pigs—Brother sells a pig to a man for a dog and so gets three dogs—Wit—Swift—Weight. The girl allies herself with a giant who has a hot coal in his mouth—The Brother and the dogs conquer him—she recovers her pigs and they pursue the Brother—he beats them as in the Battle of the Birds [*W. H. Tales*, i., No. 2] with three mystic apples—She kills her brother with a hurtful stake—The Dogs dig him up again. Wit draws out the thorn and he comes alive—The sister is burned—.'

In the Battle of the Birds, Vars. 1, 3, 6 and 7, the hero hinders the pursuing giant in the same way as the hero hinders the pursuing pigs in No. 159. But the means he employs are not three mystic apples, but things which he finds in the ear of the magic filly,[1] on which he is fleeing. The heroine does indeed

[1] Similar incidents, *Celtic Magazine*, xii., p. 475 ; *Waifs and Strays*, ii., pp. 21, 437.

But what had she in her possession but a poisoned dart that she had got from the Giant ; and one night when she had made the bed, she put the poisoned dart into her brother's pillow, and when he went to rest, the poisoned dart went into his head. He fainted away in a swoon as though he were dead, and remained in that state for three days, and then they buried him. But over the grave where he was buried his three hounds set to work to scratch. Then came his wife, and she said to them, 'What is the good of your scratching there ? He is dead, and we cannot bring him to life again.' But Knowledge said, 'If you would only take the earth away, I would try to bring him to life.' So then the earth was taken away, and Knowledge took the poisoned dart out of the back of his head and he came to life again.[1] He went home and made a great fire of green oak, and when the fire was burning well, he threw his sister on it. And the man who told me the story said that he left the man, his wife, and his hounds together in love, esteem, and playful affection.

use mystic apples in Var. 3 (as she uses mystic cakes in Var. 2, and spittle in Var. 7), but in a different manner.

Islay must have thought highly of No. 159, for he gave a fairly long summary of it in *W. H. Tales*, i., *intro.* xc. or lxxxii. He there says again that the sister 'allies herself with a giant who has a hot coal in his mouth,' and that 'This curious story seems to shew the hog and the dog as foes. Perhaps they were but the emblems of rival tribes ; perhaps they were sacred amongst rival races ; at all events they were both important personages at some time or other, for there is a great deal about them in Gaelic lore.'

Fiss, Lice and Nart (= *Fios*, *Leigheas* and *Neart*) Wit or Knowledge, Cure or Healing, and Strength, are the names of three magical dogs belonging to an Irish hero in a tale in *Folk-Lore Journal* (1884), ii., p. 193. The story does not resemble No. 159, except in the incident of Nart dragging a splinter of bone out of his dead master's body, and of Lice licking the wound, and thereby restoring him to life.

Parallels :—

(1) *Na Trì Coin Uaine*, The Three Green Hounds, *Celtic Magazine*, xiii., p. 272. Collected by Kenneth MacLeod in the Isle of Eigg, who gives a translation. The sister in this version goes away and is never seen again.

(2) *Na Trì Coin Uaine air Lomhainn*, The Three Green Hounds on Leash. *An Gàidheal* (1875), iv., p. 115 ; re-published by me with translation, *Celtic Monthly*, xxiv., p. 167. Originally contributed by 'Glasrach', but no hint is given as to where the tale was gathered. The sister reforms in this version, and all ends happily.

(3) *Fionnladh Choinneachain*. *Trans. Gael. Soc. Inverness*, v. (1875), p. 19.

In this most valuable but as yet untranslated tale of many themes, some of the incidents concerning the brother, sister, and the hounds occur. The hounds are not green nor specially magical. There are no hostile pigs or pups. After adventures similar to those of the hero in No. 151 (this book, No. 69) the hero has a great many more which do not concern us here. He shoots his sister. The story was collected by the late Dr A. Carmichael of *Carmina Gadelica*, from 'Domhnul MacCuithein,' a crofter, of Fearann-an-leagha, near Carbost, Skye.

Related stories are :—'Eisenkopf,' Andrew Lang, *The Crimson Fairy Book*. 'The Iron Wolf,' and 'The Story of Little Tsar Novishny,' R. Nisbet Bain, *Cossack Fairy Tales*.

The directions the brother gives his sister as to what she is to do or not to do while he is away hunting, differ for the different versions as under. The asterisks show which things she fails to do, or appears to fail to do. In 'Fionnladh Choinneachain' the tale is confused as to what directions are given, so that the facts can only be guessed at. We are, however, told that the sister disobeyed in every particular. In Parallel No. 2, the brother gives no directions.

Campbell's, No. 159	*Celtic Magazine*, xiii., p. 272	Fionn. Choinneachain
1. to comb her hair	*not* to comb her hair *	...
2. to sweep house	...	...
3. to keep fire in *	...	to keep fire in *
4. ...	*not* to open N. window *	*not* to open N. window *
5. ...	...	to open S. window *

'No sister should comb her hair at night, if she have a brother at sea '; *Superstitions*, p. 237. A similar belief is recorded in *Survivals*, p. 296. To comb the hair on Wednesday was taboo, as shown in the following curse :—*Galar na té chuir a' cheud chìr a' cheud aoine 'na ceann*, i.e. 'the disease that struck the woman who first put a comb to her head on a Wednesday.' The 'disease' in question was to die without leaving issue. *Trans. Gael Soc. Inverness*, xvii., p. 230 ; *Folk-Lore*, viii., p. 380 ; Rev. J. G. Campbell, *Witchcraft*, p. 296. These instances suggest that originally the brother's request to his sister was not that she should comb her hair while he was away, but that she should refrain from doing so while he was away, as in the *Celtic Magazine* version.

The command to sweep the house occurs in No. 159 only.

Shutting and opening windows. In Parallels Nos. 1 and 3, the brother orders his sister not to open the north window ; in No. 3 he probably also orders her to open the south window. Both tales are probably corrupt in these details, for there is a verse extant (*Superstitions*, p. 69) recommending that the northern, western and southern windows of a house should be kept shut, while the eastern one should be kept open, for no evil ever comes from the east.

Letting the fire out. This was a serious matter. Relighting by friction was a very laborious process, and borrowing the 'seeds of fire' from a neighbour meant borrowing what at some seasons of the year at least no one liked to give away, as so doing was supposed to give the borrower power over the lender's cows, and enabled him to spirit away the produce of the lender's dairy ; *Superstitions*, p. 234 ; *Inverness Courier*, 1876, 20th January, p. 2. Hence, no doubt, the Giant's objection to parting with his fiery ember or red-hot coal, which the sister steals from him. In the other three versions, the Giant or Giants has or have no fiery ember about them, and the sister allies herself with him or them deliberately. In Parallel No. 1, three giants enter the house because the brother forgot one day to tell his sister not to open the North window, but neither in that Parallel nor the others is any reason given for the sister's making an alliance with the monsters.

The sister's curse, *Na h-uirc 's na h-ùraindean ort*, has been translated 'Pigs and monsters come at you.' *Na h-uirc* certainly means 'pigs,' but *na h-ùraindean*, not being in dictionaries, has been provisionally rendered 'monsters'. The same curse appears in 'Mac-a-Rusgaich' (*W. H. Tales*, ii., No. 45). There, through some inadvertence, *na h-uirc* appears most often as *na h-uire*. Islay translated the curse thus, 'Adversity and calamities be upon thee.' John Dewar contributed both 'Mac-a-Rusgaich,' and 'The Three Green Dogs.' [*Ùraindean* : perhaps from *ùr*, 'new,' plus plural of *aithinne*, 'firebrand' ? The idea involved may be 'May you be burned at the stake !' ? For *uirc* compare perhaps *uirghe* ?—A. M.]

SLIOCHD AN TRI FICHEAD BURRAIDH

No. 74.

O CHIONN tìm fhada, bha aig Mac Dhùghaill Latharna deich mic, agus thug e dhaibh fearann thall 's a bhos air feadh Latharna. Bha aon diùbh do'm b'ainm Calum, agus thug Mac Dhùghaill dha baile do'm b'ainm Colgainn, agus is e Clann Chaluim Cholgainn a theirte ri a shliochd. Bha dà mhac dheug aig Mac Caluim Cholgainn, agus bha iad ro dhreachmhor, foghainteach ; agus Dòmhnach de na Dòmhnaich, chaidh Mac Caluim Cholgainn a dh'ionnsaigh na searmoin, agus bha a dhà mhac dheug aige leis. Tràth bha e féin 's a dhà mhac dheug a' dol a staigh do'n eaglais, ghabh Baintighearna Mhic Dhùghaill Dhùn Ollaigh geur-bheachd orra, cho mór dreachmhor is a bha iad. An déidh dhaibh dol dachaigh as an eaglais, dh'fharraid i de Mhac Dhùghaill, 'Có e am fear ud aig an robh an dà mhac dheug mhór, fhoghainteach ud, anns an eaglais an diugh ?' Thuirt Mac Dhùghaill, 'Is e a bha an siod, Mac Caluim Cholgainn.' Thuirt a' Bhaintighearna, 'Ma tà, cha b'fhuilear do Mhac Caluim Cholgainn an treas cuid de dh'Albainn a bhith aige dha féin.'

Chan 'eil fhios có dhiùbh a ghon no nach do ghon sùil na Baintighearna Clann Mhic Caluim ; ach thòisich galar orra, agus bha aon an déidh aoin dhiùbh a' siubhal, gus mu dheireadh nach robh beò ach an dithis. Agus bha eagal orra gun gabhadh galar an dithis sin féin, agus gun siùbhladh iad. Agus ghabh iad comhairle ciamar a dhèanadh iad. Agus b'e a' chomhairle a fhuair iad—gach fear dhiùbh a dh'fhaotainn eich, agus iad a chur shrathraichean 's chliabh air na h-eich ; agus iad a chur ge bè nì a bha iad a' dol a thoirt leò anns na cléibh ; agus iad a dh'fhalbh air an turus, agus gun iad a dhol an t-aon rathad : agus iad a bhith falbh air an turus gus gum briseadh iris aon de na cléibh, agus ge bè àite anns am bitheadh iad tràth bhriseadh iris a' chléibh, iad a thogail an taighe an sin, agus iad a ghabhail còmhnaidh anns an àite sin.

THE DESCENDANTS OF THE SIXTY BLOCKHEADS

No. 74.

A LONG time ago MacDougall of Lorne had ten sons, and he gave them land here and there throughout Lorne. To one of them, whose name was Calum, he gave a place called Colgainn, and his descendants were known as the MacCallums of Colgainn. MacCallum of Colgainn had twelve very handsome, stalwart sons, and on a certain Sunday MacCallum went to church, and his twelve sons with him. As they were entering the church, Lady MacDougall of Dunolly observed them closely, and saw how tall and fine-looking they were. After they had returned home from church, she asked MacDougall, 'Who was that man in church today with those twelve big, stalwart sons?' 'That was MacCallum of Colgainn,' said MacDougall. 'Well,' replied Lady MacDougall, ' MacCallum of Colgainn would require the third part of Scotland for himself !'

Whether the Lady's eye bewitched MacCallum's children or not, no one knows ; but a disease began to strike them and one after another they died, until at last there were only two of them left. They feared that disease would attack even those two and that they would die ; so they sought advice as to what they should do. The advice they got was this : that each of them should get a horse and saddle it with a pack-saddle and panniers, put everything they were going to take with them in the panniers, and set out on their journey. They were not to go the same way, but they were to keep on until the strap of one of the panniers snapped ; and wherever they might be when the strap of the pannier snapped, there they were to build their houses and make their homes.

Dh'fhalbh an darna fear dhiubh mu thuath agus dh'fhalbh am fear eile mu dheas. Tràth bha am fear a dh'fhalbh mu thuath a' dol troimh Ghleann Éite bhris iris aon de na cléibh, agus thuit an sac-droma bhàrr an eich. Bha, ar le Mac Caluim, gun soirbhicheadh leis anns an àite sin, agus thog e taigh ann : phòs e, agus bha clann aige : agus b'e an sliochd-san Clann Chaluim Ghlinn Éite. Dh'fhalbh am fear a dh'imich mu dheas gu dol do Chinn-tìre ; agus tràth bha e dol troimh Chnapadal bhris iris aon de na cléibh, agus thuit an sac-droma bhàrr an eich : agus thog esan a thaigh anns an àite sin, agus ghabh e a chòmhnaidh ann an Cnapadal. Phòs e, agus bha clann aige ; agus b'e a shliochd-san Clann Chaluim Chnapadail.

Bha Clann Chaluim Chnapadail agus Clann Chaluim Ghlinn Éite a' cluinntinn iomraidh mu a chéile, agus a' faotainn fios bho a chéile, agus bha iad ro thoileach an càirdean fhaicinn. Agus bhiodh iad a' cur fiosan a dh'ionnsaigh a chéile mu'n toil a bha aca air a chéile fhaicinn. Chuir Clann Chaluim Chnapadail fios a dh'ionnsaigh Clann Chaluim Ghlinn Éite ann am briathran cosmhail ri—'Thigeadh sibh-se, a Chlann Chaluim Ghlinn Éite, air chéilidh gu nar faicinn-e [sic] do Chnapadal, agus bheir sinn aoigheachd dhuibh.' Agus chuir Clann Chaluim Ghlinn Éite aig a' cheart am cuireadh a dh'ionnsaigh Clann Chaluim Chnapadail iad a dhol air chéilidh do Ghleann Éite ; agus gum faigheadh iad aoigheachd ré tamaill o Chlann Chaluim Ghlinn Éite.

Tràth fhuair Clann Chaluim Ghlinn Éite am fios-cuiridh, thog iad orra, agus dh'fhalbh iad gu dol do Chnapadal air chéilidh, a dh'fhaicinn an càirdean ann an Cnapadal. Agus tràth fhuair Clann Chaluim Chnapadail cuireadh gu dol do Ghleann Éite, cha do smaointich iad air a' chuireadh a chuir iad féin gu Chlann Chaluim Ghlinn Éite, ach thog iad orra, agus dh'fhalbh iad gu dol do Ghleann Éite. Choinnich an dà bhuidhinn a chéile air Sliabh an Tuim, aig àite ris an goirear Acha-bheann, agus cha d'aithnich iad a chéile ; bha deich air fhichead dhiùbh ann, air gach taobh ; agus bha iad 'nan daoine làidir, uaibhreach. Is ann aig àth uillt a choinnich iad, agus bha iad cho uaibhreach 's nach d'fharraid iad có e a chéile, agus chan fhanadh buidheann air bith dhiùbh air an ais gus an rachadh a' bhuidheann eile troimh an àth ; agus cha tarraingeadh

One of them went north and the other south. When the one who was going north was passing through Glen Etive, the strap of one of the panniers snapped, and the pack fell off the horse. MacCallum concluded that he would prosper in that place, and he built a house there. He married and had children, and their descendants were the MacCallums of Glen Etive. The one who went south started off for Kintyre, and when he was going through Knapdale, the strap of one of the panniers snapped and the pack fell off the horse. So he built his house there and made his home in Knapdale. He married and had children, and his descendants were the MacCallums of Knapdale.

The MacCallums of Knapdale and the MacCallums of Glen Etive used to hear news of each other and receive word from each other : both sides were eager to see their kinsfolk, and used to exchange messages about their wish to see each other. So the MacCallums of Knapdale sent a message to the MacCallums of Glen Etive framed somewhat thus : 'MacCallums of Glen Etive, come to Knapdale to visit us, and we will give you a hospitable reception.' And at the same time, the MacCallums of Glen Etive sent an invitation to the MacCallums of Knapdale to come and visit them in Glen Etive, saying that they should be entertained hospitably for a while by them.

When the MacCallums of Glen Etive got the invitation, they set off and made for Knapdale to see their kinsfolk. And when the Knapdale MacCallums got the message inviting them to Glen Etive, they never thought of the invitation they themselves had extended to the MacCallums of Glen Etive, but made themselves ready and started off for Glen Etive. The two companies met on Sliabh an Tuim, at a place called Achaveann, but they did not recognise each other ; there were thirty of them present on each side, and strong, proud men they were. It was at a ford they met, but so arrogant were they that neither asked who the other side was, and neither would stand back until the other company had crossed the ford ; nor would either draw aside until the other had passed. But both sides drew their swords to clear the way with them, and they set upon each other and buidheann air bith dhiùbh chun an darna taoibh gus an rachadh a' bhuidheann eile seachad. Ach tharraing an dà bhuidhinn an claidheamhan, gus an rathad a réiteachadh leis na claidheamhan, agus thòisich iad air a chéile, agus chog iad cath garg, gus nach robh beò dhiùbh ach aon fhear air gach taobh.

Bha an dithis seo ro bhlàth le bhith cho dian ag iomairt an claidheamhan, agus rinn iad seasamh treis gu iad fhéin fhuarachadh mun tòisicheadh iad air a chéile. B'e a bha 'san darna fear dhiubh balach òg, agus is e a bha anns an fhear eile duine leth-aosmhor, agus cha robh e cho bras ris an fhear òg. Thuirt e, 'A nis, bho nach 'eil beò de'n dà bhuidhinn ach thusa agus mise, is e an ceud nì a bu chòir dhuinn a dhèanamh na mairbh a thìodhlacadh.' 'Còrdaidh mi gu sin a dhèanamh,' arsa am fear òg. Fhuair iad caibean agus sluaisdean, agus thìodhlaic iad na mairbh. An sin, thuirt am fear a b'òige, 'Thig a nise, agus feuchamaid e, biodag air bhiodaig.' Thuirt am fear a bu shine, 'A nis, bho nach 'eil beò air an darna taobh ach thusa, agus air an taobh eile ach mise, dh'fhaodamaid sgeul a ghabhail de a chéile, agus fios fhaotainn có na daoine dh'am bheil a chéile, agus an sin, feuchamaid a' chòmhrag.' 'Agus có iad na daoine de am bheil thu, ma tà ?' ars am fear a b'òige. 'Tha mise de shliochd Mhic Caluim Cholgainn.' 'Agus tha mise de shliochd Mhic Caluim Cholgainn.' 'Ma tà, is e mise na tà beò de Chlann Chaluim Ghlinn Éite. Bha na bha sinn ann de Chlann Chaluim Ghlinn Éite a' dol air chéilidh a dh'fhaicinn nar càirdean, Clann Chaluim Chnapadail—is càirdean dìleas duinn iad, bu chlann bhràithrean sinn gu léir ; is ann an seo a choinnich sinn ris a' bhuidhinn de'm bheil thusa ; chog sinn gu h-amaideach, agus chan 'eil beò ach thusa agus mise.' 'Ma tà, is mise aon de Chlann Chaluim Chnapadail. Bha sinn a' dol air chéilidh a dh'fhaicinn nar càirdean, Clann Chaluim Ghlinn Éite, agus is e seo far an do choinnich sinn, agus an àite càirdeas a dhèanamh, is ann a mharbh sinn a chéile.' 'Ma tà, marbh mi ; is fheàrr liom a bhith marbh no beò a nise.'

Ach bha onfhadh an fhir a b'òige iar fuarachadh an sin ; agus cha mharbhadh e am fear eile. An sin, dh'iarr am fear a bu shine air an fhear a b'òige e thighinn agus gum feuchadh iad còmhrag ri a chéile, ach chan fheuchadh am fear a b'òige e. Thuirt e 'cladhaire' ris an fhear a b'òige. Ach coma có dhiùbh, fought a savage battle, until there were none of them left alive except one on each side.

These two were extremely warm plying their swords so hard, and they paused for a little to let themselves cool before they set upon each other. One of them was a young lad ; the other a middle-aged man, who was not so hot-headed as the young one. The older man said, 'Now, since there is no one left alive from either side except you and me, the first thing we ought to do is to bury the dead.' 'I agree to that,' answered the youth, and they got spades and shovels, and buried the dead. Then the younger man said, 'Come on now and let us try it, dirk against dirk !' But the older man said, 'Since you alone are left on your side, and I alone on mine, we might first exchange information and find out to what people each of us belongs ; and then let us fight the duel.' 'Who are your folk, then ?' asked the youth. 'I am of the MacCallums of Colgainn,' replied the other. 'I too am of the MacCallums of Colgainn !' 'Well then, I am the only one left alive of the MacCallums of Glen Etive. We MacCallums of Glen Etive were all of us going to visit our relations, the MacCallums of Knapdale ; they are true kinsfolk of ours, for we were all brothers' children. Here we have met the band to whom you belong, but foolishly have we fought, and there is nobody left except you and me.' 'And I am of the MacCallums of Knapdale. We were going to visit our kinsfolk the MacCallums of Glen Etive, and here indeed have we met, but instead of showing friendship, what we have done is to kill each other.' 'Then kill me. I would rather be dead than alive now.'

But the youth's frenzy had by this time subsided, and he would not kill the other. Then the older man challenged the younger to come on and fight the duel with him, but the younger would not fight. The older man called the younger a craven, yet in spite of that he refused to fight any more. When cha dèanadh am fear a b'òige tuilleadh còmhraig. Tràth chunnaig am fear a bu shine [nach] b' urrainn da am fear a b'òige a thoirt gu tuilleadh còmhraig a dhèanamh, chuir e a bhiodag ri a bhroilleach fhéin, agus thuirt e, 'Caidlidh mise an seo còmhla ri m' chàirdean' ; chuir e a bhiodag 'na bhroilleach, agus mharbh se e féin.

Chaidh an t-aon a dh'fhan beò dhiubh, agus ghabh e a chòmhnaidh aig [space in MS.], agus is e 'Bail'-a'-ghioragain' an t-ainm a theireadh feadhainn ris an àite anns an do thuinich e. Phòs e, agus bha clann aige, agus is [e] a theireadh feadhainn ri a shliochd—'Sliochd an Trì Fichead Burraidh a dhòirt am fuil aig Acha-bheann.' Is ann de an seòrsa atà Clann Chaluim Earra-ghàidheal, agus Clann Chaluim Ghlinn Falach air ceann mu thuath Loch Laomainn.

Tha Acha-bheann agus na clachan a tha comharrachadh a mach nan uaigh aig Cloinn Chaluim ri 'm faicinn air an là 'n diugh.

NOTES

The foregoing is a fusion of three versions, of which the first, the longest and fullest, was taken, and as much of the others incorporated as was consistent with the tenor of the first. This was easily done, for though the two other versions were much shorter, they agreed closely except in the following details :

The second version, which has the same name as the first, makes the rivals quarrel about which band should have the right (!) hand in passing each other, and it makes the two survivors sit down, weep, and rise up again. There it ends abruptly.

The third version, 'Comhrag an Dà Bhràthar,' says that the two septs of MacCallums dwelt in Appin and Kintyre respectively ; that they met at Christmas time, and that Sliabh-an-Tuim, where they met, was between the parishes of Melfort and Craignish, and that it was only the two greyhaired chiefs who were left alive. A version from the Canadian *Mac-Talla*, vii., p. 54, also makes the two chiefs the only persons left alive ; and says that they failed to recognize each other because it was so late in the evening when they met ; that the two bands had been resting, one on higher, the other on lower ground, and that one of those on the higher ground threw something at those on the lower, or gave other cause of offence equally trivial, whereupon they attacked each other, *gun fhios*, as the Mac-Talla version wittily says, *có bu Chalum*, which may be roughly translated, 'not knowing which was Calum, or who was who' ; indeed the legend may be the very thing that gave rise to this proverb. The last words of this version are, *Nan innsinn có iad chan 'eil fhios agam nach cuirinn mìothlachd air Cloinn Chaluim* ! 'If I were to tell who they were, there is no knowing but that I might annoy the MacCallums !'

the older man saw that he could not induce the younger to fight, he turned his dirk against his own breast and said, 'I will sleep here with my kinsfolk,' and thrusting his dirk into his breast, he killed himself.

The one who survived went away and set up his home at [space in MS.], and some called the place where he settled 'The Little Coward's Homestead.' He married and had children, and his descendants were sometimes known as 'The Descendants of the Sixty Blockheads who spilt their blood at Achaveann.' To their line belong the MacCallums of Argyll and the Mac-Callums of Glen Falloch, at the north end of Loch Lomond.

Achaveann and the stones that mark the graves of the MacCallums are to be seen to this day.

Gun fhios có bu Chalum seems to be a common or proverbial phrase (see *An Gàidheal*, ii., p. 359), and may have had its origin in this very legend.

Mrs K. W. Grant, in *Aig Tigh na Beinne*, p. 281, makes the two brothers to set out together, and that the breaking of the saddle girth of either of them was to be the sign for them to separate. In our version, the breaking was to indicate where the houses were to be built, and there is also a tale of a house being built where an ass's tether breaks, in *W. H. Tales*, iv., p. 400.

The third part of Scotland : *trian a dh'Albainn*, according to Mrs Grant, *Aig Tigh na Beinne*, p. 150, who says that the church into which MacCaluim Cholagainn and his twelve sons were going when the Lady of Dunolly noticed them was the church of Kilbride, Eaglais Chille Bhrighde.

Parallels : Sliochd an Trì Fichead Burraidh : *Mac-Talla*, vii., p. 54. Cloinn Chaluim Cholagainn : *Aig Tigh na Beinne*, p. 281 : see also pp. 118, 150. Allt na Dunach : *Trans. Gael. Soc. Inverness*, xx., p. 66. Blàr na Dunach : *Gàidheal*, ii., p. 135. Gillean Ghlinn-Comhain 's Gillean Raineach : J. F. Campbell's unpublished MS. remains : *Purple* vol. ii. Cùl-càise muinntir Ghlinn-Comhain : *Cuairtear*, i., p. 211. Itheadh càise a' Bharain Ruaidh : *Trans. Gael. Soc. Inverness*, xxi., p. 71. *Records of Argyll*, p. 304.

[J. G. Mackay does not identify the three versions mentioned at the beginning of these Notes, but the main text seems to have been No. 15 in Islay's unpublished 'Purple Volume ii,' noticed just above ; conflated with MS. vol. x., No. 165, narrated by 'a student' in Glasgow to D. Torrie.—K. H. J.]

AN TUATHANACH O'DRAOTH

BHA tuathanach ann, agus phòs e té, agus bhiodh e ag obair
roimhe a h-uile latha, agus an uair a thigeadh e dhachaigh,
siod am facal a bhiodh aig a' bhoireannach ris, 'An Tuathanach
O'Draoth.' Facal eile chan fhaigheadh e uaipe ach an Tuathanach O'Draoth. 'Is tu an Tuathanach O'Draoth.'[1] Bha e
an siod oidhche anmoch, agus is ann an cois an rathaid-mhóir
a bha e. Chunnaig e dithis mharcaiche a' dol seachad. Bha
e a' gabhail a null a choimhead orra, is chunnaig e am pocan
sin a' tuit[eam] uatha, 's air Moire fhéin! cha tug e sùil sam
bith air. An uair a bha e dol dachaigh, smuaintich e gabhail
rathad a' phocain, feuch gu dé an rud a bha ann. Dh'fhalbh
e agus togadar am pocan, 's thugar dachaigh leis 'na làimh e,
agus tilgear a dh'ionnsaigh na mnatha e an déidh dol dachaigh,
's thuirt e rithe balgan-abhrais a dhèanamh dheth.[2] Dh'fhalbh
ise, 's chaidh i do dh'àite uaigneach leis a' phocan, 's dh'amhairc
i gu dé a bh'ann, 's an uair a chunnaig i gu dé a bh'ann, chuir i
seachad e, 's thànaig i far an robh esan, 's thuirt i ris, 'O! cha
bhi thusa ris an tuathanachas; is ann a tha thu air do shàrachadh:
is ann a tha mi smuainteachadh gun cuir mi do'n sgoil thu.'
Bhuail esan air a ràdh nach rachadh e do'n sgoil gu bràth, o
nach d'fhuair e roimhe seo i ; rud a bha coltach do'n duine
bhochd. Chaith i de bheul 's de shlighe air, gus an deach e
do'n sgoil. An uair a chaidh e do'n sgoil, dh'iarr e leabhar.
Fhuair e siod, 's dh'fhaighnich am maighstir-sgoile dheth c'àite
an robh e dol.[3] Thuirt e gun robh e dol a dh'ionnsachadh sgoile.
A h-uile cothrom a gheibheadh na sgoilearan air, bhuaileadh
iad air a tharraing, 's air a rubadh, 's air spòrs a dhèanamh
dheth. Chaidh e dhachaigh mun robh an sgoil a mach, agus

---

[1] *Draoth*, good-for-nothing, humdrum, waster, spendthrift.
[2] [Mackay translates *balgan-abhrais* as 'a bag for holding materials for spinning.'
Family tradition in Skye says that the bag carried by MacDonald of Sleat's personal
attendant when MacDonald travelled to the south was *Am Balgan-amhruis*. It
contained the money for the expenses of the trip.—J. M.]

THE FARMER O'DRAOTH

THERE was once a farmer, and he got married. He used to work in the fields every day, and when he came home, his wife always addressed him thus : 'The Farmer O'Draoth !'[1] Not another word could he get from her but Farmer O'Draoth ! 'You are Farmer O'Draoth !' One late night when he was near the road, he saw a couple of riders going by. He was going over to look at them when he saw them drop a little bag, but by Mary herself, he did not so much as glance at it. But when he was going home, he thought he would go over towards the little bag to see what it was. He went and picked it up and took it with him in his hand ; when he got home, he threw it to his wife and told her to make it into a bag in which to store things.[2] She took the little bag away to a private place, and looked to see what it held. When she saw what was in it she put it away and came to him and said, 'Oh ! you must not go on with this farming. Why, you are being worn out ! I think I will send you to school.' He began to protest that he would never go to school, seeing he had not received his education earlier in life—an understandable thing for the poor man to say. But she plied him with so much flattery and craftiness that at last he went to school. When he went to school, he asked for a book. He received one, and the schoolmaster asked him where he was going (*i.e.* what he wanted). He said he was going to be educated. Every time the scholars got a chance, they would tease him and pull him about and make fun of him. So he went off home before the school came out and said to his wife that he would never go there any more. 'Why ?' asked his wife. 'The scholars have not left a single hair in my head,' said he. 'Oh, then, you shall not go there any

---

[2] *Cf.* for idiom, the question asked by the fairies of a man who entered their dwelling or *sìdhean*, to procure from them the gift of piping : *dh'fhaighneachd iad dheth c'àite robh e dol no gu dé 'n ealain a bha e ag iarraidh,* 'they asked him where he was going, or what was the art or craft he desired' ; *Celtic Review,* v., p. 345.

thuirt e ri a bhean, nach rachadh esan gu bràth tuilleadh an siod. 'Car son ?' ars a bhean. 'Cha d'fhàg na sgoilearan ribeag fuilt 'nam cheann,' ars esan. 'O', ars ise, 'cha téid thusa tuilleadh ann ; bidh tu ris an tuathanachas mar a bha thu roimhid, seach iad a bhith toirt a' chinn mar sin dhìot ; ach feuchaidh mise ris a' mhaighstir-sgoile, air son na sgoilearan a bhith riut.'

Thòisich e air an tuathanachas mar a bha e roimhid. Có thànaig mun cuairt an seo, ach gum b'e an dithis mharcaiche a chunnaig e air an rathad-mhór. 'Gu dé as misde sinn a dhol sìos far am bheil an duine bochd a tha an seo ag obair a h-uile latha fo'n rathad ?' ars an dara fear ris an fhear eile. 'O, cha mhisde,' ars am fear eile. Chaidh iad sìos far an robh e, agus dh'fhaighnich iad ris, am b'àbhaist da bhith fuireach an siod, agus thuirt esan gum b'àbhaist. 'An d'fhuair thu dad sam bith no am faca tu dad sam bith an seo ?' ars iad-san. Thuirt e gun d'fhuair. Dh'fhaighnich iad ris gu dé an rud a bha ann. Thuirt e gun robh pocan beag. Dh'fhaighnich iad dheth gu dé rinn e ris. Thuirt esan gun tug e do'n mhnaoi e. Dh'fhalbh iad còmhla ris an siod dachaigh do'n t-seòrsa bhothain a bha aige, agus is e an ceud fhacal a thuirt esan ris a' mhnaoi—'C'àite a bheil am pocan a thug mi dhuit, an uair a fhuair mi air an rathad-mhór e ?' Thuirt ise nach d'fhuair 's nach tug e pocan dhi-se riamh. Thuirt esan gun tug. 'Cuin a thug thu dhomh e ?' ars ise. 'O ! nach 'eil fhios agad,' ars esan, 'an là mun deach mi do'n sgoil !' '[? An] làimh an àidh !' [1] ars iad-san, 'mas e sin an latha a fhuair thusa am pocan, faodaidh sinne bhith falbh ; is ann a dh'fheumas tu rud fhaotainn.' Dh'fhalbh iad, 's bha am pocan 's na raibh ann aig bean an Tuathanaich O'Draoth.

[1] MS. *O'n làimh an àigh.*

From Donald MacKillop, tenant, Rusgary, Berneray. Says he learnt it from Angus MacLeod, Berneray, who died at a very advanced age about two years ago. August 1859.

more,' said she ; 'you shall farm as you did before, rather than that they should go on tearing your scalp off in that way ; but I will take the schoolmaster to task because of the scholars having worried you.'

He began farming again as before. Who should now come round but the two horsemen he had seen on the highway. 'What harm will it do to us to go down to where this poor man is working every day by the roadside ?' said one of them to the other. 'None at all,' said the other. So they went down to him and asked him if he usually lived there, and he said he did. 'Have you found or seen anything about here ?' they asked. He replied that he had, and they asked what it was. The man said it was a little bag. They asked him what he had done with it. He said he had given it to his wife. Then they went home with him to the bothy where he lived, such as it was, and the first word he said to his wife was, 'Where is the little bag I gave you the day I found it on the highway ?' She replied that he had never found and had never given her any little bag. He said that he had. 'When did you give it to me ?' she asked. 'Oh, don't you know ?' said he ; 'why, the day before I went to school !' 'By the hand of Providence !' said they, 'if that was the day you found the little bag, we may as well be off ; it is you rather who must get something.' Off they went, and the little bag and all that was in it remained with the wife of Farmer O'Draoth.

NOTES

MS. vol. x., No. 167. Scribe—Hector MacLean. In his Gaelic List, Islay has summarized this story thus—'A farmer finds a bag of money—wife sends him to school—owners come—says he found it when he went to school —wife says, "Now you see my husband is a fool."' The wife does not say so in the MS., but it is possible that she did say so in some version recited to Islay, and that he remembered the fact. For a Skye version of No. 167, see *Folk-Lore*, xxxiii., p. 382.

For a story in which a woman plays a similar trick, using a fool for her tool, see *W. H. Tales*, ii., p. 48, Var. 10. Wives fool and rule their husbands in another tale, *ibid.*, No. 48, Var. 1 ; MS. vol. xi., No. 229.

BRÀTHAIR AGUS LEANNAN

BHA tuathanach [beairteach] ann an Cinn Loch Ìnnse ann am Bàideanach, is bha duine bochd còmhla ris, is bhiodh an duine bochd a' dol a dh'iasgach an còmhnaidh, is bha farmad aig an duine bheairteach ris air son na bha e faotainn de dh'iasg. 'Tha farmad mór agam riut air son mar a tha thu cruinneachadh air son do bhùird, is tha dùil a'm gun téid mi a dh'iasgach còmhla riut,' ars an tuathanach ris an duine bhochd. Dh'fhalbh iad a dh'iasgach, agus bhuail iad air marbhadh éisg. Rinn iad iasgachd mhaith. Bha an tuathanach anabarrach toilichte na fhuair e a dh'iasg agus smuainich e gum bu chòir falbh, gun robh na leòr de dh'iasg aca, gun robh eallach an t-aon aca. Chuir iad an t-iasg air am muin, agus ghabh iad air falbh. Thuit ceò orra air an rathad, is b'éiginn daibh an t-iasg fhàgail. Chunnaig iad solus treis uatha, is an uair a rànaig iad an seo, sheall iad a staigh air uinneig chaoil a bha air an taigh a bha an sin. Chunnaig iad bòrd a staigh air a chur air dòigh, is chan fhac' iad duine ach boireannach brèagha òg, agus is ann air tùrsadh a shìn i an uair a chunnaig i iad-san a' dol a staigh. Thuirt an duine bochd nach robh e deònach air dol a staigh. 'Cha saighdear thu,' ars an tuathanach, 'feumaidh sinn biadh fhaotainn có dhiùbh, is mur a bheil 'ga chumail uainn ach an nighean, gheibh sinn e.' Dh'fhaighnich iad de'n nighinn dé as mò bha cur dragha oirre, is i cho tùrsach. Thuirt i gun robh iad fhéin a bhith 'gan cur as an rathad an ceartair. Dh'fheòraich iad dhith gu dé bha 'ga cumail fhéin an siod. Thuirt i gun robh ceò thighinn oirre mar a thànaig orra fhéin an nochd ; agus an uair a thànaig ise ann, gur e an dà mhart a bha aig a h-athair 's a bha i ag iarraidh a thug ann i, 's gun robh trì deug a' tighinn chun na cuirm a bha ise dèanamh deas ; is nach robh ach seachdain aice gus am feumadh i an ceannbhard aca a phòsadh, 's gum bu cho maith leatha an ceann a thoirt dhith 's a phòsadh. Thug i an dìol de bhiadh 's de dh'fheòil daibh. Ars an tuathanach

BROTHER AND LOVER

AT Kinlochinch in Badenoch there lived a rich farmer, and with
him there lived a poor man. The poor man was always fishing,
and the rich man envied him because he caught so many fish.
'I envy you very much the way you provide for your table, and
I think I'll go and fish with you,' said the farmer to the poor
man. They went off fishing, and they began to catch fish and
did very well. The farmer was highly delighted with the number
of fish he had caught and decided it was time to go, for they
had plenty of fish—indeed, they had a load each. They put
the fish on their backs, and off they went. But on the way a
mist fell on them, and they were forced to leave the fish. A
little way off they saw a light, and when they came up to it,
there was a house there. Looking through a narrow window in
the house, the men saw a table inside ready set ; but they saw
nobody there except a handsome young woman, and when she
saw them coming in she began lamenting. The poor man
said he did not want to go in. 'You are no soldier,' said the
farmer ; 'we must have food in any case, and if there is no one
to keep it from us but the girl, have it we will.' They asked
the girl what troubled her most, since she was so sad. She replied
that it was the fact that they themselves would shortly be killed.
They asked her what kept her there herself. She had been
caught in a mist just as they had been caught that night, she said.
And she told them that it was her father's two cows which she
was looking for that had brought her there ; that there were
thirteen people coming to the feast she was now preparing ;
and that in another week she would have to marry their chief—
and she would as soon lose her head as marry him. She gave
them as much food and meat as they wanted. 'So many men
were never gathered together without their having weapons by
them,' said the farmer to the girl, 'so show us all the secret places
of the house.' She did this, and the first room she opened was

ris an nighinn, 'Cha robh uiread siod de dhaoine cruinn riamh
gun airm a bhith aca, agus seall duinn na h-àiteannan dìomhair
a tha staigh.' Rinn i siod, agus an ceud rùm a dh'fhosgail i,
dé bha an siod ach làn de dhaoine [1] marbha! Bha rùm eile
an sin, agus cha robh i deònach a fhosgladh dhaibh idir. [Ach
mu dheireadh] dh'fhosgail i e. Gu dé a bh'ann ach dithis
òganach! Dh'fheòraich iad dith gu dé an dithis a bha an siod.
Ars i gun robh bràthair di fhéin, agus gille eile thànaig dh'a
faicinn, 's gun do chuir i am falach iad, feuch am faigheadh
iad falbh gun chur as daibh. 'A nis,' ars an tuathanach riu,
'an uair a chluinneas sibh fìdeag, freagraidh sibh mise a chuid-
eachadh liom; air neò, ma nì mise an gnothach liom fhéin,
marbhaidh mi sibh-se a rithist.' 'Nì sinn sin,' ars iad-san.
Dh'fhosgail i an sin an rùm anns an robh na h-airm. Thug an
tuathanach leis an dà ghunna a b'fheàrr a bh'ann, agus claidheamh dha fhéin, is [claidheamh eile] do'n duine bhochd. Ghabh
iad a staigh air uinneig seòmair eile a bha an sin anns an robh
feur. Dh'fhalaich iad iad fhéin fo'n fheur.

Cha robh iad fad an sin an uair a thànaig muinntir an taighe
dhachaigh, an dà fhear dheug 's an ceannbhard, agus a dhà
de chrodh an tuathanaich, agus aon de chuid an duine bhochd
leò. 'O,' ars an tuathanach ris an duine bhochd, 'tha mi
smaointeachadh gun leig mi a h-uile srad a tha 'sa' ghunna
riu,' an uair a chunnaig e iad a' leagail a' chruidh. Bha an
duine bochd 'ga chomhairleachadh, 's ag iarraidh air dàil a
dhèanamh, 's ag ràdh ris gun robh e na bu doirbhe tighinn orra
'nan seasamh mar siod na an uair a chuireadh iad na gnothaichean
gu crìch. Leig e dhaibh an siod gus an do mharbhadh an crodh.
An uair a mharbh iad an crodh, thog iad leac-an-teinntein, 's
chuir iad na seicheachan ann an sloc fodha, 's chuir iad an
fheòlach ann an sloc eile. Is ann mar sin a bha.

Dh'iarr an ceannbhard orra an siod suidhe aig am biadh, 's
air Moire fhéin, shuidh iad. An uair a bha iad treis ag obair
air am biadh, tha sibh a' faicinn, dh'iarr iad deoch. Ars an
nighean, 'Chan 'eil deur uisge a staigh.' Theann i fhéin ri falbh
do'n tobar, ach cha leigeadh iad-san a mach i. Dh'iarr an
ceannbhard air fear de na gillean falbh a dh'iarraidh uisge, agus

---

[1] MS. *ach làn dhaoine.*

full of dead men. There was another room there too, but the girl was reluctant to open it for them. [But at last] she opened it. Who were there but two youths, and the men asked her who these two were. It was her own brother, she said, and another boy who had come to see her, and she had hidden them, to see if they could manage to escape without being killed. 'Now,' said the farmer to the boys, 'when you hear a whistle, you shall answer me in order to help me ; or else, if I do the work all alone, I will kill you next.' 'We will do that,' said they. Then the girl opened the door of the room where the arms were kept. The farmer took the two best guns there were and a sword for himself and another sword for the poor man. Through a window they entered a room in the house where there was some hay, and they hid themselves under the hay.

They had not been there long when the people of the house came home : the twelve men and the leader. With them they brought two of the farmer's cows and one belonging to the poor man. 'I have a good mind to let them have every spark in the gun,' said the farmer to the poor man when he saw them killing the cows. The poor man kept counselling and urging him to wait, saying that to attack them when they were standing thus was more difficult than when they had finished what they were doing. So then the farmer let them be till the cows had been killed. When they had killed the cows, they raised the hearthstone and put the hides in a pit beneath, and they put the flesh in another pit. That's how things stood.

The leader then told them to sit down to their food, and by Mary, they did ! After they had been eating for a short time, you see, they asked for a drink. 'There's not a drop of water in the house,' said the girl. She started out to go to the well herself, but they would not allow her to go out. The leader asked one of the lads to go and fetch water ; and off he went. That's how dh'fhalbh e. Is ann mar sin a bha. An uair a chaidh am fear sin a mach do'n tobar, air Moire fhéin ! ghabh an tuathanach a mach air an uinneig, 's cha luaithe bha a cheann-san 'san tobair na bha a làmh air, 's a thug e an ceann deth. Tha sibh a' faicinn, an uair a b'fhada leis an fheadhainn a bha a staigh a bha am fear a chuir iad a mach gun tilleadh, chuir iad fear eile as a dhéidh g'a ghreasad. Air Moire fhéin ! cha bu luaithe bha ceann an fhir seo a rithist 'san tobar, na bha làmh an tuathanaich air 's thugar an ceann deth. Chuir iad an ath-fhear a ghreasad an fhir sin, agus air a' cheart dòigh, cha bu luaithe bha a cheann 'san tobar, na bha làmh an tuathanaich air, 's a thug e an ceann deth. Is ann mar sin a bha. Chuir an ceannbhard an sin a mach air fad iad, 's chaidh e fhéin a mach air an ceann, a' creidsinn gun robh a' chreach mu'n taigh. An uair a bha iad a' tighinn a mach, thug an tuathanach an dorus air, agus sheinn e an fhìdeag, 's air Moire fhéin ! cha do fhreagair duine e ; bha a' chùis cosmhail gun robh an t-eagal air a chàirdean ! Is ann mar sin a bha. Tha sibh a' faicinn, leig e fhéin orra an sin, agus mharbh e a h-uile gin, ach an ceannbhard. Air Moire, b'e an saighdear e ! Ruith an ceannbhard air falbh. Loisg e air, 's mharbh e e leis a' ghunna. Is ann mar sin a bha.

An uair a thill e air ais, bha am bodach bochd 'na laighe anns an fheur, 's e chun a bhith marbh leis an eagal. Dh'éirich e air, 's cha mhór nach do mharbh e e. 'Tha siod a nis air a chrìochnachadh,' ars esan ris an nighinn, ' 's tha do bhanais cuibhte 's am fear ud có dhiùbh.' 'Is ann liom-sa as maith sin,' ars ise. 'Is fhearra dhuit mo leigeil far a bheil an fheadhainn a tha 'san t-seòmar,' ars esan, 'gus am faic mi car son nach do fhreagair iad.' Dh'fhosgail i an dorus dha, is chaidh iad a staigh. 'O ! chaidh iad air mhìothapadh,' ars ise. Dh'fhaighnich e dhith gu dé dhèanadh e orra, gun robh e smaointeachadh gun tugadh e am beatha uatha. Thuirt ise gum b' fhearra dha leigeil leò, gum falbhadh iad leatha-se 's nach iarradh iad dad de na bh' ann. Thuirt e gun leigeadh e leò an dràsd, gus am feuchadh e gu dé bha staigh. Dh'fhosgail e [dorus] anns a' bhalla, 's air Moire fhéin ! bha àite an sin agus ionndas ann na leòr. An uair a chunnaig e a h-uile rud a bha a staigh, dh'fhaighnich e de'n nighinn có am fear a b'fheàrr leatha a leigeil beò de na gillean, chionn gum marbhadh e a h-aon diubh

it was. As soon as that fellow had gone out to the well, by Mary herself, out through the window went the farmer, and hardly was the robber's head bent down over the well when the farmer's hand was on him and he took off his head. Now, you see, when it seemed to the people inside that the man they had sent out was a long time coming back, they sent another man after him to hurry him up. By Mary herself! Scarcely had this fellow bent his head down over the well when the farmer's hand was on him and his head was taken off too. So they sent another man to hurry that one up, and in just the same way, no sooner had he bent his head down over the well than the farmer's hand was on him and he took his head off. Thereupon the leader made all the men go out, and went out himself at their head, thinking that the house was surrounded by raiders. As they were coming out, the farmer rushed to the door and whistled, but by Mary herself, not a man answered him! It seemed as if his friends were frightened. And that is how things were. So then, you see, he attacked them himself, and killed them all except the leader. By Mary, what a soldier the farmer was! The leader ran away. The farmer fired at him with his gun and killed him. That is what happened.

When the farmer returned, the poor old man was lying in the hay, almost dead with fright. The farmer fell upon him and nearly killed him. 'All that's finished now,' said he to the girl, 'You won't have to marry that man anyhow!' 'Excellent news for me!' said the girl. 'You had better let me go to those in the room,' said the farmer, 'so that I may find out why they did not answer me.' She opened the door for him, and in they went. 'Oh! their courage failed them,' said she. He asked her what he should do to them, for he was thinking of taking their lives. She replied that he had better let them go, and that they would go off with her and would not ask for anything that was there. He said that he would leave them alone for the moment, until he should find out what was in the house. He opened a door in the wall, and by Mary herself, there was a room there in which there was abundance of treasure. When he had seen everything there was in the house, the farmer asked the girl which one of the lads she would like spared, because he was going to kill one of them for their cowardice. She took her

air son mar a rinn iad, 's iad a bhith cho gealtach. Ghabh i a roghainn de na gillean, 's air Moire fhéin ! b'e sin a leannan ! agus mharbh esan a bràthair. Is ann mar sin a bha.

Thug e dhaibh na b'urrainn daibh a ghiùlan de dh'aodach, 's de na h-uile rud a b'fheudalaiche a bh' ann, 's leig e air falbh iad. Thuirt e an seo ris an duine bhochd, có aca b' fheàrr leis, fantail a ghleidheadh na bothaig, no falbh a dh'iarraidh each a bheireadh air falbh a h-uile rud a bh' ann. Cha robh aona chuid taitneach leis, tha sibh a' faicinn ; ach b'fheàrr leis falbh [agus dh'fhalbh e, a dh'iarraidh nan each, mas fhìor]. Is e an nì a bh' ann, an uair a chaidh am bodach bochd dachaigh, nach tilleàdh e gu bràth air ais, leis an eagal. B' éiginn da fhéin [an tuathanach] dol a dh'iarraidh nan each, agus an uair a rànaig e, theab e am bodach a mharbhadh. Dh'fhalbh e leis na h-eich, is thug e leis am bodach bochd. Rànaig e [bothag nam mèir-leach] is thug e leis a h-uile sìon a b' fheudalaiche na chéile a bh' ann, is chuir e teine ris a' chuid eile. Chaidh e dhachaigh, is thug e deagh roinn do'n bhodach bhochd, gealtach ged a bha e, is cha tug iad mìr dhòmh-sa ach mo leigeil air falbh falamh.

From Donald MacKillop, tenant, Rusgary, Berneray, who says he learnt it from Angus MacLeod, Berneray, a very old man who died a couple of years ago. August 1859. Scribe, Hector MacLean.

NOTES

MS. vol. x., No. 168. Scribe, Hector MacLean.

Being lost in a magic mist is usually a preliminary to adventure. Out-witting and killing robbers occurs in many tales. Giving an old man a share of the plunder and providing him for life with 'the bread of a gentleman,' occurs in 'Loch Aillse,' No. 59 (MS. vol. x., No. 111).

choice of the youths, and by Mary herself, the one she chose
was her lover. So the farmer killed her brother. And thus it was.

The farmer gave them as much as they could carry, both of
clothes and of all the most precious things there were, and then
he let them go. He now asked the poor man which he would
prefer—whether he would stay and hold the bothy or whether
he would go and get horses to carry everything away. Neither
of these alternatives pleased the old man, you see ; however he
preferred to go, [and go he did—to seek the horses, as he pre-
tended]. The upshot was that when the poor old man got home
he was so afraid that on no account would he go back. So the
farmer had to go and look for horses himself, and when he
arrived home, he nearly killed the old man. Then taking the
horses and the poor old man with him, he went back [to the
robbers' bothy], brought away all the most precious things there
were, and set fire to the rest. He went home, and he gave the
poor man a good share, faint-hearted though he had been. But
not a scrap did they give me, but let me go away empty-handed.

In Nicolson's *Gaelic Proverbs*, p. 391, there is a tale of a matron whose
husband, son, and only brother had been captured, and who got her choice
which of the three to have released. She chose her brother. [Cf. *Éigse*,
i., p. 236 ; ii., p. 24 ; vi., p. 181.—A. M.]

CAILLEACH NA RIOBAIG

BHA duine ann agus bha triùir mhac aige, is bha craobh agus tobar anns a' ghàrradh aige mu choinnimh a h-uile h-aon diùbh, is nam bàsaicheadh a h-aon diùbh, sheargadh a' chraobh is thràigheadh an tobar a bha mu a choinnimh.[1] Thuirt am fear a bu shine de na bràithrean ri càch, 'Is fhearra dhomh falbh a dh'iarraidh an fhortain, is an t-àite fhàgail agaibh féin.' Dh'fhalbh e. Rànaig e bothag am beul an anmoich, agus chaidh e a staigh. Bheothaich e an teine, agus shuidh e. Thànaig an creutair bochd sin a dh'ionnsaigh an doruis, air dha bhith treis ann. Thuirt e rithe tighinn a nuas.[2] Thuirt i nach tigeadh mura ceangladh e na coin. 'Chan 'eil rud agam a cheanglas iad,' ars esan. 'Ceanglaidh seo iad,' ars ise, is i toirt da riobaig. 'Cha cheangail,' ars esan. 'Ceanglaidh,' ars ise, 'chumadh e long mhór air acraichean.' Cheangail e an sin na coin leis an riobaig. Is ann mar sin a bha.

Bhuail a' chailleach an sin air i fhéin a cheartachadh an taobh seo is an taobh ud eile de'n teinidh, is i 'ga blàthachadh fhéin. 'Ud! a chailleach, tha thu fàs!' ars esan. 'Chan 'eil ach m'iteagan ag éirigh ris a' bhlàs,' ars ise. 'Tha thu fàs ro mhór,' ars esan. 'Tha,' ars a' chailleach, 'feumaidh tu bhith dèanamh air do shon féin, mura dèan na coin e.' An uair a chunnaig e sin, dh'éigh e air na coin. An uair a chuala ise e, ars i, 'Teann, a riobag, is thoir an ceann de bhraidean.' Theann an riobag, is thug i na cinn de na coin. Air Moire fhéin! dh'éirich iad an seo air a chéile, is dhèanadh iad bogan air a' chreagan, agus creagan air a' bhogan; an t-àite bu lugha rachadh iad fodha, rachadh iad fodha gu an glùintean; is an t-àite bu mhotha rachadh iad fodha, rachadh iad fodha gu an sùilean, gus an do smuaintich a' chailleach nach robh tuilleadh dragha aice. Chuir i fodha e an sin, agus mharbh i e. Shearg

---

[1] For trees and wells which are magically bound up with the lives of mortals, see *Survivals*, pp. 185, 189; *W. H. Tales*, i., No. 4. For the similar association of the life or soul with wreckage, see *Trans. Gael. Soc. Inverness*, xxvi., p. 297.

[2] recte, *a nìos.*

THE HAG OF THE HAIR

No. 77.   [*MS. Vol. x., No. 169*]

THERE was a man who had three sons, and in his garden there
was a tree and a well assigned to each of his sons ; if any one of
them were to die, the tree assigned to him would wither away
and the well would dry up.[1] The eldest of the brothers said to
the others, 'I had better go and seek my fortune and leave this
place to yourselves.' And off he went. At dusk, he came to a
little hut, and went inside ; he kindled the fire and sat down.
After he had been there for a while a poor creature came to the
door. He told her to come forward, but she said she would not
come unless he tied up the dogs. 'I have nothing to tie them
with,' said he. 'This will tie them up,' she said ; and she gave
him a hair. 'It will not,' said he. 'Yes, it will,' she said ; 'it
would hold a big ship at its anchors.' So then he tied up the
dogs with the hair. And that is how things were.

The hag then began to settle herself first on this side of the
fire, and then on the other, warming herself. 'Ah ! old woman,
you are getting big !' said he. 'It is only my little feathers standing
out to the warmth,' said she. 'You are getting huge !' said he.
'Yes, I am,' said the old hag, 'and you must be up and doing for
yourself, unless the dogs can do it for you.' When he saw that,
he shouted to his dogs. When she heard him, she said, 'Tighten,
hair, and take the rascals' heads off !' The hair tightened, and
took the heads off the dogs. Then, by Mary herself ! they leapt
at each other, and they would turn the stony ground into a bog
and the bog into stony ground ; where they sank least they
sank to their knees, and where they sank most they sank to their
eyes, until the hag thought that she had no more to worry about.
Then she felled him and killed him. One of the trees in his father's
garden withered and one of the wells dried up, and the next

craobh anns a' ghàrradh aig a athair, agus thràigh tobar ann,
agus thuirt am bràthair a bu mheadhonaiche gun robh a
bhràthair air bàsachadh, is gun rachadh esan air falbh air a lorg.

Dh'fhalbh e is rànaig e a' cheart bhothag anns an robh a
bhràthair. Smuaintich e gum bu chòir da tàmh a ghabhail
innte an oidhche sin. Cha b'fhada a bha e an sin, an uair a
thànaig an creutair sin mar a b'àbhaist di. Dh'iarr esan oirre
tighinn a nuas.[1] Thuirt i nach tigeadh, gun robh na coin a'
cur eagail oirre. Thuirt esan ma bha, nach robh rathad aige
air an ceangal, ach gun cumadh e uaithe iad. 'Seo riobag,'
ars ise, 'is ceangail iad, is abair "Teann, teann, a riobag, is na
leig chuige." ' Rinn e siod, is thànaig ise a nuas an sin.

Bhuail i air a ceartachadh fhéin ris an teinidh, is air a blàthachadh. 'Ud ! a chailleach ! tha thu fàs,' ars esan. 'Chan 'eil
ach m'iteagan ag éirigh ris a' bhlàs,' ars ise. 'Ud ! a chailleach !
tha thu fàs ro mhór,' ars esan. 'Tha, is feumaidh tusa bhith
dèanamh air do shon féin,' ars a' chailleach. Dh'éigh esan air
na coin, is ghlaodh ise, 'Teann, teann, a riobag is thoir an ceann
de bhraidean !' Theann an riobag, is thug i na cinn de na coin.
Dh'éirich iad air a chéile, is dhèanadh iad bogan air a' chreagan,
agus creagan air a' bhogan ; an t-àite bu lugha rachadh iad
fodha, rachadh iad fodha gu an glùintean ; is an t-àite bu mhotha
rachadh iad fodha, rachadh iad fodha gu an sùilean, gus an do
smuaintich a' chailleach nach robh tuilleadh dragha aice. Chuir
i fodha [e] is mharbh i e. Shearg craobh eile anns a' ghàrradh
aig a athair, agus thràigh tobar ann. Thuirt am bràthair a
b'òige gum biodh esan a' falbh, gun robh a bhràithrean air dol
as an rathad, is nach dèanadh e tàmh no fois gus am faigheadh
e a mach ciod e mar a chaidh iad as an rathad. Bha a chuideachd ro dhuilich air son an fhir mu dheireadh.

Dh'fhalbh e is rànaig e a' bhothag. Chaidh e a staigh, is
bheothaich e an teine. Cha robh e fad an sin gus an d'fhairich
e an creutair a b'àbhaist a' tighinn gus a' bhothag. Dh'iarr e
oirre tighinn a staigh a ghabhail a cuid de'n bhlàs. 'Chan
fhaod mise dol a staigh—tha na coin a' cur eagail orm,' ars ise.
'Bheir mise air na coin nach dèan iad dad ort,' ars esan. Cha
dèanadh seo a' chùis leatha-se, ach gum faigheadh i fhéin rud

---

[1] recte, *a nìos*.

eldest son said that his brother had died and that he would go and follow him up.

He set off and came to the same little hut where his brother had been, and he thought he ought to rest there that night. He had not been there long when that creature came, as her habit was. He asked her to come forward. She said she would not do so, that the dogs were frightening her. He said that if they were, he had no means of tying them, but that he would keep them away from her. 'Here is a hair,' said she, 'so tie them up and say, "Tighten, tighten, hair! Do not let them get near!"' He did so, and then she came forward.

She began to settle herself at the fire and warm herself. 'Ah! old woman, you are growing!' said he. 'It is only my little feathers standing out to the warmth,' she said. 'Ah! old woman, you are getting huge,' said he. 'Yes, I am; and you must be up and doing for yourself,' said the hag. He shouted to the dogs, and the hag shouted, 'Tighten, tighten, hair! take the rascals' heads off!' The hair tightened and took the heads off the dogs. They leapt at each other, and they would turn the stony ground into a bog and the bog into stony ground; where they sank least they sank to their knees, and where they sank most they sank to their eyes, until the hag thought that she had no more to worry about. She felled him and killed him. Another tree in his father's garden withered, and another well dried up. The youngest brother said that he would be off, that his brothers were dead, and that he would take neither rest nor leisure till he found out how they had died. His relatives were deeply grieved for this last man.

He set off and came to the little bothy; he went inside and kindled the fire. He had not been long there when he noticed the creature who used to come to the bothy approaching. He asked her to come in and get her share of the warmth. 'I cannot go in—the dogs frighten me,' she said. 'I will keep the dogs from doing anything to you,' he replied. This would not do for her: she herself would have to find something to tie them up with, and she gave him a black hair. He said that that would

a cheangladh iad. Thug i dha riobag dhubh. Thuirt esan
nach ceangladh siod na coin aige-san. 'Ceanglaidh,' ars ise,
'cumaidh e an long as motha air acraichean.' Is e an rud a
bha ann [gun do] chuir e anns an teinidh i. Dh'fhaighnich ise
ciod e an rud a bha an siod an uair a chuala i an riobag a'
braigheartaich. Thuirt esan nach robh fios aige.[1] Smachdaich e
na coin, is chum e dlùth ris fhéin iad air alt is nach caraicheadh iad.

Theann ise a suas [2] an seo. Bhuail i air i fhéin a cheartachadh
is a bhlàthachadh ris an teinidh. 'Ud ! a chailleach ! tha thu
fàs !' ars esan. 'Chan 'eil ach m'iteagan ag éirigh ris a' bhlàs,'
ars ise. 'O ! a chailleach, is tu tha fàs mór !' ars esan. 'O !
is mi,' ars ise, 'is tusa am fear mu dheireadh dhiubh, is feumaidh
tu bhith dèanamh air do shon fhéin.' Dh'éirich iad air a chéile.
Dh'éigh esan air na coin. 'Teann, teann, a riobag, is thoir an
ceann de bhraidean !' ars a' chailleach. Cha do thachair sin.
Chaidh na coin air chosnadh air alt is gun do chuir esan fodha
a' chailleach. 'Bàs os do chionn, a chailleach !' ars esan, 'ciod
e t'éirig ?' 'Cha bheag sin,' ars ise, 'is ann a dh'iarraidh an
fhortain a thànaig sibh : is mise a mharbh do dhithis bhràithrean
a tha marbh an siod. Tha ballan ìocshlaint is ballan pasmhuinn [3]
a staigh, is an uair a shuathas tu an rud a tha annta riutha,
éiridh iad suas cho beò is a bha iad riamh. Tha tronnc òir is
tronnc airgid a staigh anns a' bhalla an siod. O'n as ann a
dh'iarraidh an fhortain a thànaig sibh, tha fortan na leòr agaibh
gun dol na's fhaide na seo.' 'A bheil tuilleadh agad de dh'éirig,
a chailleach ?' ars esan. 'Chan 'eil tuilleadh,' ars ise. 'Ma
tà, a chailleach, ge beag sin, is liom féin e,' ars esan, agus e 'ga
marbhadh. Fhuair e a bhràithrean, is shuath e an rud a bha
anns a' bhallan riutha, is dh'éirich iad suas beò, slàn, còmhla
ris. Lìon an dà thobar, is dh'éirich an dà chraoibh, is dh'aithnich
an athair gun robh an triùir beò. Chaidh iad dhachaigh is
thug iad leò na robh an siod de dh'ionndas ; is cha tug iad òr
no airgead dòmh-sa, ach mo chur dhachaigh falamh an seo.

[1] Note on opposite page, says 'Altered,' showing that hero's actual reply had
not been recorded.
[2] So in MS.

From Donald MacKillop, tenant, Rusgary, Berneray, who learnt it
from Angus MacLeod, Berneray. August 1859. Scribe, Hector
MacLean.

not tie up the dogs that he had. 'It will,' said she, 'it would hold the biggest ship at its anchors.' What he did was to put the hair in the fire. When the hag heard the hair crackling, she asked what that was. He replied that he did not know.[1] He restrained the dogs, and kept them close to himself so that they would not stir.

Then the hag moved forward and began to settle herself and warm herself at the fire. 'Ah ! old woman, you are getting big !' said he. 'It is only my little feathers standing out to the warmth,' said she. 'Ah ! old woman, how big you are getting !' said he. 'Oh, yes, I am,' said the hag. 'You are the last of them, and you must be up and doing for yourself.' They leapt at each other. He shouted to the dogs. 'Tighten, tighten, hair ! Take the rascals' heads off !' said the hag. That did not happen. The dogs got to work so that he overthrew the hag. 'Death is over your head, old hag !' said he ; 'what is your ransom ?' 'No small ransom,' said she. 'It was to seek your fortune you came : it is I who killed your two brothers who are dead there. There is a vessel of healing salve and a vessel of curing salve in the place, and when you rub them with the stuff in those vessels, they will rise up again as much alive as ever they were. There is a trunk of gold and a trunk of silver in the wall there. Since it was to seek your fortune that you came, you have fortune enough without going any farther than this.' 'Have you anything more for your ransom, old hag ?' said he. 'I have nothing more,' said she. 'Well then, old hag, little as there is, it is mine,' said he, and killed her. He found his brothers, and he rubbed them with the stuff in the vessel, and they rose up alive and well, and there they were with him. The two wells filled up and the two trees revived ; and the father knew that the three sons were alive. They went home, taking with them all the treasure that was there ; but neither gold nor silver did they give me, they just sent me home here empty-handed.

[3] Note in MS. 'Pasmhuinn, same as pasmuinn ; what gives relief or cures in extreme cases. I am inclined to think it is derived from bàs-bhuidhinn, overcoming death.' In Dwelly's *Dictionary* I can only find *pasmunn, -uinn*, 'expiring pang.'

NOTES

See No. 69 (MS. vol. x., No. 151) notes.